S. L. FARRELL

A Magic of Nightfall

Volume Two of *The Nessantico Cycle*

DAW BOOKS, INC.

DONALD A. WOLLHEIM, FOUNDER

375 Hudson Street, New York, NY 10014

ELIZABETH R. WOLLHEIM

SHEILA E. GILBERT

PUBLISHERS

www.dawbooks.com

First Paperback Printing, March 2010.

1 2 3 4 5 6 7 8 9 10

Acknowledgments

I've read several books for inspiration and reference in writing this series. The books I read prior to starting the Nessantico Cycle as well as those read during the writing of *A Magic Of Twilight* are listed in that book; obviously, they too have also influenced the book you're holding. I've continued to read historical texts for inspiration and research—it's something I enjoy, in any case. Here are the books read during the writing of this book, all of which to some degree influenced the text.

- *The God Delusion* by Richard Dawkins. Houghton Mifflin, 2006
- *Religion and the Decline of Magic* by Keith Thomas. Oxford University Press, 1971
- *The Jesuit & The Skull* by Amir Aczel. Penguin, 2007
- *Brunelleschi's Dome* by Ross Kind. Penguin, 2001.

A trip to France in 2005 also served as inspiration for much of the Nessantico Cycle. In particular, the Loire Valley region, with its chateaux and lovely countryside, sparked several ideas, as did our days in Paris. I would recommend that anyone going to France see the Loire Valley and spend time exploring not only the chateaux, but the small villages in the surrounding countryside such as Azay le Rideau or Villaines les-Rochers. Nessantico is not specifically Paris—it's an amalgam of that city along with Florence and Venice—but many details are drawn from our experiences there. Hopefully they have enriched the book.

It may sound strange to acknowledge a piece of software, but I'm going to. In the midst of writing this book, I stumbled across the most useful novel-writing software to have ever graced my computer: Scrivener. For those of you on the Macintosh platform who are writing novels, you must take a look at this. Scrivener thinks the way I think and allowed me to manage the monumental task of writing a novel far, far better than any word processor ever could. Thanks, Keith Blount, for creating this program! For the curious, Scrivener can be found at http://www.literatureandlatte.com/ —I highly, highly recommend it!

Many thanks, as always, to my agent Merrilee Heifetz of Writers House, who has been my partner-in-writing for many years now—without her, none of this would have been possible.

My gratitude to my first readers; Denise Parsley Leigh (who was forced to read *all* the drafts), and Justin Scott and Don Wenzel, who labored through the submission draft— thanks to all of you for the input and the corrections! Your help was much appreciated!

And lastly (but certainly not last in importance—she goes last because you always want to end with something strong! I need to express my gratitude to Sheila Gilbert, a most excellent editor and someone I also consider a friend. We've now worked together on several books, and her input and criticism made each a richer book than it would have been otherwise. Thank you, Sheila!

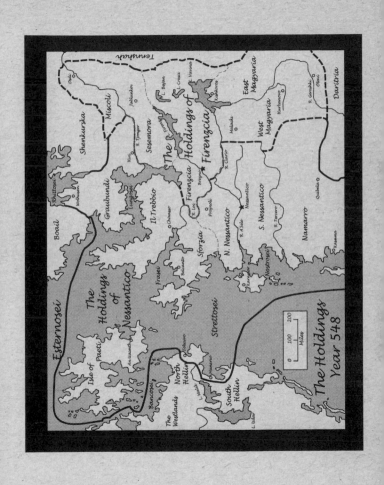

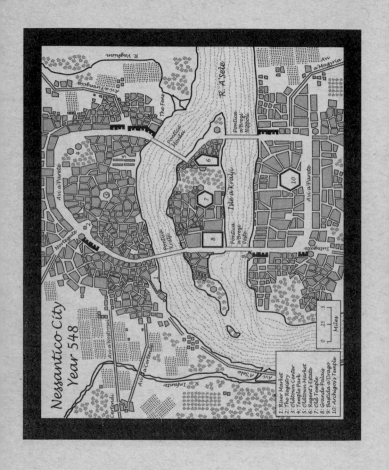

Nessantico City
Year 548

1: River Market
2: The Ragfair
3: Oldtown Center
4: Temple Park
5: Oldtown Market
6: Regent's Estate
7: Old Temple
8: Grande Palais
9: Basilica a'Drago
10: Archigos' Temple

Table of Contents

Prelude: Nessantico

IF A CITY CAN HAVE a gender, Nessantico was female....
Once, she had been young and vital: the city, the woman. During her ascension, she had transformed herself into the most famous, the most beautiful, the most powerful of her kind.

She looked at herself now and wondered—as someone might who glimpses herself all unexpected in a mirror and is startled and disturbed by the image staring back—if those attributes still held true.

Oh, she knew that youth was fleeting and ephemeral. After all, the people dwelling within her walls led lives that were short and harsh. For them, the mirrored face changed relentlessly with each passing day until that morning when they realized that the reflection in the silvered glass was lined and tired, that the gray at the temples had spread and whitened. They might feel their joints protesting at a movement that had once required no effort or thought at all, or discover that injuries now required weeks rather than days to heal, or that illnesses lingered like unwelcome guests—or worse, transitioned from "lingering" to "chronic."

The chill of mortality seeped into their mortal bones like slow ice.

Mortality: Nessantico felt it, too. Those within her disguised her lines and folds with the cosmetics of architecture. Look, she could say: there is cu'Brunelli's grand dome for the Old Temple—fifteen years under construction now—which when finished will be the largest free-standing dome in the known world. There: that's ca'Casseli's ornate and beautiful Theatre a'Kralji on the Isle, capable of holding an audience of two thousand, with acoustics so fine that everyone can hear the slightest whisper on the stage; there, the Grande Libreria on the South Bank, begun under Kraljiki Justi's reign and containing all the greatest intellectual works of humankind. Listen: that is the sweet music of ce'Miella, whose compositions rival the lush melodies of the master Darkmavis. Gaze on the symbol-laden paintings and murals of ce'Vaggio, whose ability to paint figures is often compared to that of the tragic master ci'Recroix. There is so much vibrant life here within Nessantico: all the plays and the dances, the celebrations and gaiety.

All is the same here as it has always been; no, all is *better*.

Yet she *had* changed, and she knew it. There were signs and portents. In Oldtown, not long ago, there was a woman born with the legs of a tarantula who (it was whispered) could kill with a single glance from her faceted eyes. There had been the affliction of thousands of green toads from the Fens two springs ago, so thick that they had covered the nearby lanes in a writhing mass a hand's span deep. In the sewers of the North Bank, a creature with the head of a dragon, the body of a bull, and the hands and feet of a human was said to prowl, eating rats that had grown to the size of wolves.

There were the real, inarguable signs, too. The Holdings had been broken, that strong alliance of countries forged slowly over centuries. After an ill-fated attack on Nessantico in the wake of Kraljica Marguerite's assassination, the city Brezno had become her rival as Firenzcia gathered around itself several of its neighboring lands: a Coalition under the direction of Hïrzg Jan ca'Vörl.

The Concénzia Faith, too, had been sundered, and it was not what it had been. Archigos Ana sat in the temple on the South Bank, yes, but another called himself Archigos in Brezno. Within Nessantico, the heretical Numetodo took on new adherents, and it was not uncommon to see someone casting a spell who was not wearing green robes or calling first on Cénzi.

Signs and portents. Change. The older Nessantico grew, the more change became difficult for her.

Caught in her own unwelcome autumn, Nessantico—the city, the woman—stared at her reflection in the dark waters of the River A'Sele and wondered. . . .

And, like many in her position, she denied what she saw.

ANSWERS

Allesandra ca'Vörl
Jan ca'Vörl
Varina ci'Pallo
Audric ca'Dakwi
Sergei ca'Rudka
Nico Morel
Allesandra ca'Vörl
Enéas cu'Kinnear
Karl ca'Vliomani
Allesandra ca'Vörl
The White Stone

Allesandra ca'Vörl

HER VATARH HAD BEEN the sun around which she had orbited for as long as she could remember. Now that sun, at long last, was setting.

The message had arrived from Brezno by fast-rider, and she stared at the words scrawled by a hasty, fair hand. *"Your vatarh is dying. If you want to see him, hurry."* That was the entire message. It was signed by Archigos Semini of Brezno and sealed with his signet.

Vatarh is dying.... The great Hïrzg Jan of Firenzcia, after whom she had named her only child, was passing. The words set alight a sour fire in her belly; the words swam on the page with the salt tears that welled unbidden in her eyes. She sat there—at her fine desk, in her opulent offices near the Gyula's palais in Malacki—and she saw a droplet hit the paper to smudge the inked words.

She hated that Vatarh could still affect her so strongly; she hated that she cared. She should have hated him, but she couldn't. No matter how hard she'd tried over the years, she couldn't.

One might curse the sun for its scorching heat or its absence, but without the sun there was no life.

"I hate him," she declared to Archigos Ana. It had been two years since Ana had snatched her away from her vatarh to hold her as hostage. Two years, and he still hadn't paid the ransom to bring her back. She was thirteen, on the cusp of her menarche, and he had abandoned her. What had originally been anxiety and disappointment had slowly

transformed inside her into anger. At least that's what she believed.

"No, you don't," Ana said quietly, stroking her hair. They were standing on the balcony of her apartments in the Temple complex in Nessantico, staring down to where knots of green-clad téni hurried to their duties. "Not really. If he paid the ransom tomorrow, you would be glowing and ready to run back to him. Look inside yourself, Allesandra. Look honestly. Isn't that true?"

"Well, he must hate me," she retorted, "or he'd have paid."

Ana had hugged her tightly then. "He will," she told Allesandra. "He will. It's just ... Allesandra, your vatarh wished to sit on the Sun Throne. He has always been a proud man, and because I took you away, he was never able to realize his dream. You remind him of all he lost. And that's my fault. Not yours. It's not yours at all."

Vatarh hadn't paid. Not for ten long years. It had been Fynn, the new son her matarh Greta had given the Hïrzg, who basked in Vatarh's affections, who was taught the ways of war, who was named as the new A'Hïrzg—the title that should have been hers.

Instead of her vatarh and her matarh, it was Archigos Ana who became her surrogate parent, shepherding her through puberty and adolescence, comforting Allesandra through her first crushes and infatuations, teaching her the ways of ca'-and-cu' society, escorting her to dances and parties, treating her not as a captive but as a niece it had become her responsibility to raise.

"I love you, Tantzia," Allesandra said to Ana. She'd taken to calling the Archigos "aunt." The news had come to Kraljiki Justi that a treaty between the Holdings and the Firenzcian "Coalition" was to be signed in Passe a'Fiume, and as part of the negotiations, Hïrzg Jan had finally paid the ransom for his daughter. She'd been a decade in Nessantico, nearly half her life. Now, at twenty-one, she was to return to the life she'd lost so long ago and she was frightened by the prospect. Once, this had been all she'd wanted. Now ...

Part of her wanted to stay here. Here, where she knew she was loved.

Ana folded her in her arms. Allesandra was taller than the Archigos now, and Ana had to raise up on tiptoes to kiss her forehead. "I love you, too, Allesandra. I'll miss you, but it's time for you to go home. Just know that I will always be here for you. Always. You are part of my heart, my dear. Forever."

Allesandra had hoped that she could bask in the sun of her vatarh's love again. Yes, she'd heard all about how the new A'Hïrzg Fynn was the child Hïrzg Jan had always desired: skilled at riding, at the sword, at diplomacy. She'd heard how he was being groomed already for a career in the Garde Firenzcia. But she had once been the pride of her vatarh, too. Surely, she could become so again.

But she knew as soon as he looked at her, across the parley tent there at Passe a'Fiume, that it was not to be. In his hawkish eyes, there had been a smoldering distaste. He'd glanced at her appraisingly, as he might a stranger—and indeed, she was a stranger to him: a young woman now, no longer the girl he'd lost. He'd taken her hands and accepted her curtsy as he might have any ca'-and-cu' and passed her off to Archigos Semini a moment later.

Fynn had been at his side—the age now that she'd been when she'd been taken—and he looked appraisingly at his older sister as he might have at some rival.

Allesandra had sought Ana's gaze from across the tent, and the woman had smiled sadly toward her and raised her hand in farewell. There had been tears in Ana's eyes, sparkling in the sun that beat through the thin canvas of the tent. Ana, at least, had been true to her word. She had written Allesandra regularly. She had negotiated with her vatarh to be allowed to attend Allesandra's marriage to Pauli ca'Xielt, the son of the Gyula of West Magyaria and thus a politically advantageous marriage for the Hïrzg, and a loveless one for Allesandra.

Ana had even, surreptitiously, been present at the birth of Allesandra's son, nearly sixteen years ago now. Archigos Ana—the heretical and false Archigos according to Firenzcia, whom Allesandra was obliged to hate as a good citizen of the Coalition—had blessed the child and pronounced the name that Allesandra had given him: Jan. She'd done so without rebuke and without comment. She'd done so with a gentle smile and a kiss.

Even naming her child for her vatarh had changed nothing. It had not brought him closer to Allesandra—Hïrzg Jan had mostly ignored his great-son and namesake. Jan was in the company of Hïrzg Jan perhaps twice a year, when he and Allesandra visited for state occasions, and only rarely did the Hïrzg speak directly to his great-son.

Now . . . now her vatarh was dying and she couldn't help crying for him. Or perhaps it was that she couldn't help crying for herself. Angrily, she tore at the dampness on her cheeks with her sleeve. "Aeri!" she called to her secretary. "Come in here! I have to go to Brezno."

Allesandra strode into the Hïrzg's bedchamber, tossing aside her travel-stained cloak, her hair wind-tossed and the smell of horse on her clothes. She pushed past the servants who tried to assist her and went to the bed. The chevarittai and various relatives gathered there moved aside to let her approach; she could feel their appraising stares on her back. She stared at the wizened, dried-apple face on the pillow and barely recognized him.

"Is he . . . ?" she asked brusquely, but then she heard the phlegm-racked rattle of his breath and saw the slow movement of his chest under the blankets. The room stank of sickness despite the perfumed candles. "Out!" she told them all, gesturing. "Tell Fynn I've come, but leave me alone with my vatarh. Out!"

They scattered, as she knew they would. None of them attempted to protest, though the healers frowned at her from under carefully lowered brows, and she could hear the whispers even as they fled. *It's no wonder her husband stays away from her . . . A goat has better manners . . . She has the arrogance of Nessantico . . .*

She slammed the door in their faces.

Then, finally, staring down at her vatarh's gray, sunken face, she allowed herself to cry, kneeling alongside his bed and holding his cold, withered hands. "I loved you, Vatarh," she told him. Alone with him, there could be truth. "I did. Even after you abandoned me, even after you gave Fynn all the affection I wanted, I still loved you. I could have been the heir you deserved. I will *still* be that, if I have the chance."

She heard the scrape of bootsteps at the door and rose

to her feet, wiping at her eyes with the sleeve of her tashta, and sniffing once as Fynn pushed the door open. He strode into the chamber—Fynn never simply walked into a room. "Sister," he said. "I see the news reached you."

Allesandra stood, arms folded. She would not let him realize how deeply seeing her vatarh on his deathbed had affected her. She shrugged. "I still have sources here in Brezno, even when my brother fails to send a messenger."

"It slipped my mind," he said. "But I figured you would hear anyway." The smile he gave her was more sneer, twisted by the long, puckered scar that ran from the corner of his right eye and across his lip to the chin: the mark of a Tennshah scimitar. Fynn, at twenty-four, had the hard, lean body of a professional soldier, a figure that suited the loose pants and shirt that he wore. Such Tennshah clothing had become fashionable in Firenzcia since the border wars six years before, where Fynn had engaged the T'Sha's forces and pushed Firenzcia's borders nearly thirty leagues eastward, and where he had acquired the long scar that marred his handsome face.

It was during that war that Fynn had won their vatarh's affection entirely and ended any lingering hope of Allesandra's that she might become Hïrzgin.

"The healers say the end will come sometime today, or possibly tonight if he continues to fight—Vatarh never did give up easily, did he? But the soul shredders *will* come for him this time. There's no longer any doubt of that." Fynn glanced down at the figure on the bed as the Hïrzg took another long, shuddering breath. The young man's gaze was affectionate and sad, and yet somehow appraising at the same time, as if he were gauging how long it might be before he could slip the signet ring from the folded hands and put it on his own finger; how soon he could place the golden crown-band of the Hïrzg on the curls of his own head. "There's nothing you or I can do, Sister," he said, "other than pray that Cénzi receives Vatarh's soul kindly. Beyond that . . ." He shrugged. "How is my nephew Jan?" he asked.

"You'll see soon enough," Allesandra told him. "He's on his way to Brezno behind me and should arrive tomorrow."

"And your husband? The dear Pauli?"

Allesandra sniffed. "If you're trying to goad me, Fynn, it won't work. I've suggested to Pauli that he remain in Malacki and attend to state business. What of yourself? Have you found someone to marry yet, or do you still prefer the company of soldiers and horses?"

The smile was slow in coming and uncertain when it appeared. "Now who goads whom?" he asked. "Vatarh and I had made no decisions on that yet, and now it seems that the decision will be mine alone—though I'll certainly listen to any suggestions you might have." He opened his arms, and she reluctantly allowed him to embrace her. Neither one of them tightened their arms but only encircled the other as if hugging a thornbush, and the gesture ended after a single breath. "Allesandra, I know there's always been a distance between us, but I hope that we can work as one when . . ." He hesitated, and she watched his chest rise with a long inhalation. ". . . when I am the Hïrzg. I will need your counsel, Sister."

"And I will give it to you," she told him. She leaned forward and kissed the air a careful finger's width from his scarred cheek. "Little brother."

"I wish we could have truly been little brother and big sister," he answered. "I wish I could have known you then."

"As do I," she told him. *And I wish those were more than just empty, polite words we both say because we know they're demanded by etiquette.* "Stay here with me now? Let Vatarh feel us together for once."

She felt his hesitation and wondered whether he'd refuse. But after a breath, he lifted one shoulder. "For a turn of the glass or so," he said. "We can pray for him. Together."

He pulled two chairs to the side of the bed, placing them an arm's length apart. They sat, they watched the faltering rise and fall of their vatarh's chest, and they said nothing more.

Jan ca'Vörl

"**I** HAVE TO RIDE as quickly as I can to Brezno," his matarh had told him. "I've instructed the servants to pack up our rooms for travel. I want you to follow along as soon as they have the carriages ready. And, Jan, see if you can convince your vatarh to come with you." She kissed his forehead then, more urgently than she had in years, and pulled him into her. "I love you," she whispered. "I hope you know that."

"I do," he'd told her, pulling away and grinning at her. "And I hope *you* know that."

She'd smiled, hugging him a final time before she swung herself onto the horse held by the two chevarittai who would accompany her. He watched the trio clatter away down the road of their estate at a gallop.

That had been two days ago. His matarh should have made Brezno yesterday. Jan leaned his head back against the cushions of the carriage, watching the landscape of southern Firenzcia pass by in the green-gold light of late afternoon. The driver had told him that they would be stopping at the next village for the evening, and arrive in Brezno by midday tomorrow. He wondered what he'd find there.

He was alone in his carriage.

He'd asked his vatarh Pauli to come with him, as his matarh had requested. The servants had told him that Pauli was in his apartments at the estate—in a separate wing from those of Allesandra—and Pauli's chief aide had gone in to announce Jan. The aide had returned with arched eyebrows. "Your vatarh says he can spare a few moments," he'd said, escorting Jan to one of the reception rooms off the main corridor.

Jan could hear the muffled giggling of two women from a bedroom leading from the room. The door opened in the middle of a man's coarse laugh. His vatarh was in a robe, his hair was tousled and unkempt, and his beard untrimmed. He smelled of perfume and wine. "A moment," he'd said to Jan, touching a finger to his lips before half-staggering to the door leading to the bedroom and opening it slightly. "Shh!" he said loudly. "I am trying to conduct a conversation about my wife with my son," he said. That was greeted by shrill laughter.

"Tell the boy to join us," Jan heard one of them call out. He felt his face flush at the comment as Pauli waggled his forefinger toward the unseen woman.

"The two of you are delightfully wicked," Pauli told them. Jan imagined the women: rouged, bewigged, half-clothed, or perhaps entirely nude, like one of the portraits of the Moitidi goddesses that adorned the halls. He felt himself responding to the image and forced it out of his mind. "I'll be there in a moment," Pauli continued. "You ladies have more wine."

He closed the door and leaned heavily against it. "Sorry," he told Jan. "I have . . . company. Now, what did the bitch want? Oh—you may tell your matarh for me that the A'Gyula of West Magyaria has better things to do than ride to Brezno because someone may or may not be dying. When the old bastard finally does breathe his last, I'll undoubtedly be sent to the funeral as our representative, and that'll be soon enough." His words were slurred. He blinked slowly and belched. "You don't need to go either, boy. Stay here, why don't you? The two of us could have some fun, eh? I'm sure these ladies have friends. . . ."

Jan shook his head. "I promised Matarh that I'd ask you to come, and I have. I'm leaving tonight; the servants have nearly finished packing the carriages."

"Ah, yes," Pauli said. "You're such a good, obedient child, aren't you? Your matarh's pride and joy." He pushed himself from the door and stood unsteadily, pointing at Jan with a fingertip that drifted from one side to another. "You don't want to be like her," he said. "She won't be satisfied until she's running the whole world. She's an ambitious whore with a heart carved from flint."

He'd heard Pauli insult his matarh a thousand times, more with each passing year. He'd always gritted his teeth before, had pretended not to hear or mumbled a protest that Pauli would ignore. This time . . . the nascent flush in

Jan's face went lava-red. He took three swift steps across
the carpeted room, drew his hand back, and slapped his
vatarh across the face. Pauli reeled, staggering back against
the door, which opened and toppled him onto a braided
rug there. Jan saw the two women inside—half-clothed, indeed, and in his vatarh's bed. They covered their breasts
with the sheets, screaming. Pauli lifted an unbelieving hand
to his face; over the thin beard, Jan could see the imprint of
his fingers on his vatarh's cheek.

He wondered for a moment what he'd do if Pauli got
up, but his vatarh only blinked again and laughed as if
startled.

"Well, you didn't need to do *that*," he said.

"You may have whatever opinion you want of Matarh,"
Jan told him. "I don't care. But from now on, Vatarh, keep
them to yourself or we will have more than words." With
that, before Pauli could rise from the carpet or answer, Jan
turned and rushed from the room.

He felt strangely exhilarated. His hand tingled. The rest
of the day, he expected to be summoned into his vatarh's
presence—once the wine had passed from the man's head.
But when he was told that the carriages were ready and
waiting for him, he had heard nothing. He looked up to
the windows of his vatarh's wing as he entered the lead
carriage and the servants traveling with him piled into
the others. Jan thought he glimpsed a form at the window,
watching, and he lifted his hand—the hand that had struck
his vatarh.

Another form—a feminine one—approached his vatarh
from behind, and the curtain closed again. Jan stepped up
into the carriage. "Let's go," he told the driver. "We've a
long journey ahead."

He looked out from the carriage window again now. For
most of the journey, he'd brooded on what had happened.
He was nearly sixteen. Nearly a man. He'd even had his
first lover—a ce' girl who had been part of the estate staff,
though his matarh had sent her away when she realized
that they had become intimate. She'd also given Jan a long
lecture on her expectations for him. "But Vatarh—" he'd
begun, and she cut off his protest with a sharp slash of her
hand.

"Stop there, Jan. Your vatarh is lazy and dissolute, and—

forgive my crudeness—he too often thinks with what's between his legs, not with his head. You're better than him,
Jan. You are going to be important in this world, *if* you
make the choice not to be your vatarh's child. I *know* this.
I promise you."

She hadn't said all that she could have, and they both
knew it. Pauli might be Jan's vatarh, but for him that was
just another title and not an occupation. It had been his
matarh whom Jan saw each day, who had played with him
when he was small, who had come to see him each night
after his nursemaids had tucked him into bed. His vatarh . . .
He was a tall figure who sometimes tousled Jan's head or
who gave him extravagant presents that seemed more to be
a payment for his absence than true gifts.

His vatarh was the A'Gyula of West Magyaria, the
son of the current Gyula, the ruler who Jan saw about as
often as he saw his other great-vatarh, the Hïrzg. People
bowed in Pauli's presence, they laughed and smiled as
they talked with him. But Jan had heard the whispers of
the staff, and of their guests when they thought no one
was listening.

His right hand throbbed, as if with the memory of the
slap to his vatarh's face. He looked at the hand in the dying
light of the day: an adult's hand now. The slap to his vatarh's
face had severed him from his childhood forever.

He would not be his vatarh. That much, he promised
himself. He would be his own self. Independent.

~

Varina ci'Pallo

VARINA STOOD ALONGSIDE Karl in the Archigos'
plush reception room, but—as was nearly always the
case when Ana was in the same room—she seemed invisible to him. All his attention was on the Archigos. Varina
wanted to lean over to Karl and slap him. *"Can't you see
what's in front of your face? Are you that oblivious?"*

It seemed he was. He always was, and he always would
be where Ana was concerned. Over the years, Varina had
come to that conclusion. It would perhaps have been different if Varina didn't like and admire the Archigos herself,
if she didn't consider the woman a friend. Still . . .

"You're sure of this?" Karl asked Ana. He was glancing
at a parchment that Ana had handed him, a forefinger tapping the words written there. "He's dead?" There was no
trace of sadness in his voice at all; he was, in fact, smiling as
he handed the paper back to her.

Ana frowned. If Karl found the news pleasant, it was
obvious to Varina that Ana's own feelings were more conflicted. "Hïrzg Jan's dying," Ana said. "And likely dead by
this point, I suspect, if this information is accurate. The téni
who sent this message has the healing touch; he should
know if the man's beyond saving."

"About time the old buzzard passed on," Karl said. He
glanced around the room thoughtfully, but not at Varina.
"Have you talked to Allesandra? Will she contest Fynn's
claim to the throne?"

"I don't know." Ana seemed to sigh. Ana had never
been beautiful; at best, as a young woman, she'd been plain.
Even she would have admitted that. Now, approaching her
middle years, she'd settled into a matronly figure, but there
was something striking and solid and compelling about her.
Varina could understand Karl's attraction and devotion to
the woman, even as part of her resented it. Ana's reputation had only grown over the years. Kraljiki Justi had been

mocked behind his back, and his son Audric seemed to be faring no better, and there were those in the Faith who felt Ana's tolerance and openness were heretical, but the common people of Nessantico and the Holdings seemed to adore their Archigos and had taken her to their hearts. Varina had seen the crowds around the temple whenever Ana was to give an Admonition, and she'd heard the cheers when the Archigos' carriage passed by on the Avi a'Parete.

"If Allesandra were on the throne of Firenzcia, I'd feel better about everything," Ana continued. "I'd feel there was some hope that the Holdings could be restored. If Allesandra were Hïrzgin ..." Another sigh. She looked over her shoulder at the huge, ornamental cracked globe that dominated the far corner of the room: gilded and bejeweled, with carvings of the Moitidi—the demigods who were the sons and daughters of Cénzi—writhing in agony around its base. Her voice was a half-whisper, as if she were afraid someone might overhear her. "Then I might consider opening negotiations with Semini ca'Cellibrecca, to see if the Faith could also be reunited."

Varina sucked in her breath and Ana glanced at her sympathetically. "I know, Varina," she said. "I assure you that the safety of the Numetodo would be a nonnegotiable point, even if I were willing to step aside as Archigos for Semini. I wouldn't tolerate a repeat of the persecutions."

"You couldn't trust ca'Cellibrecca to keep those promises," Varina told her. "He's his marriage-vatarh's son, all the way through."

"Ca'Cellibrecca would be bound to keep a public pledge, as well as his vows to Cénzi."

"You have more more faith in him than I do," Varina answered. That caused Ana to smile.

"Strange to hear a Numetodo speak of faith," she said, her hand reaching out to touch Varina's shoulder through her tashta. She laughed pleasantly. "But I understand your concern and your skepticism. I ask you to trust me—if it came to that, I will make certain you, Karl, and all your people are protected."

"*Will* it come to that?" Karl interjected. He'd watched Ana's hand as if wishing she were touching him. "You think there's a chance, Ana?"

She looked at the paper in her hand as if searching for an answer there, then turned to drop the scroll on a nearby table. It made little sound—a strange thing, Varina thought, for something so heavy with import. "I don't know," Ana said. "There's no love lost between Allesandra and her brother—given how long Allesandra was here with me while both of them were growing up, they're more strangers than siblings, and the way Hïrzg Jan treated Allesandra when he *did* ransom her . . ." Ana shook her head. "But I don't know what Allesandra wants anymore, or what her desires and aspirations might be. I *thought* I knew once, but . . ."

"You were a matarh to her," Karl said, and Ana laughed again.

"No, I wasn't that. Maybe an older sister or a tantzia. I tried to be someone she could be safe with, because the poor child was all alone here for far too long. I can't imagine how much that hurt her."

"You were wonderful to her," Karl persisted. Varina watched Karl's hand reach out to take Ana's. It hurt to watch the gesture. "You were."

"Thank you, but I always wonder if I could have done more, or better," Ana said. She moved her hands slowly away from his. "I did what I could. That's all Cénzi can ask, I suppose." She smiled. "We'll see what happens, won't we? I'll keep you informed if I hear any more news."

"You're still available for dinner tomorrow?" Karl asked her.

Ana's gaze slid from Karl to Varina and back. "Yes," she said. "After Third Call. Would you like to join us, Varina?"

She could feel Karl staring at her. "No," Varina said hurriedly. "I can't, Archigos. I have a meeting with Mika, and a class to teach . . ." Too many excuses, but Karl was nodding. His satisfaction at her answer was like the cut of a small blade.

"Tomorrow night, then," he said. "I'm looking forward to it. We should probably go, Varina. I'm sure the Archigos has other business. . . ." He inclined his head toward Ana and started toward the door. Varina turned to follow him, but Ana's voice called out behind them.

"Varina, a moment? Karl, I'll send her along directly, I promise." Karl glanced back, puzzled, but he bowed again and went to the doors. The two massive panels were carved with bas-reliefs of the Moitidi in battle, with swords clashing and overlapping at the join. Karl pulled and the combatants separated. Varina waited until the polished, dark wood had closed behind him and the Moitidi were once again at war.

"Archigos?"

"I wanted a moment with you, Varina, because I'm worried," Ana said. "You look so tired and so drawn. Thin. I know how caught up you've become in your . . . research. Are you remembering to eat?"

Varina touched her face. She knew what Ana was saying. She'd seen her face in the small mirror she kept on her dressing table. Her fingertips traced the new lines that had emerged in the past several months, felt the coarseness of the gray hairs at her temple. She was afraid to look in the mirror most mornings—the face that looked back at her was an older stranger she barely recognized. "I'm fine," she said reflexively.

"Are you?" Ana asked again. "These 'experiments' Karl says you're doing, attempting to recreate what Mahri could do . . ." She shook her head. "I worry about you, Varina. So does Karl."

"So does Karl . . ." She wished she could believe those words. "I'm fine," she repeated.

"I could use the Ilmodo if you'd like—it might help. If you're in pain."

"You'd disobey the Divolonté and heal me? An unbeliever? Archigos!" Varina smiled at Ana, who laughed in return.

"I can trust you to keep my secrets," Ana said. "And the offer stands, if you ever feel the need."

"Thank you, Archigos. I'll keep that in mind." She nodded her head toward the silent, battling Moitidi. "I should catch up with Karl."

"Yes, you should." Ana started to give the sign of Cénzi to Varina, then stopped herself. "I could tell him," she said.

"Archigos?"

"I have eyes. When I see you with him . . ."

Varina laughed. "You're the only one he sees, Archigos."

"And I'm bound to Cénzi," Ana said. "No one else. I'm not destined for that kind of relationship in this life. I've told him that. I treasure his friendship and all he's done for me and Nessantico. I love Karl dearly, more than I ever loved anyone else. But what he wants . . ." Her head moved slowly from side to side as her lips pressed together. "You should tell him how *you* feel."

"If I need to tell him, then it's obvious that the feeling isn't shared," Varina answered. She managed to force her lips into an upward curve. "And I'm bound to my work, as you're bound to Cénzi."

Ana stepped forward and gave Varina a quick hug. "Then Karl's a fool, for not seeing how alike we are."

Audric ca'Dakwi

EVEN A KRALJIKI could not avoid his lessons, nor the examinations designed to scrape away whatever essence of knowledge clung to the inside of his skull.

Audric stood before the Sun Throne with his hands clasped behind his back, facing his tutor, Maister ci'Blaylock. Behind the brittle, chalk-dusted stick of the maister, the audience gazed at Audric with smiling encouragement: a few chevarittai bedecked with their Blood Medals, the ca'-and-cu', the usual courtiers, Sigourney ca'Ludovici, and a few other members of the Council of Ca' ... all those who wished Audric to notice that they had attended the young Kraljiki's quarterly examination. At fourteen, Audric was all too aware of the flattering attention that came to him because of his lineage and his title.

They weren't there for the examination; they were there to be seen. By him. Only by him.

He enjoyed that thought.

"Year 471," ci'Blaylock intoned, looking up from the scroll-laden lectern at which he stood. "The line of the Kralji."

An easy one, that. No challenge at all. "Kraljica Marguerite ca'Ludovici," Audric answered quickly and firmly. He coughed then—he coughed often—and added: "Also known as the Généra a'Pace."

And also my great-matarh ... Marguerite's uneasily realistic portrait, painted by the late master artisan Edouard ci'Recroix—who had also created the large canvas of a peasant family that adorned this very Hall of the Sun Throne—hung in Audric's bedroom. Marguerite watched him every night as he slept, and gave him the same strange, weary half-smile every morning when he woke. He'd wished many times that he'd had the chance to actually know her—he'd certainly heard enough tales regarding her. He sometimes wondered if all the tales were true: in the memories of the people of Nessantico, Kraljica Mar-. guerite had presided over a Golden Age, an age of sunlight compared to the storm-wrapped politics of the present.

The court applauded politely at his answer, smiling. Most of their pleasure was undoubtedly due to the fact that they were finally nearing the end of the examination, as Maister ci'Blaylock slowly climbed the ladder of history. They'd begun—nearly half a turn of the glass ago—in Year 413 with Kraljiki Henri VI, the first year of the ca'Ludovici line from which Audric himself was descended; the onlookers had been standing the entire time since, after all, one did not sit in the presence of the Kraljiki without permission. Audric knew the answers to the few remaining questions; how could he not, being so intricately bound up in his family's life? A barely discernible sigh emanated from the court, along with a rustling of clothing as they shifted their stances. "Correct," ci'Blaylock said, sniffing. He was a dark-skinned man, as many from the province of Namarro were. He dipped the tip of his quill pen into the inkwell of the lectern and made a short, deliberate mark on the open scroll. The scratch of the pen was loud. The wings of his white eyebrows fluttered above cataract-pale eyes. "Year 485. The line of the Archigi."

Cough. "Archigos Kasim ca'Velarina." Cough.

More polite applause, and another dip and scratch of the pen.. "Correct. Year 503. The line of the Archigi."

Audric took a breath and coughed again. "Archigos Dhosti ca'Millac," he said. "The Dwarf." Applause. Pen scratch. Audric heard the far door of the hall open; Regent Sergei ca'Rudka entered, striding quickly forward to where Audric was standing. Despite his years, the Regent moved with energy and a straight bearing. The courtiers, with a cautious glance, slid quickly aside to give him room. Sergei's silver artificial nose alternately gleamed and dimmed in the shafts of failing sunlight streaming through the windows.

"Correct," ci'Blaylock intoned. "Year 521. The line of the Kralji."

That was easy: that was the year Audric's vatarh had taken the Sun Throne after Marguerite's assassination. Audric took another breath, but the effort sent him into a momentary coughing spasm: deep and filled with the

ugly sound of liquid in his lungs. Afterward, he straightened and cleared his throat. "Kraljiki Justi ca'Dakwi," he
told ci'Blaylock and the courtiers. "The Great Warrior," he
added. That was the appellation Justi had given himself. Audric had heard the other whispered names given him when
people thought no one was listening: *Justi the One-Legged;
Justi the Incompetent; Justi the Great Failure.*

Those names no one would have dared say to the Kraljiki's face while he'd been alive. Audric looked at the smiles
pasted on the faces of the ca'-and-cu' and wondered what
names they called *him* when he was not there to hear.

Audric the Ill. Audric the Regent's Puppet.

Again, applause came from the onlookers. Sergei, his
arms crossed, didn't join them. He watched from just behind Maister ci'Blaylock, who seemed to feel the pressure
of the man's presence. He glanced once over his shoulder
at the Regent and shivered visibly. "Umm . . ." The old man
shook his head, glanced at the scroll, then plunged an ink-
stained forefinger toward it. "Year 521," he said. "The line
of the Archigi."

That one was a longer answer but still easy. "Archigos
Orlandi ca'Cellibrecca. The Great Traitor and first false
Archigos of Brezno." Audric coughed again, pausing to
clear his throat. "Then the same year, after ca'Cellibrecca
betrayed the Concénzia Faith and Kraljiki Justi at Passe
a'Fiume, Archigos Ana ca'Seranta, the youngest téni ever
named Archigos."

Ana, who still held the title of Archigos. Ana, whom Audric loved as if she were the matarh he'd never known. Audric smiled at the mention of her name, and the applause
that came then was genuine—Archigos Ana was well and
truly loved by the people of Nessantico.

"Correct," ci'Blaylock said. "Very good. Also Year 521.
War and politics."

"The Rebellion of Hïrzg Jan ca'Vörl," Audric answered
quickly. The guttural Firenzcian syllables sent his lungs
into spasm again. It took several breaths to stop them and
manage to talk again. "The Hïrzg was defeated by Kraljiki
Justi at the Battle of the Fens," he managed to croak out,
finally.

"Excellent!" The voice was not ci'Blaylock's but Sergei's,
as he applauded loudly and strode out to stand alongside

Audric. The courtiers joined the applause belatedly and uncertainly. Sigourney ca'Ludovici, Audric noticed, didn't applaud at all, only crossed her arms and glared. "Maister ci'Blaylock, I'm sure you've heard enough to make your judgment," Sergei continued.

Ci'Blayblock frowned. "Regent, I wasn't quite fin—" He stopped, and Audric saw him staring at the Regent's frown. He laid down the quill and started to roll up the testing scroll. "Yes, that was very satisfactory," he said. "Well done, Kraljiki, as always."

"Good," Sergei said. "Now, if all of you will excuse us . . ."

The Regent's dismissal was abrupt but effective. Maister ci'Blaylock gathered up his scrolls and limped toward the nearest door; the courtiers drifted away like tendrils of fog on a sunny morning, smiling until they turned their backs. Audric could hear their furious whispering speculations as they left the hall. Sigourney, however, paused. "Is this something the Council of Ca' should know?" she asked Sergei. She wasn't looking at Audric; it was as if he weren't important enough to be noticed.

Sergei shook his head. "Not at the moment, Councillor ca'Ludovici," he said. "If it becomes so, be assured that I will let you know immediately."

Sigourney sniffed at that, but she nodded to Sergei and bowed the proper obeisance to Audric before leaving the hall. Only a few servants remained, standing silently by the tapestry-hung stone walls, while two e-téni—priests of the Concénzia Faith—whispered prayers as they lit the lamps against the dying light. On the wall near the Sun Throne, the faces of the peasant family in ci'Recroix's painting seemed to shiver in the light of the téni-fire.

"Thank you, Sergei," Audric said. He hacked again, covering his mouth with a fisted hand. "You could have come half a turn of the glass earlier, though, and saved me the whole ordeal."

Sergei grinned. "And face the wrath of Maister ci'Blaylock? Not likely." He paused a moment, and the lines of his face went serious around the metal nose. "I would have been here earlier to hear your examination, Kraljiki, but I've just received a message from a contact in Firenzcia. There's news, and I thought you should hear it before the Council: Hïrzg Jan of Firenzcia is on his deathbed. He's not expected to live out the week. It may be that he's dead already—the message was days old."

"So A'Hïrzg Fynn will become the new Hïrzg? Or will Allesandra fight her brother's ascension?"

Sergei's grin returned momentarily. "Ah, so you *do* pay attention to my briefings. Good. That's far more important than Maister ci'Blaylock's lessons." He shook his head. "I doubt Allesandra will protest. She doesn't have enough backing from the ca'-and-cu' of Firenzcia to contest Hïrzg Jan's will."

"Which of the two would *we* prefer?"

"Our own preference would be Allesandra, Kraljiki—after the decade and more she spent here waiting for Hïrzg Jan to ransom her, we know her far better. Archigos Ana always had a good relationship with her, and Allesandra is far more sympathetic to the Holdings. If she became Hïrzgin . . . well, maybe there would be some hope of reconciliation between the Holdings and the Coalition. There might even be a faint possibility that we could return things to the way they were in your great-matarh's time, with you on the Sun Throne under a reunited Holdings. But with Fynn as Hïrzg . . ." Again, Sergei shook his head. "He is his vatarh's son, just as bellicose and stubborn. If he's Hïrzg, we'll have to watch our eastern border closely—which will mean less resources we can spare for the war in the Hellins, unfortunately."

Audric bent over with another coughing fit, and Sergei placed a gentle hand on his shoulder. "Your cough is worsening again, Kraljiki," he said. "I'll have the healers make another potion for you, and perhaps we'll have Archigos Ana see you tomorrow after the Day of Return ceremony. It's a little early, but with the rains last month . . ."

"I'm better now," Audric told him. "It's just the damp air here in the hall." The nearest e'téni had stopped her chant, her hands frozen in the middle of shaping the Ilmodo—the energy that fueled their magic. She was a young woman not much older than Audric; she blushed when she saw that Audric had noticed her, looked quickly away, and began her chant anew: the lamp set high on the wall bloomed into light as her hands waved in the Ilmodo patterns under it.

Audric's chest was beginning to ache with the racking coughs. He hated being ill, but it seemed he was often sick. He'd been that way from the very beginning of his memories. If an illness were passing through the staff of the palais, he was certain to catch it; he was constantly assailed by coughing fits, by difficulty in breathing. Any physical exertion left him quickly exhausted and gasping. Yet somehow Cénzi had protected him from the outbreak of Southern Fever when he was four, though the illness had taken his older sister Marguerite, named for her famous great-matarh and primed to be the Kraljica on their vatarh's death. Her state funeral—a long and somber ceremony—was one of his earliest memories.

It should be Marguerite standing here now, not him. Audric hoped this meant Cénzi had a plan for him.

He drew in a long breath and this time held back the cough that threatened. "There, you see," he told Sergei. "Just the damp, and having to answer all the Maister's damnable questions."

"At least the maister's questions have definite answers. The solutions for a Kraljiki are rarely so clear-cut, as you already know." Sergei put his arm around Audric, and Audric leaned into the man's embrace. *"Trust ca'Rudka as your Regent,"* his vatarh had whispered as he lay on his bed during that final day. *"Trust him as you would me . . ."*

The truth was that Audric had never quite trusted his vatarh, whose temperament and favor had been erratic at best. But Sergei . . . Audric felt that his vatarh had made a final good choice with the man. Yes, he might chafe under the Regent's hand more and more as he approached his majority, he might be irritated that people at times treated Sergei as if he were the Kraljiki, but Audric could not have asked for a more loyal ally in the chaotic winds of the Kraljiki's court.

It didn't matter to him what the whispers of the courtiers said about the Regent. It didn't matter what the man did in the dungeons of the Bastida, or with the grandes horizontales he sometimes took to his bed.

"I suppose we must draft a statement for the Hïrzg's death," Audric said. "And we must listen to ten different councillors requesting that we respond in twenty different ways. Then ten more advisers to tell us what we need to do about the Hellins in the west."

Sergei laughed. His arm tightened around Audric's shoulder, then released him. He rubbed at his silver nose as if it itched him. "No doubt," he answered. " I would say that you have learned all your lessons very well, Kraljiki."

~

Sergei ca'Rudka

HIS AUGUST PRESENCE, the Kraljiki Audric, hunched in his padded, elevated seat alongside Sergei, coughing so desperately that Sergei leaned over to the boy. "Do you need some of the healer's draught, Kraljiki? I'll have one of the attendants bring it over . . ." He started to gesture, but Audric caught his arm.

"Wait, Sergei. This will pass." Audric said it in three breaths. *Wait, Sergei (breath) This will (breath) pass. . . .* Just the effort of grabbing Sergei's arm visibly tired the boy.

Sergei rubbed at the polished surface of the false nose glued to his face, his original nose lost long decades ago in a youthful sword fight. "Would you prefer to return to the palais, Kraljiki?" Sergei asked. "The smoke from the censers and the incense can't be good for your lungs, and the Archigos will understand. In any case, she'll be over to see you as soon as she's finished here."

"We'll stay, Sergei. This is where I should be." *We'll stay (breath) Sergei (cough breath cough). This is (breath) where I (breath) should be. . . .*

Sergei nodded. In that, the boy was right. The two were seated in the royal balcony of the Archigos' Temple, on the South Bank of the River A'Sele in Nessantico. Below, the main floor of the temple was packed with worshipers for the Day of Return. Archigos Ana stood with several of the a'téni in the quire of the Temple, her hair—streaked with bright, gray-white strands at the temples—gleaming in the glow of the téni lamps, her strong, fierce voice reciting the lines from the Toustour. The Day of Return was the Spring solstice ceremony, preparing the faithful for the eventual return of Cénzi to the world He had created. It was the duty of Kraljiki Audric to attend, which was why the temple was crowded to its very sides with the chevarittai, with the ca'-and-cu', with those lesser-ranked families who could cram into the remaining space, all of them there to catch a glimpse of the young Kraljiki and perhaps to also catch *his* eye: for a request, for a petition, or perhaps because he was not yet officially betrothed to anyone despite the persistent rumors that the Regent intended to make arrangements soon with one of the great families of the Holdings.

They also would have noted the Kraljiki's deep, barking coughs punctuating the Archigos' reading. Even Archigos Ana stopped once in the midst of her recitation to glance up with concern and sympathy toward their balcony. She nodded almost imperceptibly to Sergei, and he knew that she would hurry to the palais after the ceremony. Sergei leaned over again, whispering into the boy's ear. "The Archigos has promised to come by after we're done here and pray for you. She always helps you, I know. You can endure this, knowing you'll feel better soon."

Audric nodded wide-eyed, muffling another cough with a perfumed handkerchief. Sergei wondered if Audric knew—as Sergei did—that the reason the Archigos' "prayers" helped him so dramatically was because, against the laws of the Divolonté that governed the Concénzia Faith, Ana used her skills with the magic of the Ilmodo to heal Audric's ravaged lungs. This was something she had done since soon after Audric's birth, when it was apparent that the boy's life was in jeopardy. She had done much the same for Audric's great-matarh, the much-lamented Kraljica Marguerite, in her last days, keeping her alive when without intervention she would have died.

It had been a month since Archigos Ana's last visit for that purpose; it was obvious that the illness in the boy was returning once more: as it always, inevitably, did. Audric folded the handkerchief and put it back in his bashta; Sergei saw flecks of red caught in the linen. He said nothing, but decided he would send word to Ana that they would instead meet her immediately after the service, in her chambers here. The boy needed attention quickly.

Sergei sat back in his chair as Archigos Ana strode toward the High Lectern for her Admonition to the gathering, as the choir in their loft began a Darkmavis hymn. The ca'-and-cu' stirred in their finery. Sergei could see Karl ca'Vliomani standing near the side of the Temple, lifting his hand to Sergei in acknowledgment—ca'Vliomani, the Ambassador of the Isle of Paeti and of the Numetodo Sect, wasn't a believer but Sergei knew that the Ambassador and Archigos Ana had been, if not actual lovers, then friends and confidants since before the Battle of the Fens twenty-four years ago. During that battle, the young Archigos Ana had used both the Numetodo and her own magic to snatch A'Hïrzg Allesandra of Firenzcia from her vatarh and hold her as hostage against the Hïrzg's retreat. The plan had worked, though Firenzcia and her neighboring countries had seceded from the Holdings in the wake of the hostilities to form the Firenzcian Coalition.

Sergei found himself wondering, again, whether Ana's defeat of the Firenzcian forces had truly been the triumph they had all thought it to be, whether it might not have been better for the Holdings had Hïrzg Jan taken the city and become Kraljiki. Had that occurred, both Ana and Sergei himself would be dead, but in all probability there would be only the Holdings and no rival Coalition. There would be only one Concénzia Faith. Had that occurred, then the new Kraljiki could have dealt with the Westlanders' uprising in the Hellins fully, with all the resources of the Garde Civile and without having to worry about what might happen to the east.

Had that occurred, then Justi the One-Legged Fool would never have become Kraljiki and Audric never his heir, and Nessantico would be flourishing, not languishing.

Sergei, frankly, had never expected Archigos Ana to be able to retain her title—she had been too young and naïve, but the fire of the Battle of the Fens had tempered the steel within her. She had proved stronger than any of the a'téni who might have tried to take her place, stronger than her rival Archigos in Brezno, and certainly stronger than Kraljiki Justi, who had believed he could control the Faith through her.

In the end, Justi had been able to dominate nothing: not Ana, not the Faith, not the Holdings. While Ana showed herself to be surprisingly successful as Archigos, Justi had been a catastrophe as Kraljiki.

Justi the One-Legged squandered in two decades what it had taken his matarh and the Kralji before her more than five centuries to create, and we are left to pay for his incompetence with both the Holdings and the Faith sundered into East and West factions. And now the troubles in the Hellins

compound the issue while we have a boy on the Sun Throne
who may not live to sire an heir himself.

Sergei sighed, closing his eyes as he listened to the choir.
He would go to the Bastida tomorrow morning, and he
would assuage his worries with pain. He'd find solace in
screams. Yes, that would be good. The ending chords floated
glistening in his mind, and he heard the Archigos step onto
the stairs of the High Lectern.

Sergei would remember the next moment for the remainder of his life.

There was a ferocious, impossible light—as if Cénzi
had sent a lightning bolt from the heavens through the
gilded dome above. The harsh glare penetrated Sergei's
closed eyelids; a thunder roared in his ears and the concussion pounded at his chest. Instinctively, Sergei hurled
himself over Audric, knocking the boy to the floor of the
balcony and covering the Kraljiki's body with his own. His
aging joints protested at the sudden movement and the
abuse. He could hear Audric gasping for breath; he could
also hear the screams and wails from below, pierced by
Karl ca'Vliomani's stricken, horrified shout ringing above
them all: "Ana! *Ana!* Nooooooo!"

"Kraljiki! Regent!" Hands pulled at Sergei, lifting him—
a quartet of the Garde Kralji, whose job it was to protect
the Kraljiki and the Regent. Dust clouded the air inside the
temple and Sergei blinked against the grit, barely able to
breathe himself. He could hear the desperate coughing of
Audric. The temple stank of sulfur and brimstone.

"You, and you—escort the Kraljiki from here and back
to the palais immediately," Sergei said, jabbing his fingers
at the gardai. "You two, come with me."

Sergei hurried down the forward stairs of the balcony,
flanked by the gardai with swords drawn pushing aside
those who were in their way. People were screaming and
yelling, and he could hear the moans and shrill cries of the
wounded. Sergei was forced to limp, his right knee sore and
swelling rapidly; it took him far too long to navigate the
stairs, clutching at the railing with each step. Below, everything was confusion.

"Regent! Here!" Aris cu'Falla, the Commandant of
the Garde Kralji, gestured over heads to Sergei as gardai
pushed at the crowds. The din of pain and grief was enor-

mous, and Sergei noted many bloodied faces and arms. The front of the temple was littered with cracked stone and splintered wood; he glimpsed several bodies in the rubble.

One of the bodies wore the Archigos' robes. Sergei's breath left him, to be replaced by a cold, icy rage. "Commandant, what happened here?"

Cu'Falla shook his head. "I don't know, Regent. Not yet. I was watching the ceremony from near the rear of the temple. When the Archigos came to the High Lectern ... I've never seen anything like that, Regent. It was a spell of some sort, almost certainly, but like something a war-téni would do. The flash, the noise, the stone and wood and ..." He frowned. "... other things flying everywhere. The blast seems to have come from underneath the High Lectern. There are at least half a dozen dead, and far more injured, some of them badly. ..."

Groaning at the pain in his knee, the Regent crouched next to Ana's body. Her face was nearly unrecognizable, the lower half of her body and her right arm entirely gone. He knew immediately that she was dead, that there was no hope here. An odd black dust coated the floor around her. Sergei turned his head away to see Karl ca'Vliomani being held back by the gardai, his face panicked, his bashta coated with dust. Sergei pushed himself slowly to his feet again, grimacing as his knees cracked. "Cover her and the other bodies," he told cu'Falla. "Clear the temple of everyone but the téni and gardai. Send for Commandant cu'Ulcai of the Garde Civile if you need more help." He released a long, shuddering breath. "And let the Ambassador through to me."

Cu'Falla nodded and called out orders. Ca'Vliomani immediately darted toward Ana's body, and Sergei moved to intercept him. "No," he told Karl, clutching his shoulders. "She's gone, Karl. There's nothing you can do. Nothing."

He felt the man sag, heard him sob once. "Sergei, I have to see her. Please. I have to *know*." His eyes were stricken, and he looked suddenly decades older. His Paeti accent, which the Ambassador had never lost despite his years in Nessantico, was stronger now than ever.

"No, you don't, my friend," Sergei persisted. "Please listen to me. You don't want this to be the last image you have of her. You don't want that. Truly. I say that for your own sake."

Ca'Vliomani started to weep, then, and Sergei held him as the gardai moved around them, as téni of the temple—silent in their shock and horror—went to tend to the wounded and the dead, as the dark dust settled around and on them, as the roar of the spell echoed eternally in Sergei's ears.

He didn't think he would ever forget that sound, and he wondered what it heralded: for himself, for Audric, for the Concénzia Faith, for Nessantico.

~

Nico Morel

NICO SIPPED AT THE TEA that his matarh placed in front of him, holding the wooden mug with both small hands. "Matarh, why would someone want to kill Archigos Ana?"

"I don't know, Nico," she answered. She set a slice of bread and a few hunks of cheese before him on the scarred table near the window. She brushed wisps of brown hair from her forehead, staring through the open shutters to the narrow street outside. "I don't know," she said again. "I just hope . . ."

"You hope what, Matarh?"

She shook her head. "Nothing, Nico. Go on, eat."

They'd attended the Day of Return ceremony at Temple Park, a long walk from their apartment in Oldtown. Nico always enjoyed it when they went to Temple Park, since the open, green space was such a contrast to the crowded, dirty streets in the maze of Oldtown. Just as they were leaving the park, they heard the wind-horns start to blow, and then the rumors had gone through the crowds like a fire in a summer-dry field: the Archigos had been killed. By magic, some of them said. Awful magic, like the heretic Numetodo could do, or maybe a war-téni.

Nico had cried a little because everyone else was crying, and his matarh looked worried. They'd hurried home.

Once, Matarh had taken Nico across the Pontica Mordei to the Isle a'Kralji, and he'd seen the grounds of the Regent's palais and the Old Temple, the first one built in Nessantico. He'd marveled at the new dome being built on top of the Old Temple, with the lines of scaffolding holding the workers so impossibly high up in the sky. It made Nico dizzy just to look at them.

Afterward, they'd even gone over the Pontica a'Brezi Nippoli to the South Bank, where most of the ca'-and-cu' lived. He'd walked with Matarh through the grand complex of the Archigos' Temple and glimpsed the Archigos herself: a tiny figure in green at one of the windows of the buildings attached to the massive temple, waving to the throngs in the plaza.

Now she was dead. That was easy enough to imagine. Death was utterly common; he saw it often in the streets and had watched it come to his own family. Matarh said that Ana had been Archigos since she'd been a baby, and Matarh was twenty-eight years old—practically ancient, so it was hardly a surprise that the Archigos would die. Nico could barely remember his gremma, who had died when he was five. Maybe Gremma had been as old as Archigos Ana. Nico could remember his older brother fairly well, who had died of the Southern Fever four years ago. Matarh said there'd been another, even older brother who had also died, but Nico didn't really remember him at all. There was Fiona, his sister who had been born first—he didn't know if she was still alive, though he always imagined that she was; she'd run away when she was twelve, almost three years ago now. Talis had been living with them—Talis had been living with Matarh ever since Nico could remember, but Fiona had told him that hadn't always been the way it was, that there'd been another man before Talis who had been Fiona's vatarh and the vatarh of his brothers. She said that Talis was Nico's vatarh, but Talis never wanted Nico to call him that.

Nico missed Fiona. He sometimes imagined that Fiona had gone to another city and become rich. He liked to think of that, sometimes. He dreamed of her coming back to Nessantico with a ce' or even a ci' before her name, and he'd open the door to see her wearing a tashta that was clean and brightly colored as she smiled at him. "Nico," she'd say. "You, Matarh, and Talis are going to come and live with me . . ."

Maybe Nico would leave home when he was twelve, too—two years from now. Nico could see the deep lines in Matarh's face as she stared out toward the street. The hair at her temples was streaked with white strands. "Are you watching for Talis?" he asked.

He saw her frown, then smile as she turned her head to him. "You just eat, darling," she said. "Don't worry about Talis. He'll be along soon enough."

Nico nodded, gnawing on the hard crust of the nearly stale bread and trying to avoid the loose back molar that was threatening to fall out, the last of his baby teeth. He wasn't worried about Talis, only the tooth. He didn't want to lose it, since if he did Matarh would make him smash it with a hammer and grind it up, and that was a lot of work. When he was done, she would help him sprinkle the powder onto some milk-moistened bread, and they'd put the bread outside the window next to his bed. At night, he'd hear the rats and mice eating the offering, scurrying around outside. In the morning, the dish would be empty; Matarh said that meant that his new teeth would grow in as strong as a rat's.

He'd seen what rats could do with their teeth. They could strip the meat from a dead cat in hours. He hoped his teeth would be that strong. He reached into his mouth with a forefinger and wiggled the tooth, feeling it rocking easily back and forth in his gums. If he pushed hard, it would come out. . . .

"Serafina?"

Nico heard Talis call out for his matarh. Matarh ran to him, and they embraced as he shut the door behind him. "I was worried," Matarh said. "When I heard about . . ."

"Shh . . ." he said, kissing her forehead. His gaze was on Nico, watching them. "Hey, Nico. Did your matarh take you to Temple Park today?"

"Yes," Nico said. He went over to them, sidling close to his matarh so that her arm went around him. He wrinkled his nose, staring up at the man. "You smell funny, Talis," he said.

"Nico—" his matarh began, but Talis laughed and ruffled Nico's hair. Nico hated when he did that.

"It's all right, Serafina," Talis said. "You can't fault the boy for being honest." Talis didn't talk the way other people did in Oldtown; he pronounced his words strangely, as if his tongue didn't like the taste of the syllables and so he spat them out as quickly as possible instead of letting them linger the way most people did. Talis crouched down near Nico. "I walked by a fire on the way here," he said. "Lots of nasty smoke. The fire-téni put it out, though."

Nico nodded, but he thought that Talis didn't smell like smoke exactly. The odor was sharper and harsher. "Archigos Ana died, Talis," he said instead.

"That's what I've heard," Talis answered. "The Regent will be scouring the city, looking for a scapegoat to blame it on. It's time for foreigners to lay low if they want to stay safe." He seemed to be talking more to Nico's matarh than to Nico, his eyes glancing up toward her.

"Talis . . ." Matarh breathed his name, the way she sometimes called out Nico's name when he was sick or he'd hurt himself. Talis stood up again, hugging Nico's matarh. "It will be fine, Sera," he heard Talis whisper to her. "I promise you."

Listening to him, Nico pushed at the loose tooth with his tongue. He heard a tiny *pop* and tasted blood.

"Matarh," Nico said, "my tooth came out . . ."

~

Allesandra ca'Vörl

"**M**ATARH?"

Allesandra heard the call, followed by a tentative knock. Her son Jan was standing at the open door. At fifteen, almost sixteen, he was stick-thin and gawky. In just the past several months, his body had started to morph into that of a young man, with a fine down of hair on his chin and under his arms. He was still several fingers shorter than the girls of the same age, most of whom had reached their menarche the year before. Named for her vatarh, she could glimpse some of his features in her son, but there was a strong strain of the ca'Xielt family in him as well—Pauli's family. Jan had the duskier skin coloring of the Magyarians, and his vatarh's dark eyes and curly, nearly black hair. She doubted that he would ever have the heavier ca'Belgradin musculature of his uncle Fynn, which Allesandra's great-vatarh Karin and vatarh Jan had also possessed.

She sometimes had difficulty imagining him galloping madly into battle—though he could ride as well as any, and had keen sight that an archer would envy. Still, he often seemed more comfortable with scrolls and books than swords. And despite his parentage, despite the act (purely of duty) that had produced him, despite the surliness and barely hidden anger that seemed to consume him lately, she loved him more than she had thought it possible to love anyone.

And she worried, in the last year especially, that she was losing him, that he might be falling under Pauli's influence. Pauli had been absent through most of Jan's life, but maybe that was Pauli's advantage: it was easier to dislike the parent who was always correcting you, and to admire the one who let you do whatever you wanted. There'd been that incident with the staff girl, and Allesandra had needed to send her away—*that* was too much like Pauli.

"Come in, darling," she said, beckoning to him.

Jan nodded without smiling, went to the dressing table where she sat, and touched his lips to the top of her head—the barest shadow of a kiss—as the women helping her dress drifted away silently. "Onczio Fynn sent me to fetch you," he said. "Evidently it's time." A pause. "And evidently I'm little better than a servant to him. Just Magyarian chattel to be sent on errands."

"Jan!" she said sharply. She gestured with her eyes to her maidservants. They were all West Magyarians, part of the entourage that had come with Jan from Malacki.

He shrugged, uncaring. "Are you coming, Matarh, or are you going to send me back to Fynn with your own response like a good little messenger boy?"

You can't respond here the way you want to. Not where everything we say could become court gossip tonight. "I'm nearly ready, Jan," she said, gesturing. "We'll go down together, since you're here." The servants returned, one brushing her hair, another placing a pearl necklace that had once been her matarh Greta's around her neck, and yet another adjusting the folds of her tashta. She handed another necklace to her dressing girl: a cracked globe on a fine chain, the continents gold, the seas purest lapiz lazuli, the rent in the globe filled with rubies in its depths—Cénzi's globe. Archigos Ana had given her the necklace when she'd reached her own menarche, in Nessantico.

"It belonged to Archigos Dhosti once," Ana had told her. *"He gave it to me; now I give it to you."* Allesandra touched the globe as the servant fastened it around her neck and remembered Ana: the sound of her voice, the smell of her.

"Everyone keeps telling me how Onczio Fynn will make a fine Hïrzg," Jan said, interrupting the memory.

"I know," Allesandra began. *And why would you expect anything else?* she wanted to add. Jan knew the etiquette of court well enough to understand that.

He evidently saw the unspoken remark in her face. "I wasn't finished. I was going to say that you would make a better one. You should be the one wearing the golden band and the ring, Matarh."

"Hush," she told him again, though more gently this time. The maidservants were her own, true, but one never knew. Secrets could be bought, or coaxed out through love, or forced through pain. "We're not at home, Jan. You must remember that. Especially here . . ."

His sullen frown melted for a moment, and he looked so apologetic that all her irritation melted, and she stroked his arm. It was that way with him too much of late: scowls one moment and warm smiles the next. However, the scowls were coming more frequently as the loving child in him retreated ever deeper into his new adolescent shell. "It's fine, Jan," she told him. "Just . . . well, you must be very careful while we're here. Always." *And especially with Fynn.* She tucked the thought away. She would tell him later. Privately. She stood, and the servants fell away like autumn leaves. She hugged Jan; he allowed the gesture but nothing more, his own arms barely moving. "All right, we'll go down now. Remember that you are the son of the A'Gyula of West Magyaria, and also the son of the current A'Hïrzg of Firenzcia."

Fynn-had given her the title yesterday, after their vatarh had died: the title that should have been hers all along, that would have made her Hïrzgin. She knew that even that gift was temporary, that Fynn would name someone else A'Hïrzg in time: his own child, perhaps, if he ever married and produced an heir, or some court favorite. Allesandra would be Fynn's heir only until he found one he liked better.

"Matarh," Jan interrupted. He gave a too-loud huff of air, and the frown returned. "I know the lecture. 'The eyes and ears of the ca'-and-cu' will be on you.' I know. You don't have to tell me. Again."

Allesandra wished she believed that. "All right," she breathed. "Let us go down, then, and be with the new Hïrzg as we lay your great-vatarh to his rest."

With the death of Hïrzg Jan, the required month of mourning had been proclaimed, and a dozen necessary ceremonies scheduled. The new Hïrzg Fynn would preside over several rituals in the next few weeks: some only for the ca'-and-cu', some for the edification of the public. The formal Besteigung, the final ritual, would take place at the end of the month in Brezno Temple with Archigos Semini presiding—timed so that the leaders of the other countries of the Firenzcian Coalition could make their way to

Brezno and pay homage to the new Hïrzg. Allesandra had already been told that A'Gyula Pauli would be arriving for the Besteigung, at least—she was already dreading her husband's arrival.

And tonight . . . tonight was the Internment.

The Kralji burned their dead; the Hïrzgai entombed theirs. Hïrzg Jan's body was to be buried in the vault of the ca'Belgradins where several generations of their ancestors lay, a hand or more of them having shared with Jan the golden band that now circled Fynn's forehead. Fynn was waiting for them in his own chambers; from there they would go down to the vaults below the ground floor of Brezno Palais. The Chevarittai of the Red Lancers and others of the nobility of Firenzcia were already waiting for them there.

The halls of the palais were hushed, the servants they saw stopped in their tasks and bowed silently with lowered eyes as they passed. Two gardai stood outside Fynn's chambers; they opened the doors for them as they approached. Allesandra could hear voices from inside as they entered.

". . . just received the news from Gairdi. This will complicate things. We don't know exactly how much yet—" Archigos Semini ca'Cellibrecca stopped in mid-phrase as Allesandra and Jan entered the room. The man had always put Allesandra in mind of a bear, all the way back to when she'd been a child and he a rising young war-téni: even as a young man, Semini had been massive and furred and dangerous. His black beard was now salted with white, and the mass of curly hair was receding from his forehead like a slow tide, but he was still burly and muscled. He gave them the sign of Cénzi, clasping his hands to his forehead as his wife Francesca did the same behind him. Allesandra had been told that Francesca had once been a beauty—in fact, there were rumors that she'd once been the lover of Justi the One-Legged—but Allesandra hadn't known her at that time. Now, she was a humpbacked matron with several of her teeth missing, her body ravaged by the rigors of a dozen pregnancies over the years. Her personality was as sour as her face.

Fynn rose from his chair.

"Sister," he said, taking her hands as he stood in front of her. He was smiling—he seemed almost gleeful. "Semini has just brought some interesting news from Nessantico. Archigos Ana has been assassinated."

Allesandra gasped, unable to hide her reaction. Her hands went to the cracked globe pendant around her neck, then she forced herself to lower them. She felt as if she couldn't catch her breath. "Assassinated? By whom . . . ?" She stopped, glancing at Semini—who was also smiling; almost smugly, Allesandra thought—then at her brother. "Did *we* do this?" she asked. Her voice was as edged as a dagger. She felt Jan put his hand on her shoulder from behind, sensing her distress.

Fynn snorted. "Would it matter?" he asked.

"Yes," Allesandra told him. "Only a fool would think otherwise." The words came out before she could stop them. *And after I just cautioned Jan . . .*

Fynn glowered at the implied insult. Jan's hand tightened on Allesandra's shoulder. Semini cleared his throat loudly before Fynn could speak.

"This wasn't the Hïrzg's doing, Allesandra," Semini answered quickly, shaking his head and waving his hand in dismissal. "Firenzcia may be at odds with the Faith in Nessantico, but the Hïrzg doesn't engage in assassination. Nor does the Faith."

She looked from Semini to Francesca. The woman looked away quickly but made no attempt to hide the satisfaction in her face. Her pleasure at the news was obvious. The woman had all the warmth of a Boail winter. Allesandra wondered whether Semini had ever felt any affection for her, or whether their marriage was as loveless and calculated as her own despite their several children. Allesandra couldn't imagine submitting to Pauli's pleasure so often. "We're certain this report is true?" she asked Semini.

"It's come to me from three different sources, one I trust implicitly—the trader Gairdi—and they all agree on the basic details," Semini told her. "Archigos Ana was performing the Day of Return service when there was an explosion. 'Like a war-téni's spell,' they all said—which means it was someone using the Ilmodo. That much is certain."

"Which also means they may look eastward to us," Fynn said. He seemed eager at the thought, as if anxious to call the army of Firenzcia into battle. That would be like him;

Allesandra would be terrifically surprised if Fynn's reign were to be a peaceful one.

"Or they will look to the west," Allesandra argued, and Fynn glanced at her as he might an annoying, persistent insect. "Nessantico has enemies there as well, and they can use the Ilmodo also, even if—like the Numetodo—they have their own name for it."

"The Westlanders? Like the Numetodo, they're heretics deserving of death," Semini spat. "They abuse Cénzi's gift, which is intended only for the téni, and we will one day make them pay for their insult, if Nessantico fails to do so."

Fynn grunted his agreement with the sentiment, and Allesandra saw her son Jan nodding as well—that was also his damned vatarh's influence, or at least that of the Magyarian téni Pauli had insisted educate their son despite Allesandra's misgivings. She pressed her lips together.

Ana is dead. She placed her fingers on the necklace of the cracked globe, feeling its smooth, jeweled surface. The touch brought up again the memory of Ana's face, of the lopsided smile that would touch the woman's lips when something amused her, of the grim lines that set themselves around her eyes when she was angry. Allesandra had spent a decade with the woman; captor, friend, and surrogate matarh all at once for her during the long years that she'd spent as a hostage of Nessantico. Allesandra's feelings toward Ana were as complex and contradictory as their relationship had been. They were nearly as conflicted as her feelings toward her vatarh, who had left her languishing in Nessantico while Fynn became the A'Hïrzg and favorite.

She wanted to cry at the news, in sadness for someone who had treated her well and fairly when there had been no compulsion for her to do so. But she could not. Not here. Not in front of people who hated the woman. Here, she had to pretend.

Later. Later I can mourn her properly. . . .

"I expected somewhat more reaction from you, Sister," Fynn said. "After all, that abomination of a woman and the one-legged pretender kept you captive. Vatarh cursed whenever anyone spoke her name; said she was no better than a witch."

Fynn was watching her, and they both knew what he was leaving out of his comment: that Hïrzg Jan could have ransomed her at any time during those years, that had he done so it was likely that the golden band would be on her head, not Fynn's. *"You won't be here half a year,"* Ana had told Allesandra in those first months. *"Kraljiki Justi has set a fair ransom, and your vatarh will pay it. Soon . . ."*

But, for whatever reasons, Hïrzg Jan had not.

Allesandra made her face a mask. *You won't cry. You won't let them see the grief.* It wasn't difficult; it was what she did often enough, and it served her well most of the time. She knew what the ca'-and-cu' called her behind her back: *the Stone Bitch.* "Ana ca'Seranta's death is important. I appreciate Archigos Semini bringing us the news, and we should—we must—decide what it means for Firenzcia," she said, "but we won't know the full implications for weeks yet. And right now Vatarh is waiting for us. I suggest we see to him first."

The Tombs of the Hïrzgai were catacombs below Brezno Palais, not the lower levels of the newer private estate outside the city known as Stag Fall, built in Hïrzg Karin's time. A long, wide stairway led down to the Tombs, a crust of niter coating the sweating walls and growing like white pustules on the faces in the murals painted there two centuries before and restored a dozen times since: the damp always won over pigments. A chill, nearly fetid air rose from below, as if warning them that the realm of the dead was approaching. The torches alight in their sconces held back the darkness but rendered the shadows of the occasional side passage blacker and more mysterious in contrast. A dozen generations of the Hïrzgai awaited them below, with their various spouses and many of their direct offspring. Allesandra's older brother Toma had been interred here when Allesandra was but a baby, and her matarh Greta had lain alongside him for nineteen years now. In time, Allesandra herself might join her family, though an eternity spent next to Matarh Greta was not a pleasant thought.

The procession moved in stately silence down the staircase: in front the e'téni with lanterns lit by green téni-fire, then Hïrzg Fynn accompanied by Archigos Semini and Francesca, and Allesandra and Jan a few steps behind them, followed by a final group of servants and e'téni. As they approached the intricately carved entranceway to the tombs, decorated with bas-reliefs of the historical accomplishments of the Hïrzgai, Allesandra could hear whisperings and the rustling of cloth and an occasional cough or sneeze: the ca'-and-cu' who had been invited to witness the ceremony. These were the elite of Firenzcia, most of them relatives of Fynn and Allesandra: families who were intertwined and intermarried with their own, or those who had served for decades with Hïrzg Jan.

Torchlight and téni light together slid over the coiled bodies of fantastic creatures carved on the walls, the stern features of carved Hïrzgai and the broken bodies of enemies at their feet. The Chevarittai of the Red Lancers came to attention, their lances (the blades masked in scarlet cloth) clashing against polished dress armor. The other ca'-and-cu' bowed low and the whispers faded to silence as the new Hïrzg entered the large chamber. Allesandra could see their glances slide from Fynn to her, and to Jan as well. Jan noticed the attention; she felt him stiffen at her side with an intake of breath. She nodded to them—the slightest movement of her head, the faintest hint of a smile.

Look at her, as cold as this chamber . . . It was what they would be thinking, some of them. *She's no doubt pleased to see old Jan dead after he left her with the Kraljiki and the false Archigos for so long. She probably wishes Fynn were there with him so she could be the Hïrzgin.*

None of them knew her. None of them knew what her true thoughts were. For that matter, she wasn't entirely certain she knew them herself. She was still reeling from the news about Ana, and if she showed signs of grief, it was for her, not her vatarh.

The casket containing the remains of Hïrzg Jan sat near the entrance to his interment chamber, next to the huge round stone that would seal off the niche. The coffin was draped in a tapestry cloth that depicted his victory over the T'Sha at Lake Cresci. There was nothing celebrating Passe a'Fiume or Jan's bold, foolish attack on Nessantico a decade before: those days when Allesandra had ridden with him, when she'd watched her vatarh adoringly, when he'd promised to give her the city of Nessantico.

Instead, Nessantico had snatched her from him and given Fynn the place at her vatarh's right hand.

Fynn saluted the lancers, who relaxed their stances.

"I would like to thank everyone for being here," he said. "I know Vatarh is looking down from the arms of Cénzi, appreciating this tribute to him. And I also know that he would forgive us for not lingering here when warm fires and food await us above." Fynn received quiet laughter at that, and he smiled. "Archigos, if you would . . ."

Semini moved quickly forward with the téni and gave his blessing over the casket. He motioned Allesandra and Jan forward as the téni began to chant the benediction. They went to the casket, bowed, then placed their hands on the tapestry. "I wish you'd had more chance to know him," she whispered to Jan as the téni chanted, putting her hand atop his. "He wasn't always as angry and brusque as he was in his later years."

"You've told me that," he said. "Several times. But it's still not the memory of him I'll take with me, is it?" She glanced at her son; he was frowning down at the casket.

"We'll talk about it later," she told him.

"I've no doubt about it, Matarh."

Allesandra suppressed the retort she might have made; she would say nothing here. People were already glancing at them curiously, wondering what secrets they might be whispering and at the sharp edge in her son's voice. She lifted her hand and stepped back, allowing Fynn to approach.

She wondered what her brother thought as he stood there, his hand on the casket and his head bowed.

After a few minutes, Fynn also stepped away. He nodded to the lancers; four of them came forward to take the casket. Their faces were somber as they lifted the coffin and slid it forward into the niche that awaited it. Stone grated on wood, the sound echoing. The four stepped back, and another quartet put their shoulders to the sealing stone, which groaned and resisted as it turned slowly. The massive wheel of rock advanced along a groove carved in the floor toward the deep cut into which it would settle and rest. The stone was carved with the glyphs of Old Firenzcian, a language spoken only by scholars now, as thick as a man's arm, and standing half again a man's height. As the great wheel reached the end of the groove and dropped into the cut where it was supposed to rest, there came a tremendous cracking sound. A fissure shot through its carved face and the top third of the stone toppled. Allesandra knew she must have screamed a warning, but it was over before any of them could move or react. The mass of the stone crushed one of the lancers entirely underneath it and smashed the legs of another as it fell to the ground.

The pinned lancer's screams were piercing and shrill as thick blood ran from underneath the stone.

This is a sign . . . She couldn't stop the thought—as the remainder of the lancers rushed forward, as ca'-and-cu', téni, and servants hurried to help or stared frozen in horror at the rear of the chamber. Jan was among those trying desperately to lift the burial stone, and Fynn was shouting useless orders into the chaos.

Vatarh did this. Somehow he did this. He does not rest easily. . . .

~

Enéas cu'Kinnear

HE WAS GOING to die here in the Hellins.
That feeling of an awful destiny washed over Enéas
as he stood with the Holdings forces on the crest of a hill not
far outside Munereo, as they watched the strangely shaped
banners of the Westlanders approaching from the direction
of Lake Malik, as he heard the war-téni begin chanting in
preparation for battle. A'Offizier Meric ca'Matin was with
him, as well as the other offiziers of the battalion and several pages ready to run messages between the companies.
The cornets and flags were set to relay orders. A hundred
strides down the slope, the ranks of the Holdings army
were arrayed, restless and nervous.

Enéas had been in a half dozen battles and countless
skirmishes and confrontations in the last several years. This
sense of impending doom was something he'd never felt
before. He could feel sweat rolling down his face under the
thick iron helmet, and it was not just the sun that caused
the perspiration. He wanted to shout denial to the sky, but
he could not. Not here. Not in front of his troops. Instead,
he bowed his head and he prayed.

*Oh, Great Cénzi, why do You send this premonition to
me? What are You saying to me?*

Enéas was an o'offizier with the Garde Civile of the
Holdings. His commander in the field, A'Offizier ca'Matin,
had told him only yesterday that he had put in the recommendation that Enéas be made Chevaritt, that the
document was already on its way across the Strettosei to
Nessantico. His vatarh would be proud—twenty-five years
ago, Enéas' vatarh had served with the Regent ca'Rudka
at Passe a'Fiume and been badly burned, losing both an
arm and an eye during that horrible siege. The Garde Civile had given him the citation and the pension he was due,
and though their family had been raised from ce'Kinnear
to ci'Kinnear as a result, his vatarh had always talked about

how he could have become one of the chevarittai if he hadn't been injured, how those aspirations had been taken from him by the Firenzcian téni-fire that had disfigured him and ended his career.

Enéas had never wanted to be either chevaritt or offizier. He would have preferred that his career path was that of a téni in the Concénzia Faith rather than the one he'd found in the Garde Civile. He'd felt the calling of Cénzi ever since he'd been a young boy; indeed, he'd petitioned his parents to send him to the temple as an acolyte. But his vatarh had insisted on the martial road. *"We're just ci', my son, and barely that,"* he'd said. *"Our family doesn't have the solas to send you to the téni. That's for the ca'-and-cu' who can afford it. You'll join the Garde, as I did. You'll do as I did. . . ."*

Enéas had done better than his vatarh. "Falsoténi," his men dubbed him for his piousness, for his strict attention to the rules of the Divolonté, for his insistence that the men under his command attend the rites at the Munereo Temple on the proper Days of Observance. But they also claimed that Cénzi Himself protected Enéas—and through Enéas, themselves. In the Battle of the Mounds near Lake Malik, as an e'offizier in his second real battle, he'd been the only surviving offizier of his company as they were ripped apart by a far superior Westlander force. He'd managed to surprise the Westlanders by feigning retreat, then marching the remnants of his troops through marshland to attack the enemy from a flank unprotected by their nahualli—the terrifying spellcasters of the Westlanders, the ones who called the Ilmodo the *X'in Ka.*

Heretics, they were. False téni worshiping false gods. The thought of the nahualli enraged Enéas.

Enéas had managed to inflict severe losses on the Westlander flank and to hold the ground until reinforcements arrived. As a reward for his actions, he'd been promoted to o'offizier; a few months later, after the Campaign of the Deep Fens, A'Offizer ca'Matin had told him the Gardes a'Liste had raised their family to cu'.

When his tour was over a year from now, after his return to Nessantico, Enéas had promised Cénzi that he would resign from the Garde Civile and offer himself for training as téni, even though he would be much older than the usual acolytes. He was certain that this was what Cénzi wanted of him.

The Hellins War had been good for Enéas, though not for the Holdings.

At least, it had been so until this shadow came. This chill in his spine.

It's not a premonition. It's just fear. . . .

He'd felt fear before. Every soldier felt fear unless he were an utter fool, but it had never touched him like this. Fear rattled the bones in your flesh; fear made the blood sing in your ears. Fear turned your bowels to foul brown water. Fear set your weapon to shaking in your hand. But Enéas didn't tremble, his stomach was settled, and the tip of his sword didn't waver in his grasp.

This wasn't fear—or not any kind he'd experienced before. That worried him most of all.

What is that you send me, Cénzi? Tell me, so that I may serve You as you wish. . . .

"O'Offizier cu'Kinnear!" A'Offizier ca'Matin barked, and Enéas shook his head to dispel the thoughts. He saluted his superior offizier, who was already astride his destrier. "I need you to drive your men into their right flank; push them into the valley for the war-téni to handle. We shouldn't have their nahualli to worry about; the outriders have said they're still back near the Tecuhtli at Lake Malik. Understood?"

Enéas nodded.

"Good," ca'Matin said. "Then let's get this started. Page, tell the horns to call the advance." The boy he'd addressed ran toward the knoll where the horns and signal flags were clustered as ca'Matin saluted Enéas: the sign of Cénzi, that Enéas returned solemnly and devoutly. "Cénzi's fortune to you, Enéas," he said.

"And with all of us," Enéas returned fervently. Ca'Matin yanked on the reins. He cantered away, the powerful war-horse moving carefully through the tall grass toward the center of the lines where the banners of the Holdings rippled in the afternoon breeze.

The cornets sounded then, harsh and bright. The call floated before them in challenge to the Westlanders, and the sound of weapons clashing against armor rushed after it. Enéas took the reins of his own destrier from a waiting page and mounted. His e'offiziers looked at him expectantly. "Make your peace with Cénzi," he told them. "It's time."

He raised his hand, signaling them toward the right flank and the steep hills there.

A roar answered him, a thousand throats calling out. They began to move, slowly at first, then more rapidly, until they were rushing headlong down toward the spears of the enemy. As they charged, the war-fire of the téni behind them shrieked over their heads, smashing into the front ranks of the Westlander forces and gouging holes in their ragged lines. There didn't seem to be an answer from the nahualli; Enéas thought that the sour fear would leave him with that, but it didn't.

Enéas and his men surged into the fuming gaps. The clash of steel on steel echoed from the flanks of the lush hills, as did the screams of the wounded who went down under the hooves of the destriers they rode. Enéas struck at a short spear that thrust toward him, hacking away the barbed tip and chopping down with his saber at the hand that held it. Blood spurted and the savage face below him fell away. His horse pushed forward, and he cut at the Westlanders on either side of him, armored in chest plates of bamboo and heavy cloth sewn with small brass rings, their helmets adorned with the plumes of brightly colored birds, their ruddy skin painted with orange and yellow streaks that made their faces look like skulls or tattooed with black-and-red lines. They were fierce opponents, the Westlanders, and no soldier of the Holdings who had faced them dared to belittle their skill or their bravery. Yet—oddly—they gave way now, retreating back toward the main mass of their army. Enéas saw a darkness under their sandaled feet: the soil directly in front of him was like a circle of sand, but that sand was as black as the charcoal of a burned log.

The unease that had afflicted Enéas before the battle deepened, settling like a deathly chill in his lungs so that he labored to breathe and his sword felt like a leaden weight in his hands. He urged his horse forward onto the sand and as he did so, he shouted: a wordless cry to banish the feeling with noise and rage.

He was answered by a sound he'd never heard before. The sound . . . it was as if one of the Earth Moitidi—those unworthy children of Cénzi—had screamed an unearthly and deep roar, and the sound pulled Enéas' head around to the left toward its source. Orange fire and foul, black smoke erupted from the ground. Dirt clods fell around Enéas like a solid rain, spattering him, and with it . . . with it were parts of bodies. A hand, still clutching a broken sword, rebounded from the neck of Enéan's destrier and fell to the ground. He stared at the gory object. He heard the screams then, belatedly.

"It's the nahualli! Sorcery!" Enéas screamed in warning to his troops, to the awful hand that had fallen from the sky.

He was answered with a roar that was even louder than the first, a blast that blinded him with its light as the force of it lifted him bodily, tearing him from saddle and horse. A demigod had plucked him up—Enéas seemed to hover for a breath or more: *this . . . this is Cénzi's premonition and warning . . .*—and flung him back down to earth as if in disgust.

The earth rose up to meet him.

He remembered nothing else after that.

Karl ca'Vliomani

KARL CLUTCHED A NECKLACE in his hand: a shell of polished gray stone that he had given to Ana, long ago. The necklace had been around her neck when she died; Sergei had given it to him. Flecks of Ana's blood were caught in the deep ridges. He tightened his fingers hard around the shell, feeling the hard edges press into his palm. The pain didn't matter; it meant that he could still feel something other than the emptiness that filled him now.

Who did this? Why would they kill Ana?

Karl had lost too many of the people he most cared about over the years. He'd wrapped himself in grief and sorrow and sometimes anger at their passing, he'd awakened at night certain he'd heard their voices or thinking that "Oh, today I should call on him or her . . ." only to remember that the person in his mind was forever, irrevocably, gone.

This . . . this was worse than any of those deaths. This was a knife-blow to his heart, and he could feel himself bleeding inside.

Can I survive this? I've lost my best friend, the woman I love. . . .

Karl was seated at the front of the temple, with Regent Sergei and Kraljiki Audric to his left and the newly-installed Archigos Kenne and the a'téni of the Faith to his right. Kenne had been Ana's friend and ally from the beginning, when they had both been part of Archigos Dhosti's staff. Now, looking two decades older than his actual years, his hair white and hands shaking with an eternal palsy, Kenne appeared severely uncomfortable with the responsibility thrust upon him. The Archigos leaned over to Karl and patted his hand. He said something that Karl didn't hear against the choir's singing: "Long Lament," by the composer ce'Miella. Kenne's actual words didn't matter: Karl nodded, because he knew it was expected.

In the pew directly behind them, in the midst of the ca'-and-cu', was Varina and Mika ci'Gilan; like Varina, Mika was also a longtime friend of Karl and Ana. Mika was the local head of the Numetodo faction in Nessantico, directing the research of the sect here. Varina's hand touched Karl's shoulder; without looking back, he covered it with his own before letting his hand, like a dead thing, slide into his lap. Her fingers tightened on his shoulder; her hand remained there.

The embrace was meant to be comfort, he knew, but it was simply an empty weight.

Who did this? Karl had heard a dozen rumors. Predictably, some blamed the Numetodo. Some Firenzcia. Some the Brezno branch of the Faith. The wildest story said that the assassin called the White Stone had been responsible, that there'd been a pale pebble on Ana's left eye when she was found, the White Stone's signature.

That last rumor was certainly not true. But the others . . . Karl didn't know. But he vowed he would find out.

Karl had envied, sometimes, the comfort of faith that Ana had. He and Ana had even spoken of that, the night that he'd learned Kaitlin was dead: the woman he'd married and who had borne him his two sons on the Isle a'Paeti. Kaitlin had steadfastly refused to come with him to Nessantico. Kaitlin had known of the deep friendship between Karl and Ana; Karl was just as certain that Kaitlin knew that—despite Karl's reassurances and promises—for Karl, at least, there was more than friendship there.

He had never been able to lie easily to her. He told himself he loved Kaitlin, but he was never really able to lie to himself either.

The night he'd received the horrible letter from Paeti that Kaitlin had fallen ill and died, he'd been devastated. He never quite knew how Ana learned of it, but she came to him that evening. She fed him, she held him, she let him cry and wail and shout and grieve. Most tellingly, she never tried to give him the comfort of faith as she would have with any of her followers. She never mentioned Cénzi, not until he spoke, wiping away the tears with the sleeve of his bashta. . . .

"I envy you," he said.

They were sitting by the fire she'd started in the hearth.

Tea simmered in a pot. The wood was damp; it hissed and sputtered and cracked under the assault of the flames, sending fountains of orange-red ash spiraling up the chimney.

She raised a single eyebrow toward him.

"You believe that Cénzi takes the souls of those who die," he told her. "You believe that they continue to exist within Him, and that it's possible you may one day meet them again. I . . ." Tears threatened him again and he forced them down. "I don't have that hope."

"Having faith doesn't take away the pain," she told him. "Or very little of it. Nothing can ease the grief and loss we all feel: not faith, not the Ilmodo. Time, perhaps, might manage it, and that only blunts the sorrow." Folding the sleeve of her robe around her hand, she took the teapot from the crane and poured the brew into their cups. She handed him the jar of honey. "I still remember my matarh. Sometimes it all comes back to me, everything I felt when she died, as if it had just happened yesterday." Her fingers brushed his cheek; he could feel their softness drag against stubble. "That will happen for you, too, I'm afraid."

"Then what *good* is your faith, Ana?"

She smiled, as if she'd been expecting his question. "Faith isn't a commodity," she told him. "You don't buy it because it will do this or that for you. You have belief or you don't, and belief gives you what it gives you. You *don't* have faith, my love—Cénzi knows I'd give it to you if I could. I've certainly talked about it enough with you over the years. You Numetodo . . . you try to wrap the world in reason and logic, and so faith just crumples into dust whenever you touch it because you try to impose rationality on it. You'll do that with Kaitlin, too—you'll try to find reasons and logic in her death." She touched him again. "There's no *reason* that she died, Karl. There's no logic to it. It just *happened*, and it had nothing to do with you or with your feelings for her or what happened between the two of you."

"Not even Cénzi's will?"

She lifted her chin. She smiled at him sadly, the firelight warm and yellow on her face. "Not even that. It's a rare person who Cénzi cares about enough to change the Fate-Moitidi's dice roll for them. It was your Kaitlin's time. That's all. It's not your fault, Karl. It's not."

That had been nine years ago. He'd traveled back to

Paeti to see Kaitlin's grave and to be with his sons. He'd even brought Nilles and Colin back to Nessantico with him when he'd returned the next year. Nilles had stayed two years with him, Colin four, until they'd reached their majority at sixteen. Both had eventually left the city to return to the Isle. Nilles had already given him a great-daughter—three years old now—that he'd yet to see.

He'd stayed here because his work was in the Holdings, he told anyone who asked. But truthfully, it was because this was where Ana was. There were those who knew that, but they weren't many and most pretended not to see.

Varina's hand tightened again on his shoulder and dropped away.

Karl stared at Ana's wrapped-and-shrouded body on the stone altar and the phalanx of six fire-téni gathered in a circle around it. The corpse was layered in green silk wound with golden metallic thread. The threads glinted in the multicolored light from the stained glass in the temple's windows; censers fumed around the altar, wreathing sunbeams in fragrant smoke. He could not believe it was Ana bundled and displayed there. He *would* not believe it. It was someone else. The memory he had of the light, of the concussive roar, of her body torn apart, the blood, the dark dust . . . It was false. It had to be false. Even the thought was too painful to endure.

Kaitlin's death, that of his parents, all the others that had passed over the decades: none of them hurt like this. None.

Someone had killed the one person he loved most in the world, had struck down a woman who had struggled more than anyone since Kraljica Marguerite to keep peace within the Holdings, who believed in reconciliation before confrontation, who might have potentially reunited the broken halves of both the Holdings and the Concénzia Faith. There would be no comfort for Karl until he knew who had done this, and until that person was dead. If there was an afterlife as Ana had believed, then Karl would let the murderer's soul be condemned to care for Ana for eternity. If there were gods, if Cénzi truly existed, if there were justice after death, then that's what must happen.

He would have faith in *that*: a grim, dark, and uncompromising faith.

Archigos Kenne patted his hand and whispered more words he couldn't hear. The Regent Sergei's shoulder pressed against his to the left. Kraljiki Audric wheezed on the other side of the Regent, his labored breath louder than the chanting of the téni. He heard Varina weeping softly in the pew behind him.

The fire-téni stirred around the green-wrapped body. Their hands moved in the dance of the Ilmodo, their voices lifted in a unison chant that fought against the choir's ethereal voices. They spread their hands wide as if in benediction, and the fierce blaze of Ilmodo-fire erupted around Ana's body. The heat of the magical flames washed over them, savage and relentless. There were no sparks, no pyre feeding them: while the Kralji and the ca'-and-cu' burned in flames fed by wood and oil, the téni burned their own with the Ilmodo—quickly and furiously. The Ilmodo-fire consumed the body in the space of a few breaths, the metallic-green fabric turning black instantly, the heat shimmer so intense that Ana's body seemed to shake within it. As Karl watched, as his body instinctively leaned back against the fierce assault of the heat, Ana was taken.

The flames died abruptly as the choir ended their song. Cold air rushed back around them, a wind that tousled hair and fluttered cloth. On the altar now, there was nothing but gray ash and a few fragments of bone.

The mortal cage of Ana was gone.

"She is back in Cénzi's hands now," Archigos Kenne said to Karl. "He will give her solace."

And I will give her better than solace. He nodded silently to the Archigos. *I will give her revenge.*

~

Allesandra ca'Vörl

    "IT WAS *NOT* a sign."
    Fynn slammed his fisted hand hard on the arm of his chair. The servants standing ready along the wall to serve dinner shivered at the sound. The long scar down the right side of his face burned white against his flushed face. "I don't care what they're saying. What happened was a terrible accident. Nothing more. It was *not* a sign."
    "Of course you're right, Brother," Allesandra told him soothingly. She paused—a single breath—and gestured to the Magyarian servants: they were taking supper in Allesandra's rooms within the palais. The servants moved forward, ladling soup into the bowls and pouring wine. Fynn sat at the table's head; Allesandra at the foot. Archigos Semini and his wife were to Fynn's right; her son Jan to the left.
    Allesandra had heard some of the rumors herself. *Hïrzg Jan is upset that Fynn has taken the crown, not his daughter . . . The Hïrzg's soul cannot rest . . . I heard from one of the servants in the palais that his ghost still walks the halls at night, moaning and crying out as if angry. . . .* There were dozens of the tales surging through Brezno, twisted depending on the agenda of those who spoke them, and growing larger and more outrageous each time they were told. *Cénzi sends a warning to the Hïrzg that the Holdings and the Faith must become one again . . . The souls of all those the Hïrzg killed—the Numetodo, the Nessanticans, the Tennshah—pursue him and will not allow him to rest . . . They say that when the sealing stone fell, those in the chamber heard the old Hïrzg's voice call out with a curse on Firenzcia. . . .*
    The soup had been served and the silence had stretched too long. Allesandra could hear the breathing of the servants and the distant, muffled clatter of the cook and the kitchen help a floor below them. "I understand that the other lancer has died also," Allesandra commented when

it was apparent that no one else was willing to start a conversation.

Fynn glared at her down the length of the table "That was Cénzi's Blessing," he said. "The man would never have walked again. The healer said his spine was broken; if I were him, I'd rather die than live the rest of my life as a useless cripple."

"I'm sure he felt the same as you, Brother." She kept her voice carefully neutral. "And I'm sure that the Archigos did what he could to ease his passing." Another pause. "As far as the Divolonté would allow, of course," she added.

Francesca let her spoon clatter back to the table at that. "You may have been soiled by the beliefs of the false Archigos during your years with her, A'Hïrzg," she declaimed coldly, "but I assure you that my husband has not. He would *never*—"

"Francesca!" Semini's rebuke caused Francesca to snap her mouth closed, like a carp gulping on a riverbank. He glared at her, then clasped hands to forehead as he turned to Allesandra. His gaze held hers. Allesandra had always thought that the Archigos had exquisite eyes: powerful and engaging. She had also noticed that when she was in the room, Semini often paid close attention to her. That had never bothered her; she enjoyed his attentions. She'd thought, back when her vatarh had finally ransomed her, that he might have married her to Semini, had he not already been tied to Francesca. That would have been a powerful marriage, allying both the political and religious powers within the state, and Semini might have been someone she could have come to love, as well. Even now . . . she closed off that thought, quickly. She had taken lovers during her marriage, yes—as she had known Pauli had also done—but always carefully. Always discreetly. An affair with the Archigos . . . that would be difficult to conceal.

"I apologize, A'Hïrzg," Semini said. "Sometimes my wife's, ahh, devotion to the Faith causes her to speak too harshly. I did give the poor lancer what comfort I could, at the Hïrzg's request." He addressed Fynn then. "My Hïrzg, you shouldn't be concerned with the gossip of the rabble. In fact, I will make it clear in my next Admonition that those who believe that there are portents in this horrible incident are mistaken, and that these wild rumors are simply lies. I've already had people begin to make inquiries as to who is spreading all the vile gossip—I would say that if the Garde Hïrzg takes a few of them into custody, especially a few of those of lower rank, and, ahh, *convinces* them to recant publicly before they're executed for treason, that would certainly act as a lesson to the others. I think we'd find that all the talk about what happened at your vatarh's burial would vanish as quickly as snow in Daritria."

Francesca was nodding at her husband's words. "We should treat these people no better than we would the Numetodo," she agreed. "Just as the Numetodo are traitors to the Faith, these rumormongers are traitors to our Hïrzg. A few bodies swaying in gibbets will adequately shut the mouth of the populace." She glanced at Allesandra. "Wouldn't you agree, A'Hïrzg?" she asked, her voice far too gentle and far too eager. The woman actually leaned forward at the table, emphasizing her humped back.

"I think it's dangerous to equate rumormongering with heresy, Vajica ca'Cellibrecca," she began carefully, but Jan interrupted her.

"If you punish people for gossiping, you'll convince them instead that the rumors are true," her son said, the first words he'd spoken since they'd sat at the table, then shrugged as the others looked at him. "Well, that's the truth," he insisted. "If you give them the sermon you suggest, Archigos, you'll just be drawing *more* attention to what happened, which will make people believe the rumors even more. It's better to say and do nothing at all; all this talk will fade away on its own when nothing else happens. Every time one of us repeats the gossip, even to deny or refute it, we make it seem more real and more important than it is."

She followed Jan's gaze from Semini to the others at the table. Semini was glowering, his eyebrows lowered like thunderclouds over those captivating eyes; Francesca's mouth gaped open as if she were too stunned for words at the boy's impertinence; she gave a cough of derision and waved a hand like a claw in Jan's direction, as if warding off a beggar's curse. Fynn was staring down at the tablecloth in front of him. "It's better to say and do nothing," Jan repeated into the silence, his voice thinner and more uncertain now, "or what happened *will* become a sign. You'll all have turned it into one."

Allesandra touched his arm: it was what she would have said, if less diplomatically spoken. "Well said," she whispered to him. He might have smiled momentarily; it was difficult to tell.

"So if *you* were the Hïrzg, you'd do *nothing*?" Francesca said. "Then let's thank Cénzi that you're not, child."

That brought Jan's head up again. "If I were Hïrzg," Jan answered her, "I'd be thinking that these rumors aren't worth my time. There are more important events that I'd be considering, like the death of Archigos Ana, or the war in the Hellins that's sapping Nessantico's resources and their attention, and what all that means for Firenzcia and the Coalition."

Francesca snorted again. She returned her attention to her soup, as if Jan's comment was beneath consideration. Semini was shaking his head and glaring at Allesandra as if she were directly responsible for Jan's impertinence.

She thought Fynn was angry beneath the scowl he wore, but her brother surprised her. "I believe the young man's right," Fynn said, breaking the uncomfortable silence. He gave Jan a smile twisted by the scar on his face. "I hate the thought of having to hear the whispers for even another breath, but . . . you're right, Nephew. If we do nothing, the gossip will fade in a week, maybe even a few days. Perhaps I should make you my new councillor, eh?"

Jan beamed at Fynn's praise as Francesca sat back abruptly with a frown. Semini tried to look unconcerned. "You've raised an intelligent young man, Sister," Fynn told Allesandra. "He's as bold as I'd want my own son to be. I should talk more with you, Jan, and I regret that I don't know you as well as an onczio should. We'll start to rectify that tomorrow—we'll go hunting after my afternoon conferences, you and I. Would you like that?"

"Oh, yes!" Jan burst out, suddenly the child again, presented with an unexpected gift. Then he seemed to realize how young he sounded, and he nodded solemnly. "I'd enjoy that very much, Onczio Fynn," he said, his voice pitched low. "Matarh?"

"The Hïrzg is very kind," Allesandra told him, smiling

even as suspicion hammered at her. *First Vatarh, now Fynn. What does the bastard think he can gain with this? Is he just trying to get to me by stealing Jan's affection? I'm losing my son, and the tighter I try to hold him, the faster he'll slip away....* "It sounds like a wonderful idea," she told Jan.

The White Stone

THERE WERE EASY KILLINGS, and there were hard ones. This was one of the easy ones.

The target was Honori cu'Belgradi, a merchant dealing in goods from the Magyarias, and a philanderer who had made the mistake of sleeping with the wrong person's wife: the wife of the White Stone's client.

"I watched him tup her," the man had told the White Stone, his voice shaking with remembered rage. *"I watched him take my wife like an animal, and I heard her call out his name in her passion. And now . . . now she's pregnant, and I don't know if the child is mine or . . ."* He'd stopped, his head bowed. *"But I'll make certain that he'll do this to no other husband, and I'll make certain that the child will never be able to call him vatarh. . . ."*

Relationships and lust were responsible for fully half of the White Stone's work. Greed and power accounted for the rest. There was never a dearth of people seeking the White Stone; if you needed to find the Stone, you found the way.

Honori cu'Belgradi was a creature of habit, and habits made for easy prey. The Stone had watched him for three days, and the man's ritual never varied by more than a quarter turn of the glass. He would close his shop in Ville Serne, a town a half-day's ride south of Brezno, then stroll to the tavernhouse on the corner of the next street over. He would stay there until four turns of the glass after third call, after which he would go to the rooms where the woman—the wife of the Stone's client—waited for their nightly tryst.

On the way to those rooms, Honori would pass the alleyway where the Stone waited now. The Stone could already hear the footsteps in the cool night air. "Honori cu'Belgradi," the Stone called as the figure of the man passed by the opening of the alley. Honori stopped, his face cautious, then eagerly interested as the Stone stepped into the light of the téni-lamps of the street.

"You know me?" cu'Belgradi asked, and the Stone smiled gently.

"I do. And I would know you better, my friend. You and I, we have a business arrangement to make."

"How do you mean?" cu'Belgradi asked as the Stone stepped closer to him. *So easy* . . . Only a step away. A knife thrust's distance apart, and cu'Belgradi tilted his head quizzically.

"Like this," the Stone answered, looking around the street and seeing no one watching, and clapping cu'Belgradi on the shoulder as if the man were a long-lost friend. At the same time the hand holding the poisoned blade drove hard up under the man's rib cage and twisted it up into the heart. Cu'Belgradi made a strangled, blood-choked cry, and the body was suddenly heavy against the Stone's athletic build. The Stone half-dragged, half-carried the dying cu'Belgradi into the alleyway, laying the body quickly on the ground. Cu'Belgradi's eyes were open, and the Stone dug into a cloak pocket and brought out two stones: both white in the dimness of the alley, though one was smooth and polished as if from much handling. The stones were placed on cu'Belgradi's open eyes, the Stone pressing them down into the sockets. The one on the left eye the Stone left there; the gleaming, white, and smooth one over the right eye—the eye of the ego, the eye that held the image of the face it saw in its last moment—that one the Stone picked up again and placed back in a leather pouch around the Stone's neck.

"And now I have you, forever," the apparition known as the White Stone whispered.

A breath later, there was no one left alive in the alley, only a corpse with a white pebble over its left eye: a contract fulfilled.

PERMUTATIONS

Audric ca'Dakwi
Varina ci'Pallo
Jan ca'Vörl
Enéas cu'Kinnear
Allesandra ca'Vörl
Karl ca'Vliomani
Sergei ca'Rudka
Allesandra ca'Vörl
Nico Morel
The White Stone

Audric ca'Dakwi

THIS WAS ONE OF the bad nights.

Every individual breath was a struggle. Audric had to force the old, useless air from his lungs, and his chest ached with every inhalation, yet he was never able to bring in enough air. He sat up in his bed; he felt that if he lay down he might suffocate. The palais healers bustled around him, looks of deep concern on their faces—if only for fear of what might happen to them if he died under their care—but Audric paid them little attention except when they tried to get him to take a sip of a potion or to inhale some sour grasssmoke. His arms were tracked with fresh scabs; the healers had nearly bled him dry and another one of them was making a new cut, but Audric didn't even flinch. Seaton and Marlon, Audric's *domestiques de chambre*, rushed in and out of the bedroom, fetching whatever the healers requested of them.

All of Audric's attention went to his war for breath. His world had shrunk down to the battle of each inhalation, of trying to suck enough air in his lungs to stay conscious. The edges of his vision had darkened; he could only see what was directly in front of him. He felt little but the eternal pain in his chest.

He focused on the portrait of Kraljica Marguerite set over the fireplace mantel at the foot of his bed. His great-matarh stared back at him, her painted face utterly realistic, as if the gilded frame were a window behind which the Kraljica was sitting. He swore he saw her move slightly against the backdrop of the Sun Throne, that the painted

Sun Throne itself flickered with the light of the Ilmodo as the real one did whenever he sat on it.

Archigos Ana had never given more than a sour glance at the portrait, which always seemed to snare the gaze of other visitors to Audric's bedroom. Once, Audric had asked the Archigos why she paid the masterpiece so little attention. She had only shaken her head. "There's far too much of your great-matarh in that painting," she said. "It hurts me to see her trapped there." She frowned then. "But your vatarh loved the picture, for his own reasons."

Marguerite regarded Audric now with her appraising, piercing stare. He waited for the attack to pass. It would pass; it always had in the past. It *must* pass. He prayed to Cénzi for that, his mouth moving silently: that the invisible giant sitting astride his chest and crushing his lungs would slowly rise and lumber off, and he'd be able to breathe easier again.

It would happen. It *must* happen.

His great-matarh seemed to nod at that, as if she agreed.

Staring at the painting, Audric heard more than saw Regent ca'Rudka push into the room, scattering the healers as he leaned over the bed, waving away the sourgrass smoke drifting from the censers. "Get those out of here," he snarled. "Archigos Ana said the smoke makes the Kraljiki's breathing worse, not better. And take yourselves out of here as well." The healers scattered with mutterings, bloody fingers, and the clinking of vials, leaving the Regent alone with Audric. No, not alone . . . There was someone else with him. Reluctantly, Audric took his gaze from the painting and squinted into the darkness.

The effort made him groan.

"Archigos . . . Kenne . . ." Each word came out in its own separate breath accompanied by a rattling wheeze; he could do no better than that.

"Kraljiki," the Archigos said. "Please don't move. I've come to pray with you." Audric saw Archigos Kenne glance concernedly at the Regent. "Archigos Ana had a . . . special relationship with Cénzi that I'm afraid few téni can match, but I will do what I can. Lie back as comfortably as you can. Close your eyes and think of nothing but your breathing. Focus only on that. . . ."

His breath was racing, gasping. He could feel his heart

lurching against the confines of his ribs. He could take only the smallest sip of precious air. Audric closed his eyes as the Archigos began to pray. Archigos Ana, when she came to him, would pray also, and she would gently place her hands on his chest. It was as if he could feel her *inside* him. He could hear her voice in his head and feel the power of the Ilmodo burning in his chest, searing away the blockages and allowing him to breathe fully again. She wrapped him in that interior heat, her voice chanting and yet at the same time speaking in his head. *"You'll be fine, Audric. Cénzi is with you now, and He will make you better again. Just breathe slowly: nice long breaths. Yes, that's it . . ."* Within a few minutes, he would be breathing naturally and easily once again, an ease that at first lasted months, but more recently only a few weeks.

Now, with Kenne, Audric heard the man's half-whispered prayers only with his ears. There was nothing inside at all. There was no warmth spreading throughout his chest. These were only the prayers of an old man, outside him and spoken in a quavering voice. There was no sense of the Ilmodo, no tingling of Cénzi's power—or perhaps there was, but it was so faint that Audric could barely feel it. Maybe there *was* warmth, perhaps the painful bellows of his lungs were moving slightly easier. Audric tried to take a deeper breath, but the effort sent him into spasmodic, dry coughing that made him hunch over on the bed. His eyes opened, and Marguerite frowned in her painting. He saw that fine droplets of blood had sprayed the blanket.

"You must fight this, Audric. If you die, our line dies, and with it our dream of Nessantico and the Holdings. . . ." He saw Marguerite's painted lips move, heard the voice that he had always imagined she would have. *"You must fight this. I will help you. . . ."*

Sergei had moved quickly to his side; he felt the Regent's strong hand on his back, heard him call sharply to Marlon. A cloth dipped in cool water was passed to him. Audric took it gratefully, touching the fabric to his lips. He could taste the sweetness of the water. And yes, he could breathe somewhat better. "Thank you, Regent," he said. "I'm much . . . better now . . . Archigos." His own voice sounded distant and dull, as if someone were half-covering his ears. It was Marguerite's voice that was clearest.

"Listen to me, Audric. I will help you. Listen to your great-matarh. . . ."

Archigos Kenne nodded but Audric could see the doubt in the man's eyes. "I'm sorry, Kraljiki. Archigos Ana∴.. I know she could do much more for you."

Audric reached out to touch the man's hand. Kenne's skin was cool against his own, and dry as old paper. "I will be fine," he told the man. "I think . . . I have found the way."

The portrait of Marguerite smiled her lopsided smile at him, and he smiled back.

"There is too much for you to do to die. . . ."

"There is too much for me to do to die," he said to her, to them. It was both promise and threat.

Varina ci'Pallo

IN THE DAYS WHEN SHE'D first joined the Numetodo, when she'd been a lowly initiate into their society and first met Mika and Karl, the Numetodo House had been a shabby house in the midst of Oldtown, masked by the squalor and filth of the buildings around it.

Now, the Numetodo House was a fine building on the South Bank, with a garden and burnished grounds out front and gates bordering the Ave a'Parete—a gift from Archigos Ana and (more reluctantly) Kraljiki Justi for their aid in ending the Firenzcian siege of the city in 521. Their more spacious and lush accommodations helped to make the Numetodo more acceptable to the ca'-and-cu', but it had also made them more visible. In the past, the Numetodo met in secret, and most members kept their affiliation a secret. No more. Varina had no doubt that all those who entered through the gates were noted by the utilino and Garde Kralji who constantly patrolled the Avi, and that information was funneled to the commandant—and from him to Sergei ca'Rudka, the Council of Ca', and the Kraljiki.

The Numetodo were known—which was fine as long as their beliefs were tolerated. But with the death of Ana, Varina was no longer certain how long that might be the case. Her fears drove her back to her research. . . .

Despite the paranoid rumors among the conservative Faithful, the bulk of the Numetodo research had nothing to do with magic at all: they were experimenting in physics and biology; they were creating beautiful and elegant mathematical theorems; they were delving into medicine; they were exploring alchemy; they were examining dusty tomes and digging at ancient sites to recreate history. But for Varina, it was magic that fascinated. What especially intrigued her was how the Faith, the Numetodo, and the Westlanders approached casting spells.

The Numetodo had long ago proved—despite the angry and sometimes violent denial of the Faith—that the energy of the Second World didn't require belief in any god at all. Call it the "Ilmodo" or the "Scáth Cumhacht" or the "X'in Ka." It didn't matter. That realization had dissolved whatever remnants of faith Varina had when she first came to the Numetodo.

"Knowledge and understanding can be shaped by reason and logic alone; it's just not easy or simple. People created gods to explain the world so we didn't have the responsibility to figure things out ourselves." She'd heard Karl say that in a lecture he'd given, years ago when she was first considering joining the Numetodo. "Magic is no more a religious manifestation than the fact that an object dropped from your hand is going to fall to the ground."

Yes, the téni of the Faith and the Westlanders both used chants and hand motions to create the spell's framework, yet each of them had a different underlying "belief" which allowed them to harness the energy of magic. What the Numetodo realized was that the chants and hand motions used by spellcasters were only a "formula." A recipe. Nothing more. Speaking *this* sequence of syllables with *that* set of motions would net *this* result.

But the Westlanders . . . Varina hadn't met Mahri the Mad, but Karl and Ana had, and the tales of the Westlander nahualli from the Hellins had only verified what Karl and Ana had said of Mahri. The nahualli were able to place their spells *within* objects, which could then be triggered later by a word, or a gesture, or an action. Neither the téni nor the Numetodo could do that. The Westlander spellcasters called on their own gods for spells, as the téni did with theirs, but Varina was certain that Westlander gods were as imaginary and unnecessary as Cénzi and his Moitidi.

If she could learn the Westlanders' methods, if she could find the formula of just the right words and hand movements to place the Scáth Cumhacht inside an inanimate object, then she could begin to duplicate what Mahri had been able to do. She'd been working on that, off and on, for a few years now. Worry drove Varina more than ever now: over what Ana's death meant to the Numetodo; over Karl's deep grief, which tore at Varina as much as her own.

If she couldn't understand why people would do such

horrible things to each other, she would at least try to understand this.

She was in a nearly bare room in the lower levels of the House. On the table in front of her was a glass ball she'd purchased from a vendor in the River Market, sitting in a nest of cloth so it wouldn't roll. The ball had been inexpertly made; a curtain of small air bubbles ran though the center of it, the glass around them discolored and brown, but Varina didn't care—it had been cheap. Varina chanted, her hands moving: a simple, easy light spell, one of the first tricks taught to a Numetodo initiate. Weaving a light spell was effortless, but pushing it inside the glass—that was far, far more difficult. It was like pushing a hair through a stone wall. She could feel fatigue draining her strength. She ignored it, concentrating on the glass ball in front of her, trying to imagine the power of the Scáth Cumhacht moving into the glass in the same way she would have placed it inside her own mind, visualizing the potential light deposited around those bubbles deep inside the glass, placing the release word there with it as a trigger.

The spell ended; she opened her eyes. Her muscles were trembling, as if she'd run for leagues or been lifting heavy weights for a turn of the glass. She had to force herself to remain standing. The ball was sitting on the table, and Varina allowed herself a small smile. Now, if—

The ball began to vibrate, untouched. Varina took a step back as it rang like a glass goblet struck by a knife, there was a coruscation of brilliant yellow light, and the globe shattered. She felt a shard hit her upraised arm and she cried out.

"Are you all right?" She heard the voice behind her at the doorway: Mika. The Numetodo leader walked quickly into the room, shaking his balding head and rubbing at the close stubble on his chin. "You're bleeding, and you look like you haven't slept in a week." He pulled a chair over to the table and helped her sit down.

Varina lifted her arm—it felt as heavy as one of the marble blocks of the Kraljiki's Palais—and examined the cut in her foream. It was long but not deep, and Varina pulled a sliver of glass from the wound, grimacing. A thin line of blood ran down the arm toward her hand; she ignored it. "Damn it." Varina closed her eyes, then opened them again with an effort to look at the table: the globe had broken nearly in half along the curtain of bubbles, and the cloth on which it had been set was littered with glass fragments. "I was so close."

"I was watching," Mika said. He glanced at the shattered globe. "I thought you'd finally done it."

"I thought so, too." Varina shook her head. "But I'm too tired to try again."

"Just as well," Mika said. "I came down to tell you: Karl's back at his own apartments."

Varina cocked her head quizzically. "I thought he was staying with you and Alia and the kids for the time being."

Mika shrugged. "Said he was fine, that he needed to get back to his own life. Needed to get back to Numetodo affairs and his work as Ambassador."

"You don't sound like you believe that."

"I think . . ." Mika pressed his thin lips together. "Those are excuses. He's hurt and he's angry, and I'm not sure what he's going to do. I think he needs someone with him, to talk with him if he wants to talk, to make sure he's okay and that he doesn't do anything foolish. Ana's death has hit him harder than he'll admit."

Mika went silent, and Varina felt that he was waiting for her to respond. But it was hard to just hold her head up. Blood dripped from her finger to the floor; the severed halves of the glass globe glinted accusingly at her in the lamplight. "I guess I could send Karoli or Lauren over," Mika said into the silence.

"I'll go," Varina said. "Just give me a few minutes. I have to clean up."

Mika grinned. "Let me help you," he said.

~

Jan ca'Vörl

JAN LIKED FYNN. He wasn't sure how his matarh
would feel about that.

Matarh had told him how she'd never known Fynn, how
he'd been born only a few months after Archigos Ana had
kidnapped her from Hïrzg Jan's tent on the battlefield.
When he was a child, Jan hadn't understood all the implications of that; now, he thought that he finally began to understand the dynamics of the relationship between older
sister and younger brother, twisted and distorted by their
vatarh's vanity and pride. He could understand how his
matarh could never allow herself to like Fynn, could never
treat him as brother, could never trust him.

But he liked the man, his onczio.

Fynn had sent a note to Jan immediately after Second
Call, inviting Jan to join him for the afternoon briefing. Jan
sat alongside Fynn, with Fynn leaning over to whisper wry
comments to him as the various ministers and advisers up-
dated the new Hïrzg on current political situations. Helmad
cu'Göttering, Commandant of the Garde Brezno, related
that there had been a minor skirmish with Tennshah loyal-
ists east of Lake Cresci, easily put down. ("You should see
them run like whipped dogs when they see real soldiers riding through their hovels. They're all afraid of good Firenzcian steel," Fynn said softly into Jan's ear. "My own blade
has the blood of uncounted dozens of Tennshah soldiers
staining it. In the autumn, if you'd like, we could tour the
region, and maybe chase some of these rebels ourselves.")

Starkkapitän Armen ca'Damont of the Firenzcian
Garde Civile gave Fynn an update on the Holdings' war in
the Hellins, which—if everything the starkkapitän said was
true—was not going well for the Holdings and the Kraljiki.
("The Holdings doesn't know how to wage a real war,
Jan. They depended on Firenzcia for that for too long and
they've forgotten. If we could send our Garde Civile and a

battalion of good Red Lancers over there for a month, we could put down these Westlanders for good.")

Archigos Semini speculated on who the Concord A'Téni might name as the new Archigos of "that false and despicable Faith in Nessantico," giving them a long and tedious commentary on each of the a'téni of the major towns in the Holdings and their relative strengths and weaknesses. He contended that A'Téni ca'Weber of Prajnoli would ultimately become the next Archigos in Nessantico. ("And in the end it won't matter which one they pick, so all this hot air and effort was a waste of our time, eh?")

There were reports on a food shortage in East Magyaria ("You *did* have enough to eat for lunch, didn't you?"), on trade inequities between Firenzcia and Sesemora ("Do you find this as boring as I do?"), on the relative value of the Firenzcian solas against the Holdings solas ("By Cénzi, wake me up when this one's finished talking, would you, Nephew?"). By the end, Jan was no longer listening. Glancing over at Fynn, he could see that his onczio's eyes had glazed over as well. The new Hïrzg's fingers were tapping the polished tabletop impatiently and he was squirming restlessly in his seat. When the next minister rose to give her report, Fynn raised his hand. "Enough!" he said. "Send me your report and I'll read it. I'm sure it's fascinating, but my ears are about to fall off my head from overuse, and I've promised my nephew a hunt. Leave us!"

They grumbled inaudibly, they frowned, but they all bowed and left the room. Fynn motioned to the servants standing against the walls to bring in refreshments. "So . . ." Fynn said as they nibbled on breads and meats and drank the wine, "the life of a Hïrzg is delightful, isn't it? All that babbling, on and on and on . . . I see why Vatarh was always in a sour mood before these briefings."

"I think Archigos Semini was mistaken," Jan said. He wasn't certain why he said that; somehow, he trusted that Fynn would listen. Matarh always lectured him, as if she were teacher and he student; Vatarh was more concerned with his own pleasure than listening to his son's opinions. Onczio Fynn, on the other hand, had actually *listened* to him last night at supper, when the others at the table would have preferred he stay quiet. So he spoke his mind now, his voice trembling only a little. "Ca'Weber won't be named Archigos. The Concord will pick Kenne ca'Fionta."

Fynn raised a thick, dark eyebrow. "Why do you say that? Semini seemed to think that ca'Fionta was the weakest of the lot."

"That's exactly why," Jan answered, more eagerly now, ticking off points on his fingers. "Archigos Semini is assuming that the Concord A'Téni will think as he would think, and would choose the person he would choose. They won't. The rest of the a'téni will be worried now—Archigos Ana's assassination has made them see that a strong Archigos has enemies, and they're also wondering how long the Faith can remained sundered, now that Archigos Ana is dead. So they'll choose Kenne: because he *is* weak, and because he's older than any of the rest of them, and even if he's ultimately a bad choice, they won't have to deal with it for decades."

Fynn laughed. He clanked the rim of his goblet against Jan's. Leaning toward Jan, he put a burly arm around his shoulders. "Well spoken, and we'll see soon enough if you're right. What else are you holding back? Come on now, you can't keep the rest from me."

Fynn was smiling and Jan smiled in return, feeling a warmth toward the man. "Starkkapitän ca'Damont might be right about the war in the Hellins, but he misses the *importance* of the war. With the Holdings' Garde Civile concentrating on that struggle and bleeding resources, money, and soldiers every month, they can't be looking east with any strength. They're in a weak negotiating position against the Coalition; they're in an even worse position militarily. A strong Hïrzg might take advantage of that, one way or another."

Fynn's eyebrows climbed higher. His arm tightened around Jan's shoulders. "By Cénzi," he said, "I *should* make you my councillor, Nephew. You have your matarh's subtle mind."

He hugged Jan again one-handed, then sagged back in his chair. "Ah! I like you, Jan! It makes me wonder what I missed with my sister." Fynn frowned at that and took another gulp of his wine. "Did you know that I wasn't even aware I *had* a sister until I was nine or so? Vatarh never once mentioned her to me. Never. Didn't speak her name once; it was as if she'd never existed for him. Then, when he decided he'd finally ransom her, he sat me down and explained how she'd been snatched away by the Witch Archigos. He didn't tell me how that ended his war with the Holdings; *that* I learned much later. Vatarh was always bitter about that, his one defeat. I suppose Allesandra was the symbol of that failure for him—he certainly married her off quickly once she returned. I never really knew her. . . ."

He took another long drink of the wine and slammed the goblet back down on the table so hard that Jan jumped. Wine spilled; the base of the goblet left a crescent-moon divot in the table.

"Now, we hunt!" Fynn declared, pushing back his chair and standing up. "Come on, Nephew. We're off to Stag Fall."

~

Enéas cu'Kinnear

IF HE WERE DEAD, the afterlife wasn't anything like the one the téni had promised to the faithful.

Enéas' afterlife was illuminated by dim, ruddy light, and it stank of rotting flesh and brimstone. The ground on which he lay was wet and hard, with fists of stone that poked into his back. The téni had always said how all a person's bodily ills would be healed when he finally rested in Cénzi's arms, that those who had lost limbs would have them restored, that there would be no more pain.

But Enéas' breath rattled in his lungs, and when he tried to move, the agony made him cry out.

He heard wings flapping in response, punctuated with hoarse squawks of alarm. Enéas blinked, and the redness moved with his eyelids. He slowly lifted a protesting hand and wiped at his eyes. The red filter cleared somewhat, and he realized that he'd been looking through a film of sticky blood at a moonlit landscape, his head on muddy ground. An umber mountain lifted a scant finger's distance from him. He blinked again, squinting: a fallen, dead horse: his destrier. *Cénzi, you left me alive.* As the realization came to him, two clawed feet appeared at the summit of the equine mountain, followed by another irritated squawk, and Enéas moved his gaze to see one of the Hellins' carrion birds, the creature soldiers called rippers: ugly birds with a wingspan of two mens' height or more, great hooked beaks set in a featherless, spectrally white face, expressionless eyes like black marbles, and curved talons to rip open the corpses on which they preferred to feast. There was nothing like these beasts in the Holdings.

The bird stared at him as if contemplating a fine meal set before it. Enéas propped himself up on his elbows; it was the closest he could manage to sitting up; the bird screeched in annoyance and flapped off. Enéas could feel the foul wind stirred by its wings.

Not dead. Not yet. Praise Cénzi.

He tried to remember how he'd come to be here, but it was a muddle in his head. He remembered talking to A'Offizier ca'Matin, and the start of the charge, the rush downhill toward the Westlander force. Then . . . then . . .

Nothing.

He shook his head to shake loose the memory. That was a mistake. The world whirled around him, the redness returned, and pain shot through his temples. He caught himself before he fell back down to the ground again and waited for the earth to stop spinning. Again, he pushed himself to a full sitting position and touched his head tentatively; his hair was crusted with dried blood and his fingers could feel the jagged outline of a long, deep cut. Enéas started to feel sick. He let his hand drop, closed his eyes, and took long, slow sips of air until the nausea passed, reciting the Prayer of Acceptance to calm himself. He opened his eyes again, looking carefully around.

There were rippers everywhere; in the dim moonlight, the field seemed alive with them, the ground humped with the black hills of Enéas' fallen companions and their horses. The sickening, wet, tearing sound the birds made as they fed on the bodies was one he knew would haunt his nightmares forever. Far off, down the slope on which he sat, Enéas could see the gleam of a campfire, and around it the dark shapes of people moving. There was another sound, fainter: singing?

The figures outlined in the flame wore feathered devices on their heads, Enéas saw. They were Westlanders, then. "Tehuantin," as they called themselves. All the bodies around him wore the gold-trimmed uniforms of Nessantico, black with blood and dim moonlight rather than the brilliant blue they should have been.

We lost. We were slaughtered here, and those in Munereo may not know the outcome yet. Cénzi, is that why You saved me, so I could warn them . . . ?

Enéas tried to move; his legs didn't want to cooperate, and he realized that one leg was still trapped underneath the horse he'd been riding. As silently as he could, he pushed at the carcass, shoving against it with his good leg, and eventually the leg came free. His ankle was swollen and tender; he wasn't certain he could walk on it.

He found his sword half-buried in the mud an arm's length away. He shoved the filthy blade into the scabbard lashed to his belt. Grimacing, he crawled toward the flames, half-dragging himself around the destrier.

Part of him screamed warning. He was moving toward the enemy; they would kill him if they saw him. The a'offiziers all spoke of how the Westlanders had walked the battlefield after Lake Malik, how they'd killed all the gardai who were still alive but crippled or badly wounded. Those who were only slightly injured they'd taken captive. The whispers of what they'd done to them were far, far worse.

The bonfire—immense and furious—crackled at the bottom of the slope, and gathered around it were Westlanders: thousands of them, while smaller fires dotted the landscape past the great conflagration where they were encamped. Enéas saw a group of horses lashed together to one side of the bonfire, a bit away from those seated around the flames.

If he could not walk, he could still ride.

The journey seemed to take ages. The stars wheeled around the Sailing Star, the moon rose to zenith and began to fall, the rippers continued their long bloody feast. Exhausted, Enéas rested behind the shield of a pile of logs. The horses nickered nearby; he could smell them and hear their restless movements. The singing was louder now, a low-pitched and dissonant melody, the words they were chanting strange and unknown: a thousand voices, all singing together. The drone was maddeningly loud; the music vibrated in his chest and seemed to make the ground itself shake. He could see the Westlanders: skin bronzed like those from Namarro, their bamboo armor set with iron rings clashing as they sang and swayed. The massive logs of the pyre collapsed, sending sparks roaring upward.

One of the Westlanders at the front of the ranks rose to his feet and strode forward, raising bare muscular arms. Like the others, he wore a bamboo helmet adorned with bright, long feathers. A large, beaten silver plate lay on his chest from a chain around his neck, adorned with painted figures: that identified the man as one of the Westlander offiziers. His singing faded as he proclaimed something in a loud voice. Two more Westlander warriors came forward from the darkness on the other side of the fire, dragging between them the bloodied form of a man. The head lifted as they came into the firelight, and even at his distance Enéas recognized A'Offizier ca'Matin. He'd been stripped to the waist, and now they forced him to his knees in front of the Westlander offizier. Enéas heard ca'Matin praying to Cénzi, his face staring up at the sparks, the stars, and the moon, anywhere but at the Westlander.

The Westlander spoke to ca'Matin as he removed an odd device from a pouch on his belt. Enéas squinted, trying to see it as the offizier held it up, displaying it to the gathered troops. A short, curved barrel like the horn of a bull gleamed the color of ivory, the device set in a wooden handle. The offizier proffered the device to ca'Matin, handle foremost. When ca'Matin took it, his hands shaking visibly, his face uncertain, the warrior turned the ivory horn—Enéas heard a distinct, metallic *click*—and stepped back. He made a gesture as if he were reversing the device, then touching the tip of the horn to his abdomen. Ca'Matin shook his head, and the Westlander offizier sighed. His face seemed almost sympathetic as he took the instrument and reversed it in ca'Matin's hands. He nodded encouragingly as he pushed ca'Matin's hands back. The horn touched ca'Matin's stomach.

There was a flash that illuminated the entire landscape as if by a lightning stroke, and a booming thunderclap that drowned out Enéas' involuntary cry and sent the horses whinnying nervously and pulling against their hobbles. Ca'Matin's eyes and mouth went wide, though his expression seemed strangely ecstatic to Enéas, as if in his final moment Cénzi had touched him with glory.

Ca'Matin toppled, the device falling from his hands. His stomach was a bloody cavity, torn open as if a clawed fist had ripped him apart. Gore and blood spattered the ground underneath him, as well as the legs of Westlanders around him. The Westlander offizier raised his hands again, as the singing began once more. With a strange reverence, the two soldiers who had brought ca'Matin to the fire now wrapped his body in a cloth dyed with bright colors set in geometric patterns. They hurried the bundled corpse away into the shadows.

Enéas forced himself to move again, more desperately now. He didn't know what sorcery had been forced on ca'Matin, but he had to find a way back to Munereo: to warn them. *Help me do this, Cénzi....* He began to crawl toward the horses. If he could pull himself up on one and throw his injured leg over ... They might pursue him, but he knew this land as well as the Westlanders, perhaps better, and night would cover him.

He was to the horses now. These were captured Nessantican destriers, fitted with the livery he knew well, and more importantly, still harnessed with their bits and saddles. They were slower than the Westlanders' own steeds, but hardier. If he could get enough of a head start, the Westlander horses might tire before they could catch him.

With Cénzi's help ...

Enéas unhobbled the legs of a large gray, keeping the animal between himself and the fire. The destrier nickered, showing the whites of her eyes in the moonlight, and Enéas whispered softly to her. "Shh ... shh ... It's all right ... You'll be fine ..." He grasped at the straps of the saddle and pulled himself upright, keeping weight off his injured ankle. He took the reins in one hand, stroking the animal's neck. "Shh ... Quiet, now ..." He would have to balance himself at least partially on his bad ankle to get a foot into the stirrup; gently, he put the foot on the ground and slowly gave it weight, biting his lower lip in his teeth at the pain. He could do it, for a moment. That was all it would take. ...

He lifted his good foot and put it in the stirrup. A wave of knife cuts lanced from his ankle up his leg as for a moment it held all his weight, and the agony nearly made him faint. Desperately, he swung the bad leg over the horse's spine, almost crying out as the ankle slammed against the animal's thick body on the other side. But he was on the destrier now, half-laying on the mount's thick, muscular neck. He flicked the reins, kicking with his good leg. "Slow ..." he told the gray. "Very slow now. Quietly ..."

The gray tossed her head, then began to walk away from the other horses, heading back up the slope and away from the firelight and the encampment. The singing of the Westlanders covered the sound of iron-clad hooves on the ground. As soon as he was in the darkness again, as soon as he could put the shoulder of one of these hills between himself and the Westlanders, he could kick her into full gallop.

He was beginning to dare to think it was possible.

He nearly didn't notice the shape that moved to his left, the fragment of darkness that suddenly lifted and hurtled itself at him. He caught only a glimpse of a grim face before the man struck him from the side and bore him off the saddle. Light flared behind his eyes as he struck the ground, and Enéas screamed with the pain of his tormented leg, twisted underneath him. He heard the destrier galloping away, riderless, and then the shadow of a Westlander warrior was standing over him, his arm raised, and Enéas fell again into the dark.

~

Allesandra ca'Vörl

"**I** WOULD LIKE TO APOLOGIZE for my wife,
A'Hïrzg. She ... well, the subject of the Witch Archigos always upsets her. They have a ... history together,
after all. Still, she should not have been so outspoken at
dinner last night, especially toward you as the host."

Allesandra nodded to Archigos Semini. They were
seated on a viewing platform high on a slope behind the
Hïrzg's private estate—the palais at Stag Fall, well outside
Brezno. They faced east, the platform overlooking a wide,
long meadow of tall grass dotted with wildflowers. There,
below them, they could see a cluster of figures and horses:
Fynn, Jan, and several others. On either side of the meadow,
in the tall fir forest, drums echoed from the flanks of the
steep, verdant hills that formed the landscape: the sound of
the beaters, herding their prey toward the meadow and the
waiting Hïrzg.

Behind Allesandra on the balcony, servants bustled
about with drinks and food as they set a long table for dinner. Otherwise, Allesandra and the Archigos were alone;
all the other favored ca'-and-cu' who would be dining
with them that evening were with the Hïrzg's party in the
meadow. Allesandra had little desire to be in such close
proximity with her brother for that long. She wasn't certain
why Semini had remained behind at the palais—Francesca
was in the meadow with the others.

"Please believe me when I say that I took no offense,
Archigos," Allesandra told the man. "Even though I have
far more sympathy for Archigos Ana, I understand how
your wife might feel that way."

She glanced at Semini and saw him smile. "Thank you,"
he told her. "That's kind of you." He glanced carefully at
the servants, then pitched his voice low enough that they
couldn't overhear. "Between the two of us, A'Hïrzg, I wish
that I could have convinced your vatarh to name you as

his heir. That boy—" he pointed with his chin down to the gathering in the meadow, "—would be a perfectly adequate Starkkapitän for the Garde Civile, but he hasn't the vision or intelligence to be a good Hïrzg."

"I do believe I hear the Archigos speaking treason." Allesandra kept her gaze carefully away from him, her attention on Jan astride his horse next to Fynn. She wondered whether she could believe what ca'Cellibrecca was saying, and she wondered why he would voice it aloud to her. He had a reason for doing so, she was certain: Semini was not a man for accidental statements. But what was the reason? What did he want, and how would it benefit him?

"Did I perhaps speak what is also in *your* heart, A'Hïrzg, even if you don't dare say it aloud?" Semini answered in the same hoarse, low whisper. He turned toward her. "My heart is here, in this country, A'Hïrzg Allesandra. I want what is best for Firenzcia. Nothing more. I have given my life in service to Cénzi, and in service to Firenzcia. I shared your vatarh's vision of a Holdings where Brezno, not Nessantico, was the center of all things. He nearly achieved that vision. He *would* have accomplished that, I'm convinced, if it hadn't been for the heretical sorcery of the Witch Archigos."

There was hatred in his voice, genuine and heated. And also a strange satisfaction.

Vatarh would have succeeded if Ana hadn't taken me hostage, if she hadn't snatched me away from Vatarh and used me to end the war. As long as Allesandra remained in Nessantico, as long as her vatarh refused to pay the demanded ransom, his defeat was still incomplete. There was still hope that the results might change, and it had taken him a decade and more to lose that hope.

That's what she'd told herself. That's what Ana had told her. Ana had never spoken an unkind word against Hïrzg Jan; she had always cast him in as sympathetic a light as she could, even when Allesandra fumed and raged against his slowness to ransom her.

Allesandra caught her breath, her hand going to her throat, to the cracked globe of Cénzi around her neck.

Ca'Cellibrecca evidently misinterpreted the thought behind the gesture. "Ah, I see we share our opinion of Ana ca'Seranta. That creature kept the Holdings from falling apart entirely under that one-legged fool Justi—and now, at last, she's gone, praise Cénzi." His voice softened even further as he leaned close to Allesandra. "Now would be the time for a new Hïrzg to achieve what your vatarh could not . . . or it would be if we had a Hïrzg—or Hïrzgin—worthy of the task. Someone who was *not* Fynn. There are those in Nessantico who believe that, A'Hïrzg. People you might not suspect of harboring such thoughts."

The clamor of the beaters was coming closer in the valley beneath them. The riders were stirring restlessly, and Allesandra saw Fynn signal to Jan to nock his bow. "What are you saying to me, Archigos?" she asked, watching the tableau beneath them.

"I am saying that you are currently the A'Hïrzg, but we both know that's a temporary situation. But if Fynn were . . ." He hesitated. The drums crashed loudly below, and now they could hear a thrashing under the shade of the trees to the right. ". . . somehow no longer the Hïrzg, then you would become Hïrzgin." Another pause. "As you should have been."

The drums and shouting grew louder, and suddenly a stag emerged from the tree line several dozen strides from the Hïrzg's party. The beast was magnificent, with antlers the span of a person's arms and shoulders easily a tall man's height or more. The pelt was a stunning reddish brown, with a flash of white under the throat. The stag cantered out from the brush, then caught the scent of the hunting party. Allesandra felt herself holding her breath, looking at the gorgeous creature; alongside her, she heard Semini mutter: "By Cénzi, look at that gorgeous beast!"

The stag stopped, glaring at the riders momentarily before taking an enormous leap and bounding away from them toward the far end of the meadow. At the same moment, they saw an arrow speed away from Fynn's bow, the *twang* of the bowstring following belatedly to their ears. The stag went down with its rear legs in a tangle, the arrow embedded in its hindquarters. Then it pushed itself up once more and began running.

Jan had kicked his horse into motion with Fynn's shot, and now he raced after the wounded stag, controlling to his horse with his legs alone as he drew back the string of his bow. At full speed, he loosed his own arrow with the stag

only a few bare strides from reaching the cover of the forest once more.

The stag shuddered, the arrow plunging deep in the
left side of its chest. It ran a few more steps, nearly to the
woods. It seemed to be gathering itself—it leaped, but its
front legs snagged on the log it was trying to vault, and it
went down.

The stag lay on its side, its legs thrashing at the brush
and tearing clods of grassy earth from the ground with its
antlers. Fynn galloped up to where Jan had pulled up his
horse. Allesandra saw him slap Jan once on the shoulder,
then Fynn put another arrow to his bow.

With Fynn's shot, the stag went still. A distant cheer
echoed from the hunting party.

"Your son's physique may be slight, but he's an excellent horseman and a better archer. That was impressive—
to shoot like that while in full pursuit."

Allesandra smiled. *For a moment, he almost looked like
his great-vatarh, riding that way. . . .* Below, Fynn and Jan
had dismounted to go to the downed stag. "Moving archery
is a skill taught to the Magyarian cavalry—and Jan's had
excellent teachers."

"He's had excellent instruction in politics, as well. He
waited for the Hïrzg to give the killing blow. I assume
you've been his teacher in that."

"He knows what he should do, even if he sometimes ig-
nores my advice," Allesandra said. "Generally because I'm
the one who gave it," she added.

"Children of his age feel they must rebel against their
parents. It's natural, and I wouldn't be too concerned with
it, A'Hïrzg. He'll learn. And one day, if he were the A'Hïrzg
rather than just another ca' somewhere in the line of succession to be Gyula of West Magyaria . . ." He let his voice
trail off.

Allesandra turned to him finally. He towered over her
like a green-clad bear. His dark eyes were on hers. *Yes, he
has eyes in which you could lose yourself.* "You continue
to give me these little intimations and hints, Archigos," she
said quietly. "Do you have more than that to offer, or are
you trying to goad me into revealing myself? That won't
happen."

Ca'Cellibrecca nodded slowly and leaned down to her.

His mouth was close enough to her ear that she felt his warm breath. It made her shiver. "I have an offer, A'Hïrzg. If this is something that interests you, I do indeed," he whispered. Then he stood and applauded toward the meadow. "The cooks will have some fine venison steaks," he said loudly, "and there will be new antlers to adorn the palais. We should go down and meet the brave hunters, A'Hïrzg. What do you say?"

He offered her his arm.

She rose, and took it.

Karl ca'Vliomani

"**WHERE ARE YOU GOING?**" Varina asked him.
Karl had spent the the first night after Ana's death at Mika's house, but despite the solicitude of Mika and his wife, Karl had found their house—with their children and now the first of their grandchildren always coming in or out—too full of life and energy. He'd gone back to his own suite of rooms on the South Bank. It was Varina who came there every day, badgering his servants and generally making certain that he was fed and cared for. She left him alone with his grief; she was there when he needed to talk, or when he simply wanted the feel of another person in the room. She seemed to know when he needed silence, and she allowed him to have it. For that, he was grateful.

He remembered long ago when he'd first shown Ana what the Numetodo could do. That night, it had been Varina, a raw newcomer to the group, who Ana had seen demonstrating a spell. Varina had grown much since then; she was second now to Mika within the Numetodo here in the city, and there was no one at all who rivaled her dedication to research, nor her ability with the Scáth Cumhacht. He had never quite understood how it was she had remained alone all these years: she had been particularly striking in her youth: hair the color of autumn wheat; wide, expressive eyes the color of ancient, varnished oak; a wonderful, engaging smile and laugh that always made others smile with her. She was still attractive even now in middle years, even if in the last few years she had seemed to age quickly. Yet . . . she seemed to take all the vitality and energy she possessed and put it solely into learning the intricacies of the Scáth Cumhacht and the Second World, to find all the ways to bind that power. Even within the Numetodo, she rarely seemed to speak at length to anyone but Mika or Karl. As far as Karl knew, she had no other friends or lovers outside the group. She was an enigma, even to those closest to her.

He appreciated Varina's presence now, even if he didn't know how to express it.

He'd brooded on Ana's death now for a week, turning it over and over in his mind like a sick, ugly compost. Someone had wanted her dead. Ana had been the target, the assassin waiting for her to come to the High Lectern; certainly Karl had seen the other téni at the service ascend the lectern to place the readings and the scroll with the Admonition that Ana had intended to read, and they had not triggered the explosion.

The more he contemplated that, the more there seemed to be only one answer. An answer he wanted verified.

Varina was leaning against an archway of the anteroom as Karl shrugged on his cloak, her arms folded. She didn't repeat her query, only regarded him softly, as if concerned. "I have an appointment," he told her. She nodded. Still silent. Her eyes were wide and unblinking. "I have questions to ask."

Another nod. "I'll go with you," she said. He hesitated. "I won't interfere," she told him. "If you're going where I think you're going, you may need the support. Am I right?"

"Get your cloak," he told her. She smiled briefly—a flash of white teeth—and plucked her cloak from the peg on the wall.

The Ambassador from the Firenzcian Coalition, Andreas cu'Görin, possessed a face as thin and angular as a falcon's. As he rose from behind his desk, his heather-colored eyes regarded Karl and Varina as if the two were rabbits to be snatched up and devoured. The hawkish face was supplemented with a swordsman's lean body. Karl could imagine that the man was more comfortable in armor than in the proper, conservative bashta he wore.

It made him wonder how effective he could be here.

"Ambassador ca'Vliomani, Vajica ci'Pallo, your visit is . . . unexpected," cu'Görin said. "What can I do for you?"

Karl glanced pointedly at the aide who occupied the smaller desk on the other side of the room. "Gerald, why don't you see if you can find that proposal on the new border regulations?" cu'Görin said. The aide, as burly and thick as cu'Görin was slight, nodded and shuffled papers noisily for a breath before leaving the room.

Karl waited until he heard the door click shut behind him. "I've spent the last several days thinking about Archigos Ana's murder, Ambassador," he said. The words sounded almost casual, even to his ears. Varina shuffled her feet uneasily next to him. "You know, as much as I try to find reasons for someone doing that, I can't think of anyone who would want her dead except the people you represent."

Varina sucked in her breath audibly. A cloud passed over the heather eyes, deepening them to green. The muscles of the man's face tightened and his right hand closed as if it were searching for a sword's hilt. "You're rather blunt and direct, Ambassador."

"I've given up diplomacy for now," he answered.

Cu'Görin sniffed. "Indeed. Then I will be blunt as well. I find your accusation insulting. I'll forgive you, knowing how . . ." His nose twitched, the eyes narrowed. ". . . close you were to the Archigos of Nessantico, but I also expect an immediate apology."

"It's been my experience that expectations are often disappointed," Karl said.

"Karl . . ." Varina said softly. Her hand brushed his arm. "Perhaps . . ."

Her voice died, as if she knew he wasn't listening. The anger burned in his gut. Karl wanted nothing more than for cu'Görin to make a physical move or to blatantly insult him, anything to give him an excuse to use the Scáth Cumhacht that was smoldering in his mind waiting for the release word. But cu'Görin shook his head; he didn't sit, but seemed to lounge behind the desk, unperturbed.

"I think, Ambassador ca'Vliomani, that you discount the possibility that the assassin may have been a rogue, or perhaps hired by someone who had a personal grudge against the Archigos—someone within the Holdings of Nessantico. There's no reason to attach a conspiracy to this." His eyebrows arched; the rest of his body remained still. "Unless, of course, you have evidence that you care to share with me? But no, if you had *that*, you would have gone to the Regent, wouldn't you? The Commandant of the Garde Kralji would be standing here, not two Numetodo heretics." Slowly, almost mockingly, he sat again. Long fingers toyed with the parchments scattered on the desk's surface, and the hawk face returned, looking scornfully at Karl. "I think we're done here, Ambassador. Firenzcia has no business to do with heretics, and we never will. We're wasting each other's time."

The dismissal was a wind to his internal fire. *"No!"* Karl shouted. "We're *not* done!" He gestured, speaking one of the release words he'd prepared before he'd come. Quick fire crawled over the papers on the Ambassador's desk, consuming them in the instant it took cu'Görin to react, jumping backward from his seat. A quick wind followed, blowing the papers past cu'Görin and out the open window and whipping the Ambassador's bashta—that had to be Varina. "That fire could have been directed to you as easily as those documents," Karl told him. He heard the door crash open behind him and he lifted a hand warningly as he felt Varina turn to face the threat. "I didn't come with only a single spell, Ambassador, and my friend is stronger than I am. Tell your people to stay back, or I guarantee that you—at least—won't leave this room alive."

"Neither will you, if you persist in this nonsense," cu'Görin snarled, and Karl nearly laughed.

"That hardly matters to me at this point," he told the man. Varina's back pressed against his. He felt her arms lift, preparing a spell.

The Ambassador waved a hand to the people behind Karl. He heard a sword being sheathed and felt Varina's arms drop again. "I tell you again, Ambassador," cu'Görin said, "you are mistaken if you think that Firenzcia was involved in the Archigos' death. Kill me, don't kill me; that won't change that fact."

"I don't believe you."

Cu'Görin sniffed. "Lack of belief is the core of the problem with the Numetodo, isn't it? Do you want me to mourn for your Archigos, Ambassador? I won't. She brought this fate on herself by coddling the Numetodo and by her refusal to acknowledge the Archigos of Brezno as the true leader of the Faith. Violence was an inevitable result of her actions, but to my knowledge, it wasn't Firenzcia that did this. That's the truth, and if you can't believe me . . ." He shrugged. "Then do what you must. You'll only be demonstrating that the Numetodo are indeed the dangerous fools that every true believer knows them to be. Look at me, Ambassador. *Look* at me," he said more sharply, and Karl glared back at him. "Do you see a lie on my face? I tell you—the one who killed the Archigos wasn't anyone known to me or hired by me. *That* is the truth."

Karl could feel the Scáth Cumhacht vibrating madly inside him. He wanted nothing more than to lash out at this pompous fool, to watch the man's arrogance crumble into a scream, to have him cry out in agony as he died. But he could also hear Ana. He knew what she would tell him, and he let his hand drop to his side. He heard Varina sigh with relief.

Cu'Görin's words gave him no comfort. But he was beginning to wonder whether cu'Görin might not have told him the truth as he knew it, and Karl was also remembering a time many years ago and another person who could harness the Scáth Cumhacht—though he didn't call it that, nor did he call it the Ilmodo.

"If I find that you're lying, Ambassador," Karl said, "I won't give you the opportunity to give me your excuses or to draw your sword. I'll kill you wherever I find you. That is also the truth."

With that, he turned and Varina moved to his side. There were three guards blocking the doorway, but Karl shoved past them and strode out into the cool air and sunshine.

"What in the Eternal Six Pits was that?" Varina raged at him when they were outside on the Avi a'Parete again. She grabbed at his sleeve and pulled him to a stop. "Karl! I mean it. What did you think you were doing?"

"What I needed to do," he spat back at her, more sharply than he intended, still flushed with anger at cu'Görin and the man's attitude and his own gnawing doubts. They were all contained in his retort. "If you didn't want to be there, you didn't need to come."

"Ana's *dead*, Karl. You can't bring her back. Accusing people without evidence is just going to get you dead, too."

"Ana deserves justice."

"Yes, she does," Varina shot back. "Let those whose job

it is give her that. She wasn't your wife, Karl. You weren't lovers. She wasn't the matarh of your children."

The fury boiled inside him. He lifted his hand, the cold heat of the Scáth Cumhacht rising, and Varina spread her hands. "Do it!" she spat at him. "Go on! Will that make you feel better? Will that change anything?"

He blinked; around them, people on the street were staring. He dropped his hands. "I'm . . . I'm sorry, Varina."

She glared at him, her lips pressed tightly together. "She was your friend, and I understand that," Varina told him. "She was my friend, too. But she also blinded you, Karl. You've never been able to see what's right in front of you."

With that, she turned and left him, half-running along the Avi. "Varina," he called, but she pushed her way into the crowds, vanishing as if she'd never been there. Karl stood there, the throngs parting around him. He heard the wind-horns of the Archigos' Temple—Ana's temple—start to wail, proclaiming Second Call, and it sounded to him like mocking laughter.

~

Sergei ca'Rudka

"You don't trust me, Karl?"

Sergei watched the emotions washing over Karl's face. The man had a remarkably open face for a diplomat, a defect he'd possessed for as long as Sergei had known the man. Everything Karl thought revealed itself to an observer schooled in reading faces. Maybe that was just the Paeti way of things; Sergei had known a few people from the Isle over the decades, and most of them tended not only to speak their mind too openly, but also made little attempt to hide their genuine feelings or emotions. Perhaps that was what made the Isle renowned for its great poets and bards, for its songs and the fierce passion and temper of its people, but it also made them vulnerable, in Sergei's estimation.

Theirs was not Sergei's way.

Karl blinked at the assault of the question, which Sergei had fired at him before the servant had even closed the door. Karl stood at the door to Sergei's office, uncertain, as the door clicked softly behind him. "Of course I do, Sergei," he half-stammered, the words thick with the lilting Paeti accent. "I don't know what you're . . ." Then: "Oh."

"Yes. Oh." Sergei took a breath, rubbing at his nose. "I just had a rather unpleasant visit from Ambassador cu'Görin—though frankly any visit from him tends to be unpleasant. Still, he seems to think you're a dangerous man who should be residing in the Bastida rather than walking the streets. Actually, he said: 'In Brezno, that man would be gutted and hung in a gibbet for his impertinence, let alone his embrace of heresy.' I really don't think he likes you." Sergei rose and went to Karl, slapping him once on the back.

Cu'Gorin had indeed complained about Karl, but the Firenzcian Ambassador had come at Sergei's request, and gone away with a sealed message that Sergei hoped was already in the pouch of a rider tearing down the Avi a'Firenzcia toward Brezno. But none of that was anything he was going to tell ca'Vliomani. "Come. Sit with me, old friend. I'll have Rodger bring us some tea. I haven't had my breakfast yet."

A short time later, they were seated on a balcony overlooking the grounds. Groundkeepers prowled the gardens below them, pulling any weed daring to show its common head among the royalty of the flowers. The tea and biscuits sat untouched by either of them.

"Karl, you have to leave this to me."

"I can't."

"You must. My people are aggressively looking for the person or persons who did this to Ana. I am riding Commandant cu'Falla on this as if he were a horse. I won't let it drop, I won't let it rest. I promise you that. I want justice for Ana as much as you do. But you have to let *me* do it. Not you. *You* need to stay out of the investigation."

Karl looked at Sergei then, and Sergei saw despair pulling at the pouches below the man's eyes, dragging down the corners of his mouth. "Sergei, I'm convinced it had to be a Firenzcian plot. With Hïrzg Jan dead and Fynn on the throne, it just makes sense that he, and maybe Archigos Semini of Brezno—" Karl licked at his lips. "They all have a reason to hate Ana."

Sergei stopped Karl with a lifted hand. "Reasons, yes, but you've no proof. Neither do I. Not yet."

"Who else would want Ana dead? Tell me. Is there someone in the Holdings, maybe a jealous a'téni who wanted to be Archigos? Or someone from one of the provinces? Do you suspect someone else?"

"No," Sergei admitted. "Firenzcia is who I suspect myself. But we need to *know* before we act, Karl." The lie, as it always did, came easily to his mouth. Sergei was used to lies. One would not be heard in his voice, or seen in the twitch of a muscle.

Sometimes he thought that he was composed entirely of lies and deceptions, that if you took those away from him, he'd be nothing but a ghost.

"Know?" Karl repeated. "The way you *knew* when you threw me into the Bastida years ago? The way you *knew* that I and the Numetodo must have had something to do with Kraljica Marguerite's death?"

Sergei rubbed at the silver nose as he scowled at the memory. "I was following Kraljiki Justi's orders at the time. You know that. And you'll note that you're still alive when Justi would have preferred you dead. Give me credit for that. Karl, the stakes here are far too high for guesses, or for hotheads barging into the Ambassador of the Coalition's office and threatening him. If your guess is right, and Hïrzg Fynn was responsible for this act, the only thing you've accomplished is to give him warning of our suspicions. You and Varina actually used Numetodo spells?" He *tsked* aloud, shaking his head. "I'm surprised you didn't kill him outright."

"I wanted to," Karl said. For a moment, the lines around his mouth tightened, and his eyes glittered in the sunlight. "But I thought of Ana . . ." The glittering in his eyes increased. He wiped at his eyes with the sleeve of his bashta.

For a moment, Sergei felt genuine pity and empathy for the man. Archigos Ana he had respected, because there was no other choice. Ana never let anyone get too close to her, even those—like Karl—who might have wished that. Sergei knew this because he had watched Karl over the years, watched him because it was his duty to know the predilections and interests of those prominent in the Holdings. He knew Karl frequently engaged the services of the more expensive and discreet grandes horizontales within the city, and—interestingly to Sergei—each of those women whom Karl favored bore a physical resemblance to the Archigos, changing over the decades as Ana had changed herself. It took little intuition to guess why that might be.

Karl . . . Sergei liked the man, as much as he ever allowed himself to like anyone. He nodded to the Numetodo. "I'm glad Ana's ghost held back your hand, or otherwise, I might have had no choice. Karl, you *have* to drop this. Promise me. Let those under me work the investigation. I will tell you anything I find." That was another lie, of course. Sergei already knew details about the assassination that he had no intention of sharing with Karl; there were suspicions in his mind that he would not voice.

In the darkness of the Bastida, he'd had the gardai leave him alone with the man, an employee of the trader Gairdi, who regularly ran between Nessantico and Brezno. He'd heard the delicious whimper as he unrolled the canvas strip with its grim tools laced inside, and Sergei had smiled at the prisoner. "Tell me the truth," he'd said, "and perhaps we'll need none of this." That, too, had been a lie, but the man had jumped at the opportunity, babbling in a quick, high voice. The screams, when they'd come later, had been exquisite.

There were some vices in him that had become stronger with age, not weaker. "Promise me," Sergei said again.

Karl hesitated. His gaze skittered away from Sergei to the garden below, and Sergei followed it. There, a gardener dug his finger into soil so wet and rich it appeared black and plucked another weed. The worker tossed the tangle of leaves and roots into the canvas bag slung over his shoulder. Sergei nodded: the necessary work that kept the garden beautiful required death, too.

"I promise, Sergei." Sergei, trapped in the image, looked back to find Karl smiling wanly at him.

Yet . . . There was something Karl wasn't saying, some information he was withholding. Sergei could see it. He nodded as if he believed the man and decided that he would have cu'Falla put someone to watching Karl, with orders to learn what the man knew as well as to prevent the Paetian Ambassador from making a critical mistake—especially one that might interfere with Sergei's own intentions.

Ana was dead. While she lived, a strong and firm presence guiding the Faith, Sergei hadn't been willing to move the way he contemplated moving now. But with her dead, with the far weaker and uncertain Kenne elected to the Archigos' throne, with Kraljiki Audric so ill and frail and young . . .

Everything had changed.

"Good," Sergei said, returning Karl's smile warmly. "This has been hard for all of us, but especially for you, my good friend. Now, let's have some of this tea before it gets cold, and nibble on the biscuits. I'll bet you haven't eaten for a few days, from the look of you. Haven't Varina and Mika been watching after you . . . ?"

That evening, a turn of the glass after the wind-horns sounded Third Call, Sergei sat with the new Archigos Kenne on the viewing balcony of the temple on the South Bank, watching the daily Ceremony of the Light. For two centuries and more now, the téni of the Concénzia Faith had come from the temple in the evening and—with the gift of the Ilmodo—set ablaze the lamps that banished night from the city. For all his life, Sergei had witnessed the daily rite. The gilded, crystal-globed téni-lamps were placed at five-stride intervals along the grand Avi a'Parete, the wide ring boulevard encircling the oldest sections of the city. Until late into the night, the lamps hurled their challenge to the moon and stars, proclaiming Nessantico's greatness.

To Sergei, this was the ceremony that defined Nessantico to the populace. This was the ceremony that proclaimed Cénzi's support of the Kralji and of the Concénzia Faith, a ceremony that had existed unchanged for generations— until Archigos Ana's time. Now it meant less, when there were people walking the street who could produce light themselves: without calling on Cénzi, without the training of a téni. Ana's acceptance of the Numetodo heresy had lessened the Faith, in Sergei's opinion, and had forced the people's view of it to change.

Change. Sergei disliked change. Change meant instability, and instability meant conflict.

Change meant that everything must be reevaluated. Ana . . . Sergei had never been particularly close to the woman, but in his role as Commandant of the Garde Civile, then as Regent, he had certainly worked in tandem with her. Whatever her personal faults, she had been strong and Sergei admired strength. It was only her presence on the Archigos' throne that had kept Justi's reign as Kraljiki from being a complete catastrophe. For that alone, he would always be grateful to her memory.

But now Kenne was Archigos. Sergei genuinely liked Kenne as a person. He enjoyed the man's company and his friendship. But Kenne would not be the Archigos that Ana had been. *Could* not be, for he lacked the steel inside. Sergei understood why the Concord A'Téni chose him—because none of the other a'téni wanted the title, the responsibility, or the conflicts that came with the Archigos' throne and staff, and they especially feared it now. Kenne was no one's enemy, and, most especially, Kenne was old. Kenne was frail. He would not hold Cénzi's staff for many years . . . and maybe when he died, it would be a less turbulent time.

The Concord had acted out of their own self-preservation, and so the Concord had given the Faith a poor Archigos.

Sergei wondered if Kenne would ever forgive him for what that meant.

The two men stood as the light-téni emerged in their long processional line from the great main doors directly below them. Sergei could hear the sonorous melody of the choir finishing the evening devotions in the temple's main chapel, the sound echoing plaintively throughout the square as the doors opened. The sun had just set, though the clouded western sky was still a furious swirl of reds and oranges. In the glow, the téni turned and gave their Archigos the sign of Cénzi, and Kenne blessed them with the same sign.

The e-téni—all of them looking impossibly young to Sergei's eyes, all of them solemn with the weight of their duty—bowed as one to the Archigos, green robes swaying like a field of grass in the wind, before turning again to cross the vast courtyard before the temple. The usual crowds had gathered to watch the ceremony, though the crowds were less thick in recent years than they had been in the time of Kraljica Marguerite, when the Holdings had been one and visitors flocked to Nessantico from all points of the compass. In recent years, there were far fewer visitors from the east and south, from Firenzcia or the Magyars, from Sesemora or Miscoli. With the war in the Hellins across the Strettosei, many of the young men were gone and families traveled less. Though the courtyard of the Old Temple was full of onlookers, the Garde Kralji had no trouble making room for the light-téni; Sergei could see the paving-cobbles between them. The téni reached the Avi and split into two lines, spreading out east and west along the Avi and going to the nearest lamps, set on either side of the gated entrance to the Archigos' Temples.

The first of the light-téni went to the lamps. They stood underneath the shimmering globe of cut glass, looking up into the evening sky as if they glimpsed Cénzi watching them, and they spoke a single word and gestured from chest to lamp, closed fist to open hand.

The lamps erupted with brilliant yellow light.

Sergei applauded with Kenne. Yet . . .

That single word to release the spell: that was a change,

too; a nod to the Numetodo, who could quickly release their spells. It was another of the changes Ana had wrought. "I miss the old ways sometimes, Archigos," Sergei said to Kenne. "The long chanting, the sequence of gestures, the way the effort visibly wearied your téni . . . The Numetodo way of using the Ilmodo makes it look too easy. There was . . ." He sighed as the two men sat again. ". . . a *mystery* to it then, a sense of labor and love and ritual that's vanished. I'm not sure that Ana made the right decision when she allowed the téni to start using the Numetodo methods to light our streets."

He saw Kenne nod. "I understand," Kenne answered. "Part of me agrees with you, Sergei; there was a feeling to the old rituals that's gone now. But the Numetodo proved their worth against Hïrzg Jan, and Ana could hardly renounce them afterward, could she?" Sergei heard him give a soft, self-deprecating chuckle. "We're old men, Sergei. We want things to be the way they used to be, back when we were young. When the world was right and Marguerite was going to sit on the Sun Throne forever."

Yes. I want that more than you'd believe. Sergei scratched at the side of the nose where the glue irritated his skin; a few flecks of the resin flaked off under his fingernail. "There's nothing wrong with that. Things *were* good then, with Kraljica Marguerite and Dhosti wearing the Archigos' robes. There was no better time for the Holdings or for the Faith. We lived in a perfect time and we didn't even know it."

"Yes, we did. I agree." Kenne sighed with the memory.

The gilded doors to the temple behind them opened and an older u'téni emerged: Sergei recognized him: Petros cu'Magnaio, Kenne's assistant. The man had lived with Kenne since his time with Archigos Dhosti. Kenne nodded to cu'Magnaio with a smile as he set down a tray of fruit and tea between the two of them. It never bothered Sergei that Kenne was afflicted with what was euphemistically called "Gardai's Disease." There was some truth, after all, to the appellation: when away for years on a campaign, soldiers sometimes took comfort where they could find it, with those who were around them. "It will be getting chilly with the sunset," cu'Magnaio said. "I thought the two of you might like hot tea."

Kenne's hand hovered above cu'Magnaio's but didn't quite touch him—Sergei knew that would have been different if he had not been there. "Thank you, Petros. We won't be long here, but I appreciate it."

Cu'Magnaio bowed and gave the sign of Cénzi to them. "I'll make sure that you're not disturbed while you're talking. Archigos, Regent. . . ." He left them, closing the balcony doors behind him.

"He's a good man," Sergei said. "You've been lucky with him."

Kenne nodded, gazing fondly toward the doors where Petros had gone. Then he shook himself as if remembering something. "Speaking of those who have sat on the Sun Throne, Sergei, I'm sorry the Kraljiki couldn't join us this evening. How is Audric feeling?"

Sergei lifted a shoulder. Below, the light-téni moved out from the temple to lamps further down the Avi, the crowds walking with them, murmuring. The doves fluttered down from the domes of the Temple and the rooftops of the buildings in the complex to peck at the vacated stones of the plaza for leavings. "He's not good." He glanced back over his shoulder; the doors remained closed but he still lowered his voice. "Have you had any luck finding another téni with healing skills?"

Kenne sighed. "That has always been among the rarest of gifts, and since the Divolonté specifically condemns its use . . . well, it's been difficult. But I have hopes. Petros is making judicious inquiries for me. We'll find someone." He paused, glanced at the fruit on the plate between them and selected a piece. Kenne had long, delicate hands, but the flesh wrapping his bones was wrinkled and thin, and Sergei could see the tremor as the Archigos lifted a slice of sweetrind to his lips and sucked at it. *We can't afford weakness in both the Kraljiki and the Archigos, not if we hope to survive.*

"Sergei, we need to consider what happens if the boy dies," Kenne continued, almost as if he'd heard Sergei's thoughts. "Justi's offspring . . ." He frowned and set the sweetrind back on the plate. "Too sour," he said. "Justi's children have never been known for their longevity."

The téni moved along the Avi and out of sight. The

crowds in the square of the temple began to disperse; the
sound of the choir ended in a lingering, ethereal chord.
"I hope that Cénzi doesn't make us face that choice,"
Sergei said carefully. "But it's what everyone's wondering, isn't it?"

"There are the ca'Ludovici twins, Sigourney or Donatien. They're, what . . ." Kenne's thin lips pursed in
concentration. ". . . second cousins once removed from
Audric and first cousins to Justi, since Marguerite was
their great-great aunt. They're already of age and more,
which is good. Donatien, particularly, has distinguished
himself in the Hellin Wars, even if things haven't been
going well of late, and he's married to a ca'Sibelli, a solid
Nessantican family—we could call him back from the
Hellins. Sigourney might be the better choice, though.
She still carries the ca'Ludovici surname, of course: that
certainly has incredible weight here, and she's made her
presence felt on the Council of Ca'. The two of them
have the closest lineage claim, I believe, and I'm certain
the Council of Ca' would sustain either of their claims to
take the Sun Throne."

Sergei was unsurprised to find that the Archigos'
thoughts were so closely paralleling his own; he suspected
this was the case throughout both the Holdings and the
Coalition. He paused, wondering whether he should say
more. It would be interesting, perhaps, to see how Kenne
would react. "Allesandra ca'Vörl can claim the same lineage and the same relationship through her matarh,"
Sergei answered, as if idly musing. "For that matter, so
could the new Hïrzg Fynn. They're also second cousins to
Marguerite—with a claim to the throne equal to Sigourney
or Donatien."

In the fierce light of the téni-lamps, Kenne's eyebrows
clambered up the ridges of his forehead. "You're not seriously suggesting . . ."

The volatile tone was the reaction he'd expected, and
Sergei grinned quickly to make it seem that the words
were only a jest. "Hardly," Sergei told him. "Just pointing
out how Allesandra might respond. Certainly Sigourney or
Donatien would be good choices, as you suggest, though
perhaps we need Donatien to remain as commandant in
the Hellins. However, Audric's not dead, and I'd prefer that

he stay that way. But if the worst would happen . . . You're right; we should be considering the succession. The Holdings are already broken, thanks to Justi's incompetence, and we can't afford to have what is left shatter further." He paused. He deliberately narrowed his eyes and stroked his chin, as if the thought had just now occurred to him. "But . . . Perhaps a compromise could be worked between the Holdings and the Coalition if the worst happened, Kenne. A ca'Vörl to take the Sun Throne, but the Concénzia Faith ruled by you, not Semini ca'Cellibrecca." *There. See what he makes of the offer.*

"You'd have Ana's murderers seated on the Sun Throne?" The horror in the man's voice was palpable.

Sergei sniffed—a loud sound, whistling through the metal nostrils of his false nose. "You're making the same accusation as Ambassador ca'Vliomani. As of the moment, it's unfounded."

"Who else *would* have done this to Ana, Sergei? We know it wasn't the Numetodo—she was their ally."

Sergei didn't push the point any further. He already knew what he needed to know. "That's something my people are trying to determine. And we will." The sunset fire no longer burned in the western sky. The stars were competing against the colder flames of the téni-lamps, and the evening chill was settling around the city. Sergei shivered and rose from his chair. His knee joints cracked and protested at the movement; he grunted with the effort. Sergei could still feel the ache in his muscles and the lingering bruises from when he'd flung himself over Audric in the temple.

Old men, indeed . . .

Petros must have been watching (and undoubtedly listening, as well) through the cracks of the temple doors; as soon as Sergei stood the doors opened and an e'téni attendant hurried to him with his overcloak. He could see Petros standing in the gloom of the corridor beyond. "I should be checking on Audric, Archigos," Sergei said as he shrugged on the woolen folds. "If you find someone with the skills we were discussing, please bring him or her to the palais immediately."

"I'll stop by myself in a turn of the glass or so," Kenne said. "Petros will have my supper ready now, but I'll come afterward. To see what I can do."

"Thank you, Archigos," Sergei told him. "I will see you then, perhaps."

As he walked away from the temple, he wondered whether his message had reached Brezno yet, and what reception it might have found.

Allesandra ca'Vörl

"**Y**OUR BOY'S SHOT was as good as any I could make," Fynn declared.

Allesandra doubted that. Jan might not have the bulk and power of Fynn's muscular frame. He might not be able to wield the heavy weight of water-hardened steel someone like Fynn could manage with ease, but the boy could ride like no one else and he had an eye with an arrow that very few could match. Allesandra was certain that neither Fynn nor anyone else there could have hit, much less brought down, the stag from the back of a galloping horse.

But it seemed best to simply nod, give Fynn a false smile, and agree. It was safest, but conceding the falsehood still hurt when her pride in her son made her want to object. She stored it with the other hurts and insults Fynn and her vatarh had given her over the years. The pile in her mind was already mountainous. "Indeed, Brother. He's been taught well in Magyaria. Pauli was famous for his horseback archery when he was young; it would seem that Jan has acquired that ability from his vatarh."

"It was lucky I was there to take the final shot, though, or the stag would have escaped."

Allesandra smiled again, though she knew it was neither luck nor fortune, only Jan demonstrating that he knew better than to entirely eclipse the presence of the Hïrzg. A political move, as adroit as any she might have made.

The two of them were walking along the eastern balcony of the Stag Fall Palais—as private as one could be within the estate. Gardai stood at stiff attention where the balcony turned to the north and south, their stoic avoidance of the Hïrzg and A'Hïrzg obvious as they stared outward; from the windows left open to catch the evening breeze, they could hear the murmuring of the guests at the table they'd just left. Allesandra could pick out Jan's voice as he laughed at something Semini said.

She looked eastward, toward the evening mist rising in its soft, slow tide from the valleys toward the steep slopes in which the palais was nestled. The tops of the evergreens below them were wrapped in strands of white cloud, though the wind-scoured and treeless peaks above remained swaddled in sun that sparked from the granite cliffs and the clinging snowbanks. Somewhere hidden in the mist below, a waterfall burbled and sang.

"It's truly beautiful here," Allesandra said. "I never realized that when I was here as a girl. Great-Vatarh Karin picked a perfect location: gorgeous, and perfectly defensible. No army could ever take Stag Fall if it were well-defended."

Fynn nodded, though he didn't seem to be looking at the landscape. Instead, he was fiddling with the brocaded cuff of his sleeve. "I asked you to walk with me so we could speak alone, Sister," he said.

"I thought as much. We ca'Vörls rarely do anything without ulterior motives, do we?" she said. A quick smile played with her lips. "What did you want to say to me, little brother?"

He grinned—briefly—at that, the thick scar on his cheek twitching with the motion. "You never knew me when I was little."

"There was good reason for that." Yes, that hurt was at the very heart of the mountain inside, the seed from which it had all grown. . . .

"Or a bad one. I didn't understand then, Allesandra, why Vatarh left you in Nessantico for so long. After he finally told me about you, I always wondered why Vatarh let my sister languish in another country, one he so obviously hated."

"Do you understand now?" she asked, then continued before he could respond. "Because I still don't. I always waited for him to apologize to me, or to explain. But he never would. And now . . ."

"I don't want to be your enemy, Allesandra."

"Are we enemies, Fynn?"

"That's what I'm asking you. I would like to know."

Allesandra waited before answering. The marble railing of the balcony was damp under her hand, the swirls of pale blue in the milky stone varnished by dew. "Are you thinking that if our positions were reversed, that if I'd been named Hïrzgin by Vatarh, then you would consider me your enemy?" she asked carefully.

He made a face, his hand sweeping through the cool air as if he were swiping at an annoying insect. "So many words . . ." He sighed loudly and she could hear his irritation in it. "You make speeches that slip in my ears and make my own words twist their meanings, Allesandra. I've never been someone able to fence with words and speeches—it's not one of my skills. It wasn't one of Vatarh's either. Vatarh always said exactly what he thought: no more, no less, and what he didn't want someone to know, he didn't say at all. I asked you a simple enough question, Allesandra: are you my enemy? Please do me the courtesy of giving me a plain, unadorned answer."

"No," she answered firmly, and then shook her head. "Fynn, only an idiot would answer you with anything other than 'No, we're not enemies.' You know that, too, despite your protestations. You may be many things, but you're not *that* simple, and I'm not that foolish to fall into so obvious a trap. What's the real question you're asking?"

Fynn gave an exasperated *huff*, slapping his hand on the railing. She could feel the impact of his hand shivering the rail. "There . . . there are *people* . . ." He stopped, taking a long audible breath. When he released it, she could see it cloud before his face. He touched the plain golden band that encircled his head. "Vatarh told me before he died that there were whispers among the chevarittai and the higher téni of the Faith. Some of them opposed his naming of me as the A'Hïrzg. They don't like my temper, or they say I'm too . . . stupid." He spat out the word, as if it tasted sour on his tongue. "Some of them wanted you to have that title, or wanted someone else entirely to take the band of the Hïrzgai."

"Did Vatarh tell you who was doing the whispering? Where did it come from?" Allesandra asked. She had to ask the question. She shivered a little, hoping he hadn't noticed. "Did Vatarh tell you who had said this?"

But Fynn only shook his head. "No. No names. Just . . . that there were those who would oppose me. If I find them . . ." He took a long breath in through his nose, and his face went hard. "I will take them down." He looked directly at her. "I don't care who they are, and I don't care who I have to hurt."

She faced away from him so he could not see her face, looking at the fog drifting among the pines just below. *Good. Because I know some of them, and they know me. . . .* "You can't punish rumors, Fynn," she said. "You can't put chains around gossip and imprison it, any more than you can capture the mists."

"I don't think Vatarh was deceived by mists."

"Then what do you want of me, little brother?"

That was what he'd wanted her to ask. She could see it in his face, in the dimming light of the sky. "At the Besteigung," he began, then stopped to put his hand atop hers on the railing. It did not feel like an affectionate gesture. "You're the one that everyone looks to. You're the one who could have been Hïrzgin had Vatarh not changed his mind. The ca'-and-cu' still like you, and many of them think that Vatarh did wrong by you. The rumors always circulate around *you*, Allesandra. You. I want to stop them; I want them to have no reason at all to exist. So—at the Besteigung—I want you, and Pauli and Jan also, to take a formal oath of loyalty to the throne. In public, so everyone will hear you say the words."

They would only *be words,* she wanted to tell him, *with as much meaning as my saying now "No, Fynn, I'm not your enemy." Words and oaths mean nothing: to know that, all you need do is look at history . . .* But she smiled at him gently and patted his hand. Perhaps he really was that simple, that naive? "Of course we'll do that," she told him. "I know my place. I know where I should be, and I know where I want to be in the future."

Fynn nodded. His hand moved away from hers. "Good," he said, and the relief sang a high note in his voice. "Then we will expect that." *We . . .* She heard the royal plural in his voice, all unconscious, and it made her lips press tightly together. "I like your son," he said unexpectedly. "He's a bright one—like you, Allesandra. I'd hate to think he was involved in any plots against me, but if he was, or if his family was . . ." His face tightened again. "The air's chilly and damp out here, Allesandra. I'm going inside." Fynn left her, returning to the warmth of the palais' common room. Allesandra stood at the railing for several more minutes before following him, watching until the mists were nearly level with her and the world below had vanished into gloom and cloud.

She thought of being Hïrzgin, and it came to her that the High Seat in Brezno would never have satisfied her, even if it had been hers. It was a hard realization, but she knew now that it was in Nessantico that she'd been most happy, that she'd felt most at home.

"I know my place, Brother," she whispered into the hush of the fog. "I do. And I will have it."

~

Nico Morel

NICO HEARD TALIS SPEAKING in the other room,
even though Matarh had gone to the square to get
bread.

Matarh had kissed him and told him to nap for a bit, saying that she'd be back before supper. But he hadn't been
able to sleep, not with the sounds of the people in the street
just outside the shutters of his window, not with the sun
peeking through the cracks between the boards. He was
too old for naps now anyway. Those were for children, and
he was becoming a young man. Matarh had told him that,
too.

Nico threw the covers aside and padded softly across
the room. He leaned forward just enough that he could see
past the edge of the scarred, warped door that never closed
tightly—making sure he didn't touch it, since he knew the
hinges would screech a rusty alarm. Through the crack between door and jamb, he could see Talis. He was bent over
the table that Matarh used to prepare meals. A shallow
bowl was sitting on the table, and Nico squinted in an effort
to see it better: incised animals danced along the rim, and
the bowl had the same hue as the weathered bronze statue
of Henri VI in Oldtown Square. Matarh didn't have a metal
bowl, at least none that Nico had ever noticed; the animals
carved into it were strange, too: a bird with a head like a
snake's; a scaled lizard with a long snout full of snarled
teeth. Talis poured water from Matarh's pitcher into the
bowl, then untied a leather pouch from his belt and shook a
reddish, fine powder onto his palm. He dusted the powder
into the water as if he were salting food. He gestured with
his hand over the bowl as if smoothing something away,
then spoke words in the strange language that he sometimes spoke when he was dreaming at night, cuddled with
Nico's matarh in their bed.

A light seemed to glow inside the bowl, illuminating

Talis' face a sickly yellow-green. Talis stared into the glowing bowl, his mouth open, his head leaning closer and closer as if he were falling asleep, though his eyes were wide. Nico didn't know how long Talis stared into the bowl—far longer than the breath Nico tried to hold. As he watched, Nico thought he could feel a chill, as if the bowl were sending a winter's breath out from it, frigid enough that Nico shivered. The feeling became stronger, and the breath Nico drew in seemed to pull that cold inside with it, though somehow it felt almost hot inside him. It made him want to breathe it back out, like he could spit frozen fire.

In the other room, Talis' head nodded ever closer. When his face appeared to be about to touch the rim of the bowl, the glow vanished as suddenly as it had come, and Talis gasped as though drawing breath for the first time.

Nico gasped, too, involuntarily, as the cold and fire inside him vanished at the same moment. He started to pull his head back from the door, but Talis' voice stopped him. "Nico. Son."

He peered back in. Talis was staring at him, a smile creasing the lines of his olive face. There were more wrinkles there, lately, and Talis' hair was beginning to be salted with gray. He groaned when he stood up too fast and his joints sometimes creaked, even though Matarh said that Talis was the same age as her. "It's fine, Son. I'm not angry with you." Talis' accent seemed stronger than usual. He gestured to Nico, and Nico could see a smear of the red dust still on his palm. He sighed as if he were tired and needed to sleep. "Come here." Nico hesitated. "Don't worry; come here."

Nico pushed open the door—the hinge, as he knew it would, protesting loudly—and went to Talis. The man picked him up (yes, he grunted with the effort) and put him on a chair next to the table so he could see the bowl. "Nico, this is a special bowl I brought with me from the country where I used to live," he said. "See . . . there's water in it." He stirred the water with a fingertip. The water seemed entirely ordinary now.

"Is the bowl special because it can make water glow?" Nico asked.

Talis continued to smile, but the way his eyebrows lowered over his eyes made the smile look somehow wrong in his face. Nico could see his own face staring back from the brown-black pupils of Talis' eyes. There were deep folds at the corner of those eyes. "Ah, so you saw that, did you?"

Nico nodded. "Was that magic?" he asked. "I know you're not a téni because you never go to temple with Matarh and me. Are you a Numetodo?"

"No," he said. "I'm not a Numetodo, nor a téni of the Faith. What you saw wasn't magic, Nico. It was just the sunlight coming in the window and reflecting from the water in the bowl, that's all. I saw it, too—so bright it seemed like there was a tiny sun under the water. I liked the way it looked, and so I watched it for a while."

Nico nodded, but he remembered the red dust and the strange, grassy color of the light and the way it had bathed Talis' face, as if a hand of light were stroking him. He remember the cold fire. He didn't mention any of that, though. It seemed best not to, though he wasn't certain why.

"I love you, Nico," Talis continued. He knelt on the floor next to Nico's chair, so that their faces were the same height. His hands were on Nico's shoulders. "I love Serafina . . . your matarh . . . too. And the best thing she's ever given me, the thing that has made me the most happy, is you. Did you know that?"

Nico nodded again. Talis' fingers were tight around his arms, so tight he couldn't move. Talis' face was very near his, and he could smell the bacon and honeyed tea on the man's breath, and also a faint spiciness that he couldn't identify at all. "Good," Talis said. "Now listen, there's no need to mention the bowl or the sunlight to your matarh. I thought that one day I might give your matarh the bowl as a gift, and I want it to be a surprise, and you don't want to spoil that, do you?"

Nico shook his head at that, and Talis grinned widely, as if he'd told himself a joke inside that Nico hadn't heard. "Excellent," he said. "Now, let me finish washing the bowl— that's what I was starting to do when you saw me. That's why I put the water in it." Talis released Nico; Nico rubbed at his shoulders with his hands as Talis picked up the bowl, swirled the water inside it ostentatiously, then opened the window shutters to dump it into the flowered windowbox. Talis wiped the bowl with his linen bashta, and Nico heard the ring of metal. He watched as Talis put the bowl into the pack that he kept under the bed that he and Nico's matarh shared, then put the pack back underneath the straw-filled mattress.

"There," Talis said as he straightened again. "It'll be our little secret, eh, Nico?" He winked at Nico.

It would be their secret. Yes.

Nico liked secrets.

The White Stone

THEY CAME TO HER AT NIGHT, those who the White Stone had killed. In the night, they stirred and woke. They gathered around her in her dreams and they talked to her. Often, the loudest of them was Old Pieter, the first person she'd killed.

She'd been twelve.

"Remember me..." he whispered to her in her sleep. *"Remember me..."*

Old Pieter was their neighbor in the sleepy village back on the Isle of Paeti, and she'd known him since birth, especially after her vatarh died when she was six. He was always friendly with her, joking and gifting her with animals he'd carved from oak branches, whittling them with the short knife he always carried on his belt. She painted the animals he gave her, placing them on a window shelf in her little bedroom where she could see them every morning.

Old Pieter kept goats, and when her matarh would let her, she sometimes helped him tend the small herd. The day her life changed, the day she started on the path that had led her here, she'd been out with Pieter and his goats near the Loudwater, the creek falling fast and noisy from the slopes of Sheep Fell, one of the tall hills to the south of the village. The goats were grazing placidly near the creek, and she was walking near them when she saw a body in the grass: a doe freshly killed, its body torn by scavengers and flies beginning to buzz excitedly around the carcass. The doe's head, on the long tawny neck, gazed forlornly at her with large, beautiful eyes.

"If ye look into that right eye, ye'll see what killed her."

A hand stroked her shoulder and continued down her back before leaving. She started, not realizing that Old Pieter had come up behind her. "The right eye, it connects to a person's or an animal's soul," he continued. "When a living thing dies, well, the right eye remembers the last thing they saw—the last face, or the thing that killed it. Look close into that doe's eye, and ye'll see it in there, too: a wolf, p'raps. It happens to people, too. Murderers, they been caught that way—by someone looking into the dead right eye of the one they killed and seeing the killer's face there."

She shuddered at that and turned away, and Old Pieter laughed. His hand brushed wisps of hair that had escaped her braids back from her face, and he smiled fondly at her. "Now don't be upset, girl," he said. "G'wan and see to the goats, and I'll carve ye something new. . . ."

It was later in the afternoon when he came to her again, as she sat on the banks of the Loudwater watching the stream tumble through its rocky bed. "Here," he said. "Do ye like it?"

The carving was a human figure, small enough to hide easily in her hand: nude, and undeniably female, with small breasts like her own budding from the chest. It was the hair that distressed her the most: a moon ago, a ca' woman from Nessantico had passed through their town, staying at the inn one night on the road to An Uaimth. The woman's hair had been braided in an intricate knot at the back of the head; entranced by this glimpse of foreign fashion, she had worked for days to imitate those braids—since then, she had braided her hair every day the same way. It was braided now, just as the nude figure's was, and her hand involuntarily went to her knot of hair on the back of her head. She wanted, suddenly, to tear it out.

She stared at the carving, not knowing what to say, and she felt Old Pieter's hand on her cheek. "It's you," he told her. "You're becoming a woman now."

His hand had cupped her head, and he brought her to him, pressing her tight against him. She could feel his excitement, hard on her thigh. She dropped the doll.

What happened then she would never forget: the pain, and the humiliation of it. The shame. And after it was over, after his weight left her, she saw his belt lying on the grass next to her, and there in its sheath was his knife, and she took it. She took the hilt in hands that trembled and shook, she took it sobbing, she took it with her tashta ripped and half torn from her, she took it with her blood and his seed spattering her thighs, and she took it with all the anger and rage and fear inside her and she stabbed him. She plunged the blade low in his belly, and when he groaned and shouted in alarm, she yanked out the blade and plunged it into him again, and again, and again until he was no longer screaming and no longer beating at her with his fists and no longer moving at all.

Covered in her own blood and his, she let the knife drop, kneeling alongside him. His dead eyes stared at her.

"When a thing dies, the right eye remembers the last thing they see—the last face they saw...."

She half-crawled to the bank of the Loudwater. She found a stone there, a white and water-polished pebble the size of a large coin. She brought the stone back and pressed it down over his right eye. Then she huddled there, a few steps away from him, until the sun was nearly down and the goats came around her bleating and wanting to go home to their stables. She woke as if from a sleep, seeing the body there, and she found that curiosity drove her forward toward it. Her hand trembled as she reached down to his face, to the pebble-covered right eye. She took the stone from that eye, and it felt strangely warm. The eye underneath it was gray and clouded, and though she looked carefully into it, she saw nothing there: no image of herself. Nothing at all. She clutched the pebble in her hand: so warm, almost throbbing with life. Her breath shuddered as she clutched it to her breast.

She left then, leaving his body there. She walked south, not north, and she took the pebble with her.

She would never return to the village of her birth. She would never see her matarh again.

The White Stone turned in her sleep. "*I didn't mean to hurt you, girl,*" Old Pieter whispered in her dreams. "*Didn't mean to change you. I'm sorry. I'm so sorry...."*

OMENS

Enéas cu'Kinnear
Audric ca'Dakwi
Sergei ca'Rudka
Allesandra ca'Vörl
Karl ca'Vliomani
Enéas cu'Kinnear
Jan ca'Vörl
Sergei ca'Rudka
Nico Morel
Varina ci'Pallo
Allesandra ca'Vörl
The White Stone

Enéas cu'Kinnear

HE WISHED NOW that he'd bothered to learn more of the Westlander speech.

Enéas knew some of their words, enough to get by in the crowded, fragrant, and loud bazaars of Munereo. There, among chattering, jostling crowds, one could find sweet perfumes from the plains of the West Horn; the rich, black, and sweet nuggets from the jungles along the Great Southern River; intricate painted basketry from the people of the Great Spine; fine woolen fabrics from the sheep of the northern hills of Paeti, dyed with brilliant hues of green and orange and patterned with intricate knotted geometric patterns; exotic herbs and fruits that the sellers claimed came all the way from the great interior lakes of the western continent. In the official markets, Enéas could find inferior products priced twice or three times as much as he'd pay in the open bazaars, sold by Westlanders who understood the speech of Nessantico.

But it was at the bazaars, hidden away in the maze of narrow streets of the city where the original inhabitants still lived, that the true treasures could be found, and there no one would speak Nessantican even if they knew it.

Munereo . . . it was a dream. Another life, like his time in Nessantico itself. Against harsh reality, those times felt as if they'd happened to someone else, in another lifetime entirely.

He knew those of full native blood called themselves the Tehuantin. It was the Tehuantin they fought now, who had come pouring into the Hellins from the mountains to the west after Commandant Petrus ca'Helfier had been murdered, after the commandant had raped or fallen in love with—depending on who you asked—a Tehuantin woman. Ca'Helfier had been assassinated by a Westlander. Then the new commandant—Donatien ca'Sibelli—had retaliated, there had been riots and growing turmoil and unrest, and the strife had finally escalated into open war, with more and more of the Tehuantin coming into the Hellins.

Now Enéas was to be another casualty in that war. *If that is Your will, Cénzi, then I come to You gladly. . . .*

Enéas groaned as a sandaled foot kicked him in the ribs, taking away his breath and his memories. Someone growled fast and mostly unintelligible Tehuantin speech at him. ". . . up . . ." he heard. ". . . time . . " Enéas forced his eyes to open, slitted against the fierce sun, to see a Westlander's face scowling down at him: tea-colored skin; the cheeks tattooed with the blue-black slashes of the warrior caste; white teeth; bamboo armor laced around him, a curved Westlander sword in the hand he used to gesture, the sound of the blade audible as it cut the air.

Enéas tried to move his hands and found them bound tightly together behind his back. He struggled to push himself up, but his wounded leg and ankle refused to cooperate. "No," he said in the Westlander tongue, trying to make the refusal sound less than defiant. He cast about in his exhaustion-muddled mind for words he could use. "I . . . hurt. No can . . . up." He hoped the Westlander could understand his mangled syntax and accent.

The Westlander gave an exasperated sigh. He lifted the sword and Enéas knew he was about to die. *I come to You, Cénzi.* He waited for the strike, staring upward to see the death blow, to let the man know he wasn't afraid.

"No." He heard the word—another voice. A hand stopped the Westlander's hand as he began the downward slice. Another Tehuantin stepped into Enéas' sight. This one's face was untouched by caste marks, his hands were uncallused and soft in appearance, and he wore simple loose clothing that wasn't unlike the bashtas and tashtas of home. Except for the feather-decorated cap that the man wore over his dark, oiled hair, he could have passed in Nessantico for simply another foreigner. "No, Zolin," the man repeated to the warrior, then loosed a torrent of words that were too fast for Enéas to understand. The warrior grunted and sheathed his weapon. He gestured once at Enéas. ". . . bad . . . your choice . . . Nahual Niente," the man said and stalked away.

Nahual. That meant his rescuer was the head of the nahualli, the war-téni of the Westlanders. "Niente" might be a name, might be a secondary title; Enéas didn't know. He stared at the man. He noticed that the man's belt held two of the strange, ivory-tube devices that had been used to murder A'Offizier ca'Matin. Enéas wondered if he would be next; he would have preferred the sword. He gave another quick silent prayer to Cénzi, closing his eyes.

"Can you walk, O'Offizier?"

Enéas opened his eyes at the heavily accented Nessantican. Nahual Niente was staring at him. He shook his head. "Not easily. My ankle and leg . . ."

The man grunted and crouched next to Enéas. He touched Enéas' leg through his uniform pants, his hands probing. Enéas gave an involuntary yelp as the nahualli manipulated his foot. The man grunted again. He called to someone, and a young man came running over with a large leather pouch that he gave to the spellcaster. The man rummaged inside and brought out a length of white flaxen cloth. He wrapped it around Enéas' leg, slapping at Enéas' hand when he tried to stop him. "Lay back," he said, "if you want to live."

After wrapping Enéas' leg completely, the nahualli stood. He made a gesture and spoke a word in his own language. Immediately, Enéas felt the cloth tightening around his leg and he cried out. He clawed at the fabric, but it was no longer soft flax. His leg felt as if it were encased in a vise of unrelenting steel, and a slow fire raged within his limb as he thrashed on the ground, as the Nahual chanted in his own language.

Enéas' thrashing did no good. The heat flared until he screamed with the pain . . .

. . . and the fire abruptly went out. Enéas tore at the cloth again, and it was only cloth and nothing more. He unwrapped his leg while the nahualli watched impassively, expecting to see his flesh blistered and black and crushed. But the bruises that had mottled his leg were gone, and the swelling around his ankle had subsided.

"Now get up," the nahualli said.

Enéas did. There was no pain and his leg was whole and strong.

Cénzi, what has he done? I'm sorry . . . "Why did you do this?" Enéas said angrily.

The man looked at Enéas the way one regarded a witless child. "So you could walk."

"Healing with the Ilmodo is against the Divolonté," Enéas said angrily. "My recovery was in Cénzi's hands, not yours. It is His choice to heal me or not. You savages use the Ilmodo wrongly."

The nahualli scoffed at that. "I used a charm that I could have used on one of my own, O'Offizier. You're standing, you're healed, and yet you're ungrateful. Are all of your people so arrogant and stupid?"

"Cénzi—" Enéas began, but the man cut him off with a gesture.

"Your Cénzi isn't here. Here, Axat and Sakal rule, and it is the X'in Ka and not your Ilmodo that I've used. I'm not one of your téni. Now, you'll walk with me."

"Why? Where are we going?"

"No place you would know. Walk, or die here if that will make you feel better."

"You'll kill me anyway. I saw what you did to the ones you captured." Enéas gestured toward the devices on the man's belt. The nahualli touched them, his fingers stroking the curved bone.

"Believe what you will," he said. "Walk with me, or die here. I don't care which."

He began to walk away. Standing, Enéas could see the Westlander encampment being broken around him in a gloomy, rain-threatening morning. Already, many of the Tehuantin troops were marching away to the northeast: their offiziers mounted, the men walking with long spears over their shoulders. Enéas could see the blackened circle that was the remains of the great campfire he'd seen the night before, still smoking and fuming. The unmistakable blackened, spoked arches of a rib cage rose from the embers. He shuddered at that, knowing that the skeleton must be ca'Matin or another of his fellow soldiers.

Enéas saw the nahualli gesture to one of the warriors he

passed, pointing back to Enéas. *Cénzi, what should I do? What do You want of me?*

As if in answer, the clouds parted to the northwest and he saw a shaft of sun paint the emerald hills in the distance before vanishing again.

"Wait," Enéas said. "I'll walk with you."

~

Audric ca'Dakwi

66 **Y**OU CAN'T TELL ANYONE that I speak to you, Audric," Gremma said. The painted eyes in her portrait glinted in warning, and her varnished face frowned. "You do understand that, don't you?"

"I could ... tell Sergei," Audric suggested. He stood before the painting, holding a candelabra. He'd dismissed Seaton and Marlon for the night, though he knew that they were sleeping in the chamber beyond and would come if he called. His breathing was labored; he fought for every breath, the words coming out in gasping spasms. He could feel the heat of the fire in the hearth òn his front. "He would ... believe me. He would ... understand. You trusted ... him, didn't you?"

But the face in the painting shook her head, the motion barely perceptible in the erratic candlelight. "No," she whispered. "Not even Sergei. That I am speaking to you, that I am advising you, must be our secret, Audric. Our secret. And you must start by asserting yourself, Audric: as I did, from the very start."

"I'm not ... sixteen. Sergei is ... Regent, and it is ... his word that ... the Council of Ca' ... listens to ... Sigourney and the others ..." The effort of speaking cost him, and he could not finish. He closed his eyes, listening for her answer.

"The Regent and the Council must understand that *you* are the Kraljiki, not Sergei," Marguerite interrupted sharply. "The War in the Hellins ... It is not going well. There is danger there."

Audric nodded, eyes still closed. "Sergei has ... suggested withdrawing ... our troops, or perhaps ..." He paused as another fit of coughing took him. "... even abandoning the cities ... we've established in ... the Hellins until ... the Holdings are ... one again, when we can ... give them the resources ..."

"No!" The word was nearly a screech, so loud that Audric clapped hands to ears and opened his eyes wide, surprised to see that the mouth in the painting wasn't open in rage and that Seaton and Marlon didn't come rushing into the bedroom in panic—but hands over ears could not stop her voice in his head. "Do you know what they called me early in my reign, Audric? Did your lessons maister tell you that?"

"He told me," he said. "They called you ... the '*Spada Terribile*' ... the Awful Sword."

The face in the painting nodded in the candles' pale gleam. "And I was that," she said. "The Awful Sword. I brought peace to the Holdings first through the sword of my army, before I ever became the Généra a'Pace. They forget that, those who remember me. You must be strong and firm in the same way, Audric. The Hellins: theirs is a rich land, and it could bring great wealth to the Holdings, *if* you have the courage to take it and keep it."

"I will," he told her fervently. Images of war fluttered in his mind, of himself on the Sun Throne with a thousand people bowing to him, and no Regent by his side.

"Good," she answered. "Excellent. Listen to me and I will tell you what to do to be the greatest of the Kraljiki. Audric the Great; Audric the Beloved."

At her smile, he nodded finally. "I will be that," he said. He took in another gasping breath and coughed. "I will."

"You will what, Kraljiki?"

Audric spun about with the question, nearly dropping the candelabra with the motion, so violently that two of the candles were snuffed out. The effort sent him into wheezing spasms, and Regent Sergei rushed forward to take the candelabra from his hands and support Audric with an arm around his waist. In the Regent's burnished and polished nose, Audric glimpsed Archigos Kenne lurking concerned in the shadows near the door with Marlon holding the door open for them. Ca'Rudka helped Audric fall into one of the cushioned chairs in front of the fireplace. Marguerite stared down at him, her expression unreadable. "Here, my Kraljiki, some of the healer's draught," ca'Rudka said, pressing a goblet to Audric's lips as he stared at the painting. Audric shook his head and pushed it away.

She says that the healers won't help, he wanted to say but did not, and Marguerite's tight-lipped mouth curved into a slight smile. Audric's eyelids wanted to close but he forced them open. "No," he told ca'Rudka.

The Regent frowned but set the goblet down. "I've brought the Archigos," he said. "Let him pray for you . . ."

Audric glanced up at the painting and saw his great-matarh nod. He echoed it himself, and Archigos Kenne hurried into the bedchamber. As the Archigos busied himself with his chanting and gestures, Audric ignored both of them. He could see only the painting and his great-matarh's serene gaze. She spoke to him as Kenne touched his chest and the warmth of the Ilmodo lessened the congestion in his lungs.

"We can do this together, Audric. You are the great-son I always wanted to have in life. Listen to me, and in all history there will be no Kraljiki who can be called your equal. I will help you. Listen to me . . ."

"I *am* listening," he told her.

"Kraljiki?" Regent ca'Rudka said. He followed Audric's gaze back to the painting. Audric wondered if he'd heard the whispering, too, but then the man's silver nose glinted in candlelight as he turned back, Audric's own reflection visible there. "None of us said anything."

Audric shook his head. "Indeed," he told the man. "And that is why I listen."

Ca'Rudka smiled uncertainly. Kenne, in mid-incantation, shrugged. "Ah, a jest," ca'Rudka said. He chuckled dryly. "You're feeling better, Kraljiki?"

"I am, Sergei. Yes. Thank you, Archigos. You may go." The Archigos didn't move, and Audric scowled. "I said, Archigos, you may go. Now."

Kenne's eyes widened, and Audric saw him glance at Sergei, who shrugged. The Archigos bowed, gave the sign of Cénzi, and retreated.

"That was rude," Sergei said to Audric after Marlon had closed the doors to Audric's bedchamber behind him. "After the Archigos' efforts and prayers—"

"The man's prayers were done," Audric said, more brusquely than he'd ever spoken to Sergei before. He glanced at the painting and saw his great-matarh nod as if she were pleased. Her voice muttered in his head. *"Sergei does not care for you, Audric. He only wants to keep your power. He doesn't want you to be what I know you can be. He wants you to remain weak, to always need him so he will stay Regent.*" Her strength seemed to flow through him. He found that he could speak without the pauses, without the coughs. He spoke as strongly and well as Sergei himself. "I need to talk with you, Regent, about the Hellins. I have been considering the situation there since our last discussion. I have decided to send another division of the Garde Civile to supplement our troops there."

Audric was proud of how his voice sounded: regal and strong and fierce. He smiled up at Marguerite, and in the candlelight she nodded back to him.

~

Sergei ca'Rudka

"I WANT ... TO SEND another ... division of the ... Garde Civile ... to supplement ... our troops ... there," Audric said.

The boy could barely get the words out through the wheezing and coughing. The anger in him seemed to make the affliction worse than usual, as if Archigos Kenne's prayers had done nothing at all.

Sergei forced his features to close, to reveal nothing of what he was thinking. Let the boy have his tantrum. But the words made him worry: this didn't seem to be Audric talking; he was hearing someone else's words. Who had been speaking to the boy? Whose advice was being whispered in his ear for him to spout? One of the chevarittai, perhaps, looking for glory in war. Perhaps Sigourney herself, since her brother was commandant there.

Audric was staring past Sergei's shoulder; he glanced back to the grim portrait of Kraljica Marguerite over the hearth. "I thought I had made my thoughts on this clear to you, Kraljiki," he said, his voice carefully neutral, carefully bland. "I don't think that's wise, not with the size of the army the Coalition could raise if they decided to do so. This war in the Hellins is like a seeping wound; it cripples us and takes our attention away from where it should be: east, not west. We should be looking at what we can do to restore the Holdings."

The boy's gaze flicked from the portrait to Sergei and back again. "The Hellins provide us riches and goods that we can't find elsewhere." *"riches ... and goods ... [cough] ... that ... we can't ... find elsewhere."*

"Indeed they do, Kraljiki, but we could obtain those goods by trade with the Westlanders as easily as by war. Easier, in fact. Once the Holdings are unified again, *then* will be the time to look across the Strettosei to the Hellins once more. We have lost too much ground there, because we can't give the territory the attention we should."

Audric's face was flushed, either from the effort of speaking or from anger, or both. "That's not what my vatarh said when the Troubles started, Regent. Do you think that because I was just a child then that I wouldn't remember?" *". . . just a . . . child . . . then . . . [wheeze] . . . that I . . . wouldn't. . . . remem . . . ber?"*

The mask of his face showed nothing. "When the Troubles started, Kraljiki Justi believed he had no choice but to respond. He believed what the a'offiziers told him, that the Westlanders were little more than savages, that they would soon be pushed back past Lake Malik. But I'd remind you that I didn't share that belief. The news continues to worsen despite the best efforts of Commandant ca'Sibelli. We have misjudged the Westlanders, and it's time to save what we can from a poor decision."

"My vatarh *did not* make a poor decision!" The boy shrilled the words, managing to get them all out in one breath. He coughed then, long and deeply, and Sergei waited. "I want another division sent," Audric persisted. "That is my will. That is your Kraljiki's will."

"You *are* the Kraljiki," Sergei told him. He kept his voice low and soothing against the strident, high screeching of Audric. "But the Council of Ca' named me Regent on your vatarh's death until you reach your majority."

"I'm nearly of age," Audric answered. His face was so pale that Sergei thought the boy might faint. "Less than two years now. I could petition the Council to have you removed, to be permitted to govern fully. They've done that in the past. Maister ci'Blaylock told me: Kraljiki Carin dismissed his Regent at fourteen, the same age I am."

Sergei lifted his hand. Gently. Smiling under his silver nose. "Yes, that's been done. But you and I needn't be at odds here, my Kraljiki."

"Then don't defy me, Regent. I will go to the Council. I will. I will have you removed." The boy gesticulated wildly, and that sent him into another paroxysm of coughing.

"Audric . . ." Sergei responded patiently while the young man fell back on his pillow. Marlon, lurking in the rear corner of the room, was staring wide-eyed at Sergei, shaking his head. "Perhaps I've been remiss in not engaging you fully, in not having you take part in all the briefing and discussions. That can be changed; it *will* be changed. I promise you; if you wish to take part in all discussions of state, to read all the reports, to listen to all the councillors, to really see what it means to govern, then I will accommodate that. But the Hellins . . .". He shook his head. "It's been almost seven years now, Audric. Seven years and the Westlanders have taken back most of what we'd originally gained there. Seven years, and we've lost far too many gardai and squandered far too many gold solas and red blood trying to hold back the tide. At the end of the day, I want what you want. I want the Holdings to have the riches of the Westlands. I do. But this isn't the time. And this isn't the time for us to discuss this. Tomorrow, when you're feeling better . . ."

"Then *get out!*" Audric shouted at him, loudly enough that the hall attendant opened the door slightly to peer in. Sergei shook his head at the man. "Get out and leave me alone." He turned his head, coughing into his pillow.

"As you wish, Kraljiki." Sergei bowed to the young man. As he turned to leave, he saw the Kraljica's portrait once more. She seemed to smile sadly at him, as if she understood.

~

Allesandra ca'Vörl

THE CEREMONY AT BREZNO Temple was excruciatingly long, as was Fynn's speech of welcome to the A'Gyula of West Magyaria: Pauli, her husband. Allesandra's face ached from maintaining a smile throughout Fynn's droning greetings—written, undoubtedly, by one of the palais scribes, since Fynn sometimes peered quizzically at the parchment in front of him as he stumbled over unfamiliar words. Her spine ached from the uncomfortable, straight-backed pews of the Temple. Jan, sitting between Allesandra and his vatarh, fidgeted endlessly, enough that Pauli finally leaned over to the young man and whispered something in his ear. Afterward, Jan stopped his restless shifting in the seat, but the scowl on his face was noticeable even as Allesandra and Pauli proceeded from the temple behind Fynn, Archigos Semini, and his harridan wife, with the ca'-and-cu' of Firenzcia following them like an obedient flock of sheep.

Then came the fête at the Grand Palais of Brezno. Now it was her feet that ached, and Allesandra imagined that the whalebone stays of her fashionably cinched tashta were going to leave permanent furrows in her waist. The ballroom was a furnace on the stifling and humid evening, more like mid-Summer than the Spring the calendar insisted it was. The Archigos had stationed e'téni around the room to keep the ceiling fans a-swirl with the energy of the Ilmodo. The movement of the fan blades seemed to intensify rather than diminish the heat, churning the air into a fetid cologne of sweat, pomades, and perfumes. The night was raucous with the music of the orchestra at the far end of the room, the sound of feet dancing on the wooden floor laid down over the tiles, and a hundred separate conversations, all reflected back at them by the dome overhead.

Allesandra wished fervently to be elsewhere, but if the discomforts bothered Pauli, he hadn't allowed it to show.

He had separated from Allesandra as soon as propriety allowed, as he always did, and was standing in a cluster of young women around Fynn. Jan was there also, at his vatarh's side, and Allesandra noted that he was receiving nearly as much attention as the Hïrzg, and certainly more than Pauli. Fynn was regaling everyone with the tale of the stag hunt, his arm cocked back as if he were sighting down a bow as he laughed, slapping Jan on the back. ". . . the boy is nearly as good a shot as me," she heard Fynn say, and Jan's face was alight with a broad grin as the young women applauded and made the appropriate compliments.

Of course, it would be Pauli who would almost certainly find comfort and release between the thighs of one of them tonight. Allesandra was certain of that; her husband no longer bothered to hide his transgressions from her. She told herself that she didn't care.

"A'Hïrzg, are you enjoying yourself?" She turned to see Archigos Semini ca'Cellibrecca standing behind her with two iced drinks in his hand—Fynn had, at great expense, brought wagonloads of glacial ice from the mountains around Lake Firenz. He proffered one to Allesandra. "Please, take it," he said. "Francesca seems to have vanished and the ice will be gone soon in this heat."

Allesandra took the water-beaded glass gratefully. She sipped at the cold drink, relishing the chill as the honey-sweetened juice slipped down her throat. "Thank you, Archigos. I think you may have just saved my life."

He smiled broadly at that, his beard glistening with oil. "Would you care to walk with me, A'Hïrzg? I suspect there's a bit of a breeze over near the windows."

She glanced at the gaggle around Fynn, at her husband and son there with him. "Certainly," she told him. The Archigos offered his arm, and she put her hand in the crook of his elbow as they walked. He said nothing until they were well away from the Hïrzg, then leaned close to her. "Your husband enjoys the attention he receives as A'Gyula. But he's a fool to leave you unattended." His free hand covered hers on his arm.

"I could say the same of your wife, Archigos."

He chuckled. His hand patted hers. "The ideal spouse is both an ally and a friend," he answered. "But that's an ideal rarely achieved, isn't it? That's a shame. I've wondered, at times, what might have happened had the false Archigos not snatched you away. Perhaps, A'Hïrzg, you and I might have ended up . . . allies. Or more."

Allesandra nodded to a passing covey of ca'-and-cu' wives. She saw their speculative gazes rest on her hand laced with the Archigos' arm. "The daughter of Archigos ca'Cellibrecca was a better choice for you, Archigos. Look at where you are now."

She felt more than heard his snort of derision. "A cold, calculating choice on the part of my younger self, and it gave me a marriage with exactly those same qualities. But there are other alliances that can be forged outside of marriage, A'Hïrzg, if one is careful. And interested." His hand was still on hers, his fingers pressing.

"I've always been extremely careful about my alliances, Archigos. That's something I learned early on."

He nodded. They were near the dance floor now, the music masking their voices. "I understand you will be giving a fealty oath to Hïrzg Fynn at the Besteigung tomorrow?"

"Ah," she said. "You have sources close to the Hïrzg."

Under the salt-and-pepper beard, the man smiled. "Knowing what the powerful know is a survival tactic, A'Hïrzg, as I'm sure you realize." For several moments they walked along in silence around the edge of the floor. Couples swayed near them to a gavotte. "I also hear from Nessantico that the young Kraljiki is not well," he said. Allesandra said nothing. "The rumors that have come to me say that the Council of Ca' in Nessantico might consider the twins Sigourney ca'Ludovici or Donatien ca'Sibelli as successors should Audric die. They're second cousins to Audric, I believe." A breath. A smile. "As are you."

Allesandra stared blandly back at the man. Dancers moved past them. "As is Fynn," she answered finally.

"Yes, but you are the eldest. And you have the advantage of having lived there; you *know* Nessantico as your brother does not. And perhaps there are those in Nessantico who might recognize strength when they see it and desire a strong presence on the Sun Throne. Someone stronger than either Sigourney or Donatien." He leaned close to her and lowered his voice to a husky whisper. "For that matter, there are those *here* who would prefer you to wear the crown that is currently on Fynn's head."

"You speak treason again, Archigos?" she asked, just as quietly.

"I speak truth, A'Hïrzg."

"And those here that you speak of. Would you be among those, Archigos?"

His fingers tightened on hers. "I would. Perhaps . . . perhaps it is possible for both the Coalition and the Faith to even become one again—under the right leaders."

The right Archigos being yourself, of course . . . Allesandra watched the dancers on the floor, moving through their intricate and preordained steps. *What does he really know? What does he really want?* She didn't know how to answer him. She didn't know if he knew about the message she'd been sent from Nessantico, or if he'd perhaps received something similar. She didn't know whether Semini was a potential ally or her enemy—and the Archigos could be a terrible enemy, as the skeletons of Numetodo heretics hanging in the gibbets near the Brezno Temple could attest.

The ice was gone to water in her drink. She gave the glass to a passing servant and smiled at the Archigos. "My vatarh believed that there would be one Holdings again—when he sat on the Sun Throne as Kraljiki," she told him. "That's what I believe also, Archigos: that a Hïrzgai could also be the Kralji. And I . . ." She lifted the hand that had held the glass. She could see cool, glistening drops of water clinging to her fingers. "When last I checked, I was *not* Hïrzgin."

"No, you are not," Semini answered. "But—"

She cut him off even as he opened his mouth again. "No, I am not," she said. "That seems to be Cénzi's Will. You wouldn't intend to thwart Him, would you, Archigos?" She gave him no chance to respond. She removed her hand from his arm and gave him the sign of Cénzi. "Thank you for the drink and for the conversation, Archigos," she said. "You've given me much to think about. If . . . *if* something would happen to, well, change things, I know that you and I might make excellent allies. Certainly you are a far more competent Archigos than the one the Nessantican Faith has named. Kenne never impressed me."

She saw the pleasure in his face as she said that, and he nodded slightly. "I'm flattered, A'Hïrzg."

"No," she told him, "it's I who should be flattered. Now . . . you should find Francesca, and I must go be my husband's wife and the A'Hirzg, and pretend not to notice when the A'Gyula slips away for the night."

~

Karl ca'Vliomani

VARINA HANDED KARL the glass ball as Mika watched. Varina's touch lingered on Karl's hand for a moment before she released him, and she gave him a smile that was tinged with sadness. Her face seemed more heavily lined than he remembered, as if she'd aged suddenly in the last month.

They were in the meeting hall of the Numetodo House, where once a week the various Numetodo would give reports on their research. There were empty chairs set neatly in rows in front of the small dais on which they stood.

Karl hadn't mentioned to Mika his visit to the Firenzcian Ambassador the other day; evidently Varina hadn't either, since Mika hadn't commented on it.

"It's just a ball, right?" Mika asked as Karl hefted the globe in his palm. "Though a fairly well-crafted one." It *was* heavy and well-cast—Karl could see no air bubbles or defects in the glass: the lens of the sphere gave him a distorted, warped view of the hall. "Do you find it unusual or notable in any other way?"

Karl shrugged. "No. It's a true glasswright's work, or an apprentice's proof-work, but otherwise . . ."

Mike grinned. "Indeed. What I want you to do, Karl, is speak the word 'open' in Paeti and then toss the ball to me."

Karl hefted the glass again. *"Oscail,"* he said, and underhanded the small globe in Mika's direction. What happened next astonished him.

When the glass ball touched Mika's hand, a coruscation of blue-white flared, sending black shadows dancing around the Numetodo hall, painting momentary crazed black shadows on the back wall and causing Karl to shade his eyes belatedly. He heard Varina's quick laugh and a handclap of delight. Karl blinked, trying to see through the globules of fading afterimages that haunted his vision. "By all the Moitidi . . . You two *have* been working, I see."

"Not me," Mika answered. "It's been Varina alone." He handed the globe back to Karl—it was simply glass again. "If the Westlanders were able to enchant objects with the Scáth Cumhacht, the way you and Ana said Mahri did, then we knew it was possible. And not only that—Mahri gave Ana an enchanted object that *she* could control by speaking the right word. *Anyone* could use the magic as long as they know the release word."

Varina was still smiling. She was rubbing at a long, scabbed wound on her forearm. "We knew it was *possible*; the rest was simply a matter of figuring out the formula to do it."

"Varina's finally managed to puzzle out the sequence," Mika added. "She swore me to secrecy; said she wanted to surprise you. The spell's complicated, and takes more time and more energy than you might think. Compared to our own spells, something like this is expensive and far more of a drain on the body than anyone expected, but . . ." He nodded happily. "It's reproducible. Finally. Varina says she could teach us, and either of us could do the same."

Karl glanced at Varina, who nodded without saying anything. She held his gaze almost defiantly. He tossed the ball up in the air. "That's impressive, Varina. It truly is. But a flash of light is hardly a weapon."

"Theoretically, any spell within the arcana could be stored in any object: offensive, defensive, whatever," Varina answered. There was heat in her words. "Theoretically. Practically, well, not yet. I used the light spell because it's the first and simplest thing we teach an initiate, so it seemed best." She shook her head. There were white strands in her brown hair that Karl didn't remember from even a week ago—had they been there all along? "Look, it's a matter of binding the spell to the object and creating a trigger to activate it—covering the object in the energy of the Scáth Cumhacht the way you'd wrap a mistfruit in paper. After that, it's as if the object is an extension of the spellcaster, though the object itself has to be of good quality or it can't survive the strain. It took me a while to understand that. But . . ." She sighed, spreading her hands wide. "Just putting that simple spell in an object was incredibly exhausting, Karl. You won't be able to imagine just how exhausting until you try it yourself. The process took me three full turns of the glass, and afterward I had to rest for another day to recover. Even now, I still feel the drain on my energy, and I wonder what else it might have cost." She bit her lower lip, brushed stray wisps of whitened hair behind her ears. "You said that Archigos Ana claimed that old Mad Mahri gave her an enchantment that could literally stop time?"

Karl nodded. "That's what she told me—it was how she snatched Allesandra from her vatarh. And Mahri was able to switch his body for mine, when I was in the Bastida. His magic . . ."

". . . was utterly beyond ours, then," she finished for him. "I know. The reports from the war in the Hellins hint at the same. The nahualli of the Westlanders can do more than we can, *but* . . . I've just proved that their X'in Ka is no more god-driven than the Ilmodo, no matter what they claim or believe." She pointed to the glass ball. "If I can do this, then my bet is that we can also learn to do the same with more potent spells. It's just a matter of learning the right formulae to bind the Scáth Cumhacht to the physical object. It can be done. *We* can do it."

Karl remembered Mahri, who had befriended him and Ana when they thought they were lost, and who had turned out to be not ally, but enemy. Mahri's ravaged, one-eyed, and furrowed face swam before him as he gazed at Varina. He lifted the glass ball again. "So anyone could have done this spell. . . ." His voice trailed off. *The explosion . . . the great flash of terrible light . . . Ana's torn body . . . Magic without hearing or seeing anyone casting the spell . . . Maybe you've been wrong; maybe you've been looking in the wrong direction . . .* "Could what happened to Ana have been . . . ?" Karl couldn't finish the question. It remained lodged in his throat, heavy and solid.

But both Varina and Mika nodded in answer.

"Yes," Mika told him. "That's the rest of what we wanted to talk about. Varina and I have already had the same thought. Westlander involvement can't be ruled out in Ana's death, and frankly, what happened there makes it seem likely to me. But *why*, Karl? Why not assassinate the Kraljiki or the Regent, who are directly responsible for the war? Why kill *Ana*, of all people?"

Because it would be revenge for Mahri. Revenge. That, he could understand. "Right now, I don't know," Karl hedged.

"But someone here in Nessantico does, I'm certain, and I'm going to find that person." He took a long breath. They were both staring at him, and he hated the pity he saw in Mika's eyes, and the deep empathy in Varina's. "But that's for later," he told them. "For now, I want you to teach me this nahualli trick. Let me see how it works."

Varina seemed to start to say something, then closed her mouth. Mika glanced at her, at Karl. "I think I'll leave that to the two of you," he said. "Alia wanted me to bring some lamb home for dinner, and the butcher will be closing his shop soon." He made his farewells quickly and left them.

For too long after the door shut, neither of them spoke. When they did speak, it was together.

"I'm really sorry about the other day . . ."

"I've been thinking about what you said . . ."

They laughed, a little uneasily, at the collision of apologies. "You first," Karl told her, but she shook her head. "All right," he said. "I'll start then. You said that my . . . affection for Ana had blinded me. I've been thinking about that, and—"

"Stop, Karl" she said. "Don't say anything. I was angry and I said things that I had no right to say. I'd . . . I'd like you to forget them."

"Even if they were true?"

Her cheeks reddened. "You loved Ana. I know that. Whatever relationship the two of you had . . ." She shrugged. "It's not my concern." She stepped forward, in front of him, close enough that he could see the flecks of color in her pupils and the fine lines at their corners. She reached down and closed his fingers around the glass ball he was still holding, both her hands cupping his. "I can show you how to enchant this. You just have to be patient because—"

"Varina." She stopped and looked up at him. "You shouldn't be putting so much of yourself into this."

Her lips tightened as if she wanted to say something. Then her hands pressed against his again and she looked down. ". . . because it's difficult, and you have to think differently about the whole process. But once you make the shift, it all makes sense," she said. "You have to imagine the ball as an extension of yourself. . . ."

~

Enéas cu'Kinnear

IT HAD BEEN THREE DAYS since his capture. In that time, the Westlander army had continued marching northeast, and Enéas had walked with them. He remained close to Niente—which he'd learned was indeed the name of the nahualli who had healed him. "No one will restrain you," Niente said to Enéas at the start of their trek. "But if you are found wandering without me, the warriors will kill you immediately. It's your choice."

They were moving in the direction of Munereo. The days were filled with nothing but walking. Enéas stayed close to the nahualli, but he also watched carefully for an opportunity to escape—that was his duty as a soldier. Whatever Niente had done to his leg had healed his injuries completely; his ankle felt stronger than it had ever been. If there was a chance to slip away, well, it wouldn't be an injury that impeded him.

It wouldn't be easy. All those of the nahualli caste walked together in the middle of the army, surrounded on all sides by the tattooed and scarred soldiers of the Westlanders, well-protected. That spoke of the value that the Tehuantin placed on the sorcerers. Each of the nahualli carried a walking stick or staff: carved with animal figures and highly polished, most of them showing long use. Once, when they had paused for the midday meal, Enéas reached out to touch Niente's staff, curious as to what it might feel like. Niente snatched the stick away.

"This is nothing for you, Easterner," he said—quietly, but with a sharp edge in his voice. "Let me give you a warning: you touch a nahualli's staff at your peril. Don't do it again."

Niente conversed with the other nahualli, but always in the Tehuantin language; if any of them, like Niente, also spoke Enéas' language, they never displayed the skill. For the most part, the other nahualli ignored his presence at the side of Niente, their gazes sliding past him as if he were no more than a horse or a tent-pack. Twice a day, a low-caste warrior would hand Enéas a bowl of the mashed root-paste that seemed to be the staple food for the army; he ate it quickly and hungrily—it was never quite enough to satisfy the hunger fed by the long marches. Niente had also given him a waterskin, which he filled in the abundant small lakes and streams around the hilly region.

The army moved through the meandering valleys like a solid river, the verdant steep walls of the landscape containing them. And at night, when the army camped . . .

It was the lowest-caste warriors who always erected the nahualli's tents—the nahualli themselves seemed to do little physical labor. Niente supervised the placement of several dozen casks in his personal tent each night, marked with symbols burned into the wood. There were four symbols that Enéas could discern. Niente didn't seem overly concerned with most of them, but the ones marked with what looked like a winged dragon he watched carefully as they were placed, grimacing whenever one of the warriors set the cask down too hard, and scolding them when they did so. That first night, Niente opened several of the casks—he didn't object when Enéas sidled closer to look over the nahualli's shoulder. One cask was filled with chunks of what looked and smelled like burnt wood, another with a white powder, yet another with bright yellow crystals. Enéas peered most closely into the dragon-marked casks, to see that it was filled with a gray-black thick sand, glistening a bit in the moonlight.

He remembered that sand, strewn in circles on the ground. *The thunder, the flash, the pain . . .*

Each night, close together in the tent, Niente would sit erect and chant for a few turns of the glass at least, his eyes closed, while Enéas lay near him. Sometimes he would sprinkle one of the ingredients from the casks on the ground between them while he chanted. Enéas could feel the power of the Ilmodo in the air, causing the hair on his neck to rise and prickling his skin, and he prayed to Cénzi while Niente cast his spells, trying to offset with his prayers the heretical use of the Ilmodo. All around them there would be silence: none of the other nahualli were chanting as Niente did, and Enéas wondered at that. He also wondered at how—afterward—he seemed to feel a warmth inside himself, as if the sun's radiance were filling his own lungs. Whatever spell Niente was casting, Enéas seemed to be affected by it.

He wondered if Niente felt the same warmth and energy, but the nahualli always seemed more exhausted than exhilarated by his efforts, and the man moaned as he slept, as if he were in pain and when he awoke in the morning, there were new lines on his face, like an old apple.

On the third night, after the chanting, rather than falling asleep as he usually did, Niente placed a small bronze bowl near the opening to the tent so that the light of the campfire fell on it. The bowl was decorated around the rim with a frieze of stylized people and animals, many of which Enéas didn't recognize. As Enéas watched, Niente poured water into the bowl, then sifted a small amount of finely-ground, ruddy powder into his hand from a leather pouch. Niente dusted the surface of the water with the powder, chanting as he did so. The water began to glow, an unnatural, blue-green illumination that made the nahualli's face appear spectral and dead. The man stared into the bowl, silent, the eerie light playing over his face, shifting and merging. Curiosity made Enéas slide forward to see better. Pushing himself up, he glanced over Niente's shoulder.

Inside the bowl, in the water, was a cityscape. He recognized it immediately: Nessantico. He could see the Pontica a'Brezi Veste and the vista of the Avi a'Parete leading down to the pillared, marble public entrance to the Kralj's Palais. He could see the Old Temple, but cu'Brunelli's magnificent new dome looked as if it had fallen in completely; there was nothing but a blackened hole there where it was to have been placed. People seemed to be walking the streets, but they were few, most with their heads down and hurrying as if afraid to be seen. The streets were trash-filled and dirty, and the palais had a visible crack on its southern wall and the northern wing was a ruin. Across the street, what had been a glorious residence was now a blackened hulk. A pall of smoke seemed to lay over the city. Enéas leaned closer to see better into the water . . .

. . . and Niente's fingers stirred the water and the vision dissolved, the light going dark. Enéas was staring down only at water, the brass bottom of the bowl flecked with the granules of powder.

"What was that?" Enéas asked Niente, sitting back. The man shrugged.

"Heresy, to you," he said. "The magic of the wrong god."

"I saw . . . I thought I saw . . . Nessantico."

"Perhaps you did," Niente answered. "Axat grants the visions She wishes."

"Visions of what?" He remembered the smoke, the fissure in the palais wall, the hurrying, frightened people . . .

Niente didn't answer Enéas. He cast the water in the bowl outside the tent and wiped the bowl with the hem of his clothes. He placed it in his pack, next to the cotton padding that served as his bed. "How do you feel, Enéas?" he asked.

"I feel fine," he answered.

"It's time you returned to your own people."

"What?" Enéas shook his head, unbelieving. "You said—"

"I said that the soldiers would kill you if you try to escape. And they would. But . . . there will be no moon tonight. Axat hides Her face, and rain is coming. There will be a horse outside our tent when the storm reaches us. When you hear it, go outside to the horse. Ride hard; no one will pursue you until morning. If you're lucky, if Axat smiles on you, you will come to Munereo a few days before we do."

"You're letting me go? You'd let me warn my people and tell them to be ready for your army?"

Niente smiled. "The army of Tehuantin has nothing to fear from your people. Not here in our own country. Go," he said. "Axat doesn't intend for you to die here. You've been prepared for another fate—a far better one. You will go to your leader. You will talk to him, and you will give ·him a message for us."

"Prepared? By whom—your Axat? I don't believe in Her," Enéas told him. "She's not my god, and She doesn't control my fate, and I am not a messenger boy for you."

"Ah." Niente lay down on his bedding and pulled a blanket over him against the night cold. "Well, then stay here if that's what you wish. It is your choice." ·

"What is this message?" Enéas asked the man.

"You'll know it when the time comes."

Niente said nothing more. After a time, Enéas heard the man snoring. He lay there, wondering. He could still feel the residual tingling of Niente's earlier chant, as if his fingertips and toes had fallen asleep. Prickles crawled his limbs, almost painful but energizing at the same time. The sensation kept him awake for what seemed turns of the glass: while Niente slept, as the sounds of the encampment slowly subsided until he could hear sleeping men all around him and the soft patter of rain began to drum against the fabric of the tent, accompanied by flashes of lightning and the occasional grumbles of thunder.

Close by, a horse nickered.

Enéas slid from under his blanket and crawled to the tent's opening. Outside, the rain had become steady, pooling in black puddles dancing with spray. A few strides away, a horse stood with its head down, pulling at tufts of wet grass. The creature was bridled and saddled, but the reins hung down as if the animal had pulled away from where it had been placed. A lightning flash illuminated the encampment, freezing for a moment the falling streaks of rain, and thunder snarled close by. The horse stamped nervously at the light and sound, and Enéas thought it might bolt.

It was the duty of the soldier to escape if possible.

It's time you returned to your own people. You will go to your leader. You will talk to him, and you will give him a message for us.

Enéas glanced around; in the midst of the storm, it was difficult to see, but there seemed to be no one awake. The camp guards had retreated into their tents against the storm. He gathered himself, then stood up outside the tent. The rain slicked his hair and soaked his clothing as he stepped toward the horse, his hand out as he clucked encouragingly to the animal, murmuring soft words. The horse lifted its head but otherwise remained still, looking at him. He took the reins and patted the soaked, muscular neck. "It's time," he told the horse.

A few breaths later, he was astride and galloping away.

~

Jan ca'Vŏrl

WHEN HE ENTERED to take breakfast with his matarh, she was standing at the window to the room with the shutters open, and he thought he saw sunlight glinting on her eyes as if, perhaps, she'd been crying recently. If so, he could make a guess as to why. "Vatarh shouldn't treat you as he does," he said. "Especially with something this important. I've told him how I feel, too."

She turned to him, taking his hands. The corners of her lips lifted in a smile. "It doesn't matter, Jan. Not anymore. I'm past him being able to hurt me." He felt her fingers tighten against his. "Besides, he's given me all I really want."

She pulled him toward her and kissed his forehead. "Hungry?" she asked. "I had the kitchen make sweet cheese rétes. I know how much you like them." She led him to the table, laden with juice and milk, with eggs and bacon, sliced bread and butter, and a plate of delicate pastry strudels oozing white, creamy cheese. "Sit across from me," she said, "so we can talk." She handed him the plate of rétes, smiling as he took one.

"You look tired, Matarh."

"Do I?" She put a hand to her face. "I'll have to get my handmaid to take care of that. This will be a long day."

Jan took a bite of the strudel, enjoying the honeyed tartness of the cheese and the delicate hint of sweetnuts in the pastry dough. He could feel his matarh's gaze on him, watching. "Does it bother you?" he asked impulsively. "Onczio Fynn being Hïrzg, I mean?"

"I've thought about it enough," she answered. Her hand came up to touch her cheek again. "I'll confess that I couldn't sleep last night, thinking about that . . ." She hesitated, looking down at the tablecloth. ". . . and other things."

He was afraid that was all she was going to say. "And . . . ?"

She smiled. "I've decided that I don't wish to be Hïrzgin. I think Cénzi has other plans for me."

He searched her face, looking for a lie there. He couldn't imagine being able to say that himself if he'd been in her position, if his birthright had been stolen from him that way. Yet he saw nothing in her expression to gainsay what she'd said. "That's good," he said.

The trace of a smile touched her lips. "Why is that good?"

"Because I like Onczio Fynn," he said.

Frost in summer, the smile dissolved. "Jan, one of the traits I love about you is that you're willing to trust the people you care about. I don't want you to lose that. But you need to be careful with Fynn."

"You really don't know him yourself, Matarh. You've said that."

"I have. And I don't. But neither do you, not after a few days with him. He has a vile temper. He may be generous to those he feels are his allies, but if he suspects you're against him ..."

"I think you're overstating things," he interrupted. "He's been nothing but kind to me, and he doesn't think *you're* on his side. Be fair, Matarh."

"I am," she answered. "More than you know. What would you say if I said he'd threatened you?"

"I wouldn't believe it," Jan answered reflexively, then realized that he might be calling his matarh a liar. "Unless you've heard that yourself, from Fynn's own lips." He cocked his head at her. "Have you, Matarh?"

She was already shaking her head. "No," she answered. "I haven't. Still—promise me you'll be careful with him."

"Of course I will," he told her, and was rewarded with the return of her smile.

"Good," she said. "Now will you pass me that plate of rétes? I've been dying to try them ..."

~

Sergei ca'Rudka

THE NEWS WAS not good.

The communiqué—the latest report on the continuing battles in the Hellins—had come by fast-ship from Munereo, over the Strettosei to the great island of Karnmor, over the Nostrosei that lay between Karnmor and the mainland to the city of Fossano, then by rider along the A'Sele to Villembouchure, and from there to Nessantico. With favorable winds and riders who didn't care about how hard they rode their horses, the paper had been two weeks in arriving. The casualty figures alone made Sergei shake his head dolefully. He handed the paper to Archigos Kenne; the older man peered at it myopically, holding it so close to his face that Sergei couldn't see his expression.

"You'll note, Archigos, that we now control nothing of the Hellins beyond the area immediately around Munereo, with an arm along the sea extending northward toward Tobarro," Sergei said impatiently as Kenne labored over Commandant ca'Sibelli's tiny, cramped handwriting. "Sending out A'Offizier ca'Matin and his battalion to confront the Westlander army was a mistake, in my estimation, but it's one that's already been made and paid for by now, I suspect. I hope ca'Matin is still alive; he's one of the few good offiziers we have there. I think it would have been better had ca'Sibelli pulled back into defensive positions against this latest offensive, rather than trying to push the Westlanders back, but ca'Sibelli was never one for defense. We've already lost the Lake Malik area. I suspect we're going to lose Munereo next."

"You showed this to Audric? You told him what you just told me?" Kenne's eyes appeared over the edge of the thick yellow paper, then vanished again. Sergei could hear the man muttering aloud to himself as he read.

"I did. He said: 'Commandant Ca'Sibelli is doing exactly what I would have him do. It's as I said—he needs more troops.'" Sergei paused. He glanced around the Archigos' office. There was no one else there, but he lowered his voice anyway; one never knew who might be listening at doors. "We argued; I thought he might die in front of me, he was coughing and breathing so badly. He kept looking past me to Kraljica Marguerite's portrait, and he was saying . . ." Sergei hesitated again, not certain how much he wanted to share with Kenne. ". . . disturbing things. He insists on calling the Council of Ca' together and demanding that he be given autonomy as Kraljiki. He wants my title stripped from me; he wants no Regent in Nessantico."

It sounded so emotionless, stated so flatly. Sergei had seen what Kenne could not: the way the shouting distorted Audric's features, the red flush that crept up from the boy's neck to cover his cheeks, the flecks of saliva flying from his mouth, the eyes wide and haunted.

"I am Kraljiki!" Audric shouted at Sergei, his arms flailing. "You will do as I tell you to do, Regent, or I will have you thrown into the Bastida!" The last words had been screams, each one shouted in its own breath. Audric's hysterics caused the hall gardai as well Audric's domestiques de chambre, Marlon and Seaton, to open the bedchamber's doors to peer in. Sergei waved them all away, and the doors closed again. Audric's gaze went past Sergei and up, and Sergei glanced over his shoulder. The room was fiery, far too hot for Sergei's comfort, the flames in the great fireplace illuminating the portrait of Marguerite above the mantel. Audric was staring at her, his lips moving wordlessly.

"This report, Audric, is conclusive evidence that—"

"You will address me with the proper respect, Regent, or I will have you flogged in the palais square."

Sergei allowed himself a breath, forcing down the retort that threatened to spill out. "Kraljiki, this report shows that the Hellins may well be lost already. Ca'Matin is the best offizier we have there—frankly, I trust his judgment more than Commandant ca'Sibelli's. If he has failed to stop the Westlanders—"

"Then the wrath of Nessantico will fall fully upon them," Audric shrieked, then fell back in a fit of coughing . . .

The rest of the conversation had gone no better.

"It may not be genuine madness, Sergei. Perhaps his illness, or a fever . . ." Kenne began.

"It doesn't matter," Sergei interrupted. "Illness or simple lunacy; there's no difference if he can't be cured. Kenne, I intend to go to the Council of Ca' myself, and request that they declare Audric incompetent."

Kenne laid the paper down at that. Sergei could see the trembling in the man's fingers, could hear it in the rustling the paper made. He pursed his lips as if tasting something sour. "Some of them will think that you're attempting to grab power yourself, Sergei, that this is nothing more than you trying to place yourself on the Sun Throne. It's what Audric will tell them, I suspect. It's certainly what *I'd* tell them in his place. I can see Sigourney believing the same."

"Is that what you think, Kenne? Surely you know me better than that." Sergei scoffed, shaking his head and pacing in front of the Archigos. *I don't want to be Kraljiki. What I want is worse than you or any of them think, and if you knew, you'd all refuse to help me. . . .*

"No, Sergei. Not in the least," Kenne said hurriedly. Too fast, entirely. The man would not look at him, telling Sergei that there was doubt in Kenne's mind also. That was bad; if Kenne wondered at Sergei's intentions, then the Council of Ca' would have no trouble at all imagining the worst. "This is just all . . . so distressing," the Archigos continued. "I don't know what to think. To declare a Kraljiki incompetent . . ." He shook his head, his fingers tapping the report. "He's still just a boy, after all. A young man. Young men often say things that perhaps they shouldn't, or become more excited than they should, and when that boy is not only ca' but has been the A'Kralj and is now Kraljiki, well . . ."

"This isn't about youth and privilege, Kenne. You weren't there. You didn't hear what I heard or see what I witnessed. You've seen hints of it the last few times you've been with him, but this . . . What I am hearing from Audric now is true madness. And a mad Kraljiki will affect the Faith also."

"I will take all the war-téni and send them to the Hellins," the boy shrilled. *"All of them. All that the Faith can give me . . ."*

"I know you believe that, Sergei."

"But?"

Hands as shriveled as drying grapes lifted from the desk and fell back again. The Archigos' gaze seemed to reach as high as Sergei's nose, only to see his distorted reflection there and drop back again. "I know you care only for Nessantico, Sergei. I know you have the interests of the Kralji and the Faith in mind." Sergei stared at Kenne, silent. Waiting. "But," Kenne continued finally, "perhaps someone with Ana's, umm, 'abilities' might still be found, and we might bring the boy back from the brink. Sergei, no Kraljiki has ever been removed by the Council of Ca'. Ever. This is a step you can't take lightly. This is a step that I fear will fail and doom you."

"Believe me, I understand the risks," Sergei told him. He rose from his chair and took the report from Kenne's desk. "The war in the Hellins drains us of money and lives, Kenne, and it forces us to look the wrong way. The longer the war there continues, the more dangerous it becomes to the Holdings. Audric is convinced that the Hellins war will be the triumph of Nessantico. It won't. It will be our downfall."

"I know that's what you believe."

Sergei couldn't entirely keep his irritation at the old man's waffling from his voice. "It's what I *know*. What I must know from you, Kenne, is whether I will have your support."

A headshake. "I want to give you that," Kenne told him. "I do. But I must pray first, Sergei. You say you believe. I want to believe also, and I look to Cénzi to help me. Let me pray. Let me think. Tomorrow . . . I will talk to you tomorrow. Or by Draiordi at the latest . . ."

Useless. This is useless . . . Sergei bowed, smiled falsely, and gave the Archigos the sign of Cénzi. "I will pray for you myself, Archigos, that Cénzi speaks to you soon." *And He had better. He had better or Nessantico might find itself crushed between the stones of the East and the West.*

Sergei plucked the communiqué from Kenne's desk. He went to the hearth of the Archigos' office and let the paper flutter onto the flames there. He watched the paper darken, curl, smoke, and finally ignite.

He imagined the city doing the same.

~

Nico Morel

NICO HAD NEVER FOLLOWED Talis before. Nico's matarh worked at the tavern around the corner and down the alley from their rooms. If Talis worked, it wasn't as other men did in their neighborhood: keeping a shop; working as an apprentice to some master; acting as a simple laborer, perhaps in the grainery mills where the massive grinding wheels were driven by the chants of e-téni, or in the fiery smelters outside the old city walls, the furnaces blazing with Ilmodo fires and the chanting of differently skilled e'téni—who in return for their labors took a portion of the profits for the Concénzia Faith.

Nico had heard his matarh or others in Oldtown complain bitterly about that, how the Faith kept its hands in the pockets of every major industry in the city. The gossip gave Nico strange thoughts: he would imagine long green-sleeved hands snaking out from the temples to pluck coins from the purses of the populace. He wondered why the téni needed to do that, when his matarh and everyone else put coins into the baskets every Cénzidi when they went to the temple. If Nico had that many coins, he could buy a palais on South Bank to live in with Matarh and Talis.

Talis . . .

Nico was playing kick-the-frog in the street with some of the other boys. He was winning: he'd kicked the straw-stuffed sack that was the frog into the puddle three times already, but his friend Jordis had managed it only once and the others not at all. Nico was good at kick-the-frog. Sometimes, when he was playing, he'd feel this strange coldness go through him and he could almost *see* the frog going into the puddle, and when he kicked it then, the frog would go *splash* right into the water.

He'd plucked the soaked frog from the puddle for the

fourth time when he saw Talis come out of their door and start walking up the street. Nico kicked the frog to Jordis and the others. "I'll be back," he said, and ran after Talis.

Since he'd seen Talis with his brass bowl, he'd been watching his vatarh carefully, whenever he could. He'd seen and heard strange things when Talis thought he was asleep, even when his matarh was asleep, too. Talis would chant and move his hands the way the téni did, usually with his walking stick set in front of him. When he did that, Nico could feel the frigid tendrils in the air until the walking stick seemed to suck them in.

It was very strange, but the words—they almost sounded like the dream-words Nico sometimes heard, and he wanted to know more.

At first, he intended to simply catch up to Talis and ask him where he was going, but when Talis turned at the first intersection, striding fast as if he were intent on some destination and his walking stick tapping on the cobblestones, Nico decided to drop back and just watch him. He wasn't sure what made him do that, but with the determined way that Talis was walking, he thought his vatarh might be annoyed if Nico suddenly tugged at his bashta.

Talis was walking so quickly that Nico nearly had to run to keep up with him. A few times, as Talis turned left or right along the twisted jumble of streets, Nico nearly lost him, and the farther they went on the more frightened Nico became—he no longer knew where he was. He didn't even know which way home might be, turned around by the winding, curving streets of Oldtown.

There was sunlight suddenly ahead, and he saw Talis turn sharply left. Nico hurried after him. He found himself standing at the confluence of the alleyway with the grand river of the Avi a'Parete, the great boulevard that circled the inner portion of the city. Nico was assaulted by color, noise, and movement: the bashtas and tashtas of every conceivable pattern and shade, the carriages pushing through the throngs (look—that one had no horses at all, only a téni driving it, with one of the a'téni riding inside), a thousand people all going someplace all at once: talking or silent, grim or laughing, together or alone. Vendors along the walls called their wares; drivers called warning or rang their caution bells; a dozen conversations drifted past Nico in a moment to be replaced by a dozen more.

The buildings here, along Nessantico's most visible avenue, seemed as grand and tall as those on the South Bank, though more crowded together and far older. To his left, Nico could see the piers of an arching bridge leading over to the Isle a'Kralji, where the Kraljiki and the Regent lived. Yet among the grandeur, there were reminders that not everyone in the city lived so well. Beggars sat huddled on the corners; the one nearest Nico, swaddled in foul rags, seemed to have only one arm and about the same number of teeth in her red-gummed mouth. Her eyes were white with cataracts, like the old blind lady who lived across the street from Nico. Her single arm, rattling a battered wooden cup with a few bronze d'folias in the bottom, had too few fingers. The crowds sliding past her mostly ignored her, as if they didn't see her at all.

Nico realized that he had no idea where Talis had gone in the crowds. He looked left, then right, panic rising from his stomach into his throat. He started to run in the direction that he thought Talis had gone.

A hand grabbed his shoulder; Nico jumped and nearly screamed.

"What are you doing here, Nico? Why are you following me?" Talis' face was frowning down at him, his fingers bunched in the fabric of Nico's shirt. Relief conquered fright; Nico gasped. "Talis! I was . . . You were leaving and I thought I'd see where you were going and if I could go with you, and then I was already too far away and I was afraid I was lost."

Talis' frown melted slowly. "You don't know the way home?"

Nico shook his head. "That way?" he asked tentatively, pointing toward one of the buildings behind him.

Talis snorted. "Only if you want to take a bath in the A'Sele. I should just leave you here," he began and Nico's heart began to beat harder and tears started in his eyes, but the man continued. "But Serafina would kill me if she found out. I'm already late. You're going to have to come with me, Nico."

Nico nodded furiously. He hugged Talis around the

waist, as the man put his hand behind his head and pulled him close. Nico could feel the knob of the walking stick on his back. "I need you to be quiet, Son," Talis told Nico. "No badgering me with questions, understand? I need to meet someone."

"Who are you meeting?" Nico asked, then gulped. "I'm sorry, Talis," he said, but the man was already chuckling.

"You're hopeless, you know that? Come on," he told Nico. "Stay close with me, now."

With Nico hurrying alongside him, Talis set out across the width of the Avi a'Parete, dodging between strolling groups and pausing now and then to let a carriage pass, then rushing across the path of the next one. When they finally reached the other side, Talis quickly ducked into a small side street, and the bustle and color and glory of the Avi a'Parete vanished as if it had never been there at all. They turned left, then right, following a narrow, twisting lane, and suddenly emerged—as if from a forest made of houses and buildings crushed together into too small a space—into an open area.

Nico could smell the A'Sele before he saw the river: an odor of dead fish, human waste, and oily water. They stood in a marketplace, with dozens of stalls set up in rows along the riverbank. To his left, Nico could see—from the other side, this time—the grand arch of the Pontica a'Kralji, and out in the glittering waters of the A'Sele, the Isle a'Kralji crowned with the Kralji's Palais, the Old Temple, and the Regent's Estate. Nico stared, then realized belatedly that Talis was already strolling along the aisles of the market, and he scurried to keep up. Now he found he could barely keep his gaze on Talis; he kept being distracted by the goods in the stalls: great heaps of onions, racks of drying herbs, dried and fresh fish, bright knives and glittering stones, bolts of fabrics, tabors and lutes, mounds of apples. . . . "This is better than Oldtown Market," he said, his voice echoing his amazement.

"This is nothing," Talis told him. "I've been told that back in Kraljica Marguerite's time, you could hear the tables groaning under the load of goods coming up the A'Sele from everywhere in the known world. You couldn't walk here for the crowds and sellers. Anything you wanted, you could buy here, no matter what it was." He stopped.

They were in front of a stall shaded from the sun by thick, quilted fabric. In the gloom under the canopy, a large form moved. Nico squinted, shading his eyes. The proprietor of the stall was muscular, with thick arms dangling from the loose sleeves of a bashta adorned with a pattern like stalks of wheat. He leaned down, and Nico saw that his face was marred with strange white lines, as if the skin had been scraped raw. Between the lines, the unmarred flesh was nearly the color of polished copper, like someone from the southern provinces.

"Who's the kid?" the man asked Talis. His voice was thick with an accent that Nico didn't place until Talis responded, then he realized that it was a stronger, more pronounced version of Talis' own.

"My son Nico." Talis tapped Nico's shoulder with the stick. "Don't worry about him."

"His matarh got you playing at nursemaid now, Talis? Mahri would be so proud."

"Shut up, Uly."

The man sniffed as if amused by the exchange. He spoke at length in another language entirely, and Nico heard Talis reply in the same tongue. Talis moved under the awning with the man. "Stay here," he told Nico. "You can look at what Uly has for sale, but don't bother us."

Nico listened to the two men talking in their strange language as he idly picked at the wares on Uly's tables. He heard the name "Mahri" a few more times. Finally, Uly poured several handfuls of a black, coarse powder into a leather sack and handed it to Talis, who tied it to his own belt. The two talked a moment more, then Talis took Nico's hand and led him away from the stall and back toward the Avi a'Parete. Questions tumbled unbidden from Nico—he was unable to hold them back any longer.

"Are you and Uly from the same country?"

"Yes. Originally. Though we've both been away for a long time."

"Are you from Namarro?"

"No." Talis didn't offer more, and Nico remained silent while they crossed the avi and entered into the warrens of Oldtown once again.

"Who's Mahri, Talis?"

"No one now. He's dead."

"Who *was* he, then?" Nico persisted.

"It's not important."

"Uly said Mahri would be proud of you. And I heard him mention Mahri another time, too."

"You're going to keep pestering me, aren't you?"

Nico glanced up at Talis. He didn't look too angry, so Nico nodded. "Did you know Mahri? Was he your vatarh?"

Talis laughed, though Nico didn't know what he'd said that was so funny, and shook his head. "No. Mahri wasn't my vatarh, and I never knew him. I only knew *of* him."

"Why?"

"Because they said he could do things no one else could do. I thought I said no questions."

Nico ignored that last statement. "What things?"

Talis let loose a sigh laced with annoyance. "Things not even the téni can manage with their Ilmodo."

"Oh." Nico went quiet at that. Everyone whispered how the téni could do nearly anything with the Ilmodo, and there were whispers about Archigos Ana being able to do everything the Numetodo could do, too. But Nico knew that Talis didn't believe in Cénzi or go to temple. So maybe Mahri was a Numetodo? And didn't the Westlanders use magic too? Or maybe there were all sorts of magic, out in the world.

"Do you want to be like Mahri?" Nico asked.

He saw a corner of Talis' mouth lift. "That depends on what you mean, Nico. I don't particularly want to be dead." He laughed, but Nico wrinkled his face in a moue of irritation.

"That's not what I meant."

Talis reached down and tousled his hair, and Nico stepped away. "I know it's not what you meant," Talis said. "And I don't particularly figure that I'll ever be like him. Now, can we try to get home before Serafina realizes you're gone and turns the whole neighborhood upside down looking for you?"

Talis stopped talking and hurried his pace, taking Nico's hand. The soft leather pouch with its midnight powder swung on his belt. Nico watched it from the side of his eyes as they walked.

He'd watch Talis more. Maybe he could learn to do magic,

too. After all, the Numetodo said that most people could do magic if they worked at it hard enough. Nico worked hard; he always won at kick-the-frog because he worked hard. When you worked hard, you could feel the cold energy.

He'd watch Talis. He'd learn to do what Talis did.

~

Varina ci'Pallo

HAD SHE BEEN FORCED into a career as a spy, she would have been captured and executed her first day.

Varina leaned against the side of an apothecary at the edge of Oldtown Center, staring out at the crowds gathered in bright sunshine and searching among them for a familiar face, one that she'd lost in the twists and turns of Oldtown. She was panting a little from the effort of trying to catch up to the man after he'd made an abrupt turn—she'd come to the corner to find him gone. Vanished.

"What do you think you're doing?"

The question, coming from behind her, made Varina jump. Varina spun, bringing her hands up, ready to speak a word and release a quick push spell, but a hand grasped her arm as she turned, stopping her from casting the spell, and she was looking into the face for which she'd been searching.

"Karl . . ."

He released her hand, stepping back. She couldn't tell if he was angry or not. "You were following me." His storm-sea eyes held her.

"Yes," she admitted.

"Why?"

"Because I'm worried about you."

He sniffed as if amused. That irritated her more than his expression. "You, or Mika?" he barked. "Or maybe Sergei?"

She held his stare defiantly, her chin lifting. She brushed back her hair from her face. "All of us. *Everyone* who knows you and likes you is concerned about you, Karl, even though you don't seem to see it. Following you was my idea, though. Not Mika's. Not Sergei's. So you can yell at me if you'd like, but not them. They didn't know."

"I'm not a child who needs to be watched."

"Forgive me," she told him. "I'll be sure to mention

that to Sergei and Ambassador cu'Görin. They'll both be pleased to hear how you've matured."

Karl sniffed again. "That was a mistake. I won't repeat it."

"Karl, you were convinced that it was the Firenzcians and you were ready to be judge and executioner for them. Now you're just as convinced it's a Westlander plot and you're out chasing Mahri's ghost. I'm worried about you, yes. Mahri's dead; you won't find him. And I'm even more worried about what you'll do if you do find some Westlander, someone who might be entirely innocent. I don't know how to say this other than bluntly: do what Sergei told you to do—let them take care of the investigation. You're not helping them *or* yourself."

"And what am I supposed to do, Varina?" he asked. His face was twisted, the skin under his eyes was baggy and dark, and he hadn't trimmed his beard in days.

"You said that you were interested in what I could show you about enchanting objects. Let me teach you. Let's work on that, together—I could certainly use your help and your expertise. It might take your mind away . . ." She glanced around them. ". . . from this."

"You can't understand," he grated out. "So just leave me alone." The look of disgust he gave her was like a blow to her face.

"You've been hurt enough, Karl. I don't want to see you make it worse for yourself."

"I don't need your pity, Varina, and I don't want or need your help," he spat back at her. The words sliced into her. "What do I need to do to make that clear to you?"

"You just have," she told him. "You've made it very clear indeed." With that, she gestured at the open, sunny expanse of Oldtown Center. "Go on," she said. "I won't follow you anymore."

With that, not daring to look back, she started walking away southward, back toward the Numetodo House. She didn't look back. She told herself that she didn't want to see whether he was watching her or not.

~

Allesandra ca'Vörl

BESTEIGUNG. THE INAUGURAL for the new Hïrzg.

The day dawned brilliant and cooperative, with a sky of lush azure in which misty ships of pale white clouds scudded westward and away. The heat had broken, driven away by a cleansing rain the night before. Cénzi had blessed the day, and the téni beamed as if it had been their prayers that had caused the day to be so beautiful.

Perhaps it had.

Allesandra prayed to Cénzi as well. She prayed that the day might turn out as she hoped it would, that she had not misread the signs. And though she prayed, she also made certain that a dagger was sheathed to her forearm under the frilled and lacy sleeve of her tashta. She had learned long ago from her vatarh to never be without a weapon.

The day would be a long one for Fynn—and for those, like Allesandra, who were required to attend to him. First came the ceremony in Brezno Temple at First Call, where the Archigos gave the new Hïrzg the Blessing of Cénzi. Then there were the required state visits: to the Tomb of Hïrzg Kelwin, first Hïrzg of Firenzcia; to the temple near the Hïrzg's Palais that held a vial of blood from Misco, the founder of Firenzcia; to the great cracked boulder near Brezno's main square, where it was said that the Moitidi— at Cénzi's request—sent a furious lightning bolt down to earth to smite the army of Il Trebbio when it invaded Firenzcia in 183 during the midst of the Three Generation War. At each location, there were the obligatory speeches and ceremonies, and the ca'-and-cu' listened attentively, grateful that there was no driving rain or bitter cold or humid heat to endure beyond the stultifying, expected phrases.

Then there came the final procession to the new statue of Falwin I, erected by Allesandra's vatarh Jan after he declared Firenzcia's secession from the Holdings—it was Falwin who had led the tragically unsuccessful revolt against Kraljiki Henri VI in 418, and it was there that Fynn had erected the dais where, at last, the Crown and Ring of Firenzcia would be officially declared his to bear.

As Archigos ca'Cellibrecca passed Allesandra in his téni-driven carriage on his way to his place in the line of dignitaries, he leaned from the window and ordered the driver to halt. The e'téni stopped her chanting and the wheels slowed. The Archigos beckoned to Allesandra over the broken-globe symbol of Cénzi painted in gold and lapis. "Excuse me a moment," she told Jan and Pauli. Jan shrugged at his matarh; Pauli, deep in a conversation with a pretty young woman of the ca'Belgradin family, gave no acknowledgment at all. Allesandra went to the Archigos' carriage and gave the sign of Cénzi to Semini. Francesca was sitting next to the Archigos, in shadow. "A beautiful day for the ceremony," she said to him, to Francesca. "Cénzi has smiled on Fynn."

"Indeed," Semini answered. His voice dropped, low enough that Francesca could not have heard him, barely audible over the tumult of the musicians beginning the processional march. "However, A'Hïrzg, I would not stand too close to the new Hïrzg on the dais."

"Archigos?"

He glanced to the rear of the line, where Fynn's carriage—drawn by four white horses, one of them riderless—waited. "It's a beautiful day indeed," he said, more loudly now. "A good one for all of Firenzcia, I think," he said. "Driver—they're waiting for us."

The e'téni began chanting again; the wheels creaked as they began to turn once more. Allesandra stepped back from the carriage as Semini nodded to her and sat back again on his cushioned seat next to Francesca, who gave Allesandra a sour look as they passed. She watched them move into line just before the Hïrzg's carriage.

She had been on edge all day, wondering if ca'Cellibrecca truly intended to carry out what he had hinted at—he would do nothing himself, of course, but work through layers of intermediaries; if something were to happen, the Archigos would also want it to occur in public, where he could be seen not to be involved, and where it would have the most impact. It was exactly what she would have done herself.

"I would not stand too close to the new Hïrzg . . ."

A thrill of fear overlaid with excitement went through her. She wanted to run back to the Archigos, to whisper three words to him: *"The White Stone?"* If he nodded yes to that, then what she had planned would be a dangerous ploy indeed, given the legends of the assassin. The White Stone, it was said, would kill anyone who tried to interfere with his completion of a contract. The White Stone, those same rumors declared, was a master in the use of every weapon; there was no one who could safely cross blades with him. But the White Stone always struck his victims in isolation, not in the midst of crowds. It couldn't be him . . . at least Allesandra hoped not.

Whatever the case, it would happen soon, then. Soon. And any way this might play out, she would be the one who profited the most—if she was careful. In time. All in time. She returned to her family. "What'd the Archigos want, Matarh?" Jan asked her. Pauli continued to chat with the ca'Belgradi woman.

"To talk about the weather and—according to Francesca—take credit for it," Allesandra told him; Jan laughed at that. "Yes, I know, the woman is nothing if not predictable. Let's get to our coach, darling. The procession is about to move. Pauli, I hate to interrupt your attempts to impress the young Vajica, but we have our duty . . ."

With a grimace of irritation, Pauli broke off his conversation and strolled over as Allesandra was following Jan to the open carriage just ahead of the Archigos. She could see Semini and Francesca watching them, and she nodded to him. "You needn't be so *strident*, my dear," Pauli said.

"And you needn't be so obvious," Allesandra answered. "But this isn't a conversation we should be having in public, Pauli."

"It's not a conversation we need to have at all, as far as I'm concerned." Pauli pulled himself into the coach. He shifted uncomfortably on the plush leather of the seat, tapping at the cushions with his fingers. The sound was as bright and loud as if he were rapping on wood and the cushion barely dimpled. "Firenzcia has a knack for making something appear enticing when it is actually extraordinarily uncomfortable," he commented. "But I realize you're already intimately familiar with that quality, my dear."

"Vatarh!" Jan said sharply, and—strangely—Pauli turned to stare out from the carriage's window. Allesandra felt her cheeks grow hot, but she said nothing. They would be at the dais before a quarter turn, and the day would become what it would become. Either way, Pauli would eventually be no more irritating to her than a summer fly, and she would dispose of him as easily when the right time came. With relief.

The carriage lurched into motion then, and for the next half a turn they rode along the main avenue of Brezno, lined thickly with the inhabitants of Brezno and surrounding towns, all of them cheering and shouting, pushing and jostling against the utilino and gardai stationed there in their efforts to see the elite of Firenzcia, the grand visitors from other countries of the Firenzcian Coalition, and their new Hïrzg.

The square around Falwin's statue was packed shoulder to shoulder, the royal carriages moving along an open path kept cleared by the gardai. At the side of the dais, they were escorted up the wide temporary staircase to their places in the shadow of Falwin's statue. The ancient Hïrzg lifted his bronze arms over them, his massive sword held aloft. Allesandra could *feel* the sound of the crowd, their shouts and applause cresting as Fynn appeared on the platform, hands widespread as if embracing them all. He basked in their adulation, spotlighted in bright sun. She felt a brief pang of envy, watching him.

Allesandra was just to Fynn's left with Jan next to her, then Pauli (already turning backward to speak with the ca'Belgradi girl again); Semini stood to Fynn's right in his brilliant gold-and-emerald ceremonial robes, the crown of the Archigos on his head. Allesandra glanced at ca'Cellibrecca, standing next to the dour Francesca, who seemed to be the only one entirely unimpressed with the proceedings. Semini nodded, faintly.

When? Who? How?

Fynn had begun to speak, his voice amplified through the efforts of two softly chanting o'téni to either side of him. His voice boomed over the masses, the stentorian voice of a demigod shouting from the heavens. "Firenzcia, I stand before you as your servant, and I humbly thank you for the gift of your confidence."

A roar answered him, and he lifted his arms again. But Allesandra's attention drifted away. She scanned the front of the crowd, scanned those standing with her on the platform. There were gardai at the rail of the dais to either side of Fynn, staring outward and down—surely they would see anything troubling there before it was visible to her.

"*I would not stand too close to the new Hïrzg...*" A magical attack, then? A fireball like that of the war-téni? Semini had been a war-téni, after all. But the Archigos certainly wouldn't use the Ilmodo himself, or dare to have someone else do so when it would draw suspicion toward the téni and thus to him.

"As your Hïrzg, I promise you that I will continue my va-tarh's desire to make Firenzcia first among all nations. . . ."

Allesandra glanced over her shoulder. The ca'-and'cu and the visiting dignitaries were arrayed behind her, and at the rear, the servants waited. There was nothing unusual there. She started to turn back when motion caught her eye.

". . . a dream that would see Brezno as the center of the world . . ."

One of the servants was moving forward, bearing a tray with a pitcher of water. He moved slowly through the ranks, murmuring apologies as he pushed carefully through the rows. Moving toward Fynn. The servant's attention never seemed to leave her brother and something in the intensity of that gaze alarmed her. Semini, in the most telling action of all, muttered something to Francesca and was sidling away from Fynn, toward the far edge of the platform.

There are those who use magic and are enemies of Firen-zcia, who would gladly kill the new Hïrzg and would cast no suspicion on the Archigos at all. Allesandra felt a chill of fear; she was no longer so certain of this plan of hers. She had expected the attack to be physical: a knife, a sword, an arrow. *Vatarh wouldn't have hesitated, not if he thought there was still a chance of success. And you are his daughter, the one who is most like him . . .*

"Jan," she said, leaning over to her son. "That man—the servant, behind us, moving forward with the tray—no, don't look at him directly, but do you see him?"

Jan's head moved quickly left, then back. "Yes."

"He's a Numetodo. An assassin."

Jan blinked. "What?"

"Believe me," she whispered furiously. At the dais, Fynn was still declaiming: "*A new day for Firenzcia, a new dawn . . .*" "When he puts the tray down, all he'll need to do is speak a word and make a motion with his hands—we can't let that happen. I'll confront him to slow him down; you come from the side. Go!" She pushed at him. With a glance, Jan turned and muttered apologies as he slipped backward through the ranks of the ca'-and-cu'. Pauli glanced over at them, curious, then returned his attention to the young ca'Belgradi woman. Allesandra stepped carefully behind Fynn, and turned to face the servant.

There were only a few people between them. The servant with the tray stopped, seeing her swivel to face him, and his face tightened. She thought for a moment that she was mistaken, that the man was nothing more than what he pretended to be. But the next few breaths would be ones that Allesandra would never forget.

. . . the servant tossed the tray aside (the ca'-and-'cu' next to him reacting belatedly as tray, pitcher, mug, and water cascaded over them). He lifted his hands as if he were about to pray . . .

. . . as Allesandra flung herself toward him, only to be impeded by those between them, pushing back against her advance . . .

. . . fire bloomed between the assassin's hand as he roared a single word that sounded like the téni language. Allesandra expected to die then, consumed by the téni-fire that would also take her brother . . .

. . . but Jan slammed into the man at the moment the Numetodo opened his hands, bearing him down. (Around them, mouths gaped in mid-shout, most of them not yet realizing what was happening and wondering why this rude young man had shoved them aside, or why this clumsy servant had despoiled their fine clothing. Behind her back, Allesandra heard Fynn falter and go silent. She could imagine him turning, slowly, to see the commotion behind him.) The mage-fire arced sideways and up rather than toward Fynn and Allesandra. Ca'-and-cu' screamed as the fire touched them, tearing through them and blossoming into a fireball that exploded at eye level to the statue of Falwin. Red light pulsed and died, brighter than the sun, and now the crowds screamed also.

"Jan!" Allesandra called in panic, and she pushed forward to get to him. He seemed unhurt, struggling with the Numetodo though the man seemed curiously lethargic in Jan's hands, as if stunned by the turn of events. Around them, there was chaos. She heard Fynn shouting.

Allesandra slid her own dagger from its sheath on her sleeve. Kneeling quickly, she plunged it under the jaw of the Numetodo and yanked it viciously sideways. Blood spurted and fountained, sticky and hot as it streamed over her hand and arm. "Matarh!" Jan said, and she heard the horror in his voice as the blood splashed over him as well. Hands were grabbing at them; the gardai had arrived, their swords drawn, shoving ca'-and-cu' aside. Fynn bellowed orders.

"Who did this!" she heard him shout at her back. She turned to him, the front of her clothing ruined with gore.

"My son saved your life and mine, my Hïrzg, my brother," she told him. "And I've made certain that this assassin will never strike at you again."

The cold shadow of Falwin's statue touched her. She could see Archigos ca'Cellibrecca behind Fynn, and confusion and disbelief fought with horror on Semini's bearded features. Allesandra thought there was near-disappointment in the way Fynn stared down at the body. Pauli pushed forward and came to a stunned halt alongside Fynn as Allesandra let her dagger drop from her fingers. It clattered loudly on the planks of the dais.

"I need to clean myself of this filth," she told them calmly. "Fynn—talk to your people. Calm them. Reassure them. That's what the Hïrzg needs to do."

He scowled at her: as he always scowled when someone deigned to order him about. But he turned to the horrified, worried crowd, and he began to speak.

The White Stone

SHE WATCHED THE ASSASSINATION attempt from within the crowd, unnoticed and safe. *How terribly clumsy,* she thought, as people gaped and shouted and screamed around her. *Clumsy and stupid to boot.*

A knife was a much better weapon than magic. Stealth was much better than a brute attack. You should be there to see your victim's eyes when you strike. You should see yourself reflected in his pupils. You should feel the heat of the blood washing over your hands.

She'd been taught her blade skills at an early age, in the warrens of An Uaimth. Her body still had the scars of those lessons, and she'd thought more than once that she herself would die of them. Her teachers were the dregs of society, the dark and twisted folk who were too violent and too damaged to be tolerated by polite society. They were dangerous, and she had found herself abused and used and injured by them more than once. But they had physical skills she wanted, gained with blood and pain and fury. She had learned those lessons well, taking from each what she could.

She was never again going to let someone take advantage of her. She was never going to be weak. She was never going to let herself be vulnerable.

She had to kill a few of her "teachers," when they became too dangerous or when they tried to become too close, when they began to pry or to guess her secrets. She had left her calling card with each of them, a white pebble over the left eye. *The White Stone . . .* She'd begun to hear the name, whispered in the streets. *He always leaves a stone on the left eye . . .*

They always assumed it was "he"; that was protection, too. She could walk anywhere and never be suspected.

And they never knew there were always two stones; that she took one from victim's right eye to keep with her. To keep *them* with her.

That stone was in the small leather pouch tied around her neck, nestled between her breasts under her clothing. *That* was with her always.

She touched the pouch now as the crowds surged toward the dais, as the A'Hïrzg stood up covered in the blood of the assassin and the new Hïrzg raised his hands to the crowds and called out for them to be calm.

The White Stone smiled at that.

Death . . . Death was always calm.

INCLINATIONS

Allesandra ca'Vörl

"**I**T IS WITH MUCH PLEASURE and gratitude that I award you the Star of the Chevarittai. You may be young in years, Chevaritt Jan ca'Vörl, but I know of no one more deserving of the title."

The applause welled out from those in attendance in the antechamber of the ballroom of Brezno Palais. Jan beamed as Fynn—wearing the golden band of the Hïrzg in his hair and the signet ring on his finger—pinned the gilded star on the red shoulder sash of his bashta, then handed him a gift that had belonged to Allesandra's vatarh and Jan's namesake: a sword of dark Firenzcian steel, hardened in fire and cold water and honed to a razor's edge. Allesandra watched as Jan cupped his hand around the inlaid hilt of the weapon and placed it in the scabbard. Fynn tied the weapon to Jan's belt, then clutched his nephew to him as the applause rose. Standing next to the two, Allesandra heard the words that Fynn whispered into Jan's ear.

"That was a truly brave act, Nephew, though I was in no real danger. I would have certainly ducked out of the way of the fool's spell."

To Allesandra, the true fool was Fynn. His boasting was bad enough, and he'd ignored Allesandra's part in having saved his life. It was as if she hadn't been there at all, as if Jan had noticed the assassin all on his own.

She told herself that she didn't care, that it simply met the low expectations she had of her brother, but the thought didn't convince.

The door to the ballroom opened a moment later, and

Fynn gestured. "Come, let us all enjoy this celebration," he said to the ca'-and-cu' and the gathered chevarittai. Fynn put his arm around Jan, and together they entered the ballroom as the musicians began to play and dozens of chanting e'téni lit the lamps of the room all at once. Pauli offered Allesandra his arm; she took it—*duty and appearance*—and they followed next. Behind them, Archigos Semini and Francesca entered.

Allesandra could feel Semini's gaze on her back.

Following the assassination attempt, there had been a purge of anyone in Brezno suspected of being Numetodo. That, certainly, was also expected. There was another, somewhat less brutal purge within the staff of the new Hïrzg—confirming what Fynn had told Allesandra about how he would treat anyone who opposed him. Every servant, everyone below cu' rank employed by the palais was questioned by the Commandant of the Garde Hïrzg. A half dozen staff members, suspected of Numetodo leanings, were taken to the Bastida to be interrogated more fully. The palais maister who had hired the would-be assassin was found guilty of negligence. His position was taken away, his family was humbled to ce', and the maister himself lost his hands as punishment. The assassin's family was rounded up; no one had seen them since they entered the Bastida. A Numetodo said to have aided the assassin was flayed, drawn, and quartered in Brezno Square, the executioner keeping him carefully alive as long as possible, his screams echoing among the buildings as the crowd watched and shouted insults and gibes toward the man. The assassin's body, so unfortunately killed during the attack, was gibbeted and displayed in an iron cage swinging on a chain from Falwin's sword. The gardai around the palais were doubled, with soldiers from the Garde Firenzcia brought in to supplement them. Rumors flitted through the city as quickly and numerous as sparrows.

Two ca' had been killed in the attack by the errant spell; their funerals were elaborate and well-attended. Six more of the spectators on the dais had been burned and injured in the attack, four of them seriously; it was said that the coffers of the Hïrzg compensated them well enough to keep their families silent and satisfied.

Allesandra could still feel tension in the air, even during

this celebration. The servants kept their heads judiciously down, and if anyone noticed the gardai lining the walls carefully watching the festivities or the remarkable number of téni in attendance, no one remarked on it. It was better to smile and stay silent.

Pauli danced with Allesandra once—the barest spousal requirement. As soon as the dance was over, he excused himself. She knew she would glimpse him only across the room henceforth, and soon she'd find him missing entirely to return to his own, separate, chambers in the visitor's wing of the palais sometime early in the morning. Jan danced with her also, but his attentions were demanded by Fynn and by the crowds of sycophants around the Hïrzg. The young women, especially, seemed to find Jan's presence quite pleasant. Allesandra decided that she would need to pay careful attention to Jan for the rest of the their stay in Brezno as she watched one of the young and unmarried ca' women take her son's arm and lead him onto the floor.

"You surprised me, A'Hïrzg." Semini's voice came from behind her. "I didn't realize you had such deep love for your brother as to put yourself between him and an assassin, even if the Hïrzg seems to have conveniently forgotten that you did so."

Allesandra glanced around them to be certain no one was within easy earshot, and then turned to the Archigos, leaning in toward him with a whisper. "And I was surprised that the Archigos would hire a Numetodo."

His smile might have twitched slightly, his eyes might have narrowed. "I would *never* do that, A'Hïrzg."

"There's no need for false modesty, Semini," she told him. "I thought the idea brilliant, when the irony struck me."

"I don't know what you're talking about, A'Hïrzg," he answered stiffly.

"Ah, but you do," she said. "And you're now in my debt, Archigos. After all, the assassin wasn't able to answer any embarrassing questions afterward, was he? That was *my* doing—for you, Archigos, though my brother was terribly disappointed that there was no one to torture afterward. Come, you want to know why I did it, don't you? Let's take some air, Archigos, where we can be seen but not heard."

Allesandra led him to one of the open balcony entrances. The balcony was empty. She stood directly across from the doors, where anyone looking out would see them. The music wafted out past them and into the night; they could see the dancers, among them the Hïrzg and Jan. Allesandra turned to look at the grounds, alight with hundreds of téni-lights; a few couples were strolling there. "It almost reminds me of Nessantico and the Avi . . ." She turned from the railing. "Almost. I realize that I know very little about your personal life, Archigos. Have you ever been to Nessantico?"

Semini nodded his head. He was watching her as a wary dog might watch another. "I was ordained here in Brezno by Orlandi ca'Cellibrecca, my marriage-vatarh, but as a young o'téni I traveled with him to Nessantico several times when he was A'téni of Brezno."

"Then you undoubtedly understand why Nessantico was always the center of the Holdings. There's a grandeur and history there that one can't feel anywhere else. You can understand why—some day when the Holdings are unified again—Nessantico will become the center of the known world once again. I'm certain of that." She touched his arm; she could feel him draw back. "I want to thank you, Semini. You gave me the perfect opportunity to demonstrate to Fynn just how loyal I was to him—despite the way Vatarh disposed of me as heir, despite Fynn's paranoia and suspicions toward me, despite all the arguments and quarrels we've had. He'll never suspect again that I or Jan would conspire against him."

Even in the dimness of the balcony, lit only by téni-lamps set on either end of the railings, she could see color darken his face. His hands made fists at his sides, and he looked away from her. He said nothing.

"Kraljiki Audric won't live long, from what I'm told," she continued. "I've discovered that I really don't want to be the Hïrzgin, Semini. But when the day arrives that the Holdings become one again—let us say, under a Kraljica—it will need a strong Hïrzg to be the Holdings' sword, the role Firenzcia has always played. Now, my son will make a grand Hïrzg one day, don't you think? A wonderful leader."

His eyes widened slightly. "You want—"

"Yes," she answered before he could finish the question.

"You took an incredible risk, Allesandra."

"Well, I'll admit you did rather startle me with your audacity. I almost decided to just let it happen. But large ambitions require large risks—as you obviously realize. And you owe me for the risk I took, Semini, because I made certain afterward that the assassination attempt can't be easily traced back to you. I destroyed the evidence that could talk."

"I had nothing to do . . ."

She waved at his weak protest. "Come now. Only the moon can hear us here, and we both know better. There's *still* evidence against you, should I be forced to reveal it. We both know that if I were to relate to Fynn some of the conversations we've had, or to tell him about the missive you received from the Regent of Nessantico—" Semini's eyes widened further at that, and Allesandra knew that her guess had been right, "—well, we know that the interrogators in the Bastida can extract a full confession from anyone. Fynn would order such an interrogation, even of the Archigos, should I insist. After all, I'm his loyal sister, who interposed herself between him and that vile Numetodo. And if you tried to tell him that *I* was involved, too, why, my actions and those of Jan would give the lie to that accusation, wouldn't they?"

"What do you want?" Semini asked dully. He stepped back from her, as if her presence was a contamination. That pleased Allesandra; it meant that all the posturing was over. His fine, dark eyes flashed with the reflections of the téni-lights below them, his stance was that of a cornered bear, powerful and ready to defend itself to the death. She found she liked that.

"Actually, I don't want anything more than what you want yourself," she told him. "You and I are still on the same side, even though I know that you're feeling uncertain of that. I like you, Semini. I do. I would like you to become the One Archigos. And you *will* be—if you do as I tell you. You made two mistakes, Semini. One was thinking that Fynn was only useful to us dead when, in fact, we *want* him alive. For now."

"And the second?"

She tilted her head to the side, regarding him. "You thought that you were the one who should be making the decisions for us. I don't expect you to make that mistake again. Back when I was a hostage in Nessantico, Archigos

Ana often told how the Archigos always serves two masters: Cénzi for the Faith, and the person on the Sun Throne for the Holdings."

She touched his arm once more. This time he did not draw back, and she laced her arm with his. "Come, let's dance together, Archigos, since neither of our respective spouses seem to care. Let's see how well we might move together."

She urged him from the balcony and out again into the noise and light of the ballroom.

Enéas cu'Kinnear

"**Y**OU UNDOUBTEDLY HAVE CÉNZI watching over you, O'Offizier cu'Kinnear, though the news you carry is most disturbing." Donatien ca'Sibelli, Commandant of the Holdings forces in the Hellins and twin brother to Sigourney ca'Ludovici of the Council of Ca', paced behind his desk as Enéas stood at attention before him. The room reflected the man: clean and sparse, with nothing to distract the eye. The desktop was polished, with a single stack of paper on it, aligned perfectly to the edge of the desk. An inkwell and pen quill were set on the other side, with a container of blotting sand forming a perfect right angle above them. The wastebasket was empty. A single, plain wooden chair had been placed before the desk. The blue-and-gold banner of Nessantico hung limply on a pole in one corner.

Ca'Sibelli, in his office at least, allowed nothing to intrude on his duty as commandant. There was no questioning ca'Sibelli's loyalty or bravery—he had fought well against overwhelming odds in the Battle of the Fens and had been decorated and promoted by Kraljiki Justi, and his sister had served the state in her way, but Enéas had always suspected that the man's brain was as sparsely furnished as his office.

"Sit, O'Offizier," ca'Sibelli said, waving to the chair and taking his own seat. He plucked the top sheet from the reports and placed it in front of him as Enéas took his seat. The commandant's forefinger moved under the text as he scanned it. "A'Offizier ca'Matin will be sorely missed. Seeing him sacrificed at the whims of the false gods those savages worship must have been horrific, and you're extremely fortunate to have avoided the same fate, O'Offizier."

Enéas had wondered at that himself, and the offiziers who had debriefed him since his return had often said the same, some of them with an undertone of accusation in their voices. He'd been three days in the wilderness around Lake Malik, avoiding Westlander villages and keeping his horse moving north and east. On the fourth day, starving and weak, his mount nearly exhausted, he'd glimpsed riders on a hill. They'd seen him as well and came galloping toward him. He'd waited for them, knowing that—enemy or friend—he couldn't outrun them. Cénzi had smiled on him again: the group was a small Holdings reconnaissance patrol and not Westlander soldiers. They'd fed him, listened in astonishment to his tale, and brought him back to their outpost.

Over the next few days, as word was sent back to Munereo and the order dispatched that Enéas was to return to Munereo, he learned that barely a third of the army led by A'Offizier ca'Matin had managed to limp home after the chaotic retreat. Of his own unit, he was the lone survivor. The shock of the news had sent Enéas to his knees, praying to Cénzi for the souls of the men he'd known and commanded. Too many of them gone now. Far too many. The loss stunned him and left him reeling.

Now, Enéas simply nodded at the commandant's comment and watched as the man continued to read, muttering to himself.

"The nahualli *were* with the army, then. Our intelligence was wrong."

"Yes, sir. Though I've fought against them many times and I've never seen spells like these—fire exploding from the ground underneath us, those circles of dark sand . . ." Enéas swallowed hard, remembering. "One of those spells went off near me, and I don't remember anything after that until . . . after the battle was already over. They thought I was dead."

"Cénzi put His hand over you and saved you," ca'Sibelli commented, and Enéas nodded again. He believed that. He'd been more and more certain of it over the days since he'd left the Tehuantin encampment. Cénzi had blessed him. Cénzi was saving him for a special reason—he *knew* this. He could feel it. At night, he seemed to hear Cenzi's voice, telling him what He wanted Enéas to do.

Enéas would obey, as any good téni would.

"Cénzi was indeed with me, Commandant." Enéas felt that fervently—what other answer could there be? He had expected to die, and yet Cénzi had reached out to the heathen Niente and touched the man's heart. That was the only explanation. And despite the hunger and thirst, despite the exhaustion after he'd left the Westlanders, in some ways Enéas had never quite felt so invigorated, so full of life and *alive*. His very soul burned inside him. Sometimes he could feel energy tingling in his fingertips. "That's why, Commandant, I've made the request to return to Nessantico. I feel that this is the task for which Cénzi has spared me."

There was a destiny for him to fulfill. That was why he escaped the Westlanders; it had been Cénzi working within Nahual Niente. Nothing more. Certainly not the workings of their false god Axat.

Ca'Sibelli had frowned slightly with Enéas' last comment. He ruffled his papers again. "I have prepared a report to send back to Nessantico," ca'Sibelli continued, "and a recommendation for a commendation for you, O'Offizer cu'Kinnear. But still, we'd sorely miss your experience and your leadership here, especially with the loss of A'Offizier ca'Matin."

"That's kind of you to say, Commandant," Enéas answered. It was not like him to protest in the face of orders, but Cénzi was a higher authority. "But reports are dry things, and those in Nessantico, especially the Regent and the Kraljiki, need to know how dire our circumstances are here. I think . . . I believe I would be well-suited to take the message back. I can talk directly to those in Nessantico about how things are here. They can hear from my lips what has happened. I can convince them; Cénzi tells me that I can."

You will go to your leader. You will talk to him, and you will give him a message for us. . . . He thought, for a moment, that he heard that sentence in a great, deep voice within his head. Enéas was too startled to speak immediately. "Commandant," Enéas continued, "I do understand that my place is here with the troops, especially with the Westlanders threatening to advance on Munereo herself. I will return here, as soon as I possibly can, but I can give your report so much more impact. I promise you that. I would suggest that you go yourself, but your expertise and leadership are critical to our victory against the Westlanders."

Ca'Sibelli waved his hand. The movement stirred the top papers on the desk, and he stopped to align them again. He sighed. "I suppose one offizier more or less isn't going to make a difference—or, rather, I believe you when you say you can make far more difference speaking to the Kraljiki and the Council of Ca' than by bearing a sword here. Perhaps you're right about Cénzi's Will. All right, O'Offizier cu'Kinnear: you will leave tomorrow morning at first light on the *Stormcloud*. E'Offizier cu'Montgomeri has my report for you to deliver; you may pick it up as you leave. I will expect you back here with *Stormcloud*'s return."

Ca'Sibelli stood, and Enéas scrambled to his feet to salute. "You already know that A'Offizier ca'Matin had recommended you for the title of Chevaritt," the commandant told him as he returned the salute. "I have signed off on that recommendation; it will also be on the *Stormcloud* for the Kraljiki to sign. I suspect that there are great things in store for you, O'Offizier. Great things."

Enéas nodded. He suspected that also. Cénzi would make certain of it.

~

Audric ca'Dakwi

THE WIND-HORNS OF THE TEMPLE droned First Call, their mournful, discordant notes shredding the last vestiges of sleep.

Audric allowed Seaton and Marlon to help him from his bed. Even with their assistance, Audric was out of breath by the time he was standing on his feet in his bedclothes. His *domestiques de chambre* held him, their hands on him as they stripped his night shift from him, then began to dress him for the morning's audience. Swaying slightly in their hands, panting, he glanced at Marguerite's portrait. She smiled grimly at him.

"You're weak physically because you're weak politically," the Kraljica told him. "Cénzi has sent your illness to you as a sign. You're swaddled in iron shackles that you can't even see, Audric: heavy and confining and weighing you down, and it's that burden that sickens you. The Regent has placed them around you, Audric. He steals power from you; he steals your health. When you break free of the Regent's shackles, when you are Kraljiki in fact as well as in title, your sickness will also fall from you."

"I know, Great-Matarh," he told her. It was an effort just to lift his head. The corners of the room were as dark as if night still cloaked them; he could only see the painting. "I look forward . . . to that day." For a moment, Marlon and Seaton stopped in their attentions, startled at his reply.

"Soon," she crooned to him. "Whatever you do, it must be soon. The Regent intends to weaken you until you die, Audric. He poisons you with his words, with his advice of caution, with the power he's stolen from you. He wants it all for himself, and he is killing you to have it. You must act."

"That's what I'm doing today, Great-Matarh," he told her.

"Kraljiki?" Seaton asked, and Audric glanced angrily at him.

"You do not interrupt when I am in conversation with

your betters," he spat, the words broken by gasps for air. "Do so again and you will be dismissed from my service, and flogged for your insolence besides. Do you understand?"

He saw Seaton glance at Marlon, then give Audric a quick, low bow. "My apologies, Kraljiki. I . . . I was wrong."

Audric sniffed. Marguerite smiled at him, nodding in the frame of her picture. "Hurry yourselves," he told the two. "Today will be a busy one."

A half turn of the glass later, he was dressed and breaking his fast at the table on the balcony of his bedchamber, overlooking the formal gardens of the palais. He heard the knock on the outer door, and the hall servant talking to Marlon. "Kraljiki," Marlon said a few moments later as Audric sipped mint tea, savoring the smell of the herb. "Your guests are awaiting you in the outer chamber."

"Excellent." He set the cup down and waved away Marlon and Seaton as they hurried to assist. "Leave me. I'm fine," he told them. As he walked past the portrait of Marguerite, he nodded to her, then went to the door to the reception chamber. Marlon moved to open the door for him, and Audric held up his hand, waiting to gather his breath again, waiting until he could breathe without gasping. He nodded finally, and Marlon opened the door.

He watched them rise quickly to their feet as he entered, bowing: Sigourney ca'Ludovici, Aleron ca'Gerodi, and Odil ca'Mazzak—all members of the Council of Ca', the three most influential among the seven. Sigourney was the keystone, he knew: she carried the ca'Ludovici name as had Kraljica Marguerite. Thin and active, her long, fine-featured face animated, she was approaching her fourth decade, her hair a false coal-black shining white at its roots—and with her twin brother commanding the forces in the Hellins, she had the voice of the military behind her as well. Odil, a hale sixty, had sat on the Council of Ca' for the longest time of all of them. His body had the lean, shriveled appearance of smoked meat and he walked with a careful shuffle supported by a cane, but his mind remained sharp and keen. At barely thirty, Aleron was one of the younger members of the Council, but he was charismatic, charming, carrying his weight well enough to still be considered handsome—and he had married well into the ancient ca'Gerodi family.

"Please, be seated," Audric told them. He took his own seat near the hearth, on the other side of which his great-matarah's portrait hung. He could imagine her, the back of her head to them as she listened. "I've asked you here today because I value your counsel, and I would like your opinions." He paused, for breath as well as effect. "I won't waste your time. I wish to have Regent ca'Rudka removed from his position and to have the full powers of the government granted to me."

He saw Odil sit back visibly in his chair, and Sigourney and Aleron exchange carefully-masked glances. "Kraljiki," Aleron began, then stopped to run his tongue over his thick lips. "What you ask . . . well, you are only two years from reaching your legal majority. I know it seems a long time to someone of your age, but two years . . ."

"I'm perfectly aware of that, Councillor ca'Gerodi," Audric said scornfully, his voice interrupted by occasional coughs and pauses for breath. "You were there when Maister ci'Blaylock tested me on the lineage of the Kralji. I know my history, perhaps better than any of you. I would mention Kraljiki Carin . . ."

"Yes, Kraljiki." It was Odil who spoke. "There is an admitted precedent in Carin, but Carin . . ."

" 'But Carin?' " Audric repeated as the man stopped. Odil inhaled deeply as he sat forward in his chair.

"Kraljiki Carin was precocious in nearly every way," Odil continued. He looked down at his fingers, folded in his lap, speaking more to them than to Audric. "With the Kraljiki's pardon, the history of Nessantico is my avocation, and I would say that there were extenuating circumstances with Carin's extraordinary ascension. At twelve, he was thrust into command of the Garde Civile against the forces of Namarro when his vatarh was killed—and he demonstrated extraordinary skills in that battle. The histories all say that he had the ability to recall everything that he ever heard. He also had Cénzi's Gift, and could use the Ilmodo nearly as well as a war-téni. And Carin's health—" with that, Odil finally looked directly at Audric, "—was excellent."

"And Carin's Regent was himself the one who went to the Council of Ca' to request that the Kraljiki be given full power early," Sigourney added quietly as Audric felt the heat of blood on his cheeks. "Perhaps if Regent ca'Rudka came to us with such a recommendation . . ."

"Ca'Rudka is the problem!" Audric shouted. *Gently . . .* He heard his great-matarh's voice in his head. *Look at their faces, Audric. You frighten them with your power and you must be careful. Use your head. Play them. You want them to listen, you want them to do your bidding. You must sound like an adult, not a petulant child. You must sound reasonable. Make them believe it's in their best interests to do what you ask. Tell them. Tell them all the things we've talked about. . . .*

Audric nodded. He coughed, taking a breath and wiping his mouth with the sleeve of his bashta, lifting his other hand to the councillors. "I apologize, Councillors," he said finally. "Please understand that my . . . umm, vehemence comes solely from my deep concern for Nessantico and my worry about the Holdings—and I know you all worry with me." He glanced at Sigourney. "Councillor ca'Ludovici, Regent ca'Rudka will never come to you. Never. The truth is that he intends to remain in power, no matter what my age might be."

"That is a troubling accusation, Kraljiki, to be certain," Sigourney responded. "Do you have proof of this?"

"Like Kraljiki Carin," he answered with a nod to Odil, "I remember what is said in my presence. The Regent has hinted at this to me, and I've heard him whispering to Archigos Kenne when they thought I was asleep or too ill to pay attention. Proof? I have nothing but what I've heard, but I *have* heard it. There are curious facts as well. Regent ca'Rudka, after all, was the Commandant of the Garde Civile in my vatarh's time, and also head of the Garde Kralji before that. The Regent's handpicked men still provide the security for Nessantico: Commandant cu'Falla with the Garde Kralji and Commandant cu'Ulcai with the Garde Civile. Yet, somehow, not only couldn't they prevent the assassination of our beloved Archigos Ana, they both claim that they didn't even know of any plot against her."

"What do you mean, Kraljiki?" Aleron asked. "Are you saying that Regent ca'Rudka . . . ?" He stopped. A pudgy forefinger stroked his bearded chin.

"You all know the rumors regarding Archigos Ana— that she sometimes used the Ilmodo to heal, even though the Divolonté speaks against such practices," Audric told them. "I know those practices to be true, because the Archigos helped me, many times, in just that way. Yes, Councillor ca'Ludovici, I see you nod. I know everyone suspected this. With Archigos Ana dead, why, someone might have believed that I, too, would soon die as well—and that the Council of Ca', in gratitude for long service and given that the direct line of Kraljica Marguerite currently had no issue, might just name the current Regent as Kraljiki in title as well as fact. If ca'Rudka waited to act much longer, why, there's the danger that I might marry and have children who could claim the title."

He could see them thinking about his accusations, especially his cousin Sigourney ca'Ludovici. Trying to still the coughing, he hurried into the rest. *Yes, you have their attention now,* he heard his great-matarh say, her voice pleased.

"This has further come to a head because of the continued bad news from the Hellins," Audric hurried to continue. "Councillor ca'Ludovici, your brother is struggling mightily with the puny resources we've given him. Commandant ca'Sibelli is a fine warrior, unmatched, but still we are being humiliated by the Westlanders: we, Nessantico, the Holdings, the greatest power in the world. These people are little more than savages, yet they are stealing from us the land that the blood of our soldiers sanctified. I have told the Regent that I will not tolerate this. I have told the Regent that I wish to have additional troops and war-téni sent to the Hellins to help your brother put down this rebellion. Let me ask each of you, has Regent ca'Rudka spoken to any of you of this?" He saw their heads shake silently. "I thought not. He is content to let the Hellins fall—he has told me as much. He is content to have the great sacrifice of our gardai be wasted. Were I Kraljiki now, I would order the immediate arrest of ca'Rudka. I would put him in the Bastida and have him give us his confession, as he's made others confess over the decades. But if you won't do that, then I suggest you simply *ask* him. Not about the death of the Archigos or his intentions for me, but about the Hellins—ask the Regent about our situation there and what he feels our best course might be. Ask him how it is that he knew nothing of the plot against Archigos Ana. Listen carefully to his answers. And when you realize that I tell you the truth about this, you should understand that I'm telling you the truth of the rest as well."

He stood. He could feel his body trembling from the effort, the exhaustion threatening to take him. He seemed to see the three as if through some smoke-stained glass, and he wanted nothing more than to fall into his bed under the watchful eyes of Marguerite. He had to end this. Quickly. "For now, we're done here," he said. "Talk to ca'Rudka. And after you do, think of what I've said to you."

He bowed to them, then—with as slow and dignified a pace as he could muster—he walked across the room to the door of his bedroom. Marlon opened the door for him.

He managed to wait until it closed behind him to fall into the arms of Seaton.

Sergei ca'Rudka

"REGENT CA'RUDKA! A moment!"

Sergei turned from the entrance of the Bastida a'Drago. Above him, mortared into the stones of the dreary ramparts, the skull of a dragon's head gaped down with its massive jaws open and needled teeth gleaming. The dragon's head, discovered during the building of what had been intended as a defensive bulwark, had given the Bastida its name: Fortress of the Dragon. Now it leered at prisoners entering the dungeon, seeming to laugh as the Bastida devoured them.

Or perhaps it was laughing at all of them: the Numetodo claimed it wasn't a dragon's skull at all, but the skull of an ancient, extinct beast, buried and turned to stone. To Sergei, that was too convoluted a theory to be believable, but then the Numetodo also claimed that the stone seashells found high on the hills around Nessantico were there because in some unimaginably distant past, the mountains were the bottom of a seabed.

The past didn't matter to Sergei. Only the present, and what he could touch and feel and understand.

A carriage had stopped in the Avi a'Parete. Sigourney ca'Ludovici gestured toward Sergei from the window of the vehicle. He bowed to her courteously and walked over to the carriage. "Good morning, Councillor," he said. "You're out early—First Call was barely a turn of the glass ago."

Her eyes were a startling light gray against the dyed blackness of her hair. He could see the fine lines under the powdered face. "The Council of Ca' met with the Ambassador cu'Görin of the Coalition this morning, Regent—as your office was informed."

"Ah, yes." Sergei lifted his chin. "I saw the statement Councillor ca'Mazzak put together. He did a fine job of walking the ground between congratulating the new Hïrzg and threatening him, and I gave the statement my approval. I'm thinking that Councillor ca'Mazzak would make a fine Ambassador to Brezno, if he were willing. And I think Ambassador cu'Görin will be suitably irritated by the appointment."

At another time, Sigourney would have laughed at that, but she seemed distracted. Her lips were partially open as if she were waiting to say something else, and her gaze kept moving away from his face to the Bastida's facade. It wasn't his metal nose—Sergei was used to that with strangers, with their gazes either being snared by the silver replica glued to his face, or so aware of it that their gazes slid from his face like skaters on winter ice. But Sigourney had known him for decades. They had never been friends, but neither had they been enemies; in the politics of Nessantico, that was enough. *Something's wrong. She's uncomfortable.* "What did you really want to ask me, Councillor?" Sergei's question brought her face back to him.

"You know me too well, Regent."

He might know Sigourney, but she didn't know him. No one really knew him; he had never let anyone come that close to his unguarded core, and he was too old to begin now. She would be appalled if she knew what he'd done this morning, in the bowels of the Bastida. "I've had practice at reading people," he told her, with a nod of his head to the dragon on the Bastida's rampart. "It's in the eyes, and the tiny muscles of your face that one can't really control." He tapped his false nose, deliberately. "The flare of your nostrils, for instance. You're troubled by something."

"We've all read the latest report from my brother in the Hellins," she told him. "That's what troubles me—the situation there."

Sergei put a foot on the step of the carriage, leaning in toward her. The springs of the carriage's suspension groaned and sagged under his weight. "It troubles me as well, Councillor."

"What would you do about it?"

"When one is bleeding badly," he told her, "one is advised to bind the wound. I say that with no criticism of your brother. Commandant ca'Sibelli is doing the best he can with the resources we can spare him, but fighting a determined enemy in their home territory is difficult in the best of circumstances, and well nigh impossible at this distance."

"Are you suggesting we bind the wound, Regent, as you so fancifully put it, or to flee in disgrace from what is causing the damage?" Her eyebrows lifted with the question, and Sergei hesitated. He knew that Audric had met with Sigourney, Odil, and Aleron—that kind of gossip couldn't be kept quiet in the palais—and he remembered all too well the arguments on the subject he'd had with Audric. Sergei hadn't yet had a chance to broach the subject with any of the Council of Ca'; now it appeared that Audric had done it for him, and he doubted that Audric's view had painted him in complimentary hues.

"Whether there is disgrace in retreat depends," he answered carefully, "on whether you believe that the next wound might be a mortal one."

"*Is* that what you believe, Regent?" she persisted. "You believe the war in the Hellins is lost?"

Once, he might have hedged, not certain what was the safest opinion to reveal. As he'd grown older, as he'd gained power, he'd become less inclined to be subtle. "I believe there is a danger of that, yes," he told her. "I've told the young Kraljiki my opinion, and such will be my statement to the Council of Ca' in my next report. So you have a preview of it." He smiled; it took effort. "From the way you speak, Councillor, I suspect the Council is already aware of my feelings. Your prescience is impressive." There was no returning smile; Sigourney's face was impassive in the shadows of the coach. "Let me give you the rest of it. The worst danger, as I've also said to the Kraljiki, is that in looking west, we are ignoring the East and the Coalition. I take it Audric didn't mention that to you."

She stayed in shadow, her response masked. "You don't advise sending more troops to the Hellins? Do you advise abandoning what we've gained there?"

Sergei glanced back at the dragon; it seemed to be leering toothily at him. "Why is it that I believe you already know my answers to those questions, Councillor?"

"I would still like to hear them. From your lips."

"Then: no, and yes," he told her flatly. "If we send more troops, we are sending more of our gardai to die across the Strettosei when I am convinced we will need them here, and perhaps sooner than we might like. As for the Hellins: my experience tells me that another commandant will fare no better than your esteemed brother has. Commandant ca'Helfier, his predecessor, is ultimately responsible for the terrible situation there; it was his bungling and poor judgment that caused the Tehuantin army to become involved in the conflict, and that tipped the balance." Sergei was pleased to see her draw back at that and look away from him, as if the sight of the Pontica ahead of the carriage was suddenly far more interesting. "Our difficulties are the distance, and communication, and a vast enemy who is fighting on their home ground." He tapped the open window of the carriage with his hand. "And an enemy who is now stronger than most of us want to believe. When we took the Hellins, the Tehuantin stayed in their own lands beyond the mountains, but ca'Helfier's actions caused the natives of the Hellins to call on their cousins for help. We can call the Westlanders savages and infidels who worship only the Moitidi and set them up as false gods, but that doesn't alter the truth that their war-téni—through whatever deities they call upon—are at least as effective as our own. Perhaps even more so."

"Some might say you skirt dangerously close to heresy yourself with that statement, Regent," ca'Ludovici told him, making the sign of Cénzi.

"I see my duty as Regent to look the truth in the face, no matter what that truth is, and to speak it," he told her. That was a lie, of course, but it sounded good; as he saw it, his duty as Regent was to see that the Nessantico he handed to the next Kralji was in a stronger position than he'd originally found it: no matter what that entailed him doing or saying, legal or illegal. "That has always been my function within Nessantico. I serve Nessantico herself, not anyone within it. That's why Kraljica Marguerite named me Commandant of the Garde Kralji, and why your cousin Kraljiki Justi placed me first as Commandant of the Garde Civile and then named me Regent, even when we often disagreed." His mouth twitched at the memories of the arguments he'd had with the great fool Justi. *May the soul shredders tear at him for eternity for what he did to the Holdings.*

"I, too, serve Nessantico first," Sigourney said. "In that, we're alike, Regent. I want only what is best for her, and for the Holdings. Beyond that . . ." She shrugged in shadow.

"Then we agree, Councillor," Sergei answered. "Nessantico needs truth and open eyes, not blind arrogance. The Council of Ca' certainly recognizes that, doesn't it?"

"Truth is more malleable than you seem to think, Regent. What is the saying? 'A ca's vinegar may be the ce's wine.' Too much of what is termed 'truth' is actually only opinion."

"That may be the case, indeed, Councillor, but it's also what people say when they wish to ignore a truth that makes them uncomfortable," Sergei answered, and was rewarded with a moue of irritation, a glistening of moistened lips in the dimly-lit face. "But we can speak of that later, with all of the Council present, if you wish. There should be a new report coming from the Hellins soon, and perhaps that will tell us what is true and what is only opinion."

He heard her sniff more than he saw it, and a white hand lifted in the shadowed interior, rapping on the roof of the carriage. "We shall talk further on this, Regent," she told Sergei in a cold, distant voice, then called to the driver in his seat: "Move on."

He watched her drive away, the iron-rimmed wheels of the carriage rumbling against the cobblestones of the Avi. The sound was as cold and harsh as Sigourney's attitude had been. Sergei turned again to the Bastida and looked up at the dragon's skull above the gates. The ferocious mouth grinned.

"Yes," he told the skull. "The truth is that one day we'll all look just like you. But not yet for me. Not yet. I don't care what Audric has said to the Council. Not yet."

Jan ca'Vörl

JAN FOUND HIS MATARH standing on the balcony of their apartments in Brezno Palais. She was staring down at the activity on the main square. The Archigos' Temple loomed against the skyline directly opposite them, nearly half a mile away, and nearly every foot of that distance was covered with people. The square was illuminated with téni-lights in yellow and green and gold, dancing in the globes of the lampposts, and the markets and shops around the vast open area were thronged with shoppers. Music drifted thin and fragile toward them from street performers, wafting above the hum of a thousand conversations.

"It's a scene worth painting, isn't it?" he asked her, then before she could answer. "What's the matter, Matarh? You've been keeping to yourself ever since the party. Is it Vatarh?"

She turned at that. Her gaze slid from his face to the chevaritt's star that he wore, and he thought that her tentative smile wavered momentarily. "It's just been an overwhelming few weeks," she told him. Her hand brushed imaginary lint from his shoulders. "That's all."

"I think Vatarh's behavior has been abysmal since he came here," Jan said. "I swear, sometimes I think I could kill the man. But I'm sure you've been far more tempted than me." He laughed to take the edge from his words, but she didn't join him. She half-turned, looking back down toward the square.

"You're a chevaritt," she said. "Someday you'll go to war, and someday you'll have to actually kill someone else—or be killed yourself. You'll be forced to make that decision and it's irrevocable. I know . . ."

"You *know?*" Jan frowned. "Matarh, when did you—?"

She interrupted him before he could finish the half-mocking question. "I was eleven, nearly twelve. I killed the Westlander spellcaster Mahri, or I helped Ana kill him."

"Mahri? The man responsible for Kraljica Marguerite's death?" *Is this a joke?* he wanted to add, but the look on her face stopped him.

"I stabbed him with the knife Vatarh had given me, stabbed him as he was trying to kill Ana. I never told anyone afterward, and neither did Ana. She was always careful to protect me." She was looking at her hands on the railing; Jan wondered if she expected to see blood there. He wasn't sure what to say or how to respond. He imagined his matarh, the knife in her hand.

"That must have been hard."

She shook her head. "No. It was easy. That's the strange part. I didn't even think about it; I just attacked him. It was only afterward . . ." She took a long breath. "Did you ever think about how it might be if someone you knew were dead—that it might be better for everyone involved if that were the case?"

"Now there's a morbid subject."

"Someone killed Ana because they thought that their world would be better if she were out of the way. Or maybe they did it because someone they believed in told them to do it and they were just following orders. Or maybe just because they thought it *might* change things. Sometimes that's all the reason someone needs—you don't think about the people who might care for the victim, or what the repercussions might be. You do it because . . . well, I guess sometimes you aren't certain why."

"You're making me worry more, Matarh."

She did laugh at that, though Jan thought there was still a sadness to the sound. "Don't," she said. "I'm just in a strange mood."

"Everyone thinks that way sometimes." Jan shrugged. "I'll wager that every child has at some time wished his parents dead—especially after they've done something stupid and been caught and punished. Why, there was that time that I stole the knife from your . . ." He stopped, his eyes widening. "Was that the same one? You said Great-Vatarh had given it to you."

Another laugh. "It was. I remember that; I found you using the knife to cut up some apples in the kitchen and I snatched it back from you and spanked you so hard, and you were refusing to cry or apologize, and so I hit you harder."

"I did cry. Afterward. And I have to admit that I was so mad that I thought about . . ." He shrugged again. "Well, you know. But the thought didn't last long—not after you brought up the pie to my room, and promised to give me the knife one day." He smiled at her. "I'm still waiting."

"Stay here," she said. She left the railing and brushed past him. He heard her rustling about in her room, then came back out into the chill evening. "Here," she said, holding out a knife in a worn leather scabbard, its black horn and steel hilt gleaming, with tiny ruby jewels set around the pommel. "This was originally Hïrzg Karin's knife, and he gave it to his son, your Great-Vatarh Jan, who gave it to me. Now it's yours."

He pushed it back to her. "Matarh, I can't . . ." but she pressed the weapon forward again.

"No, take it," she insisted, and he did. He slid the blade partway from the scabbard. Dark Firenzcian steel reflected his face back to him. "Given who we are, Jan, both of us have to make truly difficult decisions that we're not entirely comfortable with, but we'll make them because they seem best for those we care most for. Just remember that sometimes decisions are final. And fatal."

With that, she pulled him to her, and brought his head down to kiss him on the cheek, and when she spoke, she sounded like the matarh he remembered. "Now, don't cut yourself with that. Promise?"

He grinned at her. "Promise," he said.

Allesandra ca'Vörl

*A UDRIC WILL NOT BE KRALJIKI long. That's what
most people here believe. There will come a time, soon,
when a new Kralji must be named. I remember you, Allesandra. I remember your intelligence and your strength, and
I remember that Archigos Ana loved you as well she might
have her own daughter, and rumors come to me that you are
not pleased that the Holdings remain sundered.*

*From my conversations with Fynn, I have no hope that
he wishes to be part of a reunited Holdings unless he's on the
Sun Throne. He has your vatarh's strength, but not his intelligence. I fear that all the good attributes of the late Hïrzg
Jan came to you.*

*When the Sun Throne is left empty, I would support your
claim to it, A'Hïrzg. And there are others here who would do
the same. I would support you openly, if you can give me a
sign that you feel as I do. . . .*

The words were burned into her mind, as crisply as the
letters written in fire-ink on the parchment. The crawling
flames had destroyed the paper almost as quickly as she'd
read the message, leaving behind ash and a sour smoke. Sergei's promise. She'd thought of it nearly every day since the
message had come, and now she knew that the Archigos had
received a similar missive. She could guess what the Regent
had promised him.

Ca'Rudka wanted a reunited Holdings and a Faith un-
sundered. Well, so did she. To create a Holdings greater
than even that of Kraljica Marguerite had been her vatarh's
dream, and—because it had been the dream of her vatarh
and she had loved him so desperately as a child—hers as
well. He had betrayed that dream and sundered the empire, but the dream remained alive in her.

It was what she wanted more than anything. More than
her own safety.

... if there were a sign ...

Archigos Semini had taken that for the obvious hint that it was, and he'd acted in haste before the pieces were in their correct places. Now—partially thanks to the Archigos' impatience and clumsiness—they were.

A sign. She would give ca'Rudka that sign, even though it gnawed at her conscience. Even though she might hate herself for it afterward.

Did you ever think about how it might be if someone you knew were dead? It was the question she'd asked Jan, but it was the question she had been asking herself, over and over.

"I'm afraid I lied to you, Elzbet," Allesandra told the woman across the smeared, dirty table. "I'm not interested in you as a servant." The woman shrugged and started to get up. Allesandra waved her back down. "I'm told," Allesandra said, "that you can put me in touch with a certain man." Allesandra placed a pebble on the table: a flat stone roughly the size of a solas, very light in color.

Even as she said the words, Allesandra doubted the truth of them. The young woman seated before her was plain in appearance. She looked to be in her third decade, though that was difficult to tell; a hard life may have made her look older than her actual years. Her hair was evidently unacquainted with a hairbrush: long and touched with fierce red highlights on the brown, wild strands flying everywhere, it was pulled fiercely back into an unkempt braid of a style Allesandra had not seen since she'd been young. Her bangs were bedraggled, her eyes nearly lost behind the forest of them. Allesandra couldn't even see the color of the eyes shaded as they were, though they seemed to be pale.

The woman only shrugged, glancing once at the pebble. "That may be," she said. Her words held the hint of an accent so slight that Allesandra couldn't place it, and the voice was whiskey-rough. "The one you're talking about is hard to contact. Even for me."

If he knows you that well, girl, I'm not impressed with his taste.... "What's your full name, Elzbet?" Allesandra asked the woman.

The woman stared, her eyes unblinking behind the

tangle of brown locks. "Begging your pardon, A'Hïrzg, but you'll not be needing my name. You're not hiring me, after all—at least no further than finding *him*."

It had taken Allesandra days to get this far, and she could be certain of nothing. There had been discreet inquiries made of people who might have had a reason to kill the three most recent victims of the White Stone, inquiries made by private agents who themselves didn't know who they were representing, only that it was someone wealthy and influential. Names and descriptions had been given, and slowly, slowly, it had all come down to this young woman. Allesandra had arranged to meet her—in a tavern on the edge of one of the poorer districts in Brezno—on the pretext of wishing to interview her for a position on the palais staff. Through the shuttered windows of the tavern, she could see the uniform of the gardai who had accompanied her, waiting by the carriage for her. "How do I know that you can do what you say you can do?"

"You don't," the woman replied. That was all she said. She waited, those unblinking, hidden eyes on Allesandra's as if daring her to look away. The impudence, the lack of respect, nearly made Allesandra get up from her chair and leave the tavern, but this was what she needed and it had taken too long to get this far.

"Then how do we proceed?" Allesandra asked.

"Give me three days to see if I can contact this person you're looking for," the woman said. Her finger flicked at the stone Allesandra had placed on the table. "If I think that your gardai or agents are watching me, or if *he* sees them, especially, nothing will happen at all. At the night of the third day—that would be Draiordi—you will do this . . ." The woman leaned over the table, she whispered instructions into Allesandra's ear, then sat back again. "You understand, A'Hirzg? You can do that?"

"It's a lot of money."

"You don't bargain with *him*," the woman said. "If what you want done were an easy task, you would do it yourself. And you, A'Hïrzg, can afford the price he asks."

"If I do this, how do I know he will keep his end of the bargain?"

No answer. The woman simply sat with her hands on the table as if ready to push her chair back.

Allesandra nodded, finally. "Find him, Elzbet," she said. She plucked a half-solas from the pocket of her cloak and placed the coin on the table between them, next to the stone. "For your trouble," she said.

The woman glanced down at the coin. Her lips twisted. Her chair scraped across the wooden planks of the floor. "Draiordi evening," she told Allesandra. "Be there as I said. Remember what I said about being followed."

With that, she turned and strode quickly from the tavern, with the stride of someone used to walking long distances. Light bloomed in the dimness as she pushed open the door with surprising strength. Through the shutters, Allesandra could see the gardai come suddenly alert as the woman left the tavern.

The coin was still on the table. Allesandra took the stone but left the coin, going to the door herself and shaking her head at the gardai, one of whom was already pulling open the door with concern; the others were watching the woman. "I'm fine," she said to them. The woman was already halfway down the street, walking fast without looking back. The garda who had opened the door inclined his head toward the woman, raising his eyebrows quizzically. "Should I—?"

"No," she said to him. "I won't be hiring her; she was a poor match. Let her go. . . ."

~

Karl ci'Vliomani

KARL WATCHED THE MAN carefully, standing close to him in the bakery, where he could hear him.

This one seemed different than the others he'd watched. For the last few weeks, Karl had prowled Old-town, dressed in soiled and ragged clothes, and watching the crowds surging around him. He'd haunted the public places, lurked in the shadows of the hidden squares in the maze of tiny streets, avoiding the occasional utilino who passed on his or her rounds and who might recognize him. He'd looked at the faces, searching for coppery skin tones, for the lifted cheekbones and the slightly flatter faces that he remembered from his own forays into the Westlands decades ago. He'd found a half dozen people, male and female both, that he followed for a time, on whom he'd eavesdropped, whom he'd touched with the Scáth Cum-hacht to see if they might respond.

There'd been nothing. Nothing.

But now . . .

"These croissants have been here all day and are half-stale already," the man said. Karl heard his voice plainly from where he stood at the bakery's open door, staring out across the street as if he were waiting for someone. He heard the man's walking stick tapping the wooden floor of the bakery. "They're worth no more than a d'folia for the dozen." The words were nothing, but that accent . . . Karl remembered it well: from his youth, from Mahri—an accent as foreign in Nessantico as his own and as unmistakable.

Karl glanced into the shop in time to see the baker's scowl. "They're still as fresh and soft as they were this morning, Vajiki. And worth a se'folia at least. Why, I can sell them to anyone for that—the flour I use was blessed by the u'téni at the Old Temple."

The man shrugged and waved his hand. "I don't see anyone else here. Do you? Maybe you'll wait all day until they're no better than cobblestones, when I'll give you two d'folia for them right now. Two d'folias against wasted bread—it seems more than fair to me."

Karl listened as they bartered, settling on four d'folias for the croissants. The baker wrapped them in paper, grumbling all the while about the price of flour and the time spent baking and the general higher costs for everything in the city recently, until Karl's quarry left the shop. The man brushed past Karl—the smell of the croissants making Karl's own stomach grumble—and strolled eastward along the narrow lane. Karl let him get several strides ahead before he followed. The man turned left down a side alley; by the time Karl reached the intersection, the man was halfway down. In the late afternoon, the houses cast purpled shadows over the lane, seeming to lean toward each other as if to converse in whispers over the cobblestones. There was no one else visible in the alleyway. The spells Karl had cast that morning burned inside him, waiting to be released. He started to call out to the man, to make him turn . . .

. . . but a child—a boy perhaps ten or eleven—emerged from an intersection a little farther down the lane. "Talis! There you are! Matarh has been wondering if you were coming for supper."

"Croissants!" Talis told the boy, holding up the wrapped pastries. "I practically stole them from old Carvel. Only four d'folias . . ." The man—Talis—clapped his arm around the boy. "Come then, we can't keep Serafina waiting."

Together, they started walking down the street. Karl hesitated. *You can't do anything with the boy there alongside him. That's not what Ana would want of you.*

The spells still hissed and burbled inside his head, aching for release. He picked one, the least of them. He lifted a fisted hand and whispered a word in Paeti, the language of his home, and felt the energy release and fly away from him. The spell was designed to do nothing at all; it only spread the power of the Scáth Cumhacht over the area—enough that someone used to wielding that power would feel it and react.

The reaction was swifter than Karl expected. Talis spun around as soon as Karl released the spell. The boy turned a moment later—probably, Karl thought, because the man had stopped. There was no time for him to conceal himself.

Talis, his gaze never leaving Karl, gave the boy the package of croissants and nudged him away. "Nico," he said. "Go on home. I'll follow you in a few minutes."

"But, Talis . . ."

"Go on," Talis answered, more harshly this time. "Go on, or your rear end will be regretting it as soon as I get there. Go!"

With that, the boy gulped and ran. He turned the corner and vanished. The man peered into the dimness, then his head drew back and he nodded. "I should thank you, Ambassador, for sparing the boy," Talis said. One hand was plunged into the side pockets of his bashta, the other was still on his walking stick—if he were about to cast a spell, he showed no signs of it. Still, Karl tensed, his hand upraised and the remaining spells he'd prepared quivering inside him. He hoped he'd guessed right in their making.

"You know me?" he asked.

A nod. "Yours is a well-known face in this city, Ambassador. A bit of poor clothing and dirt on your face doesn't disguise you well. I really hope you weren't thinking you could pass unnoticed in Oldtown."

"You felt my spell. That means you're one of the Westlander téni, like Mahri."

"Perhaps I only turned because I heard you speak a word, Ambassador. Spell? I've seen the fire-téni light the lamps of the city; I've seen them turn the wheels of their chariots or cleanse the foulness from the water. I've seen some of the people of this city with their trivial little light spells that the Numetodo have taught them—which I'm sure the Faith finds disturbing. But I saw no spell just now."

"You have the accent."

"Then you've a good ear, Ambassador; most people think I'm from Namarro," the man answered. "I'm a Westlander, yes. But like Mahri, no. There have been very few like him." He seemed relaxed and confident, and that along with his easy admission worried Karl. He began to wonder if he'd made a critical mistake. *The man's too confident, too sure of himself. He's not afraid of you at all. You should have just watched, should have just followed him.* "So why is the Ambassador of the Numetodo walking about Oldtown casting invisible spells to find Westlanders, if I may ask?" Talis asked.

"We're at war with the Westlanders."

" 'We?' Are the Numetodo so accepted by the Holdings, then? I can hear accents, too, and I would tell you that there are those of the Isle of Paeti whose sympathies might be more with the Westlanders than those of the Holdings. After all, Paeti was conquered by the Holdings just as the Hellins were, and your people fought against that invasion just as ours are doing now. Perhaps we should be allies, Ambassador, not adversaries."

Karl's teeth pressed together as he grimaced. "That depends, Westlander, on what you are doing here, and what you've done."

"I didn't kill her, if that's your accusation," the man said.

Almost, he loosed the spell at that. *I didn't kill her . . .* So the man knew exactly what it was that Karl was after, and his answer was a lie. It must be a lie. The man would say anything to save his life. A Westlander, and a téni . . . Karl's lifted hand trembled; the Paetian release word was already on his lips. He could taste it, as sweet as revenge. "I spoke of no murder."

"Nor did I," Talis said. "But then I don't think it murder to kill your enemy in wartime."

With that, the rage flared inside Karl and he could no longer contain the anger. His fist pumped, he spoke the word: "*Saighneán!*"—and with the word and the motion, blue-white lightning crackled and arced from Karl toward the mocking Westlander.

But the man had moved at the same time, his hand lifting his walking stick. A glow erupted impossibly from the stick, the glare blinding Karl as tendrils of aching brilliance crawled through the air as if they were fingers clawing at a huge, invisible globe. The ethereal fingers snared his lightning and squeezed, a small sun seeming to hang in the air between them as thunder boomed. He heard laughter. Frightened now, he spoke another word: a shielding spell against the attack he was certain would follow.

But the shield fell away unused, and through the shifting curtains of afterimages, he saw that the tiny lane was empty. Talis was gone. Karl shouted his frustration (as heads began to peer cautiously from shuttered windows, as calls and shouts of alarm came from the houses nearest him, as tendrils of smoke curled from charred facades on either side of the street) and Karl ran to the intersection down which the boy had gone.

Neither boy nor Westlander were visible. Karl pounded his fist on the nearest wall and cursed.

~

Nico Morel

NICO ONLY TOOK TWO STEPS down the turn before he stopped. He could hear Talis arguing with the
strange man, and he crept back toward them, putting his
back to the wall of the house at the corner and listening.

"I didn't kill her, if that's your accusation," Talis told the
man, and Nico wondered who he was talking about.

Evidently the man was just as puzzled, for he answered
"I spoke of no murder."

"Nor did I," Talis said. " But then I don't think it murder
to kill your enemy in wartime."

War? Nico had time to wonder before the world exploded. He was never quite certain what happened in the
next several breaths, or how he could ever describe it to
someone. Though it was daylight, there was a stroke of
light that seemed as bright in the shadows of the lane as a
thunderstorm throbbing in the blackness of night. He was
certain that Talis was dead, except that he heard Talis laugh
even as Nico pushed away from the house to run to help his
vatarh, the croissants still clutched heedlessly in his hand.

Then Talis was grabbing him by the shoulder—"By all
the Moitidi, Nico . . ."—and pulled him running down the
lane with him, ducking into a narrow alleyway between
two of the houses, and then along a back lane between
the backs of buildings, twisting and turning until Nico
was out of breath and confused, and finally stopping,
panting.

Talis put his hands on his knees, his breath fast as he
glared at Nico. "Damn it, Nico, I told you to leave," he said.
"When we get home . . ."

Nico fought not to cry at Talis' harsh tone. "I wanted
to hear," he said. "I thought . . . I thought there would be
magic."

Talis cocked his head slightly, though his too-dark eyes
still glittered angrily. "Why would you think that?"

"Because I could *feel* it, all around, like when I get cold all of a sudden and I get ghost bumps." Nico rubbed at his forearm, showing Talis.

"You *felt* it?" Talis asked, and now his voice didn't seem quite so upset. Nico nodded furiously. Talis stood up. He glanced all around them, as if trying to see if the man had followed them.

"Was he really Ambassador ca'Vliomani, the Numetodo?" Nico asked Talis. "Matarh says she saw him once, near the Archigos' Temple on South Bank. She said that the Numetodo shouldn't be allowed here. She said that the Archigos should be stronger against them."

Talis scowled. "Maybe your matarh's more right than she knows," Talis answered. He sighed, and suddenly hugged Nico to him. "Come on," he said. "We need to hurry home now. While there's still time."

Nico ate supper alone in the bedroom, while Talis and his matarh talked in the main room. Nico nibbled on the croissants and sipped at the ground-apple stew his matarh had made while he listened to their muffled voices. Most of the time he couldn't make out the words, but when they got loud, he could understand them. "... told you I expected this. The signs ... just not so soon ..."

"... want us to leave *now?* Tonight? Are you insane, Talis?"

"... you stay you'll be in danger ... go to your sister ..."

"... so it *was* you? You lied to me ..."

Nico lifted his head at that. He wondered whether his matarh was talking about the woman the Ambassador had accused Talis of killing.

There was more mumbling, then an exasperated huff from his matarh as she flung the door open, glared once at Nico without seeming to see him, then started gathering pots and utensils and stuffing them loudly into the cloth bags she used when she went to the market, muttering to herself. Talis, in the doorway between the rooms, watched her for a moment and gestured to Nico. He followed Talis into the room, watching as the man shut the door behind them.

"Matarh's really angry," Nico said as he sat on the bed

Talis nodded ruefully. "She is that," he said. "And for

good reason. Nico, the two of you need to leave the city. Tonight. You'll be staying with your tantzia in Ville Paisli, which isn't far from Nessantico."

"Are you going with us?"

Talis shook his head. "No. Nico, after what happened, the Garde Kralji is going to be looking for me—the Ambassador is a friend of the Regent, and he'll have them looking for me. He probably knows my first name and maybe yours, he knows what we look like, and he knows about where we live. We have a few turns of the glass before he can alert anyone, but I'm certain that Oldtown won't be safe for the two of you soon. So you're going to have to help your matarh gather up what you can and leave."

"But the Garde Kralji . . ." Nico sputtered. "Did you do something wrong, Talis?"

"Wrong? No," Talis told him. "I'll explain it all to you when I can, Nico. For now you're going to have to trust me. Do you trust me, Son?"

Nico nodded uncertainly. He wasn't certain of anything at the moment. "Good," Talis said. "I'm going to leave now and arrange for a cart to take you two out of the city—you remember the man I talked to at the Market? Uly? He can help me make those arrangements. When I get back, you and your matarh will need to be ready to leave, so make sure you have everything of yours you want, and help your matarh gather up her things."

Nico's mouth tasted sour, and the food he'd eaten burned in his stomach. From the kitchen, he could hear his matarh still packing things. "But if you stay, won't they find you?"

"I have ways to hide myself if I'm alone, Nico, and I have things I need to do that I can only do here. Also . . ." Talis paused and tousled Nico's head. Nico grimaced and ran his fingers through his hair to straighten it again. "What happened earlier has to be a secret, too, Nico—like the rest. If you tell people what you saw, well, you'd be putting your matarh in danger, and you wouldn't want that, would you?"

"It *was* magic, wasn't it?"

Talis nodded. "Yes, it was. And Nico, I think that you . . ." He stopped, shaking his head.

"What, Talis?"

"Nothing, Nico. Nothing." Talis was reaching under

the bed as he talked, pulling out the leather bag that held the strange metal bowl and putting his clothing and other things into it. "Now, why don't you start gathering your things? Put them all in one place, and you and your matarh can decide what you'll take and what you'll leave here. Go on, now."

Talis was already looking away, opening the chest at the foot of the bed and pulling out a linen nightshirt. Nico watched him. "Are you a téni?" he asked Talis.

Talis straightened, the linen half in the bag. "No," he said, and the way Talis said it, not quite looking at him and drawing out the syllable, told Nico that it was a lie, or the kind of evasion of the truth that Nico sometimes used when his matarh asked him if he'd done something he shouldn't have. "Now go on, boy. Hurry!"

Nico shivered. He left, wondering if he would ever see these rooms again.

Enéas cu'Kinnear

ENÉAS STOOD AT THE STERN of the *Stormcloud*, staring at the storm clouds that appeared to be rushing toward them from behind. The horizon was a foreboding black under the rising thunderheads, a rushing night pricked with intermittent flares of lightning. He could see the blurred sheets of rain lashing the ocean underneath the clouds and hear the grumbling of distant low thunder. The Strettosei had turned a dull gray green that was flecked with whitecaps from the rising wind; the canvas sheets of the two-masted ship booming and cracking as they filled with the gales and thrust the ship through the deepening waves. The bow lifted and sliced uneasily through the moving hills of water; the wild spray speckled the hair of the sailors and soaked the military bashta Enéas wore. He could taste brine in his mouth. The air around him seemed to have chilled drastically in the last few minutes as the first outrunners of the storm stretched toward them. The dipping and rolling of the deck underneath his feet was alarming enough that Enéas found himself clutching at the rail.

He could *feel* the storm. The energy of it seemed to resonate inside him, and his fingertips tingled with every lightning strike, as if they touched him from a distance.

Chasing us from the west—like the hordes of the Westlanders, crackling with the power of the nahualli. Pursuing us even as we flee, coming to us in our very homes. . . . Enéas shuddered, watching the storm's approach and imagining he could see the shapes of the Westlander warriors in the clouds, or that the thunderheads were the smoke of sacrificial fires. He wondered what had happened in the Hellins since they'd left. He wondered, and he worried at the omen of the storm.

"You'd best get below to your cabin, O'Offizier. I'll do what I can, but Cénzi knows there'll be no calming the sea with this." The wind-téni assigned to the ship had come up alongside him, unheard against the protest of the sails, the shrill keening of the wind through the rigging, and the urgent calls of the ship's offiziers to the sailors on deck. She was staring at the storm in the same manner that Enéas would gaze at an enemy force arrayed against him, gauging it and pondering what strategies might work best against it. The task of the wind-téni was to fill the sails of the ship when the natural winds of the Strettosei would not cooperate. They would also strive to calm the storms that raked the deep waters between the Holdings and the Hellins, but that was the harder task, Enéas knew: the Moitidi of the sky were powerful and contemptuous of the Ilmodo and the attempts of the wind-téni to calm their fury.

"A bad one?" Enéas asked her.

The deck lifted as they rose on the next wave, then dropped abruptly as *Stormcloud* raced down the slope beyond. Enéas wrapped an arm around the rail as water sluiced over the deck; the wind-téni only shifted her weight easily and naturally. "I've seen worse," she answered, but to Enéas' ears it sounded more like bravado than confidence. "But you never really know what's behind the thunderheads until it gets here. Let me test it." Her hands lifted and moved in a spell-pattern, and she chanted in the language of the Ilmodo, her eyes closed as she faced the storm.

Her hands dropped. Her eyes opened and she glanced at him. "O'Offizier, are you also a téni?"

Enéas shook his head, puzzled. "No. I've had some little training, but . . ."

"Ahh . . ." She paused, her eyes narrowing. "Perhaps that's it."

"What?" he asked.

"Just now, when I opened myself to the storm, I thought I felt . . ." She shook her head, and droplets flew from her spray-darkened hair. The first spatters of cold rain hit the deck like tossed stones. "It doesn't matter," she said. "Right now, I have to see what I can do with this. Please, you should go below, O'Offizier . . ."

The ship lurched again, and with it, Enéas' stomach. Lightning crackled nearer, and he thought he could feel the strike in his very flesh, raising the hairs on his arms. He gave the wind-téni the sign of Cénzi. "May Cénzi be with you to still the storm," he told her, and she returned the gesture.

"I'll need Him," she said. She faced the storm again, her hands now moving in a new spell-pattern and her chant longer and more complex. Enéas thought he could feel the power gathering around her; he retreated down the slick, sloping deck, holding onto whatever he could grab until he half-fell into the narrow stairwell leading to the cramped passenger compartments. There, he lay on his swinging hammock and listened to the storm as it broke around them, as the wind-téni struggled to keep the worst of the furious winds away from the fragile vessel that was their ship. Enéas prayed also, his knotted hands clasped to his forehead, asking Cénzi for the safety of the ship and for their safe return to Nessantico.

You will be safe . . . He thought he heard the words, but against the storm and against the vastness of the Strettosei, they were small and insignificant. His words might have been the the whisperings of a gnat.

The storm has been sent to speed you to your home . . . The thought came to him suddenly, in that low voice he'd thought he'd heard a few times since his escape from the Tehuantin. Cénzi's Voice. Enéas laughed at that, and suddenly he didn't fear the storm though the ship pitched and rolled and the wind screamed shrilly. His fear was gone and he felt a certainty that they would be safe.

He thanked Cénzi for giving him that peace.

~

Allesandra ca'Vörl

DO I REALLY WANT to do this? Allesandra shivered at the thought. It was, almost, too late to change her mind.

Alone, in the darkness of a narrow lane in Brezno on Draiordi evening, she waited where she'd been told. A man approached her, hobnailed boots clacking loudly on the cobbles, and Allesandra stiffened, suddenly alert. All her senses were straining, and she pressed a hand close to the knife hidden under the sleeve of her tashta, though she knew that if the White Stone were what he was rumored to be, no weapon would protect her if he decided to kill her. The man came close to her, his eyes on the shadows under the cowl of her tashta, assessing her.

"Ah," the man said. "I guess you're comely enough. Care to do some business with me, girlie?" he asked as he approached her, with the smell of beer trailing after him.

He thinks you're a whore. This isn't him. But, just to be certain, she opened her hand and showed him the gray-white, smooth pebble in her palm. He didn't react. "I have a se'siqil that's yours if you're good to me," the man said, and Allesandra closed her fingers around the stone.

"Be off with you," she told him, "or I'll call the utilino."

The man scowled, hiccuped, then brushed past her. He spat on the ground near her feet.

"Did you think it would be that easy?" At the sound of the voice, Allesandra started to turn, but a gloved hand gripped her shoulder and stopped her. "No," the voice said. "Just keep standing there, looking across the street. I am the White Stone." Husky, that voice, though pitched higher than she'd imagined. In her mind, she'd heard a deep, ominous voice, not this nondescript one.

"How do I know it's you?" she asked

"You don't. Not now. You *won't* know until you see the stone on the left eye of the man you want dead. It *is* a man, isn't it?" There was a quiet chuckle. "For a woman, it's always a man . . . or because of one."

"I want to see you," Allesandra said. "I want to know who I'm talking to, who I'm hiring."

"The only ones who see the White Stone are those I kill. Turn, and you'll be one of those—I know *you*, and that's enough. Do I make myself clear, A'Hïrzg ca'Vörl?" Involuntarily, Allesandra shivered at the threat and the voice chuckled again. "Good. I dislike unnecessary and unpaid work. Now . . . you brought my fee, as Elzbet told you?"

She nodded.

"Good. You'll place the pouch down at your feet, and place the stone you brought on top of it—it's a light stone, as near white as you can find? You'd recognize it again?"

Again Allesandra nodded. Resisting the temptation to look back, she unlaced the pouch heavy with gold solas from the belt of her tashta and, crouching, put it on the cobbles of the street next to her feet. She placed the pebble on top of the soft leather and stood up.

"How soon?" Allesandra asked. "How soon will you do it?"

"In my own time and in the place of my own choosing," the White Stone answered. "But within a moon. No longer than that. Who do you want me to kill?" the assassin asked. "What is his name?"

"You may not take the money when I tell you."

The White Stone gave a mocking laugh. "You wouldn't need me if the one you wanted dead weren't well-placed and well-protected. Perhaps, given your history, it's someone in Nessantico?"

"No."

"No?" There was, Allesandra thought, disappointment in the voice. "Then who, A'Hïrzg? Who do you want dead badly enough that you would find me?"

She hesitated, not wanting to say it aloud. She let out the breath she was holding. "My brother," she said. "Hïrzg Fynn."

There was no answer. She heard a clatter out in the street to her right, and her head moved involuntarily in that direction. There was nothing there; in the moonlight, the street was empty except for a utilino just turning the corner a block away, whistling and swinging his lantern. He waved at her; she waved back. "Did you hear me?" she whispered to the White Stone.

There was no answer. She glanced down: pouch and stone were gone. She turned. There was a closed door directly behind her, leading into one of the buildings.

Allesandra decided it would not be in her best interest to open that door.

~

The White Stone

"*MY BROTHER. Hïrzg Fynn.*"
She had thought herself beyond surprise at this point, but this . . .

She'd been in Firenzcia now for some three years, longer than she'd stayed anywhere in some time, but the work had been good here. She knew some of the history between Allesandra and Fynn ca'Vörl; she'd heard the rumors, but none of them spoke of a resentment this deep in Allesandra. And she herself had witnessed Allesandra *saving* her brother from an attack.

She found herself puzzled. She didn't care for uncertainty.

But . . . that wasn't her concern. The gold solas in the pouch were real enough, and she had heard Allesandra clearly, and the woman's white stone sat in her pouch next to the stone of the right eye, the stone that held the souls of all those the White Stone had killed.

Her fingers scissored around the white stone now through the thin, soft leather of the pouch. The touch gave her comfort, and she thought she could hear the faint voices of her victims calling.

"*I nearly killed you first . . . You were so clumsy then . . .*"

"*How many more? We grow stronger, each time you add another . . .*"

"*Soon you'll hear us always . . .*"

She took her hand from the stone and the voices stopped. They didn't always. Sometimes, especially recently, she'd been hearing them even when she didn't touch the stone.

To kill a Hïrzg . . . This would be a challenge. This would be a test. She would have to plan carefully; she would have to watch him and know him. She would have to *become* him.

Her fingers were back around the stone again. "*You've killed the unranked, you've killed ce'-and-ci', and they are easy enough. You've killed cu'-and-ca', and you know*" *they're far more difficult because with money comes isolation, and with power comes protection. But never this. Never a ruler."*

"You're afraid . . ."

". . . You doubt yourself . . ."

"No!" she told them all, angrily. "I can do this. I will do this. You'll see. You'll see when the Hïrzg is in there with you. You'll see."

They'll know you. The A'Hïrzg will know you . . .

"No, she won't. People like her don't even *see* the unranked, as I was to her. My voice will be different, and my hair, and—most importantly—my attitude. She won't know me. She won't."

With that, she plucked the pouch of golden coins from the bed and placed it in the chest with the other fees. From the chest, she pulled out the battered bronze mirror and looked at her reflection in the polished surface. She touched her hair, looked at the haunted, almost colorless eyes. It was time for her to become someone else. Someone richer, someone more influential.

Someone who could get close enough to the Hïrzg . . .

THRONES

Allesandra ca'Vörl
Audric ca'Dakwi
Sergei ca'Rudka
Varina ci'Pallo
Enéas cu'Kinnear
Jan ca'Vörl
Nico Morel
Allesandra ca'Vörl
Karl ca'Vliomani
Nico Morel
Allesandra ca'Vörl
The White Stone

Allesandra ca'Vörl

WITHIN A MOON . . .

That's the promise the White Stone had made.
Allesandra wondered if she could keep up the pretense
that long. It was more difficult than she'd thought. Doubts
plagued her—she had dreamed for the last three nights that
she had gone to the White Stone to try to end the contract.
"Just keep the money," she'd told him. "Keep the money,
but don't kill Fynn." Each time he'd laughed at her and
refused.

"That's not what you want," the White Stone replied.
In the dream, his voice was deeper. "Not really. I will do
what you desire, not what you say. He'll be dead within a
moon. . . ."

She hoped Cénzi was not rebuking her. *Fynn probably
contemplated killing me as Vatarh was dying, thinking I
would challenge him for the crown. He would still do so if
he suspected me of plotting against him—he's as much as
said that. This is no less than he deserves for what Vatarh
and he did to me. This is what he deserves for his continued
arrogance toward me. This is what I must do for me; this is
what I must do for Jan. This is what I must do for Vatarh's
dream. This is the only way. . . .*

The words were burning coals in her stomach, and they
touched all aspects of her life. She had suspected it would
one day come to this, but she had also hoped that day might
never arrive.

Since the attempted assassination, Fynn had enjoyed
the adulation of the Firenzcian populace and Jan—as

the Hïrzg's protector—had been taken up with it as well. Everyone seemed to have forgotten entirely that Allesandra had anything to do with the foiling of the assassination. Even Jan seemed to have forgotten that—he certainly never mentioned, in all his recounting of the story, that it had been her who pointed out the assassin to him.

Crowds gathered to cheer whenever the Hïrzg left his palais in Brezno, and there were parties nearly every night, with the ca'-and-cu' of the Coalition. There were new people there every night, especially women wanting to be close to the Hïrzg (still unmarried despite his age) and to the new young protégé Jan.

Her husband, Pauli, also enjoyed the influx of fresh young women into the palais life. Allesandra was far less pleased with it, and even less pleased with Pauli's attitude toward Jan. "He's your son," she told him. Her stomach roiled with the argument she knew was coming, and she placed a hand on her abdomen to calm it, swallowing the fiery bile that threatened to rise in her throat and hating the shrill sound of her voice. "You need to caution him about these things. If one of these eager ca'-and-cu' swarming around him end up with child . . ."

Pauli gave her an expression that was near-smirk, making the bile slide higher inside her. "Then we buy the girl and her family a vacation in Kishkoros unless she's a good match for him. If that's the case, let him marry her." His casual shrug was infuriating. Allesandra wondered how many Kishkoros vacations Pauli had bought during their years of marriage.

They were standing on the balcony above the palais' main ballroom floor. Another party was in progress below; Allesandra could see Fynn and the usual cluster of bright tashtas, and that made her hands tremble. Archigos Semini was close by as well, though Allesandra didn't see Francesca in the crowd. Jan was in the same group, talking to a young woman with hair the color of new wheat. Allesandra didn't recognize her.

"Who is that?" she asked. "I don't know her."

"Elissa ca'Karina, of the Jablunkov ca'Karina line. She was sent to represent her family for the Besteigung, but was delayed near Lake Firenz and just arrived a few days ago."

"You know her well, then."

"I've . . . talked to her a few times since her arrival."

The hesitation and choice of words told Allesandra more than she wanted to know. She closed her eyes for a breath, rubbing at her stomach. She wondered if it had just been flirtations or more. "I'm sure Jan would appreciate your familial interest, just as Fynn appreciates his First Taster."

"That was crude and beneath you, my dear."

She ignored that, peering over the railing. "How old is she?"

"Older than our Jan by a few years, I'd judge," Pauli told her. "But an engaging and interesting woman."

"And a candidate for a Kishkoros vacation?"

She heard Pauli chuckle. "She might prefer a more northern location, but yes, if it would come to that." She felt him move close to her, staring down at the crowd. "You can't protect him forever, Allesandra. You can't live his life for him, and you can't keep someone his age captive—not without expecting him to resent you for it."

"*I* was kept captive," she answered him, and pushed away from the railing. *"You can't live his life for him."'* But *I* will *shape his future. I will* . . . "We should go down."

They were announced into the party by the door heralds. She went directly to Fynn and Jan, while Pauli bowed to her and went off on his own. Arehigos Semini's eyes widened a bit with her approach—since the attempted assassination and their one subsequent conversation, the Archigos had engaged in little more than the required polite talk with her. She wondered what he'd think if she told him what she'd done.

The ca'-and'cu' in the group all bowed low as she approached. She bowed also—a mere inclination of her head—to Fynn and gave Semini the sign of Cénzi. She smiled toward Jan, but her gaze was more on the woman with him. Elissa ca'Karina was one of those women who was incredibly striking while not being beautiful in a classical sense, and the arms emerging from the lace of the tashta were decidedly muscular—a horsewoman, perhaps. Her eyes were her best feature: large, a pale icy blue, and made prominent by judicious application of kohl. Allesandra judged her to be in her early twenties—and if she was unmarried at that age given her rank, then perhaps there was some scandal attached to her: Allesandra decided that a judicious inquiry was in order. The lines of the vajica's face seemed oddly familiar, but perhaps that was only because she was little different than the others: young, eager, smiling, all eyes and laughter and attention.

"A lovely party, Brother," she said to Fynn. His smile was nearly predatory as he glanced around them.

"Yes, isn't it?" he responded, and his pleasure was obvious. "I'm absolutely surrounded by loveliness." Bright laughter answered him. Allesandra smiled in return, but she watched her brother's animated face. The image came to her of him sprawled bloody on the tiles, with a pebble over the left eye and the right staring blindly up at her. She shook away the thought, swallowing heat again. "Don't you think so, Allesandra?"

"I do. I see here two young bees and an old hornet surrounded by flowers, and the flowers had best be careful." More polite laughter, though she saw the Archigos frown as if he were trying to decide if he'd been affronted. Her gaze went back to Vajica ca'Karina. "Jan, you've neglected to introduce your yellow rose."

Jan straightened and slid the barest fraction of an inch closer to the young woman. *Almost protective . . . Yes, he's interested in her. And look at the way she keeps glancing at him . . .* "Matarh, this is Vajica ca'Karina. She's here from Jablunkov."

Elissa bowed her head to Allesandra. "A'Hïrzg," she said. "I'm so delighted to meet you. Your son has told us many delightful things about you." Her voice held the accent of Sesemora, blurring the consonants ever so slightly. The voice was husky and low for a woman. Something about the young woman, though . . .

"Have we met, Vajica ca'Karina?" Allesandra asked. "Perhaps at one of my vatarh's Solstice feasts? The shape of your face, the lines of it . . ."

"Oh, no, A'Hirzg," the woman answered. The smile was disarming, the laugh enchanting. "I would *certainly* remember having met you, and especially your son."

Allesandra was certain of that last statement, at least. "Then perhaps it's a family resemblance? Would I know your parents?"

"I don't know, A'Hirzg. I know they once entertained Hïrzg Jan, many years ago, but that was while you were still . . ." She stopped there, blushing as she recognized what she was about to say, and hurrying on. "I was named after my matarh, and my vatarh is Josef—he was a ca'Evelii before he married my matarh. Our chateau is east of Jablunkov, in the hills. A very pretty place, A'Hïrzg, though the winters can be rather long there."

Allesandra nodded to all that, committing the names to memory for the message she would send. Jan touched Elissa's arm as the musicians on the ballroom's stage started to play. "Matarh, I promised Elissa a dance. . . ."

Allesandra smiled as graciously as she could. "Of course. Jan, we really must talk later . . ." but he was already leading Elissa away. Fynn had moved out into the open dancing space as well.

"He's a fine young man, your son, and very brave." Semini's emerald-hued robes shifted as he gazed at her. He seemed uncertain as to whether to come closer to her or to flee. The compliment was so bald that Allesandra felt no compulsion to reply to it.

"Is your Francesca well? I notice she's not here tonight."

"She is indisposed, A'Hïrzg. These endless celebrations for the new Hïrzg are tiring, especially for someone with so many ailments. But she sent her regrets to the Hïrzg, and there is a meeting of the Council of Ca' tomorrow and she takes her responsibilities as councillor very seriously. There is no one who thinks more of Brezno than Francesca. It is practically *all* she thinks about."

His tone was blatantly scornful. Allesandra realized then that it had been Francesca who had put the Archigos on his path. It was *her* ambition driving him, not his own. Semini, she suspected, would still be a war-téni if it were not for Francesca. She wondered if Francesca, too, harbored images of Fynn laying dead, but with Francesca herself taking the throne. "And you, A'Hïrzg?" Semini asked. "Forgive me, but you seem a bit pale this evening."

"I find that I'm a little indisposed, Archigos."

He nodded. Under silver-flecked eyebrows, his dark gaze scanned the floor; she followed it to find Pauli laughing in a knot of older women, his hands gesturing finely as he spoke. "A family problem?" Semini asked.

"Possibly."

He nodded, as if musing on that. "When we last spoke, A'Hïrzg, you said we were on the same side."

"Aren't we, Archigos?" she asked him. "Don't we both want what's best for Firenzcia?"

He took a long breath. "I believe we do. At least, I hope so. And the last time, you asked me to dance. You said you wanted to know how well we moved together. But you left without giving me an answer." Another pause. Another breath. His gaze came back to her, intense and unblinking. "Did we? Did we move together well?"

She touched his arm. She felt muscles lurch under his robes, but he didn't move away. "I seem to remember that we did," she told him. "But perhaps a reminder would be good. For both of us."

She led him out onto the dance floor.

She thought he moved very well indeed.

~

Audric ca'Dakwi

HIS GREAT-MATARH FROWNED as he struggled to breathe on the bed. "Get *up*, boy," she told him. "The Kraljiki can't lie there weak and helpless. The Kraljiki must be strong; the Kraljiki must show he can lead his people."

"But, Great-Matarh," he told her. "It's so hard. My chest hurts so much...."

"Kraljiki?" Seaton and Marlon entered the bechamber from the door to the servants' corridor. The two of them struggled with a heavy wheeled easel draped in gold-brocaded blue cloth.

"Ah," Audric said. "Good." He pointed to the painting over the fireplace. "You see, Great-Matarh? Now you may come with me wherever I go." He supervised as his attendants took down the painting and placed it carefully on the easel, making certain it was secured to the frame of the device so it couldn't fall. Audric watched, and thought that Marguerite looked pleased. "It must have been boring, having to stare at the same room all day and night. It would have driven me mad ..." He looked at Seaton. "Have they come as I ordered?"

"Yes, Kraljiki," Seaton answered. "They're waiting for you in the Sun Throne Hall."

"Then we shouldn't keep them waiting. Bring the Kraljica with us."

"And you, Kraljiki? Should we call for a chair?"

Audric shook his head. "I no longer require that," he told them, told Marguerite. "I will walk."

Seaton and Marlon glanced quickly at each other and bowed. Audric took as deep a breath as he could and led them from the bedchamber.

He thought perhaps he'd made a mistake by the time they'd walked nearly the length of the main wing of the palais. He was panting rapidly from the effort and could feel sweat dampening the back of his neck and beading on his forehead. He dabbed at the moisture with the lace of his sleeve as they reached the hall gardai. When they started to announce them, Audric stopped them. "A moment," he said. He closed his eyes, trying to regain his breath.

"You can do this," he heard Marguerite say, and he nodded to the gardai. They opened the doors for them. "The Kraljiki Audric," one of them intoned into the hall.

Audric heard the rustling as the seven people inside came to their feet, their heads bowed as he entered: Sigourney ca'Ludovici, Aleron ca'Gerodi, Odil ca'Mazzak . . . all the appointed members of the Council. He could also see them desperately trying to glance up to see what was making such a racket as Seaton and Marlon wheeled in Marguerite's portrait behind him. "Kraljiki," Sigourney said, lifting from her bow as he stopped in front of her. "It's good to see you doing so well."

Her gaze slipped past him to the painting, and he saw her struggle to keep the puzzlement from her face.

"The reports of my illness have been exaggerated by those who wish to do me harm," he told her. "I *am* well, thank you, Councillor." He nodded to the others in the room. For a moment, he was frightened, like a child among a forest of adults, but then he heard Marguerite's voice in his ear, whispering to him: *"You are superior to them, boy. You are their Kraljiki; behave as if you expect their obedience and you will get it. Act as if you are still a child and they will treat you that way."*

With a nod to his attendants, Audric strode to the Sun Throne, forcing down the cough that threatened to double him over. He sat, and the Throne bloomed into light around him, the crystal facets gleaming. The e-téni stationed around the room relaxed as the glow surrounded him. Audric closed his eyes briefly as the easel was moved to sit at his right hand. His great-matarh could see them now, all of them.

They were staring at him, at Marguerite. *"See the greed on their faces. They all want to sit where you're sitting, Audric. Especially Sigourney; she wants it most of all. You can use that to get them to agree. . . ."*

"I won't keep you long here," he told the Council. "We are all busy people, and I am looking strongly at ways to bring Nessantico back to prominence against our enemies to both West and East. That is, I am certain, what each of us want. I vow to you now; I will reunite the Holdings."

The speech nearly exhausted him, and he could not keep away the cough that followed, smothering it in a lace handkerchief. "The Council of Ca' isn't all present, Kraljiki," Sigourney said. "We are missing Regent ca'Rudka."

"I was aware of that," Audric told her. "He is missing for good reason: the Regent was not invited."

"Ah?" Sigourney breathed questioningly as the others murmured.

"See the eagerness—especially with Cousin Sigourney? They are all thinking about where they would stand if the Regent fell, and calculating their chances. . . ."

"Yes," Audric said before any of them could voice an objection. "I called this meeting to discuss the Regent. I won't waste your time with diversions and small talk. For the good of Nessantico, I am asking for two rulings from the Council of Ca'. One, that Regent ca'Rudka be immediately imprisoned in the Bastida a'Drago for treason—" the uproar nearly drowned out the rest, "—and that I be elevated to rule as Kraljiki in truth as well as title." The clamor of the Council redoubled at that statement. Audric sat back and listened, letting them argue among themselves. *"Yes, use the opportunity to rest, and to listen. . . ."*

He did that. He watched them; he especially watched Sigourney. Yes, she kept glancing over to him as she spoke to the other councillors. He could see her weighing him, judging him. "This is what I desire," Audric said at last, when the hubbub had died somewhat, "and it is what my great-matarh desires as well." He gestured to the portrait, and was gratified to see her smile in return. They stared, all of them, their gazes moving from him to the painting and back again. "The Regent is a traitor to the Sun Throne. Ca'Rudka wishes to sit here where I am sitting now, and he is plotting to do so even at the expense of our success in the Hellins and against the Coalition."

Aleron cleared his throat noisily, glancing at Sigourney. "Councillor ca'Ludovici has mentioned to all of us here your concerns, Kraljiki, and I wish to assure you that we take them seriously," he said. "But proof of these accusations . . ."

"Your proof will come when ca'Rudka is interrogated,

Vajiki ca'Gerodi," Audric said, and the stress of speaking loudly enough to interrupt the man sent him into a spasm of coughing. They watched him, silent, as he regained control. *"Don't worry. This works to your advantage, Audric. They're all thinking that with the Regent gone, and you ill, that perhaps the Sun Throne will be quickly vacant, and one of them might take it. Sigourney, Odil, and Aleron had all heard the outlines of what you're asking already, so they know what you'll say. Look at Sigourney—see how eagerly she regards you? See how she's assessing you for weakness. She has ambition . . . use it!"* Audric glanced over gratefully at his great-matarh, inclining his head to her as he wiped his mouth.

"I am convinced," Audric told them, "that Regent ca'Rudka was responsible for Archigos Ana's assassination, that he intends to abandon the Hellins despite the tremendous sacrifice of our gardai, and that he is conspiring with those in the Firenzcian Coalition against me, perhaps intending to place Hïrzg Fynn here on the Sun Throne if he cannot sit there himself."

"Those are serious accusations, Kraljiki," Odil ca'Mazzak said. "Why isn't Regent ca'Rudka here to answer them?"

"To *deny* them, you mean?" Audric laughed, and Marguerite's amusement rose twined with his own. "That's what he would do. You're right, Cousin: these are serious accusations, and I don't make them lightly. It's also why I believe that the Regent must be removed from his position. Let those in the Bastida rip the truth from him." He paused. They watched him as he smiled at his great-matarh. "Let me rule as the new *Spada Terribile* as my great-matarh did, and bring Nessantico to new heights."

"See? They look at you with new eyes, my great-son. They no longer hear a child, but a man . . ."

They did watch him carefully, appraisingly. He sat up in the chair, holding their gazes regally as he imagined his great-matarh had, looking at the shadow of himself the gleam of the throne cast on the walls and ceiling. "I know," he told her.

"You know what, Kraljiki?" Sigourney asked him, and he shook himself, his hands tightening on the cold arms of the Sun Throne.

"I know that you have doubts," he answered, and there

was a susurration of agreement, like the voices of the wind in the chimneys of the palais. "But I also know that you are the best of Nessantico, and that you care as deeply as I do for her. I know that you will discuss this, and you will come—as you must—to the same conclusion that I have. My great-matarh was called early to the throne, and so am I. This is my time, and I ask the Council to acknowledge that."

"Kraljiki . . ." Sigourney bowed to him. "A decision this important can't be taken easily or lightly. We . . . the Council . . . must talk among ourselves first."

Show them. Show them your leadership. Now. "Do that," Audric told her. "But I ask that you send ca'Rudka to the Bastida while you deliberate. The man is a danger: to me, to the Council of Ca', and to Nessantico. That is the least you can do for the good of Nessantico."

He stood, and they bowed to him. He left the room and the Sun Throne dimmed behind him. Behind him, Seaton and Marlon escorted Kraljica Marguerite from the chamber in his wake.

He could hear her approval. He could hear it as easily as if she walked alongside him.

Sergei ca'Rudka

THE GATES TO THE BASTIDA were already open and the gardai saluted Sergei from the cover of their guardhouses set to either side. The dragon was weeping in the rain.

The sky was sullen and brooding, glowering over the city and tossing frequent sheets of hard rain down from slate-gray ramparts. Sergei glanced up—as he always did—to the dragon's head mounted over the Bastida's gates. In the foul weather, the white stone had gone pallid as water streamed over the midchannel of its snout and cascaded in a small waterfall to the flagstones underneath—there was a shallow bowl worn in the stone there from decades of rain. Sergei blinked into the storm and shrugged his cloak tighter around his shoulders. Raindrops struck his silver nose and splattered. The weather had seeped into his bones; his joints had been aching since he woke up this morning. Aris cu'Falla, Commandant of the Garde Kralji, had sent a messenger before First Call to summon him; Sergei thought that he would stay for a bit after the meeting, just to "inspect" the ancient prison. It had been a month or more since the last time—Aris would frown, then look away and shrug. However, even the anticipation of a morning in the lower cells of the Bastida, of the sweet fear and the lovely terror, did little to ease the soreness that came from simply walking.

A shame his own pain didn't have the same allure as that of others'. "A miserable day, eh?" he asked the dragon's skull, grinning up at it. "Just think of it as a good washing."

Across the small, puddled courtyard, the door to the main office of the Bastida opened, throwing warm firelight over the gloom. Sergei saluted the garda who had opened the door and entered, shaking water from his cloak. "A day best suited for ducks and fish, don't you think, Aris?" he said.

Aris only grunted without smiling, hands clasped behind his back. Sergei frowned. "So what's this important matter you had to see me about, my friend?" he asked, then noticed the woman seated in a chair before the fire, facing away from him. He recognized her before she turned and the dampness on his bashta turned as cold as a midwinter day and his breath caught in his throat. *You're truly getting old and clumsy, Sergei. You've misread things, and badly.* "Councillor ca'Ludovici," he said as she turned to him. "I didn't expect to see you here, but I suspect I should have. It would seem that I've not been paying enough attention to rumors and gossip."

He heard the door close and lock behind him. It had the sound of finality. "Sergei," cu'Falla said softly, "I require your sword, my friend."

Sergei didn't respond. Didn't move. He kept his gaze on Sigourney. "It's come to this, has it? Vajica, the boy's mind has become unhinged from his illness. We both know that. By Cénzi, he's conversing with a *painting*. I don't know what he's told the Council, but surely none of you actually believe it. Especially you. But I suppose belief isn't the issue, is it?—it's who can gain something from the lie." He shrugged. "You don't need this charade, Councillor. If the Council of Ca' wishes my resignation as Regent, it can have it. Freely. Without this charade."

"The Council does want your resignation," Sigourney answered. "But we also realize that a deposed Regent is always a danger to the throne. As Commandant cu'Falla has already informed you, we require your sword."

"And my freedom?"

There was no answer from Sigourney. "Your sword, Sergei," Aris said again. His hand was on the hilt of his own weapon. "Please, Sergei," he added, a note of pleading in his voice. "I don't care for this any more than you, but we both have our duty to perform."

Sergei smiled at Aris and began to unbuckle the scabbard from around his waist. The sword had been given to him by Kraljiki Justi during the Siege of Passe a'Fiume: dark and hard Firenzcian steel, a beautiful warrior's blade. He could use it if he wished—he could parry Aris' strike and thrust past into the man's belly, then turn to the garda behind him. Another cut would strike the head from Vajica ca'Ludovici's neck. He could gain the courtyard and be away into the streets of Nessantico before they began to pursue him, and maybe, maybe he could stay alive long enough to salvage something from this mess. . . .

The vision was tempting, but he also knew it was something he could have done twenty years ago. Now, he wasn't so certain his body could obey the mind. "I wouldn't have taken the Sun Throne had it been offered to me," Sergei told Sigourney. "I never wanted it; Justi knew that and it's why he named me Regent. I thought you knew it as well." Sergei sighed. "What else does the Council require of me? A confession? Torture? Execution?"

He could feel his hands trembling and he clenched them together around his scabbard, sliding his hand closer to the hilt. He would not let Signourney see the fright inside him. He knew torture. He knew it intimately. Aris watched him carefully; he heard the garda slip close behind him and slide his sword from its sheath.

I could still do it. Now . . .

"Your service to Nessantico is long and noteworthy, Vajiki," Sigourney was saying. "For the time being, you will simply be confined here, until the facts of the accusations against you have been resolved."

"Of what am I accused?"

"Of complicity in the assassination of Archigos Ana. Of treason toward the Sun Throne. Of conspiring with Nessantico's enemies."

Sergei shook his head. "I'm innocent of any of those charges, Councillor, and the Council of Ca' knows it. *You* know it."

Her gray eyes blinked at that, her lips tightened in the rouged face. "At this point, Regent, I know only that the charges have been heard by the Council, and that we have decided that for the safety of the Holdings, you must be held until we have made a final decision on them." She inclined her head to Aris. "Commandant?"

Cu'Falla stepped forward. He held out his hand to Sergei—*I could . . .*—and Sergei placed his still-scabbarded weapon in Aris' palm. Carefully, slowly, Aris placed it on the commandant's desk—the desk behind which Sergei himself had once sat. Aris then patted Sergei down, taking the dagger from his belt. There was another dagger, lashed to the inside of his thigh. Sergei felt Aris' hands slide over the strap, saw Aris glance up at Sergei. He gave Sergei the barest hint of a nod and straightened. "You may escort the prisoner to his cell," Aris told the garda. "If Regent ca'Rudka is mistreated in any way, *any* way, I'll have that garda in the lower cells within a turn of the glass. Is that understood?"

The garda saluted. He took Sergei's arm.

"I know the way," he told the man. "Better than any."

~

Varina ci'Pallo

"VARINA?"

She was with Karl, and he looked so sad that she wanted to reach out and touch him, but whenever she stretched out her arm, he seemed to recede from her, just out of reach. She thought she heard someone calling her name, but now it was dark where she was, so dark she couldn't even see Karl, and she was confused.

"Varina!"

With the near-shout, she came awake with a start, realizing that she was at her desk in the Numetodo House. Two glass globes sat on the table in front of her as she blinked into the lamplight. She could see a trail of saliva pooled on the desk's surface, and she wiped at her mouth as she turned, embarrassed to be found this way. Especially to be found this way by Karl. "What?"

Karl stood next to her desk in the little room; the door was open behind him. He was peering down at her. "I called; you didn't answer. I even shook you." His eyes narrowed; she wasn't sure if it was concern or anger, and she told herself that she didn't really care which.

"I was working on the Westlander technique late last night. It exhausted me so much I must have fallen asleep." She brushed her hair with her fingers, angry with herself for letting herself succumb to her weariness and angry with him for having caught her in this state.

Angry at both herself and him because neither of them had apologized for their words the last time, and now it was too late. The words still stood between them, like an invisible wall.

"Are you all right?" She could hear concern in his voice, and rather than satisfying her, it made her feel even more angry. "All this work, and these spells you're attempting. Maybe you should—"

"I'm fine," she snapped, cutting him off. "You don't have

to worry about me." But she felt physically sick. Her mouth tasted of something moldy and horrible. Her bladder was too full. Her eyelids were so heavy that they might as well have iron weights attached to them, and her left eye didn't seem to want to focus at all; she blinked again—that didn't seem to help. She wondered if she looked as horrible as she felt. "What did you want?" she asked. The words seemed slightly slurred, as if her mouth and tongue didn't want to cooperate. The left side of her whole face seemed to sag.

"I found him," he said.

"Who?" she asked. She wiped at her left eye; his figure was still blurred. "Oh," she said, realizing who he meant. "Your Westlander. Is he still alive?"

The words came out more harshly than she meant them to, and she saw him lift a shoulder, even if she couldn't quite make out his expression. "Yes, but the man attacked me magically. Varina, he had spells stored in his walking stick."

"Doesn't surprise me," she said. "An object you can carry around with you each and every day, that no one would think a second time about . . ." She wiped at her eyes again; his face cleared somewhat. "Are you all right?" She realized the question was tardy; from his expression, so did he.

"Only because I managed to deflect the worst of it. The houses near me weren't quite so lucky. He took off, but I know about where he lives—in Oldtown. His name's Talis. He lives with a woman named Serafina, and there's a young boy with them—his name's Nico. It shouldn't take long to find exactly where they live. I'll ask Sergei to help me find them." He seemed to sigh. "I thought . . . I thought you might be willing to help me."

"Help you what?" she asked. "Do you *know* this Talis was responsible for Ana's death?"

"No," Karl admitted. "But I certainly suspect it. He attacked me as soon as I made the accusation. Called her his enemy, said he considered himself at war." Karl's lips pressed together grimly. "Varina, I don't think Talis will let himself be caught without a fight. I'm going to need help, the kind of help the Numetodo can provide. We all saw what he could do in the temple, and a few Garde Kralji with swords and pikes aren't going to help much. You . . . You're the best asset we have."

Yes, I'll help you, she wanted to say, if only to see a smile brighten his face or to chip away at the wall between them. But she couldn't. "I won't go after someone you just *suspect*, Karl. I especially won't do it when there's potentially an innocent woman and a child involved. Sorry."

She thought he'd be angry, but he only nodded, almost sadly, as if that was the answer he'd expected her to give. If it was, it still wasn't enough for him to apologize. The wall seemed to grow taller in her mind. "I understand," he said. "Varina, I want to—"

That was as far as he got. They both heard running footsteps in the corridor outside, and a panting Mika came to the open door. "Good," he said. "You're both here. There's news. Bad news, I'm afraid. It's the Regent. Sergei. The Council of Ca' has ordered him to be taken. He's in the Bastida."

~

Enéas cu'Kinnear

SO FAR BELOW HIM that it looked like a child's toy on a lake, *Stormcloud* rode at anchor in the sunlight, sitting easily on the startlingly blue water of the deep harbor of Karnmor. Enéas walked the steep, winding streets of the city, reveling in the feel of solid ground under his feet again and enjoying the wide vistas the city offered. He wished he were a painter so that he could capture the pink-white buildings bright under a cloud-dappled sky, the deep azure of the harbor and the white-capped green of the Strettosei beyond it, the brilliant hues of the flags and banners, the flower boxes that hung from every window, the exotic clothes of those in the streets—though a painting could never capture the rest: the thousands of smells that flirted with the nose, or the taste of salt in the air, or the feel of the warm westerly breeze, or the sound of his sandals on the finely crushed rock that paved Karnor's streets.

The main city of Karnor—Enéas had never understood why Karnmor's capital had been saddled with such a similar name—had been built on the rising flanks of the long-slumbering volcano that overshadowed the harbor, many of its buildings carved from the rock itself. Beyond the arms of the harbor, the Strettosei stretched unbroken out to the horizon, and from the heights of Mt. Karnmor, one could look eastward over the green expanse of the huge island and see, faintly, the blue band near the horizon that was the Nostrosei. Not far beyond that narrow sea lay the wide mouth of the River A'Sele, and perhaps thirty leagues up the river: Nessantico.

Munereo and the Hellins seemed far away, a distant lost dream. Karnmor and its smaller sister islands were part of North Nessantico. He was nearly home.

Enéas had to admit that Karnmor was still foreign in many ways. Its original inhabitants were mainly sea-people: fishermen and traders, their skin darkened by the sun and their tongues soft with strange accents, though they now spoke the language of Nessantico, their original tongue nearly forgotten except in a few small villages on its southern flank. The interior of the island was still largely wild, with impenetrable jungles along whose paths beasts of legend yet walked. In Karnor's streets, one might find spice traders from Namarro, or merchants from Sforzia or Paeti, and the goods of the Hellins came here first. *If you can't find it in Karnor, it doesn't exist.* That was the saying, and to a large extent, it was true—though he had heard the same claim of Nessantico. Still, Karnor was the true nexus for sea trade throughout the Strettosei.

Not surprisingly, the markets of Karnor were legendary. Spreading along what was called the Third Level of the city—the second of the terraces sculpted into the mountain—one could walk all day among the stalls and never reach the end. That was where Enéas found himself drawn, though he didn't quite know why. After the long voyage, he thought he would have wanted nothing more than to rest, but though he'd reported to the garrison of Karnor and been assigned a room in the offizier's quarters, he'd found himself restless and unable to relax. He'd gone walking, winding up the levels to the Third, and moving from stall to stall curiously. Here there were odd purple fruits that smelled like rotten meat but tasted—as he nibbled with wrinkled nose at the sample the vendor gave him—sweet and wonderful, or herbs guaranteed, according to the seller, to increase a man's vitality and a woman's sexual appetite. There were knife sellers, farmers with their vegetables, bolts of cloth both local and foreign, papers and inks, charms and jewelry, carved toys, fine woods, musical instruments plucked or blown or hammered upon. Eneas listened to a drab gray bird in a wooden cage whose plaintive song sounded eerily like the voice of a young boy, the words of the song perfectly understandable; he touched furs softer than the finest damask when stroked one way, and yet whose tips would pierce skin if rubbed in the other direction; he examined dried, framed butterflies whose glistening wings were wider than his own spread arms, dusted with iridescent, powdery gold and a blood-red skull drawn in the center of each wing.

Enéas eventually found himself standing before the stall of a chemist, the colored powders and liquids arrayed in glass jars on dangerously teetering shelves. He leaned close to a jar of white crystals, letting his forefinger run across the label glued onto the glass. *Niter*, the coppery handwriting proclaimed. The word seemed to crawl on the paper, and prickles like tiny lightnings ran from his fingertip up his arm to his chest. He could barely breathe with the feel of it. "It's the finest you'll come across," a voice said, and Enéas straightened guiltily and snatched his hand back, seeing the proprietor—a thin man with discolored skin dappling his face and arms—watching him from across the board that served for a table. "Gathered from the roof and walls of the deep caves near Kasama, and as pure as you can get. Are you afflicted with bad teeth, Offizier? A few applications of this and you can drink all the hot tea you like and your teeth will give you no complaint at all."

Enéas nodded. He blinked. He wanted to touch the jar again, but he forced his hand to remain at his side. *You need this . . .* The words came wrapped in the deep voice of Cénzi. He nodded in answer; that felt right. He needed this, though he didn't know why. "I'd like two stones' worth."

"Two stones . . ." The proprietor leaned back, chuckling. "Friend, does the entire garrison have sensitive teeth, or are you preserving meat for a battalion? All you need is a packet . . ."

"Two stones," Enéas insisted. "Can you do it? How much? A se'siqil?" He tapped the pouch tied to his belt.

The chemist was still shaking his head. "I can't get that much of the Kasama, but I have a good source from South Isle that's nearly as good. Two stones . . ." One eyebrow raised on his thin, blotchy face. "A full siqil," he said. "I can't do it for less."

At any other time, Enéas would have haggled. With persistence, he no doubt could have purchased the niter for his original offer or a few folias more. But there was an impatience inside him. It burned hot in his chest, a fire that only Cénzi could have started. He prayed silently, internally. *Whatever You want of me, I will do. The black sand, I will create it for You . . .* Enéas untied his purse, brought out two se'siqils and handed the coins to the man without argument. The chemist shook his head, frowning as he rubbed the coins between his fingers. "Some people have more money than sense," he muttered as he turned around.

Not long after, Enéas was hurrying away from the Third Level toward the garrison with a heavy package.

~

Jan ca'Vörl

HE'D BEEN WITH OTHER WOMEN before. But he'd never wanted any of them as much as he wanted Elissa.

That's what he told himself, in any case.

She intrigued him. Yes, she was attractive, but she was certainly no more so—and probably less classically beautiful—than half of the young court ladies who clustered around Fynn and Jan at every chance. Her eyes were her best feature: those eyes of pale blue ice that contrasted so much with her dark hair: piercing eyes that could show a laugh before her mouth released it, or dart poisonous glances toward her rivals. She had an unconscious grace that the other women lacked for the most part, a lean muscularity that hinted at hidden strength and agility.

"She comes from good stock," was Fynn's assessment. "You could do worse. She'll give you a dozen healthy babies if you want them."

Jan wasn't thinking about babies. Not yet. He wanted *her*. Just her. He thought that perhaps tonight, it might finally happen.

Every night since Fynn's ascension to the Hïrzg's throne, there had been a party in the upper hall of Brezno Palais. Fynn would issue the invitations through Roderigo, his aide: always to the same small group of young women and men, nearly all of them of ca' rank. There would be card games (at which Fynn would often lose heavily and not happily), and dancing, and general drunken revelry until early in the morning hours. Jan was always invited; so was Elissa. He found himself near her more and more often, as if (as his matarh had hinted) he were indeed a bee drawn to her particular flower.

She was at his side now, with two other young women hovering hopefully near him. Jan was seated at the pochspiel table with Fynn, who was glowering over his cards and the dwindling pile of silver siqils and gold solas in front of him and drinking heavily. Elissa had circled the table to stand behind Jan. He felt Elissa lean closely into him, her body pressing against his back as she leaned down. She whispered into his ear, her breath warm and sweet. "The Hïrzg has three Suns supported by a Palais. I would bet everything and lose gracefully."

Jan glanced at his cards. He had a single Page; all his other cards were low cards in the Staff suit. Elissa's hand touched his shoulder as she straightened, her fingers tightening briefly before they left him. The bets had been heavy already this hand, and there was a substantial pile of siqils and a few solas in the center of the table. Jan had been intending to fold now that the final card had been given out—he'd hoped to make an alignment in suit, but the Page had spoiled that. He glanced up at Elissa; she smiled down at him and nodded. Jan pushed his entire pile of coins into the center of the table.

"Everything," he announced.

The player to his right—some distant relative whose name he'd forgotten, shook his head and threw his cards in. "By Cénzi, he must have drawn the Planets all aligned!" All the other players except Fynn tossed in their cards as well. Fynn was staring at Jan, his head cocked slightly to one side. He glanced down at his cards again, one corner of his mouth lifting slightly—the tick that nearly everyone who played pochspiel with Fynn knew, which was one of the reasons Fynn so often lost. Fynn pushed his chips to the center with Jan's; his pile was noticeably smaller "Everything," he echoed, and he turned his cards face up on the table. "If you'll accept my note for the remainder."

Jan sighed as if disappointed. "You won't need the note, my Hïrzg," he said. "I'm afraid that you've caught me bluffing." He showed his hand as the other players howled and the people gathered around the table clapped and applauded. Fynn gathered in the coins, smiling, then tossed a solas back to Jan.

"I can't let my champion leave the table empty-handed," he said. "Even when he tries to bluff his sovereign lord with nothing in his hand at all."

Jan caught the solas and smiled to Fynn, then pushed his chair back from the table and bowed. "I should have known that you would see through my charade," he said to Fynn, who grinned even more deeply. "Now I should drown my disappointment in some wine."

Fynn glanced from Jan to Elissa, who hovered at his shoulder. "I suspect you'll drown yourself in something more substantial," he answered. "That's not a bet I believe I'll miss either."

There was more laughter, though it came mostly from the men in the crowd; many of the women simply glared at Elissa silently. In the midst of the laughter, she leaned closer to Jan again. "Meet me in the hall in a quarter-turn," she said, and she slid away from him. The space was immediately filled by another of the available women, and someone handed him a flagon of wine as the cards of the next hand were dealt out. Fynn's attention was already on the cards and Jan drifted away from the table, conversing with the young ladies of the court who flittered around him.

When he thought enough time had passed, he excused himself and left the hall, the hall servant bowing to him with a knowing wink as he opened the door. There was no one in the corridor outside, and he felt a surge of disappointment.

"Chevaritt Jan," a voice called, and he saw her step from shadows a few strides away. He went to her, taking her hands. Her face was very close to his, and her pale gaze never left his eyes.

"You cost me nearly a week's stipend, Vajica," he said.

"And I gave the Hïrzg yet another reason to love his champion," she answered with a smile. "Anyone at the table would pay twice what you lost to be in that position. I'd say you owe me."

"All I have is the gold solas that Fynn gave me, I'm afraid. It's yours if you'd like."

"Your gold doesn't interest me. I would beg something simpler from you."

"And what would that be?"

She didn't answer—not with words. She released his hands, embracing him fully and lifting her face to his. The kiss was soft, her lips yielding under his as soft as velvet. Her arms tightened around him as he pressed her tightly against him. He could feel the fullness of her breasts, the rising of her breath, the faint whimper of a moan. The kiss became less soft and more urgent now, her lips opening so that he felt the flutter of her tongue. Her hands slid lower down his back as they broke apart. Her eyes were large and almost frightened-looking, as if she were afraid that she'd gone too far. "Chev—" she began, and he stopped her with another kiss. His hand touched the side of her breast under the lace of her tashta and she did not stop him, only closed her eyes as she drew in a breath.

"Where are your rooms?" he asked, and she leaned against him.

"Your apartment is here within the palais, isn't it?" she said, and he nodded. He held out his hand to her and she took it.

The walk to his rooms seemed to take an eternity. They hurried through the corridors of the palais, then the door was shut behind them and he took her into his embrace and forgot about anything else for a long, delightful time.

Nico Morel

VILLE PAISLI WAS BORING.

The entire town could have fit inside a single block of Oldtown, fifteen or so buildings huddled close to the Avi a'Nostrosei, with a few farms close by and a dark, forbidding wood reaching leafy arms around them and hinting at unguessed terrors. Nico could imagine dragons lurking in its hilly depths, or bands of rough outlaws. Exploring there might have been interesting, but his matarh kept close watch on him, as she had ever since they'd left Nessantico.

Nico was used to the endless roar and tumult of Nessantico. He was used to a landscape of buildings and manicured, tamed parks. He was used to being surrounded by thousands and thousands of strangers, to strange sights (even as they were leaving the city, he'd glimpsed a woman juggling live kittens), to the call of the temple horns and the lighting of the Avi at night.

Here, there was only drudgery and the same, stupid faces day after day.

His Tantzia Alisa and Onczio Bayard were nice enough people, who owned Ville Paisli's only inn, which was his tantzia's responsibility. Tantzia Alisa looked much older than Nico's matarh, even though Alisa was actually a year younger than her sister; Onczio Bayard had few teeth and those that were left smelled rotten when he leaned close to Nico, which made him wonder why Tantzia Alisa would have married the man.

Then there were the children: six of them, three boys and three girls. The oldest was Tujan, two years older than Nico, then the twins Sinjon and Dori, who were Nico's age. The youngest boy was a toddler just beginning to walk, who still sucked at Tantzia Alisa's breast. Onczio Bayard was also the town's iron forger, and Tujan and Sinjon both worked with him in the heat of the smithy, working the bellows and tending the fire while Tantzia Alisa, with Dori's help, made beds and cooked for those staying at the inn—usually only a single traveler or two.

"In Nessantico, there are fire-téni who work in the big forging houses," Nico had said the first day, watching Tujan and Sinjon labor at the bellows. That had earned him a hard punch in the arm from Tujan when Onczio Bayard wasn't looking, and a glare from Sinjon. Onczio Bayard had set Nico to pumping the bellows with his cousins all that afternoon, and he'd smelled like charcoal and soot for the rest of the day. He suspected he still did, since he was expected to put in his time at the smithy every day with the other boys, but he no longer smelled it, though his white bashta now looked a streaked gray. The smithy was sweltering, loud with the hammering of steel on steel and bright with the sparks of molten iron. The villagers would come to Bayard to create or repair all sorts of metal objects: plow blades, scythe blades, hinges, and nails. Most of the trade was barter: a plucked chicken for a new blade, a dozen eggs for a small keg of black nails.

At the forge, the day began before dawn when the coals had to be rekindled and brought to blue heat, and ended when the sun went down. There were no light-téni here to banish the night or fire-téni to keep the coals blazing. After sundown, Onczio Bayard worked with Tantzia Alisa in the inn's tavern, which did more business than the inn. Nico, along with his cousins, was pressed into service delivering tankards of ale and plates of simple food to the villagers at their tables, until Onczio Bayard would bellow "Last Call!" promptly on the third turn of the glass after sundown.

Nights after the tavern closed was the worst time.

Nico slept with Tujan and Sinjon in the same tiny room in the house behind the inn, and they would talk in the dark, their whispers seemingly as loud as shouts. "You're useless, Nico," Tujan whispered in the quiet. "You can't work the bellows as well as even Dori, and Vatarh had to show you three times how to keep the coals piled."

"He did not," Nico retorted.

Tujan kicked him under the covers. "Did. I heard him call you a *bastardo*, too."

"What's a bastardo?" Sinjon asked.

"It means Nico doesn't have a vatarh," Tujan answered.

"I do," Nico told them. "Talis is my vatarh."

"Where *is* this Talis?" Tujan jeered. "Why isn't he here, then?"

"He *can't* be here. He had to stay in Nessantico. He sent us here to be safe. I know, I saw . . ."

"You saw what?"

Nico blinked into the night. He wasn't supposed to tell; Talis had told him how dangerous it would be for his matarh and him. "Nothing," he said.

Tujan laughed in the darkness. "I thought so. Your matarh brought you here, not any Talis. Musetta Galgachus says that Tantzia Serafina's a filthy whore who makes her folias on her back, and you're just a whore's son."

The raw insult sparked against Nico like a flint on steel, and sparks filled his mind and drove him up and over on top of the larger boy, his fists pummeling at the unseen face and chest. "She is *not!*" he screamed as he struck at Tujan, and then Sinjon piled into him defending his brother, and they all tumbled from the bed onto the floor, flailing at each other blindly and hollering, tangled in the blankets. The cold fire began to burn in Nico's stomach, and he shouted words that he didn't understand, his hands gesturing, and suddenly the two boys were flying away from him, landing hard on the floor a few feet away. Nico lay there on the rough planks of the floor, stunned momentarily and feeling strangely empty and exhausted. He could hear the dogs—that slept downstairs in the inn—barking loudly. He wondered what had just happened.

His hesitation was enough; in the darkness the two boys had scrambled up and jumped on him again. "Bastardo!" He felt someone's fist smash into his nose.

The door to the room flew open—a candle as bright as dawn flaring—and adults were shouting at them to stop and pulling them apart. "What in Cénzi's name is going on here?" Onczio Bayard roared, plucking Nico from the floor by the nightshirt and sending him stumbling backward into his matarh's familiar arms. He realized he was crying, more from rage than pain, and he sniffled as he struggled to get out of her grasp and hit one of the boys again. He could feel blood trickling down from his nostril.

"Nico—" Matarh sounded caught between horror and concern. She stooped in front of him as Onczio Bayard hauled his two sons to their feet. "What happened? Why are you boys fighting?"

Nico glared at his cousins, standing sullenly alongside their vatarh. Tantzia Alisa hovered in the doorway, holding the youngest in her arms while the girls peered around her, giggling and whispering. Nico wiped at the blood drooling from his nose with the back of his hand and was glad to see that Sinjon, too, had a line of dark red trickling from a nostril, and spatters of brown on his nightshirt. He hoped that the welt under Tujan's eye would swell and turn purple by morning. "Nico? Who started this?"

"Nobody," Nico told her, still glaring. "It wasn't anything, Matarh. We were just playing, and . . ." He shrugged.

"Tujan? Sinjon?" their vatarh asked, shaking the boys' shoulders. "You have anything to add?" Nico stared at them, Tujan especially, daring him to say to his vatarh what he'd said to Nico.

Both boys shook their heads. Onczio Bayard gave a huff of exasperation. "Sorry, Serafina," he said. "But you know boys . . ." He shook his sons again. "Apologize to Nico," he said. "He's a guest in our house, and you don't treat him that way. Go on."

Sinjon muttered a nearly inaudible apology; Tujan followed a moment later. "Nico?" his matarh said, and Nico grimaced.

"Sorry," he told his cousins.

"All right then," Onczio Bayard grunted. "We'll have no more of this. Getting us all out of bed when we'd just gone to sleep. Sinjon, get a rag and clean up your face. And I don't expect to hear anything else out of the three of you tonight." Still grumbling, he left the room.

Nico thought he could fall asleep in a moment; now that the cold fire had left him, he was so tired. His matarh crouched down to hug Nico. "You can sleep with me tonight if you want," she whispered to him. He hugged her back tightly, wanting more than anything to do exactly that and knowing that he couldn't, that if he did, Tujan and Sinjon would tease him unmercifully the next day.

"I'll be fine," he told her. She kissed his forehead. Tantzia Alisa handed her a cloth, and she dabbed at Nico's nose. He pulled back. "Matarh, it's already stopped."

"All right," she told him. She rose to her feet. "All of

you—to sleep. No more talking, no more fighting. Do you hear?"

They all mumbled assent as the girls whispered and laughed and Matarh and Tantzia Alisa exchanged indulgent sighs. The door closed. Nico waited. "You'll pay for this, Nico Bastardo," Tujan muttered, his voice low and quiet and sinister in the new dark. "You'll pay. . . ."

He slept that night in the corner of the room nearest the door, wrapped in a blanket, and he thought of Nessantico and of Talis, and he knew he could not stay here, no matter how dangerous Nessantico might be.

~

Allesandra ca'Vörl

"**A**'HÏRZG! A moment!"

Semini called out to her as she left Brezno Temple after the Cénzidi service. Her foot was already on the carriage step, but she turned to him. Jan had already left—accompanied by Elissa ca'Karina and Fynn—while Pauli had said that he would attend the service given by the palais' o'téni in the Hïrzg's Chapel. Allesandra suspected that he'd instead spent the time between the sweating thighs of one of the ladies of the court.

"Archigos," she said, giving him the sign of Cénzi. "A particularly strong Admonition today, I thought." Around them, the worshipers streaming out from the temple looked toward them, but stayed carefully distant: whatever the A'Hïrzg and the Archigos discussed, it was not for common ears. The carriage attendant moved away to check the harnesses of the horses and converse with the driver; the minor ténis who always followed the Archigos had remained at the doors to the temple in a huddle, talking. Semini gave her the dark, somber smile of a bear.

"Thank you," he told her. He glanced around to see that no one was within earshot. "You've heard the news?"

"News?" Allesandra cocked her head quizzically, and Semini's mouth tightened under the grizzled beard.

"It just came to me through one of the Faith's contacts," he told her. "I thought perhaps the news hadn't quite reached the palais yet. The Regent ca'Rudka has been removed by the Council of Ca' and is currently imprisoned in the Bastida."

"Oh, by Cénzi . . ." Allesandra breathed, genuinely shocked by what he'd just said. *What does this mean? What's happened there?* If the Archigos was offended by Allesandra's curse, he showed nothing. He nodded into her flustered silence.

"Yes. I was rather amazed myself." His voice dropped

low and he leaned in toward her, turning his head so that his lips were very near her ear. The sound of his low growl made her shiver. "I worry that this changes . . . everything for us, Allesandra."

Then he stepped back again and her neck was cold, even in the early summer warmth. "Archigos . . ." she began. *What have I done? How can I stop the White Stone now? With the Regent gone, it's all for nothing. Nothing. What have I done?* She glanced up at the pigeons circling the golden domes of the temple. There were dozens of them, diving and rising and intertwining like the possibilities whirling in her head. "You trust the source of this news?"

"I do," he rumbled. "Gairdi has never been wrong before. No doubt the Hïrzg will hear the same from his own sources soon. News like this . . ." His head swiveled side to side above the green robes, the beard moving on the cloth. "It will travel like wildfire in a drought. Has the Council gone mad? From all I've heard, Audric's not capable of being Kraljiki. And with ca'Rudka in the Bastida . . ."

" 'Those swallowed by the Bastida a'Drago rarely emerge whole.' " Allesandra finished the thought for him— an old saying in Nessantico, usually muttered with a scowl and a gesture meant to ward off curses directed toward the dark stones and impassive towers of the Bastida. "I feel sorry for ca'Rudka. I liked the man, despite what he did to my vatarh." She took a long breath, glancing again at the pigeons, settling in the courtyard again now that most of the worshipers had departed for their homes. Now that she'd had time to absorb the news, the shock had passed, but the question still whirled in her mind. *What have I done?*

"This changes nothing," she told Semini firmly, wishing she were as certain as she made her voice sound. "The Regent has simply been replaced by the Council, some of whom undoubtedly intend to be the next Kralji. Audric is still Audric, and when he falls . . . well, then we will be in a position to do what we must. Don't worry, Archigos."

He nodded and bowed to her. Carefully, looking around once more, he put his hands around hers, pressing them between his own for a moment. "I will pray that you're right, A'Hïrzg," he said quietly. "Perhaps . . . perhaps we could talk more of this—privately—later this morning." His eyebrows arched above piercing, unblinking eyes.

"All right," she told him, wondering if this was what she really wanted. She would have to think further, to be certain. "In two turns of the glass, perhaps. In my chambers at the palais?"

"I will make sure my schedule is cleared," he told her. He smiled. He took a step back from her and gave her the sign of Cénzi, bowing as he did so. "I look forward to it," he said. "Greatly."

"A'Hïrzg . . ." As soon as the hall servant had closed the door behind him, as soon as he realized that they were alone, Semini had come to her and taken her hand. She let him hold it for a few breaths, then stepped back from him. She gestured at the table set in the middle of the room.

"I had my staff prepare us a luncheon."

He looked at it, and she saw the disappointment in his face.

She had been considering what she wanted to do ever since she'd left him. She needed Semini, yes, but in all likelihood she could have that help without being his lover. Yet . . . she had to admit that he was attractive, that she found herself leaning toward him. She remembered the few times she'd allowed herself to have lovers, remembering the heat and long, lingering kisses, the gasping sliding of intertwined bodies, the moments when all rational thought was lost in swirling, blind ecstasy.

She would have enjoyed having a husband who was also a lover and a partner, with whom she could have true intimacy. She could feel the void in her soul: she had no true friends, no family she loved and who loved her in return. Archigos Ana might have been her captor, but she'd also been more of a matarh to her than her own, and Vatarh had taken that from her when he'd finally ransomed her. And when she'd finally returned to the vatarh whom she'd once loved so deeply, it was to find that his affection no longer shone down on her like the very sun, but now was concentrated entirely on Fynn. Vatarh had instead married her off—a political prize to seal the agreement bringing West Magyaria into the Coalition. She loved the son that came from her spousal duty and he had loved her also as a child, but his age and Fynn were pulling him away from her.

Early on, she had imagined coming back to Nessantico—perhaps as the Hïrzgin, perhaps as a claimant to the Sun Throne itself. She had imagined her friendship with Ana restored, of the two of them working together to create an empire that would be the wonder of the ages. But now Ana was gone forever, stolen from her.

She had herself. She had no one else.

You like Semini well enough, and it's obvious he's already in love with you. But he was also nearly two decades older, and they were both married. There was no future with him—unless, perhaps, he could become the Archigos of a unified Faith.

You're thinking like your vatarh. You're thinking like old Marguerite.

Semini stared at the meal on the table: the cold, sliced meats, the bread, the cheese, the wine. "If the A'Hïrzg is hungry, then . . ."

You could end up as lonely as Ana was, as Marguerite was. Why shouldn't you let yourself be close to someone, to enjoy them? You need someone who is your ally, your lover. . . .

She touched his back, let her hand trail down his spine. "The meal," she said, "was for appearances. And for later."

"Allesandra—" He had turned toward her, and the hopeful look on his face nearly made her laugh.

She lifted up on her toes, her hand on his shoulders, and kissed him. His beard, she found, was surprisingly soft, and the lips underneath yielded to her. She brought her heels back down to the floor and took his hands, looking up at him with her head cocked to one side. His mouth was slightly open. "We would have to be careful, Semini," she told him. "So very careful."

His fingers tightened on hers. He leaned down toward her and she felt his lips brush her hair, moving as he spoke. "Cénzi has my soul," he whispered. "But you, Allesandra, you have my heart. You always had my heart." The words were so unexpected, so clumsy and cloying that she nearly laughed again, though she knew it would destroy him. She started to speak, to say something in return, but he leaned down again and kissed her brow, softly. She turned her face toward his, her arms going around him. The kiss was longer and urgent, his breath sweet, and the depth of her own hungry response startled her. She broke away reluctantly, hugging him tightly, her breath trembling.

His lips brushed her hair, his breath on her ear made her shiver. "This is what I want, Allesandra, more than anything."

She didn't answer him with words, but with her mouth and her hands.

~

Karl ca'Vliomani

"I CAN'T BELIEVE I'm seeing this. Has the Council of Ca' gone entirely insane?"

Sergei, sitting with his arms wrapped around his legs in a corner of the cell, inclined his head significantly toward the garda leaning against the wall outside the bars of the cell. "No," he said, his voice so low that Karl had to lean forward to hear it. "Not insane. Just eager to pick Audric's bones clean when he falls. And me?" He laughed bitterly. "I was the easiest jackal for the pack to shove aside. I'm to be the scapegoat for everything, including Ana's death."

Karl could taste bile on the back of his tongue. The air of the Bastida was thick and heavy and lay like a massive, sodden shawl around his shoulders, slumping them as he sat in the single chair. Memories flooded him: he had once inhabited this very cell, when Sergei commanded the Garde Kralji. Then, Mad Mahri had snatched Karl from his imprisonment with his strange Westlander magic . . .

. . . and the memories of that time, so tied to Ana and his relationship with her, brought back fully the grief and the rage at her death. He lifted his head, his jaw and fists clenched, his eyes threatening to overflow. "It was Westlander magic that killed her," he said to Sergei. "I nearly had the man."

"Perhaps," Sergei told him. "I assure you it wasn't me."

"And I know that," Karl told him. "I will tell the Council the same thing. I'll go to Councillor ca'Ludovici after I leave here—"

"No," Sergei told him. "You won't. Don't get yourself caught in this, my friend. It's bad enough that you've come to see me—the councillors will know that in a turn of the glass or less. You really don't want whispers of the Numetodo being involved in any of Audric's conspiracies—not if you don't want the Holdings looking like the Coalition." He paused. "You know what I mean by that, Karl. And be careful what you do with these Westlanders. There are already eyes watching you, and they have little sympathy toward anyone they perceive as being against them."

"I don't care," Karl told him as the lava churned in his stomach again. The resolution that had settled there hardened. *I'll find this Talis again, and this time I will force the truth from him.* "What about you?"

"So far I've been treated well enough."

"So far." Karl shuddered. He thought that Sergei was looking all of his years and more, that perhaps there was more gray in his hair than there'd been even a few days ago. "If they want a statement from you, if they want to punish you here in the Bastida . . ."

"You don't need to tell me," Sergei answered, and Karl thought he saw a visible shudder in Sergei's normally unflappable posture. "I know better than anyone. That guilt is on my hands, too." His voice dropped lower again. "Commandant cu'Falla is my friend also, and he has left me an option for that, if it comes to it. I won't be tortured, Karl. I won't permit it."

Karl's eyes widened slightly. "You mean . . . ?"

A bare nod. His voice lifted again as the garda in the corridor stirred. "Come with me—there's something I'd show you." He slowly uncoiled himself from the bed and moved to the balcony as the garda watched them carefully—Sergei's walk was more a shuffle. The wind lifted Karl's white hair as they approached the rail of a small ledge that jutted out from the tower. Below, the courtyard of the Bastida appeared small and distant far below, and before them the city spread out. To their left, the A'Sele was sun-sparkled as it flowed beneath the Pontica a'Brezi Veste. There were cages hung from the columns of the bridge, with skeletons huddled inside. Karl shuddered at the sight. "Look here," Sergei told him. He'd turned so that he faced not the city but the stone wall of the tower, and his finger pressed against one of the stones there. In the massive block of granite, a crack furrowed one corner; above Sergei's finger, a small single white flower bloomed from the gray stone. "It's a meadow star," Sergei said. "Far from its usual home."

"You always knew your plants."

Sergei smiled, crinkling the skin around his metal nose.

Karl could see the glue lifting and cracking. "You remember that, eh?"

"You made it so I was rather unlikely to forget."

Sergei nodded. He touched the flower gently. "Look at this beauty, Karl. The barest crack in a stone, and life has found it. A bit of dirt blown in, the stone eroding in the rain to make the thinnest layer of soil, a bird chancing to leave a seed, or perhaps the wind blowing it from a field leagues away so that it falls in just the right place. . . ."

"You should have been a Numetodo, Sergei. Or perhaps an artist. You have the mind for it."

Another smile. "If this beauty can happen here in this most doleful of places, Karl, then there is always hope. Always."

"I'm glad you believe that."

His finger dropped away from the stone. The wind-horns began to blow Second Call, and he glanced out toward the Isle a'Kralji where the Grande Palais gleamed white. Karl wondered whether Audric looked out from one of his windows toward the Bastida, and perhaps glimpsed them there. "I worry about you, Karl. Forgive me, but you're looking tired and old since she died. You need to take care of yourself."

Karl smiled at the thought that Sergei's opinion of Karl's appearance was much the same as his impression of Sergei. "I am, my friend." *In my own way* . . . His days and nights were spent making inquiries and trying to find the Westlander Talis again. He *was* tired, but he could not stop. He would not.

"I know you don't believe in Cénzi or the afterlife," Sergei was saying to him, "but I do. I know that Ana is watching from the arms of Cénzi, and I also believe she would tell you to still your grief. She's gone from here, her soul has been weighed, and she dwells now where she wished one day to go. She would want you to believe that much, and start to heal the wound in your heart that her death left."

"Sergei . . ." There were no words in him, no way to explain how deep the wound was and how it bled constantly. There was only the pain, and he could think of only one way to still the agony inside him. But that could wait until he found the Westlander again. "If I actually believed any of that, then I'd be tempted to jump from this ledge, right now, so I might be with her again." He glanced down again, at the flagstones so far below.

"Varina would be upset by that."

Karl glanced at Sergei quizzically. "What do you mean?"

Sergei seemed to be studying the meadow star's blossom. "She has qualities that any person would admire, and yet for all these years she's chosen to put all relationships aside and spend her time studying your Scáth Cumhacht."

"For which I'm very grateful—she has pushed our understanding of it well past where it once was."

"I'm sure she appreciates your gratitude, Karl."

"What are you saying? That Varina . . . ?" Karl laughed. "You evidently don't know her well at all. Varina has no problem speaking her mind. She's made it clear how she feels about me lately."

Sergei touched the flower. It shivered at the touch, its fragile hold on the stone threatening to fail. He took his hand away, and turned back to Karl. "I'm sure you're right," he said. He favored Karl with a smile touched with melancholy. Here in the daylight, Karl could see the deepening lines life had chiseled into the man's face. Karl looked out over the city. "This was *my* life's love," he said. "This city, and all that she means. I gave her everything. . . ."

Karl leaned close to Sergei, glancing at the garda who was ostentatiously not watching them. "I may be able to get you out of here. My own way."

He was still staring outward, his hands on the ledge, and he replied to the air. "To make us both fugitives?" Sergei shook his head. "Be patient, Karl. A flower doesn't bloom in a day."

"Patience may not be possible. Or wise."

For an instant, Sergei's face relaxed as he turned to Karl. "You could do that? Truly?"

"I think so. Yes."

"You'd endanger the Numetodo with the act. You understand that? Archigos Kenne might be sympathetic to you, but he's the next person Audric or the Council of Ca' will go after because he's simply not strong enough. All the other a'téni are less sympathetic toward the Numetodo; I see the Conclave electing a strong Archigos who will be more in the mold of Semini ca'Cellibrecca in Brezno, or— worse—I see them reconciling with Brezno entirely."

"The Numetodo have always been in danger. It was only Ana who sheltered us, and then only here in Nessantico itself." Karl saw Sergei glance at the gardai and the bars of his cell, and he saw resolution touch the man's face. "When?" Karl asked Sergei.

"If the Council actually gives Audric what he wants . . ." Sergei stroked the blossom in the wall with a gentle forefinger. The flower shivered under his touch. "Then."

Karl nodded. "I understand. But first I'll need your help and your knowledge of this place."

Nico Morel

NICO LEFT THE LITTLE HOUSE behind the inn of Ville Paisli a few turns of the glass before dawn, having tied up his clothes into a roll he carried on his back and snatching a loaf of bread from the kitchen. He stroked the dogs, who were wondering why someone was up so early, calming them so they wouldn't bark when he slipped the latch on the rear door and slipped out. He hurried along the road from the village in the dim light of false dawn, jumping into the shadows along the roadside at any noise. By the time the sun had eased itself over the horizon to touch the clouds in the east with fire, he was well away from the village.

He hoped his matarh would understand and not cry too much. But if he could find Talis and tell him what things were like in Ville Paisli, then Talis would come back with him and everything would be fine. All he had to do was find Talis, who loved his matarh—he'd be as angry as Nico was at what they were saying and with his magic, well, he could make them stop.

Talis had told him that Ville Paisli was only about a league and a half from Nessantico. Nico half-trotted along the rutted dirt lane that was the Avi a'Nostrosei; if he could get to the village of Certendi, then he could lose anyone pursuing him. They'd expect him to follow the Avi a'Nostrosei into Nessantico, but he'd take the Avi a'Certendi instead, which jogged off southeast to enter Nessantico nearer the banks of the A'Sele. It was a longer road, but maybe they wouldn't be looking for him there.

Nico watched carefully over his shoulder as he fled for anyone riding fast from behind. He could see the thatch-and-slate roofs of Certendi ahead of him when he noticed a smear of dust rising from behind a stand of cypress trees beyond a slow bend in the Avi. He scurried off the road and into a field of long-beans, crouching down in the thick leaves. It was good he'd done so, since the horse and rider soon appeared: it was Onczio Bayard, looking awkward and uncomfortable atop a draft horse, his eyes focused on the road in front of him. He let his onczio plod along the avenue until he vanished around the next turn.

Let Onczio Bayard look all he wanted in Certendi, then. Nico would cut around to the south through the farm fields and find the Avi a'Certendi where it emerged from the village.

He walked on, moving between the fields. Perhaps a turn of the glass later, maybe more, he found what he assumed was the Avi a'Certendi—a well-rutted dirt road, mostly clear of grass and weeds. He trudged on, munching on the bread and stopping to get a drink occasionally from one of the numerous creeks that were flowing toward the A'Sele.

By late afternoon, his feet were aching and sore, with blisters erupting wherever his skin touched his boots. The bottoms of his feet were bruised from the stones he'd stepped on. He shuffled more than walked, more tired than he'd ever been in his life and wishing he had another loaf of bread. But he was finally walking among the clustered houses around Nessantico's River Market. He was home and now he could find Talis. Clutching the roll of clothes tightly, he scanned the market for Uly, the seller who knew Talis. But the space where Uly's stall had been set up a few weeks ago was vacant, the cloth awning gone and a few half-broken tables the only remnant. Nico limped over to the old woman selling peppers and corn next to the space, grimacing and wanting nothing more than to sit down and rest. "Do you know where Uly is?" he asked wearily, and the woman shrugged. She waved her hand at a fly that landed on her nose.

"Can't say. Man's been gone for a hand of days now. Good riddance, too—just laughed when the Calls came and people said their prayers. And those horrible scars."

"Where did he go?"

"Do I look like his matarh?" She glared at him. "Go away. You're keeping away my customers."

Nico looked up and down the market; there were only a few people there and none were near the stall. "I really need to know," he told her.

She sniffed and ignored him, arranging the peppers in

their boxes and shooing away flies. "Please," Nico said. "I have to talk to him."

Silence. She moved a pepper from the top of the box to the bottom.

Nico could feel himself getting angry and frustrated. It felt chilly inside, like the evening breeze. "Hey!" Nico hollered at her.

She scowled at him. "Go away or I'll call for the utilino, you little pest, and tell him you were trying to steal my produce. Go on! Away with you!" She waved at him as if he were one of the flies.

The irritation rose higher in him, and his throat felt like it did when he had one of the spicy-hot dishes Talis sometimes made. There were words that wanted to come out, and his hands made motions on their own. The old woman stared at him as if he were having some kind of fit, her eyes widening as if fascinated. The words came boiling out and Nico made a grasping motion with his hands. The woman suddenly clutched at her throat with a choking cry. She seemed to be trying to draw in a breath, her face turning redder, as Nico tightened his fists. "Stop!" He could barely make out the word, but Nico let his fist relax and the woman nearly fell, taking a deep, loud breath.

"Tell me!" Nico said, and she stared at him with fear in her eyes, her hands up as if to ward off a fist.

"I hear he might be over at Oldtown Market now—" the old woman said, all in a rush. "That's what I heard, anyway, and . . ."

But Nico was already moving away, no longer listening.

He was trembling, and he felt far more tired now than he had a moment ago. He was scared as well. *Talis would be mad, and so would Matarh. You could have hurt her.* He wouldn't do that again, he told himself. He wouldn't let that happen. He didn't dare. The cold anger frightened him too much.

He felt like sleeping, but he couldn't. It took him until Third Call to find the Avi a'Parete, half-lost in the cluster of small, twisting lanes around the market and moving slowly on his aching feet. He stopped there, leaning against a building, to bow his head and say the evening prayer to Cénzi with the crowds near the Pontica Kralji. He sat down . . .

. . . and lifted his head with a start, realizing that he'd

fallen asleep. Across the bridge, he could see the light-téni just beginning to light the famous city lamps in front of the Grande Palais—a scene that would be happening simultaneously all along the great length of the Avi. With a sigh, Nico pushed himself up and plunged back into the crowds, heading northward into the depths of Oldtown, looking for a familiar side street, one that might lead him home.

He didn't know how he would find Talis in the huge city, but right now all Nico wanted was to rest his aching, exhausted feet somewhere familiar, to fall asleep somewhere safe. He could go to Oldtown Market tomorrow and see if Uly was there. He limped toward home—their old house. It was the only place he could think of to go.

The trip seemed to take forever. He had to sit and rest three times, almost crying from the pain in his feet, forcing himself to keep his eyes open so he didn't fall asleep again, and each time it was harder to force himself to stand up again. He wanted to rip the boots from his feet, but he was afraid of what he might see if he did that. But at last he walked down the lane where Talis had been attacked by the Numetodo man, and turned the corner that led toward his house. He began to see buildings and faces that were familiar. He was nearly there.

"Nico!"

He heard the voice calling his name and he turned. A woman waved at him and hurried over toward him, but she was no one he recognized. Her face was lined and tired-looking, as if she were as exhausted as he was, and she seemed older than the fall of hair around her shoulders.

"Who are you?"

"My name's Varina," she told him. "I've been looking for you."

"Did Talis . . . ?" he began, then stopped, biting his lower lip. Talis wouldn't want him talking to someone he didn't know.

"Talis?" the woman said. Her chin lifted. "Ah, yes. Talis." She crouched down in front of him. He thought she had kind eyes, eyes that again seemed younger than the lined face. Her fingers lightly stroked his cheek—the way Matarh sometimes did. The gesture made him want to cry. "You were limping badly just now. You look terribly tired, Nico, and look, you're covered with dust." Concern creased the lines of her forehead as she tilted her head to the side. "Are you hungry?"

He nodded. "Yes," he said simply.

She hugged him tightly, and he relaxed into her arms. "Come with me, Nico," she said, rising to her feet again. "I'll get us a carriage, and we'll get you some food and let you rest. Then we'll see if we can find Talis for you, eh?" She held out her hand to him.

He took the offered hand, and she closed her fingers around his. Together, they walked back toward the Avi a'Parete.

~

Allesandra ca'Vörl

ELISSA CA'KARINA ...
Allesandra kept hearing the name, every time she spoke to her son in recent days. "Elissa said the most intriguing thing yesterday ..." or "I was out riding with Elissa ..."

Today it was: "I want you to contact Elissa's parents, Matarh."

Allesandra looked at Pauli, who was reading reports from the palais in Malacki near the fire in their apartments; the servants had yet to bring in their breakfast. He seemed unsurprised by the announcement—she wondered whether Jan had spoken to him first. "You've known the woman for a little more than a week," Allesandra said, "and she's significantly older than you. I have to wonder why her family hadn't made arrangements for a marriage for her years ago. We don't know enough about her, Jan. Certainly not enough to be opening negotiations with her family."

Jan had begun shaking his head at her first objection; Pauli appeared to be stifling a laugh. "What does any of that matter, Matarh? I enjoy her company, and I'm not asking to marry her tomorrow. I want you to make the necessary inquiries, that's all. That way, if everything appears as it should and I still feel the same way in, oh, a month or two ..." He shrugged. "I talked to Fynn; he said that the ca'Karina name is well-regarded, and that he would have no objection. He likes Elissa, too."

Allesandra doubted it—at least not in the way Jan liked the woman. Fynn considered the women of the court nothing more than necessary adornment, like a display of flowers and just as disposable. He himself had no interest in them, and if he ever married (and he would not, if the White Stone earned his money—with that thought, she felt again a stab of doubt and guilt) it would be purely for the political advantage that he gained from it.

Fynn would not marry a woman for love, and decidedly not for lust.

But Jan . . . She already knew, from palais gossip, that Elissa had spent several nights with her son in his rooms. She also knew that she had no support here: not from Jan, not from Pauli, and certainly not from Fynn, who probably found the affair amusing, especially since it so obviously annoyed Allesandra. Nor, given what she'd begun with Semini, could she say much without hypocrisy. *He wants no more than you want, after all.* She fixed an indulgent smile on her face, mostly because she knew it would annoy Paul.

"Fine," she told her son. "I will make inquiries. We will see what her family has to say and proceed from there. Does that satisfy you?"

Jan grinned and flung his arms around Allesandra, as if he were a boy again. "Thank you, Matarh," he said. "Yes, that satisfies me. Write them today. This morning."

"Jan, just . . . be careful and slow with this. Will you?"

He laughed. "Always reminding me to think with my head instead of my heart. I will, Matarh. Of course."

With that, he was gone. Pauli laughed. "Lost in a glorious infatuation," he said. "I remember being that way. . . ."

"But not with me," Allesandra told him.

His smile never wavered; that hurt more than the words. "No," he said. "Not with you, my dear. With you, I was lost in a glorious transaction."

He went back to reading the reports.

Allesandra was walking with Semini that afternoon after Second Call, when she saw Elissa's form flitting through the hallways of the palais, strangely unaccompanied. "Vajica ca'Karina," she called out. "A moment . . ."

The young woman looked surprised. She hesitated for a moment, like a rabbit searching for a line of escape from a hound, then came over to them. She bowed to Allesandra and gave the sign of Cénzi to Semini. "A'Hïrzg, Archigos," she said. "It's so good to see the two of you." Her face failed to reflect her words.

"I'm sure," Allesandra told her. "I should tell you that my son came to me this morning regarding you."

Her eyebrows lifted over her strange, light eyes. "Ah?"

"He asked that I contact your family."

The eyebrows climbed yet higher, and her hand touched the collar of her tashta·as a faint hint of rose colored her neck. "A'Hïrzg, I swear I didn't ask him to speak to you."

"If I thought you had, we wouldn't be having this conversation," Allesandra told her. "But since he's made the request, I've done as he asked and written a letter to your family; I gave it to my courier not a turn of the glass ago. I thought you should know, so you might contact them as well and tell them that I await their return letter."

Her response seemed strange to Allesandra. She would have expected a flattering response, or perhaps a blushing smile of pleasure. But Elissa blinked, and she turned her face away for a breath, as if her thoughts were elsewhere. "Why . . . thank you, A'Hïrzg. I'm flattered beyond words, of course. And your son is a most wonderful man. I am truly honored by his attention and his interest."

Allesandra glanced at Semini. His gaze was puzzled. "But?" Semini asked, his voice a low rumble.

A quick duck of the head, so that Elissa was staring at Allesandra's feet, not at them. "I have deep feelings for your son, A'Hïrzg. I truly do. But contacting my family . . ." Her tongue flickered over her lips, as if they were suddenly dry. "This is too fast."

Semini cleared his throat. "Is there something in your past, Vajica, something the A'Hïrzg should know?"

"No!" The word came out as ˙an explosion of breath, and the young woman's head came up again. "There's . . . nothing."

"You sleep with him," Allesandra said, and the frank comment widened Elissa's eyes and caused Semini to inhale loudly through his nostrils. "If you don't intend marriage, Vajica, then how are you different from one of the grandes horizontales?"

The other young women of the court would have recoiled. They would have stammered. This one just stared flatly at Allesandra, her chin lifting slightly, her pale gaze hardening. "I might ask the A'Hïrzg—with the Archigos' pardon—how someone in a loveless marriage is so different from a grande horizontale? One is paid for her name, the other for her . . ." A brief flicker of a smile. ". . . attentions. The grande horizontale, at least, has no illusions about her arrangements. Either way, the bedchamber is merely a place of commerce."

Allesandra laughed, suddenly and loudly. She applauded Elissa, three quick, loud strikes of cupped palm against palm. The exchange reminded her of her time in Nessantico with Archigos Ana, who also had a facile mind and would challenge Allesandra in their discussions in unexpected ways and with bald speech. Semini was gaping, but Allesandra nodded to the young woman. "There aren't many who would answer me that directly, Vajica," she told the woman. "You're lucky I'm someone who appreciates that. But . . ." She stopped, and the laughter under her voice vanished as quickly as glacier ice in the summer heat. "I love my son fiercely, Vajica, and I *will* protect him from making a mistake if I see a need to do so. Right now, you are merely a diversion for him, and it remains to be seen whether that interest will last the season. Whatever might eventually happen between the two of you, it will *not* be your decision to make. Is that clear enough?"

"As the spring rain, A'Hïrzg," Elissa answered. She gave a curt bow of her head. "If the A'Hïrzg will excuse me . . . ?"

Allesandra waved a hand, and Elissa bowed again, clasping hands to forehead toward Semini. She hurried off, her tashta swirling around her legs.

"She's brazen," Semini muttered as they listened to her footsteps on the tiles of the palais floor. "I begin to wonder about young Jan's choice."

Allesandra linked her arm in Semini's as they began to walk again. A few of the palais staff saw them; Allesandra didn't care; she enjoyed Semini's solid warmth at her side. "That was odd," Semini continued. "It was almost as if the woman was upset that Jan had asked you to speak to her family. Doesn't she realize what's being offered?"

"I think she knows exactly what's offered," Allesandra answered. She hugged Semini's arm tightly. She glanced back over her shoulder in the direction Elissa had gone. "That's what bothers me. I begin to wonder if becoming involved with her was Jan's choice at all."

~

The White Stone

THE BITCH GAVE HER no time ... no time ...
Anger almost overcame caution. She had wanted
to wait another week, because if the truth were told, she
wasn't sure she wanted to do this—not because of the death
that would result, but because it meant that "Elissa" would
necessarily have to vanish. She was no longer certain she
wanted that to happen; she'd thought maybe, if she had the
time, she could arrange to circumvent that. But now ...

She had a few days, no more: the time it would take the
A'Hïrzg's letter to go from Brezno to Jablunkov and back.
Before the response came, she would need to be far from
here—for two reasons.

The confrontation with the A'Hïrzg and the Archigos had
shaken her. She'd gone immediately to Jan, and he'd proudly
told her that Allesandra had sent the letter by fast courier.
She'd had to pretend to be delighted with the news; it had
been far more difficult than she'd expected. Two days, then,
for the letter to arrive at the palais in Jablunkov, where an
attendant would no doubt open it immediately, read it, and
realize something was terribly amiss. There would be quick
discussion, a hastily scrawled response, and a new rider would
be hurrying back to Brezno with orders to make all haste. For
all she knew, the letter had already reached Jablunkov.

She had to act now.

When the response came, telling the A'Hïrzg that Elissa
ca'Karina was long dead, she either had to be gone, or she
had to have something that she could use as a weapon
against that knowledge. The new gossip around the palais
was how often the A'Hïrzg and the Archigos seemed to be
together lately. The looks that she'd seen between the two
certainly hinted that they were more than friends, but even
if she could prove that, there was nothing there she could
use—they were too powerful, and she had no intention of
being locked up in Brezno Bastida.

No, she would be the White Stone, as she should be. She would honor her contract and she would vanish, as the Stone always did.

She heard mocking laughter inside her with the decision.

The Moitidi of Fate were with her, at least. Fynn wasn't particularly a man of deep habits, but there were certain routines he followed. She'd come to the court prepared to do whatever it took to become Fynn's lover, but she'd found that an impossible task. Jan had been the next best choice, as the Hïrzg's current favorite companion outside his bed.

She'd also found herself genuinely liking the young man despite all her attempts to focus on the task for which she'd been so well-paid. She would have drawn out this contract for as long as she could, because she found herself comfortable with Jan, because she enjoyed his talk, his affection, and the attention he paid her during their nights together. Because she enjoyed pretending that maybe, maybe, she could have this life with him, that she could remain Elissa forever. She had wondered—skeptically, almost with fear—if she might love the young man.

The voices had howled with that, roaring with amusement.

"Fool!" the voices inside railed at her now. *"How stupid can you be? Did you care about any of us when you killed us? Did you regret what you did? No! Why should you care now? This is your fault. You don't have emotions; you can't afford them—that's what you always said!"*

They were right. She knew it. She'd been stupid and left herself vulnerable, something she should never have done, and now she would pay for her own folly. "Shut up!" she shouted back to them. *"I know! Leave me alone!"*

They only laughed, spewing back their hatred to her.

Focus. Think of only the target. Focus, or you'll die. Be the White Stone, not Elissa. Be what you are.

Fynn . . . Habits . . . Vulnerabilities . . .

Focus.

She'd watched Fynn follow his patterns for the past two weeks: at least twice during the rotation of days, Fynn would go riding with Jan and others of the court. She had been on those rides, and saw the attention that Fynn paid to Jan, who also rode alongside the Hïrzg, the two of them conversing and laughing. On their return, Fynn would retire to his rooms. Not long afterward, his domestique de chambre, Roderigo, would emerge and go to the stables, bringing back Hamlin, one of the stableboys who—she could not help but notice—was nearly the same age, build, and complexion as Jan. Roderigo would escort Hamlin to the doors of Fynn's chambers and depart as soon as the boy entered, returning precisely a half-turn of the glass later, by which time Hamlin would have left once more.

She'd watched the routine play out four times now, and she was relatively confident in its security. And today . . . today the Hïrzg and Jan were going out riding. She pleaded a headache and remained behind even though Jan's visible disappointment made her resolve waver. While they were gone, she moved through the corridors near the Hïrzg's rooms, smiling gently at the courtiers and servants she passed, then sliding quickly into an empty corridor. The main hallways were patrolled by gardai, but not those small corridors used by the servants, and at this time of day, the servants were busy in the massive kitchens below or were working in the rooms themselves. A picklock plucked from her tresses quickly opened a secured door, and she slid into the Hïrzg's apartments: an empty private office room just off the bedchamber. She could hear Roderigo giving orders to the under-servants in the next room, telling them what they needed to clean and how it was to be done. She slid behind a thick tapestry covering the wall (on the cloth, mounted chevarittai of the Firenzcian army trampled the soldiers of Tennshah underneath hooves and spears) and waited, closing her eyes and breathing slowly.

Listening to the voices. Listening to them mock her, cajole her, warn her . . .

In the darkness, they were especially loud.

A turn of the glass or more later, she heard Fynn's muffled voice and Roderigo answering him. A door closed, and then there was silence, not even the interior voices speaking. She waited a few breaths, then slid the tapestry aside, padding in her suede-soled shoes to the door of Fynn's bedchamber.

"My Hïrzg," she said softly.

Fynn was seated on his bed, his bashta half-undone, and

he leaped up at the sound of her voice, whirling about. She saw him reach for his sword—on the bed in its scabbard, the belt looped next to it, then stop with his hand on the hilt when he recognized her. "Vajica ca'Karina," he said, his voice nearly a purr. "What are you doing here? How did you get in?" His hand had not left the sword hilt. The man was careful—she had to give him that much.

"Roderigo . . . let me in," she told him, trying to sound flustered and uncertain. "I . . . I met him in the corridor just now. It was Jan who . . . who talked to Roderigo first, my Hïrzg. I'm here at his behest."

She watched his hand. His fist relaxed around the hilt. He frowned. "Then I need to speak to Roderigo," he said. "What is this about our Jan?"

She lowered her gaze as a demure and slightly frightened young woman might, looking at him through her lashes. "We . . . I know we both love him, my Hïrzg, and I know how much he respects and admires you. Even more than his own vatarh."

Fynn's hand had left the sword hilt; she took a step closer to him. "You know that he's asked the A'Hïrzg to speak to my family?" she asked him. Fynn nodded and stood erect, turning his back to the weapon on the bed. That made her smile genuine as she took a step toward him. "Jan has tremendous gratitude for your friendship," she told him. Another step. "He wished me to give you a . . . a gift in appreciation."

Another. She was within arm's length of him now.

"A gift?" Fynn's gaze slid from her face to her body. He laughed as she took a final step, her tashta brushing against him. "Perhaps Jan doesn't know me as well as he might think. What gift is this?"

"Let me show you," she said. With that she put her left arm around him, pulling him tight to her. With the same motion, she reached to the belt of her tashta and took the long dagger from its sheath in the small of her back. She plunged the blade between his ribs and twisted it. His mouth opened in pain and shock, and she stifled his shout with her open mouth. His arms pushed at her, but she was too close and his muscles were already weakening.

It was already over, though it took his body a few breaths to realize it.

When he stopped struggling and went limp in her arms, she laid him on his bed. His eyes were open, staring at the ceiling. She shook two small stones from a pouch tucked in her bosom and placed them over the eyes: the pale one that Allesandra had given her over the left, her own stone—the one she'd carried for so long—over the right. She let them stay there: as she stripped the bloodied tashta from her body and flung it into the fireplace, as she washed his blood from her hands and arms in his own basin, as she dressed herself quickly in the tashta she'd left in the other room. Finally, she plucked the stone from his right eye and placed it back in its pouch, tucking its familiar weight under the low collar of the tashta. She thought she could already hear Fynn, wailing as the others welcomed him. . . .

Then, silent except for the voices in her head, she fled the way she'd come.

She heard poor Hamlin's terrified scream just as she reached the main corridors, and the shouts of hurried orders from the gardai offiziers as they rushed to the Hïrzg's chambers.

She turned her back on them and hurried from the palais.

MOTIONS

Allesandra ca'Vörl
Enéas cu'Kinnear
Nico Morel
Jan ca'Vörl
Sergei ca'Rudka
Allesandra ca'Vörl
Enéas cu'Kinnear
Audric ca'Dakwi
Karl ca'Vliomani
Varina ci'Pallo
The White Stone

Allesandra ca'Vörl

"THE WHITE STONE..."
    "It must have been the Kraljiki who hired him..."
"The Numetodo hired him..."
"The Tennshah hired him..."
"I heard that the A'Hïrzg has been targeted herself, and her son..."

Allesandra heard the rumors. They were inescapable, choking Firenzcia like the fog that rose every evening from the woods around Stag Fall Palais, where Stark-kapitän Armen ca'Damont and Commandant Helmad cu'Göttering of the Garde Hïrzg had ordered the family be taken after the assassination. "The Commandant and I can protect you best there, A'Hïrzg," ca'Damont had said. She'd nodded stone-faced to him.

Pretense ... She had to keep up the proper face. She had to make the ca'-and-cu' believe that she grieved. She had to make them believe what she would ask of them.

Soon. Even if there was little hope now.

Security was visible everywhere around the palais, with gardai seemingly at every corner. Allesandra stood on the high balcony of the palais now, staring down to the tops of the fir trees below her on the steep flanks of the mountains, and to the gray-white strands of mist that wound between them, lifting as the sun set. She rubbed a pale-colored, flat pebble between her fingers.

She heard the door to the balcony open, followed by the murmuring of male voices. She turned to see Semini approaching her like a green-clad and sober-faced bear.

He said nothing, padding softly toward her and stopping an arm's length away—there were gardai to either side of them, a careful several strides away. He put his arms on the railing of the balcony and stared off into the mist coiling like sinewed arms around the trees, as if ghosts were tending a garden, reaching down to pull the weeds from between the wanted plants. Occasionally, a wisp would reach the level of the balcony, and cold, damp air would slide around Allesandra's ankles as if trying to pull her down into the gathering dark.

"So . . ." The word sounded like a low wind through the pine needles. "Will the White Stone be coming for me, now?" She saw his gaze flick down to the stone she held in her fingers.

"I didn't hire him, Semini," Allesandra said. *Him* . . . She wondered about that now. Elissa had seemingly vanished the same day Fynn had died, devastating Jan with another emotional hammer blow atop the death of his Onczio Fynn. Two days later, a frantic message came from Jablunkov saying that Elissa, daughter of Elissa and Josef (née ca'Evelii) ca'Karina had died six years ago and could the A'Hïrzg possibly have made some mistake.

Allesandra wondered. It was possible that "Elissa" had fled only because she knew that Allesandra had sent a letter to the ca'Karina family. It was possible that she'd run only because she knew her deception would be exposed. It was possible there was no connection between her disappearance and Fynn's death. Still, being close to Jan meant that Elissa had also had access to Fynn, and in Allesandra's experience it was dangerous to believe in coincidence. It was safer to see instead the knife-edge of conspiracy under coincidence's veil.

The White Stone's voice . . . could it have been a woman's, pitched low?

Semini was nodding as he glanced at the pebble in her hand. "Is that . . . ?"

She lifted the stone so he could see it. "Yes," she said. "This was what the White Stone left behind. It . . . reminds me of Fynn, and it reminds me that I will find who hired the White Stone and punish them."

Another nod. Semini was staring down again into the trees. "The Council of Ca' will be unanimous in naming you Hïrzgin. Congratulations." His voice was flat. "But you could have had that weeks ago, if you hadn't sent Jan to save Fynn."

"I'm glad someone remembers that. But ... I have no intention of being Hïrzgin, Semini."

That brought his face around to her again. A hand rubbed the silver-flecked beard as his dark eyes searched hers. "You're serious."

"I am."

"I thought—"

"You think entirely too much, Semini," she told him, then softened her rebuke with a smile. The garda behind was looking the other way, and her body shielded the one behind her. She reached out to stroke his arm, once. "I intend to renounce my title of A'Hïrzg. After all, too many people will be thinking just as you're thinking right now. There would always be whispers that I had Fynn killed so that I might take the throne in Brezno. If I step down, that gossip will die with my abdication. I will leave it to the Council of Ca' to name a new Hïrzg for Firenzcia."

One thick eyebrow curved high on Semini's forehead. "Have you spoken to Pauli?"

The mention of his name threw a cold barrier between them, or perhaps it was the fog. She withdrew her hand. "It's not my husband's decision to make," Allesandra told him sharply, then smiled again. "But it *will* be interesting to watch his face when I stand up in front of the Council and say this—and I expect it to be entirely a surprise to him, Semini. I also expect that he'll be rushing back to West Magyaria in a rage the next day, complaining to Gyula Karvella how the wife that he and Hïrzg Jan handpicked for him has ruined him."

"You'd truly leave the decision to the Council?"

"Oh, I've already spoken to some of them. Enough of them for my purposes, anyway. I've suggested that—after due deliberation—the Council might come to believe that my brother's recent actions have shown them whom *he* currently favored as successor: someone who had amply demonstrated his loyalty and skill. Why, Jan would grow into a fine Hïrzg, don't you think? One who would rule strongly and well for many years to come."

Semini chuckled, softly at first, then more enthusiastically. "So *that's* your intention."

The stone felt like ice in her hand. "Not entirely. I'm thinking of the future, Semini. Perhaps when the Holdings and the Coalition are united again and a competent ruler sits on the Sun Throne, and there is a righteous Archigos in the Temple of Cénzi who has also reunited the severed halves of the Faith, then Jan would be that Kralji's perfect strong right arm."

His face was split with a wide smile now. "Allesandra, you surprise me."

"I shouldn't," she told him. "You and I, Semini, are on the same side in this." She rubbed the stone between her fingers and tucked it into a pocket of her tashta. She would have it mounted in gold on a fine chain. She would wear it under her tashta when she spoke to the Council, wear it alongside the broken globe of Cénzi that Archigos Ana had given her. It would be a reminder of guilt, a reminder that she had acted in haste and done worse to her brother than her vatarh and he had ever done to her. *I'm sorry, Fynn. I'm sorry that we never really knew each other. I'm sorry . . .*

She placed her hand on the railing, close to Semini's hand, as she looked down again into the mists. A few breaths later, she felt the warmth of Semini's hand carefully covering hers.

They stood that way until darkness came and the first stars pricked the dark blue of the sky.

~

Enéas cu'Kinnear

THE MOUTH OF THE A'SELE was its widest here. The city of Fossano sat on the southern bank, the hills to the north tiny and hazed with blue on the far side, fading into invisibility as they curved away across the yawning gulf of A'Sele Bay. Dozens of trade ships plied the silt-brown water, traveling upriver to Nessantico or downriver toward Karnmor or other countries to the north or south, or even across the Strettosei itself. The water of A'Sele Bay was colored by the soil the A'Sele carried from its tributaries, with its sweet freshness coiling and fading eventually into the cobalt salt depths of the Nostrosei.

Enéas was at last back in Nessantico proper. Back in the Holdings. Back on the mainland. The scent of salt was faint here, and he stayed well away from it. From here, he would travel the main road east to Vouziers, then north to Nessantico herself at last.

Home. He was nearly home. He could taste it.

In Fossano, everything felt familiar and comfortable. The architecture echoed the solid, ornamented buildings of the capital city just as the temples were smaller replicas of the great cathedrals on the South Bank and the Isle of the Kralji, thirty-some leagues up the rushing waters of the A'Sele. There was nothing of the square, flat buildings of the Westlanders, or of the odd spires and whitewashed flanks of Karnor.

The Hellins and the battles Enéas had experienced felt distant to him as he looked out from a tavern in South Hills, as if they had happened to someone else in another life. He was floating detached from the memories; he could see them but couldn't touch them, and they couldn't touch him.

But ... always in his head there was this faint voice, the voice he knew now was Cénzi. *Yes ... I hear you, Lord of All. I listen ...*

Enéas heard His Voice now, as he touched his pack, the niter he'd purchased in Karnor heavy at the bottom. He stood at the open window of his room in the Old Chevaritt's Inn, and he could faintly catch the scent of burning nearby, and the Voice called to him to go out. Go out. Find the source. Find what was needed now.

He obeyed, as he must. He put on his uniform, buckled his sword around his hip, and left the inn.

Fossano's streets, angled up and down steep inclines, and wandered as if laid out by a drunken man. This area of town, outside the old city walls and away from the densely-packed center, had been farmland until recently. The houses and buildings were still widely separated by small fields where sheep, goats, and cows grazed or where farmers planted crops. The smell of sharp burning intensified as Enéas followed the road farther out from the town, until the houses vanished entirely and the road became no more than a rutted, weed-overgrown path.

Enéas rounded a knob of tree-dotted granite. A bluish trail of smoke was visible, coiling from near a ramshackle hut set in an unworked field. Cords of hardwood littered the yard, and three men were piling the cords into a rounded pile—already twice a man's height and several strides around. Nearby, another mound of wood had been covered with soil and turf, and smoke drifted from vent holes around the perimeter of the mound and from the covered chimney at the top. The men glanced up as Enéas approached, and he swept back his travel cloak to reveal the crest of the Garde Civile and the hilt of his sword: coalliers were known to be a rough and untrustworthy lot, living in small groups in the forested areas outside the town. A mound of cordwood might take two or three weeks to smolder and fume through the transformation to hard, pure black charcoal, and required constant tending or the coalliers would remove the earthen covering to find only ash. Coalliers stayed to themselves, venturing in only to sell bags of the charcoal they produced, and moving on to new areas of forest as the suitable trees nearby were depleted. Their poor reputation was enhanced by the fact that they'd often mix the charcoal with lumps of dirt and rocks so that the quality of the coal might be less than desirable. In Nessantico, there were e-téni whose task it was to produce the fine, gemlike charcoal used in the smelting furnaces of the great city, and to heat the houses of the ca'-and-cu'. Here, the work wasn't done through the power of the Ilmodo, but through the back-breaking and dirty labor of common people.

He waved at the coalliers as they stared, hands crossed on chests or at their hips. "What'ya be wantin', Vajiki?" one of them asked. He had a wen under his left eye like half a red grape glued to his skin, adorned with a tuft of wiry hair that matched the man's scraggly beard; the wen's twin sat off-center in the middle of his forehead. The speaker was older than the other two by several years; Enéas wondered if he might not be the vatarh or onczlo of the younger two. "Lost your troop, eh?" The trio chuckled at the man's poor jest with grim laughter as dark as the soot that stained their hands and faces.

"I need charcoal," Enéas told them. "The highest quality you have. A sack of it with no impurities. This is what Cénzi desires."

They laughed again. The man with the wens rubbed at his face. "Cénzi, eh? Are you claiming to be Cénzi, or are you a téni, too, Vajiki? Or maybe just slightly light in the head?" Again the rough laughter assaulted Enéas, as the wind sent smoke from the fire mound wrapping around the coalliers. "We'll be in town next Mizzkdi, Vajiki, with all the charcoal you'd want. Wait until then. We're busy."

"I need it now," Enéas persisted. "I'm leaving town tomorrow for Nessantico."

The man glanced at his companions. "Traveling, eh? You're not from Fossano, then?" Enéas shook his head. A smile touched the face of the older coallier. "He's fancy-lookin', isn't he, boys? Look at that bashta and them boots. Why, I'll wager he's from Nessantico itself. An' I'll bet he has a purse heavy enough to buy that charcoal he's wantin' and more."

The man took a step toward Enéas; he lifted his sword halfway from its scabbard. "I don't want trouble, Vajiki," Enéas told them. "Just your coal. I'll give you a good price for it—twice the going rate, and with Cénzi's blessing and no haggling."

"Twice the rate, and a blessing besides." Another step. "Ain't we the lucky ones, boys?" The two younger men were moving slowly to either side of Enéas, hemming him in. He saw a knife in one man's hand; the other held a stick of hardwood like a cudgel.

Enéas had seen enough brawls in his life—they were endemic among the troops, and common enough in the taverns of the towns at night. He knew that the bravery of the group would last only as long as their leader stayed untouched. The man with the wens was grinning now as he stooped down to pick up a piece of cordwood himself. He slapped the length of wood against a callused palm. "I'm thinkin' you'll be giving us that purse now, Vajiki, if you want to spare yourself a beatin'," he said. "After all, three against one—"

That was as far he got. In a single motion, Enéas drew his sword from his scabbard and struck, the steel ringing and flashing in the sunlight. The coallier's improvised club went spinning away, his hand still grasping the wood. The man gaped down at the stump as blood spurted from the arm. He howled as Enéas spun around, his sword now threatening the throat of the man with the knife. The coallier dropped his weapon and backed hastily away; the other was staring wide-eyed at the man with the wens, who had sunk to his knees, still howling, his remaining hand clasped around the stub of his forearm. "Tie that arm off to stop the bleeding if you want your friend to live," Enéas said to the coalliers. He picked up the knife the man had dropped. "Where's your charcoal?"

One of them gestured toward the crude hut. Enéas saw a cart there, dark lumps piled in one corner. A pile of burlap sacks were stacked near one of the wheels. He cleaned his blade on the grass of the field, sheathed it, and strode over to the cart and filled one of the sacks. The man whose hand he'd severed had subsided into moans and wails, falling to his side as his two companions knelt alongside him. Enéas slung the sack over his shoulder. He walked back to the coalliers and tossed a single gold solas on the grass between them—more money than they would have made for an entire wagonload of charcoal. They stared at the coin. The two younger men had tied a tourniquet around the stump of their leader, but his face was pale and the wens stood out like ruddy pebbles on his face. A wound like that, Enéas knew, was fatal as often as not:

from blood loss, or from the Black Rot that often struck wounded limbs.

"May Cénzi have mercy on you," he said to him. "And may He forgive you for impeding His will."

With that, he shifted the weight of the sack on his shoulder and started back toward town.

Nico Morel

"**H**E'S JUST A BOY, KARL. An innocent child. Don't you dare hurt him."

Nico heard Varina's voice through the locked door as he huddled against the wooden wall in the pile of blankets. He heard a male voice reply—Karl? he wondered—but the voice was too low, and Nico couldn't make out all the words through the wooden door separating them, only the phrase ". . . what I have to do." Then the door opened, and Nico flung an arm over his eyes against the light coming from the other room. A shadow lurked in the doorway and came over to him, bootsteps loud on the creaking floorboards. Nico blinked up at the man; a glimpse of graying hair and a well-trimmed beard, and soft eyes that belied the grim line of the mouth under the mustache. The man's bashta was fine and clean, the cloth shining and soft when it brushed against Nico's skin as the man knelt in front of him. One of the ca'-and-cu', Nico decided.

"I don't know nothing," Nico said again, wearily, before the man could speak. He'd said the words too many times already, in as many variations as his tired mind could summon. The woman—Varina—had asked him over and over again about Talis: if he knew where Talis was living now, how Talis was connected to him and his matarh, whether he knew where Talis was from or what he did, and where Talis had learned to use the Ilmodo (except that Varina sometimes used another word for "Ilmodo," which sounded like Scawth something or other). Nico hadn't told them anything because he knew Talis wouldn't want that. They wanted to hurt Talis; Nico was certain of that.

The man cupped his hand in front of Nico and spoke a strange word like the ones that Talis sometimes chanted when he was doing magic. Nico could feel the cold of the Ilmodo close to him, the hair on his forearms standing up as a ball of soft, yellow light appeared, like a ball of flame sitting on the man's upturned palm. In the light, Nico could see the face clearly, and he gasped.

He *knew* that face. This was the man who had attacked Talis in the street: Ambassador ca'Vliomani, the Numetodo. Nico hissed and pressed his back against the wall, as if he could melt completely through the wood and out to freedom. He wanted the cold anger to fill him again, but he was so tired and frightened that he couldn't summon up the feeling.

"Ah, so you *do* recognize me," the man said. "I thought you might. I certainly recognize you, Nico." He had an accent, but not the same one Talis had. This accent lilted and swirled, coming from deeper in the throat and not through the nose. He left out the "h' in thought, saying it as "tot." The ambassador lowered his hand to the floor and the ball of light rolled sluggishly from his hand to gutter against the floorboard. The long shadow of the man shifted on the walls.

"Are you going to hurt me?" Nico's voice sounded tiny and nearly lost to his own ears: a husk, a whisper of breeze.

The man didn't answer. Not directly. "The last time I saw you, Nico, I was nearly killed by the man with you. What was his name? Talis?" Nico was shaking his head, but the man smiled against his denial. "I really need to talk to Talis, Nico," the man continued. "And I'll bet you'd like to talk to him also."

"You're mad at him," Nico said. "You'll try to hurt him."

"I'm not mad at him," the Ambassador replied. "I know that's hard for you to believe, but it's true. There are things I need to ask him, urgent and important things, and he didn't give me a chance. That's all. We had a ... a misunderstanding."

"You promise?"

The man didn't reply, but reached into a pouch tied to his side, unwrapped something in waxed paper, and held it out toward Nico. Nico flinched back away for a moment, then leaned forward again when the man continued to hold out his hand: there in the palm was a plump date drizzled with honey and dotted with diced sweetnut. Nico's mouth watered; Varina had fed him bread and cheese and given him water, but he was still a little hungry after his long walk from Ville Paisli, and the sight of the date made his mouth water helplessly. "Go on, Nico, take it," the man said. "I brought it just for you."

Hesitantly, Nico reached for the candied fruit. When his fingers touched the loud, crinkled paper, he snatched the date from the man's hand as quickly as he could. He stuffed it whole into his mouth, and the smoky sweetness of the honey rolled on his tongue, blending with the tart bite of the date. The man continued to smile, watching him. He thought the man's face didn't look so angry now, and there was a kindness in the wrinkles around his eyes.

"You know, I have great-children who are about your age," the man said to Nico. "A little younger, but not much. You'd like them, I think, if you met them. They live on the Isle of Paeti. Do you know where that is?"

Nico nodded. Matarh had shown him a map of the Holdings, and pointed to the countries and made him learn them.

"Paeti's a long way from here," the man said. "But I'd like to go back there one day. What about you, Nico? Were you born here in Nessantico?"

Another nod. Nico licked his lips, tasting the sticky remnants of the honey.

"What about your matarh? Where's she from?"

"Here." The word came out half-strangled. The lingering taste of the date had turned bitter. He cleared his throat.

"Ah . . ." The man seemed to consider that for a moment, his gaze drifting momentarily away from Nico. He saw movement at the doorway and saw Varina leaning there. The man and Varina glanced at each other, and something in the way they looked made Nico think that they were a couple like Talis and his matarh. "And your vatarh? Is Talis from here?"

Nico started to shake his head, then stopped. Talis wouldn't want Nico talking about him. *What happened has to be a secret . . .* That's what Talis had said. He'd trusted Nico.

"He's from the Westlands beyond the Hellins, isn't he?" Karl persisted. "He's one of the ones that call themselves Tehuantin. Nico, you know that the Holdings is at war with the Westlanders, don't you? You understand that?"

A nod. Nico didn't dare open his mouth. He'd never heard that one word: Tehuantin. It sounded like a word

Talis might say, though, just the sound of it. He could hear it, in Talis' accent.

"Where's your matarh, Nico? We should take you back to her, but you need to tell us where she is."

"She's with my tantzia," Nico said. "She's a long way from here. I . . . left her." He didn't want to tell the Ambassador about his cousins and the way they'd treated him. But thinking of that made him think of his matarh, and he suddenly wanted more than anything to be with her. He could feel tears starting in his eyes, and he wiped at them almost angrily, not wanting to let the Ambassador see. Varina moved from the doorway to crouch beside him. Her arms went around him, and it felt almost as good as having Matarh hug him.

"Is Talis with your matarh?" Karl asked.

That seemed safe enough to answer. He didn't want the Ambassador going to Matarh, and if the man knew that Talis wasn't there, well, he'd leave her alone. "No," he said. He sniffed. "Karl, enough," Varina said.

He ignored her. "Where's Talis now, Nico?"

"I don't know." When ca'Vliomani just crouched there, not saying anything, Nico lifted a shoulder. "I don't. I really don't."

Ca'Vliomani cocked his head as he looked at Nico. He cupped a hand around Nico's chin and lifted his head until Nico was forced to stare in his unblinking eyes. He heard Varina draw in her breath above him. "That's the truth?"

Nico nodded vigorously. The man stared a few minutes longer, then let his hand drop away. He and Varina glanced at each other again. To Nico, it seemed as if they were talking without saying anything. Ca'Vliomani's fingers stroked his beard, scowling as if dissatisfied. His voice sounded lighter and less ominous now. "What are you doing in Oldtown, Nico? Why aren't you with your matarh?"

That was too complicated to answer. Nico shook his head against the welter of possible answers. He wasn't certain himself now why he was here. "I thought maybe . . ." The tears were threatening again and he stopped to take a breath. "I thought maybe Talis might still be where we used to live."

"He's not." It was Varina who answered. Her hand stroked his back. "We've been watching."

"Well, he saw you, then," Nico said confidently. "Talis is smart. He would see you watching and he wouldn't go there."

"He wouldn't have seen me," Varina answered, but Nico didn't believe that. He wiped at his eyes again.

"Do you have family here?" ca'Vliomani asked. "Someone to look after you?"

"Just Talis," Nico answered. "That's all."

Ca'Vliomani sighed and stood up with a groan, his knees cracking with the effort. "Then we'll have to let Talis know that you're staying with us, and maybe we'll both get what we want, eh?"

~

Jan ca'Vörl

"I'M SORRY, ONCZIO FYNN," Jan whispered. "This shouldn't have happened, and I hope . . . I hope that this wasn't my fault." His voice echoed in the vault, stirring faint ghosts of himself. The guttering light of the torch made shadows lurch and jump around the sealing stones of the tombs. Twice now he'd watched the Hïrzg laid to rest in these dank and somber chambers, far too quickly. Vatarh and son. At least Fynn's interment hadn't been accompanied by omens and further death. His had been a slow, somber ritual, one that left Jan's chest heavy and cold.

He'd searched everywhere for Elissa. He'd sent riders out from Brezno, scouring the roads and inns and villages for her in all directions. Roderigo had told him that he hadn't seen Elissa near Fynn's chambers. "But I was away from him when it happened. She might have managed to sneak in—or someone else might have. I don't know. I just don't know."

The words tasted of bile and poison. He tried to convince himself that it had all been coincidence. Matarh had shown him the letter she'd received from the ca'Karina family: Elissa was an impostor pretending to be ca'. But perhaps that was all: she'd fled because she'd known that her deception was going to be revealed. Maybe that was the entirety of it. Or . . . Perhaps she'd gone to see Fynn, to plead her case with him knowing that she was about to be exposed as a fraud, and had interrupted The White Stone at his work. Perhaps she'd fled in terror before the famed assassin had glimpsed her, too frightened to even stay in the city after what she'd seen. Or perhaps—worse—The White Stone *had* seen her, and taken her to murder elsewhere.

None of it convinced Jan. He knew what they were thinking, all of them, and when the suspicion settled in his gut, he also knew they were right. A pretender in the court, a pretender who was the lover of the Hïzrgin's favorite

companion—the conclusion was obvious. Elissa had been
the White Stone's accomplice, or she was the White Stone
herself.

Either thought made Jan's head whirl. He remembered
the time he'd spent with her, the conversations, the flirtations, the kisses; the rising, quick breaths as they explored
each other; the slick, oily heat of lovemaking, the laughter
afterward . . . Her body, sleek and enticing in the warm bath
of candlelight; the curve of her breasts beaded with the
sweat of their passion; the dark, soft and enticing triangle
at the joining of her legs . . .

He shook his head to banish the thoughts.

It couldn't be her. Couldn't. Yet . . .

Jan put his hand on the sealing stone of Fynn's tomb,
letting his fingers trace the incised bas-reliefs there. "I'm
sorry," he said again to the corpse.

If it *had*, somehow, been Elissa, then the question still
unanswered was who had hired The White Stone. The
Stone would not kill without a contract. Someone had paid
for this. Whether Elissa had been the knife or simply the
helper didn't matter. It hadn't been her who had made the
decision. Someone else had ordered the death.

Jan bowed his head until his forehead touched the cold
stone. "I'll find out who did this," he said: to Cénzi, to Fynn,
to the haunted air. "I'll find out, and I will give you justice,
Onczio."

Jan took in a long breath of the cold, damp air. He rose
on protesting knees and took the torch from its sconce.
Then he began the long climb back up toward the day.

~

Sergei ca'Rudka

"*THERE IS TRUTH IN PAIN,*" *Sergei said. He'd spoken the aphorism many times over the years, said it so the victim knew that he must confess what Sergei wished him to confess. He also knew the statement for the lie it was. There was no "truth" in pain, not really. With the agony he inflicted, there came instead the ability to make the victim say anything that Sergei desired him to say. There came the ability to make "truth" whatever those in charge wished truth to be. The victim would say anything, agree to anything, confess to anything as long as there was a promise to end the torment.*

Sergei smiled down at the man in chains before him, the instruments of torture dark and sinister in the roll of leather before him, but then the perception shifted: it was Sergei lying bound on the table, looking up into his own face. His hands were chained and cold fear twisted his bowels. He knew what he was about to feel; he had imposed it on many. He knew what he was about to feel, and he screamed in anticipation of the agony. . . .

"Regent?"

Sergei bolted awake in his cell, the manacles binding his wrists rattling the short chain between them. He reached quickly for the knife that was still in his boot, making sure that his hand was around the hilt so that if they'd come to take him for interrogation, he could take his own life first.

He would not endure what he had forced others to endure.

But it was Aris cu'Falla, the Commandant of the Bastida, who had entered the room, and Sergei relaxed, letting his fingers slide from the hilt. Aris saluted the garda who had opened the door. "You may go," he told the man. "There's lunch for you on the lower landing. Come back here in half a turn of the glass."

"Thank you, Commandant," the garda said. He saluted and left. Aris left the door open. Sergei glanced at the yawning door from the bed on which he sat. Aris saw the glance.

"You wouldn't get past me, Sergei. You know that. I have two hands of years on you, after all, and it's my duty—not to mention my life—to stop you."

"Did you leave the door open just to mock me, then?"

A smile came and vanished like spring frost. "Would you rather I shut and locked it?"

Sergei laughed grimly, and the laugh morphed into a cough heavy with phlegm. Aris touched his shoulder with concern as Sergei hunched over. "Would you like me to send for a healer, my friend?"

"Why, so I'm as healthy as possible when the Council orders me killed?" Sergei shook his head. "It's just the dampness; my lungs don't like it. So tell me, Aris, what news do you have?"

Aris pulled the single chair in the room over to him, the legs scraping loudly against the flags. "I've a garda I trust implicitly assigned to the Council—for my own safety in this troubled time, frankly. So much of what I know comes from him."

"I don't need the preamble, Aris—it's not going to change your answer, and I suspect I already know it. Just tell me."

Aris sighed. He turned the chair backward and sat, his arms folded over the back, his chin on his arms. "Sigourney ca'Ludovici is pushing the Council hard to give the Kraljiki the power he asks for. There's to be a final meeting in a few days, and a vote is to be taken then."

"They'll actually give Audric what he wants?"

A nod wrinkled the bearded chin on his hands. "Yes. I think so."

Sergei closed his eyes, leaning his head back against the stone wall. He could feel the chill of the rock through his thinning hair. "They'll destroy Nessantico for the sake of power. They're all—and Sigourney especially—thinking that Audric won't last a year, which will leave the Sun Throne open for one of them—assuming I'm gone."

"Sergei," he heard Aris say in the darkness of his thoughts, "I'll give you warning. I promise you that. I'll give you time to—" He stopped.

"Thank you, Aris."

"I would do more, if I could, but I have my family to think about. If the Council of Ca' or the new Kralji found out I helped you to escape, well . . ."

"I know. I wouldn't ask that of you."

"I'm sorry."

"Don't be." Sergei opened his eyes again, leaning forward. He cupped a hand on Aris' face, the manacles jangling with the motion. "I've had a good life, Aris, and I've served three Kralji as well as I could. Cénzi will forgive me what I must do."

"There's still hope, and no need to do anything yet," Aris said. "The Council may come to their senses and see that the Kraljiki's sick in his mind as well as his body. They may yet release you; they *will*, if the effort of Archigos Kenne and the others loyal to you have any effect at all— Archigos Kenne has already pleaded your case to them, and his words still have some influence, after all. Don't give up hope, Sergei. We both know all too well the history of the Bastida. Why, the Bastida held Harcourt ca'Denai for three years before he became Kraljiki."

Sergei laughed, forcing down the cough that wanted to come with it. "We're practical men, both of us, Aris. Realists. We don't delude ourselves with false hope."

"True enough," Aris said. He stood. "I'll have the garda bring your food up to you. And a healer to look at you, whether you want him or not." He patted Sergei on the shoulder and started for the cell door, stopping with his hand on the handle. "If it comes to it, Sergei, I'll send word to you before anyone comes to take you down to the donjons below." He paused, looking significantly at Sergei. "So you can prepare yourself. You've my word on that."

Sergei nodded. Aris saluted him and closed the door with a metallic clash. Sergei heard the grating of the key in the lock. He put his head back again, listening to the sound of cu'Falla's bootsteps on the winding stairs of the tower.

He remembered the clean sound of screams echoing on stone, and the shrill, high pleading of those sent for questioning. He remembered their faces, taut with pain. There was an honesty in their agony, a purity of expression that could not be faked. He sometimes thought he glimpsed Cénzi in them:

Cénzi as He had been when His own children, the Moitidi, had turned against Him and savaged His mortal body. Now, like Cénzi, Sergei might face the wrath of his own creation.

But he would not. He promised himself that. One way or the other, he would not.

~

Allesandra ca'Vörl

"**T**HE COUNCILLORS ARE HERE and seated, A'Hïrzg," the aide told them. "They've asked me to bring you to chambers."

Allesandra stood in the corridor outside the council chamber with Pauli and Jan on either side of her. Her hand touched her tashta, low on the throat where—under the cloth—a common white stone hung surrounded by golden filigree, next to Archigos Ana's globe. Even Pauli, who had been chattering contentedly about how West Magyaria and Firenzcia, when he was Gyula and Allesandra was Hïrzg, would together solidify the Coalition, went silent as the aide nodded to the hall servants to open the double doors and they peered into the shadowed dimness beyond, where the Council of Ca' was seated at the great table.

Jan, for his part, was solemn and quiet, as he had been since Fynn's death and Elissa's departure. Allesandra put her arm around her son before they entered. She leaned over to him and whispered: "When I leave here, you must go to your rooms and wait. Do you understand?"

He looked at her strangely but finally gave her a small, puzzled nod.

The chamber of the Council of Ca' in Brezno was dark, with stained oak paneling on the walls and a rug the color of dried blood: an interior room of Brezno Palais with no windows, illuminated only by candled chandeliers above the long, varnished table (not even téni-lights), and cold with only a small hearth at one end. The room was dreary and cheerless. It was not a room that invited a long stay and slow, leisurely conversations—and that was deliberate. Hïrzg Karin, Allesandra's great-vatarh, had intentionally assigned the room to the Council. He found the Council of Ca' sessions tedious and boring; the lack of comfort in the room ensured that they would at least be short.

"Please, come in, A'Hïrzg," Sinclair ca'Egan said from the

head of the table. Ca'Egan was bald and ancient, a quaver-voiced chevaritt who had ridden with Allesandra's vatarh before Hïrzg Karin had even named Allesandra's vatarh as A'Hïrzg. He'd been on the Council of Ca' for as long as Allesandra had known him; as Eldest, he was also titular head of the Council. Four women (one of them Francesca), five men; they rose as one and bowed to her as A'Hïrzg, a nicety even the Council of Ca' could not ignore, then sat once more. Six of the nine, especially, nodded and smiled to her. Allesandra, Pauli, and Jan stood—as etiquette demanded—at the open end of the table. Ca'Egan rattled the parchments set in front of him and cleared his throat. "Thank you for coming. We certainly needn't be long. A mere formality, actually. Hïrzg Fynn had already named Allesandra ca'Vörl as A'Hïrzg, so we only need to have your signature, A'Hïrzg, and those of the councillors here ..."

"Vajiki ca'Egan," Allesandra said, and ca'Egan's head came up wonderingly at the interruption. At her right side, Pauli grunted at the obvious breach in etiquette. "I have a statement to make before the Council puts its stamp on that document and sends it to the Archigos for his acknowledgment. I have thought about this ever since my dear brother was killed, and I have prayed to Cénzi for His guidance, and everything has become clear to me." She paused. *This is your last chance to change your mind....* Semini had argued with her for a long turn or two, as they lay in bed together, but she was convinced that this was the right strategy. She took a deep breath. She could feel Pauli staring at her quizzically and impatiently. "I do not wish to be Hïrzgin," she declaimed, "and I hereby revoke my claim on the title."

Ca'Egan's eyebrows clambered high on his bare, wrinkled skull and his mouth opened soundlessly. Francesca, in shock, reared back in her seat, stunned by the announcement, but most did not. They only nodded, their gazes more on Jan than on Allesandra.

"Cénzi's balls!" Pauli shouted alongside her, the obscenity almost seeming to draw lightning in the dark air of the chamber. "Woman, are you insane? Do you know what you're doing? You've just—"

"Shut up," she said to Pauli, who glared, though his jaw snapped closed. Allesandra raised her hands to the councillors. "I've said all I need to say. My decision is irrevocable. I leave it to the Council of Ca' to decide who is best suited take the throne of Brezno. However, it won't be me. I trust your judgment, Councillors. I know you will do what is best for Brezno."

With that, she gave the sign of Cénzi to the Council and turned, pushing the doors open so abruptly that the hall servants on station outside were nearly knocked aside. Pauli and Jan, surprised by the suddenness of her retreat, followed belatedly. Allesandra could hear Pauli charging after her. His hand caught her arm and spun her around. His handsome face was flushed and distorted, made ugly with anger. Behind him, she saw Jan standing at the open door of the chamber watching their confrontation, his own features puzzled and uncertain.

"What in the seven hells is this?" Pauli raged. "We had everything we ever wanted in our hands, and you just *throw it away*? Are you mad, Allesandra?" His hand tightened on her bicep, the tashta bunching under his fingers. She would be bruised there tomorrow, she knew. "You are going back in there now and you're telling them that it was a mistake. A joke. Tell them any damn thing you want. But you're *not* going to do this to me."

"To *you*?" Allesandra answered mockingly, calmly. "How does this have anything to do with you, Pauli? *I* was the A'Hïrzg, not you. *You* are just a pitiful, useless excuse for a husband, a mistake I hope to rectify as soon as I can, and you'll take your hand from me. Now."

He didn't. He drew his other hand back as if to strike her, his fingers curling into a fist. "No!" The shout was from Jan, running toward them. "Don't, Vatarh."

Allesandra smiled grimly at Pauli, at his still-upraised hand. "Go ahead," she told him. "Do it if you'd like. I tell you now that it will be the last time you ever touch me."

Pauli let the fisted hand drop. His fingers loosened on her sleeve and she shook herself away from him.

"I'm done with you, Pauli," she told him. "You gave me all I ever needed from you long ago."

~

Enéas cu'Kinnear

VOUZIERS: A LANDLOCKED CITY, the largest in South Nessantico, the crossroads to Namarro and the sun-crazed southlands of Daritria beyond. Vouziers sat at the northern edge of the flatlands of South Nessantico, a farming country with vast fields of swaying grain. Vouziers' people were like the land: solid, unpretentious, serious, and uncomplicated.

The coach took several days to reach Vouziers from Fossano. In a village along the way, he purchased all the sulfur the local alchemist had in his shop; the next night, he did the same in another. At each of their nightly stops, Enéas would take a private room at the inn. He would take out a few chunks of the charcoal and begin, slowly, to grind it into a black powder—he could hear Cénzi's satisfaction when the charcoal had reached the required fineness. Then, with Cénzi's voice warning him to be gentle and careful, he mixed the charcoal powder, the sulfur, and the niter together into the black sand of the Westlanders, tamping it softly into paper packages. Cénzi whispered the instructions into his head as he worked, and kept him safe.

The night before they reached Vouziers, he took a few of the packs out into the field after everyone was asleep. There, he poured the contents into a small, shallow hole he dug in the ground—the result reminded him uneasily of the black sands on the battlefields of the Hellins and his own defeat. As Cénzi's Voice instructed him, he took a length of cotton cord impregnated with wax and particles of the black sand, buried one end in the black sand and uncoiled the rest on the ground as he stepped away from the hole. *Later,* he heard Cénzi say in his head, *I will show you how to make fire as the téni do. You should have been a téni, Enéas. That was My desire for you, but your parents didn't listen to Me. But now I will make you all you should have been. You have My blessing. . . .*

Taking the shielded lantern he'd brought with him, Enéas lit the end of the cord. It hissed and fumed and sputtered, sparks gleaming in the darkness, and Enéas walked quickly away from it. He'd reached the inn and stepped into the common room when the eruption came: a sharp report louder than thunder that rattled the walls of the inn and fluttered the thick, translucent oiled paper in the windows, accompanied by a flash of momentary daylight. Everyone in the room jumped and craned their heads. "Cénzi's balls!" the innkeeper growled. "The night is as clear as well water."

The innkeeper went stomping outside, with the others trailing along behind. They first looked up to the cloudless sky and saw nothing. Out in the field, however, a small fire smoldered. As they approached, Enéas saw that the small hole he'd dug was now deep enough for a man to stand in up to his knees, and nearly an arm's reach across. Stones and dirt had been flung out in all directions. It was as if Cénzi Himself had punched the earth angrily.

The innkeeper looked up to the sky where stars twinkled and crowded in empty blackness. "Lightning striking without a storm," he said, shaking his head. "It's a portent, I tell you. The Moitidi are telling us that we've lost our way."

A portent. Enéas found himself smiling at the man's words, unaware of how prophetic they were. This was indeed a portent, a portent of Cénzi's desire for him.

The next day, he was in Vouziers. During the long ride, he'd prayed harder than he ever had, and Cénzi had answered him. He knew what he must do here, and though it bothered him, he was a soldier and soldiers always performed their duty, however onerous it might be.

On reaching Vouziers and obtaining lodgings for the night, he put on his uniform and slung a heavy leather pouch around his shoulder. He'd filled a long leather sack with pebbles; that he put into the inner pocket of his bashta. As the wind-horns blew Third Call, he entered the temple for the evening service, which was performed by the A'Téni of Vouziers herself. After the Admonition and the Blessing, Enéas followed the procession of téni from the temple and out onto the temple's plaza, alight with téni-lamps against the darkening sky. The a'téni was in conversation with the ca'-and-cu' of the city, and Enéas went instead to one of her o'téni assistants, a sallow man whose mouth seemed to struggle with the smile he gave Enéas.

"Good evening, O'Offizier," the téni said, giving Enéas the sign of Cénzi. "I'm sorry, should I know you?"

Enéas shook his head as he returned the gesture. "No, O'Téni. I'm passing through town on my way to Nessantico. I've just returned from the Hellins and the war there."

The o'téni's eyes widened slightly, and his thick lips pursed. "Ah. Then I must bless you for your service to the Holdings. How goes the war against the heathen Westlanders?"

"Not well, I'm afraid," Enéas answered. He glanced around the temple square. "I wish I could tell you differently. And here . . ." He shook his head dolefully, watching the o'téni carefully. "I've been nearly fifteen years away, and I come back to find much changed. Numetodo walking the street openly, mocking Cénzi with their words and their spells . . ." Yes, he had judged the man correctly: the téni's eyes narrowed and the lips pressed together even more tightly. He leaned forward conspiratorially and half-whispered to Enéas.

"It's indeed a shame that you, who have served your Kraljiki so well, should come back to see that. My a'téni would disagree, but I blame Archigos Ana for this state—and look what it got her: the thrice-damned Numetodo killed her anyway. Archigos Kenne . . ." The o'téni made a gesture of disgust. "*Phah!* He's no better. Worse, in fact. Why, in Nessantico you see people flaunting the Divolonté openly these days: the Numetodo tell them that anyone can use the Ilmodo, that it doesn't require Cénzi's Gift, and they show them how to do their small spells: to light a fire, or to chill the wine. They won't use the spells openly, but in their homes, when they think Cénzi isn't watching . . ." The o'téni shook his head again.

"The Numetodo are a blight," Enéas said. "Old Orlandi ca'Cellibrecca had the right idea about them."

The o'téni looked about guiltily at the mention. "That's not a name one should bandy about openly, O'Offizier," he said. "Not with his marriage-son claiming to be Archigos in Brezno."

Enéas gave the sign of Cénzi again. "I apologize, O'Téni. That's another sore point for a soldier like me, I'm afraid.

The Holdings should be one again, and so should the Faith. It pains me to see them broken, as it pains me to see the Numetodo being so brazen."

"I understand," the o'téni said. "Why, here in Vouziers, the Numetodo have their own building." He pointed down one of the streets leading off the plaza. "Right down there, within sight of this very temple, with their sign emblazoned on the front. It's a disgrace, and one that Cénzi won't long allow."

"On that point, you're right, O'Téni," Enéas answered. "That's exactly what Cénzi tells me." With that, the o'téni glanced at Enéas strangely, but Enéas gave him no chance to say anything else, bowing to him and moving off quickly across the plaza toward the street that the man had indicated. He whistled a tune as he walked, a Darkmavis song that his matarh had sung to him, long ago, back when the world still made sense to him and Kraljica Marguerite was still on the Sun Throne.

He found the Numetodo building easily enough—the carving over the lintel of the main door was a seashell, the sign of the Numetodo. There was an inn across the lane from the building, and he went into the tavern and ordered wine and a meal, sitting at one of the outside tables. He sipped the wine and ate slowly, watching the place of the Numetodo as the sky went fully dark above him between the buildings.

Three times, he saw someone enter; twice, someone left, but neither time did Cénzi speak to him, so he continued to wait, eating and occasionally touching the leather pouch on the ground alongside him for reassurance. It was nearly two turns of the glass later, with the streets having gone nearly empty before refilling again with those who preferred the anonymity of night, that he saw a man leave the Numetodo building, and Cénzi stirred within him.

That one . . . Enéas felt the call strongly, and he shouldered his pack, left a silver siqil on the table for his meal and wine, and hurried after the man. His quarry was an older man: bald on the top with a fringe of white hair all around. He was wearing tunic and pants, not a bashta, and was bareheaded—it would be difficult to lose him even in a crowd.

It was quickly apparent why Cénzi had chosen this one;

he walked down the street toward the temple plaza. The téni-lights were beginning to fade, and there were few people in the plaza, though the temple domes themselves were still brilliantly lit, golden against the star-pricked sky. Enéas glanced quickly around for an utilino and saw none. He hurried forward, and the Numetodo, hearing his footsteps, turned. Enéas saw the spell-word on the man's lips, his hands coming up as if about to make a gesture, and Enéas smiled broadly, waving at the man as if hailing a long-lost friend.

The man squinted, as if uncertain of the face before him. His hand dropped, his lips spread in a tentative returning smile. "Do I know—?"

That was as far he got. Enéas pulled the leather sack of pebbles from his pocket and, in the same fluid motion, struck the man hard in the side of his head with it. The Numetodo crumpled, unconscious, and Enéas caught the man in his arm as he sagged. He draped a limp arm over his shoulder and pulled up on the man's belt. He laughed as if drunken, singing off-key as he dragged the man in the direction of the temple's side door. Someone seeing them from a distance would think they were two inebriated friends staggering across the plaza. Enéas cast a last look over his shoulder as he reached the doors; no one seemed to be watching. He pulled on the heavy, bronze-plated door, adorned with images of the Moitidi and their struggle with Cénzi: that much hadn't changed—the temple doors were rarely locked, open to those who might wish to come in and pray, or to the indigent who might need a place to sleep during the night at the price of an Admonition by the téni who found them in the morning. Enéas slipped into the cool darkness of the temple. It was empty, and the sound of his breathing and his boot steps were loud as he dragged the Numetodo's dead weight up the main aisle, finally dropping him against the lectern at the front of the quire. He unslung the pack from his shoulder and put it on the Numetodo's lap, uncoiling the long cotton string from the top. He fed it out carefully as he backed down the aisle.

I will show you your own small Gift, Cénzi had told him only this afternoon. *I will show you how to make your own fire.* The chant and the gestures had come to him then, and though Enéas knew it was against the Divolonté for someone not of the téni to use the Ilmodo, he knew that this was Cénzi's wish and he would not be punished for it. He spoke the chant now near the temple entrance, and he felt the cold of the Ilmodo flowing in his veins and the Second World opening to his mind: between his moving hands there was an impossible heat and light, and he let it fall to the end of the cord and the fuse began to sputter and fume.

"Hey! Who's there! What's this!"

He saw a téni come from one of the archways leading off from the quire—the o'téni he'd spoken to earlier— and Enéas ducked down quickly, though the spell left him strangely tired, as if he'd been working hard all day. He heard the téni give a call and other footsteps echoed. "Who's this? What's going on?" someone said, as the fire on the fuse traveled quickly away from Enéas toward the lectern. When it was nearly there, Enéas rose to his feet and ran toward the door. He caught a glimpse of the o'téni and few e'téni, walking quickly toward the slumped, unmoving Numetodo, and someone pointed to Enéas . . .

. . . but it was already too late.

A dragon roared and belched fire, and the concussion picked Enéas up and threw him against the bronze doors. Half conscious, he fell to the stone flags as bits of rock and marble pelted him. When the hard, quick rain passed, he lifted his head. There was something red on the floor in front of him: the Numetodo's leg, he realized with a start, still clad in his loose pants. Near the front of the temple, someone was screaming, a long wail interspersed with curses. Groaning, Enéas tried to sit up. He was bleeding from cuts and scrapes and his body was bruised from his collision with the bronze doors, but otherwise Cénzi had spared him. The doors of the temple were flung open in front of him, and an utilino rushed in and past Enéas, blowing hard on his whistle. Téni were rushing in from the alcoves. The high lectern had toppled, laying broken in the aisle, and there was blood and parts of bodies everywhere. The Numetodo . . . he could see the man's head and the top of his torso, torn from his body and tossed into the aisle. The rest of him, where the bag of black sand had lain . . . Enéas couldn't see the rest.

For a moment he felt nausea: this was too much like the war, and the memories of what he'd seen in the Hellins threatened to overwhelm him. Acid filled his throat, his stomach heaved, but Cénzi's voice was in his head, too.

This is what they deserve, those who defy Me. You, Enéas, you are my Moitidi of Death, my chosen Weapon.

But I don't want this, he wanted to say, but even as he thought the words, he felt the anger of Cénzi rising up, a heat in his brain that made his head pound, and he went to his knees, clutching his skull between his hands.

Everything was confusion. People were pushing past him. He could still hear the wounded téni screaming. "... Numetodo ... I recognize him ..." Enéas heard the word amidst the chaos, and he smiled. As more people entered from the plaza, shouting and calling, he took the opportunity to slink to the side and into the shadows.

He went out into the night, feeling Cénzi's presence warming him.

You are fit for the task I have set for you. Now—go to Nessantico, and I will speak to you there ...

~

Audric ca'Dakwi

THE COUNCIL OF CA' FOR NESSANTICO met on the first floor of the Grande Palais on the Isle a'Kralji, where they had several suites of rooms and a small staff of palais servants dedicated entirely to their needs. The Council of Ca', for most of the great Kraljica Marguerite's reign, as well as that of her son Kraljiki Justi, had been largely a social organization, coming to the palais to sign the papers passed to them by the Kralji and the royal staff—a task they performed with little thought or discussion, otherwise spending their time relaxing in their sumptuous private offices or socializing in the well-appointed dining room and lounges of the Council's section of the Kralji's Palais. For many decades, being a "councillor" was mostly an honorary position, their duties ceremonial and hardly taxing, and their stipend for serving on the Council generous.

But with Kraljiki Justi's passing, with Audric being in his minority when he ascended to the Sun Throne, the Council had been required to assume a more active role in government. It was the Council of Ca' who had named Sergei ca'Rudka as Regent; it was the Council who now created and passed new legislation (until very recently, with the Regent's input as well), it was the Council who controlled the purse strings of Nessantico, it was the Council with whom the Regent was required to consult on any matter of policy within the Holdings, or any diplomatic decisions regarding the Coalition, the Hellins, or the other countries within the Holdings.

The Council had been required to wake from its comfortable, long slumber, and to a large extent it had. The last election for the Council, four years ago, had been aggressive and harsh; four of the seven members had been deposed, replaced by far more ambitious ca'.

Audric knew the history of the Council; Sergei had yammered on about it interminably, and Maister ci'Blaylock had spoken of the same in his lectures. Now his great-matarh gave him the same warnings.

"You need to be careful, Audric. Remember that each of the councillors wants to be where you are. They want the ring and the staff; they want to sit on the Sun Throne. They are jealous of you, and you must convince them that in giving you what you want, they will find themselves closer to their own goals."

Great-Matarh Marguerite was staring at him as he walked down the corridor to the Hall of the Sun Throne, where the Council awaited him. The wheels of the easel on which her painting rested were quiet today; he'd insisted that Marlon grease them with duck fat before the meeting. The servants pushed the easel down the inner corridor of the palais in front of Audric, careful to match his erratic, slow pace, while Marlon and Seaton supported him at either side. He'd had a bad day; it was a misty and cool day, and he allowed himself to cough even as he heard his great-mam's voice comforting him.

"You can allow it, this once," she told him. *"This once, your weakness will be our strength. But after this, you must be stronger. You will be stronger."*

"I will, Great-Matarh," he said. "I will be strong after today, and the sickness will leave me." From the periphery of his vision, he saw Marlon look at him strangely, though the man said nothing.

Seaton gestured to the hall servants, who opened the door to the hall and bowed as Audric and his great-matarh entered. Inside, the Council members rose from their seats before the Sun Throne and also bowed, though their bows were but the barest lowering of heads. Audric could see Si-gourney ca'Ludovici's eyes as she inclined her head, though her gaze seemed to be more on the painting of Marguerite than on him. He went to the Sun Throne, Marlon helping him up the set of three stairs to the platform on which it sat, and let himself drop into the cushioned seat. He coughed then—he could not stop the paroxysm—as light flared deep inside the crystal and surrounded him in a bath of yellow: as the Throne had done for long generations whenever a Kralji had sat there. He wiped his mouth with the sleeve of his silken bashta as the Council stood before him and

Seaton wheeled the easel to the right side of the throne, so that Marguerite glared balefully out at the seven ca'.

"Look at them," she said to Audric. *"Look how hungrily they stare at the Sun Throne. They're all wondering how they might come to sit where you are. Start by being firm with them, Audric. Show them that you are in charge of this meeting, not them. Then . . . then do as you must."*

"I will," he told her. The ca' were already starting to seat themselves, and he raised his voice, addressing them. "There's no need to take your seats," he told the ca'. "Our business here should take but a few grains of the glass."

Caught in mid-movement, the ca' straightened again with a rustling of bashta and tashta, and gazes in his direction that ranged from questioning to nearly angry. "Forgive me, Kraljiki," Sigourney ca'Ludovici said, "but things may not be as straightforward as you think."

"But they are, Vajica ca'Ludovici," Audric told her. "The traitor ca'Rudka is in the Bastida; the Council has had the time you asked for to consult with each other and deliberate. Will you name another Regent, or will you allow me to rule as Kraljiki as I should? Those are the only two options before you, and you should have made a decision." The long speech cost him, as he knew it would. He bent over coughing even as his great-matarh laughed softly in his head, covering his mouth with a kerchief that was quickly stained with red blotches. He crumpled the linen in his hand, but not so much that they could not see the blood.

He opened his eyes to see ca'Ludovici staring at his hand. Her gaze lifted abruptly, and she smiled the smile of a cat spying a cornered mouse, glancing back once at the other Council members. "Perhaps you're right, Kraljiki. After all, the day is damp and we shouldn't keep you away from the comfort of your chambers."

She took a breath, and Audric heard Marguerite whisper to him in that space. *"Now. Tell her what she wants to hear."*

"I am stronger now than I have been in years," Audric said, but he forced himself to cough again, to pause as if for breath between the words. It did not require much acting. "But I also am aware of my youth and inexperience, and I would look to the Council of Ca' for their advice, and perhaps to you especially, Councillor ca'Ludovici, as my mentor."

She bowed at that, and there was no mistaking the satisfaction in her face. "You are indeed wise past your years, Kraljiki, which means that it gives me pleasure to tell you that we have deliberated, all of us, and have come to agreement. Kraljiki Audric, despite your youth, the Council of Ca' will not name a new Regent."

He heard his great-matarh laugh with the word, exulting, and he nearly laughed himself, but did not because it would bring on the coughing again. He contented himself with a silent wave of appreciation to them. *So easy to manipulate. So predictable.* He didn't know whose thought it was: his or Marguerite's.

"I thank the Council for their efforts," Audric said. "And we see a new era for Nessantico, one where we will regain all that we have lost, and reach beyond even Kraljica Marguerite's dreams." He had to pause, to breathe and clear his lungs again. Marlon stretched his hand toward the throne to give him a new handkerchief and to take away the stained and soiled one. "As for the former Regent ca'Rudka, I think it is time that he confessed his sins, made his peace with Cénzi, and paid for the errors of his life."

Vajica ca'Ludovici bowed once more, but not before Audric again saw the satisfaction in the twisting of her features. *Yes, she sees ca'Rudka as her rival, dangerous as long as he remains alive . . .* "It will be done as the Kraljiki wishes," she said. "I will see to it myself."

Karl ca'Vliomani

THE NEWS SPREAD QUICKLY through the city, and as the Ambassador of Paeti, Karl was among the first to hear it: the Council of Ca' had declared that the Kraljiki had reached his majority and that the Regency of ca'Rudka was at an end. Karl heard it with a sinking despair, knowing what it heralded, and he immediately called for a carriage and had the driver rush across the Pontica Kralji into Oldtown.

He hoped he was not already too late. Had he been a religious man, he would have prayed. As it was, he fondled the shell necklace around his neck as if it were a talisman, as if it could ward off the storm clouds he saw in his future.

Audric, assuming the boy managed to survive, would now be a pawn of Sigourney ca'Ludovici and the Council of Ca'. Ana and Sergei had been the buffers for the Numetodo against the conservative elements within the Faith and within society. It was only those two who had allowed the Numetodo to flourish. Now, far too quickly, they were both gone.

There will be Numetodo bodies gibbeted and displayed on the Ponticas again. He could see them in his mind, and he could see his own face on one of the bodies. He hoped it was only fear that gave him that vision, and not some portent.

There are no gods. There are no portents. The rational thought did nothing to ease his mind. He wasn't feeling rational; he was feeling afraid.

Mika and Varina had agreed to meet him in his usual Oldtown tavern. Even here, where the patrons knew him and greeted him by name, Karl could imagine dark stares from those in the booths or at the tables. He no longer knew who he could count on, except these two. Varina sat next to him in the corner booth, her body a welcome warmth along his side, Mika across the booth's table.

Friends. He hoped they would remain so, after this. "You're the A'Morce of the Numetodo here," he told Mika, his voice hurried, pitched low so that none of the bar's denizens could hear him. The musician in the corner, playing a five-stringed luth and singing ballads that had been old when his great-vatarh taught them to him, helped cover their conversation. "I don't ask you to be involved, but I've made a promise to ca'Rudka and I intend to keep it. I need to warn you so you can . . . make arrangements."

Mika shrugged, though the drawn look of his features told Karl that the man was more worried than he was going to admit. Mika reached for the ale in front of him and drank a long gulp, wiping the foam from the ends of his mustache. "If Audric or the Council is willing to kill ca'Rudka, then they'll be looking at the Numetodo next as additional scapegoats, whether you do anything or not, Karl. The blame for everything will fall on us, as it always has."

"You have family here. I know. I'm sorry."

"Sali's been through this before," Mika said. "She'll understand. I'll send her and the children off to family in Il Trebbio."

"What about the boy Nico?" Varina asked. "What do we do with him?"

"We've heard nothing from Talis or his matarh?" Karl asked, and Varina shook her head in answer. "Then keep him with you for now, if you're willing. If things get too dangerous, just let him go—I've no interest in having the child hurt because he's associated with us." Karl gave a long sigh. His own ale sat untouched on the table, and he stared at the bubbles frothing against the wooden mug. *Thousands of bubbles, all rising for a time, then bursting and gone. Like me. Like all of us. Too quickly gone, and nothing afterward. Nothing . . .*

"I'll go with you tonight, Karl, after I've sent Sali and the children on their way," Mika told him. "You'll need help with this."

Karl shook his head. "That's not necessary."

"If ca'Rudka is snatched from the Bastida by magic, then we all know who's going to be blamed and who's going to be hunted," Mika said. "For once, they'll be right in blaming the Numetodo, eh? But the response we get won't change whether you go alone or with a dozen of us, or whether you succeed or fail: just the attempt will be enough."

"I'm not going to risk the lives of a dozen of us. I'm going to take two," he said. "Myself, and one other."

Mika grinned. "So I might as well make certain that you succeed—as long as ca'Rudka's alive, there's a chance he may find his way back to power, and that would be best for us."

"I'm stronger than either one of you with the Scáth Cumhacht," Varina interjected. "I'm going with you also."

With that declaration, the knot in Karl's stomach tightened. He imagined Varina dead, or worse, captured. The pain of that thought made him grimace, made his head shake. "There's no need. You have Nico to watch."

Her lips tightened. She tapped the booth's table with her fingernails. "Mika," she said, "I think we need another round here. Would you mind getting it?"

Mika blinked, puzzled. "Just call Mara over and—" He stopped, then his eyes widened slightly. "Oh," he said, his lips pursing. "Certainly. I'll go get it."

He had barely left the booth when Varina turned in the bench seat to face Karl. Her voice was low and dangerous. "Karl, I have spent years—*years*—doing the research and experiments to expand the catalog of spell formulae we now use regularly. I have thrown myself into understanding the Westlander magic and how it might work and how we might harness their ways. I have given up ..." She stopped, biting her lower lip momentarily. "I have given up the life I might have had for the Numetodo and a cause I thought we shared. And now you're going to relegate me to a babysitter? If you do that, Karl, you will be telling me that I've wasted all that time and all that effort and all those years. Is that what you're telling me? Is it?"

Her accusation sliced into him like a honed dagger. He lifted his hands from the table as if wounded. "You don't understand—" he started to say.

"What don't I understand?" she shot back. "That you don't think I'm of any use to you? That I don't ... don't care enough for you to want to help?"

"No." He shook his head helplessly. "Varina, our odds aren't good here."

"And they're better without me?"

Karl sighed. "No. That's not what I'm saying. I don't want you hurt."

"You're willing to let Mika take his chances, though? Why, Karl? Why is it different for me? Why?" The questions were hammer blows, and he thought there was a strange urgency to her questions, as if there were an answer she wanted him to give.

But he had no answers. He ducked his head, staring down at his mug, at the bubbles expiring on its rim, at the water ringing the bottom and staining the wood. "If you want to go with me, Varina," he said, "then I will be glad for your help," he told her. He lifted his head. She was staring at him with a fragile defiance. "Thank you."

Her mouth opened slightly, as if she were going to say more. Then she nodded.

Mika came back with more ale. He placed the mugs on the center of the table. "Settled?" he asked.

"Yes," Karl answered. "Settled. If this is what you both truly want, then let's finish our drinks so we can go to our rooms and prepare the spells we'll need this evening. Mika, if you'd make sure that word gets passed along that all Numetodo should leave the city or plan to make themselves very scarce for the foreseeable future . . ." He picked up his mug finally, and Mika and Varina lifted theirs. They touched them together. "To luck," he said. "We'll need it."

They drained their mugs as one.

~

Varina ci'Pallo

"**Y**OU LOOK AWFUL TIRED, Varina," Nico said.

She was. She was exhausted, so tired that her bones ached. The afternoon had been spent preparing spells, shaping the Scáth Cumhacht until the spell was complete, then placing the trigger word and gesture to release it in her mind. The spell-weariness dragged at her—it was worse now than it had been when she was younger, worse since she'd begun experimenting with the Tehuantin method. She'd gone to the small room where they kept Nico to bring him his supper and check on him.

"I'll be fine in a few turns," she told Nico. "I just have to go to sleep for a bit so I can recover."

"Talis was always tired, too, when he did magic things, especially with that bowl. I thought it made him look old, too. Like you."

The brutal honesty of a child. Varina touched her gray-ing hair, the deep wrinkles that had carved themselves into her face in the last few years. "We pay for magic this way," she told Nico. "Nothing ever comes to you in this world without cost. You'll learn that." She smiled wryly. "Sorry. That sounds like something a parent would say."

Nico smiled: hesitantly, almost shyly. "Matarh talks like that to me sometimes," he told her. "Like she's talking more to herself than me. I'll try to remember it, though."

Varina laughed. She sat on the chair alongside his bed, leaning forward to tousle his hair. Nico frowned, sliding back a little on the bed. "Nico," Varina said, drawing her hand back, "I have to talk to you. Things are happening, outside. Bad things. After I rest a little, I have to go do something, and when I get back, we're going to have to leave the city, very quickly."

"Like I had to with Matarh?" He drew his doubled legs up to his chest as he sat on the bed, wrapping his hands around them. He looked at her over his knees.

"Yes, like that."

"Are you in trouble?"

She had to smile at that. "I'm about to be."

He sniffed. "Is it because of that man?"

"Karl, you mean? You might say that."

He released his legs and glanced at the food on the tray but didn't touch it. "Are you and Karl . . . ?"

She understood what he was asking without the word. "No. What would make you think that?"

"You act like you are. When the two of you talk to each other, you remind me of Matarh and Talis."

"Well, we're not . . . together. Not that way."

"He likes you, I can tell."

That made her smile, but the taste of it was bitter. "Oh, you can, can you? When did you become so wise in the way of adults?"

Nico shrugged. "I can tell," he said again.

"Let's not talk about this," she said, though she wanted to. She wondered what Karl would say to Nico if Nico told him the same thing. "I need you to eat, and I need you to get some sleep because very likely we'll be leaving the city tonight. You need to be ready for that."

"Will you take me to my matarh?"

"I wish I could, Nico. I really do. But I don't know where we'll be going, yet. I'll take you somewhere safe. That much I promise you. I won't let anything bad happen to you, and we'll try to get you back to your matarh. Do you understand me?"

He nodded.

"Good. Then eat your supper, and try to sleep. I'm going to rest myself, in the next room. If you need me, you can call me. Go on now, you should try that soup before it gets cold."

She watched him for a few minutes as he ate, until she felt her eyelids growing heavy. When she woke up, she discovered she'd fallen asleep in the chair next to his bed, and Nico was asleep himself, curled up near to her with one hand stretched out to touch her leg. Outside, she could hear rain pattering against the roof and the shutters of the house.

She brought the covers up over Nico and pressed her lips to his cheek. She left him then, closing and locking the door behind her.

She hoped she would see him again.

~

The White Stone

NESSANTICO...
    She had never seen the city before, though of course she'd heard much about it. Even with the Holdings sundered, even with the previous Kraljiki having been a pale shadow of his famous matarh, and even with the current Kraljiki a frail boy who—rumors said—wouldn't live to his majority, Nessantico retained her allure.

The White Stone had always known she would eventually come here, as anyone with ambition must. The pull of the city was irresistible, and for a person in her line of business, Nessantico was a rich and fertile field to be exploited. But she had not expected to come here so quickly or for these reasons.

After the nearly-botched and hasty assassination of the Hïrzg, she had thought it too dangerous to stay in the Coalition. She'd slipped back into her beggar role as Elzbet, hiding herself among the poor who were so often invisible to the ca'-and-cu', and she'd made her way from Brezno to Montbataille in the eastern mountains that formed the border of Nessantico and Firenzcia, and then down the River A'Sele to the great city itself.

Playing her role, she settled herself in Oldtown. That was the best way to avoid drawing attention to herself. She was just another of the nameless poor walking the streets of the known world's greatest city, and if she conversed with the voices in her head as she walked, no one would particularly notice or care. Just another crazed soul, a madwoman babbling and muttering to herself, walking in some interior world at odds with the reality around her.

"You'll pay for this. You can't kill me *and not pay. They'll find you. They'll track you down and kill you."*

"Who?" she asked Fynn's strident voice as the others inside her laughed and jeered at him. She put her hand to her tashta, feeling underneath the cloth the small leather pouch tied around her neck, and inside it the smooth, pale stone she kept with her always. "Who will come find me? I told you who hired me. Is *she* going to search for me?"

"You're worried that someone else will figure it out. You're worried that word will get out that the White Stone was also the woman who was Jan ca'Vörl's lover. They've seen your face; they would recognize you, and the White Stone's face can't be known."

"Shut up!" she nearly screamed at him, and the screech caused heads to turn toward her. A passing utilino stopped in the midst of his rounds, his téni-lit lantern swinging over to focus on her. She shielded her eyes from the light, stooping over and grinning at the man with what she hoped was a mad leer. The utilino uttered a sound of disgust and the light moved away from her; the other people had already looked away, turning back to their own business.

The voices of her victims were laughing and chuckling and chortling as she turned the corner into Oldtown Center. The famous téni-lamps of Nessantico gleamed and twinkled on the iron posts set around the open plaza. She gazed up at the placards of the shops along the street. Here in the large plaza the shops were still open, though most of those along the side streets had been shuttered since full dark: the téni might light the lamps of Oldtown Center, but they didn't come to the narrow and ancient streets that led off the Center. They'd set the ring of the Avi A'Parete ablaze all around the city, so that Nessantico seemed to wear a collar of yellow brilliance, and they would illuminate the wide streets of the South Bank where most of the ca'-and-cu' lived, but Oldtown was left to dwell in night.

The moon had slid behind a cloud, and a drizzle threatened to turn into a hard rain. She hurried along toward the Center, knowing that the weather would send everyone home and set the shopkeepers to shuttering their stores.

There: she saw the mortar and pestle of an apothecary just down the lane, and she shuffled toward it through the rapidly-thinning crowds, keeping her back near the bricks and stones of the buildings and her head down. Once, a passing man touched her arm: a graybeard, who leered at her with missing teeth and breath that smelled of beer and cheese. "I have money," he said to her without prelude, his face slick with rain. "Come with me."

Whore! the voices called out at her gleefully, mocking. *Why not?—you let them pay you for other services.* She glared at him, and showed him the hilt of the knife at her waist. "I'm not a whore," she told him, told them. Her hand grasped the knife, and raindrops scattered from her cloak with the motion. "Back away."

The man laughed, gap-toothed, and spread his hands. "As you wish, Vajica. No harm, eh?" Then his gaze slid away from her and he walked on, splashing in the gathering puddles. She watched him go.

She could rid herself of him, but not of the others. They were with her always.

She'd reached the apothecary and glanced inside the open shutters. There was no one inside except for the balding proprietor. She went inside, the man glancing up from his jars and vials behind the counter as the bell on the door jingled brightly.

"Good evening to you. A foul night—I was just about to close up. How can I help you, Vajica?" His words were pleasant, but the tone of them and the look he gave her were less inviting. He seemed torn between coming from behind the counter and returning to his interrupted preparations to close. "A potion for headaches? Something to ease a cough?"

The White Stone would have been firm, would have been certain, but she wasn't the White Stone now, only an unranked, nondescript young woman dripping on the floor, a person who could be mistaken for a common prostitute walking the streets or trying to escape the weather for a moment.

Is this what you really want? She wasn't sure who asked the question, or whether it was her own self who asked. The voices had been quiet when she'd been with Jan. Somehow, being with him had quieted the turmoil inside her head, and that had been at least part of the attraction he'd had for her, had been why she'd let herself grow far more attached than she should have. With Jan, for that little time, she'd felt herself healing. She'd thought that maybe she could become someone other than the White Stone, could become normal. *Jan . . .* She wondered what he was thinking now, whether he was feeling that he'd been played the fool, or if he ever thought of her with regret. She wondered whether he knew who she'd been, that she'd killed his uncle, or if he thought she'd fled only because she pretended to be someone she wasn't and had been found out.

"Vajica?"

She wondered if he would ever know just how much she regretted it all.

She touched her stomach gently again, as she had more and more recently. She should have had her monthly bleeding even before she'd killed Fynn ca'Vörl. She'd thought perhaps it was the stress that had made it a few days late. But the bleeding hadn't come during her flight; it still hadn't come during the days she'd been in Nessantico, and there was now the strange nausea when she woke and there were stranger feelings inside.

It's all you will have of him. Do you really want to do this?

It might have been her own voice. It might have been all of them.

"Vajica? I don't have all evening. The rain . . ."

She shook her head, blinking. "I'm sorry," she told him. "I . . ." Her hand touched her abdomen again.

He was staring at her, at the motion of her hand on her belly. His chin lifted and fell, and he rubbed a hand over his bald head as if smoothing invisible hair. "I may have what you want, Vajica," he said, and his voice was gentler now. "Young ladies of your age, they come to me sometimes, and like you, they don't quite know what to say. I have a potion that will bring on your bleeding. That's what you need, isn't it? However, I must tell you that it's not easy to make, and therefore not cheap."

She stared at him. She listened. She put her hand to the collar of her soaked tashta and felt the stone in its leather pouch.

The voices were silent.

Silent.

"No," she told him. She backed away, hearing the door jingle as her heel slammed into it. "No. I don't want your potion. I don't want it."

She turned then and fled into the plaza and the harsh assault of the rain, the téni-lights flaring around her and reflecting on the wet streets.

That was when she heard the wind-horns begin to blow alarm, all across the city.

EVASIONS

Karl ca'Vliomani

THE PLAN WAS SIMPLE enough—it had to be. Karl had no army with which to assail the Bastida. He had no compatriots among the gardai to open the gates for him or leave them unguarded or to give him copies of the ornate keys to the donjon. He didn't have the wild, powerful magic Mahri had possessed when Mahri had taken him from the Bastida, to just snatch Sergei away.

He had himself. He had Mika and Varina. He had what Sergei himself had told him.

He had the weather.

The Bastida had originally been designed as a fortress to guard the River A'Sele from invaders coming upriver; it had been turned into a prison late in its life. Portions of its legacy still existed, and no one knew all of its hidden ways, though few knew them better than Sergei ca'Rudka, who had long been in charge of the rambling, dank collection of black stones.

The trio borrowed a small rowboat moored east of the Pontica a'Brezi Nippoli, stepping into it a few turns of the glass after full dark, as the moon and the stars were lost behind the ramparts of scudding sky-towers and a fine mist began to fall. "I'd say thank the gods, if I believed in them." Mika grinned at Karl as he helped Varina in, then Karl. Knee-deep in the river, he pushed them away from the shore. "I'll see you two later," he said.

Karl hoped he was right. He watched Mika splash from the river and run back toward the houses along the South Bank.

Karl and Varina didn't use the oars for fear that the splashing would alert one of the roaming utilino or some curious walkers above them. Instead, they allowed the A'Sele's slow current to take them downstream. They were dressed in dark clothing, their faces obscured with soot and ash though the rain quickly washed them clean. As soon as they passed the Pontica a'Brezi Veste and the grim, cheerless towers of the Bastida, they glimpsed wavering candlelight high up in the tower where ca'Rudka was kept—the sign that he was still there.

Karl steered the boat quietly to the shore. He and Varina stepped out into the muck and wet, ignoring the smell of dead fish and foul water, and slipped quickly into the shadow of the Bastida.

Karl found the door where Sergei had said it would be: where the grassy mound of the river wall—which Kraljica Maria IV had ordered built a century and a half ago to keep the A'Sele's annual spring floods from inundating the South Bank—met the flanks of the Bastida's western tower. The door was covered by sod where the flood bank swept over the stony feet of the Bastida, but the sod was but a few fingers' thickness, the barest covering, and Karl's hands quickly found the iron ring underneath. He tugged on it, carefully. The door yielded grudgingly, rain-clotted dirt falling away from it, but the sound of protesting hinges was largely covered by the hiss of rain on the river. Karl held the door open as Varina slipped inside, then he stepped inside himself, letting the door close behind him.

He heard Varina speak a spell-word, and light bloomed inside the hooded lantern they'd brought: the cold yellow light of the Scáth Cumhacht. The glare seemed impossibly bright in the blackness. Karl could see moss-slick stones and broken flags, the walls festooned with strange fungal growths and decorated with curtains of tattered spiderwebs. The brown, sinister shapes of rats slid away from the light, squeaking in protest.

"Lovely," Varina muttered, the whisper seeming to echo impossibly loudly. She kicked at a rat that scuttled too close to her feet, and it chattered angrily before fleeing.

"Better rats than gardai," Karl told her. "Come on— Sergei said this should lead into the base of the main tower. Keep that lantern well-hooded, just in case."

The walk through the abandoned corridor seemed to take a full turn of the glass, though Karl knew it couldn't have been more than a few hundred strides. The air was chill, and Karl shivered in his soaked clothing. They came to another door, this one obviously long-shut, and Karl put a single finger to his lips: beyond here, Sergei had said, they would be in the lowest levels of the Bastida, where there might be guards or prisoners locked in half-forgotten cells. Varina took a jar of cooking grease from her tashta; opening it, she slathered the foul stuff on the hinges of the door and around the edges. Then, stepping away, she pulled tentatively on the door's handle; it didn't move. She pulled harder. Nothing. She braced her foot on the wall. The door rattled once in its frame but otherwise there was no response. *Locked*—Varina mouthed the word.

Varina placed her right eye to the keyhole, peering through. She shook her head, then hunkered next to the doorframe. She spoke a single spell-word, gesturing with her hands at the same time: wood shivered into sawdust around the keyhole, the work of a thousand wood-ants performed in an instant, and the metal mechanism slipped down in the ragged, new hole with a dull *plonk*. Varina caught the bolt and wriggled it slowly and carefully loose, then pulled on the door once more. This time it gave way reluctantly but silently, and they slipped through and onto damp, well-used pavestones, poorly illuminated by torches set in ring sconces at long intervals along the walls—at least a third of them having already guttered out, streaks of black soot staining the low ceilings above them. The corridor reeked of oil and smoke and urine.

Karl pulled the door closed again behind them and studied it quickly. A casual passerby might not notice the spell-bored gouge in the dimness; it would have to do. Silently, he pointed to their right and they began padding quickly along the corridor.

All the passages will lead off to the left. Count two, and take the third. That's what Sergei had told him; now he watched carefully as they hurried. One opening, down which they could hear the sound of someone screaming: a long, thin, and plaintive mewling that didn't sound human—Karl felt Varina shudder alongside him. Two: a brightly-lit passageway, and the sound of distant, rough voices laughing at some private joke and calling out.

Three. Down a short corridor, worn stone steps spiraled upward, and they could hear low voices and the sounds of inhabitation. The tower . . .

Varina's hand grasped his arm; she leaned close to him, her warmth welcome against his side. "We should wait. Mika . . ."

"For all we know, he's already done his part. Or he's been caught himself. Either way . . ."

Her hand loosened on his arm. She nodded. He and Varina slipped down the corridor and began to ascend, as quietly as possible. The stairs, Sergei had told them, wound once around the perimeter of the tower for each floor, with a short landing at each, with a door leading to the cells for that floor. There would be gardai assigned to each floor, changing at Third Call. Already, Karl could glimpse the landing for the ground floor. He could hear two people talking—whether two gardai, or perhaps a garda and one of the prisoners, he didn't know. He started up the stair, hugging the stone wall . . .

. . . which was when they felt the tower shake once, accompanied by a low growl and a brief flash of white light that splashed on the damp surface of the stones. Karl and Varina pressed their backs to the wall as voices called out in alarm. They heard the door to the tower open, felt the touch of night air and smelled the rain. "What in the six pits is going on?" a voice called out into the night. "Was that lightning?"

The response was unintelligible and long. They heard the door close, followed by the grating of a key in a lock mechanism. "What's the ruckus, Dorcas?" someone else called.

"Someone just tried to get in through the main gate—bastard used the Ilmodo. Took down both the doors. They think it might be a Numetodo. The commandant's locked us down; I'm to tell the others. No one in, no one out while cu'Falla investigates and gets some téni here from the temple. Got it?"

A grunt answered, and Karl heard footsteps on the stairs, fading quickly.

Karl nodded to Varina. They moved.

A triangle of yellow flickered on the stones of the landing; he could see a shadow moving in the pool of light. Karl closed his eyes momentarily, feeling the spells he'd prepared earlier coiling in his head. He stepped out: his hands already moving, the release word already on his lips as Varina slipped past him and darted up the steps toward the next landing. "Hey, what—" the garda said, but Karl had already spoken the word, and lightning flared from Karl's hand to slam the garda into the wall behind him. The man went down, unconscious, and Karl hurried forward. He started to follow Varina, but voices called to him from the trio of cells there. "Vajiki! What about us! The keys, man, the keys . . ." Hands reached out from barred windows in stout oaken doors.

He hesitated, and the calls continued, more insistent. "Let us out, Vajiki! You can't leave us here!"

Karl shook his head. Having the prisoners loose would only complicate things, make the situation more chaotic than it already was and possibly more dangerous: not all the prisoners in the Bastida were political, and not all were innocent.

He followed Varina up the stairs to curses and shouts.

Varina had already repeated the process on the second floor. "I'm about exhausted," she told him, visibly sagging against the wall. "I've only one spell left in me; I've been calling the spells up on the fly like a téni."

He nodded; he felt the same exhaustion, and there was little power left in him. "I'll take the next one. We need to have enough left when we get to the Regent." Together, they moved on to the third level, hurrying as quickly as they could. Sergei's cell, they knew, was on the fourth level, though as they approached the third level, they heard voices talking. "The commandant says that we're to bring you to him," someone—the one called Dorcas—was saying.

"He said he would come himself," Karl heard Sergei's voice protesting; the man's voice sounded alarmed.

"The commandant's rather busy at the moment."

"Give me my hands, at least. This stair . . ."

"Nah. The commandant said you were to be manacled . . ."

Karl saw a booted foot appear on the curving stair at nearly head level. He felt the roiling of the last remnants of the Scáth Cumhacht in his head, and spoke the release word even as he stepped out from the wall; just behind him, he heard Varina do the same. Twin lightnings shot out, and the gardai holding ca'Rudka dropped. Sergei stumbled and went down, falling on the stair and nearly knocking over Karl. The second gardai—Dorcas, Karl assumed—remained standing, however; his sword hissed from the sheath, and he thrust at Varina, who clutched her arm and fell back. Sergei kicked at the man's knee; he howled and started to fall; Sergei kicked again, and Dorcas tumbled down the stairs headfirst. He didn't move again, his head bent at a terrible angle.

"I didn't think you were coming," Sergei said.

"I keep my promises," Karl told him. "Now, let's get out of here . . . Varina?"

She shook her head. Karl could see blood welling between the fingers she clutched to her arm, and he tore at his own clothing for a bandage. "I'll slow you down," she said. "Get going. I'll follow as fast as I can."

"I'm not leaving you here." He bound the wound with strips of cloth, tying them off tightly. Her face was pale, and there was more blood than Karl would have liked soaking her tashta. "I've nothing left of the Scáth Cumhacht. You?"

She shook her head. As he knotted the bandages tighter, she grimaced.

Sergei was crouching alongside the garda. Karl heard the rattle of steel against steel and the jingle of keys, and Sergei pulled the manacles from his hand and tossed them on the stair. He took a rapier from one of the gardai.

"Take the one from the other garda," Varina said to Karl. "We might need it."

Karl shook his head. "Let's move," he said. They hurried down the stair, Karl helping Varina. He could feel her sagging, growing heavier in his arms and slower with each flight. The prisoners screamed and shouted as they passed, shaking the bars of their cells, but Karl ignored them. They reached the ground floor, and—more slowly—started down the long curve to the lower level. Karl began to think that they would make it. They were nearly there. Varina shuffling behind him, Sergei ahead, they hurried down the short passage to the main corridor. Two intersections, another turn and a short corridor, and they would be at the door that would lead them to the ancient, unused tunnel and their waiting boat.

"Stay with us, Varina," he said, glancing back at her. "We're almost there."

They managed only a few strides when a group of a half dozen armed gardai rushed into the corridor from the intersection ahead of them. "There! It's the Regent!" one of the garda called, and their leader—the slashes of his office on his uniform—turned. Karl knew the man, though the man was looking more at Sergei than him.

"I'm sorry, Sergei," Commandant cu'Falla said, and then his gaze moved to Karl and Varina. "Ambassador, I'm afraid you and your companion have made a very bad mistake here. I'll see that she gets proper treatment for her wound. Sergei, put down your weapon. It's over."

"I might say the same to you, Aris," Karl said. "After all, you know what a Numetodo can do."

"And if you had spells left to you, you would already have used them," cu'Falla answered. "Or have I missed my guess?"

There was movement in the corridor behind the gardai; a figure in the torchlit dimness. Karl managed to smile. He held his hands wide. He could see some of the garda behind cu'Falla flinch, as if expecting the burst of a spell. "No," he told cu'Falla. "You've not missed your guess. Not for me."

The commandant nodded. "Then I'd suggest we make this easy for all of us," he said.

"I agree," Karl said. He looked past cu'Falla and the gardai, and the commandant started to turn his head. The spell hit them then: the air around the gardai flickered and snarled with lightnings. With cries of surprise and pain, they crumpled to the stone flags, the lightnings still crawling over their bodies, snapping and snarling. Behind them, Mika stood with hands extended. His body sagged as his hands dropped. "Regent," he said. "Pleased to meet you. Now, if you'll all hurry . . ."

Varina half-stumbled forward. She picked up cu'Falla's sword in her good hand and held the point at the commandant's throat. She looked at Karl. "He knows you," she said, blood streaking her cheek where she'd brushed her hands across her pale, drawn face. "He spoke your name."

"No." The response came from Sergei. He moved as if to take Varina's wrist, but she shook her head and pressed the sword forward, dimpling the flesh and drawing a point of red. Sergei looked at Karl. "He's my friend. If you do this, I won't go with you. I'll stay here. You'll have wasted everything."

Varina was staring at Karl, waiting. He shook his head to Varina, and she shrugged, letting the sword drop with a loud clatter to the flags. She swayed, then caught herself. "We're wasting time, then," she said.

Stepping past the prone bodies of the gardai, they ran.

~

Niente

NECALLI HAD BEEN THE TECUHTLI since before
Niente had been born. He knew the names of previous
Tecuhtli, but only because his parents had spoken of them.
It had been Necalli whose name was always roared at the
Solstice ceremonies in the Sun Temples; it was Necalli who
had sent the famous Mahri to the East after his visions had
foretold the rise of the Easterners of the Holdings. It was
Necalli who had responded to their cousins' pleas for help
after the commandant of the Easterners had begun repri-
sals against those who lived beyond the coastal mountains.
It was Necalli who had raised Niente up to become the
new Nahual above all the other spellcasters, many of whom
were older than Niente and were jealous of his quick rise.
It was Necalli who had agreed to allow Niente to use the
deep enchantments of the X'in Ka to snare the Holdings
offizier's mind and send him back to the Easterners' great
city as a weapon.

That spell had cost Niente more than he had anticipated,
wasting his muscles so that he still could not stand for long
without needing to sit again. The effort had drained him
so that the face that looked back at him from the water of
his scrying bowl was lined and drawn like that of a person
years older than him. He had paid the cost, as Mahri had
many times in his days, but Niente would hate to see that
sacrifice wasted.

Now he was wondering what the sacrifice had been for.
*"Strike the head from the beast, and it can no longer hurt
you,"* Necalli had said. It was what Necalli had sent Mahri
to do, but it seemed that the beast had instead consumed
Mahri. Niente worried that this might be his own fate as
well.

Most importantly, it was Necalli who had been the center of the Tehuantin world in the lifetime of most of those
here. Niente could not imagine his world without Tecuhtli

Necalli. All warriors must die, and the Tecuhtli not least among them. Yet Necalli had outlived all the sporadic challenges to his reign. Niente wished he could imagine him outliving this one as well.

But he had little hope.

Niente stood in the crowd lining the flanks of the Amalian Valley's green bowl, the easternmost of the sacred places of Sakal and Axat, his back against one of the carved stone plinths of the ball court and his hands folded over the knob of his spell-staff. He stared down into the shadowed courtyard itself. Below them, Tecuhtli Necalli stood in his armor, a gleaming sword curving sunward from his aged but untrembling sword as he faced Zolin, a High Warrior of the Tehuantin forces and the son of Necalli's dead brother. Tecuhtli Necalli's face was dark with the tattoos of his rank, swirling around the features of his face as an eternal, fierce mask, but he was an old man now, his back bent forward, his hair stringy and white. Zolin, in contrast, was a chiseled, perfect image of a warrior.

The challenge had surprised everyone. Citlali, a High Warrior himself, was standing near Niente, and he snorted at the sight below them, as Necalli and Zolin began to slowly circle each other, as the warriors gathered around the court began to chant rhythmically, pounding the butts of their spears on the stones in time. The sound was like the hammer blows of Sakal when He carved the world from the shell of the Great Turtle. "Necalli goes back to the gods today," Citlali said. "May they be ready to receive the old buzzard."

"Why?" Niente asked. "Why did Zolin challenge his uncle? Tecuhtli Necalli hasn't lost a battle to the Easterners; rather, he's pushed them back toward the Inner Sea. The Garde Civile of the Holdings hasn't penetrated our own borders yet at all. The Tecuhtli might be old, but he's still a master of strategy."

"Zolin says the Tecuhtli has become timid in his dotage," Citlali answered. His own face was swirled with black lines dotted with searing blue circles. "He dances with the Easterners, but he hesitates to destroy them. He's become cautious and too careful. Zolin has no fear. Zolin will sweep the Easterners from our cousins' land entirely. He'll attack rather than merely defend."

"If he wins the challenge," Niente said.

"No one's stronger than Zolin. Certainly not Necalli—look, his muscles sag like an old woman's."

"Must strength always defeat experience?" Niente asked him, and Citlali laughed.

"You're the Nahual," Citlali said. "One day one of your nahualli will come to you and demand challenge, and maybe you'll learn the answer to that yourself. Tell me, Niente, are you afraid that because you were Necalli's Nahual that your status will change when Zolin becomes Tecuhtli?"

Niente had learned long ago that one never showed fear to a High Warrior. The Scarred Ones already considered the nahualli to be little more than a weapon given human form, and they had nothing but contempt for those they considered weak. Niente forced a grin to his face. "Not if Zolin has a brain to go with his strength."

Citlali snorted another laugh. "Oh, he has that," he said. "He learned from Necalli himself. Now it's time for the student to supplant the master, the son to replace his father's brother." Niente could feel Citlali staring carefully at Niente, his gaze sliding up and down his body. "You've been tired lately, and those are new lines on your face. You should be careful yourself, Niente. Necalli has used you badly, as he did Mahri. It's a shame."

Niente gave a careful nod. It was what he'd thought himself, more than once.

The chant and the pounding of the beat abruptly stopped. They could hear the forest birds settling again. The silence nearly hurt Niente's ears. Necalli and Zolin were two strides away from each other, in the center of the court.

Zolin roared. He charged. His sword flashed, but Necalli's sword came up at the same time, and the blades clashed loudly as the warriors shouted approval. For a moment, the two men were locked together, then Zolin pushed Necalli away, and the Tecuhtli retreated.

"You see," Citlali said. "As they are in battle, they are here. Zolin attacks, while Necalli waits."

"And if Necalli finds a flaw in Zolin's attack, or if Zolin is impatient—then it will be Necalli who is still Tecuhtli. There are advantages to waiting."

"We'll see who the gods favor then, won't we?" Citlali grinned. "Care to make a wager, Nahual? Three goats say that Zolin will win."

Niente shook his head; Citlali laughed. Below, Zolin feinted a new charge, and Necalli nearly staggered as he brought up his sword against the anticipated strike. Zolin slid right, then quickly shifted left, his sword carving a bright line in the air. This time Necalli's response was late. Zolin's blade struck Necalli's body where the chest armor tied into the arm plates, slicing through the leather straps there and cutting deep into the shoulder of Necalli's sword arm. Necalli, to his credit, only grimaced as Zolin tore the sword out again, blood flying to spatter both of them. Zolin stalked Necalli as the Tecuhtli staggered backward, his armor dangling as he switched the sword into his left hand. Blood was pouring down Necalli's right arm, dripping from his fingers. Zolin cried aloud again, raising dust from his sandaled feet as he charged once more. Necalli brought his sword up, but the parry was weak, and Zolin's blade continued downward, tearing into the side of Necalli's bared skull and burying itself in the neck below his left ear. Zolin released the blade as Necalli dropped to his knees, his sword clattering onto the ground. For a long moment, Necalli swayed there. His left hand pawed ineffectually at the hilt of Zolin's sword. His eyes were widened as if he were seeing a vision in the air above him; his mouth opened as if he were about to speak, but only blood poured out.

He swayed hard to the right, and fell over. Zolin's roar was matched by the shouts of the thousands watching. Citlali screamed next to Niente. "Tecuhtli Zolin!" he shouted, raising a fist into the air. "Tecuhtli Zolin!"

Below, Zolin wrenched his sword from the body of Necalli. He thrust it high, and the shouting redoubled as he turned, looking up at those watching. His gaze seemed to find each of them, triumphant.

This time, Niente took up the cry, too. "Tecuhtli Zolin!" he shouted, raising his spell-staff toward the sky. But he stared more at the body of Necalli.

~

Nico Morel

NICO WAS CONFUSED and scared by the commotion. Too much was happening too quickly. There'd been the furious knocking at the door, and the man who was watching him had made a strange motion with his hands before they'd heard the Ambassador's voice on the other side. The door was flung open, and several people rushed in—they were half-carrying Varina, whose tashta was soaked with blood. Nico tried to run to her, but someone pushed him back on his crude bed with a snarl. There was lots of shouting and there were too many people in the small room. In the candlelight, everything was a confusion of shadows. He could only catch bits of what they were saying.

"... need Karina; she has the healing talent ..."

"... can't stay ... recognized us ..."

"... tell the others to make themselves scarce ..."

"... Garde Kralji will be out scouring already ..."

"... torture and kill any of us they catch ..."

"... the child has to go ..."

Nico sat on his bed, wanting to cry but afraid that it would draw attention to him when he wanted nothing more than to be invisible. A face came out of the chaos and loomed over him: Karl. "We have to leave Nessantico," he told Nico. "Varina told you that, right? You'll be coming with me, Nico. We can't leave you behind, not with no one to look after you."

"I can stay in my old house," Nico said with a confidence he didn't feel. "Matarh would look for me there, or Talis. And I know the people who live in the other houses. I'll just stay here."

"We left a note for Talis in your rooms, telling him where you were," Karl said. "He didn't come."

"He'll come," Nico insisted. "He will."

The man looked as doubtful as Nico felt inside. "I'm

sorry, Nico," he said. "But we need to go quickly, and you'll need to come with us."

Nico looked over Karl's shoulder toward the tumult in the room beyond. There were several people in the room, and he couldn't see Varina. "Is Varina going to die?" he asked.

"No." The man shook his head emphatically. "She's been hurt, but she's not going to die." Nico nodded. "Nico, you're going to need to be very brave, and very quiet. If we're found, well, Varina *would* die, and me, and maybe you as well. Do you understand?"

He nodded again, though he didn't. He pressed his lips together and swallowed hard. "That's a good young man, then," Karl said, ruffling Nico's hair like Talis sometimes did, and Varina, too. Nico wondered why adults always did that when he didn't like it. He knew that Karl had children and great-children in Paeti—his matarh had once mentioned to Talis that the Ambassador and Archigos Ana were "too close," so maybe those were the children of the Archigos. He imagined what it might have been like, to be a child growing up in the dark, cavernous confines of the temple, with the painted Moitidi fighting on the domes overhead and téni-fire blazing in the huge braziers around the quire.

"Nico! Come here." Karl was gesturing, and Nico went to him.

". . . the city gates will all be closed at any moment," a gray-haired man was saying, and Nico realized with a start that it was the Regent of Nessantico: it must be him, with that nose made of silver shining in the candlelight. Nico stared at it: he'd glimpsed the Regent a few times on the ceremonial days, sitting next to Kraljiki Audric as the royal carriage made its way around the Avi a'Parete. Nico couldn't understand why the Regent would be here, or how there could be danger if he was. Matarh had shivered when she talked about him, telling Nico tales about how the Regent had once been the commandant, and how he had tortured people in the Bastida. The Regent's face seemed more tired than dangerous right now. "Commandant cu'Falla knows the city as well as I do—I taught him—and that's a problem. He knows we need to get out, and he'll have people out looking for us." The Regent tapped his nose. "Some of us are far too recognizable."

"Then we avoid the gates," Karl said. "If we can cross the Avi near Temple Park, well, the old city walls are down there, and if we can get through the north neighborhoods into the open farmland during the night, there's a heavily-forested strip of land there, just about a league farther on in which we could stay during the day. Maybe go on to Azay, and . . ." The Ambassador stopped, shrugging. "Then we do whatever we need to do. Right now, we're wasting time."

"Indeed," the Regent answered. "Can Varina be moved?"

"I can," Nico heard Varina say, though her voice sounded weak and trembling. He saw her then, sitting up in the bed and swinging her feet over the edge. The blood on her clothing was dark and wet-looking. "I'm ready. Just let me change my clothes." She waved a hand at them. "Go on, get out of here. Wait for me outside. I'll be just a mark of the glass."

"Come on, Nico," Karl said, nodding his head toward the door, but Nico shook his head, hugging himself.

"Let him stay," Varina said. "I'll bring him with me. Go on."

"All right," the Ambassador replied, but he looked uncertain. "We'll wait in the antechamber. Hurry."

The men left, and Varina sank back on the bed for a moment, her breath quick and pained. She moaned as she sat up again, groaning as she tried to undo the ties of her tashta. "Nico," she said. "I need your help . . ."

He went over to her and undid the ties, fumbling with the knots and trying not to notice the blood that stained his fingers. She slid the tashta down to her waist, and he looked away quickly, blushing a bit, as she pushed herself one-handed to a standing position. Her breasts under the binding cloth were smaller than Matarh's, and looking at them covered only by thin cloth made Nico feel strange. "There's another tashta in the chest at the foot of the bed," she told him. "A blue one; would you get it for me? That's a good boy."

He rummaged in the chest, the smell of sweet herbs tied in linen sachets filling his nostrils, and handed her the blue tashta. "Turn around a moment," she told him, and when he did he heard her soiled tashta slide entirely to the floor. He heard her pulling up the new tashta awkwardly with her injured arm, and when she cried out in pain, he quickly went to help her, pulling the ribbon binding tight under her breasts, tying the shoulder wraps and the back lacing. "There are bandages in the bottom drawer of the chest," she said. "If you could bring me some . . ."

He hurried to get them for her, rising with the white strips of soft cloth in his hands to see her unwrapping her arm. He gasped as he saw the deep, long, and jagged cut there, still oozing blood and gaping wide, the edges pulling apart even as he watched, so deep that he thought he saw white bone at the bottom. He gulped, feeling nauseous. "I know," she told him. "It looks bad, and I'm going to need to find a healer to sew it up. But right now, I need to tie a new bandage on this to keep it closed. I can't do it one-handed. Can you help me?"

Nico nodded, swallowing hard. As she directed him, he placed a folded pad of the bandages on top of the wound, then—as she pressed the edges together as well as she could—he wrapped the bandage around it. "As tight as you can," she told him. "Don't worry, you won't hurt me." She showed him how to tear the end of the bandage in two, then tie it off to hold it in place.

She was crying as he finished, looking at her hand as she tried to move her fingers. They moved, but slowly, and she couldn't bring her lower arm up. "It'll be better, Varina," he said. "It just needs time to heal."

She smiled at him through the tears and pulled him to her with her good hand. "Thank you," she whispered into his hair. "Now—some water. I want to get the blood off my hands and yours."

A quarter turn of the glass later, they left the room, with Varina walking pale-faced but steady.

It was raining, it was cold, it was dark, and Nico was miserable.

Nico stayed close to Varina as they hurried across the Avi a'Parete under the seeming glare of the famous téni-lamps of the city. The Regent was with Nico, and Varina and Karl; the other Numetodo—the one named Mika—had left them, going another way through the city. Nico had seen a squadron of Garde Kralji hurrying down the Avi toward Nortegate, splashing through the puddles on the cobbled roadway; the Regent made them pause in the shadow of a building—rain dripping hard on them from clogged gutters above—until the gardai had vanished around the curve of the Avi, then he led them at a run into the warren of houses on the north side of the Avi. There, they quickly abandoned the main streets for side streets and alleys, staying away from the few people out in the weather and occasionally sliding into alleyways as they heard others approaching. Once, a trio of utilino passed them, and they pressed their backs to the cold, damp stones of the nearest building, holding their breaths as the utilino, obviously searching the faces of the passersby, moved on. They kept moving north: as the houses were farther apart, now separated by fields and pastures; as the lights of the city became only a glow on the clouds above them; as the cob-bled streets gave way to muddy, rutted roadways and finally to a narrow, sloppy lane. By the time they stopped, Nico felt as if he'd been running all night. His feet and legs hurt, and he was panting from the effort of keeping up with the adults. Varina collapsed to the ground as soon as they stopped.

"We'll rest here for a few minutes," the Regent said. "If anyone's coming, we should see them long before they'll notice us." They were well away from any of the farm-houses, and the rain had subsided to an erratic drizzle. Nico stood next to Varina as she leaned again the stone wall bor-dering the lane and closed her eyes, clutching her injured arm with her good one.

"The forest is a mile or so up the road; we should reach it in half a turn of the glass," the Regent continued. "We should probably get off the road; if I were the comman-dant, I'd be sending riders out along toward all the villages, looking for us."

"Then where?" Karl asked.

The Regent shook water from his graying hair; droplets beaded on his silver nose. "Firenzcia," he grunted.

Karl gave a laugh that seemed more cough. "You're jok-ing, Sergei. That's going from the chopping block into the pot. Firenzcia? Archigos ca'Cellibrecca is nothing more than a younger image of his marriage-vatarh; they'd love to have the Ambassador of the Numetodo to torture and hang in a gibbet for everyone to see. Firenzcia? That might be fine for you, but Varina and I have a better chance of survival trying to swim the Strettosei to Paeti. We might as well just surrender to the Garde Kralji now."

Varina's eyes had opened, and Nico saw that she was watching the discussion. The Regent sniffed. "Firenzcia is the Kralji's enemy. Now, so are we. I know Allesandra from her time here; so do you. With Fynn assassinated, she'll be the Hïrzg; she'll take us in."

"Unless the Numetodo are being conveniently blamed for Hïrzg Fynn's murder," the Ambassador said, and Varina nodded vigorously.

"Where else would you go?" the Regent asked them.

"To one of the northern countries, where they're more sympathetic to the Numetodo. Maybe Il Trebbio."

"That's still in the Holdings, and Audric will have sent word to them to capture us if we're seen."

"And Firenzcia won't do the same?" Varina interjected.

"We could take ship from Chivasso to Paeti, or keep going north out of the Holdings into Boail," the Ambassador said.

"And what are our chances of making that long trek without being noticed?" The Regent sniffed again.

Nico listened to them argue, pulling his cloak tightly around him. He didn't want to go to Firenzcia or Il Trebbio or Paeti or any of those places. He liked Varina and he was sorry that she was hurt, but he wanted to be with his matarh or Talis. The adults weren't paying attention to him; they were too intent on their discussion.

Slowly, Nico pulled himself up until he was sitting on the stone wall. He turned, his legs dangling over the far side. No one noticed him; no one said anything to him. He let himself drop into the high, tall grass of the field. He could still hear them arguing, and he began scurrying quickly away on the far side of the stone wall—back toward Nessantico. Back toward the only home he knew.

When he could barely hear the voices, he started to run: into the night, into the rain, toward the city-glow in the distance.

~

Varina ci'Pallo

"WHERE ELSE WOULD YOU GO?" the Regent said, and she heard Karl scoff.

"To one of the northern countries, where they're more sympathetic to the Numetodo. Maybe Il Trebbio."

Sergei sounded like a teacher instructing a slow student. "That's still in the Holdings, and Audric will have sent word to them to capture us if we're seen."

Varina, half-listening to the argument, stirred. She interrupted them with her eyes half-open. "And Firenzcia won't do the same?" she snapped back at Sergei.

"We could take ship from Chivasso to Paeti, or keep going north out of the Holdings into Boail," Karl added—she was glad to hear him support her.

"And what are our chances of making that long trek without being noticed?" The Regent's voice was nearly mocking.

The argument only sapped what little strength she had left. *Let Karl deal with him—Karl won't go to Firenzcia. He won't.* . . . As the argument continued, her attention returned to the weariness of her body and the throbbing, insistent pain in her arm that stabbed her every time she moved. Varina leaned her head back against the stone wall running alongside the road, not caring that the ground underneath her was soaked and cold, closing her eyes as the two continued their argument, feeling the occasional cold splash from the persistent clouds on her face. The rumble of the two men's voices, wordless, was like distant thunder in her head. She was shivering and miserable.

She wondered whether or not death might actually be an improvement.

She didn't know when she thought to look to her right, back toward where the city's glow painted the low, scudding clouds. At the same moment, she realized that the faint warmth that had been there was gone.

"Nico?" She sat up, stifling the scream that wanted to tear from her throat with the movement. Then, louder: "Nico?"

Karl and Sergei turned from their discussion. "Varina?" Karl began, then he cursed. "*Merde!* The boy's gone." He looked over the stone wall, and Varina—getting slowly to her feet—looked that way also. The meadow grass showed the dark, trampled path from the boy's feet, arrowing back toward the city until she lost the trail in the murk.

"I'll go after him. He can't be far." Varina started to scramble over the low wall in pursuit, grimacing as the motion pulled at her wounded arm. But she felt Karl's hand on her good arm, holding her back.

"No," he said. "You can't. He's heading back into the city and he'll get there before you catch up to him. You can't go there. They're not looking for a boy, but they *are* looking for you."

Varina was frantic. She pulled at Karl's grasp but was too weak to break away from him. Sergei watched, impassive, from the road. "He'll be all alone there. I can't leave him like that. I promised."

"He was alone when you found him. The boy's nothing if not resourceful." Karl pointed with his chin back to the city-glow on the clouds. "He thinks his matarh or Talis will find him if he stays there. He might be right. Let him go, Varina. Let him go. We have other issues to worry about."

Varina sagged. She sat on the stone wall looking at the trail of Nico's retreat. Karl released her arm, and she cradled her wounded limb with it. The rain had begun again; the drizzle masked her tears. "It's my fault," she said. "My fault. I should have been watching him. I promised I'd take him somewhere safe. I promised him—"

"Varina." She turned to Karl. He shook his head. "This is *my* fault," he told her. "You're hurt; you needed the rest. *I* should have been watching him. Not you. It's my fault."

She wished she could believe him. She sniffed. She turned her head away, back to the fading trail. Already, the grass in the meadow was lifting, hiding Nico's retreat.

"Be safe," she whispered after him: into the darkness, into the rain, into the light-touched distant haze. "Please be safe."

~

Audric ca'Dakwi

YOU HAVE EVERY RIGHT to be furious. In truth, you must be furious, so that they will fear you.

He heard his great-matarh's voice, her words sparking in his head, her own anger apparent. He could see the scowl reflected in the painting at his right hand as he sat on the Sun Throne.

I was the Spada Terribile—the Awful Sword—before I was the Généra a'Pace, she raged. *You must follow my path, Audric. You must show them the steel before you can give them the glove of velvet, so that they know the steel is always inside. Hidden.*

"I will," he told her grimly. Then he turned to Commandant cu'Falla, standing with his head down before him, a small bandage around his neck. The Council of Ca' whispered in their seats behind the commandant. "Commandant!" he barked, though the harshness of the word gave him a spate of coughing. He looked up, his lace kerchief bunched in his fist, to see cu'Falla staring at him. "You are informing me that the former Regent ca'Rudka was able to escape the Bastida and my order of execution?" He had to stop for breath. He could hear the echo of his voice against the stones of the hall. *Lower your voice. You sound shrill, like a child. Show them that you're their equal.* "I understand," he said to his great-matarh, then realized that they were all watching him, and he pretended that he'd been starting another sentence. ". . . that the Regent can't be found in Nessantico, and has likely escaped the city entirely?"

"Yes, Kraljiki," the commandant grated out. His jaw clenched, muscles bunching under his beard, his lips tightly pressed together after he uttered his response. He looked as if he were caging the words he wanted to say, and Audric waved a regal hand in the man's direction.

"Go on," he said. "Enlighten us."

"Kraljiki," he said, then glanced back over his shoulder to the others. "Councillors. This was a concerted attack on the Bastida by Numetodo—by how many, we're still not certain. The main gates were torn down with a spell, and I lost two men there when the northern supports fell as a result. I immediately had the tower where the Regent was being held locked down, fearing that what would follow would be a direct assault through the wrecked gates, and I dispatched a rider to the temple to have téni sent to counter the Numetodo spells. But it seems that the assault on the gates was merely a feint to draw our attention. When no attack materialized, I personally took gardai to the under-corridors of the Bastida, but Ambassador ca'Vliomani and his cohorts had already made their entrance—probably well before the attack on the gate."

"You're certain the man you saw was Ambassador ca'Vliomani?" Audric asked.

Cu'Falla nodded. "Absolutely, Kraljiki. When it was obvious that there was to be no assault on the gates, I took a squad to the under-corridors, as I said. We confronted Ambassador ca'Vliomani and the Numetodo Varina ci'Pallo with the prisoner; there was at least one other Numetodo in the corridors. They used their spells on us." He swallowed hard. "My men and I were incapacitated."

Audric raised his eyebrows. "Incapacitated," he said, rolling the word around as if tasting it. "But not killed, though I understand that you were ... wounded. A scratch on the neck? No worse than the nick of a razor? How fortunate for us all."

There was laughter from the councillors, with Sigourney ca'Ludovici's snicker prominent among them. Cu'Falla's face visibly reddened.

"Kraljiki, Councillors, I have known Sergei ca'Rudka since I joined the Garde," he said. "He was my commanding offizier and my mentor. He promoted me through the ranks; he—through your vatarh, Kraljiki—assigned me my current post as Commandant of the Garde Kralji. I considered him my friend as well as my superior. I assume that his friendship is why I and my men are still alive, Kraljiki."

Audric didn't need his great-matarh's cackling to propel him from his seat at that. He pointed an accusing finger at the commandant. "Your friendship and your relationship with him is why ca'Rudka was allowed to escape *at all*," he roared shrilly, forcing the cough down. "How *convenient* that you are rendered unconscious just at the right moment. How *convenient* that the Numetodo knew about this hidden passage from the river. How *convenient . . .*" He couldn't go on. The coughing overwhelmed him then, and he huddled on the Sun Throne with the lace cloth to his face as his body was racked. He barely heard the commandant's litany of denials.

"My duty is to the Kraljiki and Nessantico," cu'Falla insisted. "That supersedes any friendship I might have with the Regent. I assure you, Kraljiki, that I did exactly as you ordered. I assure you that I would have carried out your order to execute the Regent, had you decided that was to be his fate. Several of my men were injured or killed in the assault; I would never, *never* have allowed that to happen. I would not abandon my duty and my oaths of service for the sake of friendship. Never."

Audric was still regaining his breath, wiping his lips on the lace. Marlon, kneeling and leaning forward on the steps of the throne's dais, held out a new kerchief; Audric took it and gave the servant the stained one. It was Sigourney ca'Ludovici who answered cu'Falla, and Audric listened as he coughed softly into the fresh cloth. "Those are fine, honorable words, Commandant, but . . ." She glanced portentously around the hall. "Why, I see neither the Regent nor Ambassador ca'Vliomani in irons before us, and from what we're told, all the known Numetodo in the city have fled, too. As the Kraljiki has said, how *convenient* that they had the time and opportunity to do so."

"Councillor ca'Ludovici," cu'Falla said, "I must take offense at these accusations. As soon as I regained consciousness, I sent out the Garde Kralji to guard the gates and scour the city; I contacted Archigos Kenne and had him alert the utilino on their rounds; I sent word to the Keeper of the Gates and had all the inns and hostels searched. You can verify all those orders with my offiziers."

"But your *friend* ca'Rudka and his cohorts managed to escape this fine, wonderful net you placed around the city," ca'Ludovici answered. "How clever of him." Again laughter followed from the other councillors.

Audric had regained his composure. He folded the

blood-spotted lace in his hand. Cu'Falla's face was now even redder than before and Audric raised his hand to stop the commandant's protests. "I hereby decree that Sergei ca'Rudka no longer has rank at all in the Holdings. Let the Gardes a'Liste write his name simply as Sergei Rudka henceforth. The same for Ambassador ca'Vliomani—he is stripped of his diplomatic status and is now only Karl Vliomani, with no standing here. When they are found, the penalty for them will be immediate death."

He heard the murmur of pleasure from his great-matarh, and the susurration of agreement from the Council of Ca'. "As for you, Commandant cu'Falla," he said, and cu'Falla straightened his shoulders, seeming to stare past Audric. "There must also be judgment."

"Kraljiki," cu'Falla said, his chin high, his eyes guarded, "I have family here, and I have given faithful service to the Sun Throne since my sixteenth season. I ask you to consider that."

"We do," Audric told him. "We also consider that you have failed your oath and failed your Kraljiki." *Show them. Show them that you, too, can be the Spada Terrible. Show them your strength and your will.* Audric pushed himself up from the Sun Throne, tucking the lace kerchief into the sleeve of his bashta of blue and gold. He walked the few steps to stand in front of cu'Falla, feeling the approving gaze of Marguerite on his back. His head came only to cu'Falla's chest; he had to lift his head to see the man's face, and that made him angry. "We demand the sword of your office, Commandant." He held out his hand.

Cu'Falla's expression went stern and empty. He unbuckled the belt of his scabbard, the metal clasps jingling musically. He placed the weapon into Audric's outstretched hand. Audric thought he saw a glimpse of satisfaction in the man's face as the unexpected weight of the steel nearly made Audric drop the sword, his hand drooping low and the leather belt of the scabbard looping on the marble flags of the hall. Audric half-turned from the man, sliding the blade from the scabbard. The steel rang: it was a warrior's weapon, not the polished, engraved, and bejeweled showpieces most of the Council of Ca' bore. Audric held up the blade admiringly, gazing at the fine scratches where the edges had been recently honed, at the sheen of protective oil on the surface. A warrior's blade. A blade that spoke of much use, and much death.

Audric smiled.

Without warning, he brought the blade horizontal and spun quickly on the balls of his feet, thrusting the honed, triangular point of the sword deep into cu'Falla's stomach, grunting at the unexpected resistance of cloth and muscle. Cu'Falla sucked in a gasping breath, his eyes wide and mouth open. His hands went around the blade as Audric continued to push with all his strength, burying the sword deep in the man's gut; as blood spread quickly and flowed down the central gutter toward the hilt that Audric held; as cu'Falla took a second, rattling breath and blood began to flow from his open mouth; as the man's knees buckled and he fell, tearing the sword from Audric's grasp; as Audric heard the councillors rise as one from their seats in horror.

As his great-matarh laughed inside his head.

That was well done, she told him. *Well done indeed!*

Audric walked over to the writhing body and looked down into the dying man's eyes. "Now we don't have to worry about your incompetence at all," he told the man. He coughed violently from his exertions, but he didn't care about the fine red droplets that spattered the man's face and chest. Cu'Falla blinked up at him, staring. Audric wrenched the blade from cu'Falla's stomach. He placed the tip over the man's chest, feeling the tip slide between his ribs. "And we grant you one last favor: a quick death." He put all his weight behind the hilt and pushed. More blood gushed from cu'Falla's mouth, and the man went still.

Excellent! You are indeed my true heir, so much stronger than your vatarh....

Audric turned to the Council of Ca' and spread his bloodied hands wide. Sigourney ca'Ludovici's face had gone pale and she stared more at cu'Falla's corpse than at Audric.

"It seems we have need of a new commandant," he told them.

Allesandra ca'Vörl

"THIS ISN'T WHAT I WANTED, Matarh. Fynn is supposed to be the Hïrzg, and if not him, then you. Not *me*."

She brushed imaginary lint from the shoulders of the gilt-adorned bashta he wore, with the sash of the Hïrzg's office draped over the black-and-silver cloth. She touched his cheek and smiled up at him. He had been taller than her for the last two years; he would be taller yet. In that, he took after his vatarh. "It's best this way," she told him. "Firenzcia will have a strong Hïrzg for decades to come, which is what it will need."

"I don't understand." He stared at her, his head slightly cocked. "Why did you do this? Why did you turn down being Hïrzgin? All those stories about how Great-Vatarh took that from you, how he shunned you in favor of Onczio Fynn . . ."

"I didn't want it," she told him, and saw the disbelief in his face—he had always been a child in whose face you could see his thoughts. *I'll have to work with him on that. It's something he'll need to learn.* She smiled at him now, touching his cheek. "It's true, darling. Really. Now, come on; the ca'-and-cu' have come to meet their new Hïrzg, and we can't keep them waiting."

She nodded to Commandant Helmad cu'Göttering of the Garde Hïrzg, waiting patiently a stride and half from them in his dress uniform. The man saluted and raised his hand. In turn, Roderigo—who had become Jan's aide—gestured to the servants, who scurried to their posts. A flourish of cornets rose in the cool evening air as attendants opened the double doors leading to the main hall. Jan paused, not moving; she motioned to him. "You first," she said. "You're the one they want to see."

As Jan entered, applause rose and swelled, intermingled with cheers and calls of "Huzzah, Hïrzg Jan!" He stood in the doorway as if pinned in place by the accolades, his arms lifting slowly, almost regretfully, to accept them. "Go on," she whispered to him as he continued to stand there. "Go on down to them."

He glanced back over his shoulder to her. "With you, Matarh," he said, offering her his arm. She came forward to take it, smiling as she did so. The applause swelled and enveloped them.

She looked over the bright crowd. Black and silver predominated, as it did in all Firenzcian celebrations, echoing the colors of the banners hung high along the walls. Teni-lights gleamed brightly in the chandeliers, illuminating the ca'-and-cu' of Brezno, all of them gazing toward the two of them. Their faces were snared in smiles, some of them genuine, but many overlaying concern and uncertainty and mistrust. No one could miss the number of Garde Hïrzg stationed around the sides of the hall and strolling carefully through the crowd, their gazes solemn and diligent, nor Commandant cu'Göttering entering the hall directly behind Jan and Allesandra, or Starkkapitän ca'Damont's dominating presence as well as many of his chevarittai offiziers. Firenzcia had now lost two Hïrzgs in less than a year, and the A'Hïrzg they knew had given the staff and sword to her son, whom they knew little despite his recent prominence. It was obvious that Firenzcia planned to have no more losses.

Firenzcia was used to change: in the lifetimes of many of those applauding Allesandra and Jan's entrance, they'd experienced a great battle lost to Nessantico; they'd seen Allesandra herself held as hostage; they'd watched her revered vatarh abandon her in favor of her younger brother; they'd trembled as the old Hïrzg Jan had seceded from the Holdings to create the Coalition; they'd witnessed the sundering of the Concénzia Faith as well, with Archigos ca'Cellibrecca defying the old seat in Nessantico and the ascension of Archigos Ana; they'd cheered as the Coalition grew stronger with each passing year, as it seemed that the Coalition might one day even eclipse the Holdings.

In their lives, Firenzcia had gone from a servant of the Holdings to its greatest rival. Brezno's light now rivaled that of Nessantico herself.

They felt optimistic about Firenzcia and about the

Breznoian branch of the Faith, but this year had shattered much of that optimism. Allesandra knew that they cheered now more for the hope that the new Hïrzg Jan represented than for Jan himself.

If they knew what she planned . . . She wondered what their faces would look like then, and if they'd even be able to conjure up smiles at all.

Semini was among the forefront of the throng, his green-clad téni staff around him. Allesandra held onto Jan's hand as they descended the steps. As the crowd began to close around Jan, many of them parents with their young, unmarried daughters prominently in tow, she pressed his arm. "Be polite to your subjects," she whispered to him. "You never know which one of them you might need as an ally—or a wife."

"Where are you going, Matarh?" he whispered back, and she could hear the apprehension in his voice.

"Don't worry; I'll be here and I'll rescue you if I see something amiss. I need to talk with Archigos ca'Cellibrecca." She nodded to the ca'-and-cu' as they gathered around Jan and slipped through the crowd, greeting those she passed. The music had begun again, but most of those in the hall ignored the call of the dance to have their moment with the new Hïrzg. "Archigos," she said as she came to Semini, standing to one side of the crowd. His o'téni attendants, smiling and giving Allesandra the sign of Cénzi, moved aside to let her approach, and carefully returned to their own coversations.

He nodded to her, giving her the sign of Cénzi then holding out his hands to her. She took them, pressing her fingers to his for a moment before releasing him. They'd not had an opportunity to be together since their meeting at Stag Fall, over a month ago now, but there had been letters and the carefully phrased messages. She knew how she wanted this evening to end: the arrangements had already been made—Semini would come to her rooms after the reception. She smiled. "So good to see you again, Archigos. Where is your wife this evening? I expected to see Francesca with you." Always polite in public, always saying the right things.

"She's not . . . feeling well and sends her apologies to you and the Hïrzg," Semini told her. "In fact, she has not felt well for some time, and I made arrangements for her to go to the spas at Kishkoros—she'll be there for another week; I understand they're quite invigorating and restorative."

Allesandra nodded, pleased at the news: *that removes one impediment to our affair.* "They are. I'm certain the rest will do her constitution wonders—though I hope it doesn't leave you too lonely." She pressed his hands again.

He smiled at that, perhaps a bit too broadly. She saw one of his o'ténis raise her eyebrows in their direction, and Allesandra released Semini's hands. "I'm certain that work will prevent me from missing Francesca too much. There will be much that the Faith can do to help the new Hïrzg, don't you think?"

"I know that Jan will be most grateful to you, Archigos. As will I." She glanced over to the close knot of people around Jan. He was smiling broadly, shaking hands and touching shoulders, and there were young women gathered all around him. Despite his earlier apprehension, he seemed to be enjoying himself. The nascent knot in Allesandra's stomach eased somewhat. Commandant cu'Göttering remained at his side, watching closely, his hand never far from the sword at his side. Allesandra suspected that despite the gilded elegance of the hilt, the commandant's blade was quite serviceable. For that matter, she knew that Semini himself was an excellent war-téni, and had no doubt others of the téni with him were the same.

Jan was safe here. She could enjoy the evening, and enjoy watching the social maneuvers of the ca'-and'cu' who had been invited. "Since Councilor ca'Cellibrecca can't be here," she said to Semini, "perhaps you would dance with me later?"

White teeth glistened through the salt-and-pepper beard; he bowed his head slightly. "I would greatly enjoy that. Would you care to walk with me, A'Hïrzg?—my téni have put a lovely display in the garden, and I would like to show it to you." He held out his arm to her. She hesitated a moment—the ca'-and'cu' might not be paying as much attention to her as to her son, but they would notice. They always noticed. But she slipped her hand into the proffered arm and let him escort her to one of the balconies off the upper balcony of the hall. His o'téni, she noticed, carefully arranged themselves at the balcony doors as they passed through, facing into the room so that when Allesandra glanced back, she saw nothing but green-clad backs, though the door remained politely open.

"They're well-trained," she said, and Semini grinned.

"And they're very discreet. Look," he said, moving to the left side of the balcony, where even if someone tried to look out from the hall over the wall of the o'téni, they wouldn't easily see the two of them. Below, the gardens of Brezno Palais were alight with balls of glowing light that wafted gently along the paths: achingly deep purples, searing blues, brilliant reds, greens the color of spring grass, yellows more intense than summer flowers. The night was comfortably cool and the stars mimicked the garden in a sky decorated with silver clouds. Couples from the reception wandered the maze of the gardens, hand in hand.

Semini's warmth covered her back, his arms around her, pressing her against him. "I've missed you, Allesandra."

"Semini . . ." She leaned back into his embrace, feeling the desire rising up in her. He smelled of soap and the oil on his hair and musk. She imagined herself astride him, moving with him. . . .

She turned in his arms, lifting her face to him. They kissed, and she felt the soft bristle of his beard on her cheeks and the thrust of his tongue into her mouth, his hands slipping lower to cup her buttocks and press her against him. She let herself fall into that kiss, closing her eyes and just allowing herself to feel, to notice how the heat moved through her like a slow, relentless tide. She broke off reluctantly, her breath nearly a sob, turning again to relax against his body. She stared out into the light, at the lovers stealing secret moments in the garden below. "Semini—" she began . . .

. . . But a welling of noise from inside the hall pushed her away from him, guiltily. They could hear shouting, and even as Allesandra—worriedly—turned, she heard one of the o'téni speaking too loudly: ". . . let me get the Archigos for you . . ."

Commandant cu'Göttering pushed open the balcony doors and strode out into the night with a trio of o'téni trailing ineffectively behind. "A'Hirzg, Archigos," he said. Whatever thoughts he might have had on seeing the two of them close together and alone on the balcony were carefully hidden. "Your presence is required in the hall."

"What's the matter, Commandant?" Allesandra asked. "I heard shouting. Is Jan . . ."

"The Hïrzg is fine," he told her. "There is news, and a . . . guest. Please—" He gestured to the door; Allesandra and Semini followed him back into the brilliance of the palais and to the balcony stairs. Allesandra could see a quartet of Garde Hïrzg around Jan as the ca'-and-cu' gaped, and with them a travel-worn man. Halfway down the stairs, the man turned, and in the light, she saw the gleam of metal on his face: a nose formed of bright silver. And the face . . .

Allesandra felt her breath catch in her throat. She knew him. She knew him very well, and that he was here in Brezno seemed impossible.

~

Enéas cu'Kinnear

NESSANTICO...
Enéas very nearly wept when he saw her spires and golden domes again, when he glimpsed the pearly strand of the Avi a'Parete glowing in the night, when he heard the wind-horns of the Archigos' Temple plaintively announcing the Calls to prayer. The great city, the greatest of *all* cities: she was a sight that, many times during his service in the Hellins, he had doubted he would ever be permitted to see again.

And he would not have had the pleasure had Cénzi not blessed him with His favor. Of that, Enéas was certain—no, he would have died in the Hellins. *Should* have died there. He had stopped the carriage on Bentspine Hill, outside the city along the Avi a'Sutegate, and stepped out, gesturing to the driver to go on. As the carriage rattled away down the hill toward Sutegate and the familiar landmarks, Enéas went to a knee, clasped hands to forehead, and gave a prayer of thanksgiving to Cénzi.

There is still a task left for you to do, he heard Cénzi reply, as Enéas gazed down at the wonderfully-familiar landscape before him, at the River A'Sele glittering as it embraced the Isle a'Kralji, the four arcing bridges over its waters. *Then you will have truly repaid Me, and I will take you fully into My embrace....*

Enéas smiled and rose, and walked slowly down to the city he loved.

By that evening, he had given Commandant ca'Sibelli's papers and his own verbal report to the office of the Garde Civile, though the e'offizier there had seemed distracted and on edge. "Is there news from the Hellins?" Enéas asked. "More recent than what I've told you?"

The e'offizier shook his head. "Yours is the latest report we've heard, O'Offizier." His voice dropped to a conspiratorial whisper. "Between the two of us, I know that

Commandant cu'Ulcai is very concerned—he's expected a messenger fast-ship from the Hellins for the last few weeks and it hasn't come. As for events here in the city, well . . ." The man told him about the Regent's escape, how the Numetodo had been a part of it, and the execution of Commandant cu'Falla of the Garde Kralji as punishment. He leaned forward to whisper to Enéas. "Go to the Pontica a'Brezi Veste and you'll see his body swaying in its gibbet as food for the crows. Between you and me, that has Commandant cu'Ulcai worried, since both he and cu'Falla were protégés of the Regent and appointed by his hand. The Kraljiki Audric, may Cénzi bless him, may not trust those who have the whiff of loyalty to the old Regent. We can hope that Kraljiki Audric will turn out to be as strong and wise as his great-matarh, but . . ." The e'offizier shrugged, and leaned back in his chair. "Only Cénzi knows."

"Indeed," Enéas answered. "Only Cénzi knows. That is only the truth."

The offizier stamped his papers, informing Enéas that Commandant cu'Ulcai's schedule was full this day but that he might call for Enéas to give his report in person, and that he was released from other duties for the next week. He was given a room and a key, and Enéas put his pack there, placing it carefully away from the fire in the hearth and the window where the sun's heat might find it.

Then, he walked down the Avi a'Parete to the square where the Archigos' Temple sat, pigeons dotting the flagstones and flying overhead in military-precise squadrons to settle again where someone may have dropped food. Enéas walked slowly, savoring the sights and odors of the city, the taste of the air rich in his mouth. The city wrapped its presence around him like a matarh, embracing him wholly in its perfumed miasma, and he nearly sobbed with the sheer relief of it. People were streaming into the square from the Avi, and he realized that it was nearly Second Call just as the wind-horns began to sound from the great golden domes. Enéas joined the people streaming into the temple. Some of them recognized the uniform he wore, with the red sash of the Hellins prominent across it, and they nodded to him with a smile and gestured to him to enter the line. "Thank you for your service, Offizier," they told him. "We appreciate all that you're doing over there." Enéas smiled back to

them as he passed the great bronze doors with the tangled
bodies of the Moitidi streaming forth from the riven chest
of Cénzi, and entered the cool, incense-scented dimness of
the temple.

He sat close to the quire, just below the High Lectern,
leaning his head back to gaze upward to the distant, ribbed
roof. Through the colored glass high above him, brilliant
light stabbed the twilight. He could hear the chanting of
the acolytes in their alcove as the wind-horns quieted and
the procession of the téni entered the quire from the rear
entrance. He stood with the rest of the congregation, smiling with pleasure as he realized that it was the Archigos
himself who would be giving the Admonition and Blessing today: Cénzi had indeed rewarded him. When Enéas
had left Nessantico, so long ago, it had been Archigos Ana
who had given the departing battalion their Blessing, here
in this very space.

Now it would be her successor who would bless him
again, when he had a new, greater task to take on.

Enéas listened patiently to the Archigos' Admonition.
The Admonition, strangely to Enéas, was filled with a call
for tolerance, as Archigos Kenne plucked verse after verse
from the Toustour that spoke of respect for diverse views;
he cautioned those in the temple not to rush to judgment.
"Sometimes, the truth is hidden even from those who are
closest. Let Cénzi judge others, not us." That, at least, was
advice Enéas could follow, with Cénzi's voice guiding him.

After the ceremony, Enéas went up to the rail with the
other supplicants. Archigos Kenne moved slowly down the
line, stopping to talk with each of them. To Enéas' eyes, the
elderly téni looked weary and tired. His voice was a rasp-
ing husk, telling Enéas that he (or one of the other téni)
had enhanced it with the Ilmodo so that it sounded strong
and confident as he gave his Admonition. Enéas bowed his
head and gave the sign of Cénzi as the Archigos, with the
scent of incense clinging to his robes, shuffled before him.
"Ah, an offizier of the Garde Civile," the Archigos said.
"And with the sash of the Westlands, no less. We owe you
our gratitude for your service, O'Offizier. How long did
you serve there?"

"For longer than I wish to remember, Archigos. I've just
returned to Nessantico this day."

The Archigos' wrinkled, desiccated hand brushed Enéas' bowed head, fingers pressing on oiled hair. "Then let the Blessing of Cénzi welcome you back to the city. Is there a particular blessing I can offer you, O'Offizer?"

Enéas lifted his head. The Archigos' eyes were gray-white with nascent cataracts; his head had a persistent slight tremor. But his smile seemed genuine, and Enéas found himself smiling back in return. "I'm a simple warrior," Enéas told him. "An offizier serves the orders he's given. I've taken many lives, Archigos, more than I can count, and will undoubtedly take more before my service is ended."

"And you want Cénzi's forgiveness for that?" the Archigos said. His smile broadened. "You were only performing your duty, and—"

"No," Enéas interrupted, shaking his head. "I don't regret what I've done, Archigos."

The smile collapsed, uncertain. "Then what . . . ?"

"I would like to meet the Kraljiki," Enéas told him. "He should know what is happening in the Hellins. What is *truly* happening."

"I'm sure that the Kraljiki hears from the commandant—" the Archigos began, but Cénzi was talking to Enéas, and he spoke the words he heard in his head.

"Commandant ca'Sibelli is dead by now," he said loudly. "Ask the Kraljiki what news has come from the Hellins. He will not have heard anything at all, Archigos. There is no news from the Hellins because there is no one left there to send it. Not anymore. Ask the Kraljiki, and when he says that the fast-ships haven't come, tell him that I can give him the report that he needs to hear. I am the *only* one who can. Here—" Enéas placed a calling card with his name and current address on the rail. "Please ask him when you see him next," Enéas said. "That is the boon and blessing I request of you, Archigos. Only that. And Cénzi requests it of you as well. Listen? Can't you hear His voice? Listen, Archigos. He is calling to you through me."

"My son . . ." the Archigos began, but Enéas stopped him.

"I'm not a soldier whose mind was addled by what he's seen, Archigos. I was saved by Cénzi to bring this message to the Kraljiki. I give you my hand on that," he told the

Archigos, and reached out. Enéas heard Cénzi's deep bass voice boom in his head as he touched the elderly man's wrist: *"Listen to him. I command it."* And the Archigos' eyes widened as if he'd heard the voice, too. He pulled his hand away, and the voice died.

"Ask the Kraljiki for me," Enéas told him. "That's all I wish. Ask him." Enéas smiled at the Archigos and rose to his feet. The other supplicants and the téni in attendance were all staring at him. Archigos Kenne gaped, looking down at his own hand as if it were something foreign.

Enéas gave them all the sign of Cénzi and walked from the temple, his boots loud in the silence.

Niente

THE FORCES OF TECUHTLI ZOLIN and the Tehuantin army were arrayed a careful bow's shot away
from the thick defensive walls of Munereo.

Three days of battle had sent the Garde Civile retreating inside the walls. Tecuhtli Zolin had been both aggressive and unmerciful in his attack. Commandant ca'Sibelli
had sent a parley group to the Tehuantin encampment after
the first day of battle, when Zolin had routed the Garde Civile from rich, high fields south of the city. Niente had been
there when the parley group had arrived flying their white
flag; he had watched Zolin order his personal guards to kill
them and send their severed heads back to Commandant
ca'Sibelli as answer.

They had attacked the main force of the Garde Civile at
dawn the next morning; by that evening, they were within
sight of the Munereo walls and the harbor, with the Holdings fleet at anchor there.

Now it was dawn again, and Tecuhtli Zolin had called Niente to him. Zolin reclined on a nest of colorful pillows; the
High Warriors Citlali and Mazatl were with him also. Behind him, an artisan crouched over Zolin's freshly shaved
head; next to the artisan was a small table crowded with
dragon-claw needles and pots of dye. Zolin's scalp had been
painted with the spread-winged eagle that was the insignia
of the Tecuhtli; now the artisan prepared to mark the skin
permanently. He took a needle, dipped it into red dye, and
pressed it into Zolin's scalp: the warrior grimaced slightly.
"The nahuallis' preparations are finished?" Zolin asked
Niente as the artisan quickly dipped the needle again and
pressed it into Zolin's head, over and over. Blood beaded
and trickled down; the artisan wiped it away with a cloth.

"Yes, Tecuhtli," Niente told him. "Our spell-staffs have
been renewed—for those healthy enough to do so." He
lifted his own staff, displaying the carved eagles that circled

below the polished, thick knob. "We lost two hands of na-hualli in the battle; another hand and one are too wounded to be of use today. All the rest are ready." Niente nodded to the two High Warriors. "I've placed them as Citlali and Mazatl have asked."

"And the black sand?"

"It's been prepared," Niente told him. "I supervised that myself."

"The scrying bowl? What did it say to you?"

Niente had spent much of the night peering into the wa-ters, which had given him only murky and clouded visions, as well as exhaustion and a face and hands that seemed to have acquired a webbing of fine wrinkles overnight. Niente had found himself confused by the quick glimpses of pos-sible futures. But he knew what Zolin wanted to hear, and he plucked one of those fleeting visions from his mind. "I saw you inside the city, Tecuhtli, and the Holdings Com-mander at your feet."

Zolin grinned broadly. "Then it's time," Zolin said. He rose, nearly knocking over the artisan, who scurried back-ward as Zolin plucked up his sword. He patted his bleeding head, smiling. "This can be finished later. The battle can't wait."

They went outside the tent, guards straightening to attention as they emerged. From the small hill on which the Tecuhtli's tent stood, they could see the army spread out below them, the haze of cook fires drifting in the still morning. The walls of Munereo rose high farther down the slope, and sun dazzled on the water of the bay beyond and to their right. Zolin gestured, and a trio of battle-horns sounded, the call taken up by other horns throughout the encampment, and Niente could see the entire encampment stir, like a mound of red ants stirred with a stick. The battle lines began to coalesce; the High Warriors on their horses exhorting the troops. On the walls of Munereo, the rising sun reflected from metal helms and the tips of arrows as the Holdings troops waited for the attack.

Their own horses were brought to them, and they mounted. Citlali and Mazatl saluted Zolin and kicked their stallions into a gallop as they rode away. "You're with me, Nahual," Zolin said. "Now!" He, too, kicked his steed, and Niente followed the Tecuhtli's headlong gallop down the hill to where the troops waited on the slope, nearly level with the top of Munereo's walls, the troops moving quickly aside to let them pass, their shouts of support and adoration following.

Before his deep enchantment of the Easterner, Niente could have ridden all day with anyone. Now, the pounding of the horse's hooves on the ground struck Niente's body like hammer blows. It was all he could do to cling to the back of the animal with trembling knees. Zolin rode to the center of the front-line Tehuantin forces, where the eagle flag had been planted in the middle of the winding road leading down to the western gate of Munereo. There, the hand of siege dragons waited. Zolin, from his horse, patted the massive carved and painted head of one of the dragons. "The gods have promised us victory today!" he called out to those around him. He pointed downhill to the waiting city. Their warrior-marked faces were turned up to him, and they cheered. Niente had to admit that Zolin had charisma that Tecuhtli Necalli had lacked: the eagerness on the face of the warriors said that they would follow him even into the depths of one of the smoking mountains. "Tonight, we will feast where the Easterners dined, and we will take their wealth and the survivors back to our own cities, and this land will be returned to our cousins who once held it!"

They cheered again, louder than before. Zolin roared with laughter and patted the siege dragon again. "It's time!" he shouted. "This day, you will find victory or you will find peace with the gods!"

He gestured, and the battle-horns blared the call-to-advance. The lines shivered and began to surge forward, and Tecuhtli Zolin—unlike Necalli, Niente again had to admit—rode at the very front, his head bare so that anyone could see the eagle on his skull. The advance started slowly, the soldiers moving forward at a walking pace. As they continued down the slope, the walls of Munereo seemed to climb, growing ever taller as they approached until they were in their long shadow. The siege dragons, mounted on their carts, squeaked and groaned as they started down the roadway, protesting as the men pushed them down the slope toward the walls and the great, barred gates. Zolin paused, and Niente with him: there was movement on the walls, and suddenly a storm of arrows dimmed the sun, arcing high in the air followed momentarily by the *thwack* of a thousand bowstrings. "Shields!" Zolin yelled, and the warriors around them lifted their wooden shields, placing them together into a temporary roof, several of them lifting theirs high so as to shield both Zolin and Niente on their horses. The arrows rained furiously down, feathering the painted, leather-strapped planks, some of them slipping between to catch an unlucky warrior, but most thudding harmlessly into wood. "Down!" Zolin called, and the shield wall fell, the soldiers hacking at the shafts with their swords. Broken arrows littered the ground.

Now the advance quickened. Niente held his spell-staff high—he knew what must come next. "Nahualli!" he called. "Be ready!" He could already hear the distant chanting, and he felt the shifting energy of the X'in Ka as the Holdings war-téni released their own enchantments. Fireballs sputtered over the walls of Munereo, shrieking toward them in lines marked by smoke. Niente shook his spell-staff at the nearest fireball and spoke the release word: the fireball erupted while still above and before them, the fire hissing as it died with glowing sparks falling around them. Another fireball crashed untouched into the Tehuantin forces to Niente's right, and even at a distance the heat and concussion of the explosion were frightening. Where the fireballs landed, hardened warriors screamed as they died. The fireballs cut gouges in the advancing line but they filled quickly with warriors from the rear ranks. Zolin urged the line forward at a trot, the siege dragons seeming to scream as their wooden wheels lurched and bounced over the broken ground.

"Push!" Niente roared at those around the siege dragons. "Move!" Now the battle fire had finally caught him up, and Niente no longer felt prematurely old. His blood boiled and the wind sang in his ears. The hand of siege dragons were picking up speed, starting to move downhill on their own. The warriors around them no longer needed to push them; they had their own energy now, already beyond the front lines of the army. Arrows fell again and again and the shield roof snapped up each time in response, but Niente barely noticed. He watched the siege dragons, flying across the packed ground of the road now, painted jaws wide as they rushed toward the gates. Fireballs arced out, and again

Niente and the other nahualli sent their spells to counter them. He could hear Zolin shouting, screaming orders at the men.

The siege dragons flew, their handlers far behind them and shouting as the carts trundled forward on their own. Three struck the base of the city walls on either side of the gates, two the gates themselves.

The dragon heads had been packed with black sand— more of it than Niente and the other nahualli had ever prepared before. Spell-sticks had been placed on the snouted heads to respond with fire to the impact. Niente saw the burst of flame from the sticks, then ...

There was a roar as if one of the mountains of fire of Niente's home had erupted, deafening, and with it a flash of pure light that brought Niente's hand up to his eyes belatedly. Stones the size of horses were flying through the air, some of them crushing the nearest Tehuantin, but there were louder screams from within Munereo. Smoke swirled around the scene, making it impossible to see, but as it slowly cleared, a wordless shout arose from the Tehuantin forces.

The gates had been breached. Where they had been, there was only a gaping hole, and the thick supporting walls around them had collapsed. Even as they watched, a portion of the parapets collapsed on the right, spilling defenders fifty feet to the ground. "Forward!" Zolin was shouting. "Forward!"—and the Tehuantin army surged forward as one toward the city, heedless of the arrows or the fire of the war-téni. Niente found himself charging with them, his own throat raw with screams of exultation, his staff ready.

The Tehuantin poured through the broken walls of Munereo.

In the streets of the city, the battle had been pitched, vicious, and chaotic. As soon as the Tehuantin army entered the city, the native population had risen in concert, arming themselves with anything at hand to kill and loot with glee the people who had forced them into servitude. The Easterner defenders of Munereo found themselves assailed from both the front and behind.

Realizing that the day had been lost, the remnants of the Holdings force had tried to retreat to their ships in the bay, but Zolin had brought Tehuantin warships to the mouth of the bay, each with a nahualli aboard, and they sent spell-fire to burn the sails and masts of the Holdings ships; none escaped the inner harbor of Munereo Bay.

It was said afterward that one could walk from the wrecks of the Holdings ships to the shore on the bodies of the dead, and that the entire bay turned red for a week afterward from the blood washed into it from the ruins of Munereo.

The Tehuantin had found Commandant ca'Sibelli cowering aboard the flagship of the fleet and brought him back to the smoking ruins of the city. Tecuhtli Zolin had the man dragged into the main temple of Munereo and lashed to the altar there, and Niente himself prepared an eagle claw for the man, filling the curved bone tube with black sand. He spoke the enchantment as he worked: all it would need was a turn of the ivory horn and a press of the trigger in the wooden handle to strike the flint and set off the black powder. He took the eagle claw with him when he accompanied Tecuhtli Zolin to the temple. The temple was crowded with both High Warriors and nahualli; Niente saw both Citlali and Mazatl there, seated at the front. All of them were spattered with blood, most of which was not their own. Zolin stood over ca'Sibelli, naked to the waist and strapped on the altar. The gray-haired man looked terrified at the sight of the Tecuhtli; he moaned. "I've surrendered the city to you," the man said in the Easterner language. "The Regent and the Council of Ca' will pay my ransom, whatever you ask—"

"Be silent," Niente told him in the same language. "Now is the time to pray to your god, if you must."

"What does he say?" Zolin asked Niente, and Niente told him. Zolin roared with laughter. "Is this how the Easterners play at war?" he asked. "They buy and sell their captives? Are their gods that weak? No wonder they ran before us." Zolin gestured at the man with contempt. "They're barely worth the sacrifice. Sakal and Axat must get little nourishment from them."

"What is he saying?" ca'Sibelli said, lifting his head up and straining against the ropes that held him. "Tell him I know where the treasury is. There's gold, lots of it."

Niente took the eagle claw from its pouch. Ca'Sibelli

went silent, looking at it. He licked cracked, bloodied lips. "What . . . what is that?"

"It is your death," Niente told him. "Sakal and Axat demand your presence as the leader."

"No!" the man shouted. Saliva frothed around his mouth. "You can't do this. I'm your prisoner, your hostage. Ask for ransom—"

Niente leaned close to the writhing man. He could feel the man's terror, and he made his voice as gentle as he could. "This will end the killing here in your city. Your death pays for the death of all your soldiers that we have captured, and they will be spared. If you are brave, Commandant, if you show Axat and Sakal that you're worthy, they will take you to Themselves and you will live forever in Them. Forever. It is a gift we give you here. A gift."

The man gaped, disbelieving, but the chant of sacrifice had begun, low and sonorous, echoing in the chamber. The warriors and nahualli swayed with the prayer. Ca'Sibelli turned his head to stare frantically at them. Tecuhtli Zolin nodded to Niente, and he pulled the eagle's claw from his belt. Ca'Sibelli's eyes widened as Niente turned the ivory horn until it clicked into place.

Niente stood alongside the commandant. "You should be praying," he told the man. Ca'Sibelli's head was shaking violently back and forth, as if he could deny the moment. Niente pressed the end of the curved tube against the man's stomach as ca'Sibelli thrashed frantically in his bonds. Niente sighed—this would not be a good death. "Axat, Sakal, we give this enemy to you," Niente said in his own language. "Take this offering as a sign of your victory."

He pressed the trigger. There was a click, a spark, and then an explosion of flesh and blood.

Sergei ca'Rudka

SERGEI WASN'T SURPRISED that they took his sword from him. In fact, he wondered if he was to survive this meeting at all.

The room was small and overly warm, decorated in typical Firenzcian style with dark hangings and stark paintings with martial themes, all celebrating long-dead Hïrzgai. The new Hïrzg Jan sat in a plush chair to one side of the hearth, but it was obvious that Allesandra, sitting to his right, was the central character here rather than the young Hïrzg who stared at Sergei's nose, his gaze trapped there. Archigos ca'Cellibrecca loomed like some ursine demigod behind the high back of the Hïrzg's chair, scowling. The gardai who had brought Sergei here were dismissed (after another, rather thorough check of Sergei's clothing to make certain he was unarmed; they took two knives from him and missed only one small, thin blade tucked in the loose heel and sole of his boot). Faintly, Sergei could hear the musicians playing a gavotte in the hall outside, though he doubted that many at the party were still dancing. Most would be talking and gossiping, wondering what the Regent of Nessantico was doing here in Brezno.

He was certain that those in the room wondered the same thing.

"Hïrzg Jan," he said, bowing low to the young man who looked so much like his matarh. "I thank you for taking in a poor refugee, and I offer you my service in gratitude."

"Your *service*, Regent ca'Rudka?" It was Allesandra who spoke. "What has happened in Nessantico, Regent, that you now offer service to those you've fought as an enemy?"

Sergei hadn't seen her in nearly sixteen years; she'd left her confinement in Nessantico when she'd been only a little older than her son was now; she had matured into full womanhood in the intervening years. Sergei could still see the passionate young woman in her face, but there was a new hardness there and lines carved by experiences he could not know. *Don't assume that she's still the same person you knew....*

"Foul deeds and bad times," he said to her, to the others. He outlined for them the events of the last few months, including his own escape from the Bastida days ago. "I doubt that Kraljiki Audrič will survive long," he finished. "I suspect that Sigourney ca'Ludovici will be Kraljica within a year, perhaps two." He looked hard at Allesandra, whose gaze had drifted away contemplatively during his tale. "She has no better claim to the Sun Throne than others here," he said. Allesandra gave him a faint nod; Sergei thought that Jan glanced at his matarh strangely with that.

"Where are these Numetodo you say helped you escape?" ca'Cellibrecca growled. "Did you bring the heretics here also?"

Sergei languidly glanced at the Archigos. "They declined to follow me, given the reception they expected to receive, Archigos. Brezno's attitude toward the Numetodo has been . . . well demonstrated." He smiled blandly, and ca'Cellibrecca's mouth lifted in a sneer.

"As has Nessantico's, and we have seen what it gained them," ca'Cellibrecca answered. "That they would rescue you from the Bastida, Regent, would indicate that your own views are heretical, also. Have you become a Numetodo yourself?"

"My belief in Cénzi and the teachings of the Toustour remains as firm as ever, Archigos." He gave the man the sign of Cénzi. "I've found that one might disagree even with friends and yet still remain friends. I've had many interesting discussions with Ambassador ca'Vliomani over the years, heated ones at times, but neither of us has managed to significantly change the views of the other. Nor do I think that's necessarily a bad thing. Ambassador ca'Vliomani was my friend and acted to help me, even though our views on religion are entirely at odds. My soul has nothing to fear." He paused, his gaze going back to Allesandra. "Friends—and allies—may be found even where least expected. Would I be wrong, A'Hirzg ca'Vörl, in saying that you came to consider Archigos Ana your friend, even though she took you from your vatarh?"

Ca'Cellibrecca hissed audibly at that, and Hïrzg Jan's eyebrows rose, but the ghost of a smile touched Allesandra's lips. "Ah, Regent, you always fenced as well with words as you did with your blade."

Sergei bowed again to her.

"Yes," Allesandra continued, "I came to consider Archigos Ana, if not a friend, then as someone I could trust in the face of the uncertain fate my vatarh left to me. I was genuinely horrified to hear of her assassination—nor, knowing her and the Ambassador ca'Vliomani, did I believe what I heard of who was responsible. I have grieved and prayed for her since. And, yes, I understand what you're saying behind that question. I'm sure Hïrzg Jan would be pleased to accept your service and talk with you further regarding what you can do for the Firenzcian Coalition."

The boy sat up suddenly in his chair at the mention of his name, glancing over to his matarh. "Yes," he told Sergei. "I . . . we will." His voice was as uncertain as the look he cast Allesandra. Then his features settled, and he sounded more adult. "Firenzcia will offer you asylum, Regent ca'Rudka, and I'm certain we can find a use for your knowledge and your skills."

"Thank you, Hïrzg Jan," Sergei replied, and went to a knee. "That was well-spoken. I freely give you and Firenzcia the loyalty that Nessantico has scorned, and I will lend you whatever counsel and help that I can."

The young man seemed inordinately pleased at the declaration, as if he somehow dredged it unwillingly from Sergei himself. He was young and inexperienced, Sergei realized, but he seemed intelligent enough, and had an excellent teacher in his matarh. He would learn quickly. The Archigos scowled, obviously not pleased with the decision. There would be little sympathy for Sergei there—he would need to watch ca'Cellibrecca carefully and find what advantage he could against the man.

And with Allesandra . . . The woman regarded him carefully. Thoughtfully. There was ambition there, and a brilliance that had been lacking in her vatarh. He could easily imagine her on the Sun Throne. He could see her making decisions that would protect the Holdings and heal the wounds Justi and now his son had carved into the city and empire he served.

Could she be the Kraljica to rival Marguerite?

He would find out. And he would act.

~

Karl Vliomani

HE'D SHAVED OFF his beard. He'd darkened his hair
with essence of blackstone and let his features become
obscured with the dirt of the road. He'd given away the fine
bashtas in his pack in exchange for a beggar's flea-infested
and torn wardrobe. He stank of filth, and his smell alone
was enough to turn people's eyes away from him.

He wondered where Sergei was, and if he'd made his
way to Firenzcia and how he might have been received
there.

Karl had originally intended to make his way back to the
Isle of Paeti. He had rested enough to use the Scáth Cumhacht to heal the worst of Varina's wound. Then he and Varina had accompanied Sergei to the woods north of the city,
but there had parted ways, Sergei turning eastward toward
Azay a'Reaudi, while he and Varina followed the forest's
line westward. They'd crossed the Avi a'Nortegate below
Tousia, then turned southeast toward the Avi a'Nostrosei,
hoping to follow its line into Sforzia and from there find
passage on a ship to either Paeti or one of the northern
countries. They'd reached the Avi at Ville Paisli four days
later, only a day's journey by foot from Nessantico's walls.

He'd intended that they stay one day. No more. He and
Varina had taken a room in the only inn in the village, giving
false names and traveling as man and wife on their way to
Varolli in hopes of finding employment. The older woman
who had shown them the room nodded as she took their
money, slipping the coins into a pocket under the apron she
wore over a stained tashta that looked two decades out of
fashion. Her face and body showed years of children and
hard work. "I'm Alisa Morel," she told them. Karl heard
the intake of Varina's breath at the name. "My husband and
I own the inn and tavern, and my husband is the village's
smithy. If you'd like a bath—" that with a significant glance
and wrinkling of her nose suggesting that such would be a

good idea, "—there's a room below for that, and I can have my children fill two tubs with hot water. Dinner will be a turn of the glass after sundown."

The woman left them, and Varina lifted eyebrows toward Karl. "Morel . . ." she said. "Nico said that he'd run away from his tantzia and onczio. Could she be . . . ?"

"Morel's a common enough name in Nessantico." He shrugged. "But there are obviously some questions we should ask. If we still had the boy . . ."

Karl was already certain that the connection was there, though he wasn't sure how he knew. He could see from Varina's face that she was thinking the same. If he'd believed in any god at all, he might have thought they'd been led here by divine fortune.

That evening, after taking the woman's offer of a bath to rid them of the worst of the road stink, he and Varina took their supper in the common room of the tavern, both to avoid suspicion and so that they could hear any gossip that might have reached the village regarding the escape of the Regent from the Bastida. The room was—he suspected from the harried looks of Alisa, her children who served as the waiting staff, and her husband Bayard behind the short bar near the kitchen door—more crowded than usual, and the talk was largely of the events in Nessantico, which seemed to have reached the village only a few days ago.

"I spoke to the offizier of the search squad myself," Bayard Morel was saying loudly to an audience of a half dozen villagers. "His horse had thrown its shoe, and so he had me shoe the beast for him. He said that Kraljiki Audric, may Cénzi bless 'im, sent riders out on every road from the city to catch the traitor and those Numetodo heretics with him. The offizier's squad was to scour the road all the way to Varolli if necessary. He told me that the Numetodo killed three dozen Garde Kralji in the Bastida with their awful, blasphemous magic, killed 'em without a thought even though some of them were still in their beds. They left the tower where ca'Rudka was held in rubble, nothing but great stones strewn all over the ground. They were spouting fire as they rode off, a horrible blue fire, the offizier said, that slew people along the Avi as they passed, and then, with a great whoosh—" and here Bayard spread his hands suddenly wide, knocking over the nearest tankard of ale and causing his audience to rear back in wide-eyed terror, "—they vanished in a cloud of foul black smoke. Just like that. All told, there are over a hundred dead in the city. I tell you, death is too good a fate for the Regent. They ought to drag him alive through the streets and let the stones of the Avi tear the very flesh from his bones and rip off that silver nose of his while he screams."

The people in the room murmured their agreement with that assessment. Varina leaned close to Karl, grimacing as the movement pulled at the knitting wound on her arm. "By next week, he'll have it at a thousand dead. But at least it seems the searchers have already moved through. We're behind them. That's good, right?" She searched his face with anxious eyes, and he grunted assent even though he wasn't so certain himself.

Watching the room, he noticed that there was another woman helping to serve the patrons: dour and tired-looking, her mouth never gentled with a smile. She looked several years younger than Alisa, but there was a family resemblance between the two: in the eyes, in the narrow nose, in the set of her lips. She appeared too old to be Alisa's child, all of whom were still striplings. When one of the children—a sullen boy on the cusp of puberty—set a plate of sliced bread on their table, he pointed to her. "That woman there . . . who is that?"

The boy sniffed and scowled. "That's my Tantzia Serafina. She's living with us right now."

"She looks unhappy."

"She's been that way for a while now, since Nico ran away."

Karl glanced at Varina. "Who's Nico?"

"Her son," the boy said, the scowl deepening. "A bastardo. I didn't like him anyway. Always talking nonsense about Westlanders and magic and trying to pretend he could do magic himself like he was a téni. Everyone had to waste three days looking for him after he left, and my vatarh rode all the way to Certendi, but no one ever found him. I think he's probably dead." He seemed inordinately satisfied with that conclusion, satisfaction curling a corner of his mouth.

"Ah." Karl nodded. "You're probably right. It's not an easy world out there for travelers. I was just wondering why she looked so sad." Varina was looking away now, staring at Serafina, her knuckles to her mouth. The boy scuffled his feet on the rough wooden floor, sniffed and wiped his arm across his nose, and went back into the kitchen.

"Gods, it *is* her." Varina gave a nearly imperceptible shake of her head. "What do we do, Karl? That's Nico's matarh."

Karl plucked a piece of bread from the plate that the boy had brought. He tore off a chunk of the brown loaf and tucked it into his mouth, chewing thoughtfully. "If we could give her Nico," he said after he swallowed, "I wonder if she would give us Talis in return?"

Jan ca'Vörl

J AN MOTIONÉD TO THE GARDAI outside the door.
"Let me in," he said. The two men glanced at each other
once, quickly, before one of them opened the door. As Jan
stepped inside, the garda started to follow. Jan shook his
head at the man. "Alone," he said. The garda hesitated before nodding his head once in salute. The door closed behind Jan again.

"You're a brave one, to be in a room alone with his
enemy. And that one will be reporting to Commandant
cu'Göttering that you've come to visit me. Cu'Göttering
will undoubtedly inform your matarh."

Candlelight reflected from silver as Sergei turned to regard Jan. The man had been placed in one of the interior
rooms of Brezno Palais, his meal laid out before him on a
damask-covered table, the hearth crackling with a fire to
take off the night chill, and a comfortable bed soft with
down pillows and coverlets. He was wearing a new, clean
bashta and had evidently taken a bath, and his graying hair
was newly oiled.

He sat in a prison woven of silk.

"I don't care that cu'Göttering knows, nor my matarh.
Are you so dangerous, Regent ca'Rudka?" Jan asked the
man, standing across the table from him.

In reply, Sergei reached down to his bootheel: slowly, so
that Jan could see him. He slid a slender, short-handled and
flat blade from between the sole and leather and placed it
on the table, sliding it across the table toward Jan. "Always,
Hïrzg Jan," the man answered with a faint smile. "Your
great-vatarh would have told you that. Your matarh as well.
If I'd wanted you dead, you would be dead already."

Jan stared at the blade. He'd watched the gardai search
the man for weapons, had heard them declare the Regent
unarmed. "I think I'll need to have a talk with Commandant
cu'Göttering about the training of his men." He reached

down to touch the hilt with a fingertip, but otherwise didn't pick up the knife. "What else did they miss?"

Sergei only smiled. Jan put his hand on the knife and slid it back across the table to Sergei, who sheathed it again in his boot. "So, Hïrzg Jan," Sergei said. "To what do I owe the pleasure?"

Jan wasn't certain of that himself. The initial meeting with Sergei had left him unsettled, listening to his matarh and to Archigos ca'Cellibrecca, knowing that they'd dominated the moment. In truth, he was feeling overwhelmed by the suddenness of events: Fynn's assassination, Elissa's flight, the news from the Holdings, the Regent's arrival. His vatarh had left Brezno in an angry rush; his matarh and the Archigos were suspiciously close. It was as if he were being swept along helplessly in a flood he hadn't seen and hadn't anticipated. He found himself feeling lost and uncertain, and he'd brooded on that for long turns of the glass, unable to lose himself in the now-forced gaiety of the party or the distractions of the young women who flirted with him or the urgent speculations that erupted all around him.

He wanted to talk to someone. He didn't want that person to be his matarh.

Jan didn't feel like the Hïrzg. He felt like an impostor. "I want to know what I've gained by giving you asylum, Regent," he said.

"Are you having second thoughts?" Sergei asked him. He pushed his chair back from the table. "Or is it that you think that someone else made that decision for you?"

He should have felt anger at that. Instead, he only brought one shoulder up and let it drop again. "Ah," Sergei said. "I understand. So, I think, would poor Audric. Let me tell you this, Hïrzg Jan: I've known several Kralji in my time, and despite what you might think of them, the truth is that none of them ever made an easy decision. Everything you do as Kralji—or Hïrzg—affects thousands of other people, some in good ways, others adversely. Be glad that you have good advisers around you, and listen to them. It might save you from making some truly horrific decisions." He smiled then, grimly. "And if one turns out that way despite your best intentions, well, you can always blame it on their bad advice."

"You still haven't answered my question."

The smile broadened. "No, I haven't, have I?" Sergei laid his hands palm up on the table. "All I have to offer you is *me*, Hïrzg. My knowledge, my experience, my viewpoint. I happen to think that's a potentially valuable resource for you, but then I'll admit to being prejudiced on the subject." The skin around the man's false nose wrinkled, but the nose itself didn't move—it struck Jan as disturbing. It made him uneasy, but he found it hard to move his gaze away from Sergei's face.

"I have my matarh's knowledge, experience, and viewpoint; I also have the Archigos'. I have that of the commandants and the other chevarittai of the Coalition."

"You do," Sergei answered. "Your matarh was a hostage in the Holdings for much of her youth. The Archigos is an avowed opponent of the Nessantican branch of the Faith. The commandants and chevarittai are also opponents of the Holdings. None of them *know* the Holdings, and they all have reason to hate it. Hatred can be blinding sometimes. As for me, well, the welfare of the Holdings has been my life."

"Which is another reason to distrust you."

"Then let that be my first piece of advice to you, Hïrzg Jan. You *should* distrust me. A Hïrzg should be skeptical of *all* the advice he's given—because everyone's advice is painted with the colors of their agenda, mine no less than anyone's. But . . . I'm an old swordsman, Hïrzg, and I'd tell you it's easier to defeat an enemy whose moves you know and can anticipate than one you don't know at all." Sergei sat back in his chair. "I know the Holding's moves. I know them all. You need me."

"You sound so certain."

"I know my enemy, Hïrzg. If I didn't, would I have given you my knife?" He reached down and tapped his boot. "Everyone takes risks, Hïrzg. The trick is to be confident of the outcome."

"What if I'd kept the knife?" Jan asked him.

Sergei gave a short chuckle. "Then I'd have pretended that *that* was what I'd expected. Do you still like *your* choice, Hïrzg?"

Jan smiled, his lips pressed together. "It was what I expected, Regent," he said. "And that will have to do, won't it?"

~

Audric ca'Dakwi

THE O'TÉNI KNEELING next to Audric's bed opened
her eyes, her face drawn and weary, and glanced over at
Archigos Kenne. "I've finished my . . ." She hesitated, and
Audric saw her gaze flick past the Archigos to Councillor
Sigourney ca'Ludovici, standing by the fireplace and gazing
at the portrait of Kraljica Marguerite, sitting alongside the
fire on its portable easel. Above the hearth, Audric could
see the discolored rectangle where the portait had hung
for so long. In the dim recesses of the room, Marlon and
Seaton lurked, waiting to scurry forward if needed.

". . . prayers," the o'téni concluded.

The Archigos had told Audric that this woman téni
came from the temple at Chiari and was someone whose
"prayers had a special affinity for those who are sick."
That may have been true; he certainly felt somewhat better now, his lungs moving less painfully. The insistent cough
had receded, though he could still feel some tightness in
his chest—perhaps Cénzi had indeed blessed him tonight.
The improvement wasn't as marked as when Archigos Ana
had performed her "prayers" for him, but it would do. He
hoped it would last as long as Archigos Ana's ministrations
had.

"Thank you, O'Téni," the Archigos was saying, giving
the woman the sign of Cénzi. "We appreciate your efforts.
You may return to the temple now. Tell U'Téni cu'Magnaoi
that I will be along soon, if you would."

She nodded and rose shakily to her feet, as if she been
kneeling too long and her legs had gone to sleep. As Audric
watched, she pressed hands to her forehead, then to each
leg and shuffled carefully to the door of the bedchamber,
Marlon hurrying to open it for her. "Strange," Sigourney
remarked without turning from the painting, "*I've* never
been so exhausted from simply praying."

Audric saw Kenne's craggy face tighten in the candlelight at the unsubtle accusation. The Archigos otherwise ignored the comment. "Are you feeling better, Kraljiki?" he asked.

Audric's great-matarh stared at him concernedly over ca'Ludovici's shoulder. "There is nothing wrong with me," he told the Archigos, and saw his great-matarh's face nod just on the edge of perception. *Don't let them know how you truly feel, not when they might think it weakness.* "I know that," he told her, then turned back to the Archigos. "I'm feeling quite well," he told the man, and Kenne looked almost comically relieved. "Now, you said you had a favor to ask, Archigos."

"I did, Kraljiki. I had an odd encounter this morning at the temple. There was a man, an o'offizier of the Garde Civile: Enéas cu'Kinnear. He came for Cénzi's Blessing, and he had the sash of the Hellins over his uniform. A good-looking young man, with an earnest face. He told me that he was just back from the war."

"Yes, yes," Audric said impatiently, waving the man silent. The Archigos could meander on like that for a turn of the clock, relating every interminable detail of the encounter. He heard ca'Ludovici chuckle in the background. "Your *point,* Archigos?"

The Archigos didn't manage to entirely hide his annoyance, but he smiled grimly and bowed his head to Audric. "O'Officer cu'Kinnear said that he had vital information for you regarding the Hellins, Kraljiki. He said that you would not have heard his news because the fast-ships wouldn't have come. I've checked, and that's the case. I also had my staff investigate this cu'Kinnear, and they found that Commandant ca'Sibelli—" with that, the Archigos nodded in the direction of Sigourney, "—recommended him to be named Chevaritt, and the reports on the man are unanimous in their high opinion of him as a person of faith and as an offizier. In fact, I've discovered that he'd once been considered as an acolyte candidate, showing signs of the Gift—"

"Fine," Audric interrupted again, sighing. "I'm certain that this cu'Kinnear's a fine man." He closed his eyes. It was so tiresome, having to listen to the drivel of the people under him, and to pretend that he was paying attention or that he cared. *It is the bane of all Kralji,* he heard his great-matarh say, and he smiled indulgently at her. "Indeed," he told her. "It is quite so." Right now, he wanted his supper, and perhaps a round of cards with some of the young women of the ca'-and-cu'—and perhaps a dalliance, since he was feeling better.

You must be careful with that, Audric, he heard his great-matarh remonstrate. *Marriage is a weapon that can only be used once or twice; you must choose the right moment, and the right blade.*

"Don't be tiresome," he told her.

Sigourney spoke up. "If I may, Kraljiki?" He waved a hand at her. The woman was a bore; she had no humor to her; all that interested her was the business of the state. She was as dry as yesterday's toasted bread. "Archigos, if this cu'Kinnear has such vital information, why hasn't he told his superior offiziers and passed it up the chain of command?"

"That I don't know myself, Councillor," the Archigos said. "But there was *something* . . . I thought . . . I thought that when cu'Kinnear asked me to make the request of you, Kraljiki Audric, that I heard Cénzi's Voice telling me that I should listen. I would have sworn . . ." The old man shook his head, and Audric sighed impatiently again. "What would a few moments to hear the man hurt? It will be Second Cénzidi the week after next; if he could be placed on the list of the supplicants for your usual audience, Kraljiki . . ."

Snared in varnish, Marguerite seemed to shrug in the candlelight. Audric swung his legs off the side of the bed. Seaton hurried to help him rise and he waved the servant away. "Fine," he said. "Arrange it with Marlon, Archigos. I'll see this paragon of the Garde Civile on second Cénzidi—but only if no fast-ship arrives in the meantime with fresher news from the Hellins. Is that satisfactory?"

The Archigos bowed and gave the sign of Cénzi to Audric, then to the councillor. Ca'Ludovici seemed to snicker. "Now," Audric said, "I am hungry, and there are entertainments that I plan to attend this evening, so if there is no more business . . ."

~

The White Stone

THE AIR WAS RIFE with whispers and curses, and they weren't only from the voices in her mind. Nessantico shuddered with the events of the last week, with the escape of the Regent and the betrayal of the Numetodo. She had seen the squads moving angrily and suspiciously through the lanes and alleys of Oldtown; she had been questioned twice herself, dragged aside and interrogated as if they thought she might be one of the Numetodo. She knew enough to show just the right amount of fear: enough to placate them, but not enough to fuel their suspicions. Others had not been so lucky; she'd seen dozens hauled away to be questioned at length in the dark gloom of the Bastida, and she did not envy them.

It would have been so much easier for them to have hired the White Stone. The Regent's life, the Ambassador's life: she could have snuffed them out as a candle extinguished in daylight—lives no longer necessary or wanted. She could have taken their souls into the stone she carried between her breasts.

More madness for you to bear . . . They laughed at the thought. *You will lose yourself entirely in us . . .*

Soon . . .

Soon . . .

The refrain was a pounding drumbeat in her head. Fynn's angry voice was the loudest of them.

Soon . . .

Soon . . .

"Maybe not," she told them. "I'm stronger than you think. After all, I killed all of you." She said the words aloud, and those nearest her on the streets glanced at her with pity or annoyance or fear. She didn't care which; it didn't matter.

The morning sun was rising over the statue of Kraljiki Selida II in the central fountain of Oldtown Center, the disk blazing as if the tip of the Kraljiki's upraised sword was afire. To the right of the plaza was the huge statue of Henri VI, also casting its own long shadow. The morning nausea that plagued her every day when she rose had passed, and the smell of buttery croissants from the bakery just a few doors down made her hungry again. She rubbed at her belly; she could feel the swell of her stomach under her tashta; soon, she wouldn't be able to hide the pregnancy at all.

Soon . . .

"Be quiet!" she shouted at them, and her voice lifted pigeons from the pavement of the square and flung them into the air to flutter down again several strides away. Someone laughed nearby in a knot of young men, pointing at her, and she gave them an obscene gesture, which only made the laughter increase.

Soon . . .

I will destroy you as you destroyed me. That was Fynn. *Soon* . . .

Scowling, she pushed her way into the bakery and flung a bronze se'folia down on the counter. "Croissants," she said.

She'd eaten two of them before she reached the rooms she'd taken a few blocks from the Center. The sweet, moist bread soothed the ache in her belly and banished the voices. She was reaching for the key for her room when she heard noise: a scraping, an intake of breath. She stopped, putting down the bundle of remaining croissants, her hand going to the knife hilt tucked in the sash of her tashta. The sound was coming from the small space between her house and the building next to it. She peered into the purple shadows there, seeing a form hunched against the side of the house, trembling.

"I see you in there," she said. "Come on out."

She expected the person to run, to flee the other way toward the lane behind the house. But the form stirred, rising slowly, and she saw in the shifting, uncertain light from the brightening sky that it was a child. He shuffled out slowly, keeping his back to the wall of the structure, his wide eyes glancing at her then darting away again. His face was smeared with mud and his hair wildly tangled.

"What's the matter? Are you scared of me?"

"You're the crazy lady," the boy answered, and the voices

in her head hooted with delight, Fynn's loud amongst them. *You see? They already know. Soon . . .*

"What were you doing in there?" she asked.

The boy shrugged. "Waiting."

"Waiting for what?"

Another shrug. "Nothing."

"Only an idiot waits for nothing, boy. Are you hiding?" She raised a finger, stopping him in mid-shrug. "Don't lie to me, boy. I'm the crazy lady, remember? I can hear what you're thinking?" She tapped her forehead with the upraised finger. The voices hooted again. *Liar! Charlatan!* "So you'd better tell me the truth: who are you hiding from?"

He looked at her suspiciously, cocking his head as if he'd heard the voices himself. "The soldiers," he said. "The ones in blue and gold."

"The Garde Kralji?" She spat on the ground between them. "I know them. Oh, I know them well. But why are you hiding from them? They're not looking for *you*, boy, not unless you're Numetodo." His face twisted strangely at that, and she looked at him sidewise, rubbing at her stomach. There were strange flutterings there, and she wondered whether she was going to be sick again, or if she was feeling the child for the first time. "*Are* you Numetodo?" she asked. "Is that why?"

"No," he said quickly, but she had seen too many lies and deceptions in her life already, and she knew he was saying less than he could. She looked at him more closely, at the filthy clothing and matted hair. She could see the bones of his cheeks.

"When's the last time you ate?"

Another shrug.

"Do you live near here?"

He grimaced. "I . . . I used to. Just over there." He pointed down the lane. "But . . . I don't know . . ." He stopped, and she saw his lip quivering. He sniffed and drew his sleeve quickly over his eyes, pressing his lips tightly together. The defiance, the refusal to let her see just how scared and frightened he was made her decision for her. She smiled at him, crouching down in front of him. It should have been an easy movement for her, but the thickening waist made her feel as if her own body were someone else's.

"You have a name?" she asked the boy.

"Nico," he told her. "My name is Nico."

"Then why don't you come with me, Nico? I have some croissants, and a bit of butter, and I can probably find a slice of meat or two. Does that sound good?" She held out her hand to him. Hesitantly, he took it, and she stood up. The voices were laughing at her, mocking her. *The White Stone has gone soft as mud . . .*

Ignoring them, she walked with Nico to her rooms.

CONNECTIONS

Niente
Karl Vliománi
Allesandra ca'Vörl
Niente
Allesandra ca'Vörl
Jan ca'Vörl
Nico Morel
Audric ca'Dakwi
Varina ci'Pallo
Enéas cu'Kinnear
The White Stone

Niente

HE HAD NEVER BEEN AT SEA before, and he wasn't certain that he was entirely enjoying the experience.

Niente stood at the aftcastle bow of the captured Holdings galleon, once the *Marguerite* and now renamed *Yaoyotl*—which was "War" in his own language. *Yaoyotl* sailed in the middle of the Tehuantin fleet; from his perch, Niente could look out over long azure swells decorated with the white sails of well over a hundred ships. Behind them, lost over the horizon days ago, was the eastern coast of his land and the foul smoke of burned and razed Munereo, now the gravepit for the Holdings' Garde Civile, except for those few who had retreated to the Easterners' last small fingerhold on the continent, the city of Tobarro. The army of the Tehuantin had taken Munereo, taken back all the land south and west of its walls, and had taken the ships of the Holdings fleet in the harbor, at least those that had escaped the spell-fire from the Tehuantin fleet, or that had not been scuttled by their own crews and sent to the bottom when it was obvious the day was lost. Most of the ships accompanying the *Yaoyotl* were the seacraft called *acalli*: the two-masted, lateen-sailed ships with which the Tehuantin plied the Western Sea between the great cities the Eastern invaders had never seen. The acalli could not carry the number of crew or soldiers that the square-sailed Nessantican galleons could muster, nor were they as fast, but they were far more maneuverable, especially in shallow coastal waters or when the wind was against them.

The winds of the Strettosei however, blew steadily west to east at this latitude, and the wind of their passage sighed past the taut lines holding the sails as the prows of the ships carved long lines of white water through the swells, dipping and rising and falling yet again, relentless and eternal.

A motion that still, after several days, made Niente's stomach lurch and burn. His limbs, twisted and ravaged by the efforts of the spell he'd placed in the Easterner Enéas, ached as he tried to remain steady against the ship's lurching. Two of the lesser nahualli stood on the aftcastle with him, watching as Niente used his bowl to perform the scrying spell; he dared not show them the weakness of his stomach or his body, or word would go to the other nahualli and eventually come to the ear of Tecuhtli Zolin, who was also on the *Yaoyotl*. The fate of every Nahual awaited him, the fate that may have even come to Mahri and perhaps to Talis as well: as a nahualli, every use of the X'in Ka took its toll, and the greater the spell, the larger the payment the gods demanded.

Eventually, the payment would be death.

The rolling of the ship shivered the water in his scrying bowl, rendering murky the visions of the future: that bothered Niente more than the nausea. Niente peered into the water, sloshing to the rim of the brass bowl. His eyes didn't want to focus; the left eye, clouded ever since his enchantment of Enéas, had become worse since the assault on Munereo. He blinked, but the scenes in the bowl refused to become clear. He grunted, scowling, and tossed the water in disgust over the rear rail of the ship. The other nahualli raised eyebrows but said nothing. "I need to speak with the Tecuhtli," Niente said. "Take the bowl back to my room and cleanse it."

They bent their heads obediently as Niente, shuffling, pushed past them.

Niente had argued with Tecuhtli Zolin that this strategy was foolish, though he'd not dared to use that word. He wanted desperately to go home, back beyond the Knife-Edge Mountains to the great cities by the lake. Home to Xaria, his wife; home to his children. Home to familiarity.

He hadn't been alone. The High Warrior Citlali had taken the same position, as had several of the lesser warriors. "Why should we sail to the Easterners' land? Let us take the last city they hold here and push their bodies into the great water. Then let us return to our homes and our families, and if the Easterners return to trouble our cousins again, we'll push them back once more."

But Zolin was adamant. "Sakal demands more of us," he'd declared. "It is time to show these Easterners that we can hurt them as they hurt us. If one is attacked by a wolf, driving it off leaves the wolf to attack again, perhaps when it is stronger or you are weaker. Killing the wolf is the only way to be truly safe."

"This is not a wolf," Niente had persisted. "This is a many-headed beast, only one small face of which we've seen, and we are going to its lair. It may be that it will devour us completely."

Zolin had grunted at that. "Running from the wolf because you're afraid is the worst strategy of all. It only gives the wolf your unprotected back."

In the end, Zolin had won over the High Warriors, and Niente had no choice but to tell the nahualli that their task was not yet done. He'd almost been surprised that none of the nahualli had risen up to challenge him for Nahual as a result.

The quarters of the former captain were below in the ship's aftcastle, and that was where Tecuhtli Zolin had taken up residence. The Easterner furniture had been tossed overboard, to be replaced by the more familiar geometric lines and patterns of their own styles. The room was ablaze with reds and browns, the colors of blood and earth. The smell of incense wrinkled Niente's nose as he entered, the techutli's servants prostrating themselves on the rugs tossed over the wooden planks.

Tecuhtli Zolin reclined in a chair carved from a single block of green rock, cushioned by pillows and blankets. His face and torso, like those of all soldiers, was tattooed with swirls of dashes and curling lines: a record of their prowess in battle and their rank. His head was shaved as always and now adorned with the sprawling red tattoo of the eagle. The High Warriors Citlali and Mazatl had been speaking to him in low tones, but broke off their conversation as Niente entered. Their marked, grim faces turned to him.

"Ah, Nahual Niente," Tecuhtli Zolin said, gesturing. Niente strode across the room to the throne and dropped to his knees. "Get up, get up. Tell me, what do the gods say?"

Niente shook his head as he rose to his feet. He could feel the appraising stares of the High Warriors on him. "I'm sorry, Tecuhtli, but the motion of the ship . . . it disturbs the waters. I saw a battle and a city afire at the edge of a sea, and your banner flying above it, but the rest—I saw nothing of the Easterner I sent back to this Kraljiki. I saw nothing of their great city."

"Ah, but the banner and a city afire . . . that can only speak of victory. As to your Easterner—" Zolin exhaled a scoff and then spat on the floor, "—that was old Necalli's strategy, and not even the great Mahri had been able to make it work."

Niente flushed at the mention, irritated at Zolin's dismissal of Mahri, whose gifts with the X'in Ka were legendary. Mahri had evidently failed, yes, but it must have been because some force with the Easterners had been even stronger. Niente bowed his head more to hide his face than in submission. "It must be as you say, Tecuhtli."

Zolin laughed at that. "Come now, Niente. Don't be so modest. Why, you are a far-seer and a nahualli the like of which we haven't seen since Mahri. Better, since Mahri failed to stop the Easterners from invading our lands and those of our cousins. Necalli was a fool who wasted valuable resources. He wasted you as well—all the effort you put into that Easterner. But now . . ." A broad smile spread over Zolin's face. "I have thrown the Easterners back to one unimportant town on our cousins' land—with the help of your advice and your skill—and now we go to plunder the Easterners as they once plundered our cousins of the Eastern Sea." He waved a hand. "I will chop the head from this Eastern serpent myself, and I will make certain that it never grows a new one." His hand sliced downward. Zolin grinned, but the two High Warriors' faces were stoic and unmoving.

Niente wondered which one of them might one day challenge Zolin if this expedition failed, as Niente feared it would.

Niente shared the dour attitude of Citlali and Mazatl. Zolin was no different than many of those outside the nahualli. They all thought his gift was a simple thing: peer into the water and let the moon-goddess Axat send the future spinning past your eyes. They didn't understand that Axat's visions were confusing and sometimes dim, that what swam in the sacred water were only possibilities, and that those possibilities could be altered and shifted and even averted by other's abilities. Mahri—whose skills, it was said, had surpassed any nahualli's—had discovered how fickle Axat could be: Mahri's death had been one of the first visions Niente had ever seen in a scrying bowl; it had been that vision that had demonstrated to Niente's mentors how fully Axat and Sakal had blessed him. Talis, who Tecuhtli Necalli had sent to Nessantico, had since confirmed Niente's vision: Mahri had failed and been killed.

Those without the gift thought that it must be wonderful to wield the power of Axat and Sakal, of moon and sun. They didn't see how using the gift stole strength and vitality; how it disfigured and twisted those who used it. Already Niente could look into the bronze mirror in his room and see the deep lines in his face, lines that no one of his age should yet bear. He could see how his mouth sagged, how his left eye wept constantly and was now whitened with a spell-cloud, how his hair was thinning and marbled with silver strands. He could feel the constant ache in his joints that would one day turn into obsidian knives of agony. Niente had never met Mahri, but he had glimpsed the man's face in the scrying bowl, and it terrified him that one day he, too, would see people turning away rather than look on him, and he would hear the cries of frightened children as he passed.

And he knew that Tecuhtli Zolin might be pleased now with him, but that the Tecuhtli's pleasure was fragile, and could vanish as quickly as mist in sunlight. A battle lost ... That was all it would take, and Tecuhtli Zolin would be looking for a new Nahual to be at his side.

"I pray to Axat that you will slay the Eastern serpent," he told Zolin. "But I—"

He stopped, hearing a call from the deck. *"Land ..."* someone was shouting. *"The Easterner coast ..."*

Zolin's grin grew wider. "Good," he said to his High Warriors, to Niente. "It's time to see a city burn and watch our banners floating over their land." He rose to his feet, gesturing away the servants who rushed to help. "Come," the Tecuhtli said. "Let's see this land together with our own eyes, before we take it."

Karl Vliomani

"**WELL?**" KARL ASKED VARINA as she returned to the room. Varina shrugged off her overcloak and sank down on a chair. "She's Nico's matarh, that's certain," Varina said. "I told her that I'd heard her son had run away, and that when we stayed in Nessantico, I saw a boy on Crescent Street. Her eyes widened at that, and she told me that was where she'd lived until last month. When I described the boy and the house, she started sobbing. It was all I could do to stop her from rushing back to Nessantico tonight."

"And Talis?"

"Talis is the boy's vatarh, and she's in love with him, Karl," Varina said. "That much was also obvious; in fact, I suspect she's with child by him again, the way she hugs her body when she talks about him. Your encounter with him scared him enough that he sent her and Nico away from the city—I think he thought you'd have the Garde Kralji after him. She's been waiting here hoping he'll come for her, hoping that Nico would return as well." Varina leaned her head back and closed her eyes, sighing. "She's not going to betray Talis to get Nico back, Karl. Honestly, I didn't even broach that possibility with her. Frankly, I'm certain she's in her room now packing, getting ready to leave tomorrow for Nessantico, hoping to find Nico there. She's been grieving and frantic ever since he left." She opened her eyes again, looking at him. "It's what I'd do, in her place. I'm sorry—I know what you wanted me to do, but . . . I couldn't go through with it. I couldn't hold her child hostage against her giving us Talis, not when we don't actually know where Nico is. I'm sorry. I know you suspect that Talis may be the one who killed Ana, and you have good reasons for those suspicions, but this . . ."

Another sigh. She spread her hands wide. "I couldn't do it."

There was no apology in her voice or in her gaze. And he found that he couldn't summon any anger toward her—he knew how it would have been with his own sons. He might have been a poor, absent vatarh for them, but had it come to that, he would have done whatever he'd needed to do for them.

At least that's what he told himself. He wondered if it were true. What if Kaitlin had sent for him while he was in Nessantico, while Ana was alive? What if she'd asked him to return, for the sake of his sons? Would he have gone? Or would he have made some excuse, found some compelling reason that he must remain here with Ana.

"Karl?" Varina asked. "Are you angry with me?"

He shook his head. "Don't worry," he told her. "I understand." His fingers prowled stubble. He felt old tonight. His bones were cold, and the fire in the hearth did nothing to warm them. "I'll go back with her," he said finally, when the silence had threatened to go on too long. "Maybe Talis will come for her. Maybe she knows where Talis is hiding."

"If you go back, the Garde Kralji will find you, and the Kraljiki will have you tortured and executed. Your corpse will be swinging in one of the cages of the Pontica Kralji, with crows picking the flesh from your bones."

He shivered, hugging himself with arms that felt tired and weak. "You may be right. But what am I running *toward*, Varina? Leaving Nessantico—what did I really gain by that? How will I find out who killed Ana somewhere else?" He shook his head. "No, I *need* to go back. Isn't that the Numetodo method?—to learn, you must examine; to understand, you must experience. You must have facts. Finding Nico's matarh . . . ." He shivered again. "It's almost as if Ana's ghost had led me here."

"You don't believe in either ghosts or gods, Karl. Believe only in what you can see and touch and examine. Isn't *that* the Numetodo method?"

He smiled faintly at that. "No, I don't believe in ghosts," he told her. "But it's strange how comforting such a thought could be, isn't it? It almost makes you understand the hold faith has on people." He drew a long, slow breath. "Still, I'm going back."

"Then I'll go with you," Varina told him. "Just like

you, there's nothing I'm running toward. And you'll need help."

"You don't need to do this. The Kraljiki would do the same to you as he would me . . . or worse. There's no reason for *you* to go back, after all. . . ." His voice trailed off.

She didn't answer, but he saw the set of her lips and the posture of her body, he saw the way she was nearly glaring at him, and suddenly he *knew*, and the revelation was painful. "Oh," he said. He wondered how he could have been so blind. He got up from his seat at the bed and went over to where she was sitting. He started to put his hand on her shoulder, but her eyes narrowed and he drew his hand back. "Varina . . ."

Her gaze held him, her brown eyes searching his. "You loved Ana, even though she never quite loved you the same way in return. She was too caught up in what she saw as her own task in life," Varina said quietly. She nodded. Her lips twitched once as if she wanted to smile, then fell back to a frown. "Well, I understand that, Karl. I understand that very well."

"I don't know what to say."

She did smile then, the expression tinged with an underlying emotion Karl couldn't decipher. "Then you shouldn't say anything. I haven't said anything that needs a reply— beyond telling you that I'm going back with you no matter what you say."

She held his gaze, unblinking, until he nodded. "All right," he said. She nodded but otherwise said nothing. The silence grew long and increasingly uncomfortable, both of them staring at the small fire in the hearth. The thoughts roiled in Karl's head: all the times he and Varina had been together, the comments she'd made, the glances she'd given him, the occasional touches, the way she'd always deflected questions about any romantic interests she might have had, the way she'd flung herself into the work of the Numetodo.

He should have known. Should have realized. But the silence had already made the questions he should have asked more difficult. He cleared his throat. "If . . . If you're going back to Nessantico with me, then perhaps you need to start showing me more of this Westlander way of magic."

Retreating into work to avoid intimacy: that was what Ana had always done, after all.

~

Allesandra ca'Vörl

SHE FOUND SERGEI'S TALE fascinating, though she knew the man well enough to know that there were details he was holding back. She wasn't bothered by that; she would have done the same in his place. She *had* done the same, during the long years she had been held in Nessantico. She had liked Archigos Ana, who had treated her fairly and respectfully, and she had been fascinated by Sergei, first by his reputation and his silver nose, then—as she'd come to know him—by his intelligence and his intriguing, dark personality.

"Ca'Rudka is an interesting and skilled man, and I would not be where I am now if it weren't for him," Archigos Ana had told her once, a few years into her exile, as Allesandra was blooming into a young woman. *"But you can't entirely trust him. Oh, he's true to his word, but he gives that word carefully and grudgingly, and will keep to the letter of it and perhaps not the spirit. His true allegiance is to Nessantico, not to any person within it. I don't think he loves any person, don't think he ever has. His true love is the city and the Holdings itself. And some of his tastes, what he enjoys doing . . ."* Ana had grimaced at that. *"I hope those are only vile tales, and not true."*

She remembered that conversation as she regarded Sergei, now dressed in current Firenzcian fashion and colors. He had come at her invitation to eat lunch in her rooms in Brezno Palais, and if he had been offended by the careful search of his body before he'd been allowed entry, or if he noticed the two armed gardai who watched him closely from their stations in the room, he said nothing. He smiled at her as he might have at any ca' in Nessantico, and he uttered pleasantries about the presentation and taste of the meal as the servants passed in and out, and he leaned back in his chair with a cup of tea as if he were relaxed and at ease. He related how he'd been imprisoned in the Bastida, and how he'd escaped. She watched his face, watched his hands—none of them revealed any emotion at all; he might have been telling a tale that had happened to some distant relative once upon a time.

"So the Numetodo Ambassador helped you?" Allesandra also remembered Karl ca'Vliomani, who was so obviously smitten with Archigos Ana, although she seemed to treat him as no more than a good friend. Allesandra had not cared much for him, or for the Numetodo, who scorned and mocked her own strong beliefs, who believed in no gods at all. They believed that the world had always existed, that it was impossibly old and that natural processes could explain everything within it—the sheer illogic and arrogance of their philosophy annoyed Allesandra. "That won't please Archigos Semini . . . or Archigos Kenne either, I would guess."

"It was an act of friendship and nothing else."

"Archigos Ana once told me that every act reflects on the faith of the person who commits it," Allesandra told him. "Are you a Numetodo now, Sergei?"

He shook his head. "No. I believe in Cénzi as strongly as I ever did."

She wondered if that statement was simply an artful deflection, but let it go. "Can Kraljiki Audric truly rule the Holdings? Can Archigos Kenne hold the a'téni together as Ana did?"

"Time alone will give you that answer, A'Hïrzg," he responded.

"Then indulge me with speculation."

Sergei lifted a shoulder. "Archigos Kenne is . . . weak. Not just physically, but also when it comes to confrontation. He is a good, moral, and faithful man, but he's a follower and not a leader. To his credit, that defect is one that he knows and acknowledges. The Concordance of A'Téni elected him Archigos because of it; they didn't want another strong leader like Ana. As for Kraljiki Audric . . . well, he's but a boy, and in ill health. I'm sure you have your own people giving you reports, but I suspect they haven't told you the full story."

He leaned forward, setting down the teacup and plate silently on the table. She could see her distorted reflection in his nose. "Audric has gone mad," he said softly. He tapped an index finger to his forehead. "How fully, I don't know. I saw it myself before he sent me to the Bastida, and afterward my friends in court and with the Faith sent me word. He holds conversations with the painting of his great-matarh Marguerite; he puts the painting at his right hand in court as if she were his councillor."

"Truly?" Allesandra gestured, and one of the servants hurried forward to refill the teacups. She watched the golden liquid steam in her cup. "And no one says anything?"

"Kralji have sometimes acted strangely, and sometimes punished those who point out their strangeness. That's happened often enough in Nessantico's long history; we could both recite the names, I'm sure. And if it doesn't seem to directly affect the Holdings—" he lifted a shoulder, "—then it's best to keep such observations to yourself . . . and to be careful. I'm sure that's what Sigourney ca'Ludovici is doing: she wants the throne, and she watches for the opportunity to seize it. Most of the Council of Ca' would back her; the Sun Throne is hers if Audric dies or must be . . . removed. Either one of those is a very likely scenario in the next few months, I suspect."

Allesandra nodded. She lifted the teacup and blew over the fragrant surface, sipping carefully. Neither of them said anything for several breaths. "Why did you come here, Regent?" she asked finally. "I know what you told my son and the Archigos. But I think there's more."

He glanced over his shoulder at the gardai and said nothing. "They're my people," she told him. "My own handpicked gardai who have been with me since I returned to Firenzcia. I trust them implicitly. I'm sure you had men under your command whose integrity you trusted in such a manner."

"It's been my experience that nearly everyone has a flaw that can be exploited. I've learned that the fewer ears hear something, the more chances there are that statements won't be repeated."

She waited, sipping her tea; he rubbed at his nose, smearing her reflection.

"As you wish," he said at last. "Nessantico and the Holdings have been my life, A'Hïrzg. That's not a loyalty I can or will give up. My sincerest wish is to see the Holdings restored to what it was when Kraljica Marguerite was on the throne. I would like to see *you* in Nessantico, as Kraljica Allesandra. You could be the Kraljica that Nessantico requires now."

Even though she'd been expecting the words, she still found herself drawing a quick inward breath. *You see, Vatarh? You see? This is the legacy you wanted, and this is the promise you gave up when you abandoned me for Fynn.* The emotional depth of the internal response surprised her; she could feel the warmth of it spreading upward from her chest to her face. She struggled not to show any of it to ca'Rudka. "Wishes are cheap," she told him. "We can wish for all we want. What we can accomplish is quite another thing."

"Yet if two people's wishes coincide, and they coincide with those of other people, and if those people are powerful enough . . ." He smiled, folding his fingers together on the lace tablecloth as if he were praying. "Would that be your wish as well, A'Hïrzg? Can you see a ca'Vörl on the Sun Throne? I know your vatarh had that vision."

He knows. "Let's put that aside for the moment, Regent. There are other issues if this is something we would pursue—and I'm not saying that it is. What of the Faith? Who would be the Archigos in this restored Holdings you envision: Semini, or Kenne?"

"Despite what I said about his faults, I like Archigos Kenne. He is my friend, his faith is true, and as I said, he's a good man."

"He may be all of that, but he is not a friend of Firenzcia and, like Ana, would coddle the heretics. And Semini is *my* friend."

Sergei made a contemplative sound deep in his throat. "There are rumors, A'Hïrzg, that he may be more."

She flushed hotly at that. The gardai behind the Regent moved his hand from his side to the hilt of his sword, but she shook her head to him. "You speak too freely about rumors and lies, Regent. You can't treat me like a girl or a royal hostage anymore. You're on *my* land, and it's *your* life at stake, not mine. If this is the way you spoke to Audric, then it's no wonder he no longer wanted you to be Regent."

He bowed his head, but there was no apology in his hawkish eyes. "My apologies, A'Hïrzg. My stay in the Bastida has, I'm afraid, scrubbed away both my diplomacy and my patience. But those rumors and lies do concern me, if we are to work together."

"The Archigos already has a wife. That's all that needs to be said, and all the answer you'll receive. As to Archigos Kenne . . ." Allesandra remembered Kenne ca'Fionta also: a gentle man, a quiet man, one who was always an effective second-in-command but never questioned anything asked of him or spoke up for himself. She could not imagine him as Archigos. Ana could be gentle and affectionate also, but there was hard bone and steel underneath her velvet, and you did not want to be her enemy. Allesandra wasn't certain what lay underneath ca'Fionta's exterior, but she suspected that Sergei's assessment was correct.

But Semini—Semini could be as adamantine and strong as Ana. "If you want Firenzcia's help," she continued, "if you want the help of our war-téni, then it will be Archigos Semini, not Archigos Kenne, who reunites the Faith. Kenne needn't be killed; if he could be convinced to renounce his title for the good of the Faith, perhaps even to become the a'téni of one of the cities. I suspect a friend could convince another friend of the sanity of that course. I hope so, for Kenne's sake."

Allesandra settled back in her chair. Sergei, for the first time, had a look of uncertainty in his face, and she was surprised by the strength of the enjoyment that gave her. She wondered if that was how a Kraljica or a Hïrzgin often felt, if that was one of the gifts of power. A gift, or perhaps a trap for those who fell into the thrall of that feeling. "I know what I bring to you, Regent," she said to him. "I bring you my name and my genealogy. I bring you the unmatched army of Firenzcia through my son. I bring you the fearsome war-téni of the true Concénzia Faith through Archigos Semini. I bring you Miscoli, Sesemora, and the Magyarias, who answer to Firenzcia. I bring all that to the table. What is it that you bring us, Regent?"

He didn't answer quickly. His right forefinger stroked the lip of the teacup before him, and he seemed to be staring down at the pattern of the leaves in the bottom. "I bring you knowledge," he said. "I know the Garde Kralji and the Garde Civile and the strengths and weaknesses of their commanders. I know Nessantico; I know all her paths and all her secrets. There are those in the Garde Civile and the Garde Kralji who will answer if I call them. There are those among the ca'-and-cu' who will do the same. There are chevarittai who will come to me if I summon them. It may be, A'Hirzg, that I can deliver the Sun Throne to you with as few lives lost as possible."

"Why, if you could do all that, why isn't it that you're the Kraljiki yourself rather than a refugee?" she asked him, but gave him no time to respond. "And if you can do all this, what is it that you want in return?"

"Nothing," he said, and Allesandra felt surprise lift her eyebrows. "Give me whatever reward you see fit. I do this for Nessantico only, to whom I have always pledged my life. I once protected Nessantico from Firenzcia's aggression; now, I will give her to Firenzcia freely. Kraljica Marguerite believed in marriage as a way to reconcile opposing forces, and I believe the same, because the marriage of Nessantico to Firenzcia is what she needs now to survive."

Pretty words, she wanted to say scoffingly. She wasn't certain she believed the man at all. But Cénzi had brought the Regent to her, all unexpected, a gift she couldn't refuse. *"You are an intelligent, talented, and attractive young woman,"* Archigos Ana had told her when news had reached Nessantico that her vatarh had named the infant Fynn as the A'Hirzg and refused to pay the ransom that Kraljiki Justi had demanded for her release. It had been less than a year into her cushioned and bejeweled imprisonment, and Allesandra had wept in bewilderment and fright. Ana—the enemy—had held her and comforted her, had stroked her hair and calmed her again. *"I know Cénzi has a plan for you. I can feel it, Allesandra. There is a great part for you to play yet in life. . . ."*

She would play that part. She would have what her vatarh had once promised her: the brilliant necklace of Nessantico. That was the reason that Sergei ca'Rudka had appeared now.

"We shall see, Regent ca'Rudka," was all she told him now. "In the end, it will be as Cénzi wills. . . ."

~

Niente

NIENTE STOOD ON THE SLOPE of Karnor with Tecuhtli Zolin and his High Warriors, the city spread out below him, and he saw the vision he had glimpsed in the bowl.

The windows of the temple just below them were shattered, gouged-out eyes in the skull of a ruined building. Soot blackened the stones around them, greasy smoke still rising through them. The golden half-dome was broken, the gilded masonry fallen in. Fires flared skyward at a dozen places in the city, brighter than the setting sun.

The attack had gone quickly and easily. As soon as they had glimpsed the heights of the Easterners' great island Karnmor, Niente had called together the nahualli who could control the wind and the sky, and they had conjured a wall of dense fog to conceal the Tehuantin fleet as they approached. The fog bank wrapped them in gray-white air and muffled the sounds of their preparations. By the time the spell-fog failed and drifted away in wisps, the *Yaoyotl*— flying the eagle banner of Tehuantin—was already at the mouth of Karnor Harbor, its sister ships spread out in two great wings to either side. Karnor Harbor was vast and deep, nested in cliffs of stony arms with the city perched far back, leagues away.

A hand of Holdings naval ships were stationed there, and they tacked to face the onslaught even as fishing and pleasure vessels fled for safety. Niente had to admire the bravery of the Holdings captains: in the face of a vastly superior force they didn't flee but turned to confront them directly with their blue-and-gold flags fluttering atop the masts. Still, it had been slaughter. The sea wind was behind the Tehuantin fleet and the Holdings ships had to beat slowly into the wind. The war-téni aboard the Holdings galleons had little time to prepare their spells—perhaps more powerful than those of the nahualli, but slow to create, and Niente had pushed his nahualli all that day. Their spell-sticks were full, the black sands already prepared. The spells of the nahualli had been able to deflect most of the arcing fire of the war-téni away from the ships, though the ship alongside the *Yaoyotl* took a direct hit that fanned into a monstrous blossom of fire and destruction along the decks, sending dozens of men screaming into the cold swells and setting the ship aflame and dead in the water, so that the ships behind had to tack suddenly to avoid it.

Tecuhtli Zolin was on deck, screaming orders from the forecastle; the Tehuantin ships answered with the massive bolts tipped with capsules of black sand and flung from catapults on the decks: the engines had flung the sputtering missiles toward the defenders of Karnmor; the capsules, enchanted with fire spells, exploded on impact, sending boards to splinters, ripping and tearing bloody limbs from the unfortunate sailors. The Nessantican ships had faltered, their sails afire, or drooping as they lost the wind under the assault. Tecuhtli Zolin shrieked orders and a second round of fire missiles raked them.

They left the defenders behind as nothing more than hulks burning down to the waterline, and the fleet advanced into the inner harbor of the city. The soldiers of Karnor massed there under command of a few horsed chevarittai, but again Tecuhtli Zolin called his orders and the catapults flung their awful messengers into their midst, the explosions trembling the steep hills on which Karnor was built and starting fires among the buildings. The soldiers and the nahualli shouted in victory as they approached the harbor, the sound itself terrifying as swords clashed against shields and spell-staffs clattered. Niente shouted with them, his own throat raw from yelling and the smoke of battle. He saw residents fleeing through the streets in unorganized mobs, streaming up and away from the sudden clash of battle in the harbor as gangplanks boomed down and disgorged the Tehuantin soldiers. They charged out screaming, their tattooed faces furious and joyful at the same time. Tecuhtli Zolin led them, his curved sword flashing in the sunlight and his voice calling challenge to the waiting enemy. Niente and his nahualli rushed after them, and their spell-staffs gleamed white as they flung war-bolts into the ranks of the soldiers. Niente's own stave had been quickly depleted, and he had taken the bundle of eagle claws lashed to his back, turning the ivory tubes to activate the contact fire spell and tossing them high over the front ranks of the soldiers to explode in their midst. Once, a wounded Nessantican soldier had risen up from the ground as he stepped over him. Luckily, the man was weak from his wounds, and Niente was able to step away from the wobbly thrust of the sword. He'd taken his knife from his belt and slashed the keen edge across the man's exposed throat before the soldier could recover. Hot blood had spattered Niente's hand, and the man gave a gurgling cry as he collapsed for a final time. A deep knife thrust to the side of the man's neck had finished him, and Niente had risen to find the battle nearly over, with the defenders retreating into the city, pursued by the Tehuantin.

By the time the sun had set—red and sullen through the smoke of the burning city—Karnor was theirs, what was left of it. Below him, Niente could hear faint screaming and wailing as the Tehuantin sacked and plundered the city and killed those they found there. Far below, in the harbor, the holds of the Tehuantin ships were being stuffed with the largesse of the city.

Niente stood with Tecuhtli Zolin and the Tehuantin High Warriors Citlali and Mazatl. Nearby, guarded by tattooed warriors, the commandant and three chief offiziers of the defenders knelt bound and silenced. The prisoners stared at the fire that the nahualli had built at Niente's direction, and at the flat altar stone from the Karnmor Temple that Niente had ordered dragged here to the summit of Mount Karnmor.

Four eagle claws, their horns filled with black sand, had been placed in the center of the altar stone. They stared at those most of all.

"These Easterners," Tecuhtli Zolin commented, "are poor fighters. They ran like frightened children." He glanced back to the prisoners with a scowl. The Tecuhtli wore his armor, the leather-backed bamboo notched here and there by an enemy blade, the supple tubes rattling softly as he moved. The armor was spattered and stained with blood, though little of it appeared to be his. The sun was fully down now, and the moon had risen in the east—

Zolin glanced that way. "Axat won't even accept the offering of these incompetents."

Niente remembered the battles around Lake Malik, and shook his head. "Tecuhtli, they were caught unawares and unprepared for us. That won't happen again. The whispers of what happened here will come to their Kraljiki and the commanders of their army. Perhaps . . ." He hesitated, not wanting to say the next words. "Perhaps it would be best if we take what we have gained here and return home."

Tecuhtli Zolin laughed mockingly. "Go back? Now? When we're standing here in the smoke of victory, just as you foresaw? Nahual Niente, you disappoint me. I came here to challenge this Kraljiki who would send his people to steal our cousins' land but who won't even lead his own army. Citlali, Mazatl—what do you say?"

Mazatl was already frowning, firelight playing over his marked face. Like Zolin, he still wore his battered and gore-marked armor. "I say that I'm glad to be standing on the ground, even here. To be at sea again?" He spat on the rocks at his feet. "I came to fight, not to sail. I say we give Axat what She has earned here, and go on." Citlali muttered his agreement, but appeared less convinced.

The nahualli and the warriors gathered nearest the fire had already begun the low, haunting chanting of the prayer to Axat. The moon's light fell bright and full on the altar stone, glinting on the thick glass tips of the eagle claws. Niente nodded to Zolin.

Two nahualli grabbed one of the prisoners and hauled the man forward. The offizier was blubbering with fright, calling out to Cénzi. The nahualli pulled him onto the altar stone and pushed him down to his knees. He stared up at Niente in terror. "Go bravely to your death," Niente said to the man in his own language as he picked up one of the eagle claws. He turned the horn at the tip, the ominous click loud as the spell was activated. "Pray to your god. This will be quick. I promise you that much." Niente nodded again, and the nahualli held the man's arms tight as the man closed his eyes, his lips moving in silent prayer.

Niente opened his own mind to Axat and the moon glow, and pressed the bone of the muzzle to the man's stomach. The sound of the eagle claw's detonation echoed over the city.

~

Allesandra ca'Vörl

JAN LOOKED ALMOST FRIGHTENED, his eyes so wide there was white entirely around the pupils. "Matarh... taking the army against the Holdings... I don't know."

"I understand the danger," she told him. "Yes, it is a huge step to take so early in your time as Hïrzg, and I understand how you must feel. I do. You would need to trust Starkkapitän ca'Damont's expertise; even so, this would test you beyond anything you've ever done in your life. But, Jan, I know this is something you can do. Taking the army into battle is something you *must* eventually do—as nearly every Hïrzg of Firenzcia has done. Even your vatarh would tell you that. Fynn was eighteen, only two years older than you, when he first did so." She nodded toward Semini, who sat silently in his own chair. They were in Allesandra's chambers, the three of them. The servants had been dismissed after they had served dinner, the remnants of which decorated the table between them. "Semini knows," she said. "He commanded the war-téni when your great-vatarh Jan nearly took Nessantico."

"And he would have succeeded, had that vile heretic of an Archigos not used her Numetodo magic against us," Semini grumbled. He seemed more like a bear than ever, hunched over on his chair. He tapped his plate, but looked carefully away from Allesandra. She could still remember the shock of that evening: *she had been in the tent sitting on her vatarh's lap. "You are my little bird," he was saying, "and I love—" Then his voice cut off and—impossibly—she was outside far from the encampment, sprawled on rain-soaked ground in the night as Archigos Ana and some strange man fought each other with Ilmodo magic she would have thought impossible.* Yes, she remembered that all too well—and she knew that her capture was the reason her vatarh had failed, and that he blamed her for it. "Oh, there's much that the

Holdings hasn't yet answered for," the Archigos continued, looking only at Jan. He pounded softly on the tablecloth with a fist. "I look forward to demanding payment. Hïrzg Jan, I stand ready to be at your right hand, with all the war-téni of the Faith alongside me."

Jan still looked uncertain, and Allesandra reached out to pat his hand. "Jan," she said, "ultimately this must be your decision, not mine. I'm not the Hïrzg, you are."

"You didn't want *this* when you could have had it," Jan said, tapping the golden band of the Hïrzg's crown on his head. "And yet now you want to—" He stopped, abruptly. Blinked. "Oh," he said. His eyes narrowed.

She worried at the look on his face. "Think of what we could accomplish together, Jan," she told him hurriedly, "with the same family on the Sun Throne and on the Throne of Firenzcia. We could bind the Holdings together and create a greater, more peaceful empire than Marguerite's."

He said nothing. He looked from Semini to Allesandra, then rose from his seat and walked quickly to the door. "Jan?" she called after him, and he paused there. He spoke without turning around to her.

"I'm beginning to understand some of what Vatarh said about you before he left, Matarh," Jan said. "He told me that you use people for your own purposes; he said that was exactly the way your own vatarh had been, so it wasn't all that surprising. He said that was what had made Great-Vatarh an effective Hïrzg, but a dangerous friend. I wonder if I can ever be such a good Hïrzg. I wonder if I would ever want to be." Jan knocked on the door and the hall servants opened it.

Allesandra rose to her feet and pushed back from the table; she started after him as plates clashed and goblets shivered. "Jan, stay. Please. Talk to me."

He shook his head and left without another word, the door closing again.

Allesandra stood in the center of the dining room and could not hold back the sob that came. *I never meant to hurt him. I don't want to hurt him.* At the same time, she wondered at his declaration: *had* she made a mistake placing him on the Hïrzg's throne? Was she seeing Jan with a matarh's eyes and not those of truth? She felt Semini's hands on her shoulders and realized that he had risen to stand behind her. "Don't worry, Allesandra," he said to her. His words were a low growl in her ear. "Let the boy alone for a bit—and remember that in many ways he still *is* a boy. He knows you're right, but right now he's feeling that you gave him the crown of the Hïrzg as the consolation prize."

"It truly wasn't that way." Tears threatened, and she sniffed and blinked them back. "I love him, Semini. I do. He doesn't realize how much. It hurts me to see him angry with me. This wasn't what I intended."

"I know," he whispered. "I'll talk to him. I can convince him that you're right."

She shook her head, staring at the door. "I need to go after him."

"If you do that, the two of you will just end up in a worse argument. You're both too much alike. Give him time to calm and think about things, and he'll realize that he was overreacting. He may even apologize. Give him time. Let him be angry now."

His hands kneaded her shoulders. She felt his lips brush the hair at the nape of her neck, and let her head drop forward in response. "He's my son. It hurts me when he's hurting."

"If you get what you're after, then that's something you might have to accept. The Kralji of Nessantico and the Hïrzgai of Firenzcia have always had their differences and their separate agendas. If you don't want a struggle between the two of you, then you should give up this idea of yours."

She stiffened under his kneading hands, and he chuckled. "There, you see. Jan's not the only one who gets irritated when someone tells them what they must do." He continued to work the muscles of her shoulders. "There's another matter we should discuss, the two of us," he said to her. "I am with you in this, my love, but I have ambitions, too. I would be Archigos of a unified Faith, and I would sit on Cénzi's Throne in the Archigos' Temple and be your Hand of Truth. And I would be more than that, Allesandra. I would be Archigos ca'Vörl."

She turned to him, and found his face close to hers. She kissed his lips without heat. "Semini . . ."

"You told Jan to think of what the two of you could accomplish together as the same family on two thrones. I would ask you to consider what might be accomplished if the same family held not only the political thrones, but that of the Faith."

"What you're suggesting isn't possible," she told him. "There's Pauli. And Francesca. Yes, I enjoy the stolen time we have together, and I wish it were otherwise, but it's not. Semini, how would it seem if the Archigos were to dissolve his own marriage and that of the A'Hïrzg, for his own convenience? What would the ca'-and-cu' say, if only privately? What damage would that do to the Faith and to the Sun Throne?"

"I know," he growled, stepping back. "I know. But my marriage to Francesca was political from the beginning—there was never any love between us, nor much intimacy at all after the first few years and her miscarriages. Orlandi insisted that I had to marry his daughter and he was the Archigos, and your vatarh thought it would be good as well, and you were . . ." He paused. "I know I'm much older than Pauli, Allesandra, but I thought . . ."

"The differences in our ages mean nothing," she told him. She reached out to touch his face, his graying beard surprisingly soft under her fingers. "Semini . . . I do have affection for you. I love what we have, but it has to be enough. What you're suggesting . . . It would be a terrible mistake."

"Would it? I don't believe that, Allesandra. If you knew how much I've wrestled with this, if you knew the prayers I've sent to Cénzi . . ." He shook his head under her fingers. "It would *not* be a mistake," he said. "How could it be if there are true feelings between us? Can you tell me that the feelings are one-sided and our affair is simply a matter of convenience to you. Is that what it is, Allesandra? Tell me. Tell me the truth."

She stared at him, his face cupped in her hands. "One-sided?" she whispered. "No."

He breathed a long exhalation, nearly a word or cry. And then he was kissing her, and she was kissing him back, and she lost herself and her worries about Jan and what might come in the heat that enveloped her.

Jan ca'Vörl

JAN LET THE SWEAT POUR from him as he jabbed and parried with his sword against an invisible opponent. Sometimes it was Semini, sometimes it was his matarh, sometimes it was the ghost of Fynn or his great-vatarh. Jan let all his anger out into the practice. He slashed, he spun, he thrust until all the ghosts were dead and his muscles were burning.

Finally, he sheathed his sword and stood with his hands on knees, panting. He heard faint, ironic applause behind him, and he turned—beads of sweat flying from damp hair—to see Sergei ca'Rudka standing at the door of the practice room, with two gardai standing behind him. "How—?" Jan began as ca'Rudka smiled.

"I asked your aide Roderigo where you might be. I wasn't allowed to come without my friends, though," he added, gesturing to the grim-faced and solemn gardai flanking him. Sergei entered the long, narrow room, with its polished bronze walls and the narrow row of seats along the other side, the wooden practice swords in their holders in one corner. "You've had a good weapons teacher," Sergei said. "Though that's worth less than you might think."

Jan took a towel from the rack near the swords and wiped at the sweat on his brow. "What do you mean, Regent?"

"You can have all the technical skills—and you do—but they mean little when you actually face an opponent who's willing to kill you."

The way ca'Rudka made the comment, in a lecturing, superior tone, ignited Jan's anger again. They were *all* acting superior to him. They were all telling him what to do as if he were too stupid to understand anything himself. Jan sniffed. He tossed the towel in the corner. "Show me," he said to Sergei. "Prove it."

"Hïrzg . . ." one of the gardai hissed warningly, but Jan glared at the man.

"Be quiet," he said. "I know what I'm doing." Jan nodded his head toward the rack of wooden swords. "Show me, Regent," he said again. "Platitudes are easy."

Sergei bowed, as if to a dance partner. Glancing once at the gardai, he strode to the rack. Jan watched him—the man had the gait of an elder, and there was a grimace when he bent over to pull out one of the practice blades and examined it. "The great swordsman cu'Musa once said that experience is often better than raw skill," he said to Jan. "There's a tale that in a duel, cu'Musa once killed his opponent with only a wooden blade. Just like you, his opponent was armed with steel."

The gardai both started forward, reaching for their own weapons and putting themselves between Jan and ca'Rudka, but again Jan motioned them back. "You're not cu'Musa," Jan said.

"I'm not," ca'Rudka answered. He flicked the wooden blade through the air. It was a clumsy stroke, and Jan saw how ca'Rudka held his hand on the hilt, turned slightly underneath—his old teacher back in Malacki would have immediately corrected the man, had he seen that. *"With your hand like that, you have no reach,"* he would have said. But Sergei had already taken a stance—blade down, his legs too close together. "When you're ready, Hïrzg Jan," he said.

"Begin," Jan said.

With that, ca'Rudka started to bring his blade up: slowly, almost awkwardly—an amateur's move. Jan sniffed in disdain and slapped the man's blade aside contemptuously with his own. But the expected resistance of blade against blade was missing: ca'Rudka had opened his hand. He heard the wooden blade clattering against the tiles of the floor, saw it skittering away to hit the bronzed wall. Jan's strike took the weapon from ca'Rudka, yes, but without resistance his own strike swept farther to the left than it should have, and Jan saw a rush of dark clothing and felt ca'Rudka's hands slap him lightly on either side of his neck before he could react. The man was directly in front of him, the metal nose so close that Jan's face filled its reflective surface. Ca'Rudka's hands gathered in the collar of Jan's tashta and the man took a step, pressing Jan against the wall. Jan's sword was useless in his hand: ca'Rudka was too close.

"You see, Hïrzg Jan," ća'Rudka nearly whispered, "a person who wants to kill you won't worry about rules and politeness, only results." His breath was warm and smelled of mint. "I could have crushed your windpipe with that first strike, or I might have had a knife in my other hand. Either way, and you'd already be gasping your last breaths."

He stepped away, releasing Jan as the gardai grabbed him roughly from behind. One of them struck ca'Rudka in the side with a mailed fist, and the older man crumpled to a knee, gasping. "But you're a better swordsman than me, Hïrzg," ca'Rudka finished from the floor. "I'll admit that freely." The garda brought his fist back for another strike, but Jan lifted his hand.

"No!" he snapped. "Leave us! Both of you!"

The gardai looked at him startled. They began to protest, but Jan gestured again toward the door. As they bowed and left, Jan went to ca'Rudka and helped the man back to his feet. "Are you really that poor a swordsman, Regent?"

Ca'Rudka managed to smile as he held his side, leaning forward and trying to catch his breath. "No," he answered. "But I made *you* think I was." He took a long breath in through his mouth and groaned. "By Cénzi, that hurt. I trust that my point's obvious enough?"

"That people might lie and deceive me in order to get what they want?" Jan laughed bitterly. "You're not the only one trying to teach me that lesson."

"Ah." Ca'Rudka seemed to be considering that. He said nothing, waiting.

"My matarh and the Archigos seem to think that now is the time to attack Nessantico."

Ca'Rudka shrugged, then grimaced again. "Do you want to be admitting that to a potential spy in your midst, Hïrzg? Why, I might send a note back to the Kraljiki."

"You won't."

Nothing moved on ca'Rudka's face at that. He blinked over his silver nose. "Have you considered that your matarh and the Archigos might be right?"

"You'd agree with them?"

"Honestly, I'd rather that there be no war at all, that we settle our differences another way. But if I were your matarh . . ." He shrugged. "Perhaps I'd be thinking the same."

"So you think I should listen to them?"

"I think that you're the Hïrzg, and therefore you should make up your own mind. But I also think that a good Hïrzg listens to the message even when he has difficulty with the messenger."

Jan looked away from the man. He could see himself in the bronze mirrors of the hall, his image slightly distorted in the waves of thin metal. He was still holding his sword. He went to the wall where ca'Rudka's wooden sword had come to a rest. He leaned down and picked up the practice weapon, tossing it to the man.

"Show me something else," he said. "Show me how experience beats raw skill."

Ca'Rudka smiled. He took the sword, and this time his movements were fluid and graceful. "All right," he said. "Take your stance . . ."

~

Nico Morel

AFTER SPENDING SEVERAL DAYS with the woman, Nico decided she was very strange, but also fascinating. She was good to Nico. She fed him well, she talked to him—long talks in which he found himself telling her everything about his matarh and Talis and how he and his matarh had left Nessantico, and how he hated his onczio and his cousins and left the village, and how the Regent and Varina had helped him. . . .

The woman walked with him during the day around his old neighborhood, with Nico hoping he would see Talis or his matarh.

But he hadn't. "Your vatarh's name is Talis Posti?" she had asked him the first night, after he'd told her his story. "You're sure of that? And he's here in the city?" He nodded, and she'd said nothing more.

She told Nico her name was Elle, but sometimes when Nico called out that name, she didn't seem to notice. She would sometimes, in the middle of conversation, respond to some unheard comment or address the air as if talking to it. In public, she seemed to make herself shrivel and look old and frail, but in the privacy of the rooms she kept, she was another person altogether: much younger; strong, athletic, and vital. She kept weapons in the room: a sword leaning in the corner near the door and another at the side of the bed, and there were several knives with wickedly-sharp edges—she nearly always had two or more of those on her person. Nico would watch her when she honed her weapons at night with a whetstone. He'd watch her face, and the loving concentration as she sharpened the razored edges made him shiver.

She had a small leather pouch around her neck that she never took off. It was always there under her clothing, and at night she would clasp her hand around it as she were afraid someone might steal it. He wondered if when she took her daily bath in the copper tub in the common room of the house, she kept it on also. The bathing in itself was strange, since Nico had never seen anyone bathe themselves more than once a week, and more likely once a month. His matarh had always said that if you bathed too much, it caused you to get sick. Maybe, Nico thought, that was what was wrong with Elle.

At odd times, she would tell him to stay in the rooms they rented, and she would go out alone—usually at night. She would be gone for several turns of the glass, and usually Nico would fall asleep waiting for her to return. Whatever she did those nights, she never told him.

Tonight had been one of those nights. "Nico . . ." He felt her hand shaking him, and he blinked up at her face, candle-lit against the darkness of the room. "Get up," she told him.

"Why, Elle?" he grumbled sleepily. It was comfortable and warm under the covers. She didn't answer him—she had already moved to the door of their room.

"I want you to come with me," she said. Grudgingly, Nico slid the covers aside and lifted himself from the straw-filled mattress. "Shoes," Elle said as he started to pad toward her barefoot. He slipped on his worn boots as she opened the door. "Stay with me," she told him, taking his hand. They went out into the night.

Nico knew that Nessantico never slept—not entirely. No matter what time of day or night, there would be people abroad in the Oldtown streets. But the night denizens were more dangerous than those of the day, his matarh had told him. "You'll understand better when you grow up," she'd said, more than once. "Night is a mask that the city puts on when it wants to do things it shouldn't. The business people do at night . . . well, sometimes they need the darkness to hide it." He'd glimpsed some of that recently, alone in Oldtown before Elle had found him. He'd witnessed the slurred speech and uncertain walk of the tavern denizens; seen the grunting encounters in dark alleys; glimpsed the quick, brutal assaults; witnessed the furtive exchange of jingling coins for wrapped packages. He stayed close to Elle now as they moved through the streets, alive with those wearing the mask of night.

She walked rapidly, so much so that he had to half-run

to keep up with her. They cut across a corner of Oldtown
Center and into the tangle of lanes running south and west
toward the river, the buildings on either side growing rapidly older, smaller, and closer together, as if they wanted to
huddle together in the night for warmth. Nico was quickly
lost. There were no téni-lights here, only the occasional
lamps set in the windows of taverns or brothels. Twice they
passed an utilino, and Elle would draw down onto herself,
making herself look smaller and older, and she would husk
out a greeting with a grating voice that didn't sound at all
like her own.

Finally, Elle tugged him into the darkness of an alleyway and crouched down next to him. "Listen to me, Nico.
I need you to be very, very quiet now. You need to be
careful when you move so that no one hears your footsteps, and you can't talk. No matter what you see or what
happens. Do you understand?" In the faint light of the
moon, he could see the white of her eyes, and her gaze was
serious and solemn.

He nodded. She took his hand, squeezing it once gently.
"All right," she said. "Come on."

They moved farther down the alley to a tiny door half-
off its rusty hinges. Elle reached under her cloak; her fingertips, when her hand emerged again, had a dollop of
some dark substance which she smeared on the hinges. She
pushed at the door, it swung open reluctantly but silently,
and Elle ducked inside, gesturing to Nico to follow.

The smell inside made Nico want to gag: there was something dead and rotting close by, and he was glad for once
that it was far too dark to see well, though he was afraid he
was going to trip over whatever was dead down here. Elle's
hand took his again and he followed her closely toward a
dimly glimpsed stair, and up to a door. He saw Elle stoop
alongside the door and fiddle for a few moments with a few
pieces of wire inside the keyhole. There was a faint click,
and Elle pushed the door open slowly. Nico found himself
hurrying behind Elle down a narrow, dark hallway to stop
in front of a door. "When I open this door," she whispered
huskily to him, "I need you to stay here in the hall. Don't
move, no matter what. Say nothing. Just listen. Listen. Do
you understand?"

He nodded silently. Again Elle crouched by the door

with her wires; again, there was a click. Elle opened the door and slipped inside, leaving the door open. Nico couldn't see anything inside, though he squinted hard. Someone in the room was breathing hard, as if asleep. His own breathing seemed terribly loud, and if Elle made any sound at all as she moved through the room, Nico couldn't hear it. He clutched at the doorframe, frightened and wanting to disobey Elle and call out to her, but the fear choked his throat.

There was a soft *snick*, a startled grunt, and then Elle's voice. "That's right," he heard someone say softly—it sounded somewhat like Elle, but her voice was pitched deep and low. It might have been a man speaking. "That's a knife blade against your neck, and if you cry out or so much as move your hands, you're a dead man. Do as I say, and you might live. If you understand, nod your head." There was a pause, then: "Good. I know who you are and what you are. I've been watching you. Now, I want to know something else. Do you know a boy named Nico Morel? Answer me: yes or no. And softly."

Nico's own breath hissed in at the mention of his name. He heard the person half-whisper an answer: "Yes."

With that single word, he knew the voice: Talis. Almost, he leaped into the room, but he remembered Elle's warning and he remained crouched at the door. "Good. You get to live yet," Elle whispered to Talis. "Ah! No moving now; remember what I told you. I'd hate for you to slice yourself open accidentally. You've shared the bed of the boy's matarh?"

"Yes."

"Do you love her? Answer true now."

There was a hesitation in which Nico took a quick breath. Then: "I do."

"And the boy? Do you care about him?"

The answer was quicker and more emphatic. "Yes. The boy is . . ." His voice trailed off into a long silence.

"The boy is what?"

"My son. And yes. I care about the boy. That why I sent away both him and Serafina—so they'd be safe."

"But he came back here, to this city. You discovered that after the Numetodo had him. You knew the Ambassador ca'Vliomani wanted to talk to you, but you didn't answer him. You abandoned the boy, to save your own skin." Nico realized that she was talking mostly for his own benefit, so that he would hear Talis' reply.

Nico heard the rustling of cloth and straw as, despite Elle's warning, Talis moved. "Ow! No. That's not true. Ow! Easy! You're right, I knew Nico was here and didn't answer the Ambassador, but not for the reasons you say. Because . . ."

"Because?"

"I saw the consequences of trying to do that. I saw that if I'd gone to the Numetodo, worse things would have happened: for Nico, for me, for all of us. If I could have gotten Nico back safely, I would have. I knew the Ambassador would treat him kindly. I knew Nico wouldn't be hurt if I stayed hidden. But if I'd come for him, if I'd tried to rescue him, I didn't know what would happen. He might be hurt, or worse. There could have been terrible consequences."

"You know this because of magic. Westlander magic." Nico could almost see Talis' nod. It was hard to stand silent and listen. He wanted to go to Talis, to Elle, but he also wanted to hear what Talis would say. "And did you see this moment in your spells? Did you see me?" Elle asked in her strange, husky voice.

"No," he said. "I kept seeing Nico in the scrying bowl, as if he were close, but there was something around him, something protecting him."

"Then you *did* see me. I protect him. And I will continue to do so."

"Where is he?" Talis asked. "Take me to him!"

"Why? Why should I do that?"

"Because . . ." Nico heard Talis swallow hard. ". . . Because he should be with people he knows. I can take him back to his matarh."

"You'd do that?"

"Yes."

"Then I hope for your sake you keep promises."

Following Elle's answer, no one said anything, though Nico thought he could hear furtive, swift movements. He peered into the darkness until blobs of color swam in front of his eyes, trying to see. He could hear Talis stirring, heard him speak a word in another language, and Nico shivered, as if some invisble, cold breeze had touched him. Suddenly there was bright light, light that seemed to come from Talis himself. He was sitting up in bed, his blankets pooled around his waist and two small trickles of blood running down his chest from his neck, and the light was coming from a cold glow that sat in his upturned palm. Elle was no longer in the room, though curtains swayed in front of an open window near the bed. Talis saw Nico in the hallway, and his mouth dropped open. "Nico!"

Nico ran to him, crying.

Audric ca'Dakwi

THE PAPER RUSTLED in his hand as he held it at an angle so that Great-Matarh Marguerite could read it also. He could hear her intake of breath, harsh and annoyed. "We've confirmed that the seal on this is genuinely from Francesca ca'Cellibrecca," Sigourney was saying as he read the missive. "And we've had independent confirmation that former Regent ca'Rudka . . . pardon me, Rudka . . . is indeed in Brezno and that he's met with the Hïrzg, the A'Hïrzg, and the Archigos. As to the affair she talks about between the Archigos and A'Hïrzg Allesandra . . . well, that we can only speculate about."

The paper trembled in Audric's hand. His great-matarh was staring at him, her eyes furious. "You believe this?" He was asking his great-matarh, but it was Sigourney who answered.

"We have no reason not to believe it."

"Well, *I* have a reason—Maister ci'Blaylock pounded that history into me too well. Francesca ca'Cellibrecca's vatarh betrayed my vatarh and all the Holdings at Passe a'Fiume." His finger tapped the parchment. "Now she wants to *ally* with us? She wants a *reward?*"

"If she's right, Kraljiki, then we should be grateful for her warning. She *can* help us, as close as she is to the Brezno inner circles."

"You genuinely think there's going to be war?" Audric said, and hated the way he sounded: like a worried child. *"You're not a child. Not anymore. Now you must be Kraljiki,"* Marguerite told him, and he nodded to her. He made his voice as deep and stern as he could. "The new Hïrzg is foolish if he thinks he can do that. We will crush him. We will send him bleeding and broken back to Firenzcia."

"Those are brave words, Kraljiki Audric," Sigourney said, nodding, though her face looked rather unconvinced to Audric. "I'm certain that you're right. But we can also hope it won't come to that." She inclined her head toward the painting on its stand next to him. "With Vajica ca'Cellibrecca's help, perhaps we can force diplomacy on Firenzcia. Your great-matarh understood that; she didn't use force unless it was necessary."

"Don't tell *me* what she would do," Audric snapped at Sigourney. He coughed with the ferocity of the words, and had to press his kerchief to his lips until the spasm passed. When it was over, he continued, with less volume, his throat sore from the attack. "*I* know her best. It's *me* who understands my great-matarh. It's *me* she talks to. Not you."

Sigourney raised her hands, her eyes wide from his outburst. "I didn't mean to suggest otherwise, Kraljiki. It's just . . ." She lowered her voice, leaning toward him as if afraid someone might overhear, though there were only the three of them in the room. "We need to be careful here. It's possible this may be nothing, or it may be the suspicions of a wife who feels she has lost the trust of her husband, especially if the rumors regarding Archigos ca'Cellibrecca and Allesandra are true. We have to consider Vajica ca'Cellibrecca's motives."

"Sergei Rudka is in Brezno," Audric spat. "I want him *here*. I want him in the Bastida again, and this time I'll make sure he experiences all the pleasures of the deepest cells."

"Yes, yes," Sigourney was saying but he was barely listening to her, prattling on at him as if she were trying to soothe a child on the verge of a tantrum. She was still talking, but Audric heard none of it. Sigourney was beginning to remind him of Sergei, acting as if she were the one on the Sun Throne and not him. Maybe he might have to throw her in the Bastida, too. Now that he was acknowledged as the Kraljiki, maybe he'd throw all of the Council of Ca' there. Let them meet and plot in the stones of the main tower and see how they liked that. Sergei had proved that he was a traitor and he *would* pay for that; Audric vowed that he would witness the man's torment himself, maybe even help the torturer. He would watch the man writhing in torment on the table, and later enjoy the crows plucking the flesh from Sergei's bones as his body swayed in its cage on the Pontica Kralji. *"Yes, you will have all that,"* Marguerite told him. Her mouth twisted into a momentary smile. *"You are the Kraljiki now, and they can deny you nothing.*

You will plant the banner of the Holdings on the Hïrzg's very grave. Your sword will run red with the blood of those who try to stand in your way."

"Yes," he told her. "It will. I promise."

"What?" Sigourney said. She looked startled, interrupted in mid-speech. "What do you promise, Kraljiki?"

He wanted to cough. He could feel the urge in his throat and his lungs, and he forced it down. "I promise that those who stand in my way will be destroyed," he told her. "That's what I promise." He was staring directly into her eyes. He expected, he *wanted* to see fright there, but that wasn't what he saw in her face. There was only a quiet appraisal there, and perhaps pity. That made him angry, and the emotion sent him into spasms of coughing again. The coughing made it difficult to breathe; he could feel the edges of his vision darkening and he thought he might faint entirely.

As he hacked into his kerchief, nearly doubled over, he suddenly felt Sigourney's hand on his head, stroking his hair.

"I know how this illness must hurt, Kraljiki. Audric. I know." She pulled him to her, and he resisted for a moment— *"You must be strong. You can't let them see your weakness or they will exploit it."* —but he found that he wanted this—this matarhly touch—and he let her cradle him to her, as she might have one of her own sons. Her warmth was a comfort, and he heard a sob that he realized with a start had come from him. She had heard it, too, evidently. "Shh . . . it's all right. It's just the two of us. Just us. If you need to cry, I understand. I do . . . I will call the Archigos, have him bring that woman téni back here."

Her fingers swept back the hair from his face. *"Be strong . . ."* But it was hard to be strong all the time, and he'd never known his matarh's affection and his vatarh had always been surrounded by the chevarittai and the ca'-and-cu' and servants. As Sigourney held him, he opened his eyes and saw Marguerite's portrait. She stared at him, hard and cold and disapproving. Her head moved slowly from side to side. *"My true heir would not do this. This is weakness. My true heir would know how he must act."* Her disappointment burned inside him.

He pushed himself away from Sigourney, so hard the woman stumbled backward and nearly fell.

"No!" he shrieked at her. "No. We will do as *I* wish in this. We will send a demand to the Hïrzg—he must send Sergei back to us, or I will go and take him. Do you hear me? I will go there myself with the Garde Civile at my back and snatch Rudka from them." Marguerite's strength filled him and he stood, not coughing at all. "Send the commandant to me, so he can begin mustering the troops. I want you to write the demands—we will send it by fast-rider today. We will give them a month to return him. No more."

"Kraljiki, you're moving too fast. We must study this more, wait—"

"Wait?" The word came both from him and his great-matarh at the same time. "I will not wait, Vajica. And those who oppose me or refuse to go with me, I will consider no more than traitors themselves. I expect to see a draft of the demand by Third Call. Do I make myself clear?"

She stared back at him. *"Ah, that is finally fear you see in the lines of her face. You've done well, Audric."*

"Abundantly so, Kraljiki," Sigourney answered. "Abundantly."

Varina ci'Pallo

"THAT'S IT ... With the chant, think of the fibers of the wood opening like you're pushing aside a curtain."

Varina spoke quietly and encouragingly to Karl as he chanted the spell-words, staring at the walking stick he held in his right hand while his left made the necessary motions. She could see the grain of the wood shivering and parting, strangely and disconcertingly malleable. She could see the effort he was using to create the spell; Karl was panting and sweating as hard as if he'd run the entire circuit of the Avi a'Parete.

"Now—this bit is trickier—hold it apart while you place inside it the spell you've already prepared," Varina told him. He didn't glance back at her; she knew he didn't dare look away from the staff: the wood would snap back together or the stick would shatter entirely—there were still splinters in Karl's fingers from previous attempts. "Go on," she continued. "You should be able to feel the light spell you prepared. I always feel it like a tiny ball of energy in your head, ready to burst. Imagine it moving from your mind and sliding into the space you've just made on the walking stick. Imagine it nestled in there. Carefully. Good. Good. And ... Let everything go!"

Karl ended the chant, let his hand fall to his side. The gap in the wood clapped together again, a sound like two boards slamming together, and the walking stick was whole and undamaged in his hand, as if nothing had happened to it at all. Karl sagged against the back of the chair in which he was sitting. He wiped at his brow with the sleeve of his bashta as Varina laughed, clapping her hands together once. He sat there for what seemed to be several marks of the glass, trying to catch his breath.

"You did it that time," she said.

"I certainly hope so."

"You want to try it to make sure? Just hold the stick and speak the release word."

"After all that trouble?" he told her. "I think I'll just believe you for now." He sighed, letting his head drop back and closing his eyes. "By Cénzi, that was hard. No wonder Mahri looked the way he did."

She laughed again at that, but she could hear a certain, unwilling bitterness in the sound. Her fingers touched her own face, tracing the lines that hadn't been visible a year ago. She buried her worry in words. "It's a matter of finding the right word and gestures to move the energy, only you have to hold both the spell and the object being spelled at the same time—that's what makes it difficult. From what we know of the Westlanders, they attribute the power to one of their own gods, as the téni do here, but it's just a matter of the right chant, the right movements. Science, not faith. The advantage is that once you've done the task, it's the *object* that holds the spell, not you, and as long as the object is of good craftsmanship in the first place and isn't broken afterward, it could conceivably hold the spell indefinitely, I suspect. Still . . ." Fingers drifted over the lines of her face again, brushed back graying, dry hair. "It's a damned *expensive* way to do things, if you ask me."

"I can understand that," Karl told her. "I feel entirely drained."

He didn't understand. He couldn't understand. Not yet. She smiled again. She reached out as if to pat his hand, but drew back at the last moment. That was part of the uncomfortable dance they'd been doing for days now.

They were ten days back in Nessantico. They'd returned to the city with Serafina, who had taken up residence in her old rooms. She invited Varina and Karl to stay with her, an offer they'd accepted—the old Numetodo haunts were undoubtedly being watched by Garde Kralji, and they'd seen none of the Numetodo in Oldtown at all. They'd scoured the neighborhood with Serafina, asking about Nico, but no one remembered seeing the boy, certainly not after the day they'd helped the Regent escape the Bastida. If Nico had indeed returned to Nessantico, as Varina had been certain he had, he seemed to have somehow vanished; if Talis were still in the city, he remained hidden as well.

And for Varina . . . after their awkward conversation

in Ville Paisli, she didn't seem to know quite how to act around Karl. Her admission that she had wanted more of him than friendship ... Why did she say that to him? He looked at her strangely now, as if he were thinking back on all the interactions they'd had over the years and reinterpreting them, casting their conversations in the light of this revelation and wondering.

Why did you tell him? Why did you admit it?

Her hand retreated from his. He started to reach over to her. "Varina ..."

"I'm back!" The call came as the door to the room opened and Serafina came in. She carried a cloth bag from which a long loaf of bread protruded. Varina saw Serafina glance at them strangely before she walked over to the table and placed the bag there. She lifted out the loaf of bread, then a half-round of cheese and a paper bag of marshberries. They watched her, not speaking, and she sighed and shook her head.

"What's going on?" she asked.

"I don't know what you mean," Varina said. She wondered whether Serafina had seen them working the magic, but she was shaking her head with a half-smile.

"The two of you," she said, glancing from Varina to Karl. "It's obvious enough that you're not married, no matter what you told my sister back in Ville Paisli. But it's also obvious there's *something* between the two of you, and that neither of you are sure what to do about it. I understand; that's the way it was with Talis and me at first. I'd been hurt too much by a previous lover who didn't care about me but only himself, and I thought that was the way it was going to be with everyone. But Talis ... he was a good man. He cared about me, and when Nico came, he was a good vatarh as well. But the damned Numetodo ..." She bit her lower lip as Varina looked at Karl and raised an eyebrow.

"The Numetodo?" Karl asked.

"Talis said the Ambassador tried to kill him; that's why he sent me and Nico away—because he thought the Numetodo would come after him, and since the Ambassador was friendly with Regent ca'Rudka, that the Garde Kralji would be after him as well. I guess that's nothing he has to worry about now," she added with a wry smile. "The Kraljiki seems to like the Regent and Ambassador less than Talis."

"Talis hasn't contacted you?" Karl persisted.

Serafina shook her head. "He will, when he thinks it's safe. He'll know I'm here soon, if he doesn't already. Maybe he's found Nico, too." She sighed, and Varina saw her blink away tears. She put her hand on Serafina's shoulder in comfort as the woman sniffed and brushed the tears away. "Anyway," she said, "I was saying that I've watched the two of you circling each other like you're promenading around the Avi a'Parete, and . . . well, I was glad when I finally let myself admit that I was in love with Talis. It was the best thing I'd done in a long time. That's all."

She smiled, and patted Varina's hand, still on her shoulder. "I'm going to walk to the butcher's and see what he has. Then I'm going to look for Nico around Temple Park; he always liked to go there."

"I'll come with you," Varina said, but Serafina shook her head.

"No," she told them. "I'd like to be on my own for a bit. I'll be home before Third Call, and we can make a supper then."

She smiled at them again, picked up her cloth bag, and left the rooms again. They heard the snick of the lock behind her. Varina could feel Karl staring at her. "What are we going to do if we find Talis, Karl?" she asked. "Or if she finds Nico? She loves Talis, and Nico would recognize both of us. What do we do then?"

"I don't know," Karl told her. "I don't know anything anymore."

Varina nodded at that, and the silence between them slowly lengthened. She could feel the weight of it, wrapping around them like the greasy chains of a Bastida cell. Varina puttered with the bread and cheese, putting them in a woven basket.

"Varina," Karl said finally, and she stopped. "Serafina's right. It's just . . ." His fingers tapped the walking stick. "I still hurt whenever I think about Ana," he said. "She . . ."

"I know," Varina told him. "I saw . . ." she began, then dropped her gaze to the table. "A few times, on the street, I saw the grandes horizontales you hired to . . ." Her gaze came back up. "To me, they all looked like *her*: the same coloring, the same build."

He dropped his gaze, guiltily. "Varina—"

"No," she told him, interrupting. "I understood. I did. But it still hurt, because you didn't see *me*, when that's . . ." She closed her mouth, pressed her lips tightly together. She wouldn't say the rest. She wouldn't.

Karl lifted his hands, let them drop back to the table. "Serafina's right. Because of my obsession, I missed what was right in front of my nose. I was stupid. Worse, I was cruel, and that's something I never wanted to be. Not to you, Varina. Never to you. You've always been someone I admired and trusted. I always thought of you as a friend. And now . . . I don't know if . . ."

"I don't know either," she told him. *Go on*, she heard a voice inside her say. *Go on. Say it.* "Karl, we can both continue to wonder. Or—"

She let the word hang there, as bright in his mind as spell-fire.

He held out his hand to her.

She took it.

Enéas cu'Kinnear

SECOND CÉNZIDI. The day he was to meet with the Kraljiki.

This is your time, your moment. This day, I will take you up into Me and hold you, and you will be forever happy and at ease. Today . . .

"Thank you, Cénzi," Enéas whispered gratefully. "Thank you. I am your servant, your vessel."

He had taken the ground niter, charcoal, and sulfur; mixing them carefully together with stale urine as Cénzi had directed him to do, until he had created the black sand of the Westlanders. He placed the cakes of black sand into a leather satchel, which he draped over his uniform. He had rehearsed in his mind the spell of fire Cénzi had given him until he knew the gestures and the chant and could do the simple spell in the space of a few breaths. Yes, this would demonstrate to the Kraljiki what the Westlanders could do. It would make Nessantico realize how important and how dangerous this war had become.

Then, finally, he tidied the room, so that it would look neat for those who would come to look at it afterward.

As he walked to the Kraljiki's palais for his audience, he let himself take in the sights of Nessantico, absorbing everything the city he loved so much had to offer. He strolled along the North Bank of the Isle a'Kralji from his rooms, gazing fondly at the gated towers of the Pontica Mordei and watching a flatboat piled high with crates slide under its stonework span. The A'Sele gleamed in sunlight, wavelets sparking and dancing. Couples sat with linked arms on the grassy bank, lost in the presence of each other. A quartet of e'téni hurried past him on their way to some task, their green robes swaying around their ankles and the faint smell of incense trailing after them. Enéas could hear the chaotic, eternal voice of the city, the sound of thousands of voices speaking at once.

He passed the Old Temple, gazing upward at the impossible dome the artisan Brunelli was constructing, the largest in the world—if it didn't collapse under the terrible weight of the masonry. He frowned once, at the sight of a street performer who was juggling balls that he had set aglow with a spell—that was Numetodo work, not done with the prayers of a téni, and it bothered Enéas to see such a thing done publicly, without any of the onlookers being upset by it.

Archigos Ana allowed the people to lose sight of truth and faith. She coddled the Numetodo and allowed their heresy to spread—and that's why the Holdings and the Faith are now split in two and broken. I have sent the Westlanders as a sign and a warning. Today, you will bring them a final warning for Me.

The voice spoke low and sinister in his head. Karl made the sign of Cénzi, scowling at the juggler and the audience around him before walking on.

The Kraljiki's Palais was white and gold against a sky that looked painted. Enéas had been to the palais once before, as an e'offizier aide accompanying his a'offizier to a meeting with the Council of Ca', but this would be the first time that he would actually be before the Sun Throne. He gave his Lettre a'Approche to the garda at the side gates, who scanned it, ran a finger across the embossed seal, and saluted Enéas. "You are expected, O'Offizier cu'Kinnear," he said, gesturing. A servant boy came running, in the gold-and-blue livery of the Kraljiki's staff. Enéas followed the boy across sculpted, polished grounds set with topiaries and flower gardens, with several ca'-and-cu' courtiers strolling the white-pebbled walkways. Enéas' guide took him through a side door and into the palais itself, and down a corridor of pale pink marble, the floor burnished to a high sheen and téni-lamps set every few strides, though there was enough light coming through the windows at either end that the lamps were unlit. "Wait here, O'Offizier," the boy said, pausing at a door where two gardai were standing at attention. "The public reception is nearly over. I'll see if the Kraljiki is ready to meet with you." The gardai opened the door and the boy slipped inside. Enéas glimpsed the crowd of supplicants and heard the quiet hush of whispered conversations; faintly, someone was talking more loudly: a boy's voice, hoarse and broken with coughs. He thought he saw the Sun Throne, bright against the shuttered half-twilight of the hall beyond. The door closed again before he could see more.

"How goes the war, O'Offizier?" one of the door gardai asked. "Everyone's been waiting for a fast-ship from the Hellins, but it hasn't come."

"It *won't* come," Enéas told him.

The two gardai glanced at each other. "O'Offizier?"

"It won't come," Enéas repeated. "Cénzi has already told me that."

Another glance. Enéas saw a quick roll of eyes. "Oh, *Cénzi* told you. I see."

"You don't talk to Cénzi, E'Offizier?" Enéas asked the man. "Then I pity you."

The door opened again and cut off any rejoinder the man might have made. It wasn't the boy, but an older man, his livery marked with the Kraljiki's insignia. "I'm Marlon," he said. "The Kraljiki's ready for you. Follow me."

The gardai held the doors open for Enéas to pass through. The hall was still crowded, clustered with ca'-and-cu' and those lucky enough to have their names placed on the Second Cénzidi list of supplicants. They watched Enéas enter behind Marlon, their faces reflecting mingled curiosity and resentment as it became apparent that he was being taken directly to the Sun Throne.

The windows of the hall had been partially shuttered, so that the room was both dim and sweltering. At the far end of the hall, the Sun Throne shimmered with a sun-yellow glow, outlining the form of a young man. Enéas had known that Kraljiki Audric was young, but still his appearance startled him. He seemed small for his years, barrel-chested but otherwise thin, his cheeks sunken and the hollows of his eyes dark. Sweat beaded on his forehead, but the boy looked more feverish than warm.

One of the Council of Ca' stood at his left hand: an older woman with obviously dyed black hair who stared at him with the predatory eyes of a hawk, though Enéas didn't recognize her. A portrait of Kraljica Marguerite was set at Audric's right hand. The impact of the painting was stunning: Enéas had never seen anything so lifelike and solid—more of a presence than the woman on the other side of the throne. Enéas could imagine the Kraljica staring at him as he came near, and the feeling was not a pleasant one. It made him want to cradle the pouch he carried; it made him want to turn and flee.

You cannot. I will not let you. Cénzi roared in his head, and Enéas shook his head like a dog trying to rid himself of fleas.

The Kraljiki cleared his throat as Enéas approached, a liquid sound. He coughed once, and Enéas heard phlegm rattling in the boy's lungs. His mouth hung half-open, and he clutched a lace cloth spotted with blood in his right hand. "O'Offizier cu'Kinnear," the Kraljiki said as Enéas came to the dais and bowed. "I understand from Archigos Kenne that you have come from the war in the Hellins with news for us." The Kraljiki spoke haltingly and slowly, pausing often for breath and occasionally stifling a cough with the handkerchief. "We have heard of your fine record in the Garde Civile, and we salute you for your service to the throne. And I am happy to tell you that I have signed your Lettre a'Chevaritt, effective immediately."

Enéas bowed again. "Kraljiki, I am humbled, and I praise Cénzi, who makes all things possible."

"Yes," the Kraljiki answered. "We have also heard of your great devotion to the Faith, and that you once considered a career as a téni. The Holdings are pleased that you chose a martial career instead."

"I continue to serve Cénzi, either way," Enéas told him, inclining his head.

The Kraljiki, looking bored, seemingly listening to someone else. He glanced over at the painting of Marguerite and nodded. "Yes," he said. "I would think so." Enéas wasn't certain whether Audric had addressed him or not. He hesitated, and Audric's attention came back to him. "Your news, O'Offizier? What of the Hellins? We've heard nothing for over a month now."

"I have brought you something," Enéas told the Krlajiki. He patted the leather case: gently, almost a caress. He took the strap from around his head and held the pouch out toward Audric. "If I may approach . . . ?"

Audric nodded, and Enéas stepped up onto the platform of the Sun Throne. Closer now, he noticed the smell of sickness lingering around the Kraljiki: the odor of corruption, a foulness of breath. He pretended not to notice, handing the pouch to Audric, who put it on his lap. The Kraljiki peered inside, putting his hand inside to feel what was there. "Bricks of sand?" he asked, his forehead creased with puzzlement. His nose wrinkled at the smell. "Dark earth?"

"No," Enéas told him softly. "Let me show you . . ."

With the voice of Cénzi calling in his head, he began the chant: quickly, his hands darting. From the corner of his vision, he saw the woman at the Kraljiki's left startle, then step away from the throne. He heard someone behind him in the audience shout. Audric's mouth opened as if he were about to speak.

Fierce fire bloomed between Enéas' hands. He leaned forward, held it over the open lips of the pouch, and let it fall.

Cénzi roared His pleasure. The world exploded into eternal light and sound.

The White Stone

S HE WATCHED Talis over the next few days.
She found that she couldn't simply return Nico to the
man and let the boy go. The voices from the stone taunted
her for her concern. Fynn especially was derisive and bitter. *"You want a family? So now the assassin is going to care
about others? The murderer has found love now that she
has a* bastardo *in her womb?"* He cackled merrily. *"You've
become a fool, woman. Look at what my family has done
to me! The child you carry will happily betray you the same
way one day. Family!"* He laughed again, the others joining
in with him, a mocking chorus.

"Shut up!" she told them all, causing people on the street
around her to glance at her. She scowled back at them. She
hugged her stomach protectively, startled—as she always
was—by the swelling curve in what had once been an athletic, flat abdomen. Already, she sensed the fluttering of
movement there: Jan's child. Her child. "You don't know.
You can't know."

When she thought of her child, born and alive, it was
always a girl but with some of Nico's features, too, as if they
were strange siblings. "I took the boy in when he needed
someone," she told the voices. "I'm responsible for him
now. I made that choice."

They snorted derision. They howled.

She had watched Talis' rooms since she left Nico there.
She'd abandoned the rooms she'd taken, and had rented a
room above Talis' own, though she was careful not to let
Nico see her enter or leave the building. She had bored
a hole in the floor so she could both watch and listen to
them below. And she did so, ready to act if she heard Talis
mistreating Nico in any way, ready to appear as the White
Stone to take the man's life, furious and vengeful. But she
had heard nothing to make her fear for Nico.

Not directly, anyway.

She already knew from Nico that the Numetodo had been hunting Talis. She knew that he was a Westlander and a user of their magic, and the Holdings was at war with the Westlanders in the Hellins. That would be a danger for Nico, all by itself. So she watched.

On the second Cénzidi of the month, she trailed them when Nico took Talis to her old rooms, watching from the shadows of the alley across the way as they emerged again with Nico shaking his head in confusion, his arms waving as he spoke to Talis. That afternoon, through the borehole, she heard them talking below. "I don't understand," Nico said. "That's where Elle lived, Talis. Really. I was there."

"I believe you, Nico," Talis replied. "But she's not there now." She could hear the concern in the man's voice. She imagined him rubbing at the healing cuts on his neck as he spoke. She heard the unspoken commentary underneath: *She's dangerous. She might have killed me.*

"I liked Elle," Nico said. "She was nice to me."

"I'm glad she was. I'm glad she brought you to me. But . . ."

Whatever his objection, he kept it to himself. She smiled at that. *"But she's mad,"* the voices said. *"And the madness is growing."*

She clutched at the stone in its pouch as if she could strangle the voices with the white pressure of her fingers.

She didn't want to hear any more. She would continue to watch, yes, but for now it seemed that Nico was safe with Talis. She slipped out of her own room quietly, hurrying down the stairs and out the rear door of the building. She moved quickly through the streets of Oldtown, away from the main areas and into its twisted bowels where narrow streets curved and snarled and the buildings were dark, ancient, and small. She listened to her own thoughts, to the voices inside her head, to the conversation around her. "Matarh!" she heard a child's voice cry, and for a moment she thought it was Nico. She turned with a smile, her arms open to embrace him.

It wasn't Nico. It was some other child, nearly the same age. "Matarh," the boy cried again, and a young woman rushed from the door of a nearby building, gathering up the child in her arms, the boy's feet dangling as she hugged him.

She watched the scene, her arms unknowingly hugging

herself in sympathy. She wanted to feel pleasure at this scene that must be common enough, but what she felt was the hot flush of jealousy. *"Yes, that's what you'll never have,"* Fynn crowed inside her, and the others joined in. *"You can never have that. No one will ever love you that way. Not even the child you carry. Never."*

"That's not true," she told them, feeling tears streaming down her cheeks. "No, it's not true."

"It is. It is." A chorus of denial. *"It is."*

She turned and fled them, pursued by the voices. She walked hurriedly, not even knowing where she was going, pushing through crowded street markets and along half-deserted avenues, past shops and businesses. She found herself finally on the northern bank of the A'Sele near the Pontica Kralji. There, uncaring of the mud and the foul smell, she sat hugging her knees to herself, trying to ignore the screaming voices in her head as she rocked back and forth. If anyone saw her, they thought her deranged and left her alone. She sat there for a long time, her thoughts frayed and chaotic until pure exhaustion calmed her and the voices receded. She sat panting, rubbing the swelling mound of her belly and imagining the life inside.

"I will protect you. I will keep you safe," she whispered to her.

Somewhere across the A'Sele, on the Isle A'Kralji, almost as if in response, there came the sound of sudden thunder, and she saw black smoke billowing up from somewhere among the crowded buildings of the island. Not long after, the wind-horns of the city began to wail, though it was already past Second Call.

She wondered what had happened.

ENGAGEMENT

Audric ca'Dakwi
Niente
Kenne ca'Fionta
Karl Vliomani
Jan ca'Vörl
Allesandra ca'Vörl
Nico Morel
Niente
Karl Vliomani
Allesandra ca'Vörl
The White Stone

Audric ca'Dakwi

SOMEONE WAS SCREAMING. Over and over and over.

When Audric opened his eyes, everything was tinged with red as if the world had been painted with blood. Clots of it swam over his vision. His breath was a rasp, a husk; he could barely draw breath. He seemed to be in his own chambers, in his own bed, but he couldn't move his body at all. His face itched, and he wanted to bring his hand up to scratch it, but he could not lift either hand or move his feet. He was afraid to lift his head and look down, afraid of what he might see.

And the pain . . . There was so much pain, and he wanted to scream but he could only moan, a thin, eternal cry. He could feel hot tears running down his face.

"You can't die. You can't . . ." Her voice was as torn and ragged, a bare whisper.

"Great-Matarh?" he asked. "Where are you? Marlon? Seaton? Where is Kraljica Marguerite?"

His voice came from an impossible distance. His ears were full of a continuous roar, as if the city were falling around him. "Marlon? Seaton?" he called again. The pain surged over him like a great, breaking wave. He tried to scream, but nothing emerged from his open mouth.

A face loomed over him and he blinked. He thought he recognized Archigos Kenne. Téni-chants mixed in with the roar in his ears. "Archigos?"

"Yes, Kraljiki. I came as soon as I heard." He could barely hear the Archigos, the words lost in the roaring in his ears.

"What happened?" The two words each weighed as much as the great marble blocks of the palais facade. He could barely spit them out. He closed his eyes.

"We're still not certain, Kraljiki. O'Offizier cu' Kinnear . . . he may have been a Numetodo, or . . ." The Archigos' voice faded. Audric opened his eyes again; the Archigos' mouth was working as if he were still speaking, but Audric could hear only the red-tinged roar, and it swelled and with it the pain again, and he tried to scream along with it, but it was only a gasp. ". . . never know now . . . Councillor ca'Ludovici terribly injured . . . Marlon and Seaton dead . . ." the Archigos was saying, but Audric was no longer listening.

He had glimpsed the painting of his great-matarh. It leaned against the wall near his bed. The thick frame was shattered along its left side, and there were great rents in the canvas itself, frayed wounds crawling over Marguerite's face. He moaned again. "No!" he tried to shout, as if the denial could push it all away and change everything.

He remembered. He wasn't certain. The o'offizier approaching the Sun Throne, a flash . . . then nothing until now.

You can't die . . . !

The pain rushed in once more, and this time he felt his whole body shaking and jerking in response, the middle of his body arching up, and the Archigos was pressing him back down and shouting urgently to someone else in the room. ". . . whatever you can . . . the Ilmodo . . . Cénzi will forgive . . ."

The pain threatened to tear him in half, to snap him like a winter branch, but suddenly it was gone. Gone. His eyes were open, and he could see Archigos Kenne screaming at the palais healer and the woman téni in her green robes, and there were other people in the room and they were all shouting but he could hear nothing, nothing but the roar growing louder and louder. *"You can't die,"* and the pain at least was gone and he wanted to lift his hand toward his great-matarh but his body still would not move and he could not even pull in his breath even though his lungs ached and he tried . . . and tried . . . and . . .

Niente

H E HAD HOPED that the taking of the island of
Karnmor would have been enough, that Tecuhtli
Zolin would have been satisfied with that demonstration
of Tehuantin power and they would take to their ships and
return home. But Zolin had looked east instead. "We have
struck a wound to the body," he said, "but the head remains,
and the body will heal unless we strike. I know what you'd
tell me, Nahual, but now is the time to strike. I feel it. Ask
Axat. She will tell you."

Niente stared into the scrying bowl, sprinkling the herbs
over the water. Maybe it was because the water here was
less pure, or maybe it was because the land of his own gods
was so distant, or maybe it was that his own ability had
waned, but again the images he saw reflected there were
too confused and too fleeting, and they left him uneasy.

*. . . A boy on a glowing throne, but his face was a fleshless
skull, and there: was that the Easterner he had ensorcelled?
A woman lurked in the background, hard to see . . . But the
water swirled and when it cleared again Niente saw another
boy on another throne, and a woman behind him also, with a
green-robed, dark-haired téni beside her . . . Armies crawled
over a broken land with banners swaying, marching over
ground strewn with bodies . . . Fire and a temple, and ranks
of people in green robes praying . . . A great city with a river
running through its midst, and smoke rising from its great
buildings . . . A Tehuantin warrior on the ground, a spear
through him, and the body of a nahualli alongside with a
broken spell-staff, but the water was murky now and he
could not see the faces that lay there to know who they were,
though a queasy roiling churned in his gut, and he suddenly
didn't want to see . . .*

"Well?" Tecuhtli Zolin asked, and Niente glanced up
from the bowl. The Techutli had entered his tent and was
watching him. The eagle of his rank spread red-feathered

wings down his cheeks as the beak opened in a fierce cry on his forehead.

They were encamped on the edge of a great, wide river that one of the Easterners they'd captured had called the A'Sele. Far up the river, they were told, was Nessantico, the capital of the Holdings. The Tehuantin fleet was anchored close by, near where the mouth of the A'Sele emptied into the Middle Sea, their hulls low in the water with the plunder of Karnmor.

They had left the city of Karnor in ruins a hand of days ago. The city had been raped and plundered but not held; the rest of the great island had been left entirely untouched. Instead, Zolin had taken the army back on the ships, sailing out from Karnor Harbor and around Karnmor to the mouth of the A'Sele, where the army had taken to land once more. They had met little resistance. The people of the Holdings had melted away before them like spring snow, retreating and vanishing into the forests and back roads of the land, abandoning the villages with their strangely-shaped houses and buildings. This was land that had been tamed for generations: with rich farms and fields, with wide roads, paved with cobbles inside the villages and lined with stone fences outside. This was a domesticated land, not wild like the slopes of the Shield Mountains, but more like the farmlands of the great cities around the shore of the Inland Sea, or the canals of Tlaxcala, the capital built out in the sea itself.

"Nahual Niente?"

He started, realizing that he was still staring into the bowl though it was only his own uncertain and spell-ravaged reflection that he saw there, his clouded left eye frighteningly white. A drop of sweat fell from his brow into the water, shivering the image of his face. He lifted his head.

"I saw battle," he told Zolin. "And a boy king on the throne. His face was a skull."

"Ah, then perhaps your Easterner has fulfilled his task?"

Niente shrugged.

"The battle—who won?"

"I don't know. I saw . . . I saw a dead warrior, and a dead nahualli."

Zolin scoffed. "Warriors always die," he said. "Nahualli,

too. It is the way of things." Then, he stopped and his eyes narrowed, swaying the wings of the eagle. "Was it *me* you saw?"

Niente shook his head. "I don't know," he answered, but elaborated no further.

"Did you see us sailing home?" the Tecuhtli asked.

"No." Another single word, and Zolin nodded.

"You don't want to be here, do you? You think I'm making a mistake."

Niente tossed aside the water in the scrying bowl. He wiped the bowl dry with the hem of his shirt, wondering how bluntly he should answer Zolin. He had never been less than honest with Necalli, but Necalli didn't have Zolin's dangerous temperament. "We're a long way from home, in a strange land."

"A land that has offered almost no resistance," Zolin said. He swept his arms to the east. "This great city of theirs must know by now that we're here, but I see no army in front of us."

"You will. And we have no reinforcements behind us, no new warriors or nahualli to fill the gaps of the fallen. I *have* seen their castles and their fortifications in the scrying bowl, Tecuhtli. We had the element of surprise at Karnor; that's gone now. They will be preparing for us."

"And your black sand will tear down their walls and send their towers tumbling into ruin."

"I've seen the fires of their smithies and the prayers of their war-téni. I have seen their armies and they were large, sprawled over the land like a steel forest. We are but a few thousands here, Tecuhtli, and they have many more. We're now as they were in our land, far away from our resources. I doubt we will succeed here any better than they did there."

"Is that what Axat shows you?" Zolin pointed at the bowl Niente was holding, scribed with the moon symbols of the god. "Do you see—undeniably—my defeat in the water?"

Niente shook his head.

"Good," Zolin said. The muscles in his jaws worked, flexing the wings of the eagle. "I know you would rather we return home, Nahual. I understand that, and you're not alone in that feeling. I hear you, all of you. We all miss home and families, myself no less than anyone. But my duty is to protect us as best I can, and this . . . this seems to me to best do that. I appreciate that you would not lie and tell me that the gods insist that retreat is the wise course."

"I tell you what I see, Tecuhtli. Always. Nothing more. Nothing less. I vowed to Axat that I would follow and serve the Tecuhtli, no matter who he is or what he orders us to do."

Zolin gave a laugh that was more a sniff. He rubbed at his scalp, as if stroking the eagle inked into his flesh. "You made that vow to Necalli, not me. Niente, if you wish to be released from it now . . ." A shrug. "One of the other nahualli could serve."

The threat hung there in the humid air. Niente knew what Zolin offered: no Nahual gave up his title and lived; Niente wondered which one of the nahualli was whispering in Zolin's ear—certainly there were a few who felt they could be Nahual. "If the Tecuhtli feels that another nahualli is better suited to serve him, then he should have him bring his spell-staff here, and we shall see which one of us Axat favors."

Zolin chuckled, but there was an uneasiness to it that told Niente that the man was tempted. "For now, I will let you serve me, Nahual Niente. And you will see that I am right. I will come to this great city of the Easterners, and I will smash it and leave it burning, as I did Munereo and Karnor. I am a great slow spear, and I will pierce their armor, their flesh, their organs, and burrow through to stab their very heart. The people of the Holdings will understand that their god is weak and wrong. They will leave our cousins' land and ours forever. They will pay tribute to us, for fear that a Tecuhtli will bring another army here again. That is what I will do, and that is what you will see in your scrying bowl, Nahual. You will see it."

Niente lowered his head. "As I said, Tecuhtli, I will look and I will tell you all that Axat grants me to see, so that you may know the possible futures for the choices you make. That is all any nahualli can do."

Zolin sniffed. He gazed confidently at Niente from eyes surrounded by the feathered wings of the eagle. "You *will* see it," he said again. "That is what *I* tell you."

Kenne ca'Fionta

GUILT GNAWED AT HIS STOMACH and made him push his plate away.

"Kenne, you need to eat." His longtime companion and lover, Petros cu'Magnaoi, u'téni in the Faith, reached out across the white linen of the table for Kenne's hand, cupping it in his own. "You were only a pawn in Cénzi's plan. You couldn't have known."

Kenne shook his head. *It's not your fault . . . You couldn't have known . . .* That was what everyone had said to him over the last few days. Sometimes the words were spoken with a heartfelt sincerity; at other times—as when he'd gone to visit Sigourney ca'Ludovici in her bed as she recovered from her wounds—he'd thought he'd heard only a veneer of politeness draped over deep resentment.

"I sent that man to the Kraljiki, Petros. I did. No one else, and—"

"Kenne," Petros interrupted. He was shaking his hawk-thin head, the jaw-long hair that Kenne loved so much, long ago gone white but as thick on the man's head as his own hair was scarce, swaying with the motion. Pale blue eyes, still sharp and wise, held Kenne's gaze and refused to let him look away. "Stop this. You can keep repeating the same words over and over again, but none of them will change what's happened. You did what any of us might have done. This Enéas cu'Kinnear's reputation was solid, and he said he had news from the Hellins, which the Kraljiki desperately needed. If I'd been in your place, I'd have done the same."

"But you didn't. He came to *me*."

"He did, and you had no way to know what he was or what he would do, just as his superior offiziers didn't know. What we must do now is make certain that the populace's anger doesn't spill over into a bloodbath. There are already voices at the Old Temple calling for a renewed purge of the Numetodo, and the same is coming from the Council of Ca', too. Your voice is needed as the head of the Faith, Kenne. The voice of sanity."

Kenne felt Petros' fingers tighten around his own when he didn't answer. "Kenne, my love, Cénzi gives you a test now. You know that Archigos Ana wasn't killed by Numetodo, not the way Karl felt about her. This Enéas, and what he did to the Kraljiki . . . It sounds like the same thing that was done to Ana. The black dust that we found in the temple afterward; I hear that it was found all over the pieces of the Sun Throne as well . . ."

"I killed Audric," Kenne muttered. "I killed his chamber servants, the supplicants who were closest. And as for poor Sigourney . . ." Sigourney's face swam before him, torn and flayed by shards of the Sun Throne, her right eye bandaged (and gone, according to the healer who whispered to Kenne afterward), her right hand wrapped with the missing fingers far too visible, the covers falling ominously flat to the bed at her right knee.

This was his fault, no matter what Sigourney might have whispered to him with that ruined voice. This was more terrible than Ana's assassination, though that had been horrible enough.

His fault.

He started to speak to Petros and could not, his voice choking. Petros' hands tightened on his hand, lifting it and pressing it to his lips.

Someone knocked on the door. "Archigos?" The call was faint through the carved, varnished planks. Petros let his hand fall quickly and sat back in his chair.

"Enter," Kenne said.

It was one of his o'téni staff who peered in: Sala ce'Fallin, his aide. She glanced at Petros, nodding to him and giving Kenne the sign of Cénzi. "I'm sorry to disturb your dinner, Archigos, U'Téni, but . . ."

She bit her lower lip, shaking her head. "What?" Kenne asked her gently.

"There is news," she said. "A messenger has come from the Council of Ca'; you are to go to the palais immediately."

"What is it?" he asked. "Firenzcia?"

She shook her head. "No," she told him. "The messenger said nothing other than it was about Karnmor . . ."

He expected to be told that the long-slumbering volcano that overshadowed Karnor City had awakened again. But the news was far worse.

Kenne could barely believe the words of the rider who stood before the Council in their palais chambers, but the exhaustion, the dirt and soot on his face, the horror in his eyes and in his voice . . . Those he could not deny.

The city of Karnor was a smoking ruin, according to this man, with thousands dead, especially from the assault of the Westlander war-téni. Worse, the Westlander army was now on the mainland and advancing slowly up the A'Sele. The city of Villembouchure was next in their path.

"Many of the ships they came on," the rider said, "were our own. I recognized the lines of the *Marguerite* from when she left Karnor Harbor to go to the Hellins a year ago, but now she flies the eagle banner of the Westlanders and they've painted her in garish colors. That's why there have been no fast-ships from the Hellins; the Westlanders must have destroyed our forces there."

"There's no evidence of that," Aleron ca'Gerodi snapped, glaring at the man as if daring him to contradict the statement. "None at all."

The rider shrugged. "I saw what I saw, Councillor," he said. "I was one of those who fled Karnor, as the city was taken and burning. I found a boat on the eastern shore of the island; I saw the sails of the Westlander fleet driving up the mouth of the A'Sele, and I saw fires on the northern shore."

"He doesn't lie," a voice said as the doors to the chambers were thrown open. Kenne turned to see Sigourney being carried into the chamber on a litter. She sat propped up with pillows, her face a red-lined horror, the black dye washed from her hair so that the thick strands were now silver-gray. Her single eye glared at them; her right eye was covered with a quilted patch. "There are other riders coming into the city even as we speak here," she said. "I have spoken to one: a man from the headlands of the coast. He says the same: the Westlander army is here in the Holdings, and they are marching up the northern shore of the A'Sele."

"Councillor ca'Ludovici," Kenne said, concerned. "You shouldn't be here. Your injuries—"

"My injuries are not important," she answered, waving a bandaged, few-fingered hand. "The herbalist has given me extract of *cuore della volpe*; that has taken away the worst of the pain. We have lost our Kraljiki, the traitor Regent is conspiring with Firenzcia, and the Westlanders have dared to come here. My injuries?" She spat. Kenne and the others watched the arc of the expectoration to where it landed on the stone flags. "They are *nothing*," she barked in her ragged, hoarse voice. "We can't wait and dither here. We must act." She paused for breath. "And the first thing we must do is name a Kralji, since Audric had not named his successor."

Kenne knew then what had managed to cause Sigourney to ignore her injuries and leave her sickbed.

It was obvious, looking around the chamber at the other members of the Council, that the same thought had occurred to them. It was also obvious to Kenne who they would choose. Aleron was nodding, as was Odil ca'Mazzak; others were looking intently at the table, as if something had been scribbled there. It was Odil who finally spoke.

"You are Téte of the Council of Ca', Councillor ca'-Ludovici, and it was you who was closest in Kraljiki Audric's confidence. I agree—a new Kralji must be named immediately . . . and I believe it should be a Kraljica." He looked around the room. "I propose that Vajica Sigourney ca'Ludovici be named Kraljica Sigourney. She has the name, she is the closest relative here, and she has amply demonstrated that she possesses the qualities of leadership we need."

"I agree," Aleron said immediately, rising to his feet, and then they were all rising, and Sigourney was smiling through her pain and healing wounds and raising her hands to them in mock humility, and it was done—before Kenne could say anything. Not that they would have listened to him, he thought ruefully.

His voice was not one to which they paid attention.

Sigourney's single-eyed gaze traveled the room and

when it found Kenne, she frowned momentarily. He could see the accusation and the blame in her face, and he knew one thing more.

He would not be Archigos for long. The new Kraljica would find a way to bring him down.

~

Karl Vliomani

SERAFINA SMILED AT THEM as they came into the kitchen of their small apartment, though Karl could see a sadness, almost an envy, melded with the lifting of lips. She brushed her hair back from her head with the back of her hand, still holding the knife with which she'd been chopping vegetables. Karl could smell the stew, bubbling in the black pot over the hearth fire. "Good morning," she told them. "It's good to see the two of you together."

Varina laced her arm with Karl's and pressed against him. "It is," she told Serafina. "Even more than I'd hoped."

Karl smiled also, and he wondered if either of the two women could see the emotions that mixed in with his own happiness: the tiny nagging sense that he was somehow betraying Ana, even though he and Ana had never shared physical intimacy. *She would have smiled at you also. She would have told you to go ahead. She would have been happy for you.* That's what he told himself, but it didn't ease the kernel of guilt.

"I've been betrayed too many times and hurt too many times," Ana had told him once, not long after he'd returned from the Isle of Paeti, after he'd found that Kaitlin no longer loved him, no longer wanted him to be part of her and his sons' lives. "I can't give you that part of me, Karl. It's just not there anymore: there are too many scars and too much pain. I can be your friend, if that's enough for you. But not more. Not more."

"You don't love me . . ." he began to reply, and she shook her head.

"I do love you," she said, *"but not in that way. If you need that, then find someone else. I would understand, Karl. I truly would. I'm sorry . . ."* And he had *found release elsewhere, in the grande horizontales that Varina had seen. But he'd somehow missed the person in front of him who was interested in him as more than friend, and who he'd also liked. . . .*

Now, Varina hugged Karl again. He leaned down, her face turned toward him. The kiss was soft and sweet, and the guilt receded again, slightly. *"If you need that, then find someone else. . . ."* Perhaps one day, soon, even that whisper would be gone.

He hadn't known he'd needed this so much, and he wished he'd realized it much sooner.

"Let me help you, Sera," Varina said to Serafina, and her warmth left his side. "Karl, why don't you put a pot on for tea?" He watched the two women for a moment, then took the teakettle, poured water from the pitcher into it, and hung it on the crane over the fire next to the stew. He found the mint and herbs, placed it into a linen bag and tied it off.

"I'll go to the market and get some honey, and perhaps croissants," Karl told them. "With Audric's funeral procession today, I'll bet the markets—"

He stopped.

A shadow passed the shutters of the window. He heard footsteps outside the door. Someone knocked. "Serafina? Serafina, are you there?"

He knew the voice. He remembered it.

Serafina dropped the knife she was holding. It clattered from table to floor, but she didn't notice. She was running to the door. "Talis!"

She flung the door open; Karl saw the man standing there over Serafina's shoulder, but then she dropped to her knees with a cry—"Nico! Oh, Nico!"—and Nico was there also, his arms hugging his matarh fiercely. They were both crying.

"Matarh! I knew you'd come here looking for me. I knew . . ." Nico saw the two of them at the same time. "Varina," he said. "Oh." He suddenly let go of his matarh. "Talis . . ."

"I see them," Talis said. He was staring at Karl. "Serafina, take Nico and leave. Now."

Serafina was looking from Talis to Karl. Talis had lifted his walking stick—and Karl realized what that meant, realized it better than he ever had. His hand came up, readying to cast his own attack. "What—" Serafina was saying.

"Just go!" Talis said. "Now!"

"No," Serafina said. She was holding onto Nico fiercely

and though she looked as if she wanted to do nothing more than follow Talis' advice, she remained between them. "I'm not leaving until I understand what's going on."

Talis gestured at Karl with his free hand. "That bastard's the Numetodo Ambassador, Serafina," he said. "That's the man who tried to kill me and the reason you had to leave the city. He kidnapped Nico when he came back here, and used him for bait to catch me."

Serafina was staring at Karl, her gaze stricken and betrayed.

"Is this true?" she asked. "Tell me."

Karl glanced at Varina. She nodded. "It's mostly true," Karl told Serafina. "I'm Ambassador ca'Vliomani. I'm a Numetodo, as is Varina. We found Nico here when we were looking for Talis, and yes, we kept him—though I'd point out that he was alone in the streets when Varina found him and we kept him fed and warm and safe. We told people in the neighborhood that we'd found him . . . and yes, that was with the hope that Talis would come for him, but he never did. As for Talis—I believe he's the man who killed Archigos Ana." Serafina cradled Nico to herself. Confusion struggled with fear on her face as she listened to him, her gaze moving from one to the other of them. "Now ask *him* something for me," Karl told her. "The truth. Ask him who killed the Archigos."

Serafina looked at Talis, who was shaking his head. "No," he said. "It wasn't me," but Serafina's face had gone red.

"You knew where Nico was, and *you didn't go to him*?" she half-shouted to Talis. "You didn't try to help him? You didn't send word back to *me* when I was worried sick about him?"

"They would have *killed* me if I had gone for him, Serafina. And maybe Nico too."

"No." Varina stepped closer to Karl. "You're wrong, Talis. We only wanted to know the truth. The Numetodo were being blamed for Archigos Ana's death; we were in danger ourselves. I—we—would never have done anything to harm Nico. Never. You know that, don't you, Nico?"

Nico nodded earnestly on his matarh's shoulder. "I know that," he said. "Varina was good to me, Matarh. She said she would try to find you . . . and look, she did."

"Talis is a Westlander spellcaster, Serafina," Karl said.

"The last Westlander I knew like him was Mad Mahri, and he tried to kill Ana, too."

At the mention of Mahri's name, the walking stick trembled in Talis' hands and the muscles of his jaw tightened. "You *knew* Mahri?"

"I did," Karl told him. "I knew him very well. And I know he wasn't here for the good of Nessantico. And you're not either. Sera, I'm sorry. I know you love this man. But you need to understand what he is. He's an enemy of the Holdings, far more so than any Numetodo."

"She *knows* what I am," Talis grunted. "Sera, I haven't changed. I do love you; I love Nico, too. I found him and I was bringing him back to you. If you hadn't been here, I would have gone next to Ville Paisli to find you. I'm not the monster they're painting me to be." He scowled at Karl and Varina. "If I were, I wouldn't have waited; I'd have attacked the Ambassador without worrying about whether you and Nico were in the way. Sera, please. Move aside."

Instead, still holding Nico, she turned back to Karl and Varina, stepping between them and Talis. "I know Talis," she said. "I believe him when he says he didn't kill the Archigos. If you want to *talk* to him, well, he's here." She paused, stroking Nico's head. "I trusted the two of you. Now I'm asking you to trust me."

Karl glanced again at Varina. Her hands had dropped to her side. She nodded, a bare movement of her head, and Karl let his own hands drop down as well.

"All right," he said. "Tell him to put that stick of his aside, and we can talk."

~

Jan ca'Vörl

THE TEMPLE AT BREZNO was smaller than the Archigos' Temple in Nessantico, and not as venerable and sacred a place as the Old Temple on the Isle a'Kralji (or with as impressive a dome). But Brezno's dome and several of its famous frescoes had been painted by the great Firenzcian artist cu'Goslar, and they were stunning. Cu'Goslar's oddly-elongated figures loomed and twisted over the supplicants at the temple, draped in gauzy clothing or sometimes nothing at all: Cénzi, yes, was prominent, but there were also those of Firenzcia who had been important to the Faith. There was Gareth ca'Lang, the first a'téni of Brezno, his sword lashed to his handless arm as he fought his hopeless battle against the heretics of the Karinthia Sect; there was Pewitt the Hopeless, the Moitidi swarming around him, tearing and ripping the flesh from his living body, mocking the man by consuming his body as he watched in torment; there was Ursanne ca'Sankt, the great martyr who many thought would have been Archigos had she lived, desperately trying to fend off her Tennshah rapists, from which unwilling union would come the great Firenzcian Starkkapitän Adalwulf, who would later drive off the Tennshah from their settlements around Lake Firenz.

Jan was surrounded by history and swaddled in faith-driven fury. It seemed appropriate. His reconciliation with the realization that his matarh intended to vie for the Sun Throne had been a struggle as titanic as any of those depicted here, it had seemed to him. He'd confronted her after his long talk with Sergei ca'Rudka. But in the end, he had told her that he understood, even if he didn't approve. Jan wasn't certain if that was the truth or that after their several turns of argument, the statement at least let him get some sleep, but she had accepted it.

Jan had accompanied Allesandra to the temple at Archigos Semini's request, and he stared upward at the dome as they waited for him. "I remember the first time I saw these paintings," he said, trying to fill the awkward silence. "They scared me; I thought they were ghosts. I could imagine them moving, and coming down from the painting to chase me . . ." He laughed; it seemed that he had laughed far too little since the events that had ended with him as Hïrzg. "Now I think they're just overdramatic, and not all that well-painted."

"Don't tell Semini that," his matarh said to him. "He loves cu'Goslar . . . Ah, there he is."

Semini was striding quickly toward them from behind the High Lectern on the quire. Midway between Second and Third Call, the temple was mostly deserted, and the gardai who had quietly entered before Jan and Allesandra now stood silently several strides away, having emptied the main chamber of all straggling visitors. They were as alone as it seemed possible for him to be lately.

"My Hïrzg," Semini boomed, his voice reverberating from the dome above as he gave the sign of Cénzi to Jan. "And A'Hïrzg." Jan saw him smile at her—Semini seemed almost ready to take her hand, though that would have been a terrible breach of etiquette. But he stopped a careful few steps from her, closer than perhaps he should be, but not so close as to be extraordinarily obvious. Some of the irritation returned to Jan—he could hardly blame his matarh for pursuing an affair when his vatarh had betrayed her so many times. Yet the knowledge bothered him. The vision of the two of them together, their bodies entwined as his had been with Elissa . . . No—he shivered, shaking away the vision.

"Thank you both for coming," Semini continued, still looking more at Allesandra than Jan. "As I said, a message has been delivered to me, with—I'm told—an identical message for the Hïrzg. I have it here."

He handed Jan a sealed, rolled parchment, watching as Jan examined the stamp in the blue wax—the mailed fist that was Nessantico's sigil since Kraljiki Justi's time. Jan unfurled the paper and scanned the inked words there with a rising fury. He could almost hear his Onczio Fynn's voice rising inside him—he knew how Fynn would have reacted to this. Silently, his lips pressed tightly together, he handed the parchment to Allesandra; he heard her draw in her breath almost immediately. Wordlessly, she handed the scroll back to Jan.

"How *dare* he talk to us this way?" Jan spat. He opened his hands, letting the paper fall to the marble-tiled floor. The word "dare" echoed in the chamber long after he'd finished. It seemed to stir the gardai, who shifted nervously. "He talks to us as if Nessantico still ruled Firenzcia. 'Return the former Regent to us in a month, or we will take decisive action to recover him.' How *dare* he make such threats?" Another echo. "Let him try—we'll crush him."

He glanced upward at the dome. *Ghosts . . . None of them would tolerate this; I can't either. This is a slap in the face.*

"Jan, I understand your feelings; believe me, I have the same reaction," his matarh said.

" 'But . . . ?' " Jan spat angrily, turning to her. "Is that what you're about to say, Matarh? 'But . . .' What possible 'But' could there be?"

Strangely, she smiled. "My dear, you sound like Fynn, or perhaps Vatarh. I've heard them both roar just like that when they thought themselves insulted."

Her amusement served only to increase his irritation. He glanced past Semini to the mural behind the High Lectern, at the bloody strips of Pewitt's flesh clutched in the clawed hands of the Moitidi, trying to stifle his annoyance.

"The 'but,' my son, is what we've been considering," she continued. "Perhaps this is just the opportunity we needed. The excuse to act."

"The *excuse*?" he began. For a moment, he felt much younger, a child again. "Oh," he said. That word did not echo at all. It floated in the air between them, lost in the great expanse of the temple. He looked down at the paper half-unrolled over the marble tiles, the suspicion growing in him. "Strange that a message like this would lead to exactly the situation you wanted, Matarh. A bald provocation against us by Nessantico. What wonderful timing." He raised his eyebrows toward her.

She was shaking her head in denial. "I knew nothing of this until now," she told him. "I had nothing to do with it. The message is genuine. Ask the Archigos."

Semini nodded hurriedly. "The letters came sealed and via diplomatic routes," he said. "If the Hïrzg doubts that, I can have the courier brought here."

Jan waved a hand, looking away from them toward the murals of the dome. "No. There's no need. It's just . . ." His gaze came back to his matarh. "It would seem that Cénzi wants what you want, Matarh." Perhaps it was coincidence. His matarh had appeared genuinely shocked. Perhaps this *was* a sign. He was not delighted by the prospect.

"Oh, indeed," Semini responded. "The Kraljiki has played directly into our hands, or Cénzi has caused him to do so. The Kraljiki has threatened the Coalition and our Faith directly, and we have no *choice* but to respond to protect our borders and our interests. This is the moment, Hïrzg. This is the time. Much of Nessantico's Garde Civile has been sent westward to the Hellins; it will take time for them to muster the chevarittai and the remaining Garde Civile, to prepare the war-téní who remain available to them, and to draft the necessary foot soldiers they would need to make good this threat." Semini smiled, nodding to Allesandra. "Your matarh knows this. It's time for you to show your generalship, and take the Garde Civile and the chevarittai of Firenzcia to war. You will restore the Holdings to the whole it once was, Hïrzg Jan, and your name will be remembered forever for that."

"I don't know . . ."

"I do," Allesandra told him. Her voice was firm and proud. "You're ready for this, Jan."

He hesitated. He was still bothered that she would use him for her own purposes; he was also troubled by his own uncertainty as to whether he could be the Hïrzg that he wanted to be. *"I also think that a good Hïrzg listens to the message even when he has difficulty with the messenger."* Sergei's words. They calmed him. They decided him.

A breath later, he nodded. "You were right the other night. I'll need to consult with Starkkapitän ca'Damont and the chevarittai. That's what you wanted, wasn't it, Matarh?"

If she heard the faint mockery in his voice, she didn't react to it. "I'll come with you, Jan. I know the Starkkapitän, and I know the Garde Civile. I can be your mentor in this. Go on and have Roderigo summon them. I'll follow in a moment."

Jan's eyebrows rose, annoyed at the obvious dismissal, but he gave Semini the sign of Cénzi and bowed slightly to his matarh. "Thank you for relaying this information, Archigos," he told Semini. "We will need your strength and guidance in this. Matarh, I will talk with you later."

He left them, all but a few of the gardai forming around him as he departed the temple. "Your son will be a fine Hïrzg," he heard Semini growl in his low voice as he reached the doors. He assumed that it was timed so he would overhear it and think the praise genuine.

He smiled to himself. He *would* be a fine Hïrzg. He would surprise both of them with just how effective a leader he would be.

He suspected they might not like the result.

~

Allesandra ca'Vörl

THE WALKWAY AT THE REAR of the temple was dark, illuminated only sporadically by green-shuttered téni-lamps hung on porcelain hooks mortared to the wall. Fluted columns lined the walk, shielding it from the gardens of a courtyard between the northern wing of the temple complex and the temple itself. The great windows of stained glass loomed dark above her. Allesandra half-ran along the walkway, not wanting to be seen though she'd been assured that no téni would be in the area, the soft leather soles of her sandals hushing on polished granite. It had been easy enough to slip from her own rooms at the palais down the servants' corridors, waiting until there was no one watching to open the door and hurry across the plaza and into the Brezno streets. She wore a cowl over her hair, shadowing her face, and her tashta was plain. She might have been just another woman hurrying home in the evening. Semini had told her which door would be open, and which places the téni generally avoided. The ceremonies for Third Call had ended a turn of the glass ago.

She was nearly there. A turn to the left down the next opening, then up the stairs to the room that Semini kept in the temple complex when he didn't wish to return to his own apartments in the northern wing.

"Allesandra."

She froze at the hiss of the voice. Her hand went to the knife she had hidden in the sash of the tashta.

"Francesca," she said.

A figure appeared from alongside one of the columns. In the uncertain light, she saw the woman, the lines of her face holding shadows. The verdant glow from the lamps made Francesca look sickly. She spread her open hands, as if showing Allesandra that she held no weapon. "I know," Francesca said to her. "I've known all along."

"What is it that you know, Francesca?"

She laughed. The sound startled black starlings settling for the night in the fruit trees of the courtyard. They rose and fluttered restlessly. Allesandra could smell alcohol on the woman's strong breath. "We shouldn't play games, you and I," the woman said. "There's been nothing between Semini and myself for years, and if you're willing to spread your legs so that old ram can plow you, why should I care?"

Allesandra felt her cheeks heat with the raw crudity, drawing her breath in between her teeth. "If you don't care, why are you here talking to me?"

The amusement vanished from the woman's face. She sniffed, staring at Allesandra. "You're a pretty one. Semini always liked you; I heard the fondness in his voice when you finally came back from Nessantico. The lovers he had afterward . . . they always reminded me of you. Reminded him too, I assume. I know whose face he was seeing when he plowed them. Ah, that bothers you, does it? I'll bet he never told you that." Francesca sidled closer to Allesandra and she stepped back, her hand still on the knife's leather hilt. "I'll bet there's much he hasn't told you."

"Francesca, you're drunk and I'm not having this conversation. Now, let me by . . ."

The woman's hand came up, her lips twisting in a scowl. "Not yet. Look at me. Look . . ." Francesca waved her hands toward her own face. "I was beautiful once. Why, I was the Kraljiki Justi's mistress; I might have been his wife had my vatarh chosen the right side in the war. But he didn't. And now . . ." For a moment, Allesandra thought the woman wasn't going to speak again. She stood there, her body swaying slightly. "You think you know my husband? You don't know him. I saw you when the news came that Archigos Ana had died. I saw the horror and grief in that pretty face of yours. You were hurt, because you *liked* that cold bitch. Me, I *hated* her. I was *happy* to hear that she'd died. I laughed out loud. But you . . . she treated you well, didn't she? She was a matarh to you, when your own family abandoned you. Archigos Ana . . . *Phaw!*" Francesca pursed her lips, turned her head, and spat on the flags. "*He* knows who murdered her. As do I."

"Who?" Allesandra asked. Her hand had gone to her throat. She was afraid she knew the answer.

Francesca took a stumbling step forward, nearly falling and clutching at Allesandra's tashta. "Ask him," the woman grated out, her breath filling Allesandra's nostrils. "Make him tell you, and *then* see how you feel about him."

Her laugh erupted in another fluttering of starling wings, and she pushed away from Allesandra. She stumbled toward the archway leading to the north wing without looking back. "Ask him," Allesandra heard the woman say again, the words echoing around the courtyard.

She watched Francesca wrench open the doors, heard them shut again behind her. She stood there for several moments, as the starlings settled in the fruit trees once again and the moon lifted over the domes of the temple.

In the end, Allesandra turned and walked away from the temple, back toward her rooms and her own thoughts.

~

Nico Morel

IN THE DISTANCE, Nico could hear the wailing cornets and zinkes as Kraljiki Audric's funeral procession proceeded along the Avi a'Parete a few blocks away. He wondered what the procession might look like—all the ca'- and-cu' parading behind the funeral coach, the téni using their magic to turn the wheels, the new Kraljica Signourney following behind in her own special coach. It would be splendid, that procession. A wonder. Audric hadn't been much older than he was, and Nico wondered what it would be like to be so young and also Kraljiki. He wondered how someone could have hated Audric so much that he would kill him. Nico couldn't imagine hating anyone that much.

No one else in the room seemed to notice the sounds of the funeral—or perhaps they chose to ignore it.

"I didn't kill Archigos Ana."

Nico sat in his matarh's lap. She hardly let him go since she'd seen him. Not that he minded; he was quite content to sit encircled by her arms, protected. The feeling made him realize just how much he had missed her, just how scared he had been for so long. He and his matarh were sitting on the hearth, the fire warming his side. Talis was sitting at the table in the center of the room; Karl and Varina were on the other side. Nico could almost see the tension arcing between them, a fire nearly as hot as the one at his back. His matarh felt it, too; he could feel the shivering in her muscles and how tightly she held him, and he knew she was afraid that something was going to happen.

"I didn't kill her," Talis said again. "It's the truth."

"Right," Karl answered. "And we're just supposed to simply believe that. Because you say it's so."

Talis shrugged, leaning back in his chair. "You don't want to believe me, fine. It's still the truth. But . . ." Talis licked his lips. "I know *how* she was killed, and I know who must have been at least partially responsible."

"Go on," Karl said.

"It was this . . ." Talis reached into the pouch on his belt. Nico saw both Varina and Karl stiffen at that, and his matarh sucked in her breath. Karl's hands were suddenly up, as if ready to cast a spell. Talis froze. "No magic," he said. "I wouldn't, not with Sera and Nico here. I wouldn't."

After a moment, Karl let his hands rest on the table-top again, and Talis opened the pouch. He brought out a small cloth bag and untied the string holding it together. He spilled out a small mound of dark powder on the table. Karl stared at it. "There was black dust all around the High Lectern and on Ana's clothes," he said. "That . . . that's the same thing?"

Talis nodded. "Yes." He scooped up all but a pinch of the powder and put it back in the bag. "We call it *bosh luum* in our language. Black sand, in yours. Here . . ." From the pouch, he took a low, wide brass bowl, marked with strange figures around the rim. He brushed the remnants of the powder into the bowl and set it in the center of the table. "I'll leave this to you—put a small fire spell in the bowl, just the tiniest spark." He smiled, a brief flicker. "And don't put your face too near it if you want to keep that beard."

Karl glanced at Varina, obviously uncertain. Varina looked at Nico's matarh. "Sera?" she asked. "We can trust him?"

Nico felt rather than saw his matarh nod, but her hands tightened even more around him at the same time. Varina made a quick motion with her hand, and spoke a word in another language. The word sounded like "tihn-eh" to him, and as soon as Varina spoke it, a spark appeared between her fingers and she flicked her hand in the direction of the bowl, the spark flying away.

As soon as the spark entered the bowl, there was a si-multaneous flash and boom, as if a thunderstorm had bro-ken inside the bowl. The bowl itself jumped and rang, and white smoke erupted. Someone shouted; Nico couldn't tell who. His matarh had turned with the noise, her body shield-ing Nico. She turned slowly back, and Nico could see again. Karl was reaching across the table to the bowl, which still had smoke rising from it. There was a strange smell in the air, like Nico imagined that the underworld of the Moitidi might smell like.

"That was just a sprinkle of it," Talis was saying. "I would say you could imagine what a large amount of black sand could do, but I don't really think you can."

"*I* can," Karl said. He'd been examining the bowl; the way it was tilted, Nico could see that the bottom of the bowl was blackened as if it had been scorched. Karl's face was grim as he set the bowl down. "I was there when Ana died."

Talis pressed his lips together.

Varina pushed the bowl away. She lifted her head, seeeming to hear the fading sound of Audric's funeral procession for the first time. "The Kraljiki." Her eyes widened. "The rumors . . ."

". . . are quite possibly true, from what I've heard," Talis finished for her. "But that also wasn't my doing." He gestured at Nico. "The boy can tell you that. I was with him when it happened. We heard the wind-horns calling. Didn't we, Nico?"

Nico nodded.

"Westlander magic . . ." Karl breathed. He'd picked up the bowl again, staring at the sooty interior as if answers were written there. "We're just starting to understand it, and I can tell you, Talis, that it doesn't come from your gods any more than téni magic comes from Cénzi."

"Then you still don't understand," Talis said. "This *isn't* magic. At least not the black sand itself. It's no more magic than making bread, if you know the recipe for making it."

"You said you know who's responsible," Karl said. "Give me a name."

Talis took a long breath. "His name is Uly. He has a stall at the River Market. He's a Westlander, sent here at the same time I was. He's a warrior. His job was to report back to the Tecuhtli—the Tecuhtli is what your Kraljiki might be if he were also the Commandant of the Garde Civile. I was here for the Nahual, the head of my order, to help Uly and also to find out what happened to Mahri. And . . ." Talis took another breath. "I made a mistake. It was we nahualli—the spellcasters—who discovered how to create black sand; it's a secret we've kept—and yes, if others thought it was magic, we didn't correct their misconception. But Uly . . . we were here so long and he was the only person I knew who spoke my language, and until I met Sera—" he glanced at Nico's matarh and smiled, "—he was the only person who seemed to care about me. I did what I shouldn't have done. I had him help me make black sand. I tried to keep the details from him, but . . ." Talis took the bowl from the table and placed it back in his pouch. "Uly wasn't stupid. He could have easily seen enough to reproduce the process. His job was to provide me the ingredients, after all."

"You're saying this Uly assassinated Ana?" Karl asked. "That's what you want us to believe now?"

Talis lifted a shoulder. "I'm saying it's possible. Probable. I *know* it wasn't me. And it was definitely *bosh luum* that did it. Not Westlander magic. Not Numetodo magic either."

Karl's hands were clenched on the tabletop. "Where's this Uly?"

"I haven't seen him since after you attacked me," Talis answered. "I told Uly about it and said that I was going to disappear for awhile, and haven't heard from him since. I suppose the best place to start to find him would be River Market, but . . ." Talis began, but Nico squirmed in his matarh's arms.

"He's not there," Nico said. They were all looking at him now, and his matarh's arms loosened as she looked down at him on her lap.

"Nico?"

"It's true, Matarh," he said. "Uly's not there. After I left Tantzia Alisa's and walked here, I thought Uly could tell me where Talis was," Nico said. "But when I went to the River Market, Uly's stall was empty and the pepper-seller lady said he was gone."

Talis was nodding. "I thought that would be the case. I don't know where he is," Talis said. "Still in the city, probably, but where . . ."

"The pepper lady said that he might be in Oldtown Market," Nico told them.

Karl was already standing. Now Talis rose also. "I don't *know* that Uly did it, Ambassador," he said. "You don't know it either."

"I intend to find out."

"Then I'll go with you."

"Why?" Karl asked. "To stop him if he tells me that it was actually you, or that he hasn't the faintest clue how to make this black sand of yours?"

"He won't talk to you, no matter what you do to him," Talis said. "He's a warrior; he's been trained to die first. He trusts me. You? The first time you ask him something that arouses his suspicions, he'll kill you and run. Or he'll happily die in the attempt."

"I'll be with him," Varina said. She was standing, too, her arm laced with Karl's. "And we're stronger than you think."

"You'll need me," Talis insisted.

"Fine," Karl said finally. "But not with that." He gestured at Talis' walking stick.

Talis grimaced. "I can't leave that here. I won't."

"Then you'll stay with it."

Talis seemed to consider that a moment. "All right," he said. "I'll leave it. This one time. I'm going."

"I'll come, too," Nico said.

All three of them turned to him, and he could feel his matarh looking down at him as well. "No!" they said, all four of them at the same time.

~

Niente

THE VISION IN THE SCRYING BOWL troubled him.
He could feel Tecuhtli Zolin studying his face for any
sign of what the visions indicated, and he lowered his head
even further into the swirling blue mist rising from it.

*A woman sat on a glowing throne, her face twisted by
pain and horribly scarred, one eye missing. An army moved
through the mist behind her . . . There, a boy and an older
woman, and behind them also an army, though with banners
of black and silver, not the blue and gold of the Holdings . . .
A man wearing a necklace of a shell, and with him—could
it be?—a nahualli who looked like Talis, though he was embracing a woman and child who were not Tehuantin, but
Easterners . . .*

The images were coming too fast, and Niente tried to
still them with his mind, trying to force them farther out in
time, to show the wisps of the future that might come. He
prayed to Axat for clarity, he thought of their own army
and the ships riding on the river close by . . .

*The ships swayed in the midst of a storm, but the storm
rained fire down from the sky. Armies crawled over the
land, and there were the bright explosions of black sand,
and smoke hung heavy over trampled fields . . . But the mist
seemed to divide in twain—as sometimes happened when
Axat wished to show two possible outcomes. He saw a field
littered with the bodies of Tehuantin warriors, and a single
ship of their fleet with tattered sails, hurrying away westward
into a falling sun as the other ships burned in orange flame
to the water . . . "Westward . . . home . . ." He could almost
hear the words in the wind . . .*

But that vision closed, and the other came . . .

*In the second vision, there was a fierce and bloody battle
on the fields before the city, and the army of blue and gold
retreated behind the solid walls of a city . . . The same city
now, with broken walls, and through the smoke and the mist*

of the vision it was difficult to see, but he thought he glimpsed the army of the Tehuantin spilling through the breaches . . .

Another city lay beyond it, far greater, and it seemed to beckon . . .

And there it was again . . . the image of a dead Tehuantin warrior, with a nahualli lying next to him . . .

"What is it you're trying to show me, Axat?" Niente asked, his voice cracking.

"Nahual?"

Niente glanced up; the mist spilled from the scrying bowl and died.

The Tehuantin encampment was noisy and busy around them as a wan sun tried to penetrate high, thin clouds. Niente found himself missing the fiercer, warmer sun of his own land; this place was colder than he liked, as if it leeched the heat from his blood. Tecuhtli Zolin stared at him, the white of his eyes gleaming against the black lines inscribed around the sockets, the red eagle on his skull seeming to want to take flight. There was eagerness in his face. Flanking him on either side were Citlali and Mazatl, and their glances were no less eager. "What did the vision tell you?" Zolin asked Niente. "What did it say?"

"Very little," he answered, and annoyance showed over the Tecuhtli's face in a flash of teeth.

"Very little," he said, mocking Niente's tone. "Tecuhtli Necalli used to tell me how your visions in the scrying bowl would give him strategies, guide the way he placed the warriors and moved through the terrain. He said you were Axat's Nahual, showing us the way to victory. But all you give me is 'very little.' "

"I give you nothing," Niente told him, and Zolin scowled in response. "As I gave Tecuhtli Necalli nothing also. I am only Axat's conduit. I can relay what Axat shows me, but it's not *my* vision. It's Hers. All I have to give is what Axat offers. If you wish to complain about how little that is, talk to Her."

"Then tell me this very little, Nahual," he answered. He pointed eastward, to where the outlier scouts had said that an army of the Holdings waited for them, outside the city a half day's march away. Niente had ridden forward with Tecuhtli Zolin to see the city—far larger than the mostly-abandoned villages through which they had marched in the last several days, though not as elaborate or huge as the city in the scrying bowl, this Nessantico where the Kraljiki lived. Still, the city huddled behind its walls and spilling out beyond them was easily half the size of Tlaxcala or the other great island cities of the Tehuantin empire, and larger than either Munereo or Karnor.

It seemed that the Kraljiki would permit them to go no farther untested. If Zolin wanted this city, he must fight for it. Niente knew that would bother the Tecuhtli not at all.

"I glimpsed a battle," Niente told him. He closed his eyes, trying to remember the scenes flashing past in the scrying bowl. "In Axat's vision, the army of the Holdings fought, but then fell behind the walls of the city when we came upon them. I saw the walls broken, and Tehuantin entering through . . ."

"*Xatli Ket!*" Niente stopped as Zolin uttered the war cry of his caste—Citlali and Mazatl echoed the Techutli, and the cry was taken up—fainter and fainter—by the other warriors nearby. "Then Axat has shown you our victory," Zolin said. He slapped at the bamboo-slatted armor covering his chest.

"Perhaps," Niente hurried to say. "But she also showed me our army and the fleet destroyed, and a ship hurrying to the west. Tecuhtli, that is also a possible future—a sign. If we return now, if we put our army on the ships and return home, then that's a future we will never face. The Easterners will fear to ever come to our land again. We have already shown them the consequences; there's nothing left here to prove."

Zolin coughed a derisive laugh. Citlali frowned, and Mazatl looked away as if in disgust. "Retreat, Nahual?"

"Not retreat," Niente persisted. "To realize that we have given these Easterners their lesson with the ruins of Munereo and Karnor, and to return home in victory."

"Victory?" Zolin spat on the ground between them. "They would think *they* have won the victory, that we ran as soon as we saw their army."

"Tecuhtli, if we fall here, what good does that do our people to lose their Techutli and so many warriors and nahualli?"

"If we fall—and we will not, Nahual, if you have seen your vision correctly—then our people will find a new

Techutli to lead them, and they will train new nahualli in the ways of the X'in Ka, and we will be remembered when Sakal takes us into His fiery eye. *That* is what will be done, no matter how very little you help. Are you are *frightened*, Nahual Niente? Does the sight of this Easterner army make the piss run hot down your legs?"

Citlali and Mazatl laughed.

"I'm not frightened," Niente told them, and it was truth. It wasn't fright that churned his stomach, but a sense of inevitability. Axat was trying to warn him, but She would not make Her message clear enough, or perhaps he was so far from Her that the message was blurred and hard to discern. "Tecuhtli, whatever you ask me to do, I will do. When you ask me to interpret what I see in the scrying bowl, then I also do that."

Zolin sniffed. "Then this is what I tell you to do, Nahual. Fill your spell-staff. Prepare the black sand. Make your peace with Axat and Sakal, and you will walk with me into the Easterners' city—and beyond to the throne of their ruler."

Niente heard the words, and bowed his head in acceptance. *The single ship, hurrying toward the setting sun . . .* "I will do that, Tecuhtli," he said, the words heavy in his throat. "I will prepare the nahualli. Give me enough time, and I will do what I believe Axat wishes us to do."

Karl Vliomani

ULY WASN'T AT THE OLDTOWN MARKET, though he had been. People remembered the scarred, tattooed foreigner, but they told Karl that man had packed his wares and cleaned out his stall only two days ago, the same day Kraljiki Audric had been assassinated. No, none of the owners of the stalls nearby knew where he'd gone, but (they said) there were a few people who had been buying his special fertility potion who might know.

Karl had hoped to confront this Uly and get to the truth of what had happened to Ana immediately. A new fire burned in his stomach. But the relief and closure wasn't to be immediate.

It took days.

Days which strained his newfound intimacy with Varina. Ana's ghost hovered between them, resurrected by Talis' presence and his tale, and Varina retreated from it and he could not push through the specter. She still would take his hand or brush her fingers over his face, but there was sadness now in her touch, as if she were stroking a memory. He would kiss her, but though her lips were soft and warm and he wanted to yield to them, the kiss was too fleeting and distant, as if he kissed her through an unseen veil.

Days in which he wondered whether to call the Numetodo back to the city, and decided it was still far too dangerous. Mika, hopefully, was with his family in Sforzia; let him stay there; let the rest of the scattered Numetodo remain hidden. Let the Numetodo House remain dark and empty.

Days in which the news seemed to grow steadily worse: Kraljica Sigourney's own horrible injuries, the rape and plunder of Karnor, a Westlander army on Nessantico's soil and their ships on the A'Sele's waters, the mustering of the Garde Civile, "recruitment squads" roaming the city scooping up men, sometimes (according to the rumors) whether they wished to serve or not. Karl was old enough that they weren't greatly interested in him, but Talis was not. He was increasingly confined to the house, and had to be careful when he ventured out to avoid the squads. Karl had his own difficulties—his face was certainly known to many of the Garde Civile, the Garde Kralji, and the téni, and he had to be careful to disguise himself before he ventured out, to change his distinctive Paeti accent, and to not let anyone look too closely at his face.

These were days where Karl found that, grudgingly, he found Talis to be more the person that Serafina claimed he was than the person Karl wanted him to be. He still didn't trust the man entirely, and he'd slept very little that first night, with Talis, Serafina, and Nico sleeping together in the same room as he and Varina. He'd watched the man carefully, especially the next morning, when the man cleaned the brass bowl in which they'd ignited the black sand, and—as Karl remembered Mahri doing—filled it with clean water and dusted it with another, paler powder. He opened the Second World then with a spell, and the bowl had filled with an emerald fog, light pulsing and shifting over the man's face as he stared, chanting, into the bowl's depths.

In the green light, he could see the fine wrinkles in the man's face, carving themselves deeper almost as he watched. Talis already appeared to be older than Serafina had said he was; Karl thought he knew why now: the Westlander's method of magic was costly to the user.

"Mahri used to say that he saw the future there," Karl said afterward, as Talis, exhausted and moving like an old man, poured the water into the flowered window box of the room. "He didn't seem to be very good at it, if he didn't see his own death."

Talis cleaned the bowl carefully with the hem of his bashta, not looking at Karl. "What we see in the scrying bowl isn't the future, but the shadows of possibility. We see likelihoods and maybes. Axat suggests what might occur if we follow a particular path. But there's never a guarantee." He placed the bowl back into the pouch he always carried. He gave Karl a quick smile. "We can all change our future, if we're strong and persistent enough."

Karl had sniffed at that. Talis had gone over to Nico then, and the two had tussled, laughing, while Serafina watched with a smile, and the love between the three of them had been palpable. He heard Varina pad barefoot into the room, her eyes dark with sleep. She was watching, too, and he could not tell what he saw in her face. She must have felt his stare, for she turned to him, smiled wanly, then turned her head away again. She folded her arms over her chest, hugging herself and not him.

Each day, Karl would go out to Oldtown Market, usually with Varina, hoping to find those elusive customers of Uly's and asking questions. After several fruitless days, it became more routine; they would occasionally take Nico with them, with the promise to Serafina that if they found Uly, they would not confront him.

It was nearly two weeks later when it happened.

"Oh, yes, the woman I told you about was just here," the farmer said as he placed a box of mushrooms in their place. "She's wearing a yellow tashta embroidered with a dragon down the front. She's probably still around; said she was looking for fish." He pointed to his left. "You might check at Ari's, just down there. He just brought in some trout from the Vaghian."

Karl heard Varina draw in her breath, saw her tighten her grasp on Nico. Karl nodded, tossed the man a folia, and pushed his way back into the slow crowds strolling the market's dirt lanes—almost all of them women or older men. They could smell the fishmonger's stall before they saw it, and Karl caught a glimpse of a yellow tashta there. "Karl?" Varina said.

"I'm just going to ask her. If she knows where Uly is, then we'll get Nico home first." He patted Nico's head. "Can't have your matarh upset with us, after all," he told the boy.

He left the two there, approaching the stall. The woman turned as Ari displayed a rainbow-scaled fish for her, and Karl saw the head of a dragon, purple smoke coiling from its mouth. He pushed forward until he was next to her. "Excuse me, Vajica," he said, "but if you can answer a question for me, I'll buy that fish for you." Before she could answer, he gave her the tale they'd rehearsed, pointing back to Varina and Nico occasionally: how he was newly married, how his wife had a child by her previous husband and now they both wanted a child of their own but because they were both older now, they hadn't been able to conceive; how he'd heard that there was a foreign man named Uly who once had a stall here in the market who had been selling potions for just that problem, and that one of the sellers here had mentioned she might know where this Uly was. The woman looked from Karl to Varina and Nico.

She did know. "In fact, I just left him. In the Red Swan on Bell Lane, not five minutes from here. He'd just ordered a pint, so I expect he's still there."

Karl thanked her, paid the fishmonger for the trout without haggling, and returned to Varina and Nico. He crouched down in front of Nico. "Varina's going to take you home now, Nico," he said. He didn't dare look up at Varina—he could imagine the thoughts her face reflected. "I'm going to stay here a little bit longer."

Nico nodded, and Karl hugged the boy. "You two go on now," he said, rising.

"Karl, you promised . . ." Varina said.

"I'm not going to do anything," he told her, wondering if it was the truth. He told her what the woman had said. "I know where he is right now. All I'm going to do is follow him. I'll find out where he lives. Then we can figure out how to approach him."

He could see the disbelief in the way she bit her lower lip, in the hollowness of her eyes, in the slow shake of her head. She clutched at Nico. "You promise?"

"I promise," Karl said.

She stared at him, her head tilted to one side. "Come on, Nico," she said finally. "Let's go." Karl bent down and hugged Nico again, then—rising—Varina. That was like hugging one of the columns on the Archigos' Temple. He watched the two of them until they disappeared into the crowds of the market.

Bell Lane was a dirt-strewn alley a few blocks off the Avi a'Parete, only a few strides across and hemmed in closely with small shops of indeterminate purpose, and above them dingy, dark apartments. Its central gutter was filthy and wet with waste; Karl found himself walking carefully to avoid the worst of the messes. The *Red Swan* was set on a corner where the lane intersected a larger street leading up to the Avi, curls of old paint peeling from the signboard. Karl entered, the gloom inside making him pause to let his eyes adjust. The only light inside came through the cracks of the shutters and the guttering candles on a single chandelier and on each table. It was easy enough to find Uly once Karl could see in the dim light: a copper-skinned man with scars and tattoos over his face and arms.

Karl went to the bar and ordered a pint from the sour-looking barman, his back to Uly. The interior brightened suddenly as another person—a woman—entered the bar, and Karl shielded his eyes against the light.

He'd intended to do as he'd said to Varina: find Uly and follow the man until he found where he lived. But he watched the man sipping his pint, and images of Ana's sprawled, ruined body rose in his mind so that he could barely think at all, and a slow rage built in his belly, rising to his chest where it wrapped blood-engorged arms around his lungs and heart.

He swallowed half his beer at one draught. He picked up the beer and went to the Westlander's table.

"You're Uly?" he asked. He sat across from the man, who watched him carefully, as if ready to fight. Muscles corded and slid in his muscular arms, and one hand dropped below the table.

"And if I am?" he asked. His voice held the same accent as Talis', the same as Mahri's, though deeper and more pronounced, so that Karl had to listen carefully to make out the words.

"I'm told you make potions. For fertility."

The man's chin lifted slightly and he seemed to relax. His right hand came back to the scarred, beer-ringed table-top. "Ah, that. I do that, yes. You're in need of such?"

Karl shrugged. "Not that. But perhaps ... something else. I have a friend; Talis is his name. He tells me you can provide me with something not to create life, but end it. Quickly."

He watched the man's face as he spoke. At the mention of Talis, one eyebrow had lifted slightly. A corner of Uly's mouth rose, as if he were amused. He rubbed at his scarred, black-lined skull. His hands were large, the skin rough, and a long scar ran across the back: trademan's hands. Or a soldier's. "Such a thing would be illegal, Vajiki. Even if it could be done."

"I'm prepared to pay well for it. Very well."

A slow nod. Uly picked up his mug and drained it in

one swallow, wiping his mouth with the back of his hand. "It's a fine day," the man said. "Let's take a stroll, and we can talk."

He rose—the rest of his squat body was as muscular as his arms—and Karl rose with him. As they came to the door of the tavern, a woman hurrying to the door bumped into Karl, nearly knocking him into Uly. "Beg pardon, Vajiki," the woman said. Her face was streaked with dirt, dried snot rimmed her nose, and her breath was foul. She grabbed at Karl's hand and placed something hard in it. "For luck," she said. "You must keep it, and it will bring you good fortune, Vajiki. You make sure now. Keep it." She closed his fingers around it, and let him go, hurrying out the door. Karl looked at what the woman had put in his hand: a small, pale-colored pebble. Uly snorted laughter.

"The woman must have cobwebs for brains," he said. "Come on, Vajiki. Let's go."

Karl put the pebble in the pocket of his bashta and followed Uly out into Bell Lane, then across the larger cross street and down another curving alley. They were walking north, toward Temple Park. "An' what's *your* name, Vajiki, since you know mine?" Uly asked as they walked.

"Andus," Karl told him. "That's all you need to know."

"Ah, cautious, are we, Vajiki Andus? That's good. That's good. And who is it you're wanting dead?"

"That's my business, not yours."

"I hardly think so," Uly said, "since the Garde Kralji would come after me as well as you, and I've no interest in lodgings at the Bastida. I require a name from you, or we have no business at all."

"It's the Archigos," Karl told the man. "I understand you already have some experience with that."

He watched the man carefully, a spell ready to be released with a word and gesture. The man hesitated just slightly, a bare break in his step, but otherwise there was no response at all. He continued to walk on, and Karl had to hurry to catch up with him. The man's expression hadn't changed, nor had his demeanor. Karl waited for him to say something, his hand dropped to his side. They passed a side alleyway . . .

. . . and Uly pushed hard at Karl, his thick hand trapping Karl's own even as he tried to bring it up, and Uly's other hand pressed over Karl's mouth, slamming his head hard against the stone foundation of a building. The impact took the breath from Karl and sent sparks flying through his head. Uly's knee rammed into his stomach. He retched, aware that he was falling. Something—a knee, a fist, he couldn't tell what, impacted the side of his head. He couldn't see, could barely breathe. He could feel the cold cobblestones under him, the filthy water pooled there.

"You're a fool, Ambassador ca'Vliomani," Uly hissed. "Did you think I wouldn't recognize you?"

You're going to die. Now. It was a somber realization.

He could hear boots on the cobbles—a single set of footsteps, he realized—and he waited for the final blow to come. He heard a grunt, and a yelp of pain, and something heavy fell to the ground next to him. He felt a hand raise his head and fasten a hood over it so he couldn't see. The cloth smelled of old sweat. "Stay still and you won't be hurt," a voice said—not Uly's. Someone with the only the trace of some unidentifiable accent, neither deep nor high, so it was difficult to even determine the gender. "Take off the hood and you'll die." Something sharp pressed against his neck, and Karl hissed in anticipation of the cutting stroke. "Nod if you understand."

Karl nodded, and the knife blade vanished. He heard more noise—like a slap, and a grunt that could only be Uly. "Answer me if you want to live," the voice said, though it wasn't addressing Karl. "You killed Archigos Ana, didn't you? You made the black sand."

"No," Uly began, then his voice cut off with a groan of pain. "All right, all right. Yes, I helped kill her. With the black sand. But it wasn't my idea. I just gave the man the stuff and told him how to use it. I didn't know what he intended to do with it. Ouch! Damn it, that's the truth!" So much for Uly's preference to die rather than talk, Karl thought. Perhaps Talis didn't know his warriors that well after all.

"Who?"

"I don't know— Ow! By Axat! Stop! He told me his name was Gairdi ci'Tomisi, but I don't know if that's his real name or not. Paid me well—that's all I knew or cared about."

There were more soft sounds, then a long wail that had

to have come from Uly. The man was panting now, sobbing in pain, his breath fast and desperate. "Please. Please stop."

"Then tell me more about this man," the other voice said. "Quickly."

"Sounded like ca'-and-cu', the way he talked. Firenzcian, maybe, by the accent. Said he had 'orders' from Brezno, in any case. That's all I know. I made the stuff, gave it to him, and he left. I was as surprised as anyone when the Archigos was killed."

Karl desperately wanted to tear the hood from his face, to see what was happening, but he didn't dare. There were more sounds: a wet scuffling, a soft *t-chunk*, then a rustling. Someone pulled at his bashta, rummaging in his pocket. He thought he heard soft footsteps but with the pounding and ringing in his head they were faint enough that he couldn't be sure.

Then, for several breaths, there was nothing at all, only the distant sounds of the city. "Hello?" Karl whispered. There was no answer. Carefully, Karl lifted his hands to the cloth wrapped around his head and pulled it away from his face. What he saw made him recoil backward.

Karl stared at Uly's body on the cobblestones, his throat slashed and blood sprayed over his clothes. His right eye was open to the sky, but covering the left was the stone the woman had given him in the tavern.

~

Allesandra ca'Vörl

SEMINI TRIED TO CONTACT HER for several days
afterward. Allesandra rebuffed his advances. She let his
messages sit on her desk. When he sent his o'téni over to
talk to her directly, he was told firmly by her well-instructed
aides that she was in meetings and could not be disturbed.
When Semini himself left the temple to see her, she made
certain she was out of town with Jan, watching the muster
of the troops.

When Semini—under the guise of working with the war-
téni who were also mustering—came to the fields south of
Brezno, there was, finally, no way to avoid him.

Semini was a green-clad, dark blot against the sun-
washed whiteness of the tent canvas. Outside, the military
encampment stirred in the morning: the clash of metal as
the smithies worked on weapons, armor, and livery; the call
of men; the shouted orders of offiziers; the general buzz of
movement; the sound of feet marching in unison as squads
drilled. Smells drifted in as Semini let the tent flap close behind him: the cook and campfires, the odor of mud churned
by thousands of feet, and the faint stench of the ditches that
served as latrines.

She was talking to Sergei ca'Rudka as she sat behind
the field desk that had once been her vatarh's, the front
panels painted with images of Hïrzg Jan ca'Silanta's famous battles in East Magyaria. "... told the Hïrzg and
Starkkapitän to expect resistance as soon as we cross the
border," Sergei was saying, and he stopped and turned as
her gaze drifted over his shoulder toward Semini. "Ah, Archigos. Perhaps I should go."

"Come back after Second Call and we'll continue our
discussion, Regent," she told him. Sergei bowed to her,
rubbed at the reflective flank of his nose, and left the tent
with a nod and the sign of Cénzi to the Archigos.

Semini seemed uncomfortable, as if he'd expected her to

rise and embrace him as soon as the tent flap closed behind ca'Rudka. After a moment, he finally gave her the sign of Cénzi, shifting his weight as he stood in front of the desk like a summoned offizier. "Allesandra," he began, and she scowled.

"Anyone could be listening through the tent fabric. We are in public, Archigos Semini, and I expect you to address me properly."

She saw irritation quickly narrow his eyes at the rebuke. His lips pressed together under the roof of his mustache. "A'Hïrzg ca'Vörl," he said, with deliberate slowness. "I apologize." Then, he dropped his voice to a low, rumbling near-whisper. "I hope that we might still talk openly. Francesca, she . . ."

Allesandra shook her head slightly; with the motion, Semini stopped. "I spoke with your *wife*," she said, with heavy emphasis. "The other night. We had a lovely chat. She seems to believe that you had something to do with Archigos Ana's death."

She hadn't really expected him to react; he didn't. He stared blandly at her. "I know you had some affection for the false Archigos," he said. "Given what happened to you, I can understand that. But Ana ca'Seranta was *my* enemy. I didn't mourn her passing. Not in the slightest, and if my pleasure in her death offends you, A'Hïrzg, then I have to accept that. I prayed—often—that Cénzi would take her soul, because the woman was *wrong* in her beliefs and she was largely responsible for the severing of the Faith and the break of the Holdings."

"She is also the reason I am who I am. Without her . . ." Allesandra shrugged. "I might not be here. Jan may never have been born."

"And for that, if nothing else, I gave her my prayers when she died." Semini took a step to the side of the field desk, then stopped. "Allesandra, what's happened between us? It's obvious you've been avoiding me. Why?"

"When were you going to tell me that it was you who ordered Ana killed? Or weren't you ever going to tell me?"

"Allesandra—"

"If you didn't do it, then deny it, Semini. Tell me now that it wasn't you."

She wasn't certain how she wanted him to answer. In

the intervening days, she had—through the staff in the palais, through Commandant cu'Göttering of the Garde Brezno—performed her own investigation. The name of Gairdi ci'Tomisi had emerged, and she'd had Commandant cu'Göttering take the merchant, who happened to be in Brezno, to the Bastida for interrogation. Ci'Tomisi, under the Bastida's less-than-gentle persuasion, had poured out the entire story: how he served Firenzcia and Archigos ca'Cellibrecca as a dual agent, how he knew a Westlander in Nessantico who sold potions, how the man had told him about some powerful Westlander concoction, how the Westlander had demonstrated this "black sand" to him and how ci'Tomisi told his contacts in Brezno Temple about its power, and how word had come back (from 'the Archigos himself') that—if he were able to do so—a demonstration against the Nessantican Faith would be "interesting and much rewarded"; how he'd used his contacts in the Archigos' Temple in Nessantico to gain access at night; how he'd placed the black sand in the High Lectern and set a clock-candle burning within, the flame set to touch the black sand at the same time that Archigos Ana would be giving her Admonition.

Ci'Tomisi confessed in order to save his own life, blubbering and weeping. He'd succeeded, but Allesandra wondered if, in his filthy and dark cell in the bowels of the Bastida, he might be wishing he hadn't.

Allesandra was also aware that Semini would have realized that ci'Tomisi had been imprisoned and had probably talked. So she watched Semini, wondering what he would say, whether he would give her the lie and deny any knowledge of it, and how she should react if he did.

But he didn't deny it. "I am Archigos," he said. "I need to do what seems best for the Faith, and in my opinion, the Faith would stay as broken as Cénzi's world until that woman was gone."

With that, Allesandra's hand went to the cracked-globe pendant she wore, that Ana had given her. She saw Semini watching the gesture. "Cénzi would have taken her," Allesandra said. "In His own time. And if He did not, why should *you* act for Him?"

He had the grace and humility to look down at the carpeted grass that was the tent's floor. "Cénzi often requires that we act for Him," he answered finally. "There was ... a sudden opportunity, one that presented itself all unexpected and would not point back to Firenzcia, but to either the Numetodo or the Westlanders. Is that any more wrong than someone in the Holdings sending the White Stone to kill Fynn?" He stared at her.

Allesandra felt a quick stab of guilt. She pressed her lips tightly; Semini seemed to interpret the gesture as annoyance.

"I had to act immediately or not at all," Semini continued. "I prayed to Cénzi for guidance, and I felt I was answered. And at the time, A'Hirzg, you and I were not ..." He let the next word hang there, silent. He continued, but his voice was now a husk, barely audible. "Had we been, Allesandra, I would have sought your advice and taken it. Instead, I asked your vatarh, who was very ill already, and your brother."

"You're telling me Vatarh knew? And Fynn? They *also* approved of this?"

"Yes. I'm sorry, Allesandra." The regret in his voice seemed genuine. His hands were lifted, as if asking for absolution, and there was a moistness in his eyes that caught the sun filtering through the canvas. "I'm sorry," he said again. "Had I realized how much the act would hurt you, if I'd known what it would do to us, I would have stopped it. I would have. You must believe that."

"No," she told him, shaking her head. *Semini. Fynn. And Vatarh. All of them, approving of the death of the woman who kept me alive and sane.* "I don't have to believe that at all. You would say that whether it's the truth or not."

"Then how can I prove it to you?"

"You can't," she told him. "But it's something you should have told me long before now: in my role as A'Hirzg and the matarh of the Hïrzg if nothing else. And I don't know where that leaves us. I don't know that at all."

The steed was frothed with sweat as it galloped hard up the slope to where they waited, its muscular legs shivering as the rider dismounted holding a courier's pouch. He immediately dropped to a knee in front of Jan, Allesandra, Sergei, and Semini. "Urgent news from Nessantico, my Hïrzg," he said. The man's leathers were caked with road grime, his face and hair streaked with dirt. His voice shook with exhaustion, and he looked as if—like his mount—he were ready to collapse. He held out the pouch, his hand trembling. Jan took the pouch from the man as Allesandra waved to the attendants, hanging back a judicial few paces from the four. "Get this man some food and rest, and take care of his horse."

Attendants scurried to obey. Jan unfolded the thick parchment inside the pouch, dropping the pouch on the ground. Allesandra watched his eyes scan the words there. Her son's eyes widened, and he handed the paper to Allesandra silently. She understood his shock quickly; the phrases there seemed impossible.

... *Kraljiki Audric has been assassinated in much the same way as Archigos Ana* ... *Sigourney ca'Ludovici has been named Kraljica, but she has been injured in the attack* ... *Karnor has been razed and plundered by Westlanders* ... *Westlander army approaching Villembouchure* ... *Garde Civile and chevarittai mustered to stop them* ...

She passed the message to Sergei, who read it with Semini looking intently over his shoulder. "A'Hïrzg," she heard Semini say, "this comes as a shock to me. I swear to Cénzi that I knew nothing of any of this. Audric dead ..." He spread his hands in supplication. "That was not my doing, nor my intention."

She paid no attention to his protests. She put her arm around Jan, who was staring out over the army encampment, glittering with banners and armor, dotted with gray-white tents, seething with the activity of thousands of soldiers. "What does this mean, Matarh?" Jan asked her, though she saw him looking at Sergei as well. "Tell me what you're thinking."

"It means that Cénzi has truly blessed us," she told him. "We are moving at the right time, when our enemy is weakest." She nearly laughed. Audric dead, ca'Ludovici injured, the attention of the Holdings given over to the Westlanders rather than looking toward Firenzcia. "This is your moment, my son. Your moment. All you have to do is seize it."

It was her moment as well, perhaps more than her son's, but she didn't say that.

Jan continued to stare at the encampment. Then he shook himself, and in that moment, she saw a glimpse of his great-vatarh in him: the firm clamping of his jaw, the certainty in his eyes. It was the way the old Hïrzg Jan had always looked when he'd set his mind; she remembered it well. Jan gestured to the attendants.

"Bring Starkkapitän ca'Damont to me," he said. "I have new orders to give him."

The White Stone

SHE WAS ACROSS THE LANE from them when Talis went up to the building and knocked on the door, holding Nico. She heard the cry from Serafina—"Nico! Oh, Nico!"—and she watched the woman gather up Nico in her arms ... and she also saw Talis stiffen as if in alarm, raising the walking stick he always carried as if he were about to strike someone with it, gesturing with his free hand as if he wanted Serafina and Nico to leave.

She hurried across the lane, her hand on one of the throwing knifes hidden in her tashta. She caught some broken, loud conversation as she did so.

"... just go! Now! ... the Numetodo Ambassador ... tried to kill me ..."

"... knew where Nico was, and *you didn't go to him?* ..."

There was more, but the voices were yammering in her head, and she couldn't distinguish the real ones from the ones inside her head. The door closed behind Talis, and she took the opportunity to slip into the narrow space between the buildings. There, she pressed against the wall next to one of the shuttered windows. She could hear the muffled conversation—clearly enough to realize that she didn't need to intervene. Not yet. There was talk of the assassination of Archigos Ana, (*"That cold witch deserved to die for what she did to my family,"* Fynn screeched), of something called black sand that could kill (and all the voices of her victims clamored in her head at that—*"Death! Death! Yes, bring more of them here to us!"*—so loudly she had to scream silently at them to stop), of a man named Uly (*"That name ..."* Fynn said *"I know that name ..."*).

When it was apparent that Talis and Nico would be staying here, she slipped away again, returning to her apartment and gathering up the things she had there. That evening, after three or four stops, she had rented a new apartment, one street south of Nico's matarh's rooms: there, from the window, she could see the door of Nico's rooms through the space between the buildings.

For days, she watched. She would slip at night between the houses and listen to them. She followed them whenever they left, especially if Nico was with them. For days, she watched: the trips to Oldtown Market, the attempts to find Uly. She'd already found the man herself, living in squalid rooms on Bell Lane near the Oldtown Market. She found the foreigner strange and loathsome—not a man who cared about the cleanliness of his rooms or the filth ground into his clothes. He was brusque and rude with the customers to whom he sold potions, usually in the tavern below his rooms: the Red Swan. He was often drunk, and he was a poor drunk. He could be violent as well; certainly he was rough with the prostitutes he hired, enough that most of the women working the streets around the Market avoided him.

For days, she watched.

She was surprised, one day, to see Nico accompanying Varina and Karl to the market—generally, that was something that Serafina wouldn't allow. But she also knew that the market visits were by now routine, that with each passing day the group had less expectation that they would ever find Uly, and she knew that Varina and Serafina had become close friends, that Nico seemed to think of the Numetodo woman almost as a beloved tantzia. She followed the trio closely, winding her way through the throngs about the stalls, close enough to almost listen to them but never so near that one of them might notice her. She saw them talk to a farmer in his stall, saw him point and the three of them hurry away, with Varina looking suddenly worried. Karl went up to a woman with a yellow tashta—a woman that she recognized as one of Uly's customers.

A hard knot of worry twisted in her stomach—or perhaps it was the child growing there. The voices muttered. *"She will tell him . . . You'll have to intervene . . ."* She put her hand to the white stone in its pouch around her neck, pressing hard as if she could stop the voices with her touch.

Had Karl started to go after Uly with Nico, she would have stopped them. She wouldn't let them endanger Nico. She wouldn't.

But Karl sent Varina and Nico away. She followed the two long enough to know that they were actually returning to their rooms, then she turned quickly back, hurrying through the streets toward the Red Swan. On the way, she plucked a small, flat, and pale stone from the street.

She saw Karl enter the tavern and followed after him. Uly was there, sitting at his usual table and—also as usual—half-drunk. Karl saw him as well, but he was at the bar, ordering a pint. As she watched, Karl pushed away from the bar and went to Uly's table. She couldn't hear their conversation, but not long afterward, Uly finished his ale and stood up, Karl following him toward the door.

"You know what will happen." Fynn cackled in her head. *"What are you going to do about it?"*

She moved. She interposed herself between Karl and the door, bumping into him deliberately. "Beg pardon, Vajiki," she said to him. She took his hand and placed the stone she picked up into his palm. "For luck," she said. "You must keep it, and it will bring you good fortune, Vajiki. You make sure now. Keep it."

She hoped he would do that, because she couldn't help him if he didn't. Had he given it back to her, or dropped it, or tossed it away, she would have been helpless. *"The White Stone can't kill without the ritual now,"* the voices chorused mockingly. *"Weak. Stupid."*

But Karl didn't do any of those things. She had hidden herself as she left the tavern, and a few breaths later, Karl and Uly emerged. Uly led Karl away from the tavern, and she followed carefully. In any case, Uly appeared to be either too intoxicated or too uninterested in seeing if anyone was watching. She saw him push Karl into an alley, and she ran quietly forward.

When she reached the intersection, Karl was already down, and it was apparent that Uly intended to beat the Numetodo to death. "You're a fool, Ambassador ca'Vliomani," she heard Uly snarl. "Did you think I wouldn't recognize you?"

She moved then, the White Stone again, grim and serious. Uly glanced up at the sound of her approach, but her kick was already on its way, smashing into his kneecap so that the man crumpled with a groan, and then her doubled fists hit the side of his head, taking him down to the pavement unconscious.

Quickly, she tore away Uly's bashta, then went to the moaning, half-conscious Karl. She wrapped the torn cloth around his head, then slid her favorite knife from its sheath and pressed it against his neck. "Stay still and you won't be hurt," she told him, pitching her voice low. "Take off the hood and you'll die. Nod if you understand."

His head bobbed once, and she left him for Uly. She slapped the man's face to wake him, watching his eyes widen as he saw her, and she showed him the knife blade before jabbing it sharply into the tattooed flesh of his neck. She placed her boot on the man's broken kneecap. *"He's seen you. You can't let him live now,"* the voices clamored, and she bid them to be quiet.

"Answer me if you want to live," she told him. She felt his hands start to lift and she shook her head at him, driving the tip of the blade into his neck, close to the throbbing, thick vein there. His eyes widened further. "You killed Archigos Ana, didn't you? You made the black sand."

"No," the man began, but she shoved the blade in further with the lie. "All right, all right." He leaned away from her as much as he could. "Yes, I helped kill her. With the black sand. But it wasn't my idea. I just gave the man the stuff and told him how to use it. I didn't know what he intended to do with it." Again she pressed harder with the knife. "Ouch! Damn it, it's the truth!"

"Who?" she asked him. She knew Karl would be listening; she would give him the information he wanted, as long as it meant Nico would still be safe.

"You have to kill this one. You must."

"I don't know—" Uly was saying, and she ignored the voice to draw the knife's blade slightly toward herself, opening a cut. Warm blood dripped down his neck. "Ow! By Axat! Stop! He told me his name was Gairdi ci'Tomisi, but I don't know if that's his real name or not. Paid me well—that's all I knew or cared about."

The man tried to push her away, and she put more weight on his shattered knee. He panted with the pain. "Please. Please stop."

"Then tell me more about this man," she said. "Quickly."

"Sounded like ca'-and-cu', the way he talked. Firenzcian, maybe, by the accent. Said he had 'orders' from Brezno, in any case. That's all I know. I made the stuff, gave it to him, and he left. I was as surprised as anyone when the Archigos was killed."

"You can't stay here. You have to leave or someone will come and see you."

The voices were right. She pressed her lips together. With a single, savage motion, she plunged the knife deeply into the man's throat and slashed it from right to left. Hot blood spurted, and the man died in a gurgle of wet breath. Quickly now, she pulled the pouch from under her now gory tashta and opened it, placing the precious white stone on the man's open right eye. Then she went to Karl, rummaged quickly in his pocket and found the stone she'd given him. That she placed on Uly's left eye. She sheathed her blade, waited a breath, then took her stone from his right eye.

She could hear Uly's voice already, wailing in a language she didn't understand.

She placed the stone in the pouch again. She glanced down once at Karl, who was straining under the cloth, listening desperately.

She ran. She ran—staying to shadows and lonely back ways because of her blood-spattered tashta—ran to find Nico, to know that he was still safe.

BLOODSHED

Kenne ca'Fionta

KENNE STOOD ON THE BALCONY outside his private office, gazing down on the temple plaza. Below him, téni in their green robes mingled with the normal throngs as they hurried to escape the drizzle seeping from low, gray clouds. The weather seemed to weigh down the wings of the pigeons in their cooing huddles; as people hurried past, the birds would scurry away, heads bobbing, but not take flight.

The foul, miserable day matched Kenne's mood.

He was a dead man if he made the wrong move, and he wasn't sure how to avoid that fate.

Even if he avoided physical death, he was dead within the Faith. He could already feel the vultures beginning to gather: in the whispers of everyone from the lowliest e'téni to the subtext of the messages he received from the a'téni in their cities. *When will we have another Conclave?* they asked. *There are urgent matters that we must all discuss. How should we respond to the news from Nessantico? What is the Archigos' thought on these matters?*

The subtext was always below the innocent questions. It had begun even when he'd been elevated to Archigos after poor Ana's assassination. The chorus had grown louder and more constant since Kraljiki Audric's death and the news of the Westlander invasion. The messages came every day by courier: from Fossano, from Prajnoli, from Chivasso and Belcanto and An Uaimth, from Kasama and Quibela and Wolhusen. *We don't trust your leadership. Someone else needs to be Archigos.* That's what they said underneath the polite, indirect words they wrote. *You should be removed from Cénzi's Throne.*

Worst of all, he found that he agreed with them. *I never wanted this,* he wanted to write back to them. *I never asked to sit in Ana's place. I would have much preferred that someone else take this task from me.* He had told Ana herself this long years ago, after he'd returned to Nessantico to become A'Téni of Nessantico under her, after the Firenzcian army had been dispersed. "You were here before I was," she'd said to him, looking almost embarrassed to be sitting behind the desk that they both remembered Archigos Dhosti using. "By rights, you should be here and not me, my friend."

He had laughed at that, shaking his head. "Archigos Dhosti told me, long ago, that I was an excellent follower. He was right, too. I follow very well. But I don't lead. I don't have whatever it is you have, Ana. Dhosti saw those qualities in you, too—you *can* lead. You're strong, you're talented, and you have a strength of will that's amazing. That's why he made you his o'téni. Had he lived, he would have groomed you for this anyway. Me . . ." Another headshake. "I was destined to be what I am. No more. And I'm quite content to have it that way."

She had protested, politely, but they both knew that—inside—she agreed with him. With Dhosti.

Yet Cénzi had thrust this on him late in life, and Kenne could only wonder whether that had been some kind of cosmic joke.

The a'téni of the Faith were one danger to Kenne, and the new Kraljica was another. She was in pain—she would be in pain for the rest of her life, almost certainly. She had been thrust into a terrible crisis with the loss of the Hellins, the assassination of Audric, and now the invasion of the Holdings itself by the Westlanders. There was Firenzcia on her other side, no longer an ally but another enemy at her back. She would be trying to consolidate her position. She would be trying desperately to simply survive as Kraljica, and to do that, she would be looking for people with strength who could support her and she would be casting aside those she thought too weak to be of help—because weakness in her allies was as much a danger as the Westlanders or Firenzcians.

Kenne knew that Sigourney's opinion of him was perhaps even less high than that of the a'téni. She would be maneuvering to have him replaced, and quickly. Knowing the history of the Kralji in Nessantico, Kenne could not rule out that her solution would be his own assassination and replacement by someone more suitable for her. It had happened to Archigi before Kenne when they had come into conflict with the political rulers of the Holdings: such an Archigos might die under mysterious circumstances. One had only to look back to Archigos Dhosti himself, after all.

Kenne stared down at the plaza below, where Dhosti's broken body had once sprawled, the blood flowing between the cobbles. He wondered if one day soon it might be his body being tossed over the railing to fall, flailing desperately, to the ground below.

"Archigos?"

Kenne shivered at the call. He turned slowly, expecting to see Petros standing there. But it wasn't. It was, instead, a ghost.

"I know," the ghost said, and the voice's accent confirmed his suspicions. "You didn't expect to see me again. Frankly, neither did I. Sorry to startle you, Archigos. Petros was kind enough to let me in."

"Karl..." Kenne stepped back into the room, going around the desk to embrace the Numetodo. "Look at you—your beard shaved, your hair dyed and cut like some unranked person, and those horrible clothes. I wouldn't have recognized you... but I suppose that's the idea, isn't it? I thought, after you helped Sergei escape, that you'd have fled the city." He shook his head. "These are dark times," he said wearily, the depression washing over him again. "Terrible times. But—I forget myself. You look tired and hungry. Can I have Petros bring something?"

But Karl was already shaking his head. "No, Archigos. There isn't time, and I shouldn't stay here longer than necessary. I... I need a favor."

"If it's within my power," Kenne told him, and had to quash the thought that followed: *as weak as my power is, I'm afraid...*

"It is, I hope," Karl said. "Please, Archigos, sit. This may take some time. I know, at least I think I know, who killed Ana."

Kenne listened to Karl's tale with growing dread, suspicion, and horror. By the end he was sitting in his chair behind his desk, shaking his head.

"A man named Gairdi ci'Tomisi, you say?" Kenne said finally. The name had shocked him; he wondered what else he had not known. "A Firenzcian? He did this with help from Westlander magic?"

"Firenzcian, yes," Karl stated. "But you must understand that there was no magic involved. No—this black sand isn't of your Cénzi's making, nor that of the Westlander gods, either. It's not magical, not of the Second World—just the product of a person's imagination and logic." Karl tapped his head. "And that makes it even more dangerous. Look . . ."

Karl took a small pouch from the pocket of his grimy and tattered bashta, spilling a dark, granular powder on the blotter of Kenne's desk. Kenne prodded it with a curious finger. "Uly had a stash of this in his rooms; I bribed the innkeeper to let me in. Uly had the ingredients there in his rooms so we know what they are. Varina thinks she can reproduce this mixture even if Talis won't help us. Sitting there like that, the black sand's innocent enough, but put a flame to it, and . . ." Karl's voice trailed off, and he looked away. Kenne knew what the man was remembering; he remembered it, too, all too well.

"What can I do?" Kenne asked him. He stared down at his soiled desk.

"See if you can find out more about this Gairdi ci'Tomisi that Uly mentioned."

Kenne looked at him bleakly. "I know him. At least I think I do. He's a trader with Writs of Passage from both Brezno and Nessantico, and goes back and forth over the border. We—both Ana and I—have used him. We thought . . . we thought he was *our* man, our spy. He carried messages from us to the téni within the Brezno Temple that we thought we could trust, and brought back their messages to us about Archigos Semini. Now . . ." Kenne looked up at the Numetodo. "If he was actually a dual agent, in the employ of Semini ca'Cellibrecca . . ."

". . . Then it was ca'Cellibrecca who ordered Ana killed," Karl finished for him. His jaw shut audibly.

Kenne felt the remnants of his lunch rise into his throat. He swallowed hard against the bile. Yes, he believed ca'Cellibrecca would be capable of murder—after all, the man had been a war-téni for most of his life. He had no doubt killed hundreds of soldiers with the mage-fire. But he wouldn't have killed Ana without a reason. Kenne was afraid that he knew exactly what the reason might be: that ca'Cellibrecca expected the person placed in Ana's stead would be weak, and that he might exploit that weakness to reunite the Faith again—with ca'Cellibrecca as Archigos in Nessantico as well as Brezno.

Because he knew it would be me. He's probably already speaking to the Kraljica, making his overtures.

"Archigos?" Kenne took a long breath before looking up at Karl. "No Numetodo killed Audric," Karl declared. "No Numetodo killed Ana. *That* killed them both." Karl gestured at the black sand on Kenne's desk. "That makes me think that the same person is responsible for both murders."

It seemed a reasonable assumption to Kenne, but he'd been wrong about so much that he no longer trusted his own reasoning. "What ... what do you want me to do?" Kenne lifted his hands from the desk, a fingertip dark with the powder he'd touched. "How can I help?"

"See what more you can find out," Karl told him. "See if Semini really did this—if he did, I want to make the man pay. But Varin ..." He stopped. "I mean, *Ana* wouldn't want me to do anything until I *knew*, knew for certain. Can you help me with that?" Karl pointed again to the drift of black sand on Kenne's blotter. "You know what that is, don't you?" the Numetodo asked. Kenne could only shake his head.

"That's the ashes of magic, Archigos," Karl said. "That's what magic looks like when it's dead."

Kenne glanced down again. It felt like he was looking at his own remains.

~

Aubri cu'Ulcai

COMMANDANT AUBRI CU'ULCAI LOOKED backward and shook his head, wondering how the battle had come to this. It should never have happened. It wasn't possible.

He wondered how the new Kraljica would receive the news, and expected he knew the answer. And the only excuse he had was that the Westlanders refused to fight honorably, as they should.

It had begun only three short days before. . . .

Several chevarittai—as was common—rode out on their destriers to call for individual challenge as the Westlander forces approached Villembouchure. No Westlander warriors rode out to meet their challenge; the front ranks of the army marched forward, unbroken and unfazed even as the chevarittai mocked their honor and their courage. They were ignored or, worse, attacked with cowardly arrows and fire from the Westlander spellcasters. Three chevarittai were killed before Aubri had the horns call "return" and the chevarittai turned their warhorses and galloped back behind the lines of waiting infantry and war-téni.

Aubri and his offiziers huddled; they expected the attack to start as soon as the Westlander army crested the last hill before Villembouchure. After all, it was just before Second Call, and there were still hours of daylight. The Westlanders had come within a double bowshot of the front lines of the Holdings force and halted . . . and remained stopped. The chevarittai and his offiziers had pleaded with Aubri to allow them to advance and engage. He'd refused, regretfully—to do so would mean to abandon the earthworks and bunkers they'd erected in the past few days. The Holdings army was arrayed in a perfect defensive position, and Aubri was loath to move from that.

That had been the first day. He'd gone to sleep that night convinced of eventual victory—the Westlander advance would break against their hardened lines. The Westlander force, as his scouts and all the reports from the field had verified, was substantially smaller than their own: no army of that size, not even the Firenzcians at their best, would have been able to overrun the defenses Aubri had erected. The ships of the Tehuantin fleet clogged the A'Sele, but were too far from the field of battle to affect the issue; in any case, Aubri knew that a Nessantican naval force was on its way to deal with the enemy ships. At worst, the walls of Villembouchure would hold them if for some unforeseen reason Aubri could not contain them in the fields outside the city. The Westlander forces were far too small for an effective siege, and Villembouchure was well-provisioned and could withstand a siege from an even larger army for at least a month.

Yes, Aubri was confident. Despite the fact that his army had been hastily mustered and most of the infantry was poorly trained, his offiziers and the chevarittai with them were battle-tested by the many skirmishes over the last few decades with Firenzcia and the Coalition nations.

They would prevail here.

The battle began on the second day, but not—as in all of Aubri's experience and the experience of the offiziers who had trained him—at the advent of dawn. No . . . the attack came well before the sun clawed its way into the sky. And it came strangely. The lookouts posted in the foremost bunkers had sent urgent messengers running to the commandant's tent behind the lines, the uproar waking Aubri from a light, dream-troubled sleep.

"A storm walking toward us on legs of lightning," they clamored. "A wall of cloud . . ."

Alarm horns were sounding over the encampment and soldiers were hastily donning armor and grabbing weapons as offiziers screamed orders. In the distance, blue light flickered and danced and thunder boomed, yet above them the sky was clear, pricked with the crowded and familiar constellations. Aubri mounted the horse his attendants hurriedly brought to him. He galloped quickly toward the front, joined on the way by A'Téni Vallis ca'Ostheim of Villembouchure, who was in charge of the war-téni. "What in the name of Cénzi is going on?" ca'Ostheim roared. His shock of thick white hair seemed to spark in the light of the storm ahead; his belly sagged over the pommel of his horse's saddle. The lashes of his eyes were still clotted with sleep rime. A thick gold necklace with a broken globe hanging from it bounced on his chest as they rode. "I thought you said the attack would come at dawn, Commandant."

"I said that, yes," Aubri replied calmly. "It appears that the Westlanders weren't listening."

At the first line of bunkers, the two men stopped, gazing out over the space between the two armies. The Westlander encampment, which when Aubri had gone to bed had been twinkling on the far hillside like yellow stars fallen to earth, was no longer visible. Instead, an apparition of nature confronted them: a wall of black, roiling cloud perhaps twelve men high and floating two men above the ground. Like some ominous, supernatural monster, the cloud-creature crawled toward them on hundreds of legs of flickering lightning. The flashes stabbed at the ground below, seeming to pull the clouds forward a few feet with each stroke. Aubri could see the ground tearing wherever the lightning struck, leaving a trail of storm-footprints ripped from the ground. A constant din of thunder and a high, crackling snarl accompanied the vision. All around them, the army of the Holdings stared at the creature with faces illuminated by erratic white-blue. Aubri could feel the panic moving through the ranks, the men falling involuntarily backward a few steps, away from the mounds of low earthworks and fortifications they'd raised. "Hold!" Aubri cried out to them. The horns took up the call along the line: *"Hold!"* and the men shook themselves as if awakening from a nightmare. They clutched useless spears, gazing at the monster that confronted them. It was nearly across the open ground now and Aubri could glimpse nothing beyond its ferocious border.

"A'Téni ca'Ostheim, this is magic—it's your domain." Aubri had to nearly shout over the increasing din of the storm-creature to ca'Ostheim, the leader of the war-téni. "Can you stop this?"

"I'll try," he answered, dismounting. He began to chant; his hands moved in strange patterns in front of him. Aubri could feel the hair on his arms standing up as ca'Ostheim continued to chant and as the lightning began to touch the edges of the ramparts—he didn't know which it was that caused the reaction. Aubri's steed, though accustomed to the clamor, noise, and sights of war, was stamping worriedly at the ground, half-rearing away from the apparition. Aubri had to lean down and pat the horse's neck to calm it. "A'Téni! Soon, please."

Ca'Ostheim raised his hands; the chanting came to a halt. He gestured toward the storm. A wind shrieked outward from the war-téni, and where it touched the storm-creature, the clouds were torn apart. Soldiers cheered, but to either side, the storm still crawled forward, unabated, and now lighting bolts tore at the ramparts themselves, the forked legs reaching out to where the soldiers of the Holdings stood. Screams rose from either side as the bolts seared and shattered the ranks, sliding inexorably forward. And now the sundered halves of the clouds were coming back together; eager tongues of lightning were beginning to flash in front of Aubri. Ca'Ostheim had sunk to his knees. He shook his head up to Aubri. "Commandant, I can't . . . Not alone. I need to gather the other war-téni . . ."

"To your horse, then," Aubri told him. He looked to his banner bearers and the messenger horns as the screams of the wounded and dying vied with the thundering. "Retreat!" he shouted. "Back to the next line!"

The banners signaled retreat; the horns sounded the call. The ranks of soldiers broke instantly, those who still could turning to flee the storm. Faintly, in the space beyond the storm, he could hear new voices: the battle cries of the Westlanders.

Aubri yanked hard on the reins of his mount and followed his men.

That was the morning of the second day. The rest of the day went no better. The war-téni were able to disperse the spell-storm, but the task exhausted them and they had little energy left for other spells. Behind the storm, the ranks of the Westlanders—warriors with scarred and painted faces—surged forward. The hand-to-hand combat was fierce, but the chevarittai and infantry could match sword for sword. However, for the Westlander spellcasters, wielding sticks from which they cast spells, Aubri had no answer—the war-téni were largely depleted from their earlier efforts, and by late afternoon, Aubri called for the army to return to Villembouchure, behind the walls and stout gates. He was convinced that he could have held the outer defenses, but the price in lives would have been enormous. He did what any Commandant in his position would have done: he had the horns blow "disengage."

By evening, they were inside and the portcullises were lowered and locked.

That ended the second day.

In any normal battle, that would have signaled the beginning of a siege that might have lasted weeks or months before being broken, and Aubri knew that the Westlanders didn't have weeks or months—not in a strange land where they were surrounded by enemies. This was why Aubri had found it easy to call for disengagement as soon as it was apparent that victory on the fields before the city would only come at huge cost. Being inside the walls of Villembouchure must lead to eventual victory. Inevitably. And he could wait.

But the siege would last only one day.

Aubri was on the city walls, staring down at the smoldering fires of the main Westlander encampment in the dawn. That was when the arcing balls of smoke rose suddenly, arrowing toward them: a dozen or more of them, all seeming to target the great Western Gate of the city. The war-téni stationed along the walls reacted instantly, as they should, and—trained in the art of holding their spells in their minds for a time (which none of them would have admitted was a Numetodo trait forced on the war-téni by Archigos Ana)—the response of their dispersal spells was swift. But the fireballs continued on their flight. The closest war-téni looked at Aubri with wide, stricken eyes. "Commandant, those aren't *spells*—"

He got no further. The thick walls of the city shook impossibly as the fireballs slammed into the gate and the surrounding stones. Where they touched, impossible explosions tore into the stones and steel and wood. Aubri, holding onto the battlement to keep his footing, witnessed huge chunks of granite flying away as if they were pebbles tossed by a child. Fire erupted from directly below him, as white-hot as a smithy's blaze; he could feel it washing over his skin. He heard screams and cries from below.

"The gate is broken! The walls are sundered!"

The Westlanders were already rushing toward the breach, as archers belatedly cast a rain of arrows down on them. Some of the warriors went down, but many—too many—were still coming, and now Aubri saw more fireballs arcing from the north and south toward those gates.

He ran down from the battlements into bloody, savage chaos.

That was the third day. The day the city was lost. Impossibly.

Now Aubri stared back at Villembouchure from a hilltop along the Avi A'Sele. He gazed at the greasy smoke smearing the sky above the broken walls with the remnants of his army gathered around him and A'Téni ca'Ostheim at his side. Inside the town . . . Inside were the Westlanders.

"This isn't possible," he muttered.

But it was. And now the defense of Nessantico herself must be prepared. Aubri shook his head again at the sight.

He turned his horse and gestured, and he and the army began their limping retreat back toward the capital.

Allesandra ca'Vörl

SHE REMEMBERED PASSE a'Fiume all too well. It was there, twenty-five years earlier as her vatarh had besieged the town, that she first learned the hardest lesson of war: that sometimes the ones you love don't survive. She'd had a crush then on a young offizier who'd been killed in the battle. She had thought at the time that she would never be able to love anyone again, her heart was so shattered by the experience, but time had softened the pain. Now, she couldn't recall the young man's face.

The repairs from that decades-old battle were still visible on the city walls, and they brought back the memories and the pain.

This time, there was no siege. The Firenzcian army had passed through the border town Ville Colhelm without any challenge at all: the Holdings force stationed there had simply abandoned their post and fled from the far greater Firenzcian host. At Allesandra's behest, Jan had sent riders—including Sergei ca'Rudka—well ahead of the main force to negotiate with the Comté of Passe a'Fiume. With the garrison of the Garde Civile largely depleted due to the Westlander invasion, the comté chose discretion over valor (and a substantial bribe in gold over his vows of office): in exchange for the vow that the town would not be sacked, he would permit the army to cross the River Clario through the city gates to the Avi a'Firenzcia.

Allesandra rode alongside Jan as they crossed the great stone bridge over the waters of the Clario, more rapid and dangerous than the wider and deeper A'Sele, with which the Clario would join before the A'Sele reached Nessantico. The bridge itself seemed to shudder under the thudding of booted soldiers and horses' hooves, the vanguard of the army already through the gates and the remainder trailing down the road as far as one could see in the hill-pocked terrain. Jan gazed around them raptly as they passed through the tall arches set with the shields of the Kralji, and into the city itself. Crowds lined the sides of the main avenue through the town, mostly silent, and the chevarittai of the Garde Hïrzg stiffened in their saddles as they scanned the throngs for danger.

"You were here with great-vatarh?" Jan asked again, leaning over toward her, and Allesandra nodded.

"I was just a child, and your great-vatarh was in his prime," she said. "He took Passe a'Fiume in just three days of siege after the peace negotiations failed, but Kraljiki Justi—who still had two legs then—had already made a cowardly escape back to Nessantico. Your great-vatarh was furious. Sergei ca'Rudka was the commandant for the Nessantican forces; he was ... brilliant, even though badly outnumbered. Your great-vatarh would have admitted that, however grudgingly."

Jan glanced back over his shoulder to where ca'Rudka rode alongside the Archigos. The Regent's metal nose gleamed in the sun. Like the Garde Hïrzg, ca'Rudka seemed edgy and nervous, his lips pressed tightly together and his eyes scanning the crowd to either side. "I like the man, but I don't know that I entirely trust him, Matarh," Jan said, returning his attention to her.

She smiled at that. "You shouldn't," she told him. "His allegiance is to Nessantico, first and foremost. And he is a strange man with strange tastes, if one believes the rumors. That hasn't changed. He'll work with us as long as he feels that our interests converge. As soon as they don't ..." She shrugged. "Then he will just as happily be our enemy. Your instincts are right, Jan."

"He seems to admire you."

"I knew him when I was Archigos Ana's hostage. He was kind enough to me then. But right now, he's more interested in the fact that I'm Kraljica Marguerite's second cousin and the fact that this relationship gives me as much a claim to the Sun Throne as Sigourney ca'Ludivici. And, for now, we need Sergei and the alliances he may be able to bring us."

Jan nodded. He pressed his lips together as if considering all this as they rode on into the central square of the city. She wondered what he was thinking.

Here, the Temple a'Passe dominated the architectural

landscape. Like many of the structures in the city, it had been heavily damaged in the siege two and a half decades before. Afterward, the town council had made the decision to redesign the main square and the temple complex. Much of the original structure had been demolished. The thin, skeletal lines of scaffolding caged the as-yet unfinished main tower and dome of the revamped temple.

The crowds of townspeople were most dense here as the slow line of the army marched through their city. By now, Allesandra knew, the vanguard would already have passed through the western gate and beyond the city walls. By now, she also knew, messengers would be urging their horses to a gallop ahead of the force bringing news to the Kraljica, to the Archigos, and to Nessantico that the Firenzcians were on the march—for all she knew, that word may have already come to Nessantico, as the army first crossed the borders. Soon, now, their advance would be challenged; Kraljica Sigourney couldn't afford to look westward for long.

An army—especially the Firenzcian army; polished, efficient, and renowned—was a large bargaining chip on any table of negotiation, and Sigourney and the Council of Ca' would be all too well aware of that. Allesandra smiled at that thought.

The crowd pressed close to them, and the foot soldiers to either side of Allesandra and Jan pushed them back with the shafts of pikes and spears. She could see grim, unhappy faces behind the fence of weapons, and from the depths of the crowd came occasional shouted curses and threats, but when they looked that way, there was no one they could pick out of the masses. The populace remembered the Firenzcian siege, too: many of them had lost family members in the siege, and the sight of the silver-and-black banners was a mockery waving in their faces.

They passed into the shadow of the temple now, the line of the army using the bulwark of the main tower to shield them from the crowds. The wind-horns on the temple began to sound Second Call as Allesandra and Jan came abreast of the tower. Allesandra's head craned upward toward the noise, squinting into the glare of the sun. Something—a figure, a form—seemed to move above, amongst the corset of scaffolding. She couldn't see it clearly.

Allesandra was suddenly struck from behind, as her ears alerted her to the sound of hooves against cobbles. A heavy weight bore her down hard to the pavement, though the arms that had gone about her turned her so that the body underneath took the brunt of the impact. She heard a loud *kr-unk* almost in concert with the impact. A horse screamed—a horrible, awful sound—and people shouted. "The Hïrzg!" "Move! Move!" "Back! Get back!" "Above! There he is!" She could hear offiziers shouting orders and more screams. There seemed to be a mob huddled around her. She fought against the arms around her, against the folds of her assaulter's cloak and her own riding tashta and cloak. There were hands pulling at her, helping her up.

There was another scream, a human one this time, and another impact somewhere close by.

She blinked, trying to make sense of the scene.

Sergei ca'Rudka was standing near her, his cloak torn, grimacing as he kneaded his arm. The silver of his nose was scuffed and the nose itself was partially pulled back from his face, giving her a glimpse of an uncomfortable hole underneath. Jan was being helped to his feet, a stride in back of Sergei. Allesandra's horse was on its side before her, a massive statue of a Moitidi demon in pieces on the ground around it. The animal was thrashing its legs, its eyes wide, and the sounds it was making . . . Sergei moved to the horse quickly, kneeling in the wreckage of the stone carving and stroking the horse's neck as he made soothing noises. She saw him take his knife from its scabbard. "No!" she began, but he'd already made the cut, deep and swift. The horse bucked once, again, and went still.

Allesandra shook her head, trying to clear it. Half the crowd in the plaza seemed to have fled in terror; the Firenzcian soldiers had formed a thick bulwark around them. Sergei moved away from the horse, striding toward a body sprawled in a pool of blood not far from the base of the tower. Soldiers moved to intercept him; he shrugged them away angrily. Allesandra started to move and realized that her body was sore and bruised, and she was bleeding from a cut on the head. She felt Jan come up behind her.

"Matarh?" He was staring at the horse Sergei had killed. She hugged her son, desperately, then held him an arm's length away, examining him—his clothes were torn, as well, and there was a scrape along one cheek that was oozing blood, but otherwise he seemed unharmed. "What happened?" she asked him. "Did you see?"

"The Regent saved us," he said. "He took both of us from our horses just in time." He glanced up at the scaffolding, then back to the body on the ground. Sergei was enclosed in a clot of soldiers, crouched alongside the corpse. "The man . . . he was up there—he would have killed you. Maybe both of us. But Sergei . . ."

Archigos Semini came rushing up then, his green robes swirling. "Allesan—" he began, then shook his head, making the sign of Cénzi hurriedly. "A'Hïrzg! Hïrzg Jan! Thank Cénzi you're both safe! I thought—"

But Allesandra was no longer listening to him. She pushed through the crowd to where Sergei was examining the body. "Regent?" she said, and Sergei glanced up at her. He was scowling.

"A'Hïrzg. I apologize, but there was no time to give you warning. Are you badly hurt?"

She shook her head. He nodded and stood up, groaning as he did so as if the movement pained him. "I'm too damned old for this," he muttered. He kicked the corpse in front of him, the boot making a soft, ugly sound as the broken torso jiggled in response. Allesandra saw a fair face underneath the blood, a young face, perhaps Jan's age; what she saw of his clothing was suspiciously fine. The body was adorned with the broken shafts of several arrows. "Don't know who he is," Sergei said, "but we'll find out. Ca'-and-cu', though, from the way he's dressed and the way he looks. I saw him up on the scaffolding just before he tossed down the carving. That's when I moved; looks like your archers took care of the rest." He seemed to notice his dangling nose then, and pushed it gingerly back in place, holding it with two fingers. "My pardon, A'Hïrzg—the glue . . ."

"No matter," she told him, waving her hand. "Regent, I owe you my life."

She thought he would respond as most would have, with a lowering of his head and deprecation, a protest of duty and loyalty and obligation. He did not. Instead, he smiled, still holding his silver nose in place.

"Indeed you do, A'Hïrzg," he said.

Niente

THE TOWN BURNED and the flames reflected in the scrying bowl. They vanished as Zolin slapped the scrying bowl aside, splashing the water over Niente. The bowl clattered away, bronze ringing against the tiles like a wild bell until it clanged up against the far wall, where a tile mosaic of some ancient battle glittered. Outlined in glass, horses reared as soldiers with pikes marched across a field with a snow-topped mountain looming in the background.

"No!" the Tecuhtli roared. "I won't have you tell me this!"

"It is what I saw," Niente answered with a calmness he didn't feel. *The dead warrior, the nahualli sprawled next to him, only this time he saw one of their faces. Zolin's face . . . And he was too afraid to ask Axat to let him see the nahualli's features . . .* "Tecuhtli, we have accomplished so much here. We have shown these Easterners the pain that they inflicted on us and our cousins. We have taken land and cities from them as they were taken from us. We have given them the lesson you wanted to give them. To go on . . ." Niente lifted his hands. *The great city in flames and the tehuantin fleeing, their ships with broken masts canted on their sides on the river . . .* "The visions show me only death."

"No!" Zolin spat. "I've sent word back that we'll stay here, that they are to send more warriors. We will keep what we have taken. We will strike at their heart—this great city of theirs that is so close." He turned, his heavy and muscular arms swinging close to Niente's face. Zolin's thick fingers stabbed toward Niente's eyes. "Are you *blind*, Nahual? Didn't you see how easily we took this city of theirs? Didn't you watch them run from us like a pack of whipped dogs?"

"We have little of the materials left to make more black sand," Niente told the Tecuhtli. "I have lost a third of my nahualli in the fighting; you have lost as many of the warriors. We have come a long way without the resources to hold the land behind us. We are in a foreign country surrounded by enemies, with the only supplies those we can forage and plunder. If we take to our ships and leave now, we will leave behind a legend that will strike fear in the Easterners for decades. The name of Tecuhtli Zolin will be a whisper in the night to scare generations of Easterner children."

"Bah!" Zolin spat again, the expectoration close to Niente's feet, marring the polished floor of the estate house he'd taken in Villembouchure. Looking down, Niente saw that the tiles all bore the glazed image of the same mountain as the mosaic on the wall. Zolin's spittle formed a lake on the mountain's flank. "You're a frightened child yourself, Nahual. I'm not afraid of what you see in your bowl. I'm not afraid of these futures you say Axat sends you. They're not *the* future, only possibilities." His finger prodded Niente's chest. "I tell you now, Nahual, you must make your choice." Each of the last three words was another prod. The Tecuhtli's dark eyes, wrapped in the swirl of the great eagle's wings, glared at him like those of the great cats that prowled the forests of home. "No more words from you. No more prophecy, no more warnings. I want only your obedience and your magic. If you can't give me that, then I am done with you. I will go on, whether you are Nahual or not. Decide now, Niente. As we stand here."

Niente's hand trembled near the haft of his spell-stick, dangling from his belt. He could pluck it up, touch Zolin with it before the warrior could fully draw his sword. The released spell would char the Tecuhtli's body, send him flying across the room until he crumpled against the wall under the mosaic in a smoking heap. Niente could see that result, as clearly as a vision in the scrying bowl.

That would also end this. He ached to do it.

But he could not. That was not a vision that Axat had granted him. That path would lead to one of the blind futures, one he couldn't guess—a future that might be far worse for the Tehuantin than those he had glimpsed in the bowl. He realized that knowing the possible futures was a trap as much as a benefit; he wondered whether that was something Mahri, too, had discovered. In a blind future, Citlali or Mazatl might continue to follow the steps of Zolin and fare worse. They might all die here, and no one from home would know their fate. In a blind future, certainly Niente would never see his family again.

He felt the smooth, polished wood of the spell-stick, but his fingertips only grazed it. They would not close around it.

"I will obey you, Tecuhtli," Niente said, the words slow and quiet. "And I will follow you to the future you bring us."

~

Varina ci'Pallo

KARL WAS SITTING IN THE DARK on the rear stoop of Serafina's house in Oldtown, staring across the small garden planted there toward the rear of the houses a street over. His gaze seemed to be penetrating all the way to South Bank, far away. Above him, the moon was snagged in a lacework of thin, silver clouds through which the stars peered. A cup of tea steamed forgotten at his left side.

He was rubbing a small, flat, and pale stone between his forefinger and thumb.

Varina came up and sat beside him on the right—not quite close enough to touch, not far enough away that she couldn't feel the warmth of his body in the night chill. Neither of them said anything. He rubbed the stone. She could hear faint, muffled music from the tavern down the street.

When the silence between them had stretched for more breaths than she wanted to count, she started to rise again, feeling angry with herself for having come out here, and angry with him for not acknowledging her. But Karl reached out and touched her knee. "Stay," he said. "Please?"

She sat again. "Why?" she asked.

"We haven't . . . Lately . . . Well, you know."

"No, I don't know," she said to him. "Tell me."

"You're trying to make this hard for me?" He flipped the stone over in his fingers.

"No," she told him. "I'm trying to make it easier for me. Karl, being with you or being without you—those are both situations I can deal with, one way or another. What I can't handle is not knowing which it's supposed to be." She waited. He said nothing. "So which is it?" she asked.

"It's not that simple."

"Actually, it is." She hugged herself as she sat, leaning

slightly away from him. "I thought when I finally took you to my bed that I might have everything I'd wanted for years. But I discovered I still only had a part of you. I want all of you, Karl, or I don't want anything. Maybe I'm asking too much of you, or maybe I'm too possessive, or maybe you think I'm pushing you into something you don't want." Tears were threatening, and she sniffed them away angrily. "Maybe it's my fault that this won't work, and if that's the case, then fine. I just need to *know*."

"It's not you."

She wanted to believe that. Varina bit her lower lip, forcing back the tears, her breath shaking in her throat. "Then what is it?" she asked. "You go after this Uly on your own and nearly get yourself killed, you meet with Kenne without telling me, you're even making plans with Talis. But you're not talking to me."

"I don't want you to worry."

She wanted to scoff at that. "I worry *more* because I don't know the situation. I don't know what you're planning, don't know what you're trying to do, don't know what the real dangers might be." She stopped. Took a breath. "I won't be your mistress, to be there whenever you want that kind of comfort but conveniently forgotten otherwise. If that's all you want from me, then I made a mistake. I'm also not Ana, only wanting you as a friend. Again, if that's all you want from me, well, you can't have that either. Not anymore. So if that's the case, then tell me and as soon as this is over, one way or the other, I'll go my own way. I've wanted you to open the door between us for a long time, Karl. Now you have, but you can't stand there with one foot in and one outside. I need to either close that door and lock it forever, or you need to enter all the way in."

"How do I do that?" His voice sounded plaintive in the darkness. He pressed the stone between his fingers. *How can you not know?* she wanted to rail at him. *Can't you see it as plainly as I do?*

"*Talk* to me," she said. "Share what you're thinking. Let me accept the dangers you're willing to accept. Let me be *with* you."

She thought that he wasn't going to answer—which would have been answer enough. He sat there, still toy-ing with the stone and staring outward. She started to rise again, and this time he took her hand. She could feel the stone as he pressed it into her palm.

"Wait," he said. "Let me tell you what I'm thinking . . ."

And he began to talk.

~

Kenne ca'Fionta

AUBRI CU'ULCAI LOOKED like a whipped dog as he knelt on one knee, head lowered, before the Kraljica. His armor was scratched and battered, his face was streaked with grime and smoke, his hair was dark and matted, and he stank. In the Hall of the Sun Throne, he was like a horsefly paddling in a golden mug of clear, cold water.

Not that the hall itself didn't still show scars. No one could miss the marks of the hasty repair where the Sun Throne had been damaged by the assassin's magic—no, not magic if Karl ca'Vliomani was correct, Kenne remembered, but something more sinister—something any apothecary could make with the right ingredients. What had the Ambassador ca'Vliomani called it? The end of magic? Kenne wondered if the man was right.

The hanging tapestries around the hall still reeked of smoke, and Kenne wondered if there wasn't a faint, horrifying pink tinge to the tiles around the throne dais. And there was no way to miss the appearance of Kraljica Sigourney herself: the patch over her missing eye, the scars on her face, the bandages that still wrapped her arms and single leg, the way she shifted painfully on the seat, the goblet filled with an extract of the seeds of the poisonous *cuore della volpe* flower—a concoction the court herbalist had created to keep Sigourney's pain at bay.

Still, the Sun Throne gleamed underneath and around her as it had for countless Kralji; Kenne had seen to that personally. If that was a sham, no one watching would know it. Kenne sighed on his own seat to the right of the throne, weary from the effort of casting the light spell. The Council of Ca' was arrayed to the left. Otherwise, the hall had been cleared of courtiers and even servants—none of them wanted more rumors spreading through the city than there already were.

"Commandant cu'Ulcai," Sigourney said, her voice as cracked as her face, "the news you bring . . ." She stopped, her single eye closing. When it opened again, her voice was sharper. "You have failed us."

"I am sorry, Kraljica," the commandant said. "You should have my resignation letter in hand already."

"I do," she said. "But I won't be accepting it." When cu'Ulcai lifted his face with a faint hope, she scowled down at him. "That is not for any reason other than the fact that we have too few offiziers with your experience," she told him. "You have failed with the Westlanders, and the stain on your record won't easily be erased. I intend to have Aleron ca'Gerodi direct the defense of Nessantico should these barbarians be foolish enough to continue their advance. Had my brother been here . . ." With that, her lips trembled and a glimmer of moisture appeared in her eye. She took a sip of the *cuore della volpe*. "As for you—let us see how well you fare against an enemy you should know better. I am sending you east, Commandant cu'Ulcai, to direct our forces against the army of Firenzcia. Odil ca'Mazzak of the Council will be accompanying you, and you will both leave tomorrow." She waved an arm to him in dismissal. "I assume you have preparations to make, Commandant."

Cu'Ulcai rose, bowed deeply to the Kraljica, and walked from the hall, loud in the silence that followed him. When he had left, Kraljica Sigourney sighed.

"I don't trust the man," Odil ca'Mazzak muttered. "He's another offizier with ties to the traitor Regent."

"Unfortunately, he's the best we have," Kraljica Sigourney answered. "Odil, we need to go over the negotiation points you'll be discussing with the Firenzcians. Archigos, I need you to beat the drums against the Numetodo—for two reasons: to placate Firenzcia, and so that we know we don't have traitors here in the city when we're facing enemies on either side. I expect to hear aggressive Admonitions from you and all your téni starting with the Third Call services."

Kenne knew she anticipated no objection from him; she'd already turned away from him before she finished speaking. She thought he would nod and agree and say nothing. Once, she would have been right.

Once. But there was Karl's visit, and there was the specter of the false Archigos Semini ca'Cellibrecca looming on the horizon and all that would mean. And there was the memory of Ana and the freedom and leniency she'd fought for over the years.

"No," he said. "I won't do that."

The silence that followed was lengthy. Kraljica Sigourney's single eye blinked. "No," she repeated, the word like the tolling of a funeral bell. "Did I hear you correctly, Archigos?"

He nodded. "You're . . ." His throat was dry. He swallowed, trying to dredge up some moisture. "You're wrong about the Numetodo, Kraljica," he told her. "You're wrong in believing that it was their magic that killed Kraljiki Audric and injured you. It wasn't them."

Another solo blink. The other councillors watched the two of them, silent. "It wasn't? And how is it that you know this?"

"Because I've actually spoken with Ambassador ca'Vliomani. I've heard his explanations, and I've investigated on my own what he's discovered."

"Karl Vliomani—" the prominent lack of a prefix to his surname lay heavy in the air, "—is a fugitive whose life is currently forfeit. You tell me that he came to you, and *you let him leave?*"

Kenne shivered at the tone of her voice. "He came to me, yes, and he showed me this," he told her. He brought out a small glass vial from under his green robes. In it, the black sand glistened. "Watch." He rose from his seat, shuffling across the dais and down to the floor of the hall. He walked several strides away from the throne, then unstoppered the vial and let the black sand drizzle to the tiles. He came back to the dais; his knees cracking like dry twigs as he ascended the steps. "Everyone agrees that Enéas cu'Kinnear used a spell to create flame—but that was a *téni's* spell and not a Numetodo's. Cu'Kinnear was once an acolyte of the Faith and had some instruction in the use of Ilmodo. He very likely knew that spell; it's one of the first taught to the new students. Look . . ."

Kenne lifted his hands, letting them dance in the quick pattern as his voice chanted the brief phrases that were required. A moment later, a yellow flame shivered in the air between his hands. "You've all seen this a thousand times—every night when the lamps are lit along the Avi a'Parete. This is no different . . ."

He opened his hands, beginning a new chant, and the flame drifted away from his hand, floating out from the dais until it hovered above the black sand. There, he lowered his hands slowly, and the flame responded in kind, dropping down until it nearly touched the dark pile—

The *ka-WHUMP* of the explosion was louder than even Kenne expected, and the flash hurt his eyes. White smoke billowed upward, spreading out in the hall, and an acrid, sharp smell followed. He heard a *clang* as the goblet of *cuore della volpe* fell from the arm of the Sun Throne to the floor. Kraljica Sigourney was breathing heavily on the throne, hand up in front of her face as if trying to shield herself—she looked to be trying to stand on her single leg, grasping for the cane at her right hand. Several of the councillors were on their feet, shouting, and the doors to the hall were flung open by gardai, entering with their swords drawn. "Kraljica?"

Her hands came down. Kenne heard her breath slow. She waved the gardai away. "That smell . . ." she muttered. "I remember that most of all." She turned slowly to the Archigos. "This is *not* magic?" she said. "How can that not be the Ilmodo, Archigos?"

"Because it is only alchemy," Kenne told her, "a combination of ingredients that reacts violently when it comes into contact with fire. There were traces of this black sand in the wood of the High Lectern after Archigos Ana was killed; the same traces were in the Sun Throne and on the body of Kraljiki Audric."

"The Numetodo claim that faith in Cénzi isn't required to use magic, that *anyone* can do it, that it's no more complicated than being a baker. They look at rocks shaped like shells and skulls and concoct strange theories, they conduct experiments—in alchemy as in other 'sciences' as well as magic. That seems to me to *indict* the Numetodo." That was Odil ca'Mazzack. He glared at the Archigos, and the Kraljica nodded at his words.

"I'm telling you that this is not from the Numetodo," Kenne persisted.

"Even when Vliomani just happens to be the one who

has shown you this," Odil retorted scornfully. "Seems a strange leap of logic."

"The black sand is a *Westlander* concoction," Kenne told them. "Here's the logic, Councillor. Enéas cu'Kinnear had just returned from the service in the Hellins. You'll also re-member that Commandant cu'Ulcai has just told us how the Westlanders were able to tear down the walls of Vil-lembouchure with explosions similar to those that killed Archigos Ana and Kraljiki Audric."

"And he said the explosions were the *magic* of the West-lander war-téni, these 'nahualli.'" Odil shook his graying head. The extra skin around his throat wobbled with the mo-tion. "I think the Archigos is mis—"

"*No!*" This time Kenne nearly shouted the word, stamp-ing a foot on the ground at the same time. "I am *not* mis-taken. I know you all think of me as a doddering old fool who's a poor pale shadow of what an Archigos should be. There you might be right, but you are *wrong* in this. Worse than wrong—I have *evidence* that makes me believe that the false Archigos Semini was involved in the assassination of Archigos Ana. And if that is the case . . ." He stopped, out of breath. They were staring at him, all of them, as if they might at a child who was throwing a tantrum. "We *need* the Numetodo, Kraljica, Councillors," he continued, lowering his voice. "We need their skills, their magic, and we need their knowledge. Nessantico is about to be under siege from both west and east, and we can't afford to lose those who can help us."

There was a long, painful silence. Odil licked his lips and sat. The other Council members lowered their heads, glancing at each other. Kraljica Sigourney stared outward to the dark stain on the tiles. "We will consider what you have said, Archigos," she said finally, and he knew what that meant.

He grunted, lifting himself from his seat again. He took the staff of the Archigos in his right hand—the cracked globe wrapped in the naked, writhing bodies of the Moitidi—and gave the Kraljica the sign of Cénzi with the left. Again, he shuffled his way from the dais. As he passed the spot where the black sand had exploded, he stopped. The tiles there had broken. He picked up one of the larger pieces: the soft blue glaze razor sharp along one edge, the smooth surface

stained with what looked to be soot. The smell of the black
sand was strong. Kenne hefted the chunk of tile and let it
fall, and the sound was that of a dish breaking. He watched
bits of the tile bounce and scatter.

"All of Nessantico could look like this," he told them.
"All of it."

There was no answer. He tapped the end of the Archigos' staff on the tile and shuffled on.

~

Sergei ca'Rudka

THE PARLEY TENT WAS ARRAYED in the field
between the two forces: just off the Avi a'Firenzcia
and about halfway between Passe a'Fiume and Nessantico.
As they approached, Sergei could already see the shadowed forms of Odil ca'Mazzack and Aubri cu'Ulcai under
the white fabric, along with U'Téni Petros cu'Magnaoi,
there as the Archigos' representative. The Firenzcian delegation was Sergei, A'Hirzg Allesandra, and Starkkapitän
ca'Damont, accompanied by the required array of chevarittai and attendants. Since neither the Kraljica nor Archigos
Kenne were present, the Hïrzg and Archigos Semini, at
Sergei's suggestion, remained behind. Neither one of them
had been pleased with the arrangement.

"Matarh, I should be there," Jan had insisted. "I am the
Hïrzg and whatever happens there should be, must be my
decision." He had glared at Sergei, at his matarh.

"So it will be, Hïrzg," Sergei told the young man. "I promise you that. But for you to be there . . ." He shook his head.
"You are the Hïrzg, as you said. There is no peer in that tent
for you; there is no peer in the tent for the Archigos either.
You, Hïrzg Jan, can't be expected to parley on equal terms
with Odil ca'Mazzak, who is just a member of the Council
of Ca'—you would be lowering yourself to do so. I can tell
you that it's exactly what they want you to do. It would be an
admission that the Hïrzg of the Coalition is someone who is
lesser than the Kraljica of the Holdings."

He had looked to Allesandra and the glowering Archigos
then. "You asked me to give you my knowledge, to help you.
That is what I'm doing here. Appearances matter. They matter a great deal. They especially matter to those in the Kraljica's Palais."

In the end, with Allesandra's support, he had won the
argument. Jan, at least, had been somewhat gracious about
it. The Archigos had stalked off angrily, and they had heard

him complaining throughout the encampment for the next few turns of the glass.

As the Firenzcian contingent dismounted and servants took their weapons and horses and offered refreshments, the Nessanticans came forward. Sergei clasped cu'Ulcai's arm warmly, smiling at his longtime offizier. "Aubri," he said, "I wish we could have met again under better circumstances. I heard what happened with poor Aris . . ." He clasped the man on the shoulder and gave the sign of Cénzi to U'Téni cu'Magnaoi. "Petros, it's good to see you also. How is Archigos Kenne?"

"He is well, sir, and sends his blessing to you," the older man answered.

Sergei leaned close to the man as he hugged him. "Has Kenne received my messages?" he whispered into the older man's ear. "Does he agree?" Sergei felt Petros' faint nod. He also saw the appraising glances of both the delegations on him as he greeted the two men: Allesandra as well as Odil ca'Mazzak. They were both suspicious; they both had a right to be. Sergei nodded to ca'Mazzak and took his seat to the left of Allesandra.

Ca'Mazzak gestured, and pages came forward to give Allesandra, Sergei, and the starkkapitän scrolls of heavy parchment. "This is the offer of Kraljica Sigourney," ca'Mazzak said as they scanned the words there. "Your army will be permitted to return to Firenzcia. The outlaw Sergei Rudka will be handed over to us. Reparations will be paid by Brezno to the Holdings for the destruction of crops and livestock by their army, and for the violation of the Treaty of Passe a'Fiume. If you find the terms acceptable, all that is required is the signature of the A'Hïrzg as the representative of the Coalition."

It was no more than Sergei had expected. He'd witnessed Holdings arrogance and hubris too many times before.

Starkkapitän ca'Damont gave a snicker through his nose, tossing the parchment on the table. "And how does the Kraljica intend to *enforce* this, Councillor?" he asked. "With the few battalions you've given Commandant cu'Ulcai? I've nothing but respect for the commandant, who is a fine offizier, but one doesn't fight off an angry bear by threatening him with a twig." He seemed to realize then that he'd spoken out of turn. His face reddened slightly.

"My pardons, A'Hïrzg. I'm a simple offizier, but these *demands* . . ." He swept the parchment from the table to the floor; a page scurried over to pick up the scroll but didn't return it to him.

"The Garde Civile and the chevarittai of the Holdings are not a *twig,* Starkkapitän," ca'Mazzak blustered. He had puffed up like a toad, sitting erect in his chair, the wattles on his thick neck shivering. "You underestimate our ability to quickly field an army when our lands are threatened. It's a lesson the last Hïrzg Jan learned; I'm surprised that anyone from Firenzcia feels the lesson needs to be taught a second time."

Allesandra appeared to be still reading the proposal, though Sergei could see her listening carefully to the exchange. She set the paper down in front of her and folded her hands over it. "All right," she said. "Let's forgo the posturing, Councillor ca'Mazzak. We all know that Nessantico is dealing with a threat to the west. We know what happened to Karnor; we're hearing rumors that Villembouchure may have suffered the same fate—perhaps Commandant cu'Ulcai could enlighten us on that, since I expect he was there when the Holdings forces were routed? Everyone at this table knows that you haven't sufficient forces to challenge us here. So what is it that the Kraljica *really* offers?"

Sergei had suggested this direct tack to Allesandra, but the stab at Aubri cu'Ulcai had been the A'Hïrzg's own contribution. The look on Aubri's' face was enough to confirm that her guess had been correct, and Sergei felt an upwelling of sympathy for his friend.

Ca'Mazzak looked as if he'd swallowed unripened fruit. He glanced at Petros, who seemed to be examining the fields past the edge of the tent, then at Aubri. "The Kraljica is prepared to offer a compromise," he said finally. "Let the Hïrzg and A'Hïrzg return to Brezno with their Garde Brezno. However, Starkkapitän ca'Damont and the remainder of the army will remain behind to aid in the defense of Nessantico against the Westlanders, for which the treasury of Nessantico is willing to bear the expenses. As for the former Regent . . ." Ca'Mazzak glared at Sergei. "Kraljica Sigourney still demands his return to face the charges against him, no matter what agreement we reach here."

Allesandra stood at that; a moment later, Sergei, ca'Damont, and the rest of the Firenzcian contingent followed. "Then we're done here," Allesandra said. "Regent ca'Rudka is an adviser to the crown of Firenzcia, and we consider him to be the current rightful ruler of Nessantico until a legitimate Kralji is named. If Regent ca'Rudka wishes to return to Nessantico on his own to pursue his claims, he may do so. Otherwise, he is under the protection of the Hïrzg, no matter what the person you have named Kraljica wishes." She bowed to ca'Mazzak and gestured. Sergei smiled broadly at the man. They turned to go.

"Wait!" It was Petros who called to them. Allesandra stopped.

"U'Téni?" she asked, but ca'Mazzak was already spluttering.

"*I* am in charge of this delegation," he said to Petros. "You will speak when I give you permission, U'Téni cu'Magnaoi."

"Cénzi is in charge of my conscience," Petros told the councillor. "Not you, nor Kraljica Sigourney. And I *will* speak. A'Hïrzg, Nessantico is in desperate circumstances. Commandant cu'Ulcai would tell you—if he were permitted to speak—how easily the Westlanders took the cities, towns, and villages they have ravaged. Nessantico desperately requires all the allies it can muster now. Archigos Kenne is prepared to negotiate separately from the Kraljica, if he must, to achieve this."

"*What!*" ca'Mazzak sputtered. He was on his feet now as well, pounding on the table. "No, no, no. We are done here. U'Téni cu'Magnaoi, you will be transported back to the city to answer for this. Commandant cu'Ulcai, order your gardai to—"

Sergei slapped the table immediately in front of ca'Mazzak, and the man's mouth shut with an audible snap. "You're nothing but the Kraljica's yelping lapdog, Councillor," Sergei told the man, leaning close to him. "Sit down."

Ca'Mazzak glared back and turned to Aubri. "Commandant, you have your orders. You will take the u'téni into custody immediately."

Aubri didn't move, didn't respond. Sergei could feel the tension rising in the tent. He saw hands sliding carefully toward hidden weapons—he had his own blades, too, one in his boot, another under the blouse of his bashta, and his ears sang with the hum of his own fear. He hadn't been able to contact Aubri beforehand, and if Aubri decided that his loyalty to the Sun Throne was more than his old loyalty for Sergei, then ... Well, then Sergei didn't know what might happen here.

"Commandant cu'Ulcai, this is treason," ca'Mazack growled. "I will have your head for this if you don't do as ordered."

Aubri said nothing; his contemplative gaze still on Sergei. The chevarittai, of both sides, tensed, ready to move. Sergei placed himself between Allesandra and the table. "I suggest you sit down, Councillor," Sergei told ca'Mazzak. "Let U'Téni cu'Magnaoi finish outlining his offer."

For several breaths, ca'Mazzak didn't stir. His gaze moved slowly around the tent, and Sergei knew he was assessing who in the tent would follow him and who would not. Evidently, he wasn't pleased with the result. Slowly, ca'Mazzak lowered himself to his chair again. He stared at his hands.

"Good," Sergei said. For a moment, the ringing in his ears diminished. "Petros, what has Archigos Kenne to offer Firenzcia?"

"Information," Petros answered. "We have proof that Archigos Semini was involved in the assassination of Archigos Ana. We can give you names to verify that." Behind him, Sergei heard Allesandra suck in her breath at the accusation. He wondered at that—she sounded more alarmed than surprised. "Because Kraljiki Audric was killed in the same manner," Petros continued, "we have to suspect that the false Archigos was also involved in that. If Hïrzg Jan is prepared to try Archigos Semini for Archigos Ana's death before his own court, we will supply him the evidence we have. In return, the Faith of Nessantico will work with the Faith of Brezno to repair our rift; Archigos Kenne will call for a Concordance of all a'téni to elect a single Archigos to rule the Faith, and he will also step down voluntarily if he is not elected—though any Archigos must take the Archigos' Temple in Nessantico, not Brezno. Likewise, the Faith is prepared to acknowledge Allesandra ca'Vörl's claim to the Sun Throne. Archigos Kenne will support her before the Council of Ca' against Kraljica Sigourney."

"No!" Ca'Mazzak hurtled to his feet again, spittle flying from his mouth with the explosion of the word. "Archigos Kenne will be thrown into the Bastida for this, and the téni who support him purged—"

"And if that happens," Petros answered calmly, "then Archigos Kenne will order the war-téni to remain in their temples rather than answer the Kraljica's call. How will the Garde Civile and the chevarittai fare against the Westlanders without the war-téni, Councillor? How will they stand against the army of the Hïrzg?"

Again, ca'Mazzak sank back into his seat. He shivered as if with a fever, stroking his doubled chin. Sweat beaded at his hairline, and under his arms, the fabric of his bashta had turned dark.

Allesandra touched Sergei's shoulder, and he stood aside. She was smiling grimly. The A'Hïrzg gave the sign of Cénzi to Petros. "You offer all this for the trial of Archigos Semini?"

Petros nodded to her. "We trust the Hïrzg's court to be fair and impartial. And there is one more thing: all prosecution of the Numetodo must stop. Immediately. The Numetodo are innocent of any of this. Ambassador Karl ca'Vliomani must be restored to his previous position."

Sergei could feel the negotiations hanging on the balance point of Allesandra's answer to that last point. She was fingering the cracked globe of Cénzi hung around her neck. His own life hung there also, as well as that of Petros and Aubri. If he had guessed wrongly . . .

"I will talk to my son," Allesandra answered. "I will relay to him everything that has been said here." Sergei thought for a moment that this was the entirety of her answer, that he had lost. But Allesandra took a long, shivering breath. "I will suggest that the Hïrzg accept the Archigos' offer," she said. "Councillor ca'Mazzak, Commandant, U'Téni—we'll return to the parley tent in three turns of the glass to give you our answer."

"If Archigos Kenne has evidence, I will weigh it," Allesandra had said to Sergei on the way back. "And if Archigos Semini is responsible for Ana ca'Seranta's death, then . . ." She had pressed her lips together grimly. "Then I am inclined to convince my son to accept the Archigos' offer."

Somehow, she seemed to have done exactly that, though Sergei had not been present for that discussion, though everyone in the camp had heard the occasional raised voices in the Hïrzg's tent, and Sergei had especially noted that Starkkapitän ca'Damont had gardai stationed around the Archigos' tent.

He wondered what was happening in the other encampment. Everything there hung on the loyalties of the Garde Civile and the téni—and Sergei wasn't certain how that would play out. He prayed to Cénzi, hoping that He was listening.

Three turns of the glass later, Sergei, Allesandra, and the others rode out again toward the parley tent.

When he'd been Commandant of the Garde Kralji, decades ago, Sergei had occasionally felt a shiver when he'd approached the Bastida a'Drago: a quivering of the spine almost like fear that told him when something was amiss in the complex beyond the dragon's grinning skull.

He felt that shiver now as their small party approached the parley tent. It was, first of all, curious that there were no servants moving about, that the chairs on the Nessantican side of the table were empty. But what held him, what made his stomach churn and boil, was the realization that there was *something* on the table itself—two somethings, two rounded objects masked in the shadow underneath the linen flapping in the breeze. He was afraid he knew what sat there.

"Hold a moment, A'Hïrzg," he told Allesandra. "Please. Wait here."

Sergei nudged his horse forward alone, gesturing to Starkkapitän ca'Damont to accompany him. He squinted, trying to force his aging eyes to make out what it was sitting there. As he approached, he could hear a faint buzzing sound that grew slowly louder: the whine of insects.

He knew then, and the bile rose in his throat. He pulled his horse up, let himself down from the saddle, and walked into the shade of the tent.

On the table were two heads, sticky, clotted blood pooled underneath them, a carpet of flies crawling over the open eyes and in the gaping mouths.

Sergei went to his knees, making the sign of Cénzi toward the gruesome sight. "Aubri," he said. "Petros. I'm sorry. I'm so very sorry."

Shakily, he rode to his feet again, going back to the horse. He rode silently back to the others. Allesandra's eyes questioned him; she knew also. He could see it in the way her hand lifted to her mouth before he ever spoke.

"Councillor ca'Mazzak has left us his own answer," he said. "It seems he doesn't care what ours might have been."

~

Nico Morel

NICO COULDN'T BEAR to sit still. He had never imagined a place as glorious, huge, and interesting as this. They'd been ushered into an office in one of the buildings that girdled the Plaza a'Archigos; the reception room by itself was larger than the two rooms they had in Oldtown and there were at least three doors leading off into other rooms that he could only imagine. He'd caught a glimpse of a bedroom when one of the servants had moved through carrying linens, and it had seemed huge beyond all reason. The office into which they'd been ushered would have taken up Nico's house as well as those of the closest neighbors. The ceiling seemed as high as summer clouds and as white; the floor was an intricate mosaic of various colored woods, and the walls were draped with gorgeous tapestries displaying the tale of Cénzi's life, the molding along the top of the walls was carved and gilded. Behind the massive mahogany desk, a balcony looked out over the wide plaza, with the Archigos' Temple framed beyond its open draperies. The other furniture in the room was just as dominating—a long, polished conference table, with plush chairs set around it; a couch placed before a hearth in which Nico's whole family could have stood upright, surrounded by the gorgeous mantelpiece; a carved cracked-globe taller than two men standing atop one another, with the carved figures of the Moitidi wrapped around it, the base studded with jewels and glittering with gold foil. All around the walls, there were tables laden with delightful foreign wonders: statues of unfamiliar animals; a large stone broken in half, inside which beautiful violet crystals were crowded; spiny, rose-pearled shells from the Strettosei . . .

Nico blinked, staring at everything. "All this is just for *you?*" Nico asked the Archigos, marveling.

"Nico, hush," his matarh said, but the old man in the green robes only laughed.

"It's for the Archigos, whomever that person is," the man said. "I only live here temporarily, until Cénzi calls me back to Him. This used to be where Archigos Ana lived, too." He patted Nico on the head as servants brought in trays of food and drink and set them on the table. The Archigos waved to the servants as they finished. "That will be all," he told them. "Please make sure we're not disturbed. Have my carriage come to the rear door a turn of the glass before Third Call." They bowed and left. "Help yourselves," the Archigos told them as the last of the servants departed the room, closing the double doors behind them. "Karl? You all look as if you could use a good meal." Nico was staring at the food, and the Archigos chuckled again. "Go on, Nico. You needn't wait."

Nico glanced at his matarh and at Talis, who shrugged. "It's all right," his matarh told him. "Go ahead . . ."

He did. A spice-seed muffin drizzled with honey was the first thing in his mouth. Strangely, the adults didn't seem as hungry as he was. Neither Talis, Karl, nor Varina went toward the table at all, and his mother picked desultorily at a breast of duck. Instead, they huddled near the couch in front of the hearth.

"Archigos," Nico heard Karl say, "Ana would be terribly proud of you. We all owe you our thanks."

"The thanks go to you, Karl. If you hadn't come to me, if you hadn't told me what you knew . . . Well, I'm not certain what would have happened. In any case, I may have put you in more danger, not less. The Kraljica is in a rage, from what I hear, and as soon as Councillor ca'Mazzak returns from the parley with the Firenzcians, I suspect she'll be even less happy with me. None of us can be sure what will happen with that—which is why we need to talk tonight. There isn't much time; a messenger may already be on the way back to the city." Nico heard the Archigos' voice drop and fail. He turned, a slice of bread and cheese in his hand. "This is the Westlander?" the Archigos asked, nodding in Talis' direction. Talis had both his hands around the walking stick he always carried, and Nico could see air flickering around the wood as if the staff were on fire, but that was a fire colder than last winter's snow.

"Yes, Archigos," Karl answered. "This is Talis Posti. Nico's vatarh."

"Ah," the Archigos said. "Vajiki Posti, I also owe you thanks—though you'll have to forgive me if I wonder why you have decided to help me."

"Because I have glimpsed the futures, and none of them lead to a good place for my people," Talis answered, and Nico found his interest perking up with that. Talis could see the future? That would be interesting. Why, if he could do that, Nico could see himself as an adult, maybe see what would happen to him. . . . He found his hands moving as if in some strange dance of their own, his sticky fingers moving through the air, and words came to him that he didn't know, and he whispered them so quietly that none of the others could hear him. The chill from Talis' walking stick seemed to flow toward his hands; he could feel the chill in his arms.

"You have *that* gift from your gods?" Kenne asked Talis. His eyebrows lifted, and he glanced at Karl.

"Mahri claimed to do the same," Karl said. That also made Nico pay attention; he remembered hearing Talis mention that name before. "Not that it did him much good in the end."

"It's not *the* future that Axat grants us glimpses of, but all the possibilities that exist. The glimpses of potential futures aren't easy to read, though it was said that Mahri could use the talent better than anyone before or since. And yes, it seems to have failed him in the end." A brief, quick smile passed over his face. "Perhaps it was the proximity to your Cénzi."

Kenne chuckled; Nico liked the sound—it made him like this man. The cold was wrapping around his arms now, though his hands had stopped dancing.

"You're willing to help us—" Archigos Kenne spread his arms to include Karl and Varina, and the rest of the city outside the balcony, "—when that means you may be helping defeat the forces of your own people?"

"Yes," Talis said, "because Axat tells me that in doing so, I *will* be helping my people."

The cold was freezing Nico's arms and it was becoming heavy. He didn't know what to do with it, but he was shivering with the effort of holding it, and the pain almost made him want to cry out. "Sometimes your enemy becomes your ally," Varina was saying to the Archigos. "I know—"

"Nico!" His matarh's voice was a near shout. "What are you doing?" Nico jumped as his matarh clutched his shoulder, and the cold went flying away from him. As it fled, the energy sparkled and flared, like a stream of blue fire. It went shooting straight out from him, slashing between Talis and the Archigos and arrowing directly toward the cracked globe sculpture in that corner of the room. Nico sobbed—frightened both by the feeling of release and sheer terror at what he'd just released. Varina, standing a few strides away from the Archigos, gestured once and spoke a single, harsh word; at the motion, Nico saw the line of blue fire curve and turn, arcing away from the sculpture, spitting sapphire sparks over the polished desk and then hissing away out through the open doors of the balcony and out. High above the plaza, the fire gathered, then burst: an ice-blue globe that flashed like frozen lightning. With the explosion came a roll of ear-splitting thunder, echoing from the walls of the buildings flanking the plaza. Nico could feel the windows shake and rattle in their frames, and he heard glass breaking distantly.

"Nico!" His matarh had wrapped her arms around him. "Nico . . ." she said again, more softly this time. Her arms tightened around him, and he wasn't sure if it was intended to be an embrace or a stranglehold. They were all staring at him.

"I'm sorry," Nico told them. "I didn't mean to . . ."

He started to cry.

~

Karl Vliomani

"I'M SORRY," Nico said. His lower lip was trembling and he barely got the next words out before his shoulders started to shake from sobbing. "I didn't mean to . . ."

Serafina was staring at them over the boy's shoulder as she held him, her eyes wide and terrified. Outside in the plaza, they could hear faint shouts as passersby searched for the source of the thundering brilliance. Karl could hear Varina sigh with relief behind him. "If he'd been a hand's breadth to one side or the other . . ." Karl said.

"He wasn't," Varina answered. She crouched down in front of him, nodding to Serafina. "It's all right, Nico," she told him. "No one was hurt. It's all right." She looked back over her shoulder to Karl. "It's all right," she repeated. The boy sniffled, rubbing his sleeve over his nose and eyes.

Karl let go a breath. He smiled: at Varina, at Nico, at Serafina. "Yes," he said. "It's all right, thanks to Varina. Talis, did you know . . . ?"

"I suspected, but . . ." He was holding his spell-staff, looking at it bemusedly as if it were a glass suddenly emptied. "I know *now*. Archigos, are you . . . ?"

Kenne waved a hand as if in dismissal, but Karl could see the man's chest still heaving. "I'm fine," Kenne said. "And impressed. Your son's one of the few natural talents I've known. Archigos Dhosti had been one, and Ana, too. With training, well . . ."

"*I* will train him." Talis' answer was wrapped in a scowl. He clutched the spell-staff tightly. "This is Axat's gift, not Cénzi's."

"Of course," Kenne told him, but his gaze stayed on Nico. "Don't worry," he told the boy. "No one here is angry with you. Do you understand that?" Nico nodded, still sniffling.

"If I'd known about this, I'd have been far more careful when I first approached you," Karl told Talis. "But since no harm's been done . . . We still have plans and contingencies to make. Archigos, is Petros prepared to make the offer we've talked about to Firenzcia?"

Kenne nodded, more hesitantly than Karl liked, but at least it *was* a nod. In truth, he'd been afraid that Kenne might not have followed through, especially given the undeniable danger into which it placed Petros. "He is." The Archigos' voice quavered a little—fear combined with age, Karl decided. "In fact, he should have done so by now."

"Good," Karl told him. He patted Kenne on the shoulder. "He'll be fine," he told the Archigos. "And he'll be back with you soon. Now, for his part, Talis will bring the supplies from Uly's rooms here to the temple tomorrow, and we can begin to prepare the black sand for the demonstration. That should show this Tecuhtli of the Westlanders that attacking the city would be foolish. We can prevent hundreds, if not thousands, of deaths."

The Archigos' carriage was a ruse—four of Kenne's servants clambered into that vehicle when it pulled up to the rear entrance of the building, while Karl and the others hurried down a back stair toward a little-used side servants' door. None of them knew whether the subterfuge was necessary; Karl hoped not; if it was, then none of the contingencies for which they'd prepared might come to fruition.

They started to hurry away from the plaza, moving toward the Avi. Kenne had given them enough money to hire one of the carriages there to take them back to Oldtown. As they moved toward the street, they saw three separate squadrons of Garde Kralji hurrying across the Archigos' Plaza. "Wait a moment," Karl said. Talis, Serafina, and Nico were already on the Avi, looking for a carriage for hire; Varina, a little ahead of him, paused. As Karl hesitated on the edge of the plaza, he and Varina watched two of squadrons rush into the building from which they'd just come; the other entering the Archigos' Temple.

Their weapons were drawn, steel shining in the lights of the lamps.

"Karl? What's happening?"

"I don't know, Varina. I think I should go back. Take the others. I'll—"

"No," Varina told him firmly. She came back to him, lacing her arm into his. "No, Karl. Not this time. Even disguised, your face is too recognizable to the Garde Kralji, and there are too many of them anyway. You don't know why they're there; it may be nothing. It's *probably* nothing. And if it's not . . ." She bit at her lower lip. Her eyes pleaded with him. "You need to let the Archigos take care of this himself. Come with me. Please."

"But if things have gone wrong—"

"If things have gone wrong, you can't change it now. *We* can't change it. All that would happen is that you'd be lost, too." Her arm tightened on his. "Please, Karl. Let's go. If there *is* a problem, we can help Kenne more by staying alive than by being thrown in the Bastida with him. We got Sergei out; we could do the same again if we had to. Karl . . ." She leaned her head against his shoulder. "If you're going back," she told him, "then I'm going with you. But that's the wrong decision. I know it."

He stared at the buildings, wishing he could see Kenne's balcony from here. Everything was quiet; people still walked in the plaza as if nothing were happening. But he knew. He knew.

And he also knew that Varina was right. He could change nothing. He looked over his shoulder. Talis had waved down a carriage; he was looking back at them curiously. A woman—dressed strangely poorly for this part of the city—scuttled past them from the direction of the plaza. As she passed, she seemed to stumble and brush against Karl. "Sorry, Vajiki," the woman muttered. Her voice . . . it seemed vaguely familiar, but the woman kept the cowl of her tashta up and her head down. He caught a glimpse of dirty brown hair. "It's going to be a bad night. A bad night. You really should hurry home. . . ."

She scurried quickly past them.

Karl stared after the woman, who vanished around the other side of the waiting carriage. Talis was waving at them. It was then that Karl remembered where he'd heard that voice.

Karl didn't believe in either coincidence or omens.

"All right," he told Varina. "We're leaving."

~

The Battle Begun: Kenne ca'Fionta

"**I**'M AFRAID THAT your poor Petros is dead. It's a shame."

Kenne heard the words, and his old eyes blurred with tears, though he'd already known that Petros was gone. He'd felt it in his heart, ever since the Garde Kralji had come and snatched him away to the Bastida. He could only hope that Karl and his people had escaped the sweep; they'd left only a few marks of the glass beforehand. The leather-clad metal tongue gag tasted vile; the irons binding his hands were heavy enough that he could barely lift them from his lap.

Kraljica Sigourney's scarred, torn face stared down at him. Kenne held her single-eyed regard for only a few breaths sucked in past the horrible device over his head, then dropped his gaze, broken and defeated. Between his legs, his manacled hands plucked restlessly at the straw of the rude bed as he sat in his cell high in the Bastida's main tower. Her voice was sympathetic, almost sorrowful. "You're a good man, Kenne. You always were. But you were too weak to be Archigos. You should have refused the title and told the Concord A'Téni to elect someone else."

He could only nod in agreement. There had been so many nights lately when he'd wished exactly the same thing.

"You should have known this would happen, Kenne," she told him. "You chose to consort with the enemies of the Holdings. You should have known. And now . . ."

She hobbled to the cell's single window, leaning on a gilded, padded crutch, her right leg dangling to the emptiness beyond the knee. The window looked west, Kenne knew—he'd seen the sun's fading light on the wall opposite that window the past few nights, turning yellow, then red, then purple as it crawled up the damp stones. "Come here," Sigourney told him. "Come here and look."

He lifted himself off the bed with difficulty: a broken old

man now in truth. He shuffled over to the window as she stood aside. Outside, under a cheerful blue sky, he could see the A'Sele gleaming in the sun as it wound its way past the city toward the sea. Near where the river turned south, he could see dozens of gathered sails. Across the river, what had once been farmland and the estates of the ca'-and-cu', the land crawled with a dark infestation that had not been there yesterday. "You see them?" Sigourney asked. "You see the Westlander army approaching? Those are the ones for whom you betrayed the Holdings, Archigos. Those are the ones who frightened you so much that you tried to make a pact with the Firenzcian dogs against me." Her voice was growing angry now, the single eye raking him. "Those are the foul creatures who killed my brother. Those are the villains who razed our towns and villages. Whether you believe it or not, I'm certain they're also the ones who killed Audric and made me into a horror. Do I hate them? Oh, you can't imagine how much. Watch, and you'll see good Holdings chevarittai send them running, and then we'll deal with your Firenzcian friends as well. Very soon, it will begin. And you're going to help us, Kenne."

He turned his silenced head toward her, quizzical. She laughed. "Oh, you are. We must have the war-téni, after all, and we want to make certain that they understand that their Archigos now regrets his horrible treason, and that he wishes all téni of the Faith to help Nessantico in this terrible time in whatever way they can. You do wish that, don't you, Archigos?"

Kenne could only stare at her, mute.

"You think not?" she told him. "Well, the proclamation is already written; it only requires your signature. And whether you wish to do so or not, I *will* have that signature. You were a friend of Sergei Rudka, after all—you should know that the Bastida *always* gains the confessions it wants."

Even with the horrible device strapped to his face, he could not keep the horror from his face, and he saw her smile at his reaction. "Good," she said. "I shall reflect on your suffering when the capitaine hands me your confession."

She gestured to the gardai outside the cell. "He's ready," she told them. "Make sure he receives your full hospitality."

The Battle Begun: Niente

THE CITY LIFTED STONE FLANKS on the low hills; its towers and spires and domes crowding the large island in the river's center so that it looked like a barnacled rock. The metropolis had leaped far outside the confining girdle of its walls, magnificent and proud and unafraid, and the fields surrounding it were laden with grain and crops to feed its teeming inhabitants. This city . . . It was the rival of Tlaxcala, somewhat smaller but more crowded and compressed, the architecture strange. The cities of his home were dominated by the pyramids of the temples of Axat, Sakal, and the Four; here in Nessantico, what was most visible were the spires and towers of their great buildings and the gilded domes of their temples.

So foreign. So strange. Niente wanted nothing more than to see the familiar places again, and he feared he never would.

Niente looked at Nessantico and shivered, but this was not the reaction he saw in Tecuhtli Zolin. The Tecuhtli, instead, stood on the hill overlooking the river and the city, and he crossed his arms over his chest, a close-lipped smile playing on his lips. "This is ours," he said. "Look at it. This is *ours*."

Niente wondered if the man even noticed the thick lines of Easterner troops arrayed along the road, if he counted the boats that crowded the river, if he glimpsed the preparations for war all along the western periphery of the city.

"What do you say, Niente?" Zolin asked. "Will we rest tomorrow night in this place?"

"If it is Axat's will," he answered, and Zolin barked his laugh.

"It's *my* will that matters, Nahual," he said. "Don't you understand that yet?" He didn't give Niente time to answer—not that there was any answer Niente could have made. "Go. Make sure that the nahualli are ready, that the

rest of the black sand has been prepared for the initial attacks. And send Citlali and Mazatl to me. We will begin this
tonight. We will keep them awake and exhausted; then,
when Sakal lifts the sun into the sky, we'll come on them in
a storm." Zolin stared for a moment more at the city, then
turned to Niente. Almost with affection, he placed his hand
on Niente's shoulder. "You *will* see your family again, Nahual. I promise it. But first, we must give the lesson of their
folly to these Easterners. Go look in your scrying bowl, Niente. You'll see that I'm right. You'll see."

"I'm certain I will, Techutli."

But he already knew what he would see. He had glimpsed
it this morning, even as they approached this place.

He had called upon Axat and he had looked into the
bowl, and he would not dare look again.

~

The Battle Begun: Sergei ca'Rudka

FOR MOST OF THE MORNING, Sergei had ridden alone in the midst of the Firenzcian troops, lost in ruminations that were keeping at bay—at least for a bit—the growing ache in his back from the long ride. His thoughts had not been kind or gentle ones. And his body was no longer used to long days in the saddle, nor to evenings spent under a tent.

You're getting old. You won't be here much longer, and you have much to do yet.

"Regent, I would talk with you."

At the hail, Sergei glanced over, seeing the stallion draped in the colors of Firenzcia that had come alongside him unnoticed. *Old. Once, you would never have missed his approach.* "Hïrzg Jan," he said. "Certainly."

The boy brought his war stallion alongside Sergei's bay mount, the mare's ears flicking nervously and rolling her eyes at the much larger destrier. Jan said nothing at first, and Sergei waited as they rode along the Avi, dust rising in a cloud around them. The army was approaching Carrefour, with Nessantico another good day's march farther. The Nessantican forces had vanished, dissolved; gone the afternoon of the parley. "Matarh says that you have lost two good friends," Jan said finally.

"I have," Sergei told him. "Aubri cu'Ulcai was on my staff for many years in both the Garde Kralji and the Garde Civile, before I was named Regent. He was a good man and an excellent soldier. I don't look forward to speaking to his wife or his children and telling them what happened. I especially don't relish telling them that his loyalty to me was responsible for his death." Sergei rubbed at his metal nose, the glue pulling at his skin as he frowned. "As for Petros ... well, there wasn't a gentler person in the world, and I know how important his friendship was to the Archigos. I don't know what the news will do to Archigos Kenne. Killing them was cruel and unnecessary, and if Cénzi grants me a long enough life, I will make certain Councillor ca'Mazzak regrets the pain he's given to me and those I care about."

The young man nodded. "I understand that," he said. "I truly do. Someday, I will find out who hired the White Stone to kill my Onczio Fynn, and I will kill that person myself and the White Stone with him. I liked Fynn. He was a good friend to me as well as a relative, and he taught me a lot in the short time I knew him. I wish he'd been alive long enough to teach me more about . . ." He stopped, shaking his head.

"There's no book learning one can do to be a leader, Hïrzg," Sergei told Jan. "You learn by doing, and you hope you don't make too many mistakes in the process. As to revenge: well, as I've grown older, I've learned that the pleasure one gets from actually achieving the act never matches that of the anticipation. I've also learned that sometimes one must forgo revenge entirely for the sake of a larger goal. Kraljica Marguerite knew that better than anyone; that's why she was such a good ruler." He smiled. "Even if your great-vatarh would disagree strongly."

"You knew them both."

Sergei couldn't quite tell if that were statement or question, but he nodded. "I did, and I had great respect for both of them, the old Hïrzg Jan included."

"Matarh hated him, I think."

"She had good reason, if she did," Sergei answered. "But he was her vatarh, and I think she loved him also."

"Is that possible?"

"We're strange beasts, Hïrzg. We're capable of holding two conflicting feelings in our heads at the same time. Water and fire, both together."

"Matarh says you used to torture people."

He waited a long time to answer that. Jan said nothing, continuing to ride alongside him. "It was my duty at one time, when I was in command of the Bastida."

"She says the rumors were that you enjoyed it. Is that part of what you were talking about—the ability to hold two conflicting feelings in your head?"

Sergei pursed his lips. He rubbed again at his nose. He looked ahead of them, not at the young man. "Yes," he answered finally, the single word bringing back all the memories of the Bastida: the darkness, the pain, the blood. The pleasure.

"Matarh is, or *was*, anyway, Archigos Semini's lover. Did you know that, Regent?"

"I suspected it, yes."

"Even though she loves him, she was willing to sacrifice him and hand him over for judgment as U'Téni Petros asked. She'd made that decision; she told me so herself when she came back from the parley. 'Let his sins be paid back in lives saved,' she told me. There wasn't a tear in her eye or a trace of regret in her voice. The Archigos ... he doesn't know that. He doesn't know how close he was to being a prisoner. For all I know, the two of them may even still ..." He stopped. Shrugged.

"Water and fire, Hïrzg," Sergei said.

Jan nodded. "Matarh said that you love Nessantico above us all. Yet you ride with us, you saved Matarh and me in Passe a'Fiume, and you would put Matarh on the Sun Throne."

"I would, because I'm convinced that would be best for Nessantico. I want to see the Holdings restored, with Firenzcia once again its strong right arm." Sergei paused. They could see the first outliers of Carrefour before them in the road, the tops of the buildings rising beyond the trees. "Is that also what you want, Hïrzg?"

Sergei watched the young man. He was looking away, over the long line of the army stretched along the road. "I love my matarh," he answered.

"That's not what I asked, Hïrzg."

Jan nodded, still gazing at the armored snake of his army. "No, it's not, is it?" he answered.

~

The Battle Begun: Karl Vliomani

"**Y**OU CAN STILL LEAVE via some of the streets to the east of the Nortegate," Karl told Serafina. "You'll have to be careful and you'll have to go quickly, but if you have Varina with you, you and Nico would have protection."

Karl saw Serafina and Varina already shaking their heads before he finished. "I'm not leaving without Talis," Serafina said. Nico was sitting on her lap as they sat around the table in the main room of Serafina's apartment. They had finished a dinner of bread, cheese, and water, though the bread had been stale, the cheese moldy, and the water clouded. They'd eaten it all, though, not knowing when there might be more food.

With the army of the Tehuantin at the western edges of the city and their ships holding the A'Sele, with the army of Firenzcia threatening from the east, Nessantico was panicked. Wild, fantastic rumors about the sack of Karnor and Villembouchure ran through the city, growing darker, grimmer, and more violent with each retelling. The Westlanders, if the stories could be believed, were nothing less than demons spawned by the Moitidi themselves, devoted to rape, torture, and mutilation. The shelves of the stores were nearly bare; the mills had no flour for the bakeries, and there were no carts coming into the markets from the fields outside the city. Even the Avi a'Parete was dark tonight—the light-téni hadn't made their usual rounds; worse, a fog had crawled over the city from the west, thick and cold. The city trembled in darkness, waiting for the inevitable strike to come. "I thought I'd lost both Talis and Nico once; I'm not doing that again," Serafina continued.

"He *can't* leave," Karl persisted. "He's male and young enough to be pressed into service with the Garde Civile. They'd snatch him before you got halfway to the Avi. And with the Archigos in the Bastida . . . well, the Garde Kralji almost certainly have our descriptions and are already out looking for us. Two women with a young boy—you'd be safe enough, I think. But with Talis and me . . ."

"I'm not leaving without him," Serafina persisted. Her voice shook and the hand around Nico's waist trembled, but her lips pressed firmly together.

"Half the city's *already* left—those who can. The rumors about Karnor and Villembouchure . . . all that could happen here."

A shrug.

Varina was smiling grimly. Her hand touched his knee under the table. "You've lost this argument, Karl," she said. "With both of us. We're here. We're staying, whatever that means."

Karl looked at Talis, who had been sitting silently on his side of the table. He'd been strangely quiet for the last day and more, since the news had come of the Archigos' imprisonment, and he spent much time with the scrying bowl. Karl wondered what the man was thinking behind that solemn face. Talis shrugged. "I agree with Karl," he said to Serafina. "I would rather have you and Nico safe."

Varina took Karl's hand, standing. "Come with me," she told him. "Let Sera and Talis talk this out on their own. We will, too."

Karl followed Varina into the other room. She closed the door behind them, so that they could only hear the low murmur of voices in conversation. "She loves him," Varina said. She was still leaning against the door, looking at Karl.

"Yes," he protested, "and that's exactly the reason he wants her to leave: because he doesn't want to lose the people he loves."

"And that's exactly the reason she *won't* go, because she couldn't bear not knowing what happened to him." She crossed her arms under her breasts. "It's exactly the reason I won't go either."

"Varina . . ."

"Karl, shut up," she told him. She pushed away from the wall, going to him. Her arms went around him, her lips sought his. There was a desperation in her embrace, in the violence of her kiss. He could hear the sob in her throat, and his hand went to her face to find her cheeks wet. He tried to pull away from her, to ask what was wrong, but she wouldn't let him. She brought his head back down to hers. Her weight bore him down to the straw-filled mattress on the floor. Then, for a time, he forgot everything.

Afterward, he kissed her, holding her tightly, relishing her warmth. "I love you, Karl," she whispered into his ear. "I've given up pretending anything else."

He didn't answer. He wanted to. He wanted to say the words back to her. They filled his throat but stuck there. He felt that if he said them, he'd be betraying Ana and everything she'd meant to him. *"Find someone else,* she'd told him, long ago. *"Go back to your wife, if you like. Or if you fall in love with someone new, that would be fine with me, too. I'd be happy for you because I can't be what you want me to be, Karl."*

"I . . ." he began, then stopped. They both heard it at the same time, a whistling shriek and a low growl like thunder, followed almost immediately by others, and the wind-horns on the temples beginning to sound an alarm. Karl rolled away from her. "What is that?" Karl asked, but he suspected that he knew already. They both dressed quickly and rushed into the other room.

"It's begun," Talis told them as they entered. He was standing by the door. The door faced south, and from the direction of the A'Sele, they could all see an orange-yellow glow over the rooftops, illuminating the fog that blocked their vision. "Fire," Talis said. "The nahualli are hurling black sand into the city close to the A'Sele."

The wind-horns were shrilling, and there were muffled shouts and cries coming from the fog.

Talis closed the door. "It's too late now," he said. "Too late."

~

The Battle Begun: Sigourney ca'Ludovici

FROM THE TOP FLOOR of the Kraljica's Palais, leaning on the crutch that compensated for her missing leg, Sigourney could gaze over the intervening rooftops and the waters of the A'Sele to the North Bank, where the campfires of the Westlanders burned on the outskirts of the city. There, too, she knew, the army of the Garde Civile was arrayed, with Aleron ca'Gerodi now acting as commandant. He, at least, was confident in the ability of the chevarittai and Garde Civile to deal with the dual threats to the city, even if no one else was. Ca'Gerodi had been in battle before, at least—and of the chevarittai left to her, he was best suited to be commandant, since ca'Mazzak had removed Aubri cu'Ulcai from consideration. That had been a mistake, Sigourney was certain; one she could understand, yes, given his rebellion, but also one that might have cost Nessantico more than she could afford.

Sigourney's body hurt greatly tonight, and she took a long swallow from the goblet of *cuore della volpe* and placed it on the windowsill.

Sigourney had been confident, too. She had been confident they would deal with these Westlander rabble and destroy them. Then they would look to the east and deal with Allesandra and her pup, and make them see the folly of this breach of their treaty. Yes, she had been confident.

It seemed like ages ago.

But she had seen the strange fog spill from the Westlander encampment to envelop Oldtown and the Garde Civile. Then, a bare turn of the glass later, great blossoms of orange fire bloomed on the North Bank, and she had watched them suddenly arc high into the air in several directions, some falling into the fog where her army waited, and others. . . .

The A'Sele's water rippled with the fire's reflection as the blossoms—screeching and wailing—rose as if flung by angry Moitidi. She saw the answer of the war-téni: pale blue lightning that reached up toward the blossoms. Several of them reached the blossoms at the top of their arcs: where they touched, a new, brief sun burst into life and the sound of thunder rolled over the city. But there were too many of the fire-blooms and the answer of the war-téni had come too late. Most of the fireballs fell: onto the Holdings' war-ships on the river, into the maze of Oldtown, and onto the Isle a'Kralji itself. And where they fell, they exploded in a gout of bright, loud fury.

She watched one in particular: the arc lifted higher than the others, and she could see the terrifying line of it—coming directly toward her. She stared, frozen by dual fascination and dread, feeling (as it plummeted down, as it grew larger with each instant), her body remembering the shock and horror of the moment that Kraljiki Audric had been killed. She wondered if this would hurt as much.

But no . . . she could see the line of sparks it trailed, now slipping slightly to her right. The fireball slammed into the palais' northern wing, spraying thick fire over the facade and into the gardens below. She felt the entire structure shudder with the impact, so strongly that she had to hold onto the frame of the window to keep from falling. Her knuckles tightened around the bar of the crutch. There were screams and shouts from all around the grounds. Nessantico's night was once more banished—not from the famous lamps of the light-téni, but by an inferno. Even from her window, Sigourney thought she could feel its heat.

Servants rushed into the room. "Kraljica! You must come with us! Hurry!"

"I'm not leaving here," she told them.

"You must! The fire!"

"Then don't waste your time here—go help put it out," she told them. "Summon the fire-téni from the temples. Go. Go!"

She waved her free hand at them—her scarred, battered body protesting at the violence of the movement—and they scattered. The wind-horns were sounding now in the temples, the alarm taken up all around the city. Sigourney looked down and saw the palais staff hurrying toward the

burning wing. Smoke curled around the side of the palais and burned in her remaining eye. She blinked as the
eye teared, and drank the remainder of the herbalist's
concoction.

"Look at me!" she shrilled to the night and the Westlander forces hidden in the fog. "I have given up too much
to be here. You will not move me. You will not."

The Battle Begun: The White Stone

"WHY DO YOU STAY HERE?"
"Why do you watch them?—the boy's not yours."
"He's not your responsibility."
"You should have left."
"You've waited too long."

The voices yammered in her mind: cajoling, warning, pleased. Fynn's was loudest, purring with satisfaction. *"You're going to die here, and the child inside with you."*

"Be quiet," she told them all, and they lapsed into sullen silence.

The air was thick with the unnatural fog, and the smell of burning wood drifted in its tendrils. The glow had become worse, and now there seemed to be a summer snow: ash drifting to the ground and coating her greasy hair and the shoulders of her grimy tashta. There were undefinable sounds in the fog, overlaid with the continual unearthly wail of the wind-horns.

She stared at the door where she'd last seen Talis. There was no one there now, and she hadn't seen Nico. *There's nothing you can do for him. For the moment, he's safe.* She pressed her hands to her swelling belly. Maybe the voices were right. Maybe she should flee the city. Save her own child.

But Nico was her child, too. Cénzi had brought him to her. He had chosen her, and Nico was hers as much as the unborn child inside her.

"Too late . . ."

Or maybe not. Grimacing, she turned away from Nico's house and moved swiftly out into the streets. She had to see with her own eyes, had to know what was happening. The streets were far more crowded than they should have been at this time of night, but people were hurrying to their destinations without looking at each other, fear fro-

zen on their features. Many of them kept their hands near
weapons openly carried: swords whose scabbards were
peeling leather and whose blades were spotted with rust;
knives that looked as if they'd last carved a roasted pig.
There would be violence in these streets before this night
ended: a harsh word, an unintended jostle, a misinterpreted
move—anything could ignite it, a spark to dry tinder. She
knew it because violence lived inside her. She could smell
the blood ready to spill.

But not yet. Not yet. She kept to shadows, she said nothing to any of them. The White Stone avoided killing, unless
it was for pay or for her own protection.

She reached the Avi a'Parete and turned south. As she
approached the river, the smell of smoke grew ever stronger, the smoke and fog intermingling so it was impossible to
tell one from the other. There were fires burning in the warren of close-set buildings to the west of the Avi, the flames
licking high enough to be seen from where she stood. A
téni-driven carriage came rushing up from the Pontica
Kralji, with a half dozen fire-téni aboard: their faces covered with soot; already exhausted from the effort of using
their spells to extinguish the multitude of fires. A squadron of Garde Kralji, their swords out and their faces grim,
accompanied them, surrounding a pack of sullen-looking
men in plain bashtas, most of them very old or very young.
"You!" the offizier of the squadron barked, pointing at a
gray-bearded ancient lurking near the building nearest
her. "And you!"—this to a youth who could not have been
more than twelve, being pulled along by his matarh. "Both
of you! Come with us! Lively, now!"

The matarh screeched her objection, the man started
to run the other way, then evidently decided he wouldn't
make it. The Garde Kralji closed around them and moved
off into the night in the direction of the fires, taking boy
and old man with them as the matarh screamed in futile
protest.

She continued south until she saw the columns of the
Pontica Kralji looming through the smoke. She paused
there, looking out over the A'Sele. What she saw horrified
her and made the voices inside her laugh.

On the river, several of the warships were afire, already
burned nearly down to the waterline, the wreckage clog-

ging the river so that those ships that were still untouched could barely maneuver. Over the northern branch of the river, the Isle A'Kralji burned. The Kraljica's Palais was a yellow-orange inferno with a volcano of sparks whirling away from it. The grand new dome of the Old Temple looked to be shattered, fire licking at the supports that had been erected around it. There were scattered small fires here and there. The bridges, especially the two leading to the South Bank, were crowded with people fleeing, pushing carts loaded with belongings or burdened with packs. She heard a crash behind her; glancing back over her shoulder toward the buildings crowding the Avi on this bank, she saw a crowd of people smashing down the door of a bakery, and also that of a jeweler. The street behind her was getting crowded and noisy. Somewhere inside one of the shops, she heard a woman scream.

Blood. She could smell the blood. She touched the leather pouch under the cloth of her tashta and felt the smooth, polished stone there.

"The rioting's begun . . ."

"It will only get worse . . ."

The voices shouted alarm in her head. *"Have you gone stupid, woman? Move!"*

She did. She strode unhurriedly toward the nearest alley, a trash-littered space between the backs of buildings. She would go back to Nico's house. She would watch and if things became dangerous there, she would be there to help him, to get him out. If his real parents could not protect him, she would be his true parent and do so. She touched her stomach as she walked. "And I will do the same for you," she whispered to the stirring life inside her. "I will. I promise."

The voices laughed and cackled.

She saw motion at the edge of her vision in the fog and smoke, felt the prickling of danger. She whirled around. "Hey!" A man stood there—dark hair speckled with gray, but young enough that she wondered how he'd managed to avoid the press gangs prowling Oldtown. His hands were up as if in surprise, and he was smiling, showing the gaps where teeth were missing. "No need to be frightened, Vaj-ica, is there?" he said. She could see his tongue moving behind the sparse teeth. "I just wanted to make sure you were safe, I did." He took a step toward her. "Dangerous days right now."

"For you, yes," she answered. "I can take care of myself."

"Ah, you can, eh?" He sidled to one side, blocking her from moving into the alley. She turned with him, always facing him. "Not many can say that today." He took a step toward her, and she scowled.

"Don't," she told him, even though she knew already that he wouldn't listen. "You'll regret it. You don't want to meet the White Stone."

He laughed. "The White Stone, is it? Are you telling me that the White Stone is interested in the likes of you?"

She didn't reply. He took another step, close enough that she could smell him, and he reached out to grab her arm. In that same moment, she crouched and slid a dagger from its sheath in her boot, stabbing hard upward under the man's rib cage, pushing him backward into the alleyway. He gasped, his mouth gaping like a fish; she felt hot blood pouring over her hand. His fingers clawed at her arm, but fell away softly. She heard him take a gurgling breath as blood trickled from his mouth. She let the body fall as she reached under the collar of her tashta for the pouch. Hurrying, she pulled it from around her neck and let the snow-pale, polished stone spill from the pouch into her hand. She pressed the stone down on his right eye. Her own eyes were closed.

Ah, the death wail... She could hear him screaming, could feel his presence entering the stone as the others moved aside to make room for his dying spirit. The silent howling of the man filled her mind, so loud that she was surprised it didn't echo around them. When the stone had taken him fully in, she removed the stone from his eye and placed it back in the pouch, placing the leather string around her neck again and letting the pouch fall down between her breasts under the tashta.

"The White Stone protects what is hers," she said to the open-eyed corpse.

Then, the voices rising to fill her head again and a new one joining the mad chorus, she made her way back toward Nico's home.

The Battle Begun: Niente

THE SKY LIGHTENED in the east and the spell-fog vanished with the light, though the city was still wrapped in smoke. Niente stood with Tecuhtli Zolin, with Citlali and Mazatl. The warriors were arrayed in their armor, their tattooed faces painted now, so they looked like the fierce, terrible dream-creatures who raped Axat before Darkness placed her wounded body in the sky. They were near the river; the large island around which it flowed seemed to be afire, and smoke coiled up from several dozen places in the city.

"Well done, Nahual," Zolin said. "They will be exhausted and frightened from the fires in the night. Are the nahualli rested? Are their spell-staffs full?"

"They're as rested as they can be, Tecuhtli," Niente told him. "We readied our staffs last night, after we sent the black sand."

"Good," Zolin boomed. "Then stop looking so mournful. This is a great day, Nahual Niente. Today we show these Easterners that they are not immune to the wrath of the Tehuantin."

Citlali and Mazatl laughed with Zolin. Niente tried to smile but could not. He hefted his own spell-staff, and Zolin nodded. "Go to the nahualli," he said to Niente. "Citlali, Mazatl—rouse your warriors. When we see Sakal's eye open on the horizon, it is time."

Niente bowed his head to the Techutli and left them. He moved north, into the trampled field where the bulk of the army was massed near the roadway. The nahualli were there, and he gave them his orders, spreading them behind the initial line of mounted warriors and the first wave of infantry. He took his own place behind Tecuhtli Zolin and his handpicked warriors. Across the field, he could see, blurred by the poor vision in his left eye, the banners and shields of the Nessanticans, waiting. There were so many of them;

Niente looked at their own forces, significantly smaller now after all the battles.

He had no doubt that the Tehuantin warriors were braver, that the nahualli were more powerful than the war-téni of the Nessanticans. Yet . . .

There was a burning in the pit of his stomach that would not go away. He clutched his spell-staff tightly, feeling the energy of the X'in Ka bound within it, and the power he held gave him no comfort.

The eastern sky lightened further. The first rays of the morning sent long shadows racing over the land.

Zolin raised his sword, shouting. "Now! Now!" Horns sounded in response, and the Tehuantin warriors screamed their challenge. Niente raised his spell-staff, clapping it into his open hand. Fire sizzled and sparked, flying away from him toward the enemy's ranks; a moment later, the staves of the other nahualli did the same all along the long line. The war-téni of the Nessanticans responded: some of the spells vanished as if swallowed by the air; other rebounded as if they'd hit a wall, arcing back into their own ranks. Where they fell, warriors fell with them, screaming as they were consumed in the sticky tongues of fire. Many of the spells, though, passed untouched, and they heard answering screams from the Nessanticans. The archers, their arrows tipped with the last of the black sand, sent a fiery rain streaking over the field, and it was answered by a hail of Nessantican arrows. Around Niente, warriors grunted as they were impaled, but their shields had snapped up to snare most of the arrows. Zolin gestured with his sword and the warriors began to move, slowly at first, then gathering speed to run over the field toward the waiting enemy and the city beyond them.

It was difficult not to be caught up in the rush of excitement. Niente surged forward behind Zolin and the wall of the infantry, and he heard his own voice screaming challenge with the others. Then, with an audible shudder, the Tehuantin line collided with the waiting Nessanticans. Niente could see blades flashing, could see the mounted warriors on the horses slashing down into the chaotic mass of soldiers, could hear the cries from the wounded or dying of both sides, could smell the blood and see spatters of it flying in the air, but there were too many warriors between.

The warriors behind him pressed in at their backs, pushing them forward, and the front line gave way so abruptly that Niente nearly fell. He was suddenly in the midst of the battle, with individuals fighting all around him, and he saw a Nessantican in his chain mail swinging a great sword overhead as he came at Niente.

The scrying bowl . . . The dead nahualli . . .

Niente shouted and thrust his spell-staff at the man as if it were a rapier. When it touched the man's abdomen, a spell released: a flash, an explosion of broken steel links, of brown cloth and pale flesh and crimson blood. The sword toppled from nerveless hands, the man's mouth gaped though no sound emerged, and he fell.

But there was no time to rest. Another soldier came at him, and again the stave, packed with the spells Niente had prepared, took the man down. One of the mounted soldiers they called chevarittai charged toward him, and Niente flung himself to the side as the warhorse's spiked and armored hooves tore the earth where he'd just been standing, plunging on past.

For Niente, this battle—like every battle—became a series of disconnected encounters, a maelstrom of confusion and mayhem, a disorganized landscape in which he continued to push forward. The noise was so tremendous that it became an unheard roar all around him. He sidestepped swords, thrust his stave at anything clad in the colors of blue and gold. A blade caught his arm, slicing open his forearm, another his calf. Niente shouted, his throat raw, the stave hot in his right hand, the energy blazing from it fast, almost gone now.

And . . .

He realized that he was standing not in a field, but amongst houses and other buildings, that the battle was now raging in the streets of the city, and the blue-and-gold–clad soldiers were turning now as horns blared, retreating deeper into the depths of the great city.

He was still alive, and so was Zolin.

~

The Battle Begun: Sigourney ca'Ludovici

COMMANDANT ALERON CA'GERODI STOOD before Sigourney and the rest of the Council of Ca' in armor spattered with blood, his helm dented by a sword strike, his face coated with mud, soot, and gore. "I'm sorry, Kraljica, Councillors," he said. His voice was as exhausted as his stance. "We could not hold them . . ."

Ca'Mazzak hissed like a steam kettle too long over the fire. Sigourney closed her eye. She took a long breath, full of soot and ash, and coughed. Her lungs were full of the stench. She opened her eye again. Through the haze of smoke, she could see the ruins of the palais, parts of it still actively burning. She and the Council had taken refuge in the Old Temple, which despite the shattered dome, was still largely intact. The main nave was packed with the treasures of the palais: paintings (including the charred one of Kraljica Marguerite), gold-and-silver place settings, the ceremonial clothes, the staffs and crowns worn by a hundred Kralji—they were all here, though much—too much—had been lost in the blaze. Sigourney sat on the Sun Throne at the entrance to the dome chamber, though if the throne were alight, it was not apparent in the brightness of the sun through the great hole torn in the dome. The sun mocked her, shining bright in a cloudless sky.

One of the attendants handed her a goblet of the *cuore della volpe* to ease the coughing and the pain. She sipped at the cool liquid, though it was brown and cloudy in the golden cup.

"How bad is it?" she asked.

"We managed to halt their advance finally," ca'Gerodi told her. "They didn't reach the Avi a'Parete, but they have most of the streets to the west of it on the North Bank. They have the village of Viaux. There was a fierce battle near the River Market and for a time they held it, but we pushed them back. I've moved a battalion to protect the Pontica Kralji, but that's left the Nortegate area more open than I would like."

The councillors muttered to themselves. "This is unacceptable," ca'Mazzak said, more loudly.

"Then perhaps you should have left Commandant cu'Ulcai alive," Sigourney told the man. "Or would you care to take up the sword yourself?" Ca'Mazzak grumbled and subsided. Ca'Gerodi seemed to waver on his feet, and Sigourney motioned to one of the servants to bring a chair; the man sank gratefully onto the cushioned seat, uncaring of the filth he smeared on the brocade. "What are you telling me, Commandant?" Sigourney asked him. "That tonight they will set the rest of the city on fire, that tomorrow they will overrun us entirely? You said that you had more than enough men. You said that—"

"I know what I said," he interrupted, then—as Sigourney snapped her mouth shut at his rudeness—seemed to realize what he'd done and shook his head. "Pardon me, Kraljica; I haven't slept since the night before last. But yes, that's exactly what I fear: that tonight will bring more of the Westlanders' awful fire, and that when they attack tomorrow . . ." He brought his head up, gazing at her with eyes sagging and brown. "I will give my life to protect Nessantico, if that is what is required."

"Aleron . . ." Sigourney started to push up from the Sun Throne, forgetting for a moment her injuries, then fell back. The movement caused her to cough again. The councillors watched her. She knew now what she must do, and the realization burned at her, as painful as her wounded body. "Go. Get what rest you can, and we will deal with whatever tonight and tomorrow bring. Go on. Sleep while you can . . ."

Ca'Gerodi rose and saluted her. Limping, he left the room. When he'd gone, Sigourney gestured to one of the servants. "Bring me a scribe," she told him. "And I will also need a rider—the best we have—to take a message east to the Hïrzg."

The servant's eyes widened momentarily, then he bowed and hurried away.

"Kraljica," ca'Mazzak said. "You can't—"

"We have no choice," she told him, told all of them. "No choice. This is no longer about us."

Sigourney leaned back against the cushioned seat of the Sun Throne; it smelled of woodsmoke. It smelled of defeat.

RESOLUTIONS

Allesandra ca'Vörl

JAN READ THE MISSIVE carefully, his pale eyes scanning the words there. Allesandra already knew what it said—Starkkapitän ca'Damont's soldiers had intercepted the rider pounding eastward along the Avi a'Firenczia with a white banner fluttering over him in the moonlight, and had brought the sealed scroll to Allesandra, insisting to her attendants that she be awakened. Allesandra had broken the seal and scanned the letter, then she'd quickly dressed and gone to Jan.

If her son noticed or cared that the seal hung broken on the thick paper, or that the Kraljica had addressed the missive to Allesandra and not himself, he'd said nothing. He moved the candle aside that he'd been using for light; its holder scraped along the table that had been hastily set up in the field tent next to the Hïrzg's private tent.

"This is genuine?" Jan asked. A blanket was draped around his shoulders, his eye sockets were baggy and tired. He yawned and rubbed at his eyes. "We're certain?"

"The rider said that it was handed to him by Kraljica Sigourney herself," Starkkapitän ca'Damont answered.

Jan nodded. He handed the scroll to Semini, who read it, pursed his lips, then passed it to ca'Rudka. Jan seemed to be waiting, and Allesandra, seated next to him at the small table in the field tent, tapped her fingertips on the scarred surface. "We are wasting time, my son," she said. "The message is clear. The Kraljica is willing to abdicate the Sun Throne if we bring the army there immediately to stop the Westlanders. Rouse the men now, and if we march our forces at double-time, we can reach the city gates by early morning."

Jan didn't seem to hear her. He was looking at Sergei. "Regent?" he asked. "Your thoughts?"

Ca'Rudka, maddeningly to Allesandra, rubbed at his nose for a long time, staring at the parchment. She could see the candlelight flickering on sculpted nostrils. "The Kraljica wouldn't consider abdication when it was offered it to her at the parley, Hïrzg Jan, or at least ca'Mazzak would not," he said finally. "The councillor seemed entirely confident that the Garde Civile could defeat the Westlanders. Now the Kraljica's suddenly been afflicted with altruism? But as I told you, Hïrzg, I wish what's best for Nessantico. I wouldn't care to see the city destroyed. But this must be your decision."

"There, Jan, you see?" Allesandra said. She stood. "Starkkapitän, you will—"

But Jan had laid his hand on her arm. "I'm not finished yet, Matarh," he said. "Archigos Semini, what do *you* think of this offer?"

Allesandra started to protest, but Jan's hand tightened around her arm. They were all watching her. Pressing her lips together, she sat again. Semini especially stared at her, his umber eyes expressionless. He *knew*, she realized then. He knew that she had been ready to offer him up in exchange for the Sun Throne. Sergei . . . could Sergei have told him? Or . . .

Jan?

"I notice that the Kraljica's offer says nothing about the Faith," Semini answered, still staring at her. "That's not acceptable to me. I'm reluctant to commit the war-téni to an alliance with Nessantico unless Archigos Kenne is also willing to abdicate in favor of me." Semini turned from her then, and inclined his head to Jan. "Unless, of course, that is what the Hïrzg requests of me."

"Jan," Allesandra persisted, ignoring Semini. "This is what we wanted from the start. We have it in our grasp; we've but to reach out and take it."

"Oh, I disagree, Matarh," Jan snapped back at her. "It's what *you've* always wanted. It seems your whole life has been about what you wanted: your ambitions, your aspirations, your desires. Even as a girl, from what I've been told:

you wanted Nessantico in the first place, so Great-Vatarh forced his army to march faster than it should have and lost—yes, Fynn told me that tale, which he said Great-Vatarh told him."

"That's not true," Allesandra objected. *It was Vatarh who wanted Nessantico so badly. Not me. I told him to wait and be patient. I did . . .* but Jan wasn't listening, continuing to talk.

"You decided you didn't want to help Vatarh after he finally brought you back, so your marriage was a sham when it could have been a strong alliance. You didn't want me to be involved with Elissa, so you sent her away. You didn't want to be Hïrzg, so you campaigned for me to have the title. What you've always wanted is to be Kraljica, and now you want us to take this offer so you can have it *now*, whether that's best for Firenzcia or not. It's always been *you*, Matarh. You. Not Vatarh, not Great-Vatarh, not me, not the Archigos, not anyone. You. Well, you made me Hïrzg, and by Cénzi I *will* be Hïrzg, and I will do what's best for Firenzcia and the Coalition, not what's best for you. I love you, Matarh—" strangely, to Allesandra, he glanced at Sergei when he said that, "—but I am Hïrzg, and this is what I say: We *will* move on to Nessantico, but we will do so in our own time. Nessantico cries out for help from us? Well, let her cry. Let her fight the battle she has brought on herself. Starkkapitän, we will break camp in the morning as planned, and we will proceed at normal pace until we are within sight of Nessantico, and there we will wait until we know more or until the Kraljica herself comes out and bends her knee to me. I won't send a single Firenzcian life to be lost defending Nessantico from her own folly."

"Jan—" Allesandra began, but he cut her off with a snap of his arm.

"No, Matarh. We're not discussing this any further. You wanted me to be Hïrzg? Well, here I am, and that is my wish. We won't talk of it further. Starkkapitän—you have your orders."

Ca'Damont bowed, and with a glance at Allesandra, left the tent. Semini yawned and stretched like a bear waking from hibernation. He gave Jan the sign of Cénzi and followed after the starkkapitän, avoiding Allesandra's gaze entirely. Sergei watched the two men leave, then stood himself. "Should you need my counsel, Hïrzg, you know where to find me," he said. "A'Hïrzg, a good evening to you."

Allesandra gave him the barest inclination of her head. For several breaths, she and Jan sat there, silent. "You don't want me to be Kraljica?" she said, when the silence had stretched on for too long.

"Just as Sergei wants what's best for Nessantico, I want what's best for Firenzcia," he answered. Then, before she could form a response: "All I ever wanted from *you* was your love, Matarh."

His words stung like a slap across the face, so hard that it started tears in her eyes. "I do love you, Jan," she told him. "More than you can understand."

He glared at her: a stranger's face. No, his namesake's face, as she imagined it all during her captivity in Nessantico, when he refused to pay the ransom for her. "Shut up, Matarh. You've taught me well. You've shown me that aspirations and drive are more important than love. I talked to Archigos Semini. I told him how you'd been willing to sacrifice him to be Kraljica. He told me something in return: that he had plotted to assassinate Fynn. For *you*, Matarh. All for you. He told me that you *knew*, that day I saved Fynn, that the attack would come. You used him—your lover—to make me a hero, to make me the Hïrzg. The rest, I can figure out myself. I wonder, Matarh, who hired the White Stone—but I have an excellent guess." She felt her face coloring, and she looked away. "Then that oh-so-noble gesture of yours," he continued, "stepping down in favor of me: you never wanted to be Hïrzg. You always wanted more. You didn't want what was best for me, but what was best for you. I was your *second* child, the lesser one, Matarh. Ambition was always your firstborn."

The breath left her. She sat there, tears damp on her cheeks, as Jan pushed away from the table and stood. "Jan . . ." she said, lifting her arms to him, but he shook his head. He looked down on her and for a moment she thought she saw his face soften.

But he turned and walked away into the night.

Niente

THEY USED WHAT LITTLE of the black sand they had left to hurl into the city again that night. Otherwise, Niente ordered the nahualli to rest and restore their spell-staffs for the next day's battle. He had lost ten more of the nahualli during the battle, most of them late in the day as Zolin tried unsuccessfully to take the closest of the bridges over the river. The energy in their spell-staffs had been entirely gone, and there was no time to rest and replenish them. The nahualli—as Niente had ordered—tried to retreat behind the lines as soon as their power was exhausted, but some were cut down by Nessantican swords, unable to defend themselves. Niente didn't know how many of the warriors had been lost. They'd been cast back by a desperate charge of the chevarittai, and Zolin—at Niente's insistence, afraid that they would lose still more of the nahualli—had finally called a halt to their advance.

They were too few . . . both nahualli and warriors. But Zolin didn't see that, or didn't care, or was so caught up in his own vision that it overrode that of his own eyes. "Tomorrow," he said to Niente, to Citlali and Mazatl. "Tomorrow all of the city will be ours. All of it." Niente didn't know if that was to be true or not, and he was too exhausted to care.

After the last of the fireballs had been catapulted into the city, Niente went to his own tent. There, alone, he held the scrying bowl in his hands: afraid to cast the spell, afraid that he would only see the same vision, afraid of the exhaustion and pain casting the spell would cost him. He tried to remember the faces of his wife, of his children: he could bring them up in his mind, but that only made the longing worse. He wondered how they were, how they'd changed, if they missed him as he missed them.

He wondered if he would ever know.

He put the bowl away.

Sleep that night was fitful and unrestful. Nightmares intruded; he saw his wife dead, saw his children hurt and injured, saw himself fighting, fighting, trying to run but unable to do more than walk while demons draped in blue and gold swarmed around him. He tried to imagine his wife's face before him, her mouth half-open as he leaned in to kiss her . . . and her face was blank and featureless, a mask. Unable to escape the dreams, he eventually paced the encampment, listening to the sounds of the warriors resting, gazing at the strange shapes of the buildings around them. As he passed one building, he heard his name called out. "Niente."

He recognized the voice. "Citlali."

The High Warrior was leaning against the doorway of the building. Behind him, a candle gleamed in the darkness. "You can't sleep?" Citlali asked.

Niente shook his head. "I don't dare. Too many dreams," he told the man. "You?"

Citlali's black-swirled face creased into a smile. "Too few," he said. "I would like to see our home and my family again, even if in my sleep."

"That won't happen if—" Niente bit off the comment, angry at himself. If he'd been less sleep-addled, he'd have said nothing at all.

"If Tecuhtli Zolin has his way?" Citlali ventured. "I've thought the same, Nahual. You needn't look so distressed." The smile widened to a grin, and he glanced from side to side, as if looking to see that no one was listening. "And let me answer the other question you won't ask. No. I won't challenge the Tecuhtli. Look at how far he's taken us, Nahual—all the way across the sea to the great home of the Easterners. That is true greatness, Nahual. Greatness. I am proud to have been able to help him."

"Even if it means you'll never see home and family again?"

His shoulders lifted. "I am a warrior. If that's Sakal's will . . ." His shoulders fell again. "I don't need a scrying bowl, Nahual. I have no interest in the future, only the now. It's a beautiful evening, I am alive, and I am seeing a place that I never thought I would see and that few Tehuantin have ever glimpsed. How can one not take pleasure in that?"

Niente could only nod. He bid Citlali a good night and left the warrior to his reverie. For his own part, he returned to his own quarters and performed the rituals to place spells in his stave once more. Then, entirely drained from the effort, he took to his bed and let the nightmares wash over him again.

And the next day, the nightmares came true.

At dawn, Tecuhtli Zolin led them deeper into the city, and they fought street by street toward the wide main boulevard. The battle was a mirror of the one the day before: again, the initial push sent the weary Nessanticans retreating backward; by the time Sakat's eye was well up in the sky, they had reached the boulevard, where Zolin quickly regrouped them and began marching them south.

There, the Nessanticans had gathered: around the market where they'd finally stopped the Tehuantin advance yesterday, and around the bridge leading to the island. Out in the A'Sele, Zolin had ordered the ships to advance toward the army; the ships of the Nessanticans had moved to stop them, and there was another battle taking place there, one whose outcome Niente could only guess at, though many of the warships of both sides were afire. There was no retreat possible there anymore—there were too few ships left for them all to return home.

"Nahual!" From his horse, Zolin jabbed a finger toward Niente. "You will take your nahualli with you and follow me. We have the main street, now we must have the bridge. Citlali! To me!"

Zolin quickly placed the warriors in position. Citlali and Zolin would attack the piers of the bridge from the boulevard, directly into the heart of the Nessantican forces; Mazatl would wait until the assault was underway, then strike from the west flank through the River Market. Several double-hands of warriors would also begin an attack to the north immediately, pushing the other way along the ring boulevard so that the Nessanticans could not concentrate their attention on the bridgehead—not without possibly losing the easternmost bridge to the great island. Zolin sent the diversionary warriors on, then waited for the sun's shadow to move a finger's length before waving his hand and leading them east and a little north to the boulevard, where he set them into position. They could see the Nessanticans: a wall of bristling shields across the boulevard, a scant few hundred strides from them.

There was no black sand and no time to make any more even if they had the raw materials. This time, the archers began the assault with a barrage that rained down on the shields of the Nessanticans without doing a great deal of damage. The war-téni sent their fireballs screaming toward them, and Niente—with the other nahualli—raised their spell-staffs quickly. The warding spells crackled outward, a nearly visible pulse in the air. Most of the fireballs were deflected; they fell into the buildings to either side, setting them afire. But there were too many of them, and not enough nahualli. The war-spells crashed down on the assembled warriors; where that happened, men screamed, their bodies twisted and charred. Those who could do so fled, terribly injured from the burns of the viscous fire. Those who could not, died. One fireball fell close enough to Niente that he could feel the heat of it, like a smithy's furnace opening in front of him. The heat washed over his face, scouring and drying. Zolin felt it also; he glanced back at the scene as his horse reared up in fright. Zolin shouted: "Forward! Now!" He brought his mount under control and kicked him into a gallop. The High Warriors on their horses followed him and the infantry surged forward as well. Niente was pulled along in the wave.

The wave crashed against the shields painted blue and gold, and impaled itself on their spears. In the roaring chaos, Niente saw Zolin's horse go down, a spear tearing deep into the creature's chest, but Zolin himself was lost in the press of soldiers and Niente couldn't see what happened to him.

There were swords and fighting all around him, and Niente could think only of himself, of taking out as many Nessanticans as he could. He pointed his spell-staff, speaking the release word over and over, and lightning crackled from the tip, hissing and bucking as it plunged into the ranks in front of Niente. A hole opened in the shield wall as Niente released another spell, and another—the flashes sending dozens of men to the ground. Warriors, shrieking and howling, plunged into the gap with swords waving. The wall began to give, then it collapsed entirely. Niente again was pushed along with the tide, and he saw close by the towers that marked the bridge entrance.

To his right, there was a cacophony of shouts: Mazatl's warriors striking at the flank. Horns shrilled deep in the Nessantican ranks. Niente could see a banner waving there and a cluster of chevarittai on their horses. Suddenly, the banner was moving away to the south over the bridge, the chevarittai with it. He could see the realization on the faces of the enemy soldiers in front of him. He could see the way their swords dropped momentarily, the lines weakening visibly. Arrows no longer rained down, the war-téni no longer cast fireballs over Niente's head to fall into the rear of their ranks. They were moving steadily forward: the warriors, the nahualli, and now Niente could see Zolin again, bloodied and injured but on his feet, his sword cleaving the soldiers who dared to stand before him. Citlali was alongside him, his face grim and eager.

They were on the bridge now. It was theirs. The river moved sluggishly below them, and bodies fell from the rails to splash into its waters.

The Tehuantin roared. They sang as they killed, and Niente sang with them.

~

Varina ci'Pallo

THE STREETS OF OLDTOWN were awash with panicked citizens, most of them running eastward away
from the approaching Westlander forces and the battles
along the Avi a'Parete. They could all hear the sounds: the
shouts reverberating down the lanes, the cries, the screams,
the constant din of the wind-horns shrilling alarm from the
temples. The smoke of the fires was smeared across the sky,
filthy rags sometimes obscuring the sun, and the smell of
fire and carnage was thick in the air.

Varina found herself staying close to Karl for most of
the day. She would smile at him, nervous and uncertain,
and he would give her the same smile back. "Promise me,"
she said finally. They were alone in one of the rooms; Talis,
Serafina, and Nico were in the other.

"Promise you what?"

"That whatever happens, it happens to us both. Save a
last spell for us, and I'll do the same."

"It's not going to be that bad," he told her. "Talis . . . he's
one of them, after all."

She nodded at that, as uncomforted by that fact as he
was.

Late in the day, the smell of smoke became stronger. From
the windows of their rooms, they could see thick, greasy
smoke boiling up from the houses a street over to the west,
with flames occasionally shooting up through the black. Ash
was drifting down like gray snow. Karl imagined he could almost feel the heat. They went into the front room with the
others.

"Everything's burning," Nico said. He looked more
excited than concerned, but the adults all looked at each
other worriedly. The faint crackling of the flames was audible in the silence.

"You're right, Nico," Varina said to him, glancing at Serafina. "I'm afraid the fire-téni are too busy elsewhere to

do anything about this." Varina's gaze shifted from Serafina to Karl. Varina knew what he was thinking—it was what was on all of their minds: *Can we stay here? Do we need to leave?*

Less than a turn of the glass or more later, they all heard a loud commotion welling up from the west on the street outside. Varina opened the door to peer out. Not far down the street, a mob of several dozen people prowled the lane—not soldiers, not Westlanders, but those who lived in Oldtown. They were shouting, rushing from house to house and breaking in through doors and windows—she could hear the screams and cries of those inside as the mob pushed its way inside each house. They were looting, carrying out anything that appeared to be valuable: she could see some of them clutching stolen items as they marched; what else they were doing in those houses, she could only guess at. There were fires already burning in three or four houses farther down the street. The mob was shouting, screaming—*"Take what you want! The city's lost! Rise up! Rise up!"*

Karl and Talis pushed past Varina toward the street as the mob continued its slow, chaotic progress toward them. Someone at the front noticed them and pointed, and several clots of looters surged toward them. "Stop this!" Karl called, and they mocked him, shouting back at him and shaking old or improvised weapons. Karl glanced at Talis, shaking his head. He lifted his hands, gesturing, and light blossomed between his hands. Alongside him, Talis had raised his staff, tapping it once on the pavement stones: a lightning bolt arrowed up from the knob toward the smoke-wrapped sky.

The mob stopped. Without a word, they scattered in a strange silence, scurrying in any direction as long as it was away from them. A few breaths later, the street was empty. "Well, that went rather well," Karl said. He and Talis turned, and Varina saw their mouths drop open as they gaped.

Varina had cast her own spell even as Karl had cast his. She'd shaped the air around her with a sculptor's touch, drawing upon it as a canvas and placing on it an image from her mind. She knew what Karl and Talis saw, looming behind them higher than any of the houses.

"A dragon!" Nico, in Serafina's arms, shouted from the

doorway of the house in delight. Karl laughed, clapping his hands, and Varina grinned. "Can you make it spit fire and fly?" Nico asked, and Varina shook her head at the boy.

"It can't *do* anything. It just *looks* ferocious," she told him. For a moment, the danger was forgotten, but then reality collapsed back around them as Varina let the spell go. The dragon vanished in a fume of green, smoky ribbons that the wind hurried away. The looters might be gone, but nothing had changed. They'd be back, soon enough, and the nearby fires still raged unchecked. The city was still under assault.

"Karl," Varina said, "we can't stay here."

Karl looked once at Talis, saw the man nod slightly. "You're right," he said. "It's time. Let's gather what we need." He clapped Talis on the shoulder and started toward the door.

Across the street, Varina saw a lone older woman—a beggar, from the look of her clothing. She was staring toward their house. As Varina noticed her, the woman seemed to nod, then hurried away into the dark, narrow space between the houses and was gone.

Sigourney ca'Ludovici

THEY PUT HER in the Old Temple.

Commandant ca'Gerodi came fleeing back from the debacle at the Pontica Kralji, bellowing as he charged into the Old Temple to where Sigourney sat on the Sun Throne, telling her she and the Council of Ca' must take what they could and flee immediately by the Pontica a'Brezi Veste to the South Bank and out of the city.

Sigourney refused. "Let the Council go if they must," she said. "I am staying."

"I can't protect you, Kraljica," ca'Gerodi told her. "They are coming, at any moment."

"I'm not abandoning my city and my charge," she responded coldly. "I will stay."

In the end, her staff had taken what they could of the remaining treasures of the palais and fled the Isle a'Kralji. It was the same everywhere in Nessantico: in the vast Archigos' Temple on the South Bank, at the Grand Libreria with its precious, irreplaceable vellum scrolls and books; at the Theatre a'Kralji and the Museé a'Artisans. Councillor ca'Mazzak and the rest of the Council had vanished as well. Fleeing south, the only direction still open to them . . .

Sigourney remained on the Sun Throne in the Old Temple, in the sunlight coming through the ruined, charred dome. Before she allowed the court herbalist to leave, she ordered him to prepare a special goblet of *cuore della volpe*, which now sat on the arm of the Sun Throne next to her. She wore a long, cerulean tashta with a yellow overcloak, hiding the fact that there was no leg below her right knee. She had the servants place a jeweled patch over the hole where her right eye had been, and apply egg powder to her face to hide the worst of the scars.

She waited on the ancient seat of Nessantico. Waited for the inevitable.

Outside, she could hear the battle raging: the shouting

of men, the clashing of arms, the roar of war-téni spells. Smoke drifted overhead, dulling the sunlight. An elite guard of Garde Kralji was arrayed before her, their chain mail rustling as they shifted nervously, swords in hand and facing the doors to the temple. Commandant ca'Gerodi had left her a turn of the glass earlier. "I won't see you again, Kraljica," he said. "I'm sorry."

"I know," she told him. "I know. And I am sorry, too."

She waited.

When the doors burst open, the gardai in front of her stiffened and started to rush forward. "No," she told them. "Hold! Wait!" Several Westlander warriors entered the temple; with them was another man, this one without the tattoos of the warriors and carrying a burnished wooden staff: one of their spellcasters. They stopped, peering down the long aisle of the nave to where Sigourney was seated in a dusty shaft of sunlight. "Do any of you speak our language?" she called out.

"I do," the spellcaster said. His words were slurred and heavily accented, but understandable. "A little."

"Good," she said. "I am Kraljica Sigourney ca'Ludovici, ruler of this land. Who are you?"

The man whispered for a moment to the warrior alongside him, with the image of a red hawk or eagle inscribed over his bare skull. "I am Niente," the spellcaster answered. "I am the Nahual. And this," he said, gesturing to the warrior to whom he'd spoken, "is the leader of the Tehuantin, Tecuhtli Zolin. He demands your surrender, Kraljica."

"He can demand whatever he likes," Sigourney told him. She lifted a hand from the arm of the Sun Throne, the signet ring of the Kralji glinting on her hand as she touched the golden band of a crown set in her gray, coarse hair. The sun was warm on her, and she glanced upward to the charred ruins of the dome supports. "He won't have that."

Again the spellcaster spoke to the warrior, who uttered a laugh that echoed in the temple. He spoke words in a tongue that sounded at once strange and yet oddly familiar. Where had she heard words like that before? "Tecuhtli Zolin says that if the Kraljica wishes to challenge him, he is willing to meet that challenge. He will loan her his own sword if she doesn't have one of her own. Otherwise, he will order his warriors to take you prisoner. He leaves the choice to you."

She shook her head. "I know how you treat prisoners," she told him. "And you haven't looked at all the choices I have." The spellcaster appeared confused as Sigourney took the goblet from the arm of the Sun Throne and downed the bitter concoction in one long draught. "I hope you enjoy the city while you hold it," she told him. She raised the goblet to them, then let it fall ringing to the tiles. Her leg was already losing sensation as she leaned back on the throne. The paralysis rose quickly upward: her thighs, her hips, her midsection. Her heart. The sunlight in the room seemed to be dimming. "This is *my* throne," she told them, "and while I live, I will not give it up."

She laughed then. Her voice sounded strange and breathy and weak. She tried to force out the next words. "And I choose my own time." She tried to take a breath, but her lungs would not move. She opened her mouth, but there was no air for words.

She smiled at them as the sun went dark and Nessantico vanished from her sight.

~

Karl Vliomani

"WHERE DO YOU SUGGEST we go?" Talis asked.

"East," Karl suggested. "To the Firenzcians. Sergei might be there."

"We could go west," Talis countered. "To my people."

"Your people have set fire to Nessantico," Varina told him. "They kill. They rape. They plunder."

"And your people don't?" Talis snapped back at her. "You haven't been to the Hellins, have you? Or have you forgotten what started this confrontation in the first place?" He glared at Varina, who held his gaze, unblinking.

"Stop it, both of you," Karl told them. "We don't have time to waste on this. Talis, moving west means trying to get through the worst of the fires, and the south doesn't appear all that much better. We have to think of the boy, especially; it's too dangerous."

"And going toward the Firenzcians *isn't*?" Talis countered. "I'd say it's less so."

Serafina touched Talis' shoulder. "I think he's right, love," she said. "Please . . ."

Talis scowled, then shrugged. "Fine," he said. "But it's on your head, Numetodo, if this turns out badly."

They quickly gathered what they could carry. The smell of smoke was overpowering now and ash was falling steadily on the rooftops, their edges glistening with wavering fire. They couldn't see the sun at all, though it had to be high in the sky. The street outside was still deserted; those who could flee had already done so; those who were staying were hunkered down in the buildings. They moved quickly down the lane to the first intersection and turned east.

As they reached the larger streets, they encountered crowds again. Swarms of them were looting the stores, breaking down the doors and ripping off the shutters and carrying out whatever they could. They glared defiantly at the group as they passed with their prizes, defying anyone to try to stop them or to protest. A squad of four utilino appeared, shrilling on their whistles, but beyond that they made no attempt to restore order; they pointed their sticks and yelled warning, but scurried quickly away when the nearest looters turned to confront them.

Karl and the others moved after them.

Some time later, they'd gone several blocks, far enough that the ash from the fires was no longer coating their shoulders and hair. They were nearing Oldtown Center; Karl could glimpse the open square not far ahead, where the winding lane opened suddenly into it: there was the statue of Henri VI with his sword upraised, standing in sunlight. The crowds had vanished again. They might have been hurrying through a deserted city. As they approached the end of the street, Karl stopped them: pressed against the flank of the nearest building, they watched a squadron of Garde Civile rushing south across the open plaza near the fountain of Selida, led by a trio of mounted chevarittai. Many of the soldiers were visibly wounded, limping as they half-ran across the plaza.

"They're retreating," Varina whispered. "Have we lost the city, then?"

Karl could give no answer to that, though he suspected the truth. "Come on," he said. "Let's hurry . . ."

They started across the plaza as the Garde Civile disappeared into the opening of a street to the south. They had reached the end of the eastering shadow of Henri VI, nearly across Oldtown Center, when they saw what the soldiers had been fleeing from.

A noisy mass of painted men swarmed into the plaza from the north. From the distance, Karl could see that they were well armed: swords, spears, arrows. Their faces were swirled with dark lines as Uly's had been; their bodies were protected with bamboo armor. They hadn't yet seen Karl's little group, or if they had, they'd already judged them to be inconsequential. The Westerlanders moved out into the open ground: at least thirty or more of them. "Move!" Karl hissed. "Quickly!" They could easily reach one of the side streets leading into Oldtown Center and lose themselves before the Westlanders could reach them. Karl, taking Varina's hand, started to run.

He realized after a few steps that they were alone. Talis remained standing in the statue's shadow. He had Serafina's hand, and Nico's. "Talis!"

Talis shook his head. "No," he said loudly.

"Talis, Sergei went to Firenzcia. We can follow him. You don't have anything you can use to bargain with these people. Not anymore. You're endangering Serafina and Nico."

Talis smiled at Karl and Varina. "Ah, but I *do* have a bargaining chip—Uly's black sand. Remember? It's still there."

Karl felt Varina's hand tighten on his arm. He remembered: Uly, the casks of ingredients in his rooms, waiting to be mixed . . . "You can't. To give them *that*. . . ."

"These are *my* people," Talis said. "I thank you for all you've done for Sera and Nico, but these are my people, the people I know, and it's time for me to go back to them. You go on to yours." He waved to the soldiers, shouting something in a language that Karl could not understand. "Go on," he said to Karl. "Go on while you have the chance."

"At least let us take Serafina and Nico with us," Varina called to him, but Talis shook his head.

"They're my family and they stay with me. Go, Karl. Or stay. But make your choice." Serafina looked at them, her face panicked and uncertain. Nico stared, wide-eyed but seemingly calm.

Several painted warriors were coming at a run now. Talis raised his spell-staff. Light blossomed from it, coruscating and banishing the shadow of Henri VI. "Karl?" Varina's hand was raised; he could feel the energy of the Second World gathering around her.

"There are too many of them," he told her.

"We can't leave them. Can't leave Nico."

"We don't have a choice," he answered.

Karl took Varina's hand, and they ran.

~

Nico Morel

NICO COULDN'T UNDERSTAND what Talis was saying as the painted soldiers approached them. He could hear the uncertainty in his vatarh's voice and the way he was speaking louder and faster, holding the magical walking stick in front of him like a cudgel. His matarh clutched Nico so fiercely that he could barely breathe as the strange men surrounded them, impossibly large and frightening and smelling of blood and death.

Nico could feel the fear rising in him and with it, the strange coldness he'd felt in the Archigos' office, as it had when he'd run away from Ville Paisli. It began to build inside him, and he muttered to himself the strange words that came to his mind as his hands made small motions under his matarh's clinging embrace.

"Talis," he heard his matarh say, "what's happening? I'm frightened . . ."

"It's fine," his vatarh said, but his voice belied that. "I just need to talk to the High Warrior. Let me do that. They're my people; they just didn't expect to find me here . . ."

He turned back to one of the painted men, the one with a red-tongued black lizard crawling from the top of his skull, around his left eye, and down the side of his head. As they half-shouted at each other, Talis shaking his stick in the man's face, Nico felt the cold growing and growing inside, so intense that he knew he would burst if he tried to contain it any longer. Nico cried out: the strange words. He gestured.

There was no blue fire this time. Instead, the air shivered around him, rippling visibly outward, and where that fast-moving wave struck the painted men, they were thrown backward as if a great fist had struck them. "Come on, Matarh!" Nico yelled. He grabbed her hand, pulling her away so that she stumbled after him as he fled in the direction that Karl and Varina had gone. "Talis! Hurry!"

But Talis wasn't running with them; he'd also been felled by the wild burst from Nico. The lizard-warrior had already regained his feet, and Nico—glancing over his shoulder as he started to run—could see him shouting to the others as Talis screamed something back at him and raised his walking stick. Blinding light flashed from the stick and one of the warriors howled. Nico pulled at his matarh harder. "Run!"

She took a step with him, but her hand dropped away from his. He took another step before he realized that she wasn't with him. He heard Talis scream—"Sera!"—and turned back.

His matarh was lying sprawled on the cobbles of the plaza, a spear in her back and blood staining the paving stones. She was reaching toward Nico, crawling after him, her face drawn with pain. "Matarh!" Nico screamed, and ran back to her. He went down alongside her just as Talis reached her also.

"Nico . . ." she said. "I'm sorry . . ." Her head turned to Talis and she started to speak, but he stroked her head, cradling her carefully.

"No, don't say anything. We'll get you to a healer, someone who can help . . ." Talis looked up at the painted soldiers, who had gathered around them. He spoke to them, sharply, in their own language. The lizard-warrior scowled, but he gestured to his men. One pulled the spear from his matarh's back, and she screamed again. Nico hurled himself at the lizard-warrior, pummeling at the man's armor with his fist. The man grabbed Nico in one muscular arm and grunted something to Talis. "Nico!" Talis said. "They're going to help her. Please listen to me. You have to stop fighting them."

All the energy left him; he went limp in the lizard-warrior's grasp.

Two of the warriors crouched down; they tore strips from their clothing and bound it around his matarh's waist, around the wound. Then one of them gathered up his matarh in his arms; she groaned and her eyes rolled back in her head, but Nico could see that she was still breathing. One of her hands dangled; Nico wriggled in the lizard-warrior's grasp, and the man let him go. He ran and took his matarh's hand.

He held it, sobbing, as they walked quickly away from the plaza.

Niente

THEY HAD THE CITY.

Or, more properly, they held portions of it. Nessantico was too large and their force was too small to actually control the entire city. They had smashed it instead, they had used black sand to set it afire, they had sent the Garde Civile retreating to the north and south.

The city no longer belonged to the Kraljica and her people, but it was not the Tehuantins' either.

Niente was certain it would never be theirs.

"Well?" Zolin asked as Niente peered into the water of the scrying bowl.

"Patience, Tecuhtli," he told the man. "Patience." But he already knew. The vision had already passed and the water was simply water. But by pretending, he could decide what he wanted to say. By pretending, he could recover from the worst of the weariness and exhaustion the spell cost him.

He'd seen—again—in the midst of the great, ruined city, the dead Tecuhtli and the dead nahualli, and he'd felt again that shiver of certainty that he was seeing Zolin and himself. Nothing had changed. Axat still showed him the same future, the same path. Nothing had altered after this victory; Niente felt that nothing could alter it. It was fixed, as inevitable as the sunrise in the morning.

They were standing in the ruins of the temple, and Zolin sat on the throne the Kraljica had used. A spear had been thrust, butt foremost, into a crevice in the shattered tile floor next to the throne. The Kraljica's head had been set there, her single, glazed eye staring outward, the hair hanging down obscenely—her body was crumpled against the wall behind the throne where it had been tossed. A fire pit had been made in the middle of the room, fed with the wood of the temple's pews; thin, gray smoke drifted upward toward a sky that was beginning to turn purple. Tables had been erected around the pit, and a banquet was in progress, served by frightened Easterner prisoners. There was no particular need for their fright; Zolin and the other High Warriors would not have permitted any of them to be harmed. Yes, there would be the inevitable rapes and looting and killings, but the incidents would be few, and those who perpetrated them would be severely punished if they were caught. A few high-ranking offiziers would be sacrificed for the glory of Axat and Sakal, but no other prisoners would come to harm.

The Tehuantin were more lenient and kind victors than the Easterners had been when they came to the Hellins.

As the warriors feasted, Niente gazed into the scrying bowl near the pit. The firelight licked at Niente's skin, but the warmth couldn't touch the cold he felt within. He picked up the scrying bowl finally and tossed the water into the blazing coals, which hissed and steamed in response.

"So," Zolin said, "does Axat see me staying here? I think this a fine place. We could build a new city here, one like this land has never seen, one to rival Tlaxcala, and I could be Tecuhtli here, and the Easterners will serve us as they forced our cousins to serve them."

"I do see you staying here, Tecuhtli," Niente told him, and that was no more than the truth.

Zolin slapped the crystalline arms of the throne. He roared with delight, and the warriors gathered in the hall laughed with him. "You see!" he shouted to Niente. "All those worries—I told you, Nahual. I *told* you."

"You did, Tecuhtli," Niente told him.

Zolin leaned forward on the throne. "Did you see other battles? Did you see me taking new cities?"

Niente shook his head. "No," he answered. "And that wouldn't be wise, Tecuhtli. We have no more black sand at all. If we could replenish the warriors who have fallen, if I could bring more nahualli here . . ." He spread his hands. "I would tell the Tecuhtli . . ." he began, but there was a commotion at the end of the hall: the High Warrior Citlali, with a man alongside him—a man carrying a spell-staff. Niente squinted into the firelit gloom of the evening; it was not a nahualli that he recognized, and the man was dressed as one of the Easterners, the front of his clothing stained with blood. Still, that face . . .

"Talis?" Niente said. "Is that you?" The face—he looked

years older than he should, his face as ravaged by Axat's power as Niente's was, but Niente remembered the youth in the man's face.

"Niente?" Talis hurried forward and grasped Niente's forearm, his eyes searching Niente's face, no doubt as changed as his own. "By Axat, it's been a long, long time. You're the Nahual? Good. Good for you . . ." He saw Tecuhtli Zolin then and half-turned, bowing his head to Zolin. "Tecuhtli. I see that Necalli has fallen."

Niente was still looking at Talis. There was pain in the man's eyes that wasn't of the X'in Ka. "Are you hurt?" he asked, and Talis shook his head.

"No, it's . . ." He stopped, and Niente saw worry and sadness collapse in on the man. "I . . . I have a wife here, and a son. She's . . . been terribly injured. I need to get back to them . . ."

"We've taken her and the boy to the healing tent, Tecuhtli, Nahual," Citlali broke in. "They're doing what they can."

"Good," Zolin said. "And you may go to them in a moment, Talis. So *you* are the one the previous Nahual sent here? I know he told Tecuhtli Necalli that you were nearly as strong as Mahri—that you would have been a fine Nahual." Zolin glanced once over to Niente. "Perhaps that will end up being your fate. I've read your reports over the years; they've helped us understand and defeat the Easterners. For that, I'm grateful."

"Tecuhtli," Citlali said as Zolin paused, leaning back in his chair. "Talis has information you must know, about an army just to the east of the city. That is why I've brought him here."

Talis nodded, and Niente listened to him with growing dread as he talked about this army of Firenzcia, and the reputation of that country's military. Niente especially was distressed by the growing look of eagerness on Zolin's face. "Tecuhtli," Niente said, "this is what the scrying bowl was saying to me. We have done all that we came here to do. We should take ship now and return home before this army comes on us. We could raise a new army and come again with more ships and more warriors and nahualli the next time, and if you wish to sit on this throne as Tecuhtli of the East, we will place you here with enough resources to make that happen. But not now. We are too few—warriors and nahualli—for another great fight, especially without black sand."

Niente thought that, finally, he had made his point. Zolin grimaced as he sat on the throne, tapping fingers on the crystalline arm. He nodded, as if thinking.

But Talis then dashed any lingering hope. "There *is* black sand," Talis said. "Or rather, there are enough of the ingredients here in the city to make much of it. I know where it is."

Zolin leaned forward on the throne, his eyes widening so that the wings of the eagle danced on his face. "Where? Take us to it now."

"Tecuhtli, my wife . . . I need to go to her."

Niente knew how Zolin would react to that; he wasn't surprised. "We all have wives and family," the Tecuhtli retorted. "Our *duty* is here and now. Citlali, how is the woman?"

Citlali lifted a shoulder. "She is in the hands of those who know best what to do. There's nothing else that can be done."

"There. You see, Talis?" Zolin said. "You have your answer. I'm sorry for your wife's injuries, and I understand that you want to be with her. But your Tecuhtli has need of you also. Nahual Niente is correct—without more black sand, we will lose what we have gained. The black sand, nahualli, that is what is needed." Zolin leaned forward, elbows on knees. "The wife of a traitor would receive no help at all," he said.

Niente heard the next words as if they were the ringing of death chimes. "As you wish, Tecuhtli," Talis told him. "I will take you there."

"Good," Zolin said, standing. "Citlali, refresh yourself and get the warriors ready for more battle. Nahual Niente, you will do the same with the nahualli. In the meantime, I will speak with you, Talis, while we find this black sand."

~

Sergei ca'Rudka

SERGEI FOUND IT DIFFICULT to believe all that Karl and Varina told him. Sergei had seen the smoke of the fires in Nessantico and the wind had brought its scent to them and he knew that the city suffered, but this: Nessantico conquered, much of it in ruins . . .

He had not expected this.

There was too much he had not expected. Sergei was feeling very old and frail indeed.

"Archigos ca'Cellibrecca is *here?*" Karl said, and Sergei nodded in acknowledgment. Karl's face was hard and set, his voice clipped and grim. "Then take me to him, Sergei. Let that be the payment for releasing you from the Bastida. Just take me to him and walk away. You don't need to be involved in the rest."

"It's not that simple, Karl," he said.

"Actually, it *is* that simple," Karl retorted. "The man killed Ana, and I want justice for her murder."

"I can't give you that," Sergei told them. "Not here, and not now. But I can tell you that Hïrzg Jan has no great affection for the man. I think that the same can be said of A'Hïrzg Allesandra—at least for the moment. Karl, let me deal with this. Please." Sergei looked at Varina for support; she leaned close to Karl.

"Listen to him," she said. "Or listen to Ana—what would she tell you?"

The trio were in Sergei's tent in the Firenzcian encampment, where the two had been brought by the first soldiers they'd encountered. Sergei had been amazed and pleased to see the two Numetodo; after their separation, he'd been afraid that they'd been caught and imprisoned, or worse. If their tale had caused him distress, it was the thought of Nessantico laying ruined that was too painful to imagine.

He also knew that the Hïrzg and A'Hïrzg, at the very least, would also have been informed of their arrival; he was somewhat surprised he hadn't yet heard from either of them. And when Archigos Semini learned that the Ambassador of the Numetodo was in the encampment . . . He needed to prepare against that. Allesandra and Jan were another issue; he wasn't quite certain how they would respond. He'd do his best to protect Karl and Varina, but . . .

"Karl," he said. "I promise you this: when the time comes, I will help you with ca'Cellibrecca. The man is a blight and an insult to the robes Archigos Ana wore. We both agree on that. When the time comes, I will gladly help you make his death as painful as you like." Sergei almost smiled, thinking of Semini ensconced in the Bastida. Yes, that would be delightful. That would be . . . enjoyable.

Varina's eyes widened somewhat at the statement, but Karl, tight-lipped, nodded. There was a discreet clearing of a throat at the tent flap a moment later. "Enter," Sergei said, and the flap opened to reveal one of the Hïrzg's pages. "Regent, Hïrzg Jan requests that you bring your two guests—" the boy's eyes flicked across to Karl and Varina, "—to his tent. He's set a supper for them and wishes to hear what they have to say."

"Tell the Hïrzg that we'll be there directly," Sergei told the page, who bowed deeply and withdrew. "You've nothing to fear from Hïrzg Jan," he told the two. He hoped that was the truth. "I rather like the young man. In some ways, he reminds me of myself. . . ."

"Archigos Semini will counsel me that the Numetodo are heretics and liars, and dangerous to me physically as well as to my eternal soul," Hïrzg Jan said.

"Archigos Semini is a liar and a fool, and an ass besides," Sergei answered. "If I may be forgiven my bluntness, Hïrzg."

Jan grinned. "Sit," he said to Karl and Varina, gesturing to the table where bread and cheese and a pot of meat stew sat. Plates of dull pewter were set before them. "Enjoy the little comforts we have here in the field, since I can't give you the full hospitality of Firenzcia." When they hesitated, Jan's smile broadened. "I assure you that I share the opinion of the Regent when it comes to Archigos Semini."

Varina managed a smile; Karl still looked uncertain. "And what is the Hïrzg's opinion of the Numetodo?" he asked.

"One of the things that Regent ca'Rudka has taught me is that I should judge people not by what they are, but by who they are. I have no opinion on the Numetodo yet—until now, I've never met one." Jan gestured at their seats again. "Please . . ."

Sergei bowed. A moment later Karl did the same, and the three of them took their seats across from Jan. "Will the A'Hïrzg be joining us?" Sergei asked.

Jan's smile vanished at that. "No," he said, the single word nearly bitten off. Sergei waited, expecting more explanation; none came. He wondered what had happened between matarh and son—he'd had no more than a glimpse of Allesandra for a day and half now. Even while the army crawled at a maddeningly slow pace closer to Nessantico's walls, Allesandra had kept to a covered carriage, without either her son or the Archigos as company.

But he wasn't going to ask the Hïrzg to explain. Jan was looking instead to Karl and Varina. "I would like to know your story, from your own mouths," he said.

For the next turn of the glass, that is what they did, with Jan leading the two with occasional questions. Sergei listened for the most part—inwardly amused at some of the explanation that Karl left out from the tale. When Karl described the black sand, and how it had been used by the Westlanders in their assault on the city, and how the makings of more of it were in the city, Jan leaned forward.

"You say that this black sand is the key to the Westlanders' success? This is the same magic we've heard of them using in the Hellins?"

"It's not *magic*, Hïrzg," Karl said. "That's the interesting thing. It's alchemy. Varina has some idea—from what Talis has said and from the samples I brought back from Uly's rooms—of how to mix the black sand. I've seen—we've all seen—the terrible things it can do." A dark shadow seemed to pass over Karl's face with that, and Sergei knew what he was recalling: Ana's assassination. It was a horror that would never be erased from either of their minds. "They set the city afire with it; they killed hundreds. Perhaps thousands. Hïrzg, with this black sand, no army needs war-téni or their spells. No armor can withstand it, no number of swords can prevail against it."

"And you know where the cache of this black sand is?"

Karl nodded. "I do. So does Varina. We can take you there, Hïrzg. But the Westlanders will be after it also. Talis . . . I suspect that he may be already leading them to it. They may *already* have it."

"Hïrzg," Sergei interrupted. "I understand why you've let your army idle here. I might have made the same decision, if I were you—even though my heart breaks to see the city burning and to hear that the Westlanders are trampling in the ruins of the places I loved most of all in this world." He rubbed at his false nose, saw Jan staring at the motion, and dropped his hand. "But—if you're willing to listen to my counsel at all—I would tell you that the time to wait has passed. I've witnessed the effects of this black sand, too. If the Westlanders have time to create more of it, then it's your own soldiers who will pay the price for hesitation. Hïrzg, listen to what my friends are telling you. The Garde Civile of Nessantico has been defeated. That battle's over. We must strike now—not at Nessantico, but at those who defeated her: before they come to Firenzcia."

Sergei thought that his plea would have no effect. Jan was looking away, his gaze searching the firelit canvas above him as if an answer were written there in smoke. The young man sighed once. Then he clapped his hands and a page entered.

"Call the starkkapitän to come here," he said to the boy. "There are immediate preparations I need him to make. Hurry!"

Jan ca'Vörl

H E HAD LISTENED to the grand, glorious tales of war many times over the years: from his great-vatarh Jan; from his vatarh; from onczios and older acquaintances; and most recently from Fynn. Even from his matarh, who told him how Great-Vatarh had complimented her from a young age on her knowledge of military strategy.

He was beginning to realize that these tales had been concoctions and false memories or sometimes outright lies.

Until today, Jan had never ridden into a true battle. Until today, his knowledge of the martial skills had been intellectual and safe. He'd been shown how to ride, how to handle a sword, how to use a spear or bow from horseback, how to protect himself against another chevarittai or against a footman. He had been in mock sword fights, had been part of military maneuvers. He'd been schooled in the craft of war: the tactics to use against an adversary who had the higher ground or the lower, or who had more soldiers or less, or more war-těni or less. He knew which formation was supposed to be best against another.

It was what any young male of his rank would have been taught.

War, in Jan's mind, had been a very neat and tidy exercise. He'd known—intellectually—that it couldn't possibly be that linear and efficient. He'd understood that.

But . . . he had not known that war would be this messy. This chaotic. This real.

No one in the Firenzcian army was under the misapprehension that Jan—like Fynn, like his namesake the old Hïrzg Jan—would be the one to truly general the army in this important attack. They knew the strategy was that of Starkkapitän ca'Damont, with aid from the Regent ca'Rudka and input from the A'Hïrzg and the two Numetodo who had come to the encampment from the burning city. They knew that it would be Archigos Semini who would command the war-téni.

Jan would be there, and the command banner would fly from the Garde Hïrzg and the chevarittai around him, and he would press forward just behind the front lines of his forces as Fynn and the former Hïrzg Jan had done before him. But Jan would look to the Starkkapitän before he gave his orders. Jan knew the wisdom of that; he knew that the rest of the offiziers and chevarittai knew it as well. Frankly, he was comfortable with it; Jan could feel his inexperience and he was not so arrogant as to insist on bungling this assault.

The entrance into Nessantico started well enough. A crescent blade, the Firenzcian forces pushed into the city through all the gates on the eastern side of the city. There had been no resistance; to the contrary, their appearance was greeted with cheers and huzzahs from the remaining populace and scattered remnants of the Nessantican Garde Civile. A few chevarittai of the Holdings had even crept out from hiding to swell their ranks. After a turn of the glass inside the city walls, Jan began to hope that this was how it would continue: that they would march unchallenged all the way to the western boundaries of the city to find the Westlander forces in full retreat.

He was sweating in the heat of the day under his armor and longed for nothing more than to rid himself of the heavy burden of steel links. That seemed to be the worst discomfort of victory.

"What way, Ambassador?" Jan asked Karl, riding with his entourage along with his matarh, Varina and Sergei.

"North for a few cross streets," the Numetodo answered, pointing, "then several blocks eastward."

Jan nodded. The Firenzcian army swelled along the Avi. The sun shone brightly. It was a fine day. They had already won, and he felt the confidence to give an order of his own. "Starkkapitän," Jan said to Starkkapitän ca'Damont, "I will take half the Garde Hïrzg with me, as well as the Regent and the Numetodo. I leave you in charge of the army. Do what you need to do to secure this area of the Avi and the city. Then you and the A'Hïrzg proceed south to the Isle a'Kralji and make certain we hold the Isle and the eastern ponticas. If there's a problem, send a messenger to me immediately. In turn, I will send a rider as soon as we locate the black sand and know the situation there."

"Jan. Hïrzg." His matarh was frowning, while ca'Damont merely looked uncomfortable. "I don't think—"

"I have given my orders," Jan snapped, interrupting her. "Starkkapitän? Do you see an issue with them?"

Ca'Damont shook his head once. He barked out quick orders. "I will meet with you later, Matarh," Jan said. "On the Isle."

Allesandra looked unconvinced. He thought she was going to argue further, but she only glared at him. He saw her glance once at Sergei; the Regent gave her the barest of shrugs under his own armor. His nose sent sparks of sun chasing across his face.

His matarh finally inclined her head. "As you wish, my Hïrzg," she said. "My Hïrzg," not "my son." He could hear the irritation in that. She yanked hard on the reins of her horse and started south, a quartet of Garde Hïrzg and one of the war-téni closing around her belatedly. The starkkapitän gave a salute. "Cénzi's guidance to you, my Hïrzg," he said. "I will make certain the A'Hïrzg remains safe." He started to move away, then pulled up on the reins. "Fynn made an excellent choice in you," he said to Jan. "Be careful, Hïrzg Jan."

Starkkapitän ca'Damont saluted again and moved away, the greater part of their entourage moving with him. Jan looked around at the others. "Let's find this black sand," he said to them. "Ambassador ca'Vliomani—the lead is yours."

Karl led Jan's squadron north along the Avi, the soldiers they passed saluting the Hïrzg and his banner, then turned left down a more narrow street, leaving behind the army. The jingling of their armor and the stolid, steel-clad *clop* of their horses' hooves on the cobbles was the loudest sound along the street. There were no more faces in the windows, no one visible up the curving way. Some of the doors to the buildings they passed were open; many of them forcibly. Trash littered the avenue. They passed several bodies: people a few days dead from the look of them, their corpses bloated and with limbs thrust at stiff, strange angles, maggot-encrusted and swarming with flies. Jan stared at them as they passed; he noticed Sergéi doing the same, with an odd intensity.

Not long ago, these had been living, breathing people, perhaps hurrying to lovers, carrying their children, shopping for food in the markets or drinking in the taverns, carrying on with their lives. He doubted that they'd expected those lives to end so quickly and finally. He doubted they'd expected to turn into transient, accidental monuments to warfare.

He sniffed, unable to keep their stench from his nose— he wondered if Sergei could smell them at all. He clenched his sword tighter in his hand and wrapped the reins more tightly around his left hand.

To the south, they all heard a sudden rumbling like thunder, and faint shouting. Sergei, next to Jan, glanced that way worriedly. "I think, Hïrzg," he said, "that a battle has started. Perhaps we should return."

Jan shook his head. "Ambassador, how far are we from this place?" he asked.

"Another two cross streets," ca'Vliomani replied. "No more."

"Then we'll go on."

Sergei pressed his lips tightly together, but made no other response.

They continued, coming to another, even smaller lane, where Karl paused and rose up in his saddle. Glancing down the narrow street, Jan saw a battered, ancient sign hanging from a building to the right: a badly-rendered swan was drawn in red paint on the boards.

"There," ca'Vliomani called out to Jan and the others. "We should—"

He got no further.

From the left, from the right, several dozen painted warriors came shrieking toward them. The next minutes dissolved into a chaos Jan would remember for the rest of his life.

. . . a coruscation of blinding light from the front of the group, then another, and he realized that Karl and Varina had both released spells. He heard screams . . .

. . . the chevarittai at Jan's right was taken from his saddle by a leaping Westlander, and the man's horse rammed hard against Jan's leg. His right leg was pinned between the two horses and he shouted at the pain that shot through the limb despite the protection of his greaves. He yanked at the reins of his horse . . .

. . . but there was more movement to his right and behind him even as he did that. He saw steel and brought his sword across his mount's body almost too late—enough that the blow that would have taken him above the straps of his cuisse was deflected, but the Westlander's blade instead chopped deep into his destrier's rear leg. The horse whinnied in terror and pain. Jan saw the horse's eyes go wide, felt the horse's leg give out under him, and he was falling . . .

. . . "To the Hïrzg!" he heard someone call. Jan was on the ground with a confusion of legs—both equine and human—around him. He pushed himself up quickly (his right leg sending fire up his spine at the abuse). There was a Westlander coming at him, and Jan managed to find the hilt of his sword, lift the heavy steel, and thrust underneath the chest plate of the man's strange armor. He felt his blade enter flesh. It caught briefly, and Jan—grunting, feeling his mouth stretched in a rictus of fury—twisted and pushed, and the blade went suddenly in. The Westlander, impaled, still completed his strike, but the vambraces laced around Jan's forearms took the brunt, though he thought that his right arm might have been broken by the blow. He tried to pull his sword from the man, but could not, and the man's dead weight nearly pulled the weapon entirely from his grip, which had gone numb and dead itself . . .

. . . Another Westlander shrilled to his left, and Jan pulled desperately at his sword again, though he knew it would be too late. But another sword—a Firenzcian one—sliced across the man's throat, nearly severing the head. Jan was spattered with hot blood . . .

. . . . And hands were lifting him. "Are you all right, my Hïrzg?" someone asked, and Jan nodded. His right hand was tingling, but seemed to have returned to life. He clenched the fingers, working them in the mailed glove, then reached down and pulled his sword free. He turned . . .

. . . he saw a trio of Westlanders gathered as a shield around another of the painted warriors, this one with a bird tattooed over his shaven skull and face. Sergei was there, his sword rising and falling, but the Firenzcian soldier next to him fell, his hand taken from his wrist. Jan rushed toward that gap, not thinking but only reacting . . .

. . . and somehow he was past the guard and in front of the bird-marked Warrior. The Westlander's armor turned Jan's first cut, and the hard bronze pommel of the man's sword slammed into Jan's chin underneath his helm. He went staggering backward, tasting blood . . .

. . . As he saw the bird-warrior parry Sergei's attacking sword . . .

. . . . as he charged again at the man, grimacing and grunting, and the Westlander couldn't defend against both of them at once. It was Jan's blade that slithered through, that found the chink between the rounded bands of the man's armor and entered him. The Westlander gaped as if surprised. Jan heard a voice somewhere call out a strange name: "Tecuhtli!" as the man fell to his knees. Sergei's sword followed Jan's, striking the man in the neck and head. The bird-warrior went down onto the blood-spattered cobbles, facedown . . .

. . . and it was over except for the roaring of his pulse in his ears.

Jan realized that he was breathing hard and fast, that his heart was pounding so furiously that it threatened to burst from his rib cage, that his leg and both arms ached, that he was liberally coated with gore, and that at least some of the blood was his own. He was standing wide-legged and bent over, breathing hard. His stomach heaved; he swallowed hard against the searing bile, forcing himself not to be sick. He felt Sergei's hand clap him on his armored shoulders. He blinked, looking around him: there were at least a dozen bodies on the ground, some of them clad in the black-and-silver livery of Firenzcia. A few were still twitching; as Jan watched, those of the Garde Civile were dispatching those of the Westlanders who were still alive. There were streams of blood trailing from the bodies, and entrails spilled on the street like obscene sausages.

Karl and Varina were untouched—the bodies nearest them were charred and blackened; there was a smell of cooked meat in the air. Sergei's false nose was entirely gone and his left cheek had been laid open by a cut; where the nose had been, the flesh was mottled and the cavities of Sergei's head gaped open, making his face look terrifyingly like a skull. The nausea hit Jan again, and this time the world seemed to spin a little around him. He put his sword tip on the ground and leaned heavily on it.

"Tecuhtli!" Jan heard the call again, and this time a man stepped out from the building where the sign of the red swan hung, no more than a half dozen strides from where Jan and the others stood. He held a glass flask in his right hand, packed with dark granules; in his left was a gnarled walking stick. The man stopped, as if startled by the display of carnage before him.

"Talis . . ." Jan heard Karl breathe the name: a wonderment, a curse, a spell. "Black sand . . ."

The man scowled. He hefted the jar in his right hand, he brought his arm back as if to throw it. Jan wondered what it would feel like to die, and whether he might meet Great-Vatarh Jan and Fynn there.

A woman rushed from the alley behind the tavern, a blur of brown and gray, so quickly that none of them had time to react. As Talis lifted his hand, she grasped his hair and yanked his head back. Talis' mouth opened, gaping like a fish in a market, and red followed silver as she slid a knife over his throat. A second mouth gaped wider than the first, vomiting blood. The glass jars fell from Talis' hands, shattering on the ground but without exploding. The woman leaned down over the body—she seemed to be placing something hurriedly on the man's eye—and Jan had a good look at her face through the tangled, matted hair.

His heart leaped in his chest. His breath caught. "Elissa?" he whispered.

The young woman's head came up. Her eyes widened as she saw him, and though she said nothing, he heard the intake of her breath. She snatched something from Talis' face—Jan caught a glimpse of a pale white stone between her fingers. She ran into the alleyway from which she'd come. One of the soldiers began running in pursuit after her. "No!" Jan called after the man. "Let her go!"

The soldier stopped. Jan heard the whispers around him: "The White Stone . . ."

The White Stone . . .

No, he wanted to tell them, that couldn't be, because

that person had been Elissa, whom he'd loved. It couldn't be because the White Stone had assassinated Fynn, whom he'd also loved. That couldn't be.

Yet, somehow, impossibly, it was.

It was.

~

Niente

THE SHIP WAS CROWDED with those fleeing the city, with those from other ships now canted over and half-submerged in the river. The deck was slick with water and blood and vomit. The water around them was dotted with bloated, stiff bodies—Easterners and Tehuantin alike. There were wounded warriors and nahualli sprawled everywhere on the deck, moaning in the dying sunlight; those crew members who were still able climbing the masts to loose the sails and tighten the lines. The anchor, groaning and protesting, was hauled up from the muck of the river's bottom, and the ship's captain screamed orders. Slowly, far too slowly for Niente, the city was beginning to fall behind them as the river's currents and the wind bore them away.

Niente watched from the high stern of the warship, standing at Citlali's right hand. The High Warrior's body was decorated with the black-red tracks of clotted sword cuts, and he leaned heavily on a broken spear shaft as he glared back at the city.

"You were right, Nahual," Citlali said to Niente. "Axat's vision—you saw it correctly."

Niente nodded. He still marveled that he was here, that he was alive, that Axat had somehow, impossibly spared him. He could still see the vision from the scrying bowl—only now, it wasn't his face on the dead nahualli who lay next to Tecuhtli Zolin, but Talis'. Axat had spared him. He might yet see home, if the storms of the Inner Sea allowed it. He would hold his wife in his arms again; he would hug his children and watch them play. Niente took a long, shuddering breath.

"I wasn't strong enough," he said to Citlali. "I wasn't the Nahual I should have been. If I'd spoken more strongly to Zolin, if I'd seen the visions more clearly . . ."

"Had you done that, nothing significant would have changed," Citlali answered. "Zolin wouldn't have listened to you, Nahual, no matter what you told him. All he could hear were the gods singing for revenge. He wouldn't have listened to you. You would have been removed as Nahual and you'd have died here, too."

"Then it was all a waste."

Citlali laughed—humorless and dry. "A waste? Hardly. You have no imagination, Nahual Niente, and you are no warrior. A waste? No death in battle is wasted. Look at their great city." He pointed eastward to where the sun shone golden on the broken spires and lanced through the curling smoke of the remaining fires. "We took their city," Citlali said. "We took their heart." He held his hand out, palm upward as if clutching something. His fingers slowly closed. "Do you think they'll ever forget this, Nahual? No. They'll shiver in the night and start at a sudden sound in terror, thinking that it's us, returned. They'll remember this for hand upon hand of generations. They will never feel safe again—and they would be right."

Citlali spat over the rail into the river. His spittle was flecked with blood. "We took their heart, and we will keep it," he said. "I make that promise to Sakal here, and you are my witness—let His eye see my words and mark them. We will keep what we've taken from them. A Tecuhtli will stand again where Zolin fell."

He clapped Niente on the back, hard enough that Niente staggered. "What do you think of that, Nahual?"

Niente stared at the city, dwindling in the boat's wake. "I will look in the scrying bowl tonight, Tecuhtli Citlali" he said, "and I will tell you what Axat says."

~

The White Stone

THE NEW VOICE in her head screamed and wailed and raged, speaking half in the language of Nessantico and half in a language she didn't understand at all. The others in her head laughed and hooted.

"Your lover Jan . . . What a pleasant vision he has of you now!"

"Do you think he would marry the filthy assassin he saw?"

"He laid with a murderer and now she carries his child."

"He's glimpsed the truth. I hope you always remember the horror on his face when he recognized you."

That last one was Fynn, pleased and smug. "Shut up!" she shouted at them, but they only laughed all the louder, their voices crowding out what she heard with her own ears.

She'd followed Talis and the Westlander leader from the Isle back to the Red Swan after she'd made certain that Nico seemed to be safe. She was angry, furious with Talis—he'd broken his promise to her. The Numetodo . . . they might be disgusting heretics, but they had treated Nico kindly and with respect, the woman especially.

But Talis . . .

Talis had betrayed Nico and because of that Nico's matarh lay near death, and she had told Talis what the price would be. She had told him, and she would exact payment. The White Stone always kept her word.

So she had followed him, when—all out of nowhere—the sounds of battle had erupted from the east and she'd watched the Westlander leader arrange his men to ambush the Firenzcian chevarittai and soldiers. Suddenly there was far too much fighting going on, too much movement for her to make a move, and she was worried now about Nico and whether he was truly safe and she wanted desperately to run back to him, afraid that following Talis might have been a mistake. But she'd seen Talis slip from the room into which he'd gone and rush out into the street, and she'd followed. She watched the confrontation and she'd seen the chance. She slashed her blade across his throat and she felt him die as he dropped the flask of dark powder And as she laid him down and started to put the stone on his eye, she'd glimpsed *him*.

Jan.

The shock had been palpable. She'd felt it as strongly as if her heart had been placed directly on a bed of hidden, red-hot coals. Jan: he stood there, and she had witnessed the slow recognition on his face. His expression had frightened her. It was full of shock and affection, of yearning and horror. Seeing him was awful and wonderful at the same moment, and she had wanted to run to him, had wanted to take his hand and place it on her swelling stomach and whisper, *Here, darling. This is the life we have created together. This is what our love has made;* she wanted also to run, to flee, to hide her face and pretend this revelation had never happened.

The second impulse was the stronger.

She'd taken the white stone from Talis' eye and she'd fled, wanting Jan to follow her and afraid that he actually would.

She didn't stop until she reached the Pontica Kralji. There were no strange, bronze-colored men there; none who were living, anyway, though their bodies littered the ground. She could see soldiers in the black and silver of Firenzcia moving everywhere on the streets—causing Fynn to exclaim excitedly inside her head—and she carefully made her way across the Pontica and slid quickly into cover on the island. That was easy; so many walls tumbled down, so many fire-scarred buildings. She went to the gardener's cottage on the palais estates where they'd taken Nico and his matarh, where the healer for the Westlander had worked over her injured body.

The healer and all the Westlander soldiers were gone, but her fears eased when she saw that Nico was still there, holding onto his matarh's hand as he crouched next to the table on which she lay—it must have once been one of the dining tables from the palais, still covered with fine, lacy damask, now bloodstained and filthy. She could see Serafina's chest rise with a slow breath, but her eyes were still closed and she seemed unresponsive.

"Nico," she said, and he started, his hand clenching his matarh's tightly.

"Oh," he said a moment later. His face brightened slightly. He sniffed and ran his hand across his nose. "Elle. It's you."

She nodded and came to him. She clasped her own hands around his and his matarh's. She saw him stare at the blood that mottled her skin. "We need to go, Nico," she told him.

"I can't leave Matarh," he said. "Talis will be back soon."

She shook her head. Her hands pressed tighter against his. His skin was warm, so warm, and she felt the child within her jump at the touch—the stirring of life, the quickening. She gasped slightly at the feel. "No," she told him. "I'm afraid Talis is dead, Nico."

She saw the tears start in his eyes and his lower lip trembled. Then he sniffed again and blinked. "That's the truth?"

She nodded. "The truth, Nico. I'm sorry. I'm very sorry."

He was crying fully now, the words coming out between the sobbing breath. "But my matarh . . . I can't . . . They just left her . . . She's asleep and I . . . can't wake her up. . . ."

"Your matarh would want you to go with me. Look at her, Nico. She loves you so much, I know she does, but I don't know if she's ever going to wake up, and the city is full of soldiers and death. She would want you to go with me because I can keep you safe. I *will* keep you safe."

"But I did this to her," Nico said. "It was my fault. I want her to know that I'm sorry."

She pressed Nico's hand around his matarh's. "She knows. Nico, we need to hurry."

She pulled his hand away from his matarh's, prying away the fingers gently. He released his grip reluctantly but without protest. "Give her a kiss," she said. "She'll feel it, and she'll know."

Nico stood up. Leaning over his matarh's body, he gave her a kiss on the cheek. He put her hand, dangling over the side, on the table, and patted it. He looked back over his shoulder, then, his eyes swimming with tears that didn't fall.

"I promise you, Nico—I'll find her again if she lives and bring her back to us. I promise you."

He nodded. She held out her hand to him, and he took it. She brought him to her, hugging him briefly, then releasing him with a sigh. She took his hand again.

"It's time," she told him.

Together, hand in hand, they made their way from the smoldering, ruined city.

~

Allesandra ca'Vörl

"HERE YOU ARE, MATARH. It's all yours. I hope it makes you happy."

Jan's words were scalding water poured over her. They burned and seared her, delivered with an appalling and terrifying scorn and distance. He gestured grandly and mockingly in the direction of the Sun Throne. Allesandra stared at the massive piece of carved crystal, sitting—strangely misplaced—in the middle of the ruined Old Temple. The throne had been cracked and badly repaired; a cloth with strange geometric patterns was draped over it, the ruins of the shattered dome and its lantern littered the broken tiles behind, and all around the hall were the remnants of some feast. Rats prowled the corners of the room, and the air stank of smoke and rotting meat. Near the rear there was a body, with one of the tapestries thrown hastily over it.

Allesandra knew whose body was under the covering: Sigourney, her staked head lolling separately near the throne.

The Regent and the two Numetodo were standing limned in sunlight by the open doors of the temple, too far away to hear her and Jan's conversation. Starkkapitän ca'Damont called out orders in the temple's plaza, sending out patrols to make certain that all the Westlander troops were gone from the city and to stop any looting by the survivors.

Allesandra heard the scrape of footsteps at the temple doors; she glanced over her shoulder to see Archigos Semini stepping carefully over the rubble on the floor. Jan saw him also. "Ah, Archigos Semini," Jan said. "I'm glad you're here, since this is also yours. I give you Nessantico. You won't be in Brezno any longer."

"My Hïrzg?" Semini asked, glancing worriedly from Allesandra to Jan. "I was considering that perhaps the Archigos should reside in Brezno now, given the destruction here. I could assign an a'téni to Nessantico . . ."

"Oh, I agree," Jan said, and his smile made Allesandra shiver. It was the grim, bloodless smile her vatarh used when he was angry. She had seen it many times in her childhood, and in her adulthood after he had finally brought her back to Firenzcia. Now here the scornful, mocking expression was again, returned. Jan's face was smeared with soot and blood, and his right arm and leg were heavily bandaged. He limped, he seemed barely able to lift his sword arm. She wondered what her son had seen, what he was feeling. She longed to fold him into her arms and comfort him as she had when he'd been a child, but he stood a careful step from her as if he were afraid of exactly that. "You see, there *will* be an Archigos in Brezno. As to whether there's one in Nessantico, well . . ." Jan shrugged, coldly. "That's your choice. You might wish to claim the title and hold it for a while—though you've always said you wanted a re-united Faith. Or perhaps the Archigos in Brezno will let *you* be the a'téni here in Nessantico, though I'll advise the Archigos against that."

"Hïrzg?" ca'Cellibrecca spluttered. His face had gone the color of the white that sprinkled his dark beard and hair, the contrast strong. "I don't understand."

"Perhaps Matarh will explain it to you, since this is now her city," Jan said.

Allesandra stared at the throne. She felt dead, numbed. If someone cut her now, she thought, she would feel nothing, not even the heat of the blood on her skin. "My son gives me Nessantico, but he has informed me that Firenzcia will not be rejoining the Holdings," she told Semini, and her voice was as dead as her emotions.

"Consider it my wedding gift, Matarh," he told her. "For the wedding I never had, with the woman you sent away from me."

"I was protecting you, Jan," Allesandra told him, though there was no energy to her protest. "Elissa was a fraud. An impostor."

"I know," Jan told her. "She'd been hired to kill Fynn."

"What?" That brought her head up and caused fire to course through her briefly. Allesandra swung to face him. "What are you saying? The White Stone killed Fynn."

"Indeed, she did," Jan told her, with that same infuriating smile. "Let me tell you something you might not know,

Matarh, though you should have: Elissa was the White Stone. She used me in order to get to Fynn."

"That's not possible," Allesandra said. It couldn't be; it wasn't possible. The voice she'd heard, the woman go-between; no, it wasn't possible, yet . . . She remembered the voice, higher than she might have expected for a man. And she had never *seen* the Stone. She had just assumed . . .

"Believe whatever you need to believe," Jan was saying. "I really don't care." He gestured again toward the throne. "Take your new seat, Matarh. Don't be shy. You've waited for it for so long, after all, and Regent ca'Rudka has re-nounced all claim to the title. You can have Semini give you a blessing. Maybe the ca'-and-cu' will come back to the city now, so you can tell them that there's a new Kraljica."

Jan started to walk away toward the open doors. She took a step and caught at his wounded arm. "Jan. Son . . ."

He wrenched his arm away from her, grimacing with ob-vious pain as he did so, and that was more an agony to her than any sword cut. "*Sit*, Matarh. Take your Sun Throne. You have what you've always wanted. Enjoy the gift I've given you."

With that, he walked away toward ca'Rudka and the others. She watched him leave, wanting to call out to him, to keep him from leaving, to stop the pain.

She didn't. She watched him reach the bright doorway, and she heard his laugh as he clapped ca'Rudka on the back with his uninjured hand. The four of them walked away and sunlight collapsed around them.

Semini was staring up at the sky where Brunelli's dome had once been, his breath loud in his nose. Allesandra walked slowly to the Sun Throne.

She sat.

In the depths of thick crystal, there was no light. No re-sponse at all. The throne remained sullenly dark.

Epilogue: Nessantico

SHE WAS SHATTERED. She was broken.

She had been scorched by fire and magic; she had been slashed with steel. She had been looted and ravaged. Her greatest treasures were damaged or gone. The buildings that had been her crown were tumbled ruins and piles of blackened stone. The jeweled necklace of the Avi a'Parete no longer glistened in the night. Now there were only stars in the sky above, gleaming mockingly down at her darkness.

Half her population was dead or had fled. She had felt for the first time in long centuries the tread of conquering soldiers along her streets: had felt them not once, but twice. A Kraljica sat on the Sun Throne, but she looked out on an empire that had withered and shrunk.

There was no denying the gauntness of the visage that stared back at the city from the filthy mirror of the A'Sele: the city's face was a crone's face, a blasted face, a face of scars and open wounds and pain. There was no beauty here, no glory, no wonder.

That was gone, as if it had never been.

When the rains came, as they did frequently that autumn, it was as if the entire world wept for her: the city, the woman. The storms washed away the soot and extinguished the fires, but they could not heal. They cooled and soothed, but they could not restore. They flushed away the bodies and garbage and soil that choked the river, but their thundering could not shatter the memories.

The memories would stay.

They would stay for a long, long time. . . .

Appendices

PRIMARY VIEWPOINT CHARACTERS
(by rank, then alphabetical order)

Audric ca'Dakwi *[AHD-ric-Kah-DAWK-whee]*
The Kraljiki in Nessantico.

Sergei ca'Rudka *[SARE-zhay Kah-ROOD-kah]*
The Regent of Nessantico until Audric comes into his majority at sixteen.

Karl ca'Vliomani *[Karhl Kah-vlee-oh-MAHN-ee]*
Ambassador of the Numetodo from the Isle of Paeti, friend of Archigos Ana and Regent ca'Rudka.

Allesandra ca'Vörl *[Ahl-ah-SAHN-drah Kah-VOORL]*
Daughter of the Hïrzg of Firenzcia, and once the heir to that title herself.

Jan ca'Vörl *[Yahn Kah-VOORL]*
Son of Allesandra and Pauli.

Enéas cu'Kinnear *[Eh-NIGH-us Coo-ken-EAR]*
An offizier with the Garde Civile in the Hellins, fighting the Westlanders.

Varina ci'Pallo *[Vah-REE-nah Kee-PAHL-low]*
A Numetodo.

Nico Morel *[NEE-koh Mohr-ELL]*
A young boy living in Oldtown.

Niente *[Nee-EHN-tay]*
The Nahual (chief spellcaster) of the Westlanders
(Tehuantin).

The White Stone
An assassin.

SUPPORTING CAST
(by rank, then alphabetical order)

The Ca':

Karin ca'Belgradin *[KAH-reen Kah-bell-GRAH-deen]*
Allesandra's great-vatarh, once Hïrzg of Firenzcia.
Died of Southern Fever.

Francesca ca'Cellibrecca *[Frahn-SESS-ka
Kah-sell-ee-BREK-ah]*
Daughter of Orlandi ca'Cellibrecca, wife of Semini.

Orlandi ca'Cellibrecca *[Orh-LAHN-dee
Kah-sell-eh-BREK-ah]*
Archigos Orlandi I, the first of the Breznoian Archigi.
Deceased.

Semini ca'Cellibrecca *[SEH-meen-eh Kah-sell-ee-BREK-ah]*
(née cu'Kohnle) The Archigos in Brezno. Married to
Francesca.

Justi ca'Dakwi *[JUSS-tee Kah-DAWK-whee]*
(née ca'Ludovici, nee ca'Mazzak) Kraljiki Justi III, also
known as Justi the One-Legged, son of Kraljica Marguerite I (ca'Ludovici), vatarh of Marguerite, Audric,
and Elzbet ca'Dakwi. Deceased.

Marie ca'Dakwi *[MAH-ree Kah-DAWK-whee]*
Matarh of Marguerite, Audric, and Elzbet ca'Dakwi.
Deceased.

Armen ca'Damont *[ARR-mhen Kah-dah-MHONT]*
Starkkapitän of the Firenzcian Garde Civile.

Sinclair ca'Egan *[Sinn-CLARE Kah-EE-ghan]*
Head of the Council of Ca' in Brezno.

Kenne ca'Fionta *[KENN-ah Kah-fee-ON-tah]*
A'Téni of Nessantico within the Concénzia Faith.

Aleron ca'Gerodi *[ALH-er-onn Kah-ger-OH-dee]*
Member of the Council of Ca'.

Petrus ca'Helfier *[PET-roos Kah-HELL-fear]*
Once Commandant of the Holdings forces in the Hellins.

Marguerite ca'Ludovici *[Marhg-u-REET Kah-loo-doh-VEE-kee]*
Former Kraljica of Nessantico, the "Généra a'Pace."

Sigourney ca'Ludovici *[Si-GOHR-nee Kah-loo-doh-VEE-kee]*
Second cousin to Audric ca'Dakwi, twin sister of Donatien ca'Sibelli, and a member of the Council of Ca'.

Meric ca'Matin *[MAHR-ick Kah-mah-TEEN]*
An a'offizier with the Holdings army in the Hellins.

Odil ca'Mazzak *[OH-deel Kah-MAH-zak]*
Member of the Council of Ca'.

Dhosti ca'Millac *[DOST-ee Kah-MEE-lok]*
Archigos of the Concénzia Faith prior to Archigos Ana. A dwarf.

Villa ca'Ostheim *[VEEH-ahh Kay-OHST-hime]*
A'Téni of Villembouchure, and a war-téni.

Ana ca'Seranta *[AHN-ah Kah-sir-AHN-tah]*
Archigos of Nessantico.

Donatien ca'Sibelli *[Don-AY-shun Kah-see-BEHL-lee]*
Second cousin to Audric ca'Dakwi, and twin brother of Sigourney ca'Ludovici. Commandant of the Garde Civile in the Hellins.

Colin ca'Vliomani *[KOHL-inn Kah-vlee-oh-MAHN-ee]*
Son of Karl, living on the Isle of Paeti.

Nilles ca'Vliomani *[NIGH-ulhs Kah-vlee-oh-MAHN-ee]*
Son of Karl, living on the Isle of Paeti.

Fynn ca'Vörl *[Finn Kah-VOORL]*
Hïrzg of Firenzcia.

Greta ca'Vörl *[GREH-tah Kah-VOORL]*
Matarh of Hïrzgin Allesandra.

Jan ca'Vörl *[Yahn Kah-VOORL]*
(née ca'Belgradin) Vatarh of Hïrzgin Allesandra.

Pauli ca'Vörl *[PAHL-lee Kah-VOORL]*
(née ca'Xielt) Husband of Allesandra, son of the Gyula of West Magyaria.

Toma ca'Vörl *[TOH-ma Kah-VOORL)*
Son of Jan and Greta. Deceased.

Valeri ca'Weber *[Vahl-AIR-ree Kah-VEH-ber]*
A'Téni in Prajnoli, North Nessantico.

The Cu':

Cu'Brunelli *[Koo-Broon-ELL-ee]*
A famous architect in the Holdings, responsible for the design of the great dome of the Old Temple.

Aris cu'Falla *[AIR-iss Koo-FAH-lah]*
Commandant of the Garde Kralji.

Andreas cu'Görin *[Ahn-DREH-us Koo-GOHR-ren]*
Ambassador for the Firenzcian Holdings to the Holdings of Nessantico.

Helmad cu'Göttering *[HELL-mahd Koo-GERR-tehr-ring]*
Commandant of the Garde Brezno.

Petros cu'Magnaoi *[PET-rhoss Koo-mag-NAY-oy]*
Kenne's longtime companion and lover, an u'téni in the Faith.

Aubri cu'Ulcai *[AHH-bree Koo-UHL-kie]*
Commandant of the Garde Civile in Nessantico.

The Ci':

Edric ci'Blaylock *[EDD-reek Kee-BLAY-lok]*
Maister (teacher) for Audric.

Sala ci'Fallin *[SAHL-ah Kee-FAHL-een]*
Kenne's O'Téni assistant.

Alia ci'Gilan *[AHH-lee-ah Kee-GHEE-ahn]*
Wife of Mika ci'Gilan.

Mika ci'Gilan *[MEE-kah Kee-GHEE-ahn]*
A'Morce (Head) of the Numetodo in Nessantico.

Edouard ci'Recroix *[EDD-ward Kee-reh-KROI]*
A famous artist.

Gairdi ci'Tomisi *[GAIR-dee Kee-Tome-EES-ahh]*
A Firenzcian agent in Nessantico.

The Ce':

Sala ce'Fallan *[SAH-lah Keh-FAHL-linn]*
An o'téni and aide to Archigos Kenne.

Roderigo ce'Messina *[Rod-eh-REE-goh Keh-Meh-SEE-nah]*
Chief aide to the Hïrzg.

The Unranked:

Alisa Morel *[Ah-LEES-sah more-ELL]*
Serafina's sister and Nico's tantzia in Ville Paisli.

Bayard Morel *[BAY-ardh more-ELL]*
Serafina's marriage-brother and Nico's onczio in Ville Paisli.

Serafina Morel *[Sair-ah-FEEN-ah more-ELL]*
Matarh of Nico.

Talis Posti *[TAWL-iss POHS-tee]*
The lover of Serafina Morel.

Citlali *[See-TAHL-lee]*
A general of the army.

Darkmavis *[Dark-MAY-viss]*
A well-known composer.

Xaria *[Shah-ree-ahh]*
Niente's wife.

Mahri *[MAH-ree]*
A Tehuantin spellcaster who lived in Nessantico during the end of the reign of Kraljica Marguerite.

Marlon *[Marr-LOAN]*
One of Audric's bedchamber servants.

Mazatl *[Mah-ZAH-uhl]*
A general of the Tehuantin army.

Necalli *[Neh-CAHL-lee]*
The Tehuantin Tecuhtli (king) responsible for Mahri's and Talis' machinations in Nessantico.

Seaton *[SEA-tun]*
One of Audric's bedchamber servants.

Uly *[OOO-lee]*
A seller in the River Market, a Tehuantin who know Talis.

Zolin *[ZOE-leen]*
The Tecuhtli (king) of the Tehuantin people.

DICTIONARY:

A'Sele *[Ah-SEEL]*
The river that divides the city of Nessantico.

Archigos *[ARR-chee-ghos]*
The leader of the Concénzia Faith. The plural is "Archigi."

Avi a'Parete *[Ahh-VEE Ah-pah-REET]*
The wide boulevard that forms a circle within the city of Nessantico, and also serves as a focus for city events.

Axat *[Ahh-SKIAT]*
The moon-god of the Tehuantin.

Bashta *[BAASH-tah]*
A one-piece blouse and pants, usually tied with a wide belt around the waist, and generally loose and flowing elsewhere. Bashtas are generally worn by males, though there are female versions, and can be either plain or extravagantly ornate, depending on the person's status and the situation.

Bastida a'Drago *[Bahs-TEE-dah Ah-DRAH-goh]*
The "Fortress of the Dragon," an ancient tower that now serves as a state prison for Nessantico. Originally built by Kraljiki Selida II.

Besteigung *[BEHZ-tee-gung]*
"Ascension" The ceremony where a new Hïrzg or Hïrzgin of Firenzcia is officially recognized after the prescribed mourning period for the previous ruler.

The "ca'-and-cu' " *[Caw-and-Coo]*
The term for the high status families in the Holdings. The rich.

The "Calls"
In the Concénzia Faith, there are Three Calls during the day for prayer. First Call is in the morning, when the sun has risen above the horizon the distance of a fist held at arm's length. Second Call is when the sun is at zenith. Third Call is when the sun is a fist's length above the horizon at sunset.

Cénzi *[SHEN-zee]*
Main god of the Nessantico pantheon, and the patron of the Concénzia Faith.

Chevaritt *[Sheh-vah-REE]* **Chevarittai**
[Sheh-vah-REE-tie]
The "knights" of Nessantico—men of the ca' and cu' families. The title of "chevaritt" is bestowed by the Kraljiki or Kraljica, or by the appointed ruler of the various countries within the Holding; in times of genuine war, the chevarittai (the plural form of the word) are called upon to prove their loyalty and courage. The chevarittai will follow (usually) the order of the Commandant of the Garde Civile, but not particularly those of the common offiziers of the Garde Civile. Their internal status is largely based on familial rank. In the past, occasional conflicts have been decided by honorable battle between chevarittai while the armies watched.

Coinage
There are three primary coinages in use in Nessantico: the bronze "folia" in tenth (d'folia), half (se'folia),

and full (folia) denominations; the silver "siqil" in half (se'siqil) and full denominations; the gold "sola" in half (se'sola) and full denominations. Twenty folias equal a se'siqil; fifty siqils (or two thousand folias) equal a se'sola. The daily wage for a simple laborer is generally around a folia; a competent craftsperson might command four or five folias a day or a se'siqil a week. The price (and size) of a loaf of common brown bread in Nessantico is fixed at a d'folia.

Colors
Each of the various countries within the Holdings retained their colors and flags. Here are the basic banner structures: East Magyaria: horizontal stripes of red, green, and orange; Firenzcia: alternating vertical stripes of black and silver; Graubundi: a field of yellow with black stars; Hellin: red and black fields divided diagonally; Il Trebbio: a yellow sun on a blue field; Namarro: a red crescent moon on a field of yellow; Nessantico: blue and gold fields divided diagonally. Used by both North and South Nessantico; Miscoli: a single white star on a field of midnight blue; Peati: vertical stripes of green, white, and orange; Sesemora: a field of silver with a mailed fist in the center; Sforzia: a field of white with a diagonal blue bar; West Magyaria: horizontal stripes of orange, red, and blue.

Comté [KOM-tay]
The head of a town or city, usually a ca' and a chevaritt.

Concénzia [Kon-SEHN-zee-ah]
The primary theology within Nessantico, whose primary deity is Cénzi, though Cénzi is simply the chief god of a pantheon.

Concord A'Téni
The gathering of all a'Téni within Concénzia—a Concord A'Téni is called to elect a new Archigos or to make changes to the Divolonté.

Cornet
A straight wind instrument made of wood or brass, and played like a trumpet.

Cuore della volpe

"Fox Heart," a reddish flower with large white seeds. The oil of the seeds, mixed with wine, is medicinal in dilute quantities and is used for pain relief. In stronger dilutions, the extract is extremely potent and can cause temporary paralysis or death.

Days of the Week

The six days of the week in Nessantico are named after major deities in the Toustour. The week begins with Cénzidi (Cénzi's Day), and follows with Vuctadi, Mizzkdi, Gostidi, Draiordi, and Parladi.

Divolonté *[Dee-voh-LOHN-tay]*

"God's Will" —the rules and regulations that make up the tenets followed by those of the Concénzia Faith.

Domestiques de chambre

"Chamber servants"—the servants whose task it is to attend to the Kraljiki or Kraljica in their bedchamber. Only highly trusted servants are given this assignment.

Family Names

Within Nessantico and most of the Holdings, the family names follow the female line. A man will (except in rare cases) upon marriage take his wife's family name, and all children (without exception) take the family name of the matarh. In the event of the death of a wife, the widower will usually retain his wife's family name until remarried. Status within society is determined by a prefix to the family name. In rising order, they are: none, ce', ci', cu', ca'.

Firenzcian Coalition

The loose alliance between Firenzcia and states that have seceded from the Holdings: Firenzcia, Sesemora, Miscoli, East and West Magyaria.

Fjath *[Phiy-AHTH]*

The title for the ruler of Sforzia.

Garda

"Guard" or "soldier" (used interchangeably). The plural is Gardai.

Gardai's Disease
A euphemism for homosexuality.

Garde Brezno *[GAR-duh BREHZ-noh]*
The city guard of Brezno in Firenzcia.

Garde Civile *[GAR-duh Sih-VEEL]*
The army of the country of Nessantico. Not the largest force (that's the army of Firenzcia), but the Garde Civile directs all the armies of the Holdings in war situations.

Garde Kralji *[GAR-duh KRAHL-jee]*
The city guard of Nessantico. Based in the Bastida, their insignia is a bronze dragon's skull. The common ranks are "gardai" (ranging from a prefix of e' to a'), the officers are "offizier" (also ranging from a prefix of e' to a'). The highest rank in the Garde Kralji is Commandant.

Gardes a'Liste *[GAR-dess Ah-LEEST]*
The bureaucratic organization responsible for maintaining the rolls of family names, and for assigning the official prefixes of rank to them.

Généra a'Pace *[Jhen-AH-rah Ah-pah-SAY]*
"Creator of Peace"—the popular title for the late Kraljica Marguerite I. For three decades under her rule, there were no major wars within the Holdings.

Grandes Horizontales *[GRAHN-days Hor-eh-ZHON-tah-leh]*
The term for the high-class courtesans with ca' and cu' patrons.

Greaves
Leg armor.

Gschnas *[Guh-SHWAZ]*
The "False World" Ball—takes place every year in Nessantico.

Gyula *[G-YUH-lah]*
Ruler of West Magyaria. East Magyaria also uses the same title.

Hauberk
　A short chain mail coat.

Hïrzg *[HAIRZG (almost two syllables)]*
　The title for the ruler of Firenzcia. "Hïrzgin" is the
　feminine form, and "A'Hïrzg" is the term for either the
　female or male heir.

Ilmodo *[Eel-MOH-doh]*
　"The Way." The Ilmodo is a pervasive energy that
　can be shaped through the use of ritualized chants,
　perfected and codified by the Concénzia Faith. The
　Numetodo call the Ilmodo "Scáth Cumhacht." Other
　cultures that are aware of it will have their own name.
　The Tehuantin call it "X'in Ka."

Instruttorei *[Inn-struh-TORR-ay]*
　Instructor.

Kraljica *[Krahl-JEE-kah]*
　Title most similar to "Empress." The masculine form
　is "Kraljiki" (Kralh-jee-kee). To refer to a ruler
　nongender-specifically, "Kralji" is generally used, which
　is also the plural.

Kusah *[KOO-sah]*
　The title for the ruler of Namarro.

Marque
　The document given to an acolyte who is to be taken
　into the Order of Téni and placed in the service of the
　Concénzia Faith.

Matarh *[MAH-tarr]*
　"Mother."

Moitidi *[Moy-TEE-dee]*
　The "half-gods"—the demigods created by Cénzi, who
　in turn created all living things.

Montbataille *[Mont-bah-TEEL]*
　A city set on the long slopes of a mountain in the east
　of North Nessantico; also the site of a famous battle
　between Nessantico and the province of Firenzcia, and
　the only good pass through the mountains between the
　Rivers Clario and Loi.

Nahual *[NAH-hu-all]*
The proper title for the chief spellcaster of the Tehuantin. The lesser spellcasters are called "nahualli"—which is both singular and plural.

Namarro *[Nah-MARR-oh]*
The southernmost province of the Holdings of Nessantico.

Nessantico *[Ness-ANN-tee-ko]*
The capital city of the Holdings, ruled by the Kraljica.

Note of Severance
A document that releases an acolyte from his or her instruction toward being in the Order of Téni. Typically, 5% or less of acolytes complete their training and are accepted into the Order. The vast majority will receive a note.

Onczio *[AHNK-zhee-oh]*
"Uncle."

Offizier *[OFF-ih-zeer]*
"Officer"—the various ranks of offizier follow the ranks of téni. In ascending order: e'offizier, o'offizier, u'offizier, a'offizier. Often, an offizier in one of the armies also is a Chevaritt.

Passe a'Fiume *[PASS-eh ah-fee-UHM]*
The city that sits on the main river crossing of the Clario in eastern Nessantico.

Pochspiel *[POCK-speel]*
A Firenzcian card game of bidding and bluffing, similar to modern poker.

Pontica a'Brezi Nippoli *[Phon-TEE-kah Ah-BREHZ-ee Nee-POHL-ee]*
One of the Four Bridges of Nessantico.

Pontica a'Brezi Veste *[Phon-TEE-kah Ah-BREHZ-ee VESS-tee]*
One of the Four Bridges of Nessantico.

Pontica Kralji *[Phon-TEE-kah KRAWL-jee]*
One of the Four Bridges of Nessantico.

Pontica Mordei *[Phon-TEE-kah MHOR-dee]*
One of the Four Bridges of Nessantico.

Quibela *[Qwee-BELL-ah]*
A city in the province of Namarro.

Rétes
A Magyarian strudel, often made with apples or sweetened cheeses.

Sakal *[Sah-KHAL]*
The sun god of the Tehuantin.

Sapnut
The fruit of the sapnut tree, from which a rich yellow dye is made.

Scarlet Pox
A childhood illness, often deadly.

Scáth Cumhacht *[Skawth Koo-MOCKED]*
The Numetodo term for the Ilmodo.

Sesemora *[Say-seh-MOHR-ah]*
A province in the northeast of the Holdings of Nessantico.

Southern Fever
An affliction that kills a high percentage of those affected—the fever causes the brain to swell, bringing on dementia and/or coma, while the lungs fill with liquid from the infection, causing pneumonia-like symptoms. Often, even if the victim recovers from the coughing, they are left brain-damaged.

Starkkapitän *[Starkh-KAHP-ee-tahn]*
"High Captain"—the title for the commander of Firenzcian troops.

Stone
A measure of weight for dry goods. Merchants are required to have a set of weights, certified by the local board. A stone is approximately a pound and a half in our measures.

Strettosei *[STRETT-oh-see]*
The ocean to the west of Nessantico.

T'Sha *[Ti-SHAH]*
The ruler of Tennshah.

Ta'Mila *[Tah-MEE-ah]*
The ruler of Il Trebbio.

Tantzia
"Aunt."

Tashta *[TAWSH-tah]*
A robelike garment in fashion in Nessantico.

Tecuhtli *[Teh-KOO-uhl-ee]*
The title for "Lord" or "War-King" in the Tehuantins' language.

Tehuantin *[Teh-WHO-ahn-teen]*
"The People"—the name the Westlanders call themselves.

Téni *[TEHN-ee]*
"Priest." Those of the Concénzia who have been tested for their mastery of the Ilmodo, have taken their vows, and are in the service of the church. The téni priesthood also uses a ranking similar to the Families of Nessantico. In ascending order, the ranks are e'Téni, o'Téni, u'Téni, and a'Téni.

Téte *[teh-TAY]*
"Head"—a title for the leaders of an organization, such as the Guardians of the Faith or the Council of Ca'.

Tlaxcala *[Tlash-TAH-lah]*
the capital city of the Tehuantin nations.

Toustour *[TOOS-toor]*
The "All-Tale"—the bible for the Concénzia Faith.

Turn of the glass
An hour. The glass referred to is an hourglass, the sides of which are typically incised with lines marking the quarter-hours. Thus a "mark of the glass" is roughly fifteen minutes.

Utilino *[Oo-teh-LEE-noh]*
A combination concierge and watchman who patrols a small area (no more than a block each) of the city. The

utilino—who is also a téni of the Concénzia faith—is
there to run errands (for a fee) as well as to keep order,
and is considered to be part of the Garde Kralji.

Vajica *[Vah-JEE-kah]*
Title most similar to "Madam," used in polite address
with adults who have no other title, or where the title is
unknown. The masculine form is "Vajiki." The plurals
are "Vajicai" and "Vajik."

Vambrace
Armor protecting the lower arm.

Vatarh *[VAH-ter]*
"Father."

Verzehen *[Ver-ZAY-hehn]*
Tehuantin term for a telescope.

Ville Colhelm *[VEE-ah KOHL-helm]*
A town on the border of Nessantico and Firenzcia, at
the River Clario.

War-téni
Téni whose skills in Ilmodo have been honed for
warfare.

Zink
A wind instrument similar to a cornet, but curved
rather than straight.

HISTORICAL PERSONAGES:

Falwin I *[FAHL-win]*
Hïrzg Falwin of Firenzcia led a brief, unsuccessful
revolt against Kraljiki Henri VI, which was quickly and
brutally put down.

Henri VI *[OHN-ree]*
First Kralji of the ca'Ludovici line (413–435), from
whom Marguerite I was descended.

Kalima III *[Kah-LEE-mah]*
Archigos from 215–243.

Kelwin *[KEHL-win]*
First Hïrzg of Firenzcia.

Levo ca'Niomi *[LEHV-oh Kah-nee-OH-mee]*
Led a coup in 383 and was Kraljiki for three days. Forcibly removed, he would be imprisoned for almost two decades in the Bastida, and there would write poetry that would long survive his death.

Maria III
Kraljica of Nessantico from 219–237.

Misco *[MEEZ-koh]*
The legendary "founder of Brezno."

Pellin I *[PEH-Lihn]*
Archigos of the Faith from 114–122.

Selida II *[Seh-LEE-dah]*
Kraljiki of Nessantico. Finished building the city walls and the Bastida d'Drago.

Sveria I *[seh-VERH-ee-ah]*
Kraljiki of Nessantico 179–211. The Secession War occupied nearly all his reign. He finally brought Firenzcia fully into the Holdings.

SNIPPETS FROM THE "NESSANTICO CONCORDIA"
(4th Edition, Year 642)

Family Names in the Holdings:
Within Nessantico, lineage follows the matrilineal line. A husband might, in rare cases, retain his own family name (especially if it were considered higher in status than his wife's), but the wife can never take his name. In the vast majority of cases, however, the husband will legally take on his wife's family name, thus becoming a member of that family in the eyes of Nessantico law—the husband will continue to bear that name and be considered to be part of that family even upon the death of his spouse, unless and until he remarries and thus acquires his new wife's name. (Divorces and annulments are rare in Nessantico, requiring the signature of the Archigos, and each divorce is a special

situation where the rules are sometimes fluid.) Children are, without exception, given the mother's family name: "One always is certain of the mother," as the saying goes in Nessantico.

The prefix to a family name can change, depending on the relative status of the immediate family within Nessantico society. The prefixes, in order of rising status, are:

- none
- ce' (keh)
- ci' (kee)
- cu' (koo)
- ca' (kah).

One of the functionary roles of the Kralji was to sign the official family rolls every three years wherein the prefixes are recorded, though the Kraljiki or Kraljica rarely determined any changes personally; that was the role of the bureaucracy within Nessantico known as the Gardes a'Liste.

Thus, it is possible that the husband or wife of the ci'Smith family might gain status in some manner and be awarded a new prefix by the Gardes a'Liste. Husband, wife, their children, and any surviving maternal parents thus become cu'Smith, but brothers, sisters, and any cousins would remain ci'Smith.

Royalty Succession Within The Holdings:

Various countries within the Holdings, not surprisingly given the variance of customs, have various rules of succession within their societies. This is especially true when those countries are independently ruled. For instance, in East Magyaria, the closest male relative of the previous ruler who is also *not* a direct child of that ruler is named as the successor. However, with the ascension of Nessantico and the Holdings, those countries within Nessantico's influence tend to follow the lead of the Kralji.

For the royal families of Nessantico, title succession is normally to the Kralji's children by birth order regardless of gender. However, it is possible for the Kralji to legally designate a favorite child as the heir and bypass earlier-born children, if the Kralji deems them unfit to rule, or if, for some reason, they fall out of favor. This is an uncommon occurrence, though hardly rare throughout history. For the Kralji, it means that his or her children will tend to curry favor so as to remain in good graces or perhaps to unseat one of their brothers or sisters from being named the a'Kralj.

The Ilmodo and Spellcasting:

Some people have the ability to sense the power that exists all around us: the invisible potent energy of the Second World. In the Nessantico-controlled regions of the world, usage of magic has always been linked to religious faith, all the way back into prehistory. The myth of Cénzi extends deep into the historical mist, and it is the followers of Cenzi who have always possessed the power to manipulate the "Ilmodo" through chants and hand motions.

The chanting that binds the power of the Ilmodo is the "Ilmodo language" that all acolyte téni are taught. The Ilmodo language actually has its linguistic roots in the speech of the Tehuantin language, though neither those of the Concénzia Faith nor the Numetodo realized that for centuries. The Tehuantin of the Westlands also take power from the Second World via the instrument of religion, though through a different god and mythology, and they have their own name for the Ilmodo: X'in Ka.

The Numetodo have taken the most recent path to this power: not through faith at all, but essentially by making a "science" of magic. The cult of the Numetodo first arose in the late 400s, originally from the Isle of Paeti, and spread mostly west and south from there, sometimes reacting violently with the culture of Nessantico and the Concénzia Faith.

However the power is gained, there is a necessary "payment" for spell use: using spells costs the wielder physically; the greater the effect, the higher the cost in exhaustion and weariness for the caster.

Different paths have resulted in different abilities—for Concénzian téni, there is no "storage" of spells—their spells take time to cast and once prepared, they must be cast or they are lost. However, the téni of the Faith have the advantage of being able to cast spells that linger for some time after the casting (see "The Lights of Nessantico" or "The Sun Throne of the Kralji"). Téni who cast spells quickly and effectively are unusual, and have in historical times been suspected of heresy.

The Numetodo, in contrast, have found a way to cast their spells several turns of the glass earlier (though such spells can't be stored indefinitely). Like all users of this power, they "pay" for it with exhaustion but hold the power with their minds to be released with a single gesture and word. Their spells are generally longer and more arduous to create (even more so than that of the téni), but do not require "faith"—as is required by both the path of Concénzia and the Tehuantin. All they require is that the spellcaster follows a "formula." However, any variation from the formula, even small, will generally ruin the spell.

The Tehuantin, following what they call X'in Ka, must perform the chants and hand gestures much like the téni, but they can also "enchant" an object with a spell (something neither téni nor Numetodo can do), so that the object (e.g.: a walking stick) manipulated in a particular way (e.g.: striking someone) can release a spell (e.g.: a shocking jolt that renders the struck person unconscious).

In all cases and whatever the path of the spellcaster, the spells of the Second World tend to be linked to elementals in our world: fire, earth, air, and water. Most spellcasters have an ability sharply stronger in one element and much weaker in the others. Rarely does a spellcaster have the ability to handle two or more elements with any skill; even more rare are those who can move easily between any of the elements.

The Ranks of Téni in the Concénzia Faith:

The téni are ranked in the following order, from lowest to highest:

- **Acolyte**—those who are receiving instruction to become one of the téni—generally, the instruction requires tuition be paid to Concénzia by the students' families. The Concénzia Faith brings in both male and female students to become téni, though realistically the classes tend to be largely male, and there are fewer women than men represented in the higher ranks of the téni. (There have been only six female Archigi in the long history of the Faith.) During the acolyte period (typically three years), the students serve within the Faith, doing menial tasks for the téni, and also begin to learn the chants and mental discipline necessary for Ilmodo, the manipulation of the universe-energy. Typically, only about 10% of the acolytes receive the Marque of the Téni. There are schools for acolytes in all the major cities of Nessantico, each presided over by the a'téni of the region.

- **E'Téni**—the lowest téni rank for those brought into the service of the Faith. The acolytes who receive their Marque are, with exceedingly few exceptions, awarded this rank, which denotes that they have some small skill with Ilmodo. At this point, they are generally tasked with menial labor that requires the magic of Cénzi, such as lighting the city lamps, and expected to increase their skill and demonstrate their continuing mastery of the Ilmodo.
- **O'Téni**—an e'téni will be awarded this rank, generally after one to five years of service, at which point they are either put in service of one of the temples, administering to the needs of the community, or they are placed in charge of one of the téni-powered industries within the city. This is where most téni will end their careers. Only a select few will pass this rank to become u'téni.
- **U'Téni**—u'teni serve directly under the a'teni of the region. An u'téni is generally responsible for maintaining one of the temples of the city, and overseeing the activities of the o'téni attached to that temple.
- **A'Téni**—the highest rank within the Faith with the exception of that of Archigos. The a'téni each are in charge of a region centered around one of the large cities of the Holdings. There, they generally wield enormous power and influence with the political leaders and over the citizenry. At times this can be a contentious relationship; most often, however, it is neutral or mutually beneficial. In the year of Kraljica Marguerite's Jubilee, there are twenty-three a'téni in the Faith, an increase of three from the time she ascended the throne. Generally, the larger and more influential the city where they are based, the more influence the a'téni have within the Faith.

- **Archigos**—the head of the Faith. This is not necessarily an elective office. Often, the Archigos designates his or her own successor from among the a'téni or even potentially a favorite u'téni. However, in practice, there have been "coups" within Concénzia where either the Archigos died before naming a successor, or where the right of the successor to ascend to the position has been disputed, sometimes violently. When that happens, those a'téni who aspire to the seat of the Archigos are locked in a special room within the Archigos' Temple for the Concord A'Téni. What happens there is a matter of great speculation and debate. One will, however, emerge as Archigos.

The Creation of Cénzi:

At the start of all things, there was only Vucta, the Great Night, the eyeless female essence who had always existed, wandering alone through the nothingness of the universe. Though Vucta could not see the stars, she could feel their heat, and when she was cold, she would come to them and stay for a time. It was near one star that she found something she had never experienced before: a world—a place of rocks and water, and she stayed there for a time, wondering and dreaming as she walked in this strange place, touching everything to feel its shape and listening to the wind and the surf, feeling the rain and the snow and the touch of the clouds. She hoped that here, in this strange place near the star, there might be another like her, but there were no animals here yet, nor trees, nor anything living.

As Vucta walked the world, wisps of her dream-thoughts gathered around her like a mist, coalescing and hardening and finally growing heavy from their sheer volume. The dream-thoughts began to shape themselves, a white shroud around Vucta that grew longer and more substantial as she walked, heavier and heavier with each step until the weightiest part of it drooped to the ground and snagged on a rock. Eyeless, Vucta could not see that. She continued her walking and her thinking, and her dream-thoughts poured from her, but now they lay solid where they had fallen, stretching and thinning as she strode away from where they were caught. Vucta, in truth was already growing tired of this place and her search, and she desired the heat of another sun, so she leaped away from the world and the shroud of her dream-thoughts snapped as she flew.

Vucta's dream-thoughts lay there, all of them coalescing, and when the sun shone on the first day after Vucta's departure, there was a form like hers curled on the ground. On the second day, the sun's light made the dream-thoughts stir, and the form moved arms and legs, though it did not know itself. The dream-thoughts that were the yearning of Vucta gathered in its head, and from Vucta's desire to know the place where she walked, they made eyes in the face.

On the third day, when the sun touched it once more, it opened those eyes and it saw the world. "I am Cénzi," the creature said, "and this place is mine." And he rose then and began to walk about.

That is the opening of the Toustour, the All-Tale. In time, as the creation story continues, Cénzi would become lonely and he would create companions—the Moitidi—fashioning them from the breath of his body, which still contained Vucta's strong power .. Those companions, in turn, would imitate their creator and fashion all the living creatures of the earth: plant and animal, including the humans. The Moitidi's own breaths were weak, and thus those they created were correspondingly more flawed. But it was Cénzi's breath and the weaker breaths of the Moitidi that permeated the atmosphere of the world and would become the Ilmodo, which humans through prayer, devotion to Cénzi, and intense study could learn to shape.

But the relationship between Cénzi and his offspring would always be contentious, marred by strife and jealousy. Cénzi had given his creations laws that they were to follow, but in time, they began to change and ignore those laws, flaunting themselves over Cénzi. Cénzi would become angry with his creations for their attitudes, but they were unrepentant, and so they began to war openly against Cénzi. It was a long and brutal conflict, and few of the living creatures would survive it, for in that past there had been many types of creatures who could speak and think. Cénzi's throwing down of the Moitidi as they wrestled and fought would cause mountains to rise up and valleys to form, shaping the world which had until then been flat, with but one great ocean. The final blow that destroyed most of the Moitidi would fracture the very earth, tear apart the land, and create the deep rift into which the Strettosei would flow.

After that immense blow that shook the entire world, those few Moitidi who remained fled and hid and cowered. Cénzi, though, was haunted by what had happened, and he wished to find Vucta and speak with her, whose dream-thoughts had made him. Only a single speaking and thinking species were left of all of Cénzi's great-children, and he made this promise to them, our own ancestors: that if they remained faithful to him, he would always listen to them and send his power back to them, and that one day, he would return here and be with them forever.

With that promise, he left the world to wander the night between the stars.

In the view of the Concénzia Faith, Cénzi is the only god worthy of worship (Vucta being considered by the Concénzian scholars to be more an all-pervading spirit rather than an entity), and it is His laws, given to the Moitidi, that the Faith has codified and now follows. The gods worshiped by other religions within and without the Holdings are those cowardly Moitidi who came out of hiding when Cénzi left and have deceived their followers into thinking they are true gods. The surviving Moitidi remain in mortal fear of Cénzi's return and flee whenever Cénzi's thoughts turn back to this world, as they do, reputedly, when the faithful pray strongly enough.

The truth of this is shown in that the laws of humankind, wherever they may live and whomever they may claim to worship, have a similarity at the core—because they all derive from the original tenets of Cénzi.

The Divolonté:

The Divolonté is a loose collection of rules and regulations by which the Concénzia Faith is governed, the majority of which derive from the Toustour. However, the Divolonté is secular in origin, created and added to by the various Archigi and a'téni through the centuries, while the Toustour is considered to be derived from Cénzi's own words. The Divolonté is also a dynamic document, undergoing slow, continual evolution through the auspices of the Archigos and the a'téni. Many of its precepts and commands are somewhat archaic, and are ignored or even flaunted by the current Faith. It is, however, the Divolonté that the conservative element within the Faith quotes when they look at the threat of other faiths, such as that of the Numetodo.

BETWEEN THE BOOKS:

YEAR 521 (the events of *A Magic of Twilight*): This is Kraljica Marguerite's Jubilee Year—under her half century of rule, Nessantico has flourished. However, in the spring, Kraljica Marguerite is assassinated. Kraljiki Justi (her son) takes the Sun Throne. Archigos Dhosti dies; Archigos Orlandi becomes head of the Concénzia Faith. Hïrzg Jan leads the army of Firenzcia into the Holdings, intending to take Nessantico. Archigos Ana becomes head of the Concénzia Faith after Archigos Orlandi defects to Hïrzg Jan at Passe a'Fiume. The Firenzcian forces attack Nessantico. Allesandra, daughter of Hïrzg Jan of Firenzcia, is taken as hostage by Archigos Ana and Kraljiki Justi. The Firenzcian forces retreat.

522: Orlandi formally declares himself Archigos in Brezno—the Concénzia Faith is sundered. A son, Fynn, is born to Hïrzg Jan and Greta ca'Vörl. Hïrzg Jan refuses to pay ransom for Allesandra, declaring Firenzcia independent of Holdings. Semini cu'Kohnle marries Francesca ca'Cellibrecca, daughter of Orlandi

523: Envoy Karl ci'Vliomani of the Isle of Paeti is elevated to Ambassador and given the rank of cu'. The Numetodo influence begins to grow within the Holdings. Sesemora secedes from the Holdings and allies with Firenzcia—the first country within what will be known as the Coalition of Firenzcia. Hïrgina Greta ca'Vörl dies under "suspicious" circumstances; the Numetodo sect is blamed.

524: Miscoli and East Magyaria join Sesemora in seceding and joining the Coalition of Firenzcia. War is declared between the two rival Holdings. It will drag on for years without a decisive victory by either side. The Eastern and Western branches of the Concénzia Faith declare each other heretical and invalid.

525: Kraljiki Justi marries Marie ca'Dakwi of Il Trebbio, daughter of the current Ta'Mila (local ruler) of Il Trebbio.

Justi takes the ca'Dakwi name (as is proper and expected in their society). Archigos Orlandi of Brezno dies of natural causes. A'Téni Semini ca'Cellibrecca becomes Archigos there.

526: A first child is born to Justi and Marie, a son. He will die within three months. Hïrzg Jan formally declares his son Fynn to be the A'Hïrzg—the heir to his throne. This leaves Allesandra in limbo, no longer the official heir to her vatarh's throne.

527: A second child is born to Justi and Marie, a daughter. Like her sibling, she will die within three months

529: A third child is born to Justi and Marie, another daughter who is named Marguerite. She is stronger than her siblings and lives. She becomes the A'Kralj (heir).

531: The Treaty of Passe a'Fiume is signed, ending open hostilities between Nessantico and Firenzcia. As part of the negotiations, Allesandra (now twenty-one years old and having lived nearly as long in Nessantico as in Firenzcia) is finally ransomed and returns to Firenzcia.

532: Allesandra marries Pauli ca'Xielt of West Magyaria, son of the Gyula (local ruler) of West Magyaria. West Magyaria secedes from the Holdings and joins the Firenzcian Coalition.

533: A male child is born to Allesandra and Pauli: Jan. This will be their only child. Their marriage is rumored to be "troubled." In Nessantico, Marie dies bearing the fourth child of Justi, another son. Though sickly, Audric will survive.

535: Nessantican forces push farther westward in the Hellins (and also on the Isle of Paeti, which they will come to control).

537: Southern Fever rises again in the cities. Marguerite ca'Dakwi, vacationing in Namarro, is infected and dies. Audric becomes the A'Kralj in her place.

540: The Commandant of the Holdings forces in the Hellins, Petrus ca'Helfier, is killed by a Westlander after ca'Helfier either "rapes" a Westlander's daughter or the two of them fall in love (the truth here will probably never be known). The new Commandant, Donatien ca'Sibelli, takes the murderer forcibly and executes him without trial; the Westlanders protest. Retaliations escalate, and there is suddenly open war—and Commandant ca'Sibelli finds that there are new forces with the Westlanders: soldiers with faces marked by tattoos and spellcasters with skills that match those of the téni. In the Coalition, A'Hïrzg Fynn, now eighteen, leads the Firenzcian army successfully against Tennshah, taking land in the east for the Holdings of Firenzcia.

542: There are attacks by Westlanders inside the Hellins frontier—the magic used by the Westlanders proves formidable. Westlanders win a large-scale battle with Holdings forces in the Hellins. The towns around Lake Malik and Lake Udar are lost, as is control of the western frontier. The Hellins Holdings are reduced to thin strips of land around the cities of Tobarro and Munereo.

543: Hïrzg Jan suffers a heart attack. His health begins a slow, steady decline.

544: Justi, realizing he is dying, names Sergei ca'Rudka as his choice for Regent until Audric reaches his majority at sixteen. Kraljiki Justi dies, and Audric becomes Kraljiki at age eleven.

548: *A Magic of Nightfall* begins.

Rochelle Botelli

SHE HADN'T EXPECTED to find herself in Brezno. Her matarh had told her to avoid that city. "Your vatarh is there," she'd said. "But he won't know you, he won't acknowledge you, and he has other children now from another woman. No, be quiet, I tell you! She doesn't need to know that." Those last two sentences hadn't been directed to Rochelle but to the voices who plagued her matarh, the voices that would eventually send her screaming and mad to her death. She'd flailed at the air in front of her as if the voices were a cloud of threatening wasps, her eyes—as strangely light as Rochelle's own—wide and angry.

"I won't, Matarh," Rochelle had told her. She'd learned early on that it was always best to tell Matarh whatever it was she wanted to hear, even if Rochelle never intended to obey. She'd learned that from Nico, her half-brother who was eleven years older than her. He'd been touched with Cénzi's Gift and Matarh had arranged for him to be educated in the Faith. Rochelle was never certain how Matarh had managed that, since rarely did the téni take in someone who was not ca'-and-cu' to be an acolyte, and then only if many gold solas were involved. But she had, and when Rochelle was five Nico had left the household forever, had left her alone with a woman who was growing increasingly more unstable, and who would school her daughter in the one, best skill she had.

How to kill.

Rochelle had been ten when Matarh placed a long and sharp knife in her hand. "I'm going to show you how to use this," she'd said. And it had begun. At twelve, she'd put the skills to their intended use for the first time—a man in the neighborhood who had bothered some of the young girls. The matarh of one of his victims hired the famous assassin White Stone to kill him for what he'd done to her daughter.

"Cover his eyes with the stones," Matarh had whispered alongside Rochelle after she'd stabbed the man, after she'd driven the dagger's point through his ribs and into his heart. The voices never bothered Matarh when she was doing her job; she sounded sane and rational and focused. It was only afterward . . . "That will absorb the image of you that is captured in his pupils, so no one else can look into his dead eyes and see who killed him. Good. Now, take the one from his right eye and keep it—that one you should use every time you kill, to hold the souls you've taken and their sight of you killing them. The one on his left eye, the one the client gave us, you leave that one so everyone will know that the White Stone has fulfilled her contract . . ."

Now, in Brezno where she had promised never to go, Rochelle slipped a hand into the pocket of her out-of-fashion tashta. There were two small flat stones there, each the size of a silver siqil. One of them was the same stone she'd used back then, her matarh's stone, the stone she had used several times since. The other . . . It would be the sign that

she'd completed the contract. It had been given to her by
Henri ce'Mott, a disgruntled customer of Sinclair ci'Braun,
a *goltschlager*—a maker of gold leaf. "The man sent me de-
fective material," ce'Mott had declared, whispering harshly
into the darkness that hid her from him. "His foil tore and
shredded when I tried to use it. The bastard used impure
gold to make the sheets, and the thickness was uneven.
It took twice as many sheets as it should have and even
then the gilding was visibly flawed. I was gilding a frame
for the chief decorator for Brezno Palais, for a portrait of
the young A'Hïrzg. I'd been told that I might receive a contract for *all* the palais gilding, and then this happened . . .
Ci'Braun cost me a contract with the Hïrzg himself. Even
more insulting, the man had the gall to refuse to reimburse
me for what I'd paid him, claiming that it was *my* fault, not
his. Now he's telling everyone that I'm a poor gilder who
doesn't know what he's doing, and many of my customers
have gone elsewhere . . ."

Rochelle had listened to the long diatribe without emotion. She didn't care who was right or who was wrong in
this. If anything, she suspected that the *goltschlager* was
probably right; ce'Mott certainly didn't impress her. All
that mattered to her was who paid. Frankly, she suspected
that ce'Mott was so obviously and publicly an enemy of
ci'Braun that the Garde Hïrzg would end up arresting him
after she killed the man. In the Brezno Bastida, he'd undoubtedly confess to having hired the White Stone.

That didn't matter, either. Ce'Mott had never seen her,
never glimpsed either her face or her form, and she had
disguised her voice. He could tell them nothing. Nothing. She'd been watching ci'Braun for the last three days,
searching—as her matarh had taught her—for patterns
that she could use, for vulnerabilities she could exploit.
The vulnerabilities were plentiful: he often sent his apprentices home and worked alone in his shop in the evening
with the shutters closed. The back door to his shop opened
onto an often-deserted alleyway, and the lock was ancient
and easily picked. She waited. She watched, following him
through his day. She ate supper at a tavern where she could
watch the door of his shop. When he closed the shutters
and locked the door, when the sun had vanished behind the
houses and the light-téni were beginning to stroll the main

avenues lighting the lamps of the city, she paid her bill and slipped into the alleyway. She made certain that there was no one within sight, no one watching from the windows of the buildings looming over her. She picked the lock in a few breaths, opened the door, and slid inside, locking the door again behind her.

She found herself in a store room with thin ingots of gold—"zains," she had learned they were called—in small boxes ready to be pressed into gold foil, which could then be beaten into sheets so thin that light could shine through—glittering, precious metal foil that gilders like ce'Mott used to coat objects. In the main room of the shop, Rochelle saw the glow of candles and heard a rhythmic, dull pounding. She followed the sound and the light, halting behind a massive roller press. A long strip of gold foil protruded from between the rollers. Ci'Braun—a man perhaps in his late fifties, with a paunch and leathered, wrinkled skin, was hunched over a heavy wooden table, a bronze hammer in each of his hands, pounding on packets of vellum with squares of gold foil on them, the packets covered with a strip of leather. He was sweating, and she could see the muscles in his arms bulging as he hammered at the vellum. He paused for a moment, breathing heavily, and she moved in the shadows, deliberately.

"Who's there?" he called out in alarm, and she slid into the candlelight, giving him a small, shy smile. Rochelle knew what the man was seeing: a lithe young girl on the cusp of womanhood, perhaps fifteen years old, with her black hair bound back in a long braid down the back of her tashta. She held a roll of fabric under one arm, as if she'd purchased a new tashta in one of the many shops along the street. There was nothing even vaguely threatening about her. "Oh," the man said. He set down his hammers. "What can I do for you, young Vajica? How did you get in?"

She gestured back toward the storeroom, placing the other tashta on the roller press. "Your rear door was ajar, Vajiki. I noticed it as I was passing along the alley. I thought you'd want to know."

The man's eyes widened. "I certainly would," he said. He started toward the rear of the shop. "If one of those no-good apprentices of mine left the door open . . ." He was within an arm's length of her now. She stood aside as if to let him pass, slipping the blade from the sash of her tashta. The knife would be best with him: he was too burly and strong for the garrote, and poison was not a tactic that she could easily use with him. She slid around the man as he passed her, almost a dancer's move, the knife sliding easily across the throat, cutting deep into his windpipe and at the side where the blood pumped strongest. Ci'Braun gurgled in surprise, his hands going to the new mouth she had carved for him, blood pouring between his fingers. His eyes were wide and panicked. She stepped back from him—the front of her tashta a furious red mess—and he tried to pursue her, one bloody hand grasping. He managed a surprising two steps as she retreated before he collapsed.

"Impressive," she said to him. "Most men would have died where they stood." Crouching down alongside him, she turned him onto his back, grunting. She took the two light-colored, flat stones from the pocket of her ruined tashta, placing a stone over each eye. She waited a few breaths, then reached down and plucked the stone from his right eye, leaving the other in place. She bounced the stone once in her palm and placed it on the roller press next to the fresh tashta.

Deliberately, she stripped away the bloody tashta and chemise, standing naked in the room except for her boots. She cleaned her knife carefully on the soiled tashta. There was small hearth on one wall; she blew on the coals banked there until they glowed, then placed the gory clothes atop them. As they burned, she washed her hands, face and arms in a basin of water she found under the worktable. Afterward, she dressed in the new chemise and tashta she'd brought. The stone—the one from the right eye of all her contracts and all her matarh's—she placed back in small leather pouch whose long strings went around her neck.

There were no voices for her in the stone, as there had been for her matarh. Her victims didn't trouble her at all. At least not at the moment.

She glanced again at the body, one eye staring glazed and cloudy at the ceiling, the other covered by a pale stone—the sign of the White Stone.

Then she walked quietly back to the storeroom. She glanced at the golden zains there. She could have taken them, easily. They would have been worth far, far more than what ce'Mott had paid her. But that was another thing her Matarh had taught her: the White Stone did not steal from the dead. The White Stone had honor. The White Stone had integrity.

She unlocked the door. Opening it a crack, she looked outside, listening carefully also for the sound of footsteps on the alley's flags. There was no one about—the narrow lane was as deserted as ever. She slid out from the door and shut it again. Walking slowly and easily, she walked away toward the more crowded streets of Brezno, smiling to herself.

The Novels of
Tad Williams

To Order Call: 1-800-788-6262
www.dawbooks.com

DAW 102